GESELL DOME

GESELL

Guillermo Saccomanno

DOME

Translated from the Spanish
by Andrea G. Labinger

OPEN LETTER
LITERARY TRANSLATIONS FROM THE UNIVERSITY OF ROCHESTER

Copyright © Guillermo Saccomanno, 2013
Translation copyright © Andrea G. Labinger, 2016
First published in Argentina as *Cámara Gesell*

First edition, 2016
All rights reserved

Epigraph trans. by Johanna van Gogh-Bonger, ed. by Robert Harrison.
Letters to Theo van Gogh, Sept. 24, 1888, www.webexhibits.org.

Library of Congress Cataloging-in-Publication Data: Available.
ISBN-13: 978-1-940953-38-0 / ISBN-10: 1-940953-38-3

*This project is supported in part by an award from
the National Endowment for the Arts.*

ART WORKS.
arts.gov

Printed on acid-free paper in the United States of America.

Text set in Caslon, a family of serif typefaces based on the designs
of William Caslon (1692–1766).

Design by N. J. Furl

Open Letter is the University of Rochester's nonprofit, literary translation press:
Lattimore Hall 411, Box 270082, Rochester, NY 14627

www.openletterbooks.org

For Anselmo

Translator's Introduction

Villa Gesell exists. With the click of a mouse you can easily find it on any detailed map of Argentina, a beachside resort town some 200 miles south of Buenos Aires. Though this novel is a work of fiction, Villa Gesell, which serves as a model for the town depicted in it, is quite real. In fact, for approximately the past two years, I've inhabited author Guillermo Saccomanno's Villa, virtually, to be sure. Unlike Saccomanno however, who literally—and literarily—has made Villa Gesell his home for several decades, I've never actually set foot on its "streets of sand," strolled along the tree-lined boulevards of Pinar del Norte, or trod the grittier streets of El Monte or La Virgencita. I've never shaken the hand of a single flesh-and-blood denizen of the Villa, nor have I patronized its shops, rented a beach cabana for the summer, or endured a bleak, drizzly, lonely winter season in one of its apart-hotels. Instead, my experience of Gesell has been exclusively that of an outsider peering in, unobserved, as if gazing through the very device that lends its name to the title: the Gesell Dome. Saccomanno explains how this invention, created by American psychologist Arnold Gesell, functions:

The Gesell Camera [more commonly known as Gesell Dome] . . . *was conceived as a dome for observing children's behavior without their being disturbed by the presence of strangers. The Gesell Dome consists of two rooms with a dividing wall in between in which a large, one-way mirror allows an observer in one room to see what is happening in the other, but not vice-versa. Both rooms contain audio and video equipment for recording different experiments. It is frequently used for observing suspects during interrogations and also to ensure the anonymity of witnesses. The camera is considered to be the ideal instrument for taking legal testimony from children.*

In other words, the Gesell Dome—or filming chamber—that Saccomanno has created for us, his readers, theoretically affords an unobstructed, uncensored, panorama of a complex society, populated by numerous characters, many of whom we are invited to follow as they go about their daily lives. At times these lives inevitably intersect; sometimes they remain apart: isolated, searching, intermittently elated or depressed, peaceably complacent or violently desperate. We watch them, fascinated, but by no means dispassionately, for these are not Arnold Gesell's children at play, nor are we objective, scientific observers.

The person for whom Villa Gesell was named, however, has nothing to do with psychology or child behavior, but rather with its founder, Carlos Idaho Gesell, a descendant of German immigrants who, as an inventor and entrepreneur in his own right, was also responsible for the forestation of the sand dunes in the area and the establishment of the seaside vacation spot that Villa Gesell eventually was to become. Saccomanno's title is an amalgam of these two, unrelated Gesells: the German developer and the North American psychologist. He uses both of them to make his point: the first as historical artifact and the second as literary device.

Literary references, both subtle and obvious, abound in this lengthy text. From its very first sentence, a tribute to Baudelaire's *Les Fleurs du Mal* ("Tonight, *hypocrite reader, my double . . .*"), *Gesell Dome* draws the reader into a world of greed, lust, hypocrisy, envy, racism, and social inequity. *The Inferno*, too, makes its presence known unabashedly and overtly: one of the protagonists, the editor of the local newspaper and cynical commentator on the town's foibles, is named Dante, and allusions to the hellishness of the place are not infrequent. When true innocence surfaces—as it does, rarely—its impact is therefore all the more astonishing. Saccomanno's use of an omniscient, undifferentiated narrator with a panoramic sweep is yet another (and quite possibly unintentional) literary nod to Dos Passos's *U.S.A.* trilogy, with its multiple voices, incorporation of newspaper articles, song lyrics, advertisements, and other forms of intertextuality. And, of course, as Saccomanno has acknowledged on many occasions, William Faulkner and his paradigmatic Yoknapatawpha County make their influence known throughout the vast scope of this work.

But by far the most pervasive literary presence in *Gesell Dome* is generic: that of noir, or more explicitly, neo-noir fiction and the challenges it presents, particularly for the translator. Noir is inherently transgressive and hermetic: transgressive because of the nature of its subject matter and hermetic because it often depends on private linguistic codes and specialized argot with which the general public may not be familiar. In translating the novel, I relied heavily on the linguistic and cultural expertise of a friend and native informant, the much-acclaimed Argentine noir novelist Alicia Plante, whose familiarity with *lunfardo* in all its permutations was invaluable in deciphering pervasive, encoded language that I might have otherwise found impenetrable. *Lunfardo*, whose origins can be traced to the late nineteenth and early twentieth century in the Río de la Plata area, is a form of popular speech originally associated with immigrant groups, especially with the influx of working-class Italians at that time. Over decades it has become entrenched in general parlance and has insinuated itself into everyday speech: many *lunfardo* expressions, once the private domain of a very specific population and social class, have become commonplace, even standardized. In turn, a new lexicon of street-speak has come to take the place of these now quaint-sounding expressions. I have no doubt that these, too, will inevitably be supplanted by yet others. Since the novel is not a period piece, Plante and I have attempted to maintain a contemporary English slang idiom that reflects the corresponding *lunfardo* terms of the original without either reverting to archaic slang (e.g., 1940's "gumshoe" jargon, entirely inappropriate here) or committing the equally egregious error of trying to sound too cutting-edge or place-specific (e.g., North American urban hip-hop of the early twenty-first century). Thus, "cool," "dude," and even "bro" will be found in this translation, as they have endured over time, while other, more ephemeral slang expressions have been avoided. Similarly, the novel is peppered with examples of *vesre*, a feature of *lunfardo* that involves the reversal of syllables, e.g., *Monra* for *Ramón* or *tordo* for *do[c]tor*, creating a cryptolect comparable to Pig Latin, back slang, or—a distant cousin, perhaps—Cockney English. In deliberating over how to contend with these syllabic permutations, we considered reversing syllables in the translation or possibly even inventing neologisms to reflect the distortions in the original, but ultimately concluded that the effect in English would be too jarring, even bizarre, and not at all akin to the comfortable familiarity of such language among Spanish speakers in the Río de la Plata area.

Linguistic issues aside, *Gesell Dome* presents an even more fundamental challenge for the translator: that of tone. While Saccomanno adheres closely to the traditional noir diet of relentless violence and mayhem, he tempers his sinister tale with outrageous humor and compassion as well. Much of the grisliness is over-the-top, clear evidence of the author's background as a writer of comic strips. *Gesell Dome* is by no means a tale for the squeamish, but its humor, brutal honesty, and the tenderness concealed in its murky heart make it irresistible, at least to this reader. How best to capture Saccomanno's unique voice and make it accessible to the English-speaking world became my personal obsession as I sat before my computer screen day after day and experienced the perverse joy of slipping into the skins of the myriad characters who populate this abundant novel, speaking in their voices and occupying, albeit momentarily, their place in the universe. The Villa beckons: I invite you to join me there.

Andrea G. Labinger

"*But what makes those people stay where they are is precisely the feeling of the house, the reassuring, familiar look of things.*"
—*Vincent van Gogh*

Some Inhabitants of This Place

DON KARL: As his Alpine-style seaside resort grew, he filled his coffers. Italian and Spanish immigrants arrived to give shape to the place. People say that at the Hotel Austria there was a transmitter, that lights shone on the sea at night, that German submarines unloaded the Reich's gold and carried away passports. Everyone talks about the myth, but no one will offer you any evidence beyond pure gossip. Today the Villa is a city, and the portrait of the deceased, our venerable founder, is displayed in card and almanac form in every store, from delis to auto repair shops. Even the *criollos* who came from Macedo, Juancho, Madariaga and beyond, think of themselves as German descendants. That's the story of the origin of our Villa, today inhabited by 40,000 souls. I won't say anything more: take a stroll around and you'll see.

THE QUIROSES: Better known as the Kennedys, heirs of Don Evaristo, Don Karl's attorney, his long arm of the law. Alejo, Braulio, and Julián were all brought up to be honchos, and they are, especially Alejo, the eldest. Corruption, murder, drugs. Owners of the Villa's destinies. They're no worse than we are, but they represent us. You can ignore them, but they won't ignore you. And sooner or later you'll find yourself involved in a lawsuit and you'll go to them for help. If you run into a Kennedy on the street, you'd better greet him. You never know when you'll need to drop by his legal office. You never can tell. Especially in this Villa.

DANTE: Publisher and editor of *El Vocero*. He arrived at the Villa in the seventies. Fleeing from terror, like so many others. The left-wing journalist who came here on the run and sold Don Karl on the idea of a newspaper that would extol his personality and his accomplishments. Everything you need to know to stay on top of things, Dante already knows, but he doesn't publish it all. And whatever he doesn't know, he'll certainly find out through Remigio the limo driver, his Virgil, who knows and shares with him all the secrets and mysteries of this inferno.

ALBERTO CALDERÓN: *Cachito,* to everyone. Son of a *criollo* farm worker. Our mayor. Smiling, paternal, a good ol' boy politician who does favors for everyone. Don't ask how he made his money. Two terms of office don't seem to be enough for him. Not a single scandal mars his reputation. Beti, his esteemed spouse, works hard to protect their happy family image, just as it appears in the photos in *El Vocero*, while Gonzalo, his offspring, is a drug dealer and a blackmailer.

ATILA DOBROSLAV: *Our Speer.* The Croatian builder who erected the greatest number of buildings by cutting down the trees Don Karl planted. Power covers up everything: ecological disaster and the deaths of Bolivian workers on his construction sites. And his son Fito, the toady who gave him a granddaughter who should have been a grandson. A family in which incest and parricide might be more than mere town gossip. But we all turn a blind eye before the power of this partner and ally of Cachito and the Kennedys.

EL MUERTITO: They say the anguished scream of a child that we hear on certain nights, nearly always when the moon is full, that blood-curdling howl, belongs to Camilo, the son of Alba, the woman no one mentions, the guerrilla Kennedy sister, murdered in a military operation during the last dictatorship. They say it's the cry of the incestuous child of Alejo and his sister. But they also say—and why not?—that it's the spirit of all the children in our Villa, the mistreated, the abused, those who've been shot, those who are no longer here. They say.

VALERIA STEIN: Another respectable spouse, wife of Marconi the pharmacist. If adultery is the Villa's favorite siesta-time sport, Valeria could be a champion. And Alejo knows it all too well.

PRIESTS: Fathers Fragassi, Beltrán, Azcárate. The succession of parish priests in our Villa, praying to protect us and protect themselves. Nearly identical to one another; accomplices to the secrets of their flock. Their mission in this vale of tears is to listen to our sins and forgive them as we, too, forgive them because you've gotta keep on living, know what I mean?

DIEGO FRUGONE: *The Captain.* As a boy he must have dreamed of becoming a sheriff, but he was born in this country. He was with the Provincial Police, who sent him to this Villa, and here acts of heroism don't count, even if you own a badge and a .38. Besides, honesty is unprofitable. His subordinates, Renzo and Balmaceda, are an example.

CLAUDE FOURNIER: He keeps a low profile. He could be our Van Gogh, but he's got one ear too many; that's how alienated he is. In his paintings, reproductions of this landscape, there's always nature, only nature; the human species is notable for its absence. Maybe because we're more like some animal species than members of the human race.

MALERBA: The Capo. You can hire him to teach a lesson to a guy who's become a nuisance or get him off your back. Also, if the need arises, he can sell you the weapon you need at a good price. Absolute confidentiality, we speak from experience. He lives out on the edge of town with his dogs, far from the hand of God—if, in fact, he never was near it. He arrived at the Villa after the seventies. They say he belonged to the People's Revolutionary Army, but also that he was part of a band of French mercenaries. A fugitive from the army and the police. A consummate professional. Although he used crack and then got cancer, but he's still trustworthy. Just ask the Kennedys.

CRAZY HEINRICH: The madman who's on top of that eucalyptus tree with a mechanical saw. Don Karl's great-nephew. He's decided to cut down, one by one, the trees planted in his great-uncle's forestation project, a task that will take him some time, but Crazy Heinrich is in no hurry. If you're looking for the truth in this community, he thinks, don't let the tree block your view of the forest. And that's what Crazy Heinrich's doing up there.

DEBORAH MILLER: The shrink. From the couch to alternative therapies, touching on Lacan and Bach drops along the way, more than one desperate soul has come to her office. As her list of patients dwindles, she changes residence, as evidenced by the changing phone numbers she includes in the ads offering her services.

HORACIO ZAMBRANO: Physician at the hospital. Former soldier in the Malvinas War. He treats as many of the destitute and humble as he can. An abortionist for poor girls. He has seen war. And he questions the sense of bringing more lives into this Villa, which is to say the world.

MONI: No town can escape the local poet. She came to us with her verses at the end of the seventies. And set anchor. Relentlessly honored by the City and the Rotary Club, among other institutions. No doubt more people have come between her legs than have read her poetry.

WE: All of us. More than 40,000 souls. We're not bad people. We are what we can be. It isn't much, but it's quite a lot considering the possibilities in a community that lives from whatever it can earn in two months. If you think about it, it's not so terrible that barely 10% of the inhabitants have a criminal record. It could be worse.

GESELL DOME

Tonight, *hypocrite reader, my double,* as you're about to start reading this book, novel, stories, chronicles, or whatever you prefer to call these bits of prose, pieces of nothing, on this freezing night, with the sea so close and so alien, right here in this Villa, May, June, July, August, September, what difference does it make, in any of the off-season months, here, in his chalet in Pinar del Norte, a left of center surveyor is fucking his kid, someone, a mechanic, in a tin-roofed house in La Virgencita, is beating his girlfriend, someone, a drunken laborer in a vacant lot, tries to break another drunken laborer's neck during a game of *truco,* someone at the terminal, a night watchman in canvas espadrilles, after the last bus has gone, drinks *mate,* the steak of the poor, someone, an AIDS victim, hangs himself in a shanty in the south, someone, a foreman at the cement plant, is burying his girlfriend's body at a construction

3

site, someone, a young officer, is applying an electric cattle prod to a juvie thug at the police station, someone, a loser wrapped in cardboard, dies of cold in the doorway of a building near the docks, someone, a radio-taxi driver, balls his sister-in-law while his brother works as a security guard in a warehouse, someone, a little hoodlum, runs along the boulevards with a police car in pursuit, someone, a city councilman, does a line of coke while the poker game drags on, someone, a frightened old woman, lets her dogs out at night, someone, an FM operator, plays Pink Floyd and rolls a joint, someone, behind a temple, an evangelist in a mystical trance, splits his sinful fiancée's skull open with an ax, someone, a cashier from Banco Provincia, emerges from bingo having lost not only his salary, but also a sum he won't be able to justify, someone, the rotisserie owner from the next block, takes off his belt and walks into his son's room, projecting his shadow, someone, your neighbor the builder, jerks off watching a porn flick, someone, one of the gunmen from El Monte, is selling crack to a bunch of kids, and those boys and girls, dressed in hoodies, have just finished poisoning your Rottweiler and in a minute will be pointing a gun at you, forcing your wife to suck them off, fucking your daughter, and you'd better tell them where you keep your cash because you don't know what they're capable of with that iron you won with supermarket bonus points, the iron they've plugged in and is starting to heat up.

One morning, the bus leaves the main road and turns into the roundabout. The entrance to the Villa. Alpine-style constructions. Tiled roofs. Real-estate offices. Farther on is the tourist information cottage. Now that the bus has slowed down, you can take in the grove on both sides of the road. For a moment you feel like you're entering an enchanted forest. The wood and stone totem pole takes you by surprise. Some say it's a reproduction of an Inca totem. It has the head of an eagle. Others claim that if you look carefully at the hieroglyphs, you can read a Tibetan message. At the tourist office they'll tell you that the totem is a symbol of hospitality and advise travelers that they'll find spiritual peace in this place. The older residents, the pioneers, those who settled here toward the end of the Second World War, Germans and Central Europeans, offer another version; they interpret the symbols and hieroglyphs differently. But they haven't got the nerve to translate them. The totem has a function: to protect the residents from foreigners. When the newcomer's eye meets the eagle's, he feels intimidated. It's a Nazi symbol, say the Villa old-timers. And they say it in a low voice, fearfully. Some say there never were any Nazis here. And when they say it, you think it's themselves they want to convince even more than the visitors. What matters is spiritual peace. Everyone comes here, to our Villa, looking for that: spiritual peace.

Classes recommence with a strike, El Vocero *reports on the front page of this Friday's issue. The teachers' unions launched 24-, 48-, and 72-hour strikes, halting all activities. As a result, classes that were to begin on Tuesday at certain schools, Wednesday at others, and Thursday at most of the rest, will not resume again till Friday or even next week if a salary agreement between union members and the authorities cannot be reached. There has been a 98 percent compliance rate with this demonstration of force.*

A great number of parents has participated in a protest against the strike, claiming that it's not just a matter of knowing how to deal with their children's excess free time. It's a question of their future, they argue.

Meanwhile, a march punctuated by environmental and left-wing flags came out in defense of the teachers. We support the teachers in their demands for higher salaries and better-quality education.

Opposing groups of marchers came together in Plaza Primera Junta, escalating into verbal assaults and fistfights. At last, thanks to police intervention, tempers were soothed and everyone returned home.

On this side, by the coast, the hotels have exotic names: Capri, Cadaqués, Belvedere, San Diego, Malibu, Aloha, Nice, Buzios, Acapulco,

Hawaii, Bahia, Mallorca, Aegean, Taormina, Samoa, Mediterranean, Venice, but if you walk about ten blocks into town toward the Boulevard, you'll find a different Villa. The landscape becomes grittier. Urbanized, as they say. The periphery encroaching on an architecturally pretentious Villa that's no longer what it used to be. It's presumptuous to call this broad avenue, with its pockmarked asphalt and median with grass and bicycle paths, a boulevard. Each green belt is under the auspices of some benevolent association: parents who've lost their children, cancer patients, jovial grandparents, charitable women, sports fans. The names of the businesses don't matter much anymore: there might be a woman's name for a hair salon, a family name for a pharmacy, a clever quip for an auto shop, or the name of a planet for a computer service. A couple of stores interspersed between a chalet with peeling paint and a squat little house. Here you can find auto shops, auto parts stores, brakes, mattresses, tools, veterinary clinics, paint stores, plumbing fixtures, lube and oil centers, hair salons, used clothing stores, butcher shops, wholesale food markets, metal sheeting stores, lumber shops, exterminators, kiosks, lots of kiosks, little ones, big ones, limo services, small appliance stores, impounds, hardware stores, rental halls for parties, warehouses, political party headquarters, freight carriers, bakeries, grills, service stations, more kiosks, little ones and big ones.

The division of the landscape by class, bourgeoisie and petty bourgeoisie, distributed between the pine groves and the proximity of the beach on one side and behind them the landscape of the poor, goes back to the Villa's original design. In the earliest blueprints, this zone had been designated the Workers' Quarters. Which, when seen through the eyes of nostalgia, suggest the notion of an optimistic future. And as you continue across the Boulevard, a few blocks beyond, you'll find the other Villa, the shantytown. But don't try to go in. You won't be able to. Unless you need a fix and, impelled by a need to score some dope, you pay the toll exacted by the stoned, armed kids waiting at the entrance.

6

When the season ends, when the beach empties out, the surfers arrive. The rental stands have already dismantled their tents. The coast is a horizon of wind, sand, and sea. Then come the surfers. They seem to have always been there, a few arm strokes from shore, at the breakers, waiting. Now the sea belongs to them. And there they'll stay, crouching in the water despite omens of a southeaster.

You have to watch them from here, from the beach, for the duration of their wait, their wait for a wave. Sometimes they're out there early. Even if it's a gray morning with a storm hovering. Suddenly you ask yourself why they didn't catch that particular wave. But a wave the observer deems appropriate might not be the one the surfer is waiting for. That long-awaited wave is a personal dream. And if the sea is too tame, that calm might hold a premonition. After the lull, the waves start to build. There's that suspense of the body over the board, muscles tensed, ready for the leap and the journey along the wave. But to catch a suitable wave, in addition to reflexes you also need that special stroke of luck to let you balance dizzily on the crest of foam. Because the sea is treacherous here. Just the same, for that stroke of luck to occur, you have to be there, in the water at all times, waiting.

You wonder how to explain that thing that is within, yet not within, in the wave. Maybe the mystery is explained in the wait.

You probably wonder what I'm talking about.

Writing. I'm talking about writing.

It came out in El Vocero: *The Catholic community, led by Father Martín Fragassi, is preparing a new version of the Living Via Crucis, the main event of Holy Week in our Villa. This week there have been two rehearsals of the procession, which includes an impressive theatrical performance along our main avenue. The dramatization of religious scenes will be directed by Norberto Brandsen, coordinator of La Marea Theater Group. The performance will include the usual troupe of actors and also seeks the collective participation of neighbors, according to our mayor, Alberto*

Cachito Calderón, thereby encouraging the spontaneous creativity of young and old alike with the religious zeal that marks our place in the world.

Now, one week after the start of classes at middle school on a Monday afternoon, Melina D'Angelo, barely fifteen and three months pregnant, though not yet showing, entered Nuestra Señora del Mar Church without being seen, kneeled at the altar, and shot herself twice in the belly with a Bersa pistol belonging to her father, Roberto Liberio D'Angelo, owner of El Bulón Repair Shop, located at the corner of the Boulevard and Avenida 137. There was no room for doubt about the girl's intention to end both the life growing inside her and her own.

It was barely the end of March. And people could talk about nothing but Melina's suicide. No matter how much they tried to avoid it, Melina slipped into every conversation. The weather: summery. You could still walk around in shirtsleeves. Nights were just cool enough for a sweater. It was on one of those nights. At middle school: that's where it happened. And what happened distracted us from Melina for a while.

At night school, I was saying, a kid gutted another kid. The murderer, they claimed, was a scrawny little half-breed who kept to himself, and the other one, the victim, another half-breed, a big guy who used to beat up the whole class, including the other guy, the weakling, always teasing him. Until one night last week the bully threw a wad of paper at his target. Not a peep out of the shy one. At his desk, minding his own business. But then he stands up, walks over to the other one, and stabs him with a kitchen knife. Then he splits. A clumsy oaf looking for a hideout, he sneaks into a little shed in back of his house. And what does his saintly mother do? She hauls his ass over to the police station; she turns him in. The cop took him to Dolores, but they say the kid will go free. Because of how meek he was, they say, they're going to let him go. Because he acted under

8

emotional pressure. And yet they say the kid wasn't so meek after all, nor did he come from as normal a family as some people swear. Brawlers, the father and the uncles. I was with them at a few *asados*. I remember a lamb we were carving up at a stand in La Polaca. A drunk hassled one of the uncles. The uncle's knife was a flash of light. In the end they let the kid go, someone says. And when he returns to night school, the whole gang grabs him and crushes him. Not one bone left unbroken. He's in the hospital now. In a body cast. Now it seems like there's going to be a protest in the Villa to make them lock the kid up again. His father's going to be at the march, too, he said. With his knife. To skin alive the ones who want the kid put away again. Mano a mano or in a mob, he'll skin them alive, he promised.

And of course it was Moure, the veterinarian, who offered this opinion: Half-breeds shouldn't be sent to school. They should be sent to gas chambers. He said it with conviction.

Tuesday morning, sitting at the computer as he downed another mug of instant coffee, Dante, the sixtyish publisher and only reporter for *El Vocero*, our Friday newspaper, after editing the story about the kid who got knifed in a classroom at middle school, wondered how to write about Melina's suicide, the topic that had brought him there.

Solid gold, that girl. Her father, el Negro Berto, was a likeable, well-regarded guy, but he also had a strong, even irritable, disposition. He would take off his thick glasses, anticipating a fight that never came to pass. Because every outburst was over almost before it began, and he quickly reverted to his good-natured *gaucho* self. These outbursts, they said, began when he lost his wife and was left alone with Melina, who was three at the time. Since then, although several females fluttered their wings at him, Berto had no romantic history to speak of. Melina was, as they say, the light of his life. My friend, my companion, my sweetheart, he called her. The light of my life. If Berto killed himself working night and day at the shop, it was

9

because he had sworn to himself that the girl would never lack for anything. Only the best for her, he repeated. And when she finished high school, he vowed, Melina would study law. Melina would have a degree. Melina wouldn't be some common girl like so many in La Virgencita and El Monte. Melina would be someone. And when she got serious about a boy, he would have to embody all the favorable and proper conditions to share his life with a real young lady. All the conditions. And more.

The kids at middle school. First the girl's suicide. Then the stabbed little half-breed. Murder, Dante thought, was within the realm of normalcy. Why not? Marginality, violence, et cetera. And that et cetera contained a sort of wretchedness that wasn't his problem, though it was what inspired the crime section of *El Vocero*, he had to admit, which was running a bit short today. But Melina's suicide was something else. He couldn't put aside the secret. The secret, an open secret, was known throughout middle school and also in the neighborhood. The suspense was growing. Not only for Dante. We all wondered how El Negro Berto would react when he found out about his daughter's romance.

Sharpshooting champion, El Vocero *reports. A distinguished and very large Villa crowd attended the traditional Sharpshooting Pistol Competition, sponsored and promoted by the Chamber of Commerce and the Beer Lovers' Association. It should be noted that the crowd on this occasion was larger than in previous years, which proves that interest in this contest is growing, especially on the part of young people. More than 80 marksmen from Buenos Aires, Madariaga, Mar del Plata, Necochea, and Bahía Blanca were in attendance. There were seven very fluid events, consisting of 9, 16, 18, 19, 20, 21, and 31 shots apiece. The winner in the Unmodified Gun Division was our dear Esteban Armada, 18. The champion received congratulations from our mayor, Alberto Cachito Calderón, who presented him with the trophy. A big shot, Esteban.*

The end of March, the air of March, the light of March. I'm at an *asado* with the Melitóns in the park of the Transatlantic Building. Juan Melitón is a street cleaner contracted by the city lumberyard. Mariela, his wife, is the custodian of the building. The couple is there with their son, Kevin, along with guests, three of Kevin's young friends. Like Kevin, they're all fifteen. And there's no way around it: it's hard to move the conversation away from a pregnant girl's suicide.

One of the kids makes an attempt: I'm glam, says the one in red pants. Not me, says the one with a pierced lower lip. I'm punk. But we all wear skinny jeans. Stovepipe pants—in my day we called them stovepipes. One of the kids, the long-nosed one, is an orphan, Melitón the Gaucho tells me. The pimply one, the one who looks like a wanker, has parents who are separated. We're reggae, says the kid. And he points to Kevin: I'm gonna be Rasta, Kevin promises. With dreads and everything, he smiles.

And I'll beat the living shit out of you, his father replies, adding soda to his red wine. He takes a swallow, returns to the grill, and brings *chinchulines*. As he serves them, the conversation turns to the murder at night school. In addition to Melina's death, the kids have been hit hard by the knifing at night school. They hadn't yet gotten over Melina's tragedy when they were struck by another. Struck, I say. No, grazed. Maybe because at their age these dramas seem like a novel; they get swept up in them. And who doesn't like to feel he's part of a novel, right?

A kid knifed another kid, they said. The murderer was shy. He looked like a wuss. And the other guy, a bully, on his case all the time. Till the nerd stuck a knife in him. The zit-covered guy reflects: You gotta watch out for the quiet ones. The one with the big nose says: That dude could really draw. An artist. Cities blown up by death. Vampires, he drew. Skeletons.

And you? Melitón asked. You wanna be like that?

What do you want me to be—a street cleaner like you?

We don't have the money to pay for a school like Nuestra Señora for you, Mariela tells him. So you'll have to behave yourself and do okay in middle school.

To be someone, Melitón tells him. Anyone can be a bully with a knife. In workman's sandals, that's how I want to see you.

For people from around here, this is the Villa, and when they say Villa, they trace this place back to its origins, the Central European pioneers. Italians, Galicians, those who came from other parts, like the majority, because the majority here came from other parts, not just from Austria, as if Austria was a big deal. Everyone, I'm saying, including the natives, calls this town the Villa. And when they say "Villa," they feel like a superior, chosen race. The kids, on the other hand, those who were born here, almost all share the single goal of getting the hell out. The stoner snobs who want to keep on kicking back take their surfboards to Costa Rica. The blue-collar kids who are looking to earn some cash go to Spain to become dishwashers or to the States to scrub toilets. Wherever it is, they'll be better off. Anywhere but the Villa. This damn town, they call it. They've got plenty of reasons. Wait till winter and you'll understand, Dante predicts.

Nicolás Parenti, seventeen, repeating his next-to-last year of high school, was famous for the number of warnings and absences he was able to accumulate soon after the beginning of the school year. That first week he had already racked up twenty warnings, cut classes four times, and wasn't about to change, even though his father, José Luis Parenti, owner of El Ropero Moderno clothing store, made a significant donation to the school co-op so his son wouldn't be expelled.

Limits, he needs limits, said José Luis, wiping his hand nervously across his bald spot. Yeah, sure, what limits can you set when you have no character, his wife said. You're responsible for his lack of control. Because, according to Lidia, it was José Luis who needed to set Nico on the right course. If they'd had another child, Nico would be different, she said. But no—Nico was an only child. Only and last. Because a second delivery would have been fatal, the doctors told her. Her frustration turned to bitterness, and the bitterness into a constant resentment against José Luis. By the first day of class, Nico had already gotten into a fistfight with a couple of classmates, cursed out a teacher, and run off to God knows where. Suddenly vanished. He'll come back when he's hungry, his father said. And that's how it turned out. Nico returned early one morning while his parents were sleeping and the house was dark, and raided the fridge. His father woke up; they argued. Shouting. They swore at one another. The mother was slow to intervene. It was hard for her to conceal how much she enjoyed watching Nico humiliate José Luis. She stepped in only when Nico knocked his father down by smashing a bottle against his head.

Dante, our reporter, is a devoted client of Josema's, and not only because of the stylistic efforts the barber expends on his high-and-tight. If he's missing a piece of information to finish an article, he goes to Josema Unisex Stylist to find it. Because there's not a single rumor, true or false, that doesn't get teased out here. Obviously, Melina's suicide also came out. They talked about it, sorrowfully. There was nothing more to say, they said.

I just listen, said Josema. We're alike that way, added Dante. We know more about the Villa than the Villa knows about itself, Josema remarked. Thing is, he writes, while I don't have a proper education. I talk, he says, and Dante writes. If he ever decided to write for TV, we'd blow the ratings sky-high. What connects us, Dante says, isn't so much our interest in other people's stories. It's a strong stomach for digesting garbage. Sometimes I think we've eaten so much shit that we've acquired a taste for it.

And Josema offers the example of the military regime, almost forty years ago, when random corpses would wash up on the beach early in the morning. Some of them tied up with wire. Eaten by fish, nearly all of them. In those days, Police Commissioner Vidal, the mayor, came to the barbershop every other day. He'd ask me to trim his mustache like General Videla's. I know as much about you as about my daughter, Vidal would tell me. But he wasn't referring so much to the strict control he had over the girl as to her origins: Vidal would tell anyone who wanted to listen that the girl was the daughter of subversives. And at his city office, he would stroke his 45 on his desktop. Because Vidal greeted you with a pistol on his desk. Since his wife was impotent—that's what Vidal used to say, his wife was impotent—they had decided to adopt. And so they got that little girl from guerrillas and they were reacclimating her, because even though she was very young, she still carried her parents' vices in her blood, and they had to be careful. On those occasions Vidal would also remind Josema of his militant past in the Communist Party. We know you aren't a threat to anybody; you make a hell of a racket, yeah. But you don't have the balls to pick up a weapon.

Vidal would boast: When I came to the Villa I already had files on everyone. But I also did some intelligence work. Like with my little girl. Deep down the girl and the Villa are alike. You have to keep them both on a short leash, because when you get careless, Vidal said, and he didn't finish the sentence. On those occasions Josema sharpened the razor, shaved the Commissioner, and couldn't take his eyes off his neck. Tell me the truth, Josema, am I right or wrong. Or are you going to tell me you don't feel like slitting my throat, Vidal would taunt him. When he left, I would stand there with knots in my stomach, Josema recalls. I had to digest that humiliation.

How happy I was when he was diagnosed with cancer, Josema recalls. Remember, Dante, how drunk we got celebrating Vidal's prostate cancer? Then the wife and daughter moved to Córdoba. The wife was an alcoholic. Both of them were killed in an accident at La Cumbre. The car veered off the road in the mountains. Unstable, the wife was. That time we got drunk out of sadness. The girl deserved better.

Why sweet, gentle, lovely, and outstanding Melina, as everyone memorialized her after her death, had fallen in love with an awful creep was a mystery. What she could have seen in Nico was a total enigma. The truth is that when he was with her, Nico seemed like a different kid. With her he was well mannered: he said hello, was pleasant, and acted gentle, docile. You don't understand him, Melina would say. He's not what you think. He's such a *sweetie*, Melina said in English—she took private English lessons. With me he's different, she said. The Nico who goes out with me isn't the one you want to see. And at that point, when we all knew about Melina and Nico's romance, we couldn't help making conjectures and bets. How El Negro Berto would react, how he'd get his hands on Nico, and— the million dollar question—what he'd do when he found out about his daughter's betrayal. Because for Berto it would be nothing but a betrayal. He'd kill himself; Berto would kill himself. No, he'd kill her. But first he'd kill the boy. Don't exaggerate, you guys, someone said, he'll lock her up in a convent. The entire Villa was breathlessly waiting to find out what would happen when El Negro Berto found out. What nobody could have imagined was that he would find out with the girl killing herself with two shots to her belly. Whoever said "belly" and not "baby bump" was sensitive, one of a group of sensitive souls that later on, just a few weeks later, when the accusations of child abuse against the kindergarteners at Nuestra Señora came out, used diminutives like someone telling a story to a child: coochie, wienie, tushie. They even called the victims the abused little ones, *los abusaditos*. But that's another story, one more, like all of them, and there are even more to come. Let's not get ahead of ourselves.

Several assaults, you can read on the cover of this Friday's edition of El Vocero. *In the last week seven armed robberies were reported. Four of businesses, two of private residences, and one in the street.*

Recently I ran into Jorgelina, the teaching assistant at middle school. She tells me she's requested a psychiatric leave of absence:

I can't stand it anymore, she tells me. Did you hear about the kid who stabbed another kid in class? He stuck him several times with an ordinary kitchen knife. The boy died in my arms. I can still see his eyes, feel his blood between my fingers. In my twenty-three years at the school, twenty-three dead kids. I don't want any more.

When March turns into autumn, the street cleaners get to work early in the morning at the entrance of Nuestra Señora del Mar Institute. By 7:30 you can see them gathering the dry leaves and branches knocked down by the latest storm. Soon the 4x4s will pull up.

The mommies bring their children to Nuestra Señora. Blondes. Purebreds. Very strong. Lots of iron. And soy cutlets. Never stew. The half-breeds, ever more slowly, drag their brooms along the sidewalk and rake sand off the street. Ever more slowly. They dawdle with their shovels, their wheelbarrows. They work in slow motion, watching out of the corner of an eye, as though spying. Because more than one mommy has an important name in the Villa. It's wise to observe them discreetly. Valeria the Jew, Marconi the pharmacist's wife, sluttier than a bitch in heat, they say, showed up one morning with nothing on underneath. Not even panties. No doubt she was on her way to screw Quirós.

Then they disperse, raising a dust cloud that renders them invisible.

El Negro Berto found out about Melina and Nico's romance at the same time he learned of her pregnancy. Another father would have fallen apart. The Bersa his daughter had used wasn't the only weapon

16

he owned. In his workshop he kept an old Ballester-Molina, a relic. He loaded the gun, climbed into the F100 and minutes later pulled up in front of El Ropero Moderno. Frightened, Parenti came out to the street. Behind him, Lidia. We're part of the tragedy, too, Berto, Parenti greeted him, pale and trembling, and not just from fright. Us, too, he said. It happened to all of us. El Negro Berto didn't say anything. It was a kid thing, Lidia said. What happened didn't just happen to you. Your daughter wanted it, too. She must have enjoyed it. This drama affects two families, Parenti said. Yours and ours. I have no more family, said El Negro Berto. Nico's not here, Lidia quickly interjected. If you find him, bring him here, the mother begged. We'll know what to do. He won't get away with it. This time we're sending him to reform school.

With his hand on his forehead, Parenti cried: I knew this would end badly.

It hasn't ended yet, said El Negro Berto.

And he got back into his F100.

But let's not kid ourselves; the Villa today isn't exactly Dubai, man. The buildings are known for their inferior quality. In order to save on material and draw the maximum benefit from the space, the apartments are narrow—but that's not all. Their walls are thin, the windows not strong enough to withstand a southeaster. The elevators can't take intensive use. And every so often one of the cables breaks. Or the floor gives way. Not to mention the rotted balconies. Who doesn't remember the balcony that collapsed with five drunken kids on it. Three died.

Because, on account of the high rents, the apartments have two or three times as many people as they can hold. An example: during high season, a one-room apartment might be occupied by two couples with kids and in-laws included, or even eight adolescents. But tourists couldn't care less about construction. They've come to the seashore and they try to spend as much time as possible on the beach. They get by with fruit and sandwiches and skip lunch. But at night the building turns into a beehive where you can breathe the aroma of burgers and steaks along with après-sun cream.

The construction is so cheap that you can hear everything going on in the pigsty next door. In the one upstairs. In the one downstairs. You can hear voices and shouting, laughter and arguments. Insults and the bawling of a baby. The creaking of a bed where people are fucking and the clamor of pots and pans. A din of broken glass and the cursing of some drunks. The howl of an orgasm and the angry crash of a venetian blind. Doorbells ringing, knocks on doors. Anyone watching TV has to turn up the volume because the cumbia playing next door makes it impossible to hear. One complaint by a neighbor is enough to start an argument. The kids with their music going full-blast argue that they're on vacation. The couple protesting because their kids can't sleep with that racket threatens to call the police.

When the season is over, if you want to rent a room for the winter, the real estate agencies and owners will give it away to you for a few pesos, as long as you cover taxes. In one of these single-room dwellings lives Dante, our reporter from *El Vocero*. As long as my books and records fit and I can listen to Mozart's *Requiem* without bothering anybody, I'm satisfied, he says. There's not much more to life. More than Mozart, I mean. And with the building empty for nearly ten months, no one's going to hassle me to lower the volume.

On Tuesday night Nico Parenti was playing pool at Poolenta, the El Monte bar, near Cirunvalación, the only light on that pitch-black street. Nico was playing with the Vicuñas, those scourges. Seeing El Negro Berto walk in was enough to make the Vicuñas disperse. El Negro didn't even give him time. He fired at his forehead. Blew his head off.

Then he vanished into the darkness. He got into his F100 and followed the main road. He didn't stop till he reached the cliffs of Mar del Plata.

The pioneers prefer to keep their mouths shut. And yet there is testimony about Nazis hidden in the Villa. There's that story from the photo album some tourists found when they rented the chalet from old Don Manfred—a photography buff—in Pinar del Norte. Before renting out the chalet, Don Manfred closed off the basement. But the renters' kids removed the padlock and opened the door to the basement. People say that when they found the photos they were so shocked they didn't know what to do.

They closed the door. They had come for a vacation. Not to embitter their lives.

This Thursday morning, for two hours now, almost 11 o'clock, just about time to put the paper to bed, Dante has been sitting at the computer. He tries out various versions of the article. Nothing works for him. Melina D'Angelo. Age fifteen. Daughter of a prestigious mechanic in our community. He writes disjointed phrases that he plans to connect later. Finally he opts for a box, an obituary. And the hell with it. In a few days we'll all have forgotten the whole business. One more stripe on the tiger. *Deepest sorrow*, he titles it. *Our Villa was saddened last Tuesday by news of the death of a beautiful young lady, a diligent student, and a loyal and generous friend. We all mourn your absence, dear Melina*, he writes. That's it. Now he just needs to get his hands on a photo of Melina. He'll call the middle school, ask some of her friends for a picture.

But he still has one other piece of news to report: *Suffering enormous pain at the loss of his daughter, Melina, Roberto D'Angelo, known to all as El Negro Berto, consumed with anger, sought revenge by attacking the girl's boyfriend, Nicolás Parenti, whom he killed at a pool hall in our Villa. Hours later, D'Angelo lost his life in a ravine in Mar del Plata.* Dante hesitated over the title: *Double family tragedy*. That's enough, he said to himself. Enough.

He hits "delete," erasing both stories. He won't publish anything. It isn't necessary. No need. As usual in the Villa, all 51,068 residents were up to date on everything. And by the time a news item was published in *El Vocero*, it was already ancient history. Each man, each woman, related the facts in their own way and according to their convenience, almost always embellishing them, offering a casual explanation, introducing an anecdote that had gone unnoticed, giving the matter an extra turn of the screw, and, in that invention, there was often more truth about the event than in the generally oblique, presumably objective article that Dante was able to give us on Fridays.

To me, who will never be a father, they come and say Father, like the male who gave them his blood along with his semen, the one they abhor, their vigilant shadow, a shadow those miserable cowards hope to free themselves from, but they wait, carefully counting the years, months, weeks, days, minutes the wretch still has left so that they can lock him up in the back room or in the dank prison of a nursing home with his meals on a tin plate, and they wait, calculating their inheritance, whether a small fortune or a hovel, they wait, consulting the almanac, the clock, the second hand, for that night when they'll have to come to the chapel looking for me so I can give the old man his last rites, and they'll gaze at me with heads bowed, a grieving, bovine expression, just like when they meekly show up at the confessional, momentarily given over to submission and silence, convincing themselves of the fear projected onto a punishment which, whenever I command it, Our Fathers and Hail Marys, they know will be less of a punishment than a formality, the necessary purification required of an abstract god with the ability to grant them the freedom to continue exercising their baseness with impunity, a Rosary of abjection, always the same, because they always make the same mistakes, and when they softly stammer the reckoning of their nasty deeds, they imagine that a dozen prayers will rinse away the filth that defines them as a flock, because there's no other way to be accepted in the flock than by sharing the dung, grime, fluids, and stench of this Villa, mired in its swamp, but then they're cornered by guilt and come to me, deluding themselves into thinking they can overcome their instincts, make me their accomplice, and both of us, the absolver and the absolved, collude in a hypocritical pact, confession and forgiveness, a contract of fleeting purity, a consent required by the Sunday worshippers when I see in their faces, fragrant with fancy soap and shaving cream, that grimace of provincial kindliness that will last till the noontime binge of *carne asada*, savoring innards, free once more, their souls freshly prepared to screw over their neighbors. No, I would never touch their offspring. And if I did—may God free me of such temptation—I wouldn't confess it.

Fátima was the prettiest waitress who worked last summer at Las Camelias, the little grill Betina owns at the roundabout. From the first day, around November, Fátima had us. A blonde with a sweet, little-girl expression, though her curves dissolved any tenderness inspired by that overgrown baby-faced smile. She didn't look like a Santiagueña. We placed bets on who would be the first. All of us wanted to sit in Fátima's section. Even Dante, always composed, trying not to lose the self-control that, according to him, is second nature, a kind of addiction imposed on him by the profession. A reporter has to be neutral, he used to say. He observes without judging. Yeah, but you make sure to sit in the chick's section so you can look at her ass, we told him.

Fátima must have been under twenty. If you gave her a compliment, flirted with her, Fátima would melt you with that gentle smile. But it was hard to get beyond that smile. Because then Betina would step in. Someone mentioned that there was something going on between them. They also said that after Betina dumped the Cobra, her last kept man and an incurable gambler, she preferred women. But that was much later, in winter. A dirty lie spread by the Cobra.

When we asked Betina why she kept such a close eye on Fátima, she told us that she had promised her parents. The little girl had to reach the altar a virgin. We remember: she called her "the little girl." It wasn't just a matter of love and purity. She had a good catch waiting for her: a nice lawyer. A condition for the wedding was that he had to be the first.

No one had a go. But when the season ended, after Holy Week, Fátima got on the bus back to Santiago. She was three months gone. Not showing yet. We also found out that the story about the wedding was a lie. Fátima had three kids in Santiago. And this baby bump was her fourth.

Also, we found out more than one person had fallen for the purity story. Negotiating with Betina first, of course. We found out, I say. We found out what we had always known, but what had seemed too obvious to be true: the girls handed over a percentage of the "virgin surcharge" they made to Betina. If they wanted extra pay, that was the condition. And Fátima was no exception. With that baby face, imagine. It's just that purity these days is worth more than euros.

Dante leaves the office of *El Vocero* and walks toward the beach. Sea air cleanses, they say. Although Dante is skeptical, he decides to determine if it's true. It's a sunny, warm afternoon. In a little while the sun will set. On an afternoon like this, on Monday, Melina fired two shots into her belly. There is no suicide that isn't at once a question and an accusation. It's easy to accuse: a widowed father, hermetic, stubborn, who turned the girl into a personal vindication of his frustrations. He never took his eyes off her.

Another father would have broken down in his widowhood, El Negro Berto used to say. But he didn't need to say it. Just like he didn't need to keep her on such a short leash. Melina had been a model child by nature, one who attracted the admiration and envy of many parents. If Melina was as she was, an ideal girl, it wasn't because of the discipline with which her father had raised her. It was her nature to be that way. Therefore, Dante thinks, accusing the father, blaming it on the daughter's fear of her father's discovery of her pregnancy, becomes a theory like any other, but it doesn't answer the question that's been poisoning the entire Villa: Why?

Suddenly, an intuition. Melina's suicide is a foretaste of what we will live in the months between the end of last season and the beginning of the next. Eight months, almost nine. The gestation period of the new season. If Melina left us with a question, the answer can only be found among all of us. If anyone cares to find an answer.

Unaware of his surroundings, Dante suddenly notices that night has fallen and the Villa lies behind him. His meandering thoughts have led him farther than he'd planned. It's going to be a tough trip back, walking along the sand. My tobacco, he curses. Standing atop a dune, Dante watches the lights of the Villa. A lovely scene.

And it's just beginning, he thinks.

The scandal at Nuestra Señora del Mar, the eleven, because now there were eleven abused kindergartners, exploded the following Tuesday at noon. By Wednesday there were sixteen. On Thursday, nineteen. The pediatrician found irritation in one little girl's vagina. As I anticipated, diminutives and euphemisms formed part of the rumor that spread throughout the entire Villa: heiny, wienie. And just as the diminutives helped emphasize the victims' drama with manipulative tenderness, it also seemed to reduce the crime to a lesser category. But the capital letters pushed to the forefront in the flyer that the parents wrote; indignation was spelled out, just like in the title: THE RAPE OF INNOCENCE, all caps. There are no fewer than eleven physically abused children in the four-year-olds' room and the two-year-olds' room, as verified by professional psychologists and doctors, plus ten other little ones who may have witnessed the abuse and exhibitionism.

And so the abuse oscillated between diminutives and capitals. Dante noticed this detail. But it was no time for semiotics. Besides, the article left a great deal to be desired: exhibitionism is spelled with an "h," observed Anita López de Campas, language teacher at

Nuestra Señora as well as at middle school. Spelling is the least of our worries right now, a father bristled. A committee was formed and everyone took their 4x4s over to the TV station. But the station owners, Salvatore of Hogarmar Appliances, Barbeito of Galería Soles, and Rinaldi, the supermarket impresario, refused to broadcast the news that ignited the Villa's fury. It's not just that this incident will be bad for tourism, Salvatore said. It's also a matter of the little boys and girls, Martínez explained. And Rinaldi, in a sensible tone: We have to act cautiously while the police investigate. By late afternoon the national media were also expected to get on board. In total, between the original eleven children and the other ten mentioned in the flyer, there were now twenty-one victims. At first rumors centered on the school's kiosk owner. Then on a friend of his. Both of them had disappeared: the kiosk guy and his friend, vanished. By curfew two kindergarten teachers were also under suspicion. By nighttime the news was on every channel. On top of all this, in addition to the DA who was sent from Dolores to intervene, a priest had now been dispatched to the Villa by the archbishopric to mediate. It was said: Father Fragassi, our parish priest, the principal of the school, had a history. Two years before, he had made advances on the kid who was filling his tank at the Shell station. If the rumor was false, that was yet to be proved. But there must have been some reason that this particular rumor, and no other, had spread. Where there's smoke, there's fire.

And what if our dear little priest is innocent, asked Carbone.

Even though Dante kept wondering about Melina's suicide, he had to admit that he'd been thinking about it less. And the same thing was happening with the night school case, that little half-breed who had knifed a classmate.

The worst that can happen to you is for a gigantic wave to hit you from behind by surprise. The right thing to do, if you don't want it to destroy you, is to face it head-on, diving into it before it crests. The scandal at Nuestra Señora del Mar was one of those waves. One of those huge ones, typical of southeasters, that rise and rise till they take on the threatening shape of a claw, and, once they reach that size, begin to collapse on you and sweep you away.

Last Wednesday the parents were still meeting. The school was to remain closed until the case was solved. According to the parents, the investigation wasn't getting anywhere. Since it was a religious school, they said, the crime would go unpunished. Priests always cover each other's asses. In the afternoon more parent groups were formed. Armed, in their 4x4s, they patrolled the Villa, looking for the kiosk owner and his friend, the two of them a couple. Another group entered the school and cornered the principal, Father Fragassi. When they emerged, their knuckles were skinned and they were spattered with blood.

The photos are in black and white, turned sepia by time, enclosure, humidity, saltpeter. Women walk clinging to their husbands' arms, holding their children by the hand. All of them wear that armband with the star. Up close one can see the sign of a train station, platforms, railroad cars. Everywhere, uniformed soldiers with dogs. In other photos, some of those uniformed soldiers stand at attention while the prisoners clamber off the trains. There's a building that looks like a factory, a smoking chimney. By way of contrast, some festive pictures, officers and women dancing, an orchestra, an officer sitting at a table raises his glass in a toast, and in another he sings, his arm around a woman's waist. In another photo, skeletal corpses in a mass grave. In yet another, the same officer who was toasting and singing now fires at the head of a fallen boy. The photos are in a box in the basement of Don Manfred's chalet. Don Manfred, that skinny, angular officer who's firing his gun against the boy's skull, almost unrecognizable if you compare him to the pale, fat guy he's become. Gout, he suffers from gout. And never stops complaining.

It troubles him that his gout keeps him from maintaining the chalet as he'd like: if only he could keep it as splendid as on the day he moved in and store the past in the basement. One of these days he's going to burn all that stuff that gives the Jews so much to talk about, always going on about being persecuted. Who would've thought that the Moishes would become his bread and butter? Because when the season arrives and he has to rent out the place, the majority of renters are always the same, Moishes. The Libermans, a well-known psychiatrist's family. The Feldmans, furriers. The Kleins, clothing manufacturers from the Once District. Every summer he rents to Moishes. Who can understand what pleasure the Moishes take in coming to this Villa, where the history of the Nazis and submarines during the war was no fairy tale.

Early this morning just four drivers remained at Remises del Mar Limousine Service, more than enough. And four is a whole fleet on a frozen night in May. Dead hours at the limousine service run from two till just past seven, when the Villa begins to stir a little with kids on their way to school. That's how it goes in winter, long as the hopes of the poor, and even longer are the early morning hours at the limousine service.

Those few drivers who are there show up because they can't stand sleeping with their wives, because they're insomniacs, or, more often, because they're flat broke and need some cash to feed their families tomorrow. Remigio is a nighttime regular. But for other reasons. If Remigio works several nights a week, it's because he desperately needs to recoup the dough he lost on Bingo, and if he doesn't, he'll have to put up with the cursing of that witch of his, Daniela, when he gets home. Another reason for his being at the limousine place this morning is that he's got some bitch to keep happy while her hubby works as night watchman at a hotel or a construction site, making sure no one swipes the building materials and tools. One of his newest babes, it seems, is Neli, Commissioner Frugone's wife.

It's astonishing and even envy-inspiring that Remigio, with a fox like Daniela at home, goes sneaking around with whatever old hag crosses his path. Because no broad is turned off by Remigio. When it comes to getting laid, Remigio doesn't mind taking risks. If he has one talent, it's speed; he could fuck a hare on the run. He knows that screwing Frugone's wife has its risks, that he might turn up with a bullet in the back of his head, face down in the beach grasses on a southern dune, but no—up till now the cuckold doesn't realize that he is one. And if he doesn't find out, it's because Emi, the kid, his own offspring, covers up for his old lady. A bit of a faggot, that kid, dyed hair, with that earring and the tattoo he goes around showing off. Because he resents his father so much, he enjoys covering up his mom's affair. She's got a certain something, the Commissioner's wife: not a very attractive face, but in the veteran category, well past forty, her body isn't one you'd turn down. The thing is, says Remigio, to get away with certain tricks in the Villa, you gotta know how to move. Move in every sense of the word.

At night there was a lamb barbecue at Nacho's country house. Abril, the little one, was three. Toddling from table to table, tipsy. Abril held a plastic glass in her hand, asking for pan-pam, pan-pam. But Mariana and Toto ignored her. Lolly lolly. Too caught up in arguing. Although there were hints of autumn, we were lucky, and it was a warmish night. The moon walked among the pines. We'd left off the wine and had moved on to champagne. Abril had just learned to walk. And to talk. Those were the days when Toto went around with Wanda, the Uruguayan, who helped him at his business, and also with Moni, the poet, who came by often. Toto had separated from little Vivi, with whom he had five kids. Vivi was at the birthday party, too. Toto always cared about keeping good relationships in the family. We're nature, he would say. We're trees; we grow branches. Toto, spreading his arms, also encompassed Wanda and Bárbara's kids. But this isn't Toto's story. Pan-pam, pan-pam, Abril begged. It was comical to see her; she wanted to lick the bottom of the glasses. There were around fifty of us that April evening. Nothing was left of the grub, not even a sausage. But there was plenty of booze. With Toto you never ran out of booze.

Just then the kids brought in Toto's birthday cake with sixty candles, and the girl went back to her parents. For a change they were arguing and cursing at one another. No doubt about it, from the way they poked their noses at each other. Finally Mariana one-upped Toto: Where you gonna find someone else to suck you off like I do? It caught Toto off-guard. He had to admit it. When you're right, you're right, honey. The little one grabbed her mother's glass. It wasn't empty. She *was* right. Pan-pam, pan-pam, said Abril, licking her lips. Mariana and Toto laughed. All three of them toasted. If only you knew how that munchkin was conceived. Line after line, and some booze. She's not going to want chocolate milk anymore. Buy her champagne.

In those days, as the Allies were winning the war, the three or four measly cabins started to multiply. Soon there were a dozen; the settlement grew, taking the shape of a Villa that was recommended by one friend to another among the Buenos Aires German community. During that same period the Hotel Wagner was built, with a movie theater, which, according to the old timers, showed *The Triumph of the Will*. It had a radio and a transmitter, which, they say, communicated with submarines along the Huns' route. Here, at night, a twinkling of light could sometimes be seen where the sea met the sky. Nazi bigwigs disembarked, bringing with them the Führer's gold; they carried passports, like I said, allowing them to return to Hamburg and come back again with more fugitives. Odessa, let's call it. Everyone knows. No one tells.

The Villa guaranteed a healthy, natural life. The German women bathed naked in the sea. And the natives jerked off spying on the bare-ass Valkyries. The men were devoted to the hunt. The wild pigs ran away toward Mar de las Pampas. There, with nothing but a Luger and a knife, you could liquidate them.

Like I was telling you, the first suspicions fell on Ramiro, the school's gay kiosk owner with dyed-blonde hair and that little earring—of course you know who. And they also suspected his partner, Gabriel, the buff P.E. teacher, personal trainer of all the snobby chicks in the Villa. The Kennedy women trained with him. Also Beti Calderón, the mayor's wife. And Valeria, the wife of the pharmacist. We all thought Gabriel was finished when two young thugs whacked Floreal, the lottery ticket vendor who was his partner last year. Some even said that the robbery and murder had been instigated by Gabriel, who was into young kids. After Floreal's murder, Gabriel hooked up with Ramiro, but the relationship didn't look serious. Roxana, the gardener and Ramiro's close friend, thought they were well-suited, that their relationship had a future. Even though for Ramiro it was less like love and more like a crutch. But after a while it got serious, and they even went around saying they hoped the same-sex marriage law would be passed. In his free time between classes, Gabriel would go to Ramiro's kiosk for a Gatorade. Sometimes they'd be joined by Noelia, Roxana's close friend; the two of them were so tight that people thought there was something more between them. People said that those two, Ramiro and Gabriel, together with Noelia and Roxana, threw parties at the kindergarten. That they filmed the things they did with the kids. And that Father Fragassi, another gay, but closeted, was involved. The priest turned a blind eye, he covered up for them, people said. They said all that. The thing is, the four of them—Ramiro and Gabriel on one side, Roxana and Noelia on the other—had to disappear into thin air in order to avoid the posse of parents who patrolled the Villa looking for those responsible for the abuse. What an array of weapons was unearthed: from 22s and 9-millimeters to 45s and 357s, sawed-off 12-calibers, carbines, rifles with telescopic lenses. And hunting knives. Who would have imagined there was such an arsenal in the Villa. That's how those groups of parents went around, with their boots and their bomber jackets, ready for the hunt. As if the suspects were wild pigs.

When the last tourists disappear, those who had hoped that the season's two months' worth of work would save them must go and beg the manager of Banco Provincia for mercy. It's true, though: at the end of the season, few people are in the same place they were at the beginning of the story. And you can see couples regrouping. Between dumping and getting dumped lurks a silence that brings on gloomy thoughts: now loneliness is even lonelier. And so: alcohol. Or a line of coke. By the time you react, it's too late. You've got to let off steam with someone. Suicide starts dogging you. So close at hand. Some folks reject the idea of financial motives, blaming emptiness instead. Before we realize it, one morning the Villa is a grayish blue. Deserted houses, deserted hotels, deserted shops, deserted streets. And on top of that, the fog, the drizzle. Melancholy rots the spirit like humidity on fallen leaves. Women choose gas, pills, or opened veins. Men, in general, hang or shoot themselves.

Suicides increase when temperatures begin to drop. Dante can prove it. He doesn't need to keep track of the suicides he reports on in *El Vocero*. An elderly couple. A retiree. A grandfather with aches and pains. It's not true that winter only carries off the old folks. It also sweeps away the kids. Loaded with dope, drag racing while high, screwing around with guns. There are also those attention-seeking kids. Hanged from the cross in church or with their brains blown out by swallowing a gun on top of the German's grave. Two methods that are becoming quite popular these days. And they're trying to say something. I'll bet winter cleans out more teens than seniors, Dante ventures.

And while the cabins were multiplying, Don Evaristo Quirós, the shyster, the crow, came to the Villa, he who never turned down a lawsuit no matter how sleazy, as long as it promised to be juicy. A real visionary, Doctor Don Evaristo Quirós: in fifteen, twenty years at the most, the dunes would pay off. And who better than Alejo, his nephew, putative son, and future heir to his law practice. Alejo, his right-hand man, skillfully trained in all bureaucratic shady deals. Alejo: shiny new law degree, which evil tongues said was purchased by his uncle, framed in gilded wood and placed beneath his Uncle Evaristo's diploma.

It's like Dante wrote here: *The Villa is a labyrinth that not even the pioneers control*, Remigio reads this morning. There's no denying that our reporter is a cultured man. Every so often he cranks out one of these articles. I don't know if it's to educate the simple people or to show off that he's been to school and is a great reader. Avid reader, as he likes to say. You may have heard him: I'm an avid reader, Dante always says.

The other drivers, nodding off or drinking a watered-down *mate*, don't pay too much attention to Remigio's reading.

Dante had written: Despite having lived here for decades, many residents of our Villa still get lost. The winding streets of sand, which follow the zigzagging foot of the dune, form a genuine labyrinth where streets cut each other off, come together, twist and turn. And whoever gets lost might well fear an encounter with the mythical and terrifying Minotaur.

Remigio repeats that: Minotaur. And then: Anybody who's heard of the Minotaur, raise your hand. Not one of the drivers responds. Remigio lets them stare at him, intrigued. It was a monster from Crete, he explains, the capital of Ancient Greece. Very avant-garde, those ancient Greeks. More advanced than us. They already had gay marriage. But let me tell you, they were no ordinary faggots. Homosexuals, but serious homosexuals, not fairies like the ones today. And philosophers, too. Warriors, that's what they were. Once in a while they boned the women. Mostly just to preserve the species, keep them happy for a while so they could occupy themselves with the kiddies while the men discussed important matters. There, in the labyrinth, lived the monster, half man, half fierce bull. The lower part, up to the waist, was a man, and the upper part a bull. But the human part had something of the bull: that Minotaur had a pretty good-sized sausage on him. Anyone who committed a crime—no kidding—they stuck him in the labyrinth. As soon as the condemned man began to lose his way in the labyrinth, the meat-locker smell would nauseate him. From outside, the cries of the crowd, screaming, applauding. The shouting was a sign to the monster that they'd tossed in his food. And he acknowledged it with a roar that made your blood run cold. And so the Greeks, once the Minotaur had responded to them, called for silence. And they waited and waited and waited. As soon as you entered the labyrinth, the shouting outside began. Then the roar. The monster could've been on the other side of the wall, in the passageway on one side, in a corner, lying in wait. You had to walk with lead feet. And that stench of entrails, of blood. The only thing you could hear was the buzzing of the flies. As you walked, you jumped over human remains. The condemned man would be saved if he found the exit from the labyrinth. But hardly anyone ever escaped. Because when you turned down a passageway, there was the Minotaur. It was the Minotaur's habit to fuck the condemned man's ass wide open and then gobble him up.

After a thoughtful silence, Remigio pronounces:

That's what should be done to the people who raped the kindergarteners. Throw them to the Minotaur.

Maybe it's a good story to tell some other time, if anybody cares, says Dante. It seems that Don Evaristo and Doña Pola, his wife, had no children. Don Evaristo blamed Doña Pola, who had turned out to be as dry as an old raisin. And she, in turn, replied that if they didn't have a baby it was because of that bullet that had split open one of his testicles when he was working in Ayacucho. Don Evaristo never explained to her where that shot had come from. It wasn't necessary, considering that he had amassed a fortune by rescuing crooks from their involvement in shady politics. Don't clarify, Eva. You make things more obscure, said Doña Pola. I told you not to call me Eva, Don Evaristo bristled.

But then there was that nephew of his. His brother Justo had baptized him with the same name: Alejo's middle name was Evaristo. The fact that Justo had honored his brother by giving the boy his name marked his destiny. The nephew would compensate for Evaristo's lack of a little calf of his own.

Rumor had it that Alejo's parents had burned to death trying to put out the fire at the ranch in General Guido. But it wasn't true, like so many stories that don't tell how things really were. It came out that the fire had been no accident. Alejo told Dante the truth, the whole truth late one night after dinner at the German Club. It was closing time. But no one was about to kick out Dr. Alejo Quirós and his scribe, Dante.

The way it went down was that Justo, his father, had found Leonor, his mother, on all fours beneath a laborer. He walked into the room, pistol in hand; didn't say a word. Neither did the lovers. It wasn't yet time to wake up the kids. The laborer silently allowed himself to be tied up. He knew it: for him there would be no mercy. Then Justo shoved him under the bed. Leonor was emotionless, not resisting what was about to come. Justo ordered his wife to wake the kids, dress them, and pack their bags. Alejo and Alba would go to Madariaga, where Uncle Evaristo lived. Composed, the mother stifled her distress while the father prepared the carriage. After the mother had given them a kiss, the father sent them off into the darkness of night. He forced the woman back into the house. He tied her to the bars of their marriage bed. And next to her, also bound, he laid the laborer. He was gone a long time. He took his time irrigating the foundations of the house with gasoline and kerosene. He went back inside and walked to the bedroom. He poured fuel on the lovers. He sat down to watch them as he took a swig of gin from the mouth of the *porrón*. The fire enveloped them. The bodies in the bed, shrieking, scorching, writhing. The roar of the flames and the screams. Justo watched them calmly as the crossbeams began to collapse. By the time the fire had consumed the roof, exposing the open sky, it would be nearly daybreak. And the children would be far away. That's what he must have been thinking when a burning beam fell on top of him.

Alejo once told this story to Dante. How at dawn, when they turned back to look, they saw the glow of the fire. How Alba wanted to go home. But he, Alejo, seemingly aware of what that fire meant, tugged on the horse's reins. They had to obey their father, he told his sister.

Without irony, Alejo said to Dante:

There's some truth to it when they call me a son-of-a-bitch.

Since the Villa pins its mission on the forestation of what had been once only sand and wind, many people take credit for participating in that imaginary pioneering effort, because here even someone who arrived just last month feels like a pioneer, worrying, like everybody else, about protecting nature, preserving a harmonious life and a deep relationship between human beings and the landscape. That's how some folks talk. To recap: It was decreed that anyone who cuts down one tree during construction must plant two. Four or five businesses devoted to macrobiotics and homeopathy have prospered in the last few years. The hippie legacy of the seventies has now combined with New Age tendencies and Eastern thought, alternative medicine and yoga. Meditation and martial arts alternate with floral and musical therapy. One curative technique that's both mental and physical is listening to oneself through the reverberations of bowls. To a greater or lesser extent, we are all supporters of a healthy, quality lifestyle. That's why we oppose the construction of the Twin Towers. If the thundering din of Dobroslav's—our Speer's—machinery deafens us, imagine the terrible effect it will have on the birds in the forest, forcing them to migrate. Most of us, I'd say some eighty percent of the Villa, came here to get away from concrete. And now those two huge skyscrapers are an assault on our quality of life. Because if there was one reason for our migration to the Villa, it was to find a better quality of life. Sure, what happened to the *los abusaditos* at Nuestra Señora also compromises the quality of life by generating negative energy. But that mess, like everything else in this Villa, will be forgotten. The Twin Towers, on the other hand, are turning out to be a more serious abuse because they're forever. God knows how many birds will lose their homes because of concrete.

We still have to tell this story, and it's important that we do: Alejo, the boy, made two important friends in the Villa: Julián Mendicutti, the son of Don Néstor the hardware dealer, now an official who supervises the shenanigans at City Hall; and Braulio Ramos from the real estate office, who, with information supplied by Julián, can tell you which house or lot you can arrange to take over for a few pesos. The entire Villa, from one end to the other, belongs to the Kennedys, as some people call the three of them, a nickname, we should emphasize, that makes them proud. We're more like brothers than if we really were, Braulio, the weak one, likes to say.

It's interesting to see how identities are formed in a family. Don Evaristo soon recognized his nephew's aptitudes. Alejo had turned out to be a crouching little *criollo*, lying in wait, who wouldn't leap out till he found the best opportunity. Silent, slippery. It was hard for Don Evaristo to fault him for anything. That boy ought to have been his son. Then, Don Evaristo says to himself, the dynasty would be well-served. And he set Alejo up to train in legalistic tricks and to succeed him. He took the boy everywhere. He was his shadow.

The Villa's business community is shocked by the heavy fines imposed by the Provincial Ministry of Labor following safety and health inspections.

In a meeting between representatives of our Chamber of Commerce and Industry and Ministry officials, it was alleged that the amount of the fines was an attack on the Villa and its expansion. After a heated discussion between the parties, it was agreed to establish an interim period in which the businesses involved would commit to improving health and safety conditions within 48 hours.

In their own way, our local Kennedys have blood ties. As kids, romping in the dunes, they swore a blood oath. They cut themselves with a little knife, a gift from Don Evaristo to Alejo. The legend the three kids wanted to establish claims that on a November noon, atop one of the dunes, on the burning sand, Alejo took out the knife and cut the palm of his right hand. Then he passed it to Braulio. And Braulio grabbed it. Clenching his teeth, he cut himself. With his bloody hand, he shook Alejo's. Julián, not to be left behind, slashed his own palm. And so the three of them comingled their blood. Then they looked toward the Villa, the red roofs of the chalets peeking out between the green groves. Suddenly, Julián recalls, it grew dark and night descended in the middle of the day. The sky began to crackle. Thunder, too.

They didn't have to say so, but Braulio, the most timid, who always needed to emphasize things to boost his own self-confidence, did: Three against all. No one will stop us.

The need to add two additional lanes to Route 11 between the Villa and Mar del Plata is urgent. And it doesn't tally with the sixteen-year period established by the contract awarded by the Provincial government. If the number of cars in our Villa continues to grow and tourist affluence keeps increasing every season, transit along this route will become intolerable. Driving the road under these conditions, with all the bumps and potholes, represents a danger for travelers. This section, we must emphasize, has become a death trap. In addition to these dangers, its condition signals a

vital need: that our Villa must not remain isolated from the great neigh-
boring metropolis, the Pearl of the Atlantic.

Like I was telling you, Quirós, Mendicutti, and Ramos feel like the Kennedys. Imagine—there was no way Don Evaristo, Dr. Evaristo Quirós, could've passed up the opportunity that the German's sons had served him on a silver platter by hiring him to file a lawsuit against their father, who at that point was over eighty. The suit, based on the grounds of senile dementia, couldn't fail. And Don Evaristo went right ahead and drew up the suit against the German. And who helped him with the legal mumbo-jumbo, eh? His little chick, Alejo, who was already a young rooster. He might not have graduated from law school in La Plata with the best grades, but he was sharp in carrying out orders.

An impressive starting line of four-wheel beach bikes. For three days the Endurance Festival brought together nearly one hundred thousand people to witness the greatest motorcycle race in Latin America. The tournament, with more than five hundred entrants, set the Southern dunes vibrat-ing. Dicky Garramuño, our beloved local treasure, owner of Garra Cross, emerged champion with his excellent performance in one of the first races. His triumph is even greater considering the participation of important international figures.

This morning Don Evaristo, an in-patient at the Clínica del Mar, is dying, hooked up to a tangle of tubes, waiting to descend at any moment to his well-deserved hell.

From outside came sobs, snot, and prayers. The Kennedys were stationed in the room at the Clínica del Mar. At the foot of the bed, giving moral support to Alejo. I can't stand seeing him like this, said Julián. God is unfair, sniveled Braulio, the same softie as ever. This doesn't happen in developed countries, Julián declared. Euthanasia and on to the next thing. So much suffering, and what for. This guy's not your protector anymore, Alejo, said Braulio. And you, you fucking piece of shit, don't act like my *compadre*, Alejo thought but didn't say so. If the old man regained consciousness and strength, he'd whip the bejeezus out of them, he thought.

A chip off the old block, like I was saying about Alejo. He didn't need more than a few seconds. Alejo grabbed the pillow from underneath his head, put it over Don Evaristo's face, and pressed. He didn't have to apply much weight. Easier than he thought.

He replaced the pillow beneath his head. He arranged it gently. He leaned over the dead man. He kissed him on the forehead.

Forgive me, *Tatita*, he said. And that was the first time he'd ever called his uncle *Tatita*.

And he crossed himself.

Did you hear what happened at Nuestra Señora?, someone gossiped to José María, the guy from the car dealership. The parents beat the shit out of Father Fragassi. They're saying your wife is involved in that business of *los abusaditos*, too. They're gonna pulverize the degenerates, they say. The degenerates being, in addition to Noelia, his wife; Roxana, her best friend; and two fag buddies of theirs, Ramiro and Gabriel. José María's reaction was more instinct than paranoia. He didn't wait for the parent posse to break down the door to his house. He packed Noelia and the kids into the car and they got the hell out of the Villa without saying where they were going. But first they stopped at Roxana's place, so she could go with them. At least until the storm passed. But Roxana refused: she had nothing to feel guilty about, she said; she had no reason to flee. She'd stop those fancy-ass motherfuckers in their tracks with her head held high: who'd they think they were, anyway, the owners of the Villa, the owners of justice? When the 4x4s passed by the auto dealership, José María was gone. And since they didn't find anyone at home when they smashed in the front door of their house in Pinar del Norte, frustration led them to burn it down. After the fire, the hunting party made its way to Roxana's—the other kindergarten teacher's—place. They blocked the entrance with the 4x4s head on. They kicked at the door. Don Lucho sent his daughter to hide at the back of the house. Like I said, Don Lucho and La Chacha, people from around here, life-long residents, self-sacrificing, working people. Good people, decent. Don Lucho, even at age eighty-something, stood up to those guys. More than one was high, and those who weren't had a few whiskeys in them. With one good smack they knocked the poor old guy down. They stepped over him. They decided to tie up La Chacha. The girl, Roxana, managed to hide in a little shed in back. When she heard the old folks screaming, she leaped over the wall into a neighbor's yard. She hid out a few blocks down the street, at Malvina the dress-maker's house. From there she called Ramiro and Gabriel. The two of them already knew about the hunting party. Ramiro refused to run away. Gabriel couldn't convince him to get on the motorcycle. They argued. It was growing dark. And Ramiro wouldn't go. We're innocent, he said. According to them, we're guilty, Gabriel replied. Guilty of what, argued Ramiro. Guilty of our love, he said. You're an idiot, Gabriel told him. Finally he revved the motor. Good luck, babe. And he took off on his bike, looking for a side road that ran parallel to Route 11 toward Mar del Plata. A few minutes later Ramiro saw the headlights of the 4x4s advancing along the sand-covered street. He snatched a windbreaker and jumped out a back window. Running through vacant lots without stopping, without even turning around to see the house ablaze as he disappeared into the night and the Villa became countryside.

Everything I am I owe to Uncle Evaristo, Alejo said in the doorway of the Neri Funeral Home. A mentor. He taught me life.

At this time of night visitors are sparser. From the social climbers to the poor devils, from the blowhards of Pinar del Norte to the *comadres* of La Virgencita, no one would think of missing it: Don

Evaristo's wake is a social event. Alejo asks Dante to walk him out to the street for a smoke. He owes it all to the old man.

He didn't just teach me that one hand washes the other, he says. People accused him of being in cahoots with the cops and getting people out of jail. Tell me, if he hadn't taken pity on those poor jerks, who else would've done it? In his eyes they were all innocent. When one guy's got too much and others have nothing, he used to tell me, justice for the poor has to step in. And it *is* justice, like the Bible says, to rob another crook, a hundred years of forgiveness. They say the same thing about me, that I protect hoodlums. Tell me, where's the injustice if a kid who lives in a tin and cardboard shack breaks into chalets and robs them. As long as he doesn't whack a baby or rape a pregnant chick, I've got no objection. Let's say they beat up the owner. No big deal, either. You should see how grateful those poor kids are. On Judgment Day they'll be the forgiven ones. But before Judgment Day there'll come a day when they all rise up from their hellholes and head this way and they'll knock everything to the ground. And *then* there'll be justice. Damn right. Why're you looking at me like that? You think it's funny that someone like me, with the reputation I've got in the Villa, can think this way. Believe it or not, I'm more of a leftist than my late sister.

Around blue midnight, the cold wind from the sea brings raindrops like Thelonius's keys.

My sister. What can I tell you, Dante. Alba did her name proud. She had a special light. Among her many virtues, the greatest was this: she made you feel less shitty in this world. A transfusion of hope. From the start she understood that our aunt and uncle had adopted us for the sake of convenience. Uncle Evaristo, *tatita*, because he needed someone to leave his law practice to. Proud, I made him proud. The only way he could maintain the respect he'd earned in the Villa, a respect held up by thumbtacks, was by leaving it to someone with the same last name, and particularly, because this was the trait he most appreciated in me, such a person had to be as crafty as he was. Because while I may not be intelligent, I'm no dummy, either. Crafty, yes. I'm crafty. Shrewdness, more than intelligence, that's me. Instinct. Quick reflexes.

Alba, on the other hand, was intelligent. She liked to say that love was a sign of intelligence. I argued with her about this. When someone does a good deed, he does it for expedience. Because he expects that love to be paid back with interest. There's nothing greedier than generosity, I'd tell her. Sometimes I thought Alba loved me because it made her feel guilty to look down on me. I had the impression that loving me took a lot of effort for her. But I was wrong. That's just the way she was.

To get back to the subject. If Uncle Evaristo needed a successor, Aunt Pola dreamed of a little girl. She was very religious, my Aunt Pola. Till the end of her life she never stopped going to church. As if with that faith of hers, which was so much like fear, she could keep God from seeing her as complicit in her husband's sins. Even though she would drag Alba to church, my sister was more of a bookworm. From *Little Women* to *Das Kapital*, she read everything that fell into her hands. And whatever didn't fall into her hands, she searched for. She found *Das Kapital* at Trudy's, a friend whose parents were Germans. Can you believe it, Dante—she studied German in order to understand that book. A crucial book, as we would discover. Because Alba, kind as she was, had everything it took to become a nun. And yet she turned to the other side. She went to Buenos Aires, studied sociology. She became a guerrilla. Which turns out to be the same thing. A nun and a guerrilla have a lot in common.

There are days and nights when I can't do anything but think of her, as if by thinking of her I could bring her back. It's just that Alba, even though she's no longer with us, is still my conscience.

The sun comes up later this time of year. If it's a foggy dawn, it'll surely be a bright day. These days it's pleasant to come to the dunes and watch the sun rise over the sea. The horizon turns red, and it looks as if the sky is bleeding. Slowly, it grows pinkish. The clouds are long, dark stains. You see the sunrise and you feel like everything that happened last night has been left behind. For a moment, just as long as dawn lasts, you're neither a victim nor a victimizer. It gives you the feeling that the pain has moved on to someone else. Outlines begin to take shape. And in the same way, your feelings and thoughts now turn to reconciliation and peace. You realize that this state is more or less an illusion, that in a while you'll turn your back to the sea and return, and then—but it's best not to think about then. A few seagulls fly over the breakers.

Another news item this week was Dr. Alejandro Quirós's presentation in defense of Father Martín Fragassi, the accused school principal. Let us recall that when this case erupted in our community, Father Fragassi was brutally beaten by the students' parents, resulting in his admission to the Villa Hospital in serious condition. Following this incident, the Church dispatched Father Joaquín Azcárate to our community, a young, charismatic priest who quickly earned local favor.

In the russet late afternoon, Don Carneiro stands at the entrance to Neri Funeral Home. He makes note of each and every man and woman present for the funeral of Doctor Evaristo Quirós, prominent leader of our Villa, as his obituary in *El Vocero* defines him. They've known one another since the 40s. Don Evaristo, then a lawyer in the Madariaga district, freed Don Carneiro, a police corporal, from a jail cell where he awaited sentencing for a violent crime. Dr. Quirós was also the legal representative of the ranchers back when the conservatives were the government.

In his influential days, Don Evaristo always carried his riding crop in hand. Many were the times he used it on someone's face. All the Villa's deed titles passed through Dr. Quirós's law office. He was the intellectual author of more than one application of pressure, as well. Dr. Quirós took charge of the pressure. Of the paperwork. And Don Carneiro, following Don Evaristo's orders, was responsible for keeping the poor wretches in line.

Now Don Evaristo has kicked the bucket at about age ninety. And his funeral is being held at Neri Funeral Home. The entire Villa comes to the wake. To put it accurately, we're all in his debt. He's gotten more than one of us out of a scrape. The slickest shyster on the coast, Don Quirós. That's why so many people are lined up to view the casket and say their farewells on this frozen night. You should see the number of palms, wreaths, floral offerings, and even scraggly bunches of flowers from the poor. Who doesn't have a son who Don Quirós has helped spring from the police station. Even in Batán the old man had plenty of clout when it came to reducing somebody's sentence. No way the poor folk wouldn't come and say goodbye. At one side of the entrance to Neri Funeral Home stands Don Carneiro, who must be over seventy by now, but he stands tall. He commands respect. Although he's retired from the police force, Don Carneiro helps out when necessary at the Quirós Law Offices, now under the direction of Alejo, the putative son.

Now the sun is up. And still Don Carneiro stands there, program in hand, noting who has come to bid goodbye to the Esteemed Departed. Some say he's doing this in order to see who the grateful ones are. A reckoning that also factors in those who are absent. Those who didn't show up, too bad for them. The no-shows, as is well known, will go on a blacklist: those who hate Quirós. And, in fact, many have good reason to. Better hurry up and let Don Carneiro see you and mark down your name before the caravan of cars, station wagons, jeeps, pickups, and minivans takes off for the cemetery. The fire truck leads the way.

Look at Alejo. The spitting image of the deceased, as if he were his own offspring. His uncle's double. He doesn't shed a tear. You'll never know what he's thinking, what he's feeling. But he's got us all figured out, that's for sure. Rumor has it he put the old man of his misery. Could be.

You're not gonna walk to the cemetery. C'mon, I've got room in my pickup. Going to the burial gives you points.

After Holy Week, the last long holiday, summer's final death throes, the last frantic attempt to make ends meet by those who weren't saved along with the tourist season, it always rains. And in May, when the sun rises around 6:30, if it's not pouring, it's drizzling. An occasional sunny day, but mostly the threat of a storm, a southeaster, and lots of water. That gray, dense sky is the harbinger of what's to come. Cold, drizzle, saltpeter. After the last wave of tourists, the restaurants, bars, and shops shut down. The Villa turns into a ghost town. Many of the locals, who depend on the summer season to live, take their vacations in May, true, but it's not only their exodus that makes the Villa seem like it was devastated by a plague. It's when the long *garúa* and the fog set in, and now you notice the saltpeter corrosion in the door and window hinges, the humidity that stains the buildings, both inside and out. Saltpeter corrosion also dulls the soul. Lives fold in on themselves. You walk along the main drag at seven in the evening and it's already dark; no one except little cliques of girls and boys gathered in the doorways of video arcades. On Fridays and Saturdays, in their cars with doors wide open, music blaring, they smoke and drink. Others, dying of cold, light bonfires on the dunes. In the morning the remaining coals and empty bottles will be left on the sand. Autumn has turned into winter, and the vacuum creeps in. Corrosion. Saltpeter. Here, nothingness tastes like salt. Bodies and hearts grow dull, too. On nights like this, when you walk around here, the corrosion overcomes you, penetrates your bones, and all you want is to go back to your little cave, a glass of gin, the TV. You don't have anything to talk about with your wife anymore, assuming you have one, and you'd better have one when winter sets in. The local FM station plays Janis Joplin in these early hours of the morning. It's not the cheeriest stuff in the world, but at least it cleans the saltpeter off you. Then you too, like Janis, ask God to buy you a Mercedes Benz.

Nuestra Señora del Mar was still closed that morning. But the fifth-graders cut the wire fence, filtered in through the playing field, and headed for the kiosk. They looted it. Didn't leave a piece of candy. Then they set it on fire. A neighbor called the firefighters. They arrived before the blaze could spread to the classrooms.

Poor guy, one of them said as he packed up the hose. If he's innocent, who'll pay him back?

And what about the damage to his reputation, asked another.

Reputations can be recovered, remarked Commissioner Frugone, who knows about such things. Cash can't.

Meanwhile the parents from the co-op, armed and in their 4x4s, continued the search for the suspects, Ramiro and Gabriel, a search that extended till this Friday morning. Now people were saying that the kindergarten teachers, Noelia and Roxana, had filmed every-thing they did to the kids. The mothers also split up into groups and went off in their 4x4s looking for the teachers. But it seemed as though the teachers, having heard the rumors, had been swallowed up by the earth.

The 4x4s still patrol the town. They come and go along the pop-lar groves, disappear along the boulevard and return to the center of town.

Dante, sitting at the computer, saw him walk down the middle of the passageway between the dark, dusty booths that open only dur-ing tourist season to offer stolen jeans, crafts, cheap sweaters, cos-tume jewelry, prints, and tattoos. Alejo ambled along, the lapels of his black overcoat turned up. In that overcoat he looked like he was coming from a wedding or a funeral. He was coming to ream

45

Dante out, for sure. If Quirós was the money behind *El Vocero*, it was inevitable that now, with the scandal of *los abusaditos*, he would drop by the newsroom—this place infused with humidity and tobacco, warmed by an infrared heater. For sure he was coming to ream him out. Regarding the scandal, Dante had gone too far in his last editorial: No one is innocent, he had written. But no. Alejo wasn't there to launch into one of his lectures.

Tell me, do you believe what some people are saying, Alejo blurted out as he took a seat. What which people are saying about what, Dante retorted. I'm talking about euthanasia, Alejo said. And he lit a cigarette. What do you think? I'm for it, said Dante.

Don't play dumb, Alejo went on. I'm talking about what people are saying, that I killed the old man. While my brothers were moaning and groaning about how long it was taking him to die, they say I was the one who cut him loose. Alejo stared at Dante. You heard the rumor. You can't deny it. There's not one drop of shit that doesn't splash the walls of my law firm, and that's even truer of this rag here. I just want to know. What's your opinion.

I express my opinion through my editorials, Dante said. And these days, if you'll pardon my bluntness, there's a more important subject than euthanasia: child abuse.

Alejo kept staring at him.

Finally Dante took a breath and asked: You killed the old man?

I'm the one who leads the family, manages its affairs, and the one who says which way this town should go. Not just because I'm the oldest in the family. I am who I am because I look death in the eye. It's a question of balls. Sometimes they're heavy. Today they're dragging me down. Some days more than others, Alejo said.

And he asked: Where's your ashtray.

I'm trying to quit, Dante said. Use the cup.

Alejo ground it out right on the floor:

I ought to quit too, he said. And he stood up: That piece you wrote was good, Dante. A kick in the ass for the holier-than-thou.

Your editorial, I mean. A dose of morality isn't such a bad thing every once in a while, dammit. Every so often you make me feel like I'm not sorry I set you up working at this rag. But don't go overboard. I'll let you know when to put on the brakes. This mess could fuck up the season for us pretty good. Keep it up for now. I'll let you know when you need to lay off the sermons.

That's what you came to tell me.

No, I was just passing by.

Alejo winked as he turned to go:

Chau, Pulitzer. See you.

Dante didn't reply.

He watched him walk away down the middle of the passageway, just as he'd come, slowly, the lapels of his black overcoat raised. He was in no hurry.

The alleged parricide, Dante thought.

Just now when Adriana is involved with the project of setting up her Pilates studio, the business at Nuestra Señora has to happen. If the uproar is driving her crazy it's not so much because of the seriousness of what took place; it's that, with school closed, she can't put up with Felicitas and Luz at home anymore. Mama, Mommy, look at Feli, Luz shouts from the playroom. Adriana has to interrupt her meeting with the architect, Durand, who's proposing a fantastic corner for the place: where Alameda 306 meets Avenida del Mar. She's anxious to see the plans, but with classes suspended she has to deal with the girls—a real pain—and Felicitas and Luz aren't exactly two little angels she can bring to the architect's studio. Impulsive, loud, hyper: that's what they're like. And they end up driving her crazy. With classes on hold, when they're not in front of the TV all day long, they invite their little friends, who are just as manic as they are. Adriana pops in earplugs so she won't hear the shouts, shrieks, squeals, coming from the playroom. Luz got hurt, Mommy, shouts Felicitas. As she tugs on the girl's arm, Adriana notices a bloodstain on her dress. That's all I needed this afternoon, to go running to Clínica del Mar. Luz, stunned, that gash on her head, the blood, is slow to react. Adriana can't wait till the day she has the Pilates place set up once and for all and can recover her muscle control, relaxation. She takes a deep breath. She fell from the top of the armoire, Ma. You two are the bane of my existence, says Adriana, fetching ice cubes, dumping them into a plastic supermarket bag, applying them to Luz's head, running to the medicine cabinet, looking for alcohol, bandages. Ohmmm.

God punishes. He always punishes. Sometimes it takes Him a while; sometimes He does it in a way that takes us a while to understand. But sooner or later divine justice catches up with us. And no sin or sinner can escape His penetrating gaze. Don Evaristo Quirós, the old shyster, instigator of the shady deals that laid the foundation of this Villa, creator of a corrupt dynasty, was punished by the Lord in the form of Alba, his subversive stepdaughter, who robbed banks, kidnapped rich people, attacked army barracks, and killed members of the military. God punished her, too. When the bloodthirsty she-wolf found herself surrounded by the military, she had to wrap her cub in blankets and hide him in a piece of furniture to keep him from being riddled with bullets. And the Quirós family couldn't understand why that kid screamed. We don't let him lack for anything, Doña Pola said. Crazy like his mother, pronounced Don Evaristo. We'll just have to send him to boarding school. But they didn't. Alejo forbade it: The only thing the boy needs is a change of direction. And I'm going to get the best out of him. He took him home to live with him and Jackie. Before becoming a father to his own children, he was a father to his sister's son. And, truth be told, you'd never know he wasn't the father, so great was the resemblance between those two. The nephew was a juvenile version of the uncle. If in fact he *was* the uncle, as many people in the Villa wondered.

Braulio and Julián laughed at those screams Camilo produced.

But Alejo didn't find them funny at all. And once he nearly boxed their ears.

Alejo brought him up in his image and likeness. Pretend you had a son, he told Jackie. He'll turn out all right with us, Alejo promised. What this boy needs is love.

It would be unfair to say Jackie didn't try: loving that boy who grew up silent and mute till the craziness struck him and he let out that scream that could be heard throughout the Villa.

Be patient, Alejo said to her. Soon we'll have our own.

And so you find out. In the end you find out. And in the end everyone finds out. Even if you don't want to. I'll give you an example: you have a neighbor that you never said hello to in all your life, and without wanting to, you find out: something he's hiding, because we're all hiding something, a humiliation, a vice, a sorrow, and that something comes to light when you least expect it, and the one you least expected to find out will find out, and after a while the whole town knows, because there are no secrets to be kept here. Of course, some people think that marriage can be a hiding place, but no, not that, either. Not even by being alone till the last of your nights on earth will you be able to conceal something you don't want to make known. It's found out. Always. Everything is revealed. Because you'll overhear a conversation at the supermarket, or a limo driver will tell you. You mustn't trust limo drivers, those guys who are up on all the details concerning each and every soul in this place, which now, in winter, seems to be buried in the fog that comes from the sea, that fog that seems to absorb all secrets. Maybe you find out when you go to the bank or to City Hall to pay a fee. Pay attention; be careful. Never let your guard down, not even when you're walking in the woods, wandering among the poplars with only the sound of your own footsteps in the sand and without a soul in sight as you look around you, blinds closed in the chalets and cabins, and that intimidating silence. Don't let your guard down, not even if the weeds have grown tall around a house, blocking access; despite its abandoned appearance, don't let your guard down. People are always watching you here. That venetian blind just crept up a few inches, that curtain moved, someone is spying from behind that privet hedge. You're being watched. Always. And just as they observe you without your noticing, soon you're going to start observing us. But don't tell anyone I said so. No one at all.

We found out from Beto, the guy from La Vaca Gorda butcher shop, the one across from the police station, that the first formal complaint of child sexual abuse was filed at that station by Fito Dobroslav the albino, our Speer's heir. His little girl, Mechi, was the first victim of abuse. Ten others followed. That is, if there weren't more than ten: eventually people said nineteen. Because after that . . . we all know what happened. A string of formal complaints. Among those who beat Father Fragassi most savagely were the Dobroslavs, our Speer and his heir. Our Speer was the one responsible for the plan to mess up the priest, the principal of Nuestra Señora del Mar. He should be castrated, they say Fito roared as he tried to flip open a Victorinox while our Speer kicked the fallen man. The Bible-Thumper had a God in reserve, Dante remarked. It was a pure miracle he saved his hide, thanks to some folks who reacted at the last moment, when Father Fragassi was already unconscious, and decided that enough was enough. It was tough to drag Fito out of the school. His fists were skinned. And his father congratulated him with pats on the back. For once his son, the servile kid that obeyed his orders with a *heil*, had shown a hidden backbone.

Around that time Commissioner Frugone remarked to Dante that only one formal complaint had been verified, a little girl with vaginal irritation and depression. The child, we discovered, was Mechi Dobroslav. Later on, after a few months had gone by and the scandal of *los abusaditos* was becoming old news while the Paradise Towers, our Speer's dream project in the middle of the forest, were going up,

Beto told us that Fito had retracted the accusation. The rumor began to circulate that our Speer had abused his own granddaughter. Let's keep this just between us. There's been no proof, as far as anyone knows. As always around here, the rumor had more repercussions than did the lack of proof. Where there's smoke, somebody said. And Dante recalled that all happy families are alike, and the unhappy ones, too, in their own way. But in spite of what happened with Mechi, the Dobroslavs didn't appear unhappy and were getting ready for the dedication of the towers. Which would be blessed by the new parish priest, Father Joaquín Azcárate, in a ceremony attended by our power brokers. Following the blessing, Cachito, the mayor, will say a few words in praise of the progress that a work of this magnitude represents for the Villa.

Seen on a map, the Villa is an amoeba of irregular squares extending along the coast. If you arrive in May you'll find a peaceful town, a deserted vacation destination, swept by wind, dullness, and cold. In the morning, walking along the hillocks of the coastal sand road, seeing the closed-down rows of tents, the walled-up beachfront bars, the tall apartment buildings overlooking the sea with blinds lowered, faded billboards creaking and twisted by southeasters: it all reminds you of a ghost town; it's intimidating. The Villa is buried in solitude. And its scant activities are reduced to a few blocks on the main drag, two or three bank branches, a currency exchange booth, a sweets shop, City Hall, and the few bars where merchants discuss business, grousing, as usual, about the last season.

There are grocery stores and a few shops open for business where hardly anyone buys anything, since in the off-season no one has a peso to spare.

And even less if you go to bingo.

While the secondary school kids at Nuestra Señora were entering the school through the sports field and wrecking Ramiro the fag's

51

kiosk, while the police were searching for him, trying to get one step ahead of the posse that patrolled the Villa from one end to the other, Ramiro was hiding in a shack near Macedo. He didn't even peek out at the countryside. Fatigue, hunger, and thirst had cornered him among a rusty plow, a rusty scythe, and a couple of shovels. He wrapped himself in some burlap bags and lay down. But he could hardly sleep a wink. The night sounds frightened him. On the fourth night he heard movement and curled up against the wall. A dark, bulky shape advanced toward him, snorting. It took him a while to figure out it was a cow. He wouldn't last long there, dying of hunger and thirst. Without a doubt—he was going crazy.

One night he heard the sound of the engines. Engines coming closer and closer. Headlights lit up the shack. He grabbed a shovel, ready to face whatever might be out there. The headlights, a couple of flashlights, blinded him. He was able to make out the figure of Police Commissioner Frugone. It wasn't the posse. It was the police. And they were aiming at him. I'm innocent, Ramiro cried. In the line of fire, he dropped the shovel. Stumbling, he allowed himself to be handcuffed. Frugone shoved him toward a police car, pushed his head down, heaved him in. Don't waste your breath now—you'll need it later.

At the police station the commissioner took him to the cells. There was a large one, full. Men, kids. One of the Reyes brothers, the oldest, was there. A beast. Also two of the Vicuñas. Not to mention the juvie thugs, in addition to a Chilean laborer who had battered his wife. Two half-breeds waiting for their rap sheets to be checked. Gems, all of them. About twenty, Frugone estimated. He knew what was in store for Ramiro if he put him in with those guys. The fate that awaited him. The fate of a short-eyes.

He ordered a cell to be emptied and locked Ramiro up in there alone. He felt sorry for him. With that dyed hair and the little earring, he reminded him of his own son.

Thirteen- and fourteen-year-old pregnant girls, grandparents responsible for raising their grandchildren, Hilda tells Dante. Hilda is a surgical assistant at the hospital. And she wants Dante to write on this subject. Listening to Hilda's litany, Dante exhibits the patience of a Buddha.

You should see the number of D&C's and childbirths we get every day, every night, in the hospital. Not to mention the kids who come in with knife or gunshot wounds. At school, the middle-class teenagers mix with the kids from the lower classes or the classless ones. Same thing at the hospital. In the ICU you might have a kid from Pinar del Norte in one bed and right next to him a Bolivian from the Mar Azul shantytown. For both it's a point of pride to be the wild kid. And I won't even tell you what happens if the middle-class kid steals a girl away from the tough little thug from El Monte or La Virgencita. On and on it goes, all winter long. And then, when tourist season arrives, all the girls and guys dream of picking up a girl or guy from the capital and getting the hell out of town.

Hilda falls silent. Then:

Promise me you'll write about it, Dante.

Dante looks at her, doesn't say a word.

Neither of us made the money we expected during the season. Not Paula with her incense, not me with the ceramics. Nothing happened during Holy Week, either, the final long holiday, our last chance, the last drag of weed. Now eternal months loom before us. Not a tourist till December. No matter that we're vegetarians—it still won't be easy for us. Those who managed to earn a few pesos go on vacation. Those of us who got screwed stay here alone, with nothing. We'd better resign ourselves to ecological consolation. You've gotta put some heart into it, Mike, Paula tells me. After all, we're vegetarians and members of the Humanist Party. We've got the beach to ourselves, the still-warm sun peeking out from behind cottony

clouds, the yellow leaves of autumn, the birds, the silence of the poplar groves, a silence that's both the Villa and ourselves. The silence
is a solid mass. You bump into it when you walk. Weeks can go by
without us exchanging a word. Last year, when they cut off our electricity, we spent a hundred twenty-three days not talking to each
other. I remember because I counted them. One hundred twenty-
three days of silence. Two thousand nine hundred fifty-two hours.
One hundred seventy-seven thousand, one hundred twenty seconds
of silence. Which could bring you wisdom if you meditated. On the
other hand, true enough, you might commit suicide. You don't screw
around with silence.

The dead girl, says Dante. You're talking about your sister.
    You're no dummy, huh, Alejo replies. You're pretty sharp.
    The rain falls harder and harder. Even though *El Vocero*, our
newspaper, has the same writer for its editorial, arts, economy sections, society pages, horoscope, and as if that weren't enough, the
obituaries, joyous events, and advertisements all come from a single
pen—Dante's—he took it as a joke: I contain multitudes, he said.
    El Vocero's office is located at the back of Galería Soles, Barbeito
el Gallego's mini-mall. It occupies the last space, a 9-by-12 foot
area that barely holds a desk, a computer screen, a hard drive, and a
printer, all made in China, and to this cubicle that reeks of tobacco,
humidity, and stale coffee, the rain now brings cold air, the smell of
damp earth. The storm seems to offer some relief, but not for Alejo,
who, sitting across from Dante, slowly begins to tell the story:
    My sister, yes. We rode at night, many a time. Galloping at first,
then racing, and we dismounted at the beach. We rode by the light
of the moon and the stars. First toward the southern dunes. Then
toward the wash. Uncle Evaristo smelled something fishy: What can
the two of you be doing, he would ask us, sarcastically. If I ever catch
you, he'd threaten. It infuriated him to see the horses all exhausted
in the morning. The old man knew the whole time.

I've come to get the tires on this wheelchair inflated—my grandson's. It's because of that damn bar he's in a wheelchair. For the rest of his life. He keeps going to the bar just the same. To think that in our day we were happy just lighting bonfires on the beach. We used to love coming here. We've been coming to the Villa since we were twenty. When Oscar and I were in college. Then we got married, our first kid was born, and I quit school. Oscar took a while to graduate because I got pregnant again right away. I had my little girl. Oscar brought his work home from the law office. He also worked at a notary's office. He graduated by getting credit through examination. Even when we had financial problems, we always kept coming here. In a tent, for years. Till we were able to buy some land and build. Seems like yesterday. The Villa was different then. Fun was different, too. And we were more idealistic. We were satisfied with fewer things. It was enough for us just to come to the sea, which isn't enough for kids nowadays. They want nightlife. They take pills. They get drunk. Then there are accidents. That's how it was with Maxi. A wonderful kid, our grandson. He played basketball. Until what happened, happened. Coming out of a bar. Two gangs of kids got into a fight. When the police arrived Maxi was unconscious; his head was shattered. Since then he's been in a wheelchair. He hardly speaks. You can't stay locked up indoors all day, we tell him. But there's nothing doing. There's nothing we can do during the day. At night, yes. On Saturdays he asks one of us to take him to the bar. He likes to stay in the car, watching the other kids go inside. He wants to stay there till dawn, staring at the bar and the parade of kids. When it starts to get light, he asks us to bring him home. That's it, Maxi says. And we bring him home. Every Saturday, till dawn. And then we leave. I told you, he doesn't like people to see him.

The storm won't let up. It whips the Villa. And here, in the narrow, fetid office of *El Vocero*, Alejo continues talking to himself. If this office stinks, if this newspaper office smells bad, thinks Dante, for sure it's because all the shit of our beloved community ends up here.

I always wonder, says Alejo. Why Alba and not me. Why not me, Alejo asks himself. He doesn't ask Dante. Why not me. He asks himself. And at times he doesn't appear to be talking to Dante, but rather to his sister, Alba. One of those nights my dapple tripped over a chinchilla burrow. I could have been killed in the fall, but I wasn't. Why Alba and not me. In those days, in the early seventies, I was a newly minted lawyer. A little right-winger, Alba used to rib me. Because at the university, in La Plata, I hung out with the right-wingers. And what about you?, I'd tease her. You're going to change the world, I'd say. Lay off me, sis. You'll always be a small-town rich girl. If you want to help the half-breeds, go back to your family and volunteer at Caritas. Charity work is the best thing for a rich girl like you.

I had plenty of brushes with death: that drug-related accident at the casino in Pinamar. I had gotten loaded at the casino. I was driving with a bottle of whiskey and a hooker I picked up at the roulette table. The chick was blowing me. When I saw the Costamar bus coming straight at me, I reacted as best I could. The bitch died and I got away. When I opened my eyes, I was in a hospital in Mar del Plata. Alba was at the foot of the bed. What you did was nauseating, she said to me. And that was the next-to-last time we saw one another. Because she had already gotten involved with guns.

People around here are very hospitable. Sure, in order for them to accept you completely, first you have to live here for a year, pay your dues for a year, which isn't so long. Time enough for your particular vice to emerge. Because we all have one. And you'll be no exception to the rule. Vice unites people. When yours surfaces, you'll find out who else shares it with you, and you'll be in the same boat. You'll see how fast they'll open their doors to you, and their hearts, too. And you'll fit in just like me. Look at me. You see, we're all very human here.

Months before what happened, happened, says Alejo, Alba phoned me. The low-level militants were dropping like flies. And she was just one more. We met in Chascomús. We spent a night at the Automobile Club hotel. It was the last time we were together, Alejo says.

It's still raining.

Dante doesn't ask. He lets the other man go on.

Then Vidal, the military quartermaster, sent for me. They'd finished her off. The military surrounded the block where the operatives' house was. It happened at daybreak. With helicopters and all. Alba and her *compañeros* exchanged gunfire with the military. They found the baby in a closet, wrapped in a blanket. His birth certificate was pinned to him with a safety pin. They left him at Casa Cuna. And then, and then, and then. You watched Camilo grow up, Dante. He looks like me. More and more. Draw your own conclusions. And if you feel inspired, write yourself a Greek tragedy.

It's true that Remigio knows the Villa, this labyrinth. The shortcuts, the forks in the roads, the hidden passageways, and the streets that end as soon as you turn the corner, giving you no way out. Knowing each stretch doesn't just allow him to find a place for sneaking around with a married woman like Neli, quite the filly, the wife of Police Commissioner Frugone. Mastering the Villa in each and every one of its hidden nooks and being well aware of the lines between civilization and the world of the half-breeds assures him that he can't be pigeonholed. Though you can't always trust appearances, either. Remember the swanky gang? That's what they were called: the swanky gang. Dante wrote the article: Teenagers from wealthy families in our Villa, he wrote. One night they picked up Remigio, and pointing a pistol at his head they took him past Circunvalación. Since he hadn't collected more than a few miserable pesos that night, they made him strip; they took his car, a Sienna he was still paying for, and left him there, naked. It was pure wickedness: when the police found the limo, it was on fire. Evil, just plain evil.

Remigio knows the Villa inside out. He can show you the abandoned building site, a chalet that never got built, where the kids go to buy drugs. Not weed. From coke to any kind of pills you want. And it's not just the half-breeds from El Monte or La Virgencita who go there. The kiddos from Nuestra Señora go there, too. The building has no water or electricity. They throw parties; they get hammered. One rainy afternoon, Remigio saw some naked girls, like sleepwalkers, among the pines. They didn't feel the cold. They didn't feel. And yet there they were, within reach. But Remigio puts it like this: A house is one thing; a kid is another. If you go near that house at night, you might see some candles. Many's the time I've driven girls and boys from Nuestra Señora there. They usually ask me to drop them off a block before or past it. But they don't fool me. I can see where they're heading through my rear-view mirror.

The other place where the kids score dope is behind that club, Acid, Remigio says. On Saturday night, you know, Dante. Just take the 306, the one that runs parallel to the club, and you'll see a whole herd of kids turning down that street and standing in line. Their connection is Gonza Calderón. Any kind of crap you're looking for, Gonza sells it. He works for El Capo Malerba, they say. The only thing I can tell you for sure is that if he didn't have a deal going with the cops, he wouldn't be dealing, period.

A totally unoriginal name for a bar: Moby-Dick. For folks from around here, just plain Moby. It's on the beach. A wooden structure on piles. In the daytime during the high season, it's the bar belonging to the cabana rental stand of the same name. A happening place. At night, a restaurant and pub. From April on, it's closed all day and opens secretly for just a few folks, the gamblers. Though secrecy is relative. Everyone knows all the hopeless junkies gather here, those capable of risking not only their cars, but their homes, too, on a single poker hand, leaving themselves and their families in the street. At night Moby is one of those few faint lights you can see on the beach, a yellow glow in the fog, and it's open to anybody who needs conversation, a whiskey, and if he gets lucky, a body to drag off to bed in this season of southeasters, the sea and its furious waves, the gale winds that threaten to knock down trees, rip out shutters, and blow roofs away.

By accepting the demand for discretion imposed on you by a drunk with his elbows propped up on the bar, you can find out everything. Affairs, the most common thing. Thefts. Swindles. The truth about a murder. The reason behind a suicide. Predictably, many versions of the case of *los abusaditos* have emerged from here. No two alike. The wheeling and dealing of the Kennedys, of course, the strings that never stop moving. Bet you don't know who they screwed over this time. Nature. They're involved up to their necks in razing the forest so they can build a couple of twin towers. And since Alejo is the city's legal advisor, Cachito, the mayor, is going to take his advice and sign off on the project. Fuck ecology.

Welcome to the belly of the whale. What'll you have?

At half past five in the afternoon, shortly after it opens its doors, the law office fills up. Men and women stand in the waiting room. And the line snakes out to the street, where they wait under the eaves. From probation to divorce, division of assets, bankruptcy, with things like a conflict over a partition wall. Alejo can solve anything for you, from a labor dispute to a suit for damages. Naturally, to win the suit, no matter how serious, you've got to show up ahead of the other party. Because if it turns out you're the one being sued instead of the one suing, you're done for. Rattling off his contacts, his influence, Alejo calms you down, gets you some coffee, explains how he's going to use his connections, and when you leave the office, you leave feeling that tonight you'll be able to sleep well. With all the influence he has, you think to yourself. Friends at the Madariaga courthouse, clout at the courts in Dolores, not to mention the weight of the Quirós name here in the Villa. All legal, Alejo explains. And even though you can tell by the wink in his eye that it's not true, it doesn't worry you. What matters to you is to get the trial over with as fast as possible. How could it *not* interest you? And the amount you have to spend doesn't worry you, either. Let's not talk about money right now, says Alejo, slapping you on the back, walking you to the door. Go home, relax, he tells you. How are the kids, he asks. They must be huge. And give your wife my best. One of these days we'll have to have a nice *asadito* at the Deportivo, he smiles. The official letter you received that morning, with which you rushed to the law office, has now lost its transcendence. Don't get upset, Alejo tells you. Everything will be all right. A little while ago you were one more anxiety-ridden face in line, waiting for an appointment, and now, on your way out, after you shake Alejo's hand and the next client walks in, your expression changes. You smile. It's a fact, you'll sleep well tonight. And with any luck, before you close your eyes you'll have a quickie with your wife after all this time.

As soon as the posse discovered that the Commissioner had captured one of the suspects, they gathered in front of the police station. It was still nighttime when the 4x4s braked to a halt at the station. Commissioner Frugone came out to meet them. Dobroslav was the one to speak for the group. He demanded that the Commissioner hand over Ramiro. They'd get a confession out of him. Insecurity had its limits, they said. And that you don't screw around with kids. They were prepared to enter the police station by force. Over my dead body, Frugone said. And he pulled out his 9 millimeter. You people can take me down, but I'll pick off a few of you first. Then the members of the posse noticed the gun barrels pointing at them from the ground floor and second floor of the police station. That's the way it happened, Dante said with precision. They must've gotten scared. They left, cursing Frugone under their breath.

Their retreat didn't reassure Frugone. He knew they'd be back, that they'd snort and swig to pump up the courage they were lacking.

Not one of them was brave by himself. But together they'd egg each other on.

They'd be back. He knew it.

This Saturday at 3 P.M. there will be a celebration of the 48th anniversary of the Evangelical Christian Churches of our Villa and of the 5th anniversary of the Plazoleta of the Evangelical Christian Churches. On Idaho Boulevard, between Calles 134 and 135, a monument to the Bible will be unveiled.

Concrete's my thing, says Dobroslav, our Speer. Indestructible like me—that's concrete. Dobroslav is the Villa's main builder. Dobroslav has constructed more than fifty buildings, in addition to that apartment hotel facing the woods, two pretentious resort hotels in the North, as well as the spa in Mar de las Pampas. And he used concrete in all of them. Just as he'll use it in the construction of the Paradise Towers, his great project. To make it happen, he's joined forces with the Kennedys. Julián Mendicutti greased some palms at City Hall. Alejo Quirós prepared the necessary paperwork. Braulio Ramos designed the sales plan for the apartments at his real estate office. Three strong cards that acted as one. The transaction closed on all sides.

And while the scandal of *los abusaditos* held the Villa rapt, Dobroslav ordered the center of the forest razed, flouting laws that forbade cutting a single weed in Pinar del Norte, and despite protests by the Greens. By the time we ecologists reacted, it was too late. Dobroslav assigned Fito, his architect son, who appears in small type in the Paradise Towers billboard, to deal with the protests: They criticize us for stimulating private investment, generating work and creating jobs, argued Fito. Cachito the mayor said the same thing when he was asked for an explanation at the City Council meeting. This project was approved by the majority, and negotiations were absolutely transparent, he says. Besides, I might point out that there's no violation of the Villa's interests, since the buildings won't affect our prized ecology. The towers will be built in the forest, but in the middle of the forest, without affecting nature. A real wellspring of work, Dobroslav's project currently employs a large labor force, Cachito continues, alluding to the Bolivians and Peruvians who work on scaffolds on the twentieth floor, swaying furiously in the southeasters. He doesn't mention those who can't work anymore.

From lethal falls to amputated limbs. The list of workers injured in accidents is an open secret. More than one person will be able to spot some worker flying in a southeaster, the wind sucking up his screams.

Then Fito says: The condor passes. And he laughs his head off.

Adriana Perrone de Mendicutti, daughter of Raúl Perrone, the first underwriter of the Villa, had a husband, and then children, so she wouldn't feel like a loser. You gotta have what you gotta have. And she also had what Julián wanted to have, and by so doing earned the preposition "de," because around here if a woman isn't "de" somebody, she isn't "de" anyone. And if you're not "de" anyone right now, you once were. De Mendicutti, I'm Adriana de Mendicutti, she introduces herself, evading her paternal surname, Perrone. As if that evasion would make her more of a Kennedy. And besides the "de," she's got the girls, both of them lovely: Felicitas and Luz, who turned out just as pretty as their mother, but with their father's bullying nature. Adriana can't stand to see them fawning over her husband. When she sees the girls acting all lovey-dovey with their father, her stomach roils a little: two treacly dolls that take after her, enraptured with that guy who, she realizes, she's been fed up with for a long time.

I'm not them, she tells Julián. And I'm not like your dear little sisters-in-law, either, those blissfully betrayed wives. You think I was born yesterday: Braulio has that Mimi from the boutique, and Alejo has Valeria, the pharmacist. For my part you can get yourself some little half-breed from the Tropicana; as long as it's all low profile, I'm good. You taught me yourself: low profile, like with the Paradise Towers scam; just as long as one hand doesn't know what the other is doing. Do your own thing. I'm not interested in cheating on you. There's nothing tackier than adultery. I'm not like your partners' hoodwinked wives, who'd kill for a man. I don't need one. I've got my own life, see? I'm a human being, Julián. I'm thirty-five years old. I have ideas; I have projects, too, and I'm not going to end up like all those other women. Adriana takes a breath. She tries to relax and breathe more softly, deeply. She can't wait till her Pilates studio is up and running. And don't even think of screwing me over with a divorce. You're not about to play me for a fool and you're not going to leave me in the street, you hear me? If I find out you're plotting to divorce me and leave me in the street, I'll go to the media and open my mouth; I'll spill everything about what's going on in the Pinar del Norte Hotel, and you and your buddies will fall from the top floor of the towers, just like the Bolivians. Fuck your partners. I'll get all three of you with a single shot. Nobody screws with me. You think I don't have the ovaries to go to the radio and TV stations right now.

You can't, Adri. Calm down, Julián begs. You're upset. Think about the family. How can you even think of going against my friends. You know we're like brothers.

They're not your brothers. They're your partners.

They're my family. Like you.

I'm me, asshole. Wake up. I'm a human being.

We watched the Moure Veterinary Clinic minivan swerve up and down the road and pull up in front of Galería Soles. We saw Moure, crazy drunk, walking with the sham *hauteur* of alcohol. We saw him heading straight toward the office of *El Vocero*.

How could you, Dante, Moure rebuked him. My girl had nothing to do with it. How could you think that my girl, a highly regarded person in the Villa, loved, appreciated, respectable, an outstanding gym teacher at Nuestra Señora, could be involved in that filth, that shit about *los abusaditos*. I didn't say she was connected, Dante cuts him short. I just wrote, literally, what she said: That at Nuestra Señora, like everywhere else, there are decent people and others who leave something to be desired. That's what I published. You shouldn't have published anything, Moure shouted. And all because she testified, that fool. And you included her name. You published her name. My family name, an important family name. Betina Moure, my girl. You smeared her, like she was some cheap whore. Nothing good will come to her from that article. But she's testifying in the police proceedings, Dante explains. Whether she's in the proceedings or not, she's innocent, understand? An innocent young girl. Okay, she's had a few boyfriends. She's made mistakes in love because she's innocent. And yeah, she's passionate. This publicity doesn't do my girl any good. Not my girl or my veterinary clinic. You know how hard it was to have my clinic earn the excellent reputation it has.

Unfazed, Dante continued to concentrate on writing a new piece of unconfirmed information: Mayor Cachito Calderón would be offering a public works contract for the new sewer system to a relative.

All I did was to transcribe information from the DA's office, says Dante. You have to publish a retraction, or . . . Moure starts to say. Dante interrupts: Or what?

Or I'll cancel the veterinary clinic ad in your rag, Moure threatens.

Alejo used to brag that although Camilo wasn't his child, he and Jackie, his wife, would straighten him out. While the couple was raising their nephew, Mili and Juan Manuel were born. It must be admitted that even though he wasn't a child of hers, Jackie devoted as much energy to Camilo as if he were her own. In spite of her affection for him and the attention she lavished on him, Camilo hardly uttered a word, and when he did, it was gibberish. Until he let loose that blood-curdling scream. We never quite got used to that hair-raising shriek. It was just a matter of time, Alejo said. Suddenly time turned into almost thirty years. Since the day the military handed him over to Alejo and he brought him home, almost thirty years. They'd cure him of it, Alejo promised. They would change his disposition, even though the nephew was no longer a kid. According to Alejo, they would do it: Camilo would stop being a shadow, a silent introvert who, when you least expected it, emitted one of those screams that stretched out into a war cry and froze your blood, even though we grew accustomed to the fact that, at the most unlikely moments, and not just in the black silence of dawn anymore, that scream would cut through the Villa like a vulture, filtering through any crack, a red-hot knife piercing your eardrums. What do we mean, a kid? Because Camilo never was a kid, not even when he *was* a kid. In those days, remember, word got around that Camilo was El Muertito, the Dead Little One. Or maybe it was a sick joke started by the kid, who, let's be clear, yes, let's be perfectly clear, wasn't such a kid anymore, though he looked like a big, retarded angel, with a saccharine expression in his eyes that occasionally, before his attacks—the scream, the shriek—took on an evil little glow, which didn't descend as far as his androgynous smile. Although he didn't look it, he must have been around thirty. Let's do the math: if he wasn't quite two when the military murdered his parents, and that was in '78, Camilo must have been around thirty. But with that face of his, like an androgynous teenager, he gave the strong impression of being trapped at a younger age. No doubt if he had wanted to, the kid could've had all the chicks in the Villa. Young girls and older women all fell for him. But the kid didn't seem to be aware of his own magnetism. Not a fag—more likely a virgin, someone observed. He's a pure soul; it's just that you guys don't believe in purity. They say Alejo took him to the Tropicana one afternoon at siesta time. To get him deflowered, that's what he wanted. They say that whores believe that deflowering a kid brings good luck. According to Jennifer, nothing happened. It was like fucking a saint. Fucking El Muertito is a sin, they said.

When he has to get around in the Villa, Dante calls Remises del Mar Limousine Service and asks for Remigio. Let's concede that he's not just his chauffeur. Like Josema the barber, Remigio is his deep throat. When Dante has to report his sources, he calls him "someone close to the facts." Every time Remigio finds himself quoted in that way, he winks an eye and boasts: Yours truly, Mr. Close-to-the-Facts.

Just as there isn't a corner Remigio's unfamiliar with, there's also not a face that escapes him. Fact is, I'm a good psychonomist, says Remigio. And he explains: I said it right. Because Remigio, besides never forgetting a face, always remembers the impression that face made on him. In his rear-view mirror Remigio has read the soul of quite a few men and women in the Villa. And he remembers. He always remembers. I don't know what I'd do without you, Dante jokes. And in the joke there's a lot of truth. You're Virgil, Dante often tells him. Remigio feels flattered to think that Dante identifies him with the Greek heroes. What we've got here is a cultural exchange, Remigio likes to say. Dante teaches me Classical culture and I teach him popular culture. One of Remigio's contributions, Dante admits, was to wise me up to the gut trucks. You know that there are a few trucks that handle the waste from the butcher shops. These trucks carry fat and sell it in Mar del Plata. Theoretically they should come back empty. But they don't. They come back loaded with cartons of beer that they sell illegally. If the cops don't stop them along the way and confiscate the new load it's because they've made a deal with them. They enter the Villa on Circunvalación and head straight for El Monte and La Virgencita, where they sell the beer to the half-breeds for a few cents. And later you see the darkie kids tooling around the Villa, passing the bottle of Quilmes from hand to hand. They walk along, casing a particular kiosk.

If Dante didn't write about it, you can imagine why. The cops aren't the only ones involved in collecting revenue from the gut-truck drivers: Cachito and Alejo have a hand in it, too.

A beam hits a Bolivian in the back of the head, knocks him down, leaves him blind. A weak rung, a Peruvian steps on it and falls thirty feet: his life is spared but he's left paralyzed. Trying to get out of the way of a crane with planks that are about to hit him, a Paraguayan jumps aside, trips over a pail, loses his balance, and falls from the scaffolding: a broken back. A Chilean loses his arm to an electric saw. The accidents mount. Mishaps, Dobroslav calls them. Who today remembers the slaves who died building Cheops's pyramid, he asks. And Fito, his albino son, nods. He always nods. We hardly know what his voice sounds like. And that smile. He has a forced smile, as if his father had him by the balls, squeezing him tight. And yet, there's Cheops, Dobroslav says. A real symbol, Fito nods. Dobroslav shoots him a sober look. Go take care of pouring the concrete, he orders. We don't want another retard screwing us up today, Heil, says the son. To every order from his father: Heil. Then, more kindly, Dobroslav looks at Fito with pity as he walks away. He's not a eunuch, but he lacks initiative. Like he's Italian. Let's not forget what laughing-stocks the Italians were at El Alamein. They're like the locals here. Although I don't have too many locals on my jobs. Foreigners, most of 'em. And I've got no choice but to hire foreigners, from the Andes. You've gotta admit it: they're more willing to work than the locals. Sure, they built Machu Picchu. Nobody asks how many lives were needed to build Machu Picchu. The locals lack nobility, Speer says, Albert Speer. My obsession with each job is the appearance of the Villa, to save the spirit of the Villa that was being lost because of inferior people.

This afternoon, after a fuck, Alejo nods off, seems different, a big, helpless lunk, Valeria thinks. She likes to watch him sleep. She asks herself how they ever happened to hook up, and it's hard for her to determine which one of them saw the other first three years ago at the Selva Negra Hotel, during Winterfest, between waltzes, polkas, and German choirs, and what she ever saw in him, squat, pudgy, more stocky than athletic, with those squinty eyes, that fleshy mouth. Or maybe he was the one who came up to her: If religion didn't separate us, he charged. I didn't know you were a believer, she replied. We Kennedys all are. All are what, she said. And added, emphatically: All sinners. Therefore, we're all believers. Alejo defied her: I'm the least sinful of all, he said with a wink. You must be the worst, she replied. You're one of those people who get turned on by the forbidden—the more forbidden, the better. How would you know, he asked. Because you're so horny it's killing you. I'm the forbidden, she said, and asked: Am I wrong? Not at all, he responded. Soon after they were killing each other in a hotel room. Now, this afternoon, watching him nap, Valeria feels tenderness. A tenderness that closely resembles loneliness. If it could only be like this all the time. If the two of them could only be like this forever, she says to herself. More like the two people they are now. Better not to think, better not to dream. Dreams spoil everything. She has to live in the present, as Deborah, the psychotherapist, recommended. Valeria strokes Alejo's hair. He's sound asleep. He hardly moves. Then he turns over in bed.

Her cell phone rings: it's her husband. Valeria texts Marconi back. I'm coming, she writes. And adds: I love you. Valeria stands up, checks the time. She grabs her dildo, rinses it in the sink, gets dressed. As she leaves the apartment hotel, the wind sweeps across the dunes. She gets into her 4x4. She hits the gas. Right now she should already be in her lab coat, waiting on customers at the pharmacy with her husband. The last thing she wants at this point is a scene. If Marconi, because she calls her husband by his last name, asks her where she was, she'll tell him she got sidetracked chatting with some mothers from Nuestra Señora. That they're planning to go to court to protest the delay in the case of *los abusaditos.*

Neli couldn't believe that her husband, Police Commissioner Frugone, had brought the Villa's most wanted criminal to their home. Ramiro looked at her, frightened. You're completely nuts, Frugone,

Neli said. Bringing your work home. If I didn't bring him here, they'd kill him, Frugone explained. They won't dare come here.

You're out of your mind, Neli said.

Don't raise your voice, the kid's asleep, he said.

You're putting us in danger, she said, try to understand that. You didn't think of Emi.

Nothing will happen, he said. Let him toughen up.

He's a child, she said.

All the more reason, because he's a boy and not a girl. Let him toughen up.

There you go again. Emi is sensitive. But it's not what you think.

I don't think anything.

Yes, you think that because he dyed his hair and wears an earring, he's queer. He's sensitive. That's what's it is with him. Sensitive. And you treat him like a homo. Like this prisoner here.

I'm sensitive, too, Frugone replied. But when I was a kid I didn't wear an earring or dye my hair.

Frugone wanted to calm down, not get embroiled in the same old argument. Ramiro kept quiet.

It was midnight when a voice, Dobroslav's, resounded from the street:

It's not about you, Commissioner. Be reasonable, Frugone. We just want the pervert.

Hand him over, Neli told him. Those lunatics are capable of anything.

You're just doing your duty, we know that. But we're doing our duty as parents. Give us the perv, shouted Dobroslav, and it's all good, Commissioner.

Frugone grabbed Ramiro by one arm, pulled on it, and took him to his son's room. Don't even think of looking out, he said. He locked the door. Neli and Emi stared at him, astonished. He wanted to hear his son ask for a weapon and say, I'm with you, Pop. Instead he said, Hand him over.

You two, hide, Frugone ordered. Under the bed.

Then, with his 9 millimeter, he went out into the night. The headlights of the 4x4s beamed on the front of the house. Frugone could hardly see. Dobroslav came toward him.

Enough, he said. Go away, all of you, and it's all good, he said.

He raised the 9 millimeter and pressed it against Dobroslav's forehead.

I won't count to ten. Just to three.

One, he began.

He didn't make it to two. Fito surprised him from behind, pushing his weapon down. They fell upon him. They kicked him tirelessly.

Emi shoved his way through with jabs and bites to reach the bloodied, sand-covered, destroyed body of what was his father.

The posse, trampling one another, entered the house with a howl.

One week after meeting Jennifer at the Tropicana, that dump with little purple lanterns at the side of the road, a place that can be seen at night from a distance because of the enormous neon sign in the shape of a red, stiletto-heeled shoe, Garrido brought her home to live with him. It must have been more than a year ago that we saw her for the first time at Garrido's house, next door to La Ola Eléctrica, his store. A statuesque Dominican girl. And she sang boleros, too. A little off-key, but with style. Maybe that style was due to her accent. A real homebody, that Mulatto chick, Garrido said. She helped him with his spare-parts business, cooked, kept his house clean, and took pains waiting on us at the Friday night *asados*, as if she were the hostess. After the meal, Jennifer sang for us. *Nochie*, her voice enveloped you. Because Jennifer pronounced it *nochie* instead of *noche*. And she looked right into your eyes.

Whenever Garrido had to travel to the Interior, Jennifer hopped into the truck and went with him. She had stamina for driving, had once driven from Patagonia to the Quiaca. Why wouldn't she have stamina, Garrido said, with the hunger she must have suffered. What really made him fall for Jennifer was how delicately she cut his toenails. She's got a real knack for pedicures, Garrido remarked. It's a shame she's about to fly the coop, he regretted in advance. And I'll have to go out and find me another one along the road. It seems every one of the girls Garrido brought home to live with him, he picked up at the Tropicana. Not one of them lasted two years. It's not like I let them want for anything, he said. And he added: For me, love is like medicine. Even though it has an expiration date. He let Jennifer go well before the two years were up. Better to do it before I get too attached, he said.

Jennifer didn't set herself up as a pedicurist. She returned to the Tropicana. And once more she put on the red, super-tight dress with that plunging neckline. Gimpy Argibay had been waiting for his chance ever since the first time he saw her at Garrido's place. But now, although she was back at the shack, she wasn't the same Jennifer. She cut Gimpy short: Anyone but Garrido's friends, she stopped him.

Conduct, like they say. Then Garrido changed his mind. And he went looking for her. But this time Jennifer wasn't about to run off with him without making it official. What a party that wedding was! Jennifer's Dominican friends were there. And not one of us stayed away.

Until some time ago the residents of Pinar del Norte went around ranting and raving about middle school, that it was a den of juvenile delinquents, that the kids emerged from that lair as lowlifes. All that's missing is for them to practice sharpshooting, they said. The big shots presented a project to the city: they wanted to shut down the school. They looked down their noses at us. These days I enjoy hearing them whisper about what happened at Nuestra Señora, the scandal of *los abusaditos*. They discuss it *sotto voce* because you might have a family member nearby with a little girl, a little boy, that it happened to. Now that what happened at the swankiest school in the Villa has come out everywhere, we just love it: it's quite clear who's who. We slice each other open with knives or blow each other away with guns, but we don't go around fucking kindergarten babies.

Crazy Heinrich lives in the woods, past the Idaho campgrounds. He must be around forty, but he looks younger. At first he gives you the impression he's a bum. Later, after watching him for a while, you realize he's trying to pass for a country man. But it's just an act. No doubt he's inherited many hectares of land, but in addition he got his ancestors' craziness, especially from his Austrian grandfather. He built himself a bunker in a storage bin, with no electricity or running water.

When Crazy Heinrich comes up to you, the first thing you smell is a mixture of grass and sweat. Like an animal. When he shows up at Marconi's grill, at the entrance to the Villa, and sits down at the counter, he eats in a corner, far away from everyone else. With his hands. He chews dog-style, leaving the bones stripped. No, he doesn't drink. Just as well that wacko doesn't go for alcohol. But in his animal behavior, there's still a deliberate, provocative air. You sense it when he casts a sidewise glance at the rest of the room, defiantly studying some customer. He strips the rib bare with his teeth and stares at you. He nails you with his gaze, those green eyes, half in jest and half looking for trouble. The wacko tries to pass himself off as a hermit, but the way I see it, I tell you, he's just play-acting and just a plain slob. Because, even though he lives cheaply, imagine what kind of income the land he inherited from his grandfather must bring in with the rent from the campgrounds alone.

No, he has no family. Inge, his mother, went bed-hopping in the sixties. So no one ever learned who his father was. A child of life, Inge used to say, quoting Khalil Gibran. A pity, Inge. She killed herself when she was older, after Lennon's death. An overdose.

But in spite of his hermit-like appearance, Crazy Heinrich has a certain magnetism with women. Last time, Yoli the hairdresser, Josema's ex, remarked: If you bathe him, shave him, and spray on a little cologne, that wacko is Brad Pitt. You should see him climb trees, hatchet in hand. He can chop down a eucalyptus by himself. He laughs when people tell him that his Austrian grandfather planted trees, while he's stubbornly cutting them down instead, waging a personal battle against himself. The leaves keep you from seeing the sky, he says. The forest is a hiding place. But it's also a trap. My grandfather didn't trust the sky. He had good reason. I'm his curse, the emissary of Pan he says, laughing boisterously, the laugh of one possessed. And he grabs his fly, suggesting he has a hard-on.

You have to pay attention to the sky, the wacko says to anyone who wants to listen. Because that's where whatever's coming will come from. It won't take me by surprise. That's why I want to keep it in my sights.

But how about the attack old lady Schwartz had, the mother of Sergio the optometrist whose store is opposite Plaza 9 de Julio? The first summer she was here, she went to buy a strudel for her daughter-in-law, who was eight months along and had a craving. She went into the Viena Bakery. Just as Fat Frida was about to wait on her, old lady Schwartz ran out of the place. She returned home with her heart in her throat: she had a coronary and went mute. Dr. Cohan took care of her at the hospital. As he was examining her, he saw the brand from the concentration camp, the number. Since Cohan is a *Landsman*, he was able to translate what old lady Schwartz was saying. She had recognized the Kapo from Buchenwald. The next day the bakery was closed. And it didn't open again till recently, when Tuquita, the lifeguard who came back from Ibiza with a Swedish chick and lots of cash, bought it. Nobody heard another word about Frida. A real shame. Because the strudel was delicious.

All the kids go around in tracksuits, with hoods. The half-breeds wear hoodies to make themselves look tough. And they are—they're dangerous. Just look at the way they walk, swaggering like they were Black giants from the Bronx. But they're not; they're a pack of puny little scarecrows. Even though they look malnourished and you might think you could take them down in a scuffle, be careful, don't count on it. They may be malnourished, but what if they're high and packing heat? Just look how they're watching you. Trying to see if you can take their stare. If you lower your eyes, you lose. If you keep your gaze steady, prepare yourself, because two things can happen. One, they crack up and make a fool of you. Two, they gang up on you. That's what I'm saying: the hoodie is part of a code. The half-breeds wear it to intimidate you. And those who aren't half-breeds use it as protection, too, so the half-breeds can't tell who's a half-breed from who isn't. There are blond kids who dye their eyebrows black. And pass themselves off as half-breeds. They don't turn their backs on me anymore. I bought myself a 22 caliber Bersa. No matter where they cross my path, I'll get 'em. And if they come into my house again, I'll shoot. Shoot first and ask questions later.

I'll tell you what I think, and you know I'm not a racist, I was an activist in the 70s, I went into the shantytowns to teach them how to read, all that pedagogy of the oppressed stuff, but now it's different—oppressed, my balls. Because you don't know where the shots are coming at you from. Here's what I think: danger is a half-breed and fear is a blond. But fear is no fool. And a half-breed's a half-breed.

Around here outsiders aren't the only ones who try to be someone else. Those who were born and raised here also want to be someone else. Listen, that's what happened with Alberta Vázquez. Sure, you won't be able to place her by name. Her girlfriends teased her. And if she was nasty to guys, it was because of her name. One fine day Alberta went to Adriana and Susi, her closest friends, and told them:

Call me Jacqueline. From now on I'm someone else; I'm Jackie. She was already of age, she flirted with Alejo, and it was his influence at the Civil Registry that allowed her to change her name. There you go, he said. Now all you need to be a Kennedy is to get married. She wasn't worried that her parents might be offended by her name change. Jackie no longer cared about her Galician shopkeeper ancestors in the southern part of the Villa. Because Jackie aspired to greater things, just as she aspired to coke, and that's how she hooked Alejo. Later it was Jackie who introduced Adriana and Susi to the other Kennedys, Julián and Braulio. Adriana and Susi were just as quick on the uptake. One of them, Adriana Perrone, nabbed Julián, and the other, Susi Rodríguez, nabbed Braulio. All three of them had always aimed high. But Jackie got herself the grand prize. That was in the days when old Don Evaristo was planning his retirement and Alejo was already in charge of the whole legal practice. Alejo promised to make great strides.

If Jackie was unrecognizable to those who met her when she was a student at Nuestra Señora, it was also because of her surgeries. And you should see how important she thinks she is. Imagine, two trips a year to wherever she wants. Not to mention her checkbook and the 4x4 that she crashes every so often to get her husband to buy her a new one. So no way is she going to separate from Alejo just because he's fucking Valeria, the pharmacist's wife. No matter how much serious money she might bleed from Alejo in a divorce, it'll never be as much as she'd get by sticking with the same old story. Alejo, for his part, is no dummy, either. He knows that a separation from Jackie could make things intolerable. Not because of what she would shave off his fortune. On account of the kids, on account of how much he loves Mili and Juan Manuel. And Camilo, the nephew he raised as his own, although some say he *is* his own, that he did it with his sister, the militant. Let them say what they will. No matter what you may want to call him, to Camilo he's a hell of a dad. And Jackie appreciates it.

There must be no greater humiliation for a father than for his son to see him crawling on all fours, his face smashed, destroyed. They beat the shit out of me, those sons of bitches, Frugone would tell Dante. They knocked out some of my teeth, they broke a couple of ribs. My kid was crying: Don't die, Papi. The two of them, him and my wife, helped me into a police car. They took me to the hospital. Just like what happened to Marlon Brando in that movie where he tries to save Redford, who escapes from jail and comes back to town. Everybody, for whatever reason, wants to give Redford hell. Brando wants to save him from a lynching. He protects him. But the fancy-asses in the town take over the police station from Brando. They beat the shit out of him. Like me. But I still got my way: they never caught the little fag. He jumped out of the window of Emi's room. It probably wasn't too hard for him to hitch a ride along the road.

While I'm recovering, those two cutthroats, Renzo and Balmaceda, will fill in for me. Everybody thinks I was more of an asshole than a hero. I know I lost face. And now those two will get the credit; they'll rule with an iron fist. And when I recover, for sure they'll transfer me, because they're gonna transfer me, even though I'd rather resign. But where will I go, huh? Tell me, where will I make the dough I'm making. The car, the house, private school for the kid, trips to Disneyland—the cost of living's no joke. Work as a security guard? No, give me a break. If I quit, where will I go. Outside of the Provincial Police Corps I'm nobody, Dante. And I can't quit. They won't let me. I know too much. When the pie comes in, it's divided up. So much from dope, so much from whores, so much from hits. You get your percentage of the take. And you can't refuse. If you quit, you know what's in store for you.

María is forty-eight but you'd take her for over sixty, easy. Hair whiter and whiter all the time, fewer and fewer teeth, and a curvature of the spine that keeps getting more twisted. With what she earns from cleaning houses, she supports her whole family, who live with her in La Virgencita: five kids—three girls and two boys. In addition, six grandkids: four girls and two boys. And let's not forget the three great-grandkids, two girls and a boy. María would rather have had boys than girls because the girls get knocked up and the family keeps multiplying. Sebas, the oldest, wants to carve out a future for himself working at El Atlético and training as a boxer with Cannonball Santoro. Martín works on and off at an auto shop. And the girls, Verónica, Cinthya, and Vanesa, help out by doing odd jobs that don't last because they never stop breeding. Vanesa, the youngest, takes care of the household and cooks for everyone. The grandkids are a disaster, too. As for Facundito, better not to know what he's into. Augustito, poor angel, has a mental problem. That's what María calls it: a mental problem. The boy stays holed up in his room for weeks at a time, mute, and no one can get him out. Till a thunderstorm comes along: then he starts in with the howling and all of them together have to grab him and take him to the emergency room for an injection. As far as the rest of them are concerned, the grandkids and great grandkids, she's tired of disowning them. One day the police will show up and tell her they killed one as he was climbing over a wall. When winter comes, all María asks is that God protect her job at the houses where she cleans and that she won't get caught when she pinches a few coins she's found lying around. She's already lost two houses because of this. And she doesn't want the rumor to spread, lest she end up with nothing. Besides, they're about to kick her out of Cachito's house. For a while now, Beti, Cachito's wife, has been suspecting her. Now María cleans house for her sister-in-law Valeria. Marconi the pharmacist's wife. A big cuckold, Cachito's brother-in-law. Valeria the Jew is Dr. Alejo Quirós's lover: who doesn't know that? If the whole Villa knows that the pharmacist is a cuckold, María wonders, how come his sister Beti doesn't wise him up. Beti or Cachito, she thinks, could easily tip him off. Although if Marconi hasn't gotten wise by now to the horns he's sporting, it must be for convenience's sake. He'd rather be a cuckold than lose Cachito and Alejo's financial backing. That's what María thinks when she sees a few bills, three fifties, sticking out from under the lamp on the nightstand. María hesitates before taking them. She thinks of everything she could buy with fifty. She hears the engine of the 4x4. María hesitates with the money in her hand. To these people, she tells herself, money is more important than honor. And since they're calculating types, no doubt they've kept a record of these bills. I wonder if they left them there to test me. I wouldn't put it past them.

Full selection of religious articles. Artistic plasterwork. Sculptures. We work miracles with restoration.
  La Sucursal del Cielo, Calle 4, No. 107. Tel. 469070.

When we arrived at the Villa in '76, we had nothing but the lot. Papa had bought it a few years earlier with the idea of building there one day, but it wouldn't be easy for him, considering what he earned at the factory. He worked in a metallurgical plant in Munro. He was a union delegate. And Mama was an English teacher at a commercial secondary school in Boulogne. Both of them were militants. Papa was on the list. It seems we were spared miraculously because the night they came for us, we were already on the Antón bus on our way here. Nicolás was four, Matías three, and I was two. But I remember. They say I can't possibly remember, I was very small, but I remember. We had spent a few days at the Villa that summer; we'd set up a tent on the lot. Now that we were returning, my brothers and I thought we were going on vacation again. But no: we stayed. Mama found a job more easily. Because they needed teachers. And besides, she was blonde. Blonde, tall, and thin. It was harder for Papa. Because Papa is dark-skinned, like us. He looks Indian. First he worked at the cement factory. Then at the lumberyard. We raised the tent and camped for a while. Camping in the middle of winter, you can't imagine. And afterward in a rented tent, while we were building the house. Because everything Papa and Mama earned went into bricks. In a year it was built. You don't seem like a *criollo,* Ibáñez, the manager at Banco Provinicia said to him. You bust your butt like an immigrant. Papa didn't reply. He lowered his head, shook his hand. When he left the office, Papa went to the beach and washed his hand.

They say that to prove they weren't racists, the Germans brought in many Jews, like Don Salo Katzman, the Auschwitz survivor. And I'm telling you, like my Papa taught me, don't believe the Germans were Schindler: they just trusted Jews more than half-breeds because they were blond.

If there's any advantage to a nighttime farewell at the terminal, it's that afterward both the one who leaves and the one who stays behind have the whole night and the consolation of sleep before them. The sadness of goodbye will be erased, at least for a few hours. The departing one will nod off against the window, looking out at the dark fields, every so often a light. At last fatigue will overtake his body, and no matter how uncomfortable the seat may be, he'll sink into sleep. The one left behind, in turn, will go back home, knock around for a while, and eventually go to bed because tomorrow is another day. Tomorrow will be the Villa again. Tomorrow he'll go back to the routine that will plunge him into oblivion. Tomorrow we will *be* oblivion. And it'll be a relief.

A sizeable throng, Dante said. Sometimes he talks to us as if he were writing. Especially when he's just put an edition to bed. During the afternoon hours, a sizeable throng from the Dolores Squad arrived at our Villa, he said. We don't make fun of his rhetoric. Get to the point, we told him. He needed to down a whiskey before going on. To the business at Nuestra Señora, he said, like it was a toast. But he meant the re-opening of the case. He knew for a fact that the subject would dominate the conversation at Moby tonight. Dante had just arrived from *El Vocero*'s office after working late on an article about the school's closing. He came into the bar just after midnight. We had been waiting for him.

How could we go to bed without getting the latest on what had happened. He told us what he wrote, the scoop. In the afternoon, a sizeable throng from the Dolores Squad and the Federal Chamber arrived at the Villa to carry out investigations connected to the reports of abuse filed shortly after the start of the school year by more than fifteen parents of Nuestra Señora del Mar kindergarten children.

Let's see if you can guess where the first raid took place. Place your bets, gentlemen. The church. And it's no rumor that they raided the chapel and the priest's residence.

They say we Kennedys are Mafia, Braulio says whenever he gets plastered. So what, if nobody has the guts to accuse us up-front. He smiles a twisted smile with his thin lips. They say Alejo controls the Villa from his law office. That Julián is the City government. And me, Braulio, from my real estate agency, that we share power between us, that we buy off politicians, and that both the Peronists and the Radicals are our puppets. We've got Cachito in our pocket. And as a result we govern with the Peronist bunch. And if it all comes together tomorrow, we'll do it with the Neighbors' Union. Because we can even bribe Miguens, the guy from the Civic Front opposition. That one would kill his mother for a few pesos. No matter who's in office, they'll have to do their duty as we see fit. Mafia, they call us. If being a prominent, traditional, and respectable family is being Mafia, then we're Mafiosos. Well, you know, to live, a person needs a family. And a family like ours means support. Nobody survives alone for very long in this world. If you want to be somebody in the Villa, it's to your advantage to belong to some family. It could be the German Club or the Rotary, the Police Cooperative or El Atlético. And what's the first thing they tell you when you become a member: We're one big family, they tell you. And you have to understand what it means to belong to this family: watch out if you change your mind and want to get away; watch out because you're carrying off all our secrets.

We've had the hots for Senta, the Montenegrin girl, since the first time we saw her. We've had the hots for her ever since Federico, Rinaldi's kid, introduced her to us. My fiancée, the kid boasted. Had we been in his shoes, we would've been all puffed up too. We knew it: the same motives for his vanity would be those of his misfortune. An unpronounceable last name, Senta's. She worked at Banco Nación in Madariaga. Soon after they met, Federico and Senta set the date. A good catch, the Rinaldi kid. Heir to Los Médanos supermarket chain. The reception was a bacchanal. Old Rinaldi rented the Ocean Hotel, the whole place. Rooms for friends and family from outside the Villa. A Cuban salsa band. Mariachis. All of us slobbering fools danced with the bride.

Then the new Señora Rinaldi managed to get the Nación to transfer her to the Villa. Whenever we ran into her, she held our gaze. Old Rinaldi had to admit it: If you could only see how hard it is for me to keep my eyes off Senta when we're at family gatherings. If Rinaldi had no qualms about stocking the supermarket with merchandise stolen from carjackers, we wondered, how long would it take him to make a play for the daughter-in-law? He replied before we could ask: She's not my daughter, he interjected. It's not incest. Around that time someone remarked: There's something going on between Lanari, the branch manager of the Nación, and Senta, his secretary, because, yeah, now she was his secretary. The gossip didn't faze him. His honor wasn't at stake: She's my kid's wife, he said. Not mine. But we found out that Rinaldi kept an eye on her. Until he caught them by surprise in Mar del Plata, coming out of a hotel. Lanari and the Montenegrin, in sunglasses.

The usual malcontents attributed the credit and loans Rinaldi got at the Nación to his daughter-in-law's influence. Rinaldi never tried to hide it: My daughter-in-law is influential. And she only thinks about the family. Because it's all in the family.

Then, the kid's suicide. Shot himself right in the head. Federico caught the Montenegrin. But not with Lanari. With his old man.

The photos found in Don Manfred's basement, it was said, were of Dachau.

We also know how to appreciate kindness, because kindness exists, too. And if you don't agree, just look at Juan, the guy from Venado Tuerto. He arrived here in the 60s, dead broke. Selling hot dogs on the beach during the day and sleeping in sheds at the terminal. Until he opened his little bar. Remember, he was nearsighted: when he looked at you it was so pathetic that you lowered your eyes. After the little bar, a luncheonette. In a few years he turned the corner and opened up the restaurant. He married Hilde, the Austrian. They had two kids. Juan was crazy about his family. And he didn't deserve what Hilde did to him: running off with one of the waiters after emptying out his accounts at the Nación and the Provincia plus the safety deposit box. Juan came to terms with the blow. He dealt with raising the kids alone. He spoiled them too much. When they were barely of age, they left him, too: Rodrigo, the older boy, to Costa Rica with his surfboard, and Ramiro, the younger one, to Mallorca. Juan faced his loneliness bravely. When the last crisis came, every night of the rawest winter, he fed the kids from La Virgencita. The kids came to the restaurant at closing time and Juan gave them the leftovers, wrapped up for take-out. He had a huge heart, that Juan. Then he took on the project of the kids' dining room. He didn't even ask the Rotary politicians for help. They wanted to show off what a guy like that had accomplished. But Juan didn't get involved with anyone. He kept on going. Even when a gang of kids, the same ones he used to feed, broke into the restaurant with guns, Juan didn't waver. He didn't report them. And besides continuing to feed the kids, he started feeding dogs. He began to shelter homeless dogs on a parcel of land behind his house. He had more and more of them. And then the neighbors reported him, saying it was illegal to keep all those dogs, it was filthy, it was dangerous. The politicians tried to make him pay. Same with the Rotarians: they demanded an investigation. And the most fucked-up thing of all: the rumor that he was fattening up the dogs for the restaurant. And he went broke. He went broke, just like that. What a shame; such kindness. It's a fact that good folks are taken for fools. And fools don't win. Around here, those who turn out all right are—don't laugh—are the fuckers like you guys who get off on other people's misfortune. We'll miss that fool. To die like that. His heart. Because the fool was all heart.

There are more people who've heard El Muertito at night than those who swear they've seen him. The power of suggestion, Dante scoffs. And yet, those who've seen El Muertito say it's a bird with a little boy's head, a little boy no more than two years old. If we consider what the head of a child that age weighs, the bird's body must have been able to support it in the air. I'm not saying a condor, but a substantial bird in any case. A kind of super-sparrow, say those who saw it. You'd need power to take flight with that head. Now go believe those who say they've seen it, impressionable kids, possibly frightened by their parents, strung-out druggies, drunks in a frenzy of DTs, retards, and for sure we've got a few, the superstitious half-breed bunch who, when they're suffering from liver problems or cancer, go to the folk-healer. And not only did they see it, they say. Some of them heard it screech like a seagull. Others heard it singing something like a lullaby on the roof of their house and when they went out to see, El Muertito flew off, startled by the presence of humans. Me, the only thing I can say for sure, is if it comes screwing around here, I'll fill it with buckshot and pickle it.

On Sunday at dawn an 18-year-old youth was murdered at the corner of Calle 119 and Avenida 15. The crime took place during a quarrel that erupted at the quinceañera party of a girl from a family with a well-established criminal history. The party, according to witnesses from the neighborhood known as El Monte, spun out of control at several points: shouting, fighting, and excessive alcohol consumption alerted the neighbors to the possibility of violence. At the dance, two inebriated youths fought with knives over the young birthday celebrant. During the melée several shots were heard, causing the neighbors to phone the police. When the patrol cars approached the area, they saw a male individual lying in the street in a pool of blood. As they drew closer, they were attacked with rocks, insults, and aggression. Several additional patrol cars arrived for reinforcement, allowing arrests to be made and for the victim, who had suffered gunshot wounds, to be taken to the hospital. But the violence continued at the public hospital. Friends and enemies of the victim, who died in the ambulance, launched a fight in the lavatories, destroying the sanitary facilities. The birthday girl, in an alcohol-induced coma, was admitted shortly thereafter. When she was discharged hours later, she was taken into custody to investigate the young man's death. Meanwhile, the perpetrator remains at large.

The first thing we tell a young couple that's looking into coming here to live: This is an ideal place to raise children. The landscape. Where else will they find surroundings that combine the forest, the sea, and right there, behind us, the countryside, the *pampa* in all its range. Ideal for settling down and starting a family.

But what we're not so careful to tell them is that we don't know what to do when the kids grow up. That the three public schools, where the laborers' kids and the ones from the shantytown go, are pathetic and full of lowlifes. That the private school, Nuestra Señora, where the snobs send their progeny, is a reform school for the privileged. That by the age of twelve they're already druggies. In the winter, at nightfall, just look at the mob of kids congregating on the corner in front of Acid: beer, Coke with Fernet, weed and acid.

On Avenida 3 and 106. Also at Pibeplay, the electronic games kiosk. Stoned out of their minds, they eventually head for the woods. You see them crossing the poplar groves with bottles. Don't even think about cutting through the woods at night, where the kids practice their rituals. And at night, the beach. You can see the bonfires, hear their shouts in the wind. After midnight, the ones from La Virgencita head for home, strung out and armed. They've already held up a bus driver twice. These are the same kids who stop the bus the next morning on their way to middle school.

Andrea is an architect, four months pregnant. Diego is a designer. They're no more than thirty. And they're dying to come and live here. They've told this to Braulio, the agent from Ramos Real Estate: they're hunting for a place to bring up their son, because it's going to be a little boy. Braulio shows them a house in the north. Look around, Braulio tells them. The privileged space where the baby will grow up, he tells them, spreading his arms as if unfurling the landscape, acacias, pines, eucalyptus. Listen, he says. Birds.

At this stage of life, says Dante resignedly, a person starts repeating himself. It's always the same old story: no matter how much you may think you're investigating variations on the same theme and might be able to find something different, a new perspective on the story, it isn't so, because your thoughts have grown calluses, you're overcome by complacency, and, as they say, in the suspicious calm of the Villa your will begins to stagnate, and when the time comes to interpret a fact, you end up choosing the most conventional view of the matter, because as we turn it over and over in our heads, at some point we might be surprised to learn that probing commits us, that each and every one of us, no matter how much distance we try to establish, wherever we go, leaves traces of blood or shit from our shoes.

Today's news item in *El Vocero:*

News has leaked that the Provincial Director of Private Education, Sr. Jorge Giusti, has declared his intention of closing Nuestra Señora del Mar Institute before a group of parents that handed him a note at the entrance of the assembly hall, demanding mass dismissal of the school's administrative staff, including the parish priest. The new management of the establishment remains in the hands of the two inspectors in charge of preparing a preliminary report—a thorough investigation including copies of all the parents' testimonies. An instructor will arrive at the Villa shortly to develop an overview of the institution in order to investigate the responsibility of the school and its staff for the irregularities: sexual abuse involving a dozen kindergarten pupils.

At the same assembly, amid cries of protest and accusations against the school, police authorities confirmed that no arrests have been made and that the investigation will continue under the auspices of the DA's office. Let us recall that the case exploded when the community became aware of more than twenty complaints of sexual abuse affecting 4- and 5-year-old children who attended kindergarten, the entry level grade. The crime apparently dates from one month earlier and may have been covered up or minimized by school authorities, which has provoked the parents' indignation.

Representatives of several national media attended the assembly, among them TN, Channel 8, and Channel 10 (Mar del Plata). Newspapers including *La Nación*, *La Capital* (Mar del Plata), and *El Día* (Mar del Plata) also reported on the case.

Every day there are more vagrants who sleep wherever night catches them: in an abandoned construction site, at the back of a warehouse, on a bench at the bus terminal. We know what winter nights are like here on the coast: sleet, frost, a cold that breaks your heart. Arno is different. Not only because of the way he's put up with it through the years. Because he's of a different race. Superior. He must be around eighty. Speaks a thick, fluent German. And around here everything German still means something. We're not saying it's like a family crest or something, but people look at you differently if you have German ancestry. That's why Arno's different from so many other homeless folks or vagrants who wander around town. Sometimes they pick on him. Out of pure spite. Fucking half-breeds.

Arno was a sailor on the *Graf Spee*. And yet nobody remembers a different Arno from the one we see on the main drag, looking for a place to lounge in the sunshine and spend hours there with a bottle, greeting everyone who goes by. Because Arno's got class. He still keeps his dignity in spite of his poverty. He begs with refinement, as if doing you the favor of letting you demonstrate your kindness.

Because Arno knows that we treat him differently from the other tramps, like that pair of drunken half-breeds, him and her, who come at you with attitude. Violence, practically. If we toss them a coin, it's more out of fear than pity. We give alms to many others out of disgust, to get them away from us. They stink with their filth, the stench of their wounds. It's not like Arno doesn't smell or that he lacks infected cuts and scrapes. It's enough to see him close up: the scabs he has on his face! More like from a beating than a fall. The half-breed kids, those pieces of shit. They can tell he's different. And they beat him up. Regardless, even though he's crippled, Arno smiles when he comes up to you, extending an open hand. A grimy, wounded hand. You can appreciate that class of his. Not like the half-breeds. It's with them that the Villa started to decay. And later with the Moishes.

The times I've smoked watching the stars.

The atmosphere breathed in the house is dense. The girls leave the house holding their papa's hand. You'd wear down anybody's energy, Adriana says to the back of Julián's head. Her husband doesn't respond. He loads the girls into the 4x4. As Nuestra Señora del Mar is still closed and the girls go to Nuestra Señora, before leaving for City Hall, Julián is going to drop them off at Alejo's place; it's best if they spend the morning with Jackie. Ever since Adriana's been obsessed with her Pilates studio, she says she has no time to deal with the girls, that the girls are a shared responsibility. It's karma, she says. And change your expression, will you. You're not going to get very far with that low astral.

Julián and the girls in the 4x4. The sun filtering through the golden branches of the forest. It's a pleasure to see it reflected in the windshield. The girls half asleep. Julián looks at them in the rearview mirror: two angels. It's one thing that Adriana's closed her legs to him. But it's fucked up that she's closed her heart to the girls. They may be angels, but they're not stupid. Felicitas and Luz can't stand their mother, either. They wait for him to come home to tell him everything Adriana did or didn't do to them. For example, she tells them off and punishes them, sends them to their room for causing a commotion, but it doesn't occur to her to entertain them. Till he gets home and they tell him. At least they have someone to tell, people say.

And to top it all off, Adriana is so crazy that she pressures him with the threat of the business about Dobroslav's towers if he even thinks of asking for a divorce. He believes she's capable of that. And more. Julián feels more defenseless than the girls. And he wonders whom he can tell about this living nightmare. Braulio: impossible. The only thing Braulio's interested in is getting shitfaced and fucking that chick from the boutique. What would Braulio say? Susi's closed her legs to me, too—so what. I've got Mimí to do everything I ask for and more. Mimí asks me to leave Susi. Imagine me leaving Susi for a little Jewish slut. No way, man. It's amazing how chicks can smell it, I swear. Every time I bang the Jew, that night Susi wants to fuck. One cunt smells another. They get off on each other. Find yourself a chick and you'll see. You're gonna tell me you can't hook one. That's what Braulio will tell him. Besides, Braulio will go and blab the story to Alejo, that Adriana and I have hit the skids. And even if Braulio doesn't say anything to Alejo, eventually Alejo will find out anyway. Because Alejo always knows everything. As he pulls up in front of his friend's house, he realizes that the best thing would be to go directly to Alejo, ask him for help, like that time when they were kids, in the ocean, and the tide dragged him out and he was terrified, as if he'd forgotten his swimming lessons at the German Club, and he started to drown and he would have, too, if it hadn't been for Alejo swimming out to him.

The drowsy girls clamber out of the car and disappear into Alejo's house. Jackie offers him coffee, but no thanks, I've just had some. Alejo slaps him on the back. What a face, bro. What kind of face, Julián asks.

Like you could use a fuck, Alejo replies.

Rubén is a musicians' agent. Now he's brought a jazz quintet to the Villa. They're all staying at the Acapulco. He's been a jazz fan since he was young. He always tells people how jazz changed his life when he was a kid and his uncle put some ragtime music on the stereo. It was a sign from destiny. First he became a record collector. And then a distributor. He hosted radio shows, interviewed musicians, both foreign and national. Here in the Villa he stays at a hotel belonging to Melvin, a pianist who played for Radio El Mundo in his youth. He accompanied Johnny Ray. Melvin's like that because he had an embolism. But the doctor allows Melvin his whiskey anyway when he listens to jazz in the afternoon. And Sharon serves it to him. You can tell there's love between those two. Sharon used to be a blues singer. Now she handles the front desk at the hotel. They named the Hotel "Acapulco." A southeaster twisted the sign. And that's how it remained. Forever. Twisted. Just like Melvin after the embolism.

Here's the story: Sharon sang at a dive on 25 de Mayo. As she knew several languages, she performed for sailors in whatever language they requested. She was the nightclub owner's lover. The place was called Nevada, and the boss, the Greek, was a smuggler. Melvin was going downhill. He ended up at the Nevada. Sharon introduced him. He was her brother, she said. The Greek took him on. It didn't take long for him to realize there was something more between those two. Their relationship was as false as their stage names. One early morning, before closing, while Melvin was drawing a blues number out of the piano and Sharon sang along, the Greek sidled up to the piano and lowered the cover on his hands. He broke his fingers. Melvin never played again.

Later, Rubén tells me, they came here to the coast.

And their real names, I ask.

What does it matter, Rubén replies. The names are variations. Not the theme.

It seemed like the late Fina had been reincarnated in her daughter. She's as beautiful as her mother was when you stole her, said his compatriot to Pascual, who, as soon as he arrived, had gone to live in San Justo, at the home of some bricklayer uncles. That's where he met Fina. The girl was fifteen. They fell in love at first sight. Pascual asked for her hand. Her parents laughed at his pretensions. Fina was studying to be a secretary. She had a future. She'd marry a doctor. Pascual had tried not to dishonor the family, but the family had dishonored him with their disdain because he was a simple bricklayer. Pascual and Fina eloped. They fled toward the sea.

Here in the Villa, Pascual was an important bricklayer and Fina was a dressmaker. Fina became pregnant in 1970. She died in childbirth. Later, in the mid-eighties, the Fina we all saw was her daughter. She had been reincarnated in her daughter. Seeing her with her father at Sunday Mass was like seeing a May-December couple. Evil tongues, as usual, said that they really were a couple.

Fina became pregnant. We thought it was by her father, but no. Some little *criollo* from the lumberyard. It was tough to get Pascual to spit out the boy's name. Hilario, his name was, a laborer from the sticks, a *criollo* from Madariaga. He told Fina to bring him home. He wanted to talk to him.

Some stories are repeated. We all thought the same thing happened to Pascual as to his uncles. Hilario and Fina disappeared. No one had the nerve to ask Pascual about it. Hilario had stolen his daughter, just as he, Pascual, had stolen her mother.

Pascual concentrated on his garden. As lush as a cemetery, his garden was. Every Sunday instead of going to Mass he brought flowers to his dead wife. No Mass, though: he never went back. From the time he was left alone, he didn't return. God, we thought, had disappointed him. He soon grew old. White hair, bent back, coughing more and more. He refused to see the doctor. He died of sadness, people said. In his will he left the house to some distant relatives in Italy. He asked that the money from the sale of his property be used to transport his remains back to the village. He wanted to be buried there, in his homeland.

Ramos Real Estate kept the house; they knocked it down. There were plans to build an inn. When Dobroslav Construction began excavating to put up an apartment house, they found the couple's bones in the place where the garden had been.

On the front page of *El Vocero:*

A traveling circus has set up camp in La Virgencita, on a lot at the intersection of Circunvalación and 105th. Neighbors have complained about the dirt generated and the presence of dangerous, large animals, enclosed in precarious conditions. Opposition council members maintained that circuses are prohibited within city limits, to which City Hall replied that the circus has been inspected and everything is in order.

Two photographs accompanied the report: one of an old, skinny, bored lion and one of a languishing tiger. Regardless, the circus is quite the rage. Everyone from snobs to *criollos*, and all those in between, our neighbors to the south and beyond, those from Mar de las Pampas. Visitors even came from Madariaga.

But the enthusiasm was short-lived. Besides, winter fell early. Winter pushes us into our dens. A movie, a pizza, some beer, and right back indoors. And once the attraction of the circus had ended, you could feel the silence of the night, with no dogs barking. Someone said that first the feral ones in the dunes disappeared. Then, the guard dogs in Pinar del Norte. Costs a lot to feed wild beasts.

If man is no friend to man, somebody said pensively, how can you expect him to respect the animal he calls his best friend.

Published in *El Vocero*: *The city has again suffered a fatality among its younger population. This time it occurred in the neighborhood of 115th and 15th, at dawn on Sunday the 28th, when, in the middle of an argument and before several witnesses, one Peruvian minor shot another. The autopsy report determined that one of the bullets entered through the left armpit and exited through the shoulder blade, resulting in a mortal wound. A neighbor attempting to intervene in the struggle was also wounded. It was reported that there had been repeated previous confrontations between the youths. The assailant was apprehended two days later, early Tuesday morning, as he was about to leave a property in Pinar del Norte with a water heater. After arresting the assailant, police transferred him to a facility for juvenile offenders. While the investigation is underway, focus remains on the search for the murder weapon. Additionally, police reported that they continue to search for two other minors who were involved in the unfortunate incident. These events are being investigated by the DA's Office.*

At the first hint of a southeaster, the TV station issues a weather alert. Parents are advised to bring their children home from school. Businesses shut down. Those who live near the beach watch the sea with suspicion. Black clouds grow blacker. Gale winds begin shaking doors and windows. It's a good idea to secure gates and shutters. Children indoors. Soon the Villa is leveled and deserted. Those who live in the woods shut themselves inside their houses, fearing that a eucalyptus might fall on the roof. And those who live where the Villa turns into countryside bring their animals indoors with them.

Animals and country folk alike silently listen to the first whistling of the storm, peer out of the corners of their eye like Don Argüello's horses, and prepare for what's about to come. We don't know how long it will last. Because last year we had a whole spate of them. On Thursday it was punishing. With any luck, it seemed like it might abate on Tuesday. Even if a timid sun peeked out on Wednesday, it wasn't wise to be too optimistic. At night the gusts resumed. Thursday dawned black again. By afternoon it was lashing at us once more. If we consider the force of the storm that's blowing now, it won't be just a harbinger, but rather the confirmation that another series is on its way. It's not so much the water we fear. What's destructive is the wind. The southeaster knocks down trees, posts, street lights. It lifts roofs, snaps tree limbs, whips electric cables. Be careful opening the car door because it'll shear off on you. A flying roof tile crushed somebody's head. Nothing to do but huddle inside, and, in the warm intimacy of every house, every apartment, every pre-fab hut, every shack, wait and wait while listening to the echoes of a metal sheet flying, a trunk cracking apart, windows shattering, those temblors that seem to let up for a moment but then return with renewed force. It's hard to sleep at night with that racket going on. The weather alert continues on TV for the four days of the southeaster. Don't let your children go outside, they recommend. As if they were in less danger at home. You just have to look at them when they go back to school: a black-and-blue mark, a bruise, a cast. My mom will get mad if I tell you, señorita.

Who doesn't remember the Kennedys when they were young? The fights would always break out at a dance, a party at the German Club or at the Pink Panther, the whorehouse that preceded the Tropicana. The reason was invariably some broad. Julián, always the sloppy drunk. Braulio, always the instigator. Alejo, always the quiet one: his distant manner hid a calculating personality. Never expose your underbelly unless necessary. Braulio was the one who provoked, attacked and started throwing punches. Julián followed. And just as his buddies were divvying things up, Alejo intervened to cover their backs. When the brawl ended his pals looked like they had come from Thermopylae. Alejo, imperturbable, kept his cool and appeared to be the winner, as if it had been his gaze alone that determined the result of the battle. All of that was twenty years ago, but to him it feels like yesterday. Now there's Julián, blinded by Adriana. If she were his wife, Alejo would have stopped her in her tracks long ago. And then there's Braulio, back and forth with that twisted gait of his, stinking of alcohol, unbearable, because Mimí, the boutique clerk he's been banging for a while now, dumped him this afternoon, leaving him with a boner, her hysterical, sick way of controlling him, making him hysterical, and then Braulio has no choice but to get it out of his system any way he can, so he usually goes to El Atlético to hit the punching bag. He doesn't even change clothes. He puts on his gloves and hits the bag. But after hitting it drunk for ten minutes, he falls over, unconscious. And they call Alejo. At El Atlético they fear a heart attack. Weeds never die, says Alejo.

Exclusive interview with Anita López for El Vocero. *Our middle school language teacher and a local militant of the Radical Party presented a project for stimulating our youth at the Forum for a Non-Violent Villa:*

In the classroom you see children who are terribly distraught, and if they're afraid, they obey. If they're not, they lose control. But I don't work from the perspective of fear; I try to generate other methods instead by admitting that the children aren't enjoying school because they're over-loaded with aggression. Minor details end up leading to highly violent situations. Here at our school at the beginning of the year, one boy knifed a classmate. That's why we have proposed to create workshops that stimulate reflection. In the first place, the kids are so accustomed to violence that it doesn't bother them. Being beaten is a part of their lives. But when you encourage them to reflect, they realize that no one has fun by attacking or being attacked. What I see is that the kids who resort to violence in

school are those who suffer from it at home, and logically they reproduce
the same behavior in the educational arena. Also, the kids are very hooked
on consumerism. Whatever they can't get legally, they want to get through
illegal channels. A child sees nice things on TV that he might want to have,
and he sees his father working like a slave just to bring home a paycheck.
There's also another factor to consider: you can't make a child understand
that he should follow a moral path when he hasn't got a chance of entering
the work force. A first step in this project is to promote music. And so today
we're going to present a modern musical group made up of three students
from our dear institution, this middle school. And we're committed to the
development of these young artists: "The Skinheads."

My Dears:

   It would have been in bad taste to leave without saying goodbye.
That's why, before I go to my death, I am writing you these lines. I
don't want you to feel that I'm leaving because of you. Nor because of
anything stupid I did. Things weren't so bad with you, surrounded
by affection and good feelings. But I was as bored then as I am now,
as I write you this letter. There's nothing more boring than explaining why one fine day a person makes up his mind to leave. One
should just leave, and *chau*. But I don't want my decision to cause you
remorse. When I brought you to the Villa to live, I thought the scenery would lift my spirits. Since I didn't want to leave your mom alone
with you still being so young, I couldn't make the decision I've now
made and I just put up with the situation. Now that you're grown up
and can manage on your own, I'm leaving you the business and the
two limos. There's also money left in the account at Banco Provincia,
which I'd like you to use to pay for my grandchildren's education. For
quite a while now, all my days have been the same. Every day the
same as the one before. Tomorrow will be the same as next Tuesday.
As boring as staring at the sea. One wave follows another. You might
argue that not all waves are the same, that no two waves are identical. And even though you may be right, ask yourselves how long you

can look at the same spectacle. If it was as wonderful as the people who go and see it claim, they'd stay here their whole lives long. But no, there comes a time when a person gets bored, stands up, and leaves. Which is what I'm doing. I ask you not to worry or argue or blame one another. Understand that one day you'll stop missing me. Because missing someone can also get boring. And going to the cemetery. So throw my ashes into the sea, which is the most practical thing, and *chau*.

> Yours truly,
> Coco

As the scandal of *los abusaditos* spread, as parents kept patrolling the Villa in their 4x4s and summoned the media—there were quite a few who advocated castration or lynching, or even both at once—Alejo left his office one morning with some files, climbed into his Audi and took off full speed toward Dolores—people said—to use his influence to expedite the investigation, and we all thought his concern about the case and quest for justice were authentic, because Alejo might be a lowlife, but even a lowlife is moved at the sight of innocence violated. That's what people said. That's what we thought. That was the reason for his silent, urgent trip to the DA's office in Dolores. But Alejo didn't stop in Dolores; he continued on to La Plata.

On Saturday afternoon there was a gunfight between members of two notorious families of undesirables operating in the Villa. The incident was reported at Calle 147 and Avenida 4 when family members exchanged insults and gunshots from inside two cars. Long-time enemies, these two families have caused, and continue to cause, outbreaks of violence. This time the confrontation involved a gray Volkswagen Golf and a blue Peugeot 206 that was stopped by local police when it turned onto Avenida del Mar. Police officers managed to subdue the attackers, including two men, a woman, and a minor. From inside the vehicle police confiscated a 9-mm pistol stolen right from Mar del Plata, 11 caliber cartridges, a walkie-talkie, cell phones, and marijuana. Those arrested are all residents of our Villa, and all have criminal records.

Our Villa, our dear Villa, the place where nature has a place, as the Municipal Tourism Board ads say, our Villa, with its forest, its poplar groves, its sea, terrain prized by ecologists, those defenders of all things green, because here nobody dares chop down a tree without a city permit, our Villa was now falling into disrepute due to the media smear campaign, and the sooner the case of *los abusaditos* at the most elite school, Nuestra Señora del Mar, was resolved, the sooner it was taken care of, the better for everyone because it could end up ruining the tourist season. That's why we were waiting for Alejo, in his high-speed, hush-hush journey to La Plata, to push the paperwork through. But that didn't happen. Because Alejo's urgency had to do with approval of the construction of Dobroslav's towers in the heart of the forest, which of course meant cutting down trees, bribing municipal officials, and to hell with ecology. He bribed two or three bigwigs. And he returned with approval for Dobroslav's project, which he had started some time ago. One more business venture for the Kennedys, like I told you: Julián, at City Hall, had drawn up the specs, and Braulio, from the real estate office, took care of selling the half-built super-apartments.

And yes, while all of us were searching for the guilty parties, and parents were on the hunt in their 4x4s, while local authorities and upstanding institutions affected indignation, Alejo (no fool, he), instead of expediting the investigation of the case, got approval of the specs for Paradise Towers.

Our power brokers are opposed to even considering the idea that our myth of origin also has to do with the wild boars that inhabit the area. They prefer a different version of the story: it was no accident, they say, that the priest Thomas Falkner, who ran around here when it was all swamplands, baptized it The Land of Storks. If it's true that storks bring babies into this world, it's a shame those poor kids drop to earth only to be butt-fucked by wild boars.

Me, I've never cared about politics. Don't bug me with power, man. In the seventies they talked a lot about socialism, but communes were the thing. I spent five years in a commune in El Bolsón. Everything was shared there. But it wasn't like they said, endless orgies. Orgies are for the desperate middle class. No, our thing was just the opposite: gentleness. Our thing was experimentation. If you've read *The Teachings of Don Juan*, you'll get what I mean. *The Yagé Letters*, the interior of your mind. I saw what's inside me, you know. *The Doors of Perception,* that kind of thing, know what I mean? In those days I concentrated a lot. Taoism, the path. I went Tao all the way. And the whole time I went without sex. A purification. Because that could also be part of it. But in the end I quit because all extremes are bad. At El Bolsón I fell in love with Lila. We got pregnant. We liked the idea of a Mapuche childbirth. But our folks wanted to be there. Lila's parents sent us a money order. Mine lent us a small apartment in Plaza San Martín. We started selling our crafts to some guys in Galería del Este. City life didn't suit me. Those were the black days of the *Proceso*. Lila and I used to love rolling a joint and taking Ayelén out at night in her little carriage to the area where the banks are. We used to fantasize about all the cash in those deserted fortresses and how people went crazy over the dark energy of the dollar. Early one morning, I remember, a green Falcon came for us. *Give peace a chance,* we sang to them. And it was cool; the dudes went on their way. But I nearly shit my pants. Lila didn't want to go back to El Bolsón. Ayelén would be too far from her grandparents, she said. We were getting bitter. And one night the pigs nabbed us. Lila's old man and old lady had ratted us out. The cops went straight for the pot. They picked me up. They left Lila and our baby girl alone. For two years I hung in. When I got out I looked like Gandhi. But

I didn't lose my positive energy, and even though Lila was hooked up with a guy from Silo, I told her we could start over again here in the Villa if she wanted. And we came here. More than thirty years here with the crafts booth. But not all three of us. Because whenever Ayelén went to visit her grandparents, they brainwashed her. I want to go to the city, she told us. There was no way to convince her. And she went to Buenos Aires. A Citibank yuppie. According to Lila it wasn't so much the grandparents as those nights in the baby carriage around the area where the banks were that hooked Ayelén. What kind of incense do you want?

At thirty-four Anita López has everything she needs to be happy, they say. A language teacher at our Villa's middle school for more than fifteen years, a secure job, as secure as her marriage to Campas, the owner of Campas Plumbing Supplies. And one hell of a chalet in Pinar del Norte.

When that business of the swastika on The Skinheads' drums happened, it drove Campas crazy that Anita might have been involved in the matter. They're my students and they're kids, Anita said. To anybody who wanted to listen, Anita said: I don't think we should pay too much attention to the issue. They're kids—they think one way today and tomorrow another. When I was a girl in La Plata, I might have been part of the Night of the Pencils, but here I am. We all grow up. Times change.

The Skinheads—Tobi Mendaña, Melanie Ortiz, and Lucas Iriarte—had always been troublemakers, with attention and behavior problems. Unmanageable for all the teachers except Anita. Because, convinced that arts education could save those kids condemned to drugs, self-destruction, and marginality, she started out by giving them Homer and didn't stop till Artaud. Children of broken families, raised with domestic violence, alcohol and drugs, regarded with suspicion by their middle school teachers, the three youngsters astonished the Villa the night they introduced themselves as a band, giving a concert at Plaza 25 de Mayo. For Anita, the Skinheads' presentation felt like a personal triumph. But the lyrics nearly ended up costing her her job. She had to explain the swastika on Lucas's drum set. Everyone knows I'm from a Radical Party family, Anita later defended herself in a statement to *El Vocero*. We've got to salvage whatever's of value in what these kids are expressing. They're children and they're confused, Anita said. Instead of demonizing them we should understand them. According to Anita, it was necessary to look around, to look at the world, at the country, at the Villa, at the families, the whole context.

It would have all gone away that Saturday night in May if the Skinheads hadn't played a new song, "Bolita Bug." And if later, on Monday, a worker from the garden center hadn't discovered an incinerated Bolivian infant in the forest.

Joseph Pilates was a sickly child, which led him to study the human body and devise a method of strengthening it through exercise. Thus, in time he became a great athlete. It was in England where he would begin to develop his method, while being detained in a concentration camp during the First World War due to his German nationality. While working as a nurse, he developed a method to improve other detainees' health through exercise. For the weaker and sicker patients he devised a system of pulleys and cords over the beds in order to exercise muscles, the origin of some of the machinery he later invented, like the reformer, the trapeze, the chair, and the barrel. In time he would develop a large repertoire of exercises to be carried out on this equipment, along with others that could simply be practiced on the floor, on a cushioned pad. Over the years Pilates has evolved, creating new machines, support apparatus and ways of utilizing them, although the essence is retained by all of them. Other systems have been developed, combining different disciplines, like Yogalates, which incorporates yoga and Pilates, or Chi-Pilates, which introduces the concept of chi or vital energy, characteristic of traditional Chinese medicine, into the method. Very close to you, in our Villa, Adriana de Quirós will soon be offering you the best in Pilates at her studio on Avenida del Mar and Alameda 306. Telephone 416089.

For a life more your own.

Although there isn't any proof to implicate them, no one can get it out of our heads that they, those snobby upper-class kids, were the ones who burned the Bolita baby, the one that was found half-buried in the forest. If the baby's parents didn't file a formal complaint it's because they're undocumented. Besides, who cares what happens to a Bolita, even if it's a burned baby. Least of all Commissioner Frugone, who's deep in the throes of depression, medicated, a zombie, thinking only that he'll be transferred to another department after the beating he got from the parents of Nuestra Señora.

Nobody paid any attention to that Bolita business because at that same time, federal agents were also snooping around here, searching for a kidnapped businessman connected with the trafficking of ephedrine, which, according to the media, might be located in a hideout along the coast. But let's admit that even if the police don't find proof to incriminate those responsible, that doesn't mean we don't know. Juan Manuel and Matías Quirós, Nico Martínez Gálvez, Facu Sergione, Gonza Calderón, and also, it seems, the Porter twins, all laugh every time the business of the Bolita baby is mentioned. Openly. We even heard Facu Sergione say who gives a damn about a little bug like that. Because Bolitas were bugs. And bugs didn't belong in the Villa. An ecological problem, said Mati Quirós. The planet will be better off with one less Bolita bug, pronounced Gonza Calderón.

Even if we had suspected that sooner or later they would pull something, no one ever thought they'd be capable of roasting a Bolita baby, even though it's not a big deal. Because something serious, I mean really serious, would be, like, kidnapping a blond baby and then setting it on fire.

You want me to tell you about terror? I'll tell you if you like. But then don't say I didn't warn you. Terror isn't so much what might happen as what already has. Or rather, what might happen again. Because you know it can happen again. And the next time will be worse. The next time is always worse. Then, night. You toss and turn in bed. Thought you heard a noise. Your wife sits up; you can hear her frightened breathing. Did you hear that, she asks you. It was the wind. Turn on the light, she asks. No, better not. What time is it. You look at the hands of the clock in the darkness. Almost two-thirty. You wonder if you should get up. The wind. For a long moment nothing can be heard but the wind, bringing the sea closer. Maybe what the two of you heard was the cat jumping in the eaves. No, it wasn't the cat. Let's sleep, you say. She struggles against going back to sleep. It must've been in the kids' room, you say. One of them talking in his sleep. No, it wasn't one of the kids. She's still sitting up in bed. She's terrified. She doesn't need to say so. One hand on her chest, over her heart. After what happened to them, the thing that happened to all of them and could never happen to you until it did, what happened to you, later, when you realized that all those it happened to—and *all* didn't mean just a few, but the whole neighborhood, all of them, I say—it happened to them again. When you think that since it already happened to you, it won't happen again, you relax. Your heartbeat returns to normal. You let yourself slip into the swamp of sleeping pills. And that's when it happens again. And it happens more often than you'd think. Which explains the locks, the gates, the guard dogs. Look: there's not a house without that little yellow sign in front: Property under Surveillance. Security Alarm. Police Patrol. But there's no guarantee it won't happen to you again. A lock can be picked. The gate can be yanked off. The guard dog can be poisoned. And the alarm, between the time it goes off and the patrol car arrives, it's happened to you. What you're thinking now, she's thinking too. Now it's nearly four. Again. So, what was that, she asks. You sit up. What was what, you ask. A bird, you tell her. Warbling. Warbling, she repeats. You hear birds, I hear noises, she says. Now you're both sitting up in bed, in the darkness. Again. Did you hear that, she asks. No, you lie.

It's true that the scandal at Nuestra Señora, that whole brouhaha over *los abusaditos* distracted us from our ecological concerns. What do we, the Greens, who are also defenders of public schools, gain by paying attention to the case and joining the marchers to demand justice? After all, it wasn't our kids who were abused because we don't send them to parochial school. We don't believe in dogma or authoritarianism. We had nothing to gain by being part of that march. In fact, we lost. Because we knew, we always knew, that nothing would come of it. And worst of all, while the entire Villa was outraged by the case of *los abusaditos*, about thirty of them at the time, the town VIPs took advantage of the situation to carry out another huge real estate fraud: they cut down the forest, raised two concrete skyscrapers, and, when we tried to make our voices heard, it was already too late: the plans had been approved, the documents were in order, and Cachito refused to receive us in his government office. We even planned a hunger strike on the sidewalk in front of City Hall. This type of protest worries Cachito. They conspire against the Villa's image, he says. No sooner had we set ourselves up on the sidewalk in front of City Hall, Cachito called us inside. Without losing his typical good-ol' boy smile, he pressured us: if we didn't stop screwing around, he would report the marijuana plots each one of us has at home. Two or three people proposed that we needed to discuss our strongarm tactics. We're counterculture and anti-power. We're not the kind to allow ourselves to be extorted by a corrupt politician. And if we lifted our tactics, if we didn't go on a hunger strike, it was because a polar mass was coming from the southeast and that night we were expecting a massive freeze. Twenty below. Olas FM predicted. Sleet started to fall. Luckily, I keep my plants in a greenhouse at the ideal temperature.

Exclusive interview with The Skinheads:

We Skinheads don't just shave our heads. We also shave off consumerism. What we do is a fusion of reggae with a kind of dark country. Which is what the soundtrack of the Villa would be if it was a film. Reggae and dark country, darker than anything else, is what you feel here in the off-season. The lyrics are Melanie's, they're all Melanie's. Melanie's our muse. "Blood in Your Eye" is the number we get asked to play the most because it's a love song and a song of rage. And it talks about what's happening to us. We're bald as a tribute to Luca: your society turns our stomachs. Because we're skinheads they say we're Nazis: prejudice, like everything else. What we believe is that Hitler had his positive vibe; he wanted to do away with borders and for all of us to be superior. We say the same thing in "Phoenicians," which has our most social lyrics. But basically what matters to us is that the group sounds supercool and the lyrics stick. One that's very popular is "Superior Feelings," which is our opening number. People criticize the swastika on our drums because they don't understand what we're all about: the gammadion is a symbol of energy that comes from India. That's why our dream is to play in Katmandu. In the seventies, when our parents were into the counterculture, we would've picked up a submachine gun. But the weapon of our generation is music. Let the guitar sound like an Uzi.

But after writing up the interview, Dante decides not to publish it. It would just be throwing more fuel on the fire.

We spent several summer vacations here. We've always enjoyed it. The scenery, the forest, the dunes, the beach, and the sea. Edith and I always said that someday, when I retired, when we had enough saved up, we'd come here to live. But that day never came. Till we had no choice but to move. We were pressured by circumstances. Adapting, I mean really adapting, was very hard for us. It's true we didn't arrive at the Villa under the best conditions. And it's also true that no one arrives here a winner, to take over the town, but rather in ruins, looking for a truce if not a getaway. We had a boy with Down syndrome, Felipito. And Edith was getting over cancer. I quit the Bank. We sold the house we had in Almagro. And so we settled in the Villa. We rented a small chalet and I converted the car into a private taxi, while Edith set up a kiosk on 3rd. Felipito lent a hand as best he could. But nobody bought from us. Felipito spooked them.

We would get up early, drink some *mates,* and leave the house. After I dropped Edith off at the kiosk with Felipito, I would pick up my first passengers: school kids. Starting my morning off with the kids didn't exactly make for a happy day. Why wasn't Felipito like them, normal, I'd wonder. Why did this misfortune happen to *us?* Why, God? But it did me no good to think about that.

My co-workers at the limo rental agency kept their distance. You're not suited for this, Sergio, the owner, told me one day. Why don't you go find something else, he asked. He didn't offer any other explanations. Things weren't going much better for Edith. She couldn't even make one friend on the block. Our savings were dwindling. Too many kiosks, a cookie vendor told her. You guys are new. And people prefer what's familiar. Besides, you've got the boy with that problem. You should take him to one of those special places.

The neighbors made us feel the same indifference. Our greetings were returned with a grumble or a nod, avoiding us.

Till that morning when the swastika appeared on the side wall. Get out dirty Jews, the painted letters said. That night Edith asked if we could move somewhere else. I was opposed. We're going to fit in here, no matter what it takes. I went to the police station to file a complaint. Pérez is spelled with a "z," the cop behind the counter told me. My last name has no "z." It's an "s." Then you're a Jew. No, I'm not a Jew, I lied. And I challenged him: If you want, I'll show you, bringing my hands to my fly. The cop laughed. It's not necessary, *amigo.* I believe you.

The following Sunday we went to church. They stared at us. As if they knew what had happened at the police station. But they stared at Felipito even more. Christian piety. That Sunday our relationship with the people began to change. They even started to like Felipito; they gave him gifts all the time.

Alejo doesn't recall seeing Julián so despondent since that late April afternoon when, as twelve-year-old boys, they walked into the sea, and before the breakers the claw of an enormous wave swallowed up his friend. It took a few, seemingly eternal, seconds before he spotted him again. Julián slapped and swallowed water. He knew how to swim, but he was paralyzed by fear, and now the current was carrying him away. Although Julián was the most solid of the three, he seemed smaller, dragged off by the undertow. Alejo was about sixty feet away when he noticed that the other one was terrified, had lost his ability to react, and was sinking; he rose to the surface, paddling desperately, only to sink again as if his swimming lessons at the German Club, where he had been designated second-place champion, were of no use whatsoever. Alejo swam toward his friend. The more he stroked against the current, the more it moved against him. Until he was able to reach him. Don't do anything, he said. Leave it to me—just don't do anything. Leave it to me. And that was how he managed to bring him to shore, Julián, standing on the beach, trembling, the sound of his teeth chattering, his tears. I don't know what happened to me, Ale. What matters is that you don't cry, don't let them see you crying. And he clapped him on the back. Julián couldn't stop crying. Stop, Alejo ordered. And gave him a slap. Julián looked around. What worried him most now was no longer fear, but rather that someone might have witnessed the slap. No one was there. Alejo seemed to understand his reaction. There's nobody around, Julián. Nobody saw you drowning; nobody saw the slap. You've got to learn: For some things you've got to learn to be invisible. Then he helped him put on his T-shirt. He slipped an arm around his shoulder. Let's go to your house.

Since then, from that afternoon till this one, the two of them, alone at the law office, Alejo can't recall seeing Julián weak as he is now, on this other afternoon when he tells him about his latest argument with Adriana. She's half crazy over the Pilates studio, which is the only thing that matters to her, to be herself. And there's not enough cash in the world to keep that business going. She won't see reason. And don't even think about the business, she says. She threatens, she threatens me all the time. If we get divorced, Julián, she'll tell; she's prepared to sell us out. She's not interested in an arrangement. Just like we squeeze everybody, she's gonna squeeze us, she says. She's got it into her head. She says if she feels like it, she'll go to the media and report our deals. Starting with Dobroslav's towers. She's out of control. The crazy part is that I'm not even thinking of divorce. I love her. I really love her, you know?

Imagine, blackmailing us, says Alejo. She's crossed the line, bro. The towers? So that's what she told you, Alejo goes on, thoughtfully. And you think she'll have the nerve. Julián nods. And then: You think she'll have the ovaries to risk airing our business in public, Alejo asks. You don't know what Adriana's like when she's out of control. You don't know her, Julián. It's impossible to make her see reason. You don't know Adriana.

We'll have to talk to her, Alejo says. She'll have to understand that we're a family.

How, asks Julián, frightened.

Leave it to me, says Alejo. I'll think of some way to calm her down.

I'll have to swim, he thinks, but doesn't say it. To swim again to save you.

Last Wednesday night police raided a residence in the Circunvalación area. Occupied by a large Chaqueña family of limited means, the dwelling was used as a hideout for a gang of juvenile delinquents who stashed the haul from their robberies there. In addition to plasma TVs and cell phones, fire-arms and top-quality cocaine were found there. The father justified the situation, claiming that he was unemployed and had nine mouths to feed that social services could not provide for adequately.

The scandal of *los abusaditos* was quieting down. And by the time the Greens reacted, it was too late: the Twin Towers, as we began to call Dobroslav's structures, rose above the pine grove. All useless: the demonstration before City Council, the graffiti cursing Dobro-slav the builder and Cachito the mayor, who had signed off on the project. For a few weeks the whole Villa buzzed with talk of ecology. There was a street meeting, with debates about the effect of concrete and cement on nature. No one mentioned the dead bricklayers at the construction site. And the hippies, so terribly worried about the endangered natural world, didn't mention them either. We're just as much at risk as the snow leopard, said Marzio, the ecologists' leader. Soon humanity will be an endangered species. Look at Chernobyl, someone added. You've got to admit no one pays too much atten-tion to the Greens; they're all artisans, all potheads. Men come and go, but concrete is forever, Dobroslav liked to say, and Fito, stand-ing beside his father in admiration, nodded. Nevertheless, a furious debate erupted in City Council. If tourists are drawn here by our nature, a Radical argued, these masses of concrete are going to kill the goose that lays the golden eggs. There was a proposal by the Humanist Party: Stop the project. The Radicals were opposed: What our Villa needs is affordable housing, roofs for those who've been overlooked. Nature does define us, it's true, Cachito countered, but we can't stop progress. Progress means investment. And with invest-ment we'll give roofs to those who live out in the open.

Dante restricted himself to transcribing. From the front page of *El Vocero*, Dobroslav smiled: Facing the future, read the caption below his photo, the photo of a winner, raising his arm in a victo-rious salute. Real fascist, the Croat's gesture. One night, while we were downing our last whiskeys at Moby's, someone chided Dante: Sellout, he called him. This is what you wrote: Facing the future. Why didn't you caption it Facing the sun, attacked another. Dante didn't flinch. If it pisses you off so much, go and read Walsh. Sooner or later crime takes the form of a public document. Look for the list of the owners of the Towers apartments, he suggested. File a formal complaint and I'll publish it, he said. Let's see which of you has the guts to get involved.

He was right: among the owners there were five Council members, and, of course, Cachito. Quirós Real Estate had allotted apartments to two deputies and three provincial legislators. The investigation was carried out by Marzio of the Green Party. But he didn't get as far as filing a complaint against them. Before that could happen, he received a visit from El Capo Malerba. Afterward, Marzio emerged with a badly bruised face, a broken arm and leg. And a brace on his neck. His Jeep had overturned, the Green later explained. That's what I get for driving stoned, he explained.

And no one ever mentioned the incident again.

Dante doesn't let up with his notes on the abused children. Though elliptically, he works out a way to publish something that has to do with the case he seems to have taken on as a personal matter.

Thinking about Gesell, Dante titled a note of interest published this week in *El Vocero*:

Arnold Lucius Gesell was born in Alma, Wisconsin in 1880, the son of a photographer and a teacher, both interested in the field of education. The fact that he had been able to observe his siblings' growth and learning motivated him from youth to become interested in child development. The Gesell Camera, his creation, was conceived as a dome for observing children's behavior without their being disturbed by the presence of strangers. The Gesell Dome consists of two rooms with a dividing wall in between in which a large, one-way mirror allows an observer in one room to see what is happening in the other, but not vice-versa. Both rooms contain audio and video equipment for recording different experiments. It is frequently used for observing suspects during interrogations and also to ensure the anonymity of witnesses. The camera is considered to be the ideal instrument for taking legal testimony from children. In his research Gesell studied hundreds of children, including Kamala, the case of a feral girl who was raised by wolves near Calcutta. He also carried out investigations with young animals, including monkeys. As a psychologist, Gesell understood the great importance of each of the components of the inheritance-environment relationship in the nature-nurture polemic. He emphasized the importance of not jumping to hasty conclusions regarding specific causes of mental disabilities. He believed that many aspects of human conduct, like temperament, are inheritable. Children and young people in contemporary culture were two obsessions that stimulated his fieldwork. A seminal figure in youth culture in the 40s and 50s, he died in Cambridge, Massachusetts in 1961.

It's been so long since we got together, girls, says Adriana, surprised and happy. Susi and Jackie are smiling too. This gathering at the German Club's café has them all worked up. For a moment they've returned to what they once were: the *enfants terribles* of La Almeja Roja. 'Cause we may be married women, but we haven't lost our spirit, Adriana says. You look fantastic, Jackie tells Susi. Workouts, Susi says. And a balanced diet. Susi regards both of them. And you two, old-timers that keep it up. Hold on, girl, what do you mean old-timers, Adriana asks. She means we were warriors, Jackie laughs. I still am, says Susi. A girl never gives up everything, says Jackie. You always were too much, Susi, says Jackie. And every so often, whenever I can, I go to Mar del Plata by myself, she says, for a quickie, and stops short. And I suppose *you* were born yesterday, Jackie, Susi retorts. I'm the most Kennedy of all, Jackie feigns offense. A real lady. First lady, practically. Let's avoid certain topics, Adriana pleads.

Like what, Susi asks. Marital ones, Adriana says. They sap your energy, she explains.

After the initial outburst of joy and all three talking at once, now there's silence. They look at each other.

This idea of yours for a get-together was so great, Adriana tells Susi. It wasn't my idea, Susi replies, nodding in Jackie's direction. Not mine, either, Jackie says. Sorry to disappoint you, Adri. It was Alejo's idea.

What do you mean, Alejo's, Adriana asks.

And Jackie starts telling her what she has to tell her, that she should stop screwing around and threatening to separate from Braulio and air family business matters, that if she makes a stink, if she opens her mouth, if she even thinks of ratting on the Kennedy business, it's the end of everything. If she needs to set up the Pilates studio to feel like a big shot, she should go right ahead, but stop being so cocky. Because anyone can have an accident on the highway. What if you're driving with the girls, imagine, and your brakes give out. It can happen to anyone.

Adriana can't believe what is coming out of Jackie's mouth. Susi remains silent. She nods. She simply nods. With a little smile, she nods. Then, as if to herself, she remarks: Braulio, as a widower, would be a great catch.

Don't play dumb with us, Adri, says Jackie. We've always been all for one and one for all. We're not just friends, Adri. We're family. If you take this too far, all three of us lose.

What, you've got nothing to say, Susi asks.

Yes, says Adriana.

What, Jackie asks.

I feel like taking up smoking again, says Adriana.

Say what you will about Moure, the veterinarian, but he takes his natural science classes at the middle school very seriously. And he knows how to capture the attention of teenagers. Here's one of his note cards for tomorrow's class:

Bats (scientific name *Chiroptera,* from *chiro,* hand, and *ptero,* wing), usually a symbol of night and nature's mysteries, are mammals whose upper extremities develop like wings. They can fly unlimited distances and are the only animals capable of flying blind at night. They build nests for their young in the hollows of trees or crevices in buildings. Many females give birth in these same areas. Bats have a lifespan of fifteen years or more. The majority subsists on fruit or insects. Attacks on humans are infrequent, but not unheard of. Only three species consume birds, and only the common vampire bat feeds on large mammals, both cattle and human beings. A bat bite is not very harmful in and of itself, but diseases like histoplasmosis, ringworm, Japanese encephalitis, or parasites can be transmitted through the saliva, and because these are not easily detectable they can cause serious damage. The most obvious example is rabies.

If Dicky Garramuño considered it as great a victory that Rosita Müller, the Winterfest Queen, cast her eye on him as it was for him to win the local motocross competition, you have no idea what it meant to him when she got pregnant. Dicky never lacked for girls. Not one broad resisted him. Cigarette girls, whatever. But Rosita was on a different level: the Winterfest Queen, the Claudia Schiffer of our German community. Sublime, Dicky would say. Sublime. Not only that: when he impregnated Rosita, he had such fantasies of having a boy, the continuation of the line. Garramuño has always been an important name in the Villa. Garra Cross, from bicycles to competition motorcycles, with quads in between, is at the entrance to the Villa; you should see the models Dicky displays on the sidewalk: flashy, shiny, gleaming in the sunlight. For motorcycle freaks—and others, too—Garra Cross is one of the most famous businesses in the area. They come from Madariaga and even from Ayacucho and Tandil to buy motorcycles. No kidding, because Dicky earned his reputation from the time he was a little lamb, racing, competition after competition. There's not one province where he hasn't raced.

And he always brought back a cup. No one knows as much about motorcycles as he does. A winner, you might say. But he still needed one thing to be a real winner, a winner with a capital W. And that was being a father. When Rosita and Dicky left the office of Dr. Pausini, the gynecologist at Clínica del Mar, Dicky had tears in his eyes. And Rosita embraced him tenderly and gave him little kisses. You should have seen them. Dicky, slipping his arm around her shoulder and with one hand on her belly. They had left the Harley at the entrance to the Clinic, but they didn't return on the motorcycle. Now you have to take care of yourself, Mamita, Dicky told her. And he called for a limo to take her home.

If, on the one hand, it was joyous news for Dicky, it was a letdown for Rosita. Because now Dicky didn't touch her. Her colleagues at Huerta Accounting Services, Malena the accountant and Tini the secretary thought that what was happening to Dicky was common. A woman gets knocked up and the guy starts sticking it in any hole. But that wasn't the case. For Dicky the pregnancy was heaven-sent. Now fucking became a dirty act. One night at Moby he opened up: the pregnancy had turned him spiritual.

Moure, the veterinarian, told him that going so long without relations would affect his mind. An organ that isn't used, atrophies, he told him. But Dicky was firm in his resolve. Besides, if I penetrate her with a tool like mine, I'll hurt the baby for sure, maybe even deform him. We're going to start attending Mass every Sunday. To pray that the kid comes out whole. You've gotta put some muscle into your spirituality, he said.

We imagined that after his kid, Fede, committed suicide, Rinaldi would never take off his dark glasses. The manager at Banco Nación was transferred to a branch in Patagonia, and Senta, the Montenegrin girl, too, although to a different destination: a branch in Formosa.

One night at Moby somebody said that Rinaldi wouldn't survive his son's death. Dante, with his thirty years' experience writing obituaries, ventured: I'll bet you anything you want the old guy doesn't kill himself.

And we lost.

Within a few months old man Rinaldi brought a supermarket cashier back to the mansion. A little *criolla* from Macedo. She smells like grass after the rain, the old man remarked. A wild perfume.

Deborah the psychologist helped me a lot, old man Rinaldi said. Grief can't last forever. One morning the sun comes out. And you realize that the sun is always there. And you have to take off your dark glasses. The life force.

Nine months later, the new heir to Los Médanos supermarket chain was born. Rinaldi baptized him Federico, like the other one. You should see how happy he is pushing the new Federico along the main street in his carriage.

From the Society pages of *El Vocero*:

The grand opening cocktail party for "Adriana Pilates" was attended by many important public figures of our Villa, including Mayor Alberto Calderón and his wife, Beatriz Marconi. Calderón casually remarked that all the criticism launched against public works under his administration, such as the construction of Paradise Towers and the bidding to lay the new sewer system, are futile maneuvers by the opposition to stymie the Villa's progress. He also declared that he has decided to ignore rumors about corruption in the department run by his planning advisor, Julián Mendicutti. "This might be the best place to discredit those mediocre, resentful voices because this establishment, which is being launched today, is just one more example of the growing pains of a family, the great family that is our community. And now, enough words. Let's put politics aside. I propose a toast to our hostess and wish her all the success she deserves and will certainly achieve in this endeavor."

Moni is fifty-seven, but looks forty. She lives by leasing out an event space which, in the Villa's prehistoric days, was a music hall. She doesn't earn much in rent, but by combining it with what she collects from her literary workshop at Casa de la Cultura, she gets by. Moni doesn't complain. Nobody believes her age, and she can still sing Piaf songs barefoot at a party. Five years ago Moni lost Heiner, a surveyor, one of the first to come to the Villa when the German began to auction off land. Heiner had twenty years on her. And died of cirrhosis. Demián and Paloma, the couple's children, are in Atlanta and Sydney, respectively. It wasn't so much a question of looking for a more placid fate in a less unstable country as of putting some distance between them. Demián was embarrassed that his mother's lovers were younger than he was. Paloma, for her part, never got over the fact that he stole her girlfriend. Even though they earn good money, Demián as an economist and Paloma as a chef, neither one ever returned to the Villa. Not even when Heiner died. They never offered to pay Moni's airfare to visit them, either. They can't forgive me for being so free, Moni thinks this afternoon as she enters the cemetery. She stops at the *Angelitos* section, where the children lie. She observes the graves. She takes notice of the names. Responding to an impulse, she sits down on the lawn. She takes out her notebook and writes a poem: "*Sleep, my Brian / Sleep Ayelén / and Manuel, too / One fell off the dapple horse / AIDS led the other away / and a lung buried the third / The grass sings the* criollito *lullaby / Dead / Heavens, / don't grow bright, / for night is falling.*

Then Moni cries. She realizes something: She's not crying for the dead *criollitos*.

For a baby to be born healthy, with no defects, with all its little fingers and toes, is, despite the advances of science, a divine matter, Dicky tells her. And if you want the miracle to happen, you've got no choice but to go to Mass. Every Sunday. From now on we're going to Mass every Sunday, darling. Rosita couldn't believe her ears. If Dicky ever had a reputation, it was for being a seducer and whoremonger. He'd laid a few of her friends and acquaintances. If she had fallen madly in love with Dicky, she now thought, it was because the two of them made a perfect couple. The Winterfest Queen and the motocross champion. You're very fast, she told him when they started dating. I've been around the track a few times. But with you I'm gonna put on the brakes, baby, he'd promised. Who would've guessed it: Dicky would keep his promise to hit the brakes. And the one to rev her own engine would be Rosita.

This Tuesday police apprehended a 52-year-old man, a Paraguayan national, in possession of two marijuana plots at a residence located at Calle 108 and 115th in La Virgencita. The operation took place as part of the investigation of several robberies, some of which were recorded last year. Although no related evidence was found, the subject was tried on charges of violation of Drug Law 23737, since an envelope containing 60 grams of marijuana packaged for sale was found at the home. Agents from the First Precinct, as well as members of the Department of Investigation and Narcotics Bureau, participated in the arrest.

Things aren't so simple with the nephew, Alejo said. He never said *my* nephew. The nephew, he said. That's what he called Camilo. Using the definite article to establish distance. Even though he screams less, whenever he goes mental, if he doesn't start trembling, he pierces your eardrums with that shriek. Then it passes. But you should see how awful that screaming is: it lodges in your soul and you can't turn it off for days.

According to this Friday's edition of El Vocero:
Last Tuesday at dawn, frightened neighbors called the police after hearing a single gunshot at a home located at Calle 134 between 15th and 16th. Agents arrived in time to save a woman who had attempted suicide with a firearm. In order to protect the victim's identity and her motives for such a dramatic decision, Commissioner Frugone restricted his remarks to

reporting that the victim, a young woman, is an addict who is currently recovering at the local hospital.

You know why we are the way we are. Because there are more houses here with an *I Ching* than a Bible.

I have to tell you about the first time our little girl saw the sea and fainted from the impact. It was during the dictatorship. A big night out the night before. We took the Citroën and went to a movie in Flores and then to a pizzeria. When we got home we could see the whole operation from the corner. I turned the corner on Bacacay, looking for a major avenue. The little one fell asleep in the back seat. She woke to the quiet of the car and the sound of the waves. It was daylight. The little one got out of the car; the sun hit her full in the face. She walked a few steps on the sand. And when she saw the sea, she fainted. Well, that's the story. No more. There can't always be a moral.

Sometimes adolescents irritate and frighten us, and can even give us a heart attack. As they grow and pass through one of the most complex stages of the family relationship, they mire us in helplessness. Approaching their problems from the vantage point of psychotherapy can prevent or free more than one family group from critical situations. Establishing a dialogue with them instead of waiting for them to tell us what's wrong can be quite a challenge. Love and understanding are essential. Teaching them to love and establish satisfactory relationships, allowing them to communicate and, for us adults, learning to listen to them, are some ways to deal with cases that cause anxiety and imbalance. It's crucial to offer them affection, to validate their feelings, and to be aware of their vulnerability. Deborah Miller. Family therapy and harmony. 418061. Mention this ad and receive a free diagnostic consultation. Insurance accepted. Financing available.

Sometimes Cachito wonders not only how he got where he is—such an exalted place—but also how it happened that he, a nice neighborhood boy, a Peronist boy, a Perón Peronist, as he likes to make clear every time he's asked what kind of Peronist he is, without realizing it, gradually gave up his auto shop, started getting involved, aimed high, and was elected mayor. Sometimes he thinks he's living someone else's dream. And when he wakes up, it won't be his anymore; it'll be the other guy's. But, he wonders, is the cost of the dream fulfilled really worth it? A marriage crippled by rancor, a druggie son whom he has to save from the police all the time, he himself a user. When Cachito has these thoughts, when fear slams him up against the wall, his mouth starts to tremble. But he calms down right away by telling himself he needs these thoughts to convince himself that he's not a bad guy. That he's still the mechanic who gave everyone a credit line, the guy always ready to do favors, even if it could be expected that sooner or later those favors would be repaid in kind and turn into votes. Someone who's aware of his sins, they say, is less of a sinner than he seems.

When he can't take it anymore, like now, he consults Alejo, the only one who understands him:

If the Bolitas haven't made a stink about that roasted baby business yet, Alejo reassures him, it's because they're immigrants and most of them are illegals, Cachito. Like at our Speer's construction sites. Besides, let's not kid ourselves, if nothing's happened after all that commotion about *los abusaditos*, nothing's gonna happen because of some barbecued Bolita.

Cachito settles down for a while. But he knows those thoughts will return. More and more often, they return.

On Monday afternoon there was an assault at a private residence located at Calle 133 and Avenida 28. According to police information, two armed individuals knocked at the door of the house. Inside, a meeting of several youths with abundant police records for various crimes was taking place.

One of them, the youngest, only 17 years old, got up and opened the door.
This was followed by a barrage of at least five gunshots, which, miracu-
lously, missed the youth. The minor, a Peruvian national, quite well
known in the neighborhood and with an extensive criminal history, fled
through the back of the house while his friends took refuge nearby. Inves-
tigators suspect that the assault was part of a settling of affairs between
rival gangs of Peruvian and Bolivian immigrants, a confrontation that
could happen in any neighborhood. The event can be related to an episode
of fifteen days ago, when a member of a family with a criminal history was
shot in the leg, producing a wound that seriously affected the groin area.
According to reliable information obtained by El Vocero, *police cannot*
rule out the possibility of similar confrontations in the future.

Rosita Müller, granddaughter of Friedrich Stegman, old Don Friedrich, the man responsible for bringing the first water pumps to the
Villa and later the owner of Stegman Pressurized Pumps. His wife,
Doña Tea, a stunning Austrian who, at age sixty-something, still
has an enviable figure. They had a daughter, Gisela, one of the most
sought-after beauties in the Villa in the 1960s. The family dynasty,
uncontaminated by other immigrant or *criollo* bloodlines, was extended when Gisela, their daughter, married Freddy Müller, the engineer
and director of the Electrical Cooperative. Gisela and Freddy had
Rosita, our Claudia Schiffer, the prettiest little girl, most admired
teenager, and later, when she became a young woman, a beauty whom
the Villa's Aryans crowned Winterfest Queen. Rosita represented the
beauty and superiority of her race. Anyone who knew Doña Tea, her
grandmother, says that Rosita is her spitting image. Somebody, one
of the old Aryans, of whom there are fewer and fewer these days, on
learning that Rosita was going to marry Dicky Garramuño, remarked
that God, if He existed, would be sure to punish that defiling of
blood. In all likelihood the Garramuños, no matter how popular
they may have been in the Villa and in the world of motocross, were
part Gypsy. And everybody knew what the Führer thought of that

sallow race. No argument could convince the old Aryans that Dicky came from a Sevillian grandfather who had mixed his blood with the daughter of Galician grocery store owners from Madariaga. The fact that Dicky was dark-skinned was a warning of how the chosen race that characterized the founding families of the Villa would degenerate. Practically cast into exile, Rosita went to live with Dicky in a chalet in the south. Nonetheless, Dicky would organize the Villa, whether the Müllers liked it or not. The Garramuños, all of them, weren't going to tolerate such a huge insult. The Müllers can suck my dick, said Dicky to anyone he pleased.

On this May afternoon, Rosita walks into the chapel and asks for Father Joaquín. The priest lays his hand on her shoulder and guides her to the confessional. Darkness, silence, lowered voices. It's hard for Rosita to speak. I have erotic dreams, Father, she says. Her cheeks are on fire. I'm pregnant and I have these dreams.

Tell me, says the voice of the priest. Tell me everything.

That week, after another Bolivian flew off a scaffold at Dobroslav's construction site, Moni went to see Dante so that he might publish her poem: *Scaffold*, she titled it. It went like this: *They die on scaffolds / They die flying / Like condors*. You think so, Dante asked her. What do you have against protest poetry, Moni replied. Nothing, girl. I didn't think it was your style, he said. I'm a nonconformist about so many things, Dante. Publish it and I'll buy you a drink. It tickled Dante to think of the fit Dobroslav would have when he read it. What do you have against poetry, Don Speer, he would say when the Croat showed up to confront him.

One morning Gerardo, the lifeguard, comes back from rowing. He's dragging the kayak when he spots the cormorant. The cormorant is dead. What's a cormorant doing here, he wonders. Gerardo has seen cormorants in Patagonia, but never here. He's fascinated by two rings on its leg. One made of metal, the other plastic. With numbers, he notices. This is an elite cormorant. It must belong to a flock that's being studied. Gerardo picks up the cormorant and runs; he hurries upstairs to his room at Luna Lunera. He wraps it in a Disco bag and pops it in the fridge. Can't let nature spoil, he thinks. Then he calls the Wildlife guys. The Wildlife Department is in charge of the sea lions, seals, and penguins that end up on this beach. They even dealt with a killer whale last winter. But now no one answers. Gerardo tries again at midday. Nothing. Later in the afternoon. Still nothing. He opens the fridge. He looks at the cormorant. He closes the fridge. His heart races; his hands sweat. By nightfall he can't stand it anymore. The sky is red. A storm is coming. Then it occurs to him to call Moure, the veterinarian. We've got to save the planet, Gerardo tells him. Bring it to me, Moure says. Gerardo takes the cormorant out of the fridge, gets on his motorcycle, and races off to the veterinarian. Moure is about to close. However, he tells him, he'll make the sacrifice. He has his contacts. Not to worry, Moure reassures him. With his contacts he'll take care of the matter.

Gerardo hops back on his cycle. Lightning's already started. He needs a beer, he tells himself. And speeds toward Moby.

Moure plucks the cormorant. The first thunderbolts. He's never tried it, he tells himself. It can't be too different from duck, he thinks. That night he invites Yoli, the beautician, Josema the barber's ex, to dinner. Rain and white wine: a perfect evening.

At last the Müllers had to give in, and even though they had just barely started acknowledging the Garramuños, there was a wedding, after all. After a few whiskeys, Alejo, the guest of honor (who could hardly fail to be present at such an event), Alejo, as I was saying, opening his heart among friends, said in an aside: If you manage the whole Villa's dirty dealings, from the wheeling and dealing of the co-ops and arrangements with the police to lines of succession and divorces, a zipped lip and a poker face are as essential as a suit and tie. Make friends with the judge, Alejo is now saying, no longer Dr.

Quirós but Alejo, and by calling him Alejo they not only feel like big shots, but also safe, protected. Patriarchal, that smile of his as he considers the wedding crashers. That smile, half good ol' boy and half cunning fox, legacy of the late Don Evaristo. Who doesn't like acting important just because he's a friend of one of the Villa's VIPs, Alejo remarks. It happens everywhere; it happens here. And the wedding crasher also feels like a proprietor; he imitates the bosses' attitudes. How many are there around us who talk like hicks, like ranchers, act like snobs when they're really just a bunch of pathetic nobodies.

Alejo always boasts of telling it like it is: Because those of us who are conservatives don't have to go around hiding it. We walk with our heads held high. Just because human rights may be in style, it's not going to change history. Go to court and see if some human rights lefty will get a kid off if he's a juvie thug. I'd like to see what you'd do without a right wing friend in this world.

You can see Rosita's baby bump, someone says, in a louder-than-appropriate voice. And we give him the elbow.

And when the bride and groom start making the rounds of tables, greeting their guests, we change the subject.

The prettiest girls are of noble birth, Alejo says. He says it before giving the bride a kiss.

She'll be a great breeder, Alejo says. I could always tell by her rump.

We were about to ask him if, in addition to the groom, he hasn't boned her, too. But there are times when knowing too much is dangerous.

Anita wakes up at dawn. She dreamed of a Bolivian baby crying in her arms. She couldn't find a way to make him go to sleep. Suddenly she couldn't take it anymore. She grabbed the baby by the feet and started to knock his head against the wall. Then she woke up. And now, moving around the kitchen, she thinks she can still hear the baby crying. She goes out into the night. The cold of winter, the starry sky. She stays out for a while looking at the stars. Then she goes inside.

She takes a Valium. She goes to bed. Every night, the same thing.

Mabel, the teller at Banco Provincia, wife of Mario Pertuzzi of Electromar, wasn't pregnant when she and Daniel became lovers. When the pregnancy became impossible to hide, they kept on meeting. They met at her house or at his real estate office. Elvira, his wife, didn't suspect anything—least of all her best friend. All Elvira's tests came out negative. And sometimes envy ripped her apart. Why is it she can have one and not me, she said to herself. And she concealed her bitterness by intensifying the relationship between the two couples. When all four of them got together for their Sunday *asados*, Mabel and Daniel touched one another under the table. And if they sometimes ended up alone in a corner, Mabel took advantage of the opportunity to rub his cock and Daniel to lick her nipples. Meanwhile Elvira and Mario chatted about movies.

Marianito was born in June. And Elvira got pregnant in July. So Elvira could, after all, Daniel rejoiced. Now the two couples were more alike and closer than ever. What Daniel didn't know was that it was Mario who had impregnated his wife. Don't ask me how Mabel found out. The fact is that, instead of a scandal or separations—fuel for gossip—Mabel proposed a civilized arrangement that everyone could live with. To become swingers. The thing is that Mabel, in addition to being a great reader, has always been very modern.

Who knows how long the arrangement will last. They don't exactly look unhappy. The kids will grow up together, Mabel says. Like brothers, says Elvira.

Milena arrived for winter vacation. Her mother had taken her to Retiro Station, put her on the bus, and walked her to her seat. She should have gone with her, she blamed herself. She doubted Pablo had stopped drinking. And it wouldn't have been a surprise if he forgot to meet the child at the Villa terminal.

But Pablo was there, waiting for her. Walking around and around the bus station in the afternoon sun. Bathed, perfumed, clean clothing. He'd cut himself shaving. His hands felt cold, clammy, and frozen. He hadn't seen his daughter in two years. She was almost six now.

For the two weeks that the little girl stayed with him in the cabin he'd borrowed, he took her on outings in the forest, strolls along the beach, horseback riding through the dunes. They explored, they went for walks, and they rode horses in silence. When he tried to make conversation, the child answered in monosyllables. He bought her a storybook. He read it to her every night, again and again, every night. And those were the only words he exchanged with her. He missed alcohol the most when the child was sleeping. But he could take it. Two weeks. He'd never imagined that two weeks could last so long. Until the night before her departure, when the child asked him, What're you thinking about, Pa? Nothing, sweetheart, he replied. He couldn't say that the only thing he'd been waiting for the last few days and nights was for her to return to her mother. Go to sleep, my love, he said. He kissed her on the forehead.

It was safer for the child to go home in the daytime, his ex had told him. And now that the bus is starting to leave the terminal behind, he glances at his watch. He has the whole day ahead of him. The whole week. The whole month. The whole year. Until, with any luck, in summer, if Pablo is still going to school, his ex might let the little girl come back. But there's still plenty of time. He walks into the bar.

All of your sexual preferences, including those that seem the strangest, are the result of experiences that happen from birth through the age of four. During this period the so-called erotic map is drawn, on which all pleasurable behaviors, emotions, and objects surrounding the child are inscribed. Later these behaviors become latent, with education activating some and

repressing others. The repressed behaviors can pass into unconscious obliv-
ion, only to re-emerge with great force as something desired but forbidden,
something we call morbidity. Or they can become compulsive behaviors
associated with anxiety, fear, shame, and guilt. Sexual fantasy is therapy's
best ally because the impossibility of fantasizing, that is, of giving oneself
permission, is precisely the nucleus of the problem. Working with fantasy,
no matter how aberrant, and accepting as natural those behaviors that are
considered perversions, eliminates guilt and thus the associated morbidity.
Deborah Miller, MA, 418061, Psychoastroanalysis. Mention this ad and
receive a free initial consultation.

Adrián, alias Condorito, is a shadow running along the streets of
sand. Every so often a dog crosses his path. Snapping. He can't catch
his breath. A stabbing pain in his chest. He can't stop. Although
he can't hear the police siren nearby, he doesn't stop. Now there are
several dogs charging after him. He still has a few bullets left, but
he can't shoot at the dogs. The discharges will be heard all through
the neighborhood. And then the siren will start again. He must get
rid of the weapon, the kid thinks. He must throw it away. Without a
weapon, there's no proof against him. But he's afraid to go unarmed.
The cops are practically on top of him. But the cops are the least
of his problems. The Bolitas are more fucked up. The last one to
be offed by the Bolitas was the Worm. They found him with his
balls stuffed in his mouth, in the garbage dump on Circunvalación.
Adrián manages to get the dogs off him, but when he turns onto the
avenue, he sees the patrol cars. As if he'd been looking for the police,
like in a dream where you try to do one thing and it turns out to be
another. He's blinded by the headlights. They aim at him. He raises
his hands. But they shoot him anyway. The shots ring out, enclosed
between the walls in the Pinar del Norte night. A policeman squats
down, verifies that the kid is dead. He gropes for the pistol in his
waistband, points at the sky, shoots. Twice, he shoots. Then he sticks
it in the corpse's hand. Case closed.

Tell me what doesn't sag at this age, *gorda*. Ass, boobs, everything. At our age the only thing that rises are the gums. The worst is when you realize that things sag on them, too, the guys. If they need Viagra, you need something more than enthusiasm. Everything sags, everything. No matter how many boob jobs you get, don't think you're gonna be the same. All that surrounds your boobs are you and the years. The only option you've got left is to go around like the Duchess. Every Saturday she goes out to drink and pick up some kid. She's no fool, that Duchess. She never leaves the kid more than a hundred peso bill under the pillow. For services rendered.

According to statistics, the number of residents hovers around twenty thousand souls. Many live along the boulevard, far from the beach. Around there you can also find another kind of villa: a *villa miseria*, the slums. On both sides of downtown, more silent chalets. The thud of a poorly secured shutter. A bark. Because what you see most now are skinny dogs sniffing around in garbage cans. A random seagull. You can hear your own footsteps on the sand.

And if walking in the south, by the dock, offers nothing but low-slung, unmatched structures, alternating with apartment buildings, the north at least maintains the charm of the forest, warbling hidden in the foliage that spills over the gabled roofs, evoking an Alpine construction, although, every so often, interspersed, a pretentious California-style residence can be seen, exuding sweet money and nouveaux riches.

In summer, when the season starts heating up, nearly a million tourists pass through the Villa. Then it's impossible to have a long conversation with the locals. Each one immersed in his business. On the other hand, now, in winter, though the days are shorter, they seem eternal.

And no, nobody likes eternity. I don't want to end up frozen like Walt Disney. All my life I've preferred summer.

It was a crack of lightning. Don't tell me it wasn't a crack of lightning. And it changed many people's lives. You may say that the idiots who ran out of the asylum were cracked to begin with, but no. Not possessed, either. They saw the light. Lots of them saw the light here. And you can tell, you can sense it. It's enough to see the gleam in their eyes.

I'm more than five months along, Father, Rosita whispers in the confessional. I'm burning up, but Dicky doesn't want to do it. He says it's not right. So then I have these dreams. Rosita goes around and around, she can't find the words and when she does, she holds back. Penis, she says. Vagina, she says. Anus, she says. Sperm, she says. As she gets caught up in the telling, a flush of heat ignites her and she doesn't care anymore, she can't contain herself, and she utters cock, cunt, asshole, cum, he rubs it against her, she dreams, and he jerks himself off, she dreams that she likes to stick a finger in her ass when his cock is inside her cunt, then she dreams that another cock is entering her, she's dripping, she says. I'm all wet, Father. Right now I'm dripping. From the other side, silence. Rosita thinks she can hear Father Joaquín breathing. The thing is, I love my husband, Father. I love him. I really love him. The silence inhibits her. There's movement on the other side. The Father peeks out. He's grabbing his hard-on. Rosita brings it to her mouth.

They say Condorito was whacked by the Peruvians from Mar de las Pampas, who were out for his blood. They murdered him. No, don't say we cops didn't do anything. We do what we can, what's within our reach. Never let it be said we don't do anything. I'd like to see what you guys would do with three mobile units to patrol the whole Villa. It's a sure thing we'll find the responsible parties, for sure, because we use intelligence. But then they let 'em go. You put those kids in jail and wham, they're right back on the street. It's our job to make sure they comply with whatever they promised the judge. We keep them under surveillance. And when we go after them at home in El Monte or La Virgencita, there they are, wasted. Of course they're gonna commit offenses again. Because these types are already hardened criminals. A firm hand, that's what people want from us. But with all this human rights business, we're limited. And we're the ones who end up under investigation. They're minors, people say. Unless they resist and use a weapon, we can't eliminate 'em. In the Condorito case, things weren't the way the media said, that we whacked him with no resistance on his part. All we need now is for them to charge us with Condorito's death. We do use intelligence, like I said. And if we were gonna put the weapon in the dead guy's hand, we wouldn't have put it in his right hand, knowing he was a lefty. And that human rights lawyer representing the mother accuses us of executing him. Four shots don't make an execution. Just between us, I wish we *had* done it. But it wasn't us. Let me be honest with you: The Villa will be a better place without Condorito. Luckily, there are honest people on our side. Look at the collection the Rotary took up for the police association. Look what a success it was.

The bit about a round bed, I dunno. Could be. I'm not about to put my hands in the fire for anyone. Least of all for them, Basualdo's girls. Everyone knew them as Basualdo's girls. Clarita, the oldest, must have been around seventy. And Blanca wasn't far behind. In the 70s both of them were on the cover of *People*, remember. They were photographed there, on the beach, where Charlie's bar used to be. Clarita had a thing going with Charlie, but it didn't last long. That was the new wave. Hippies, artists, lefties, lots of Bohos, all got together. Summer ended and Clarita stayed in Bebe's cabin. But later she moved to Schmidt's place. In the spring she hung out at Pepe Regueiro's. She was really something, that Clara was. But Blanquita was no slouch, either. Blanquita arrived in '76, running away, of course. Then they set up the Black Forest, a German sweet shop. Evil tongues claimed that the name came from the fact that they didn't shave their legs. The Villa was a small town in those days. And Basualdo's girls, as refined as they seemed, fucked more than half the town. Not even the Rotarians got a pass. Very freewheeling for those times. The House of Tarts, or the tarts' house, as some called it, fell apart on account of the Rotary women, who made the sign of the cross in their direction. They worked it out so that Banco Provincia would refuse them a loan when they were squeezed for cash. The girls didn't give up: they built a few rooms on the back of their property, nailed up a Rooms Available sign, and rented them out to the kids during high season. Sometimes they didn't even charge them. Suspicious generosity.

Last summer, in bikinis, they inaugurated their new tits. But summer passes in a sigh. And winter came. Suddenly we stopped seeing them. They must have gone on a trip, we thought. Until the neighbors were drawn by music from the chalet. A drizzle was falling. The same song, over and over: "Bye Bye Love." They'd teased their hair. Dressed in miniskirts and flats, like in the 60s, there they were. Lying in the round bed. They wore that Valium smile.

It really happened: Gálvez the sculptor, the one who comes every winter, told Dante about it in an interview. And Dante verified it later with one of the artist's daughters. One fine day he rounded up his wife and all his kids and told them he didn't want to be a father anymore, that he was giving up his relationship, charge, title, or whatever you want to call it. He had enough problems being a father to his creations. Around eight boys and girls, he had. None of them was more than fifteen when the father announced his decision. And he up and moved. What nerve. Because after that he devoted himself to the bottle and didn't even make one more fucking piece of pottery. Maybe if he'd been Henry Moore, the family would have forgiven him.

One of the pleasures Dante offers us every so often on the back page of *El Vocero*:

Our neighbors in the Villa are accustomed to spending lots of time, even months, without going near the beach, but those who do can enjoy the solitary pleasure of the magnificent, unparalleled landscape offered by living in this place. Tuesday afternoon: In addition to the unexpected mid-May heat wave and the vision of a calm sea, one could also spot a giant orca. The splendid marine animal was swimming placidly only three hundred feet from shore, heading south. Glorious, my friends.

This morning Alejo called Don Carneiro to his office and told him he needed to take care of a transaction. Those government properties beyond Mar de las Pampas, he said. Trespassers. He gave no further explanations. Don Carneiro knew what Alejo expected of him. The office has the paperwork for the assignment of lots, Alejo told him. We can't lose that land. I need your help, Don Carneiro. A simple transaction. Alejo emulates his deceased father's ways when he gives an order. He doesn't order. It seems like he's asking a favor. When Alejo asks him to take care of a transaction, Don Carneiro is transported back to the old days.

At your service, Don Carneiro says.

And now, Don Carneiro and Gancedo, the two of them in the darkness, the lights of their 4x4s extinguished. They remain silent. Gancedo lights a cigarette. And Don Carneiro asks him to put that thing out. He quit smoking long ago. Gancedo obeys. He rolls down the window and tosses the cigarette out. For a few seconds the chill invades the vehicle. Don Carneiro coughs, annoyed. There, in front of them, about sixty feet away, shadows move in the night. The structure is a house, half wood and half metal sheeting. The sooner they finish this business, the sooner he'll get back home. It's not a night for being outdoors.

A flame lights up the flank of the house, then the fire spreads. Now the shadows are running toward the 4x4. There are two of those shadows. Two men. Their silhouettes are outlined against the glow of the flames surrounding the house, climbing. The two shadows, the two men, climb into the 4x4. They stink of gasoline.

Soon the flames will consume everything. Gancedo is nervous. He doesn't like this situation that Don Carneiro calls a transaction. He hopes the Bolivians will wake up and get out once and for all. Imagine if they stay there.

The first to leave the house is the woman. She emerges with a baby in her arms and another holding her hand. Then the man. With another baby in his arms.

The 4x4 pulls away, leaving the fire, the screams, the children's crying behind.

End of transaction.

They say that during the days and nights when armed parents patrolled the Villa, the mothers, for their part, wanted to find out what had become of the kindergarten teachers. Alejo, in turn, kept mum and headed for the courts in Dolores. He was going there to put pressure on the DA's office, people said. You don't screw around with Quirós. He hadn't participated in the beating that the parents gave the priest. Neither did he go to his desk and pull out the 3.57 that the employees at his law office had given him for his birthday. From his stepfather, Don Evaristo, Quirós had suckled the cold blood that allows him to manage murky affairs like this without losing control. The case exploded in the media, and the news, spreading through the entire country, splashed on us. Let's agree: that kind of shit stains us, and we'll pay the consequences when high season comes around. What a lovely image of the Villa with all this, he told Dante. Don't give more play to the business at Nuestra Señora. Let's hope we can still have a summer season.

Later, as days and weeks, and even months, went by, the investigation began to stall. At this point the archbishop had removed the church authorities from the school. There were two new kindergarten teachers. If parents were still sending their kids to that school it wasn't just because they hadn't found openings elsewhere. They had to admit it: Nuestra Señora, despite what happened, had always been a reputable institution attended by the children of the Villa's finest folk. But it wasn't just the power of the Church that covered everything up. It seems that, contrary to what was said at first, Alejo didn't go to Dolores to expedite the case, but rather to bury it. And afterward he continued on to La Plata to get the paperwork approved for Paradise Towers. Paperwork: the thing that turned him on the most. Confidential; I got it from Marta, Don Gauna's daughter, who's been a secretary at the courthouse in Dolores for years. It's just that in the long run, scandals like the one at Nuestra Señora end up tainting us all and can bring the season down.

Massage therapy can change your life. The theoretical portion offers excellent images and instructive explanations of the fundamentals of massage therapy techniques. The content includes: Massage therapy and its concepts. Back massage. Lower extremities. Shoulder, thorax, and the cervicothoracic area. Esthetic and sports massage. Injuries. Massage therapy for common illnesses. Special massage therapy techniques: traditional Chinese medicine, Shiatsu, acupuncture, anesthesia, and pain relief through acupuncture. Acupuncture for pain management. Graphic atlas of acupuncture. Auriculotherapy. Lymphatic drainage. Bach Flowers. Osteopathic studies. Sacroiliac articulation, pelvis. Treatments: cervical, dorsal, and lumbar spine. Mitchell's sacral techniques: semi-direct techniques. Chiromassage. Reflexology. Reiki. Plus relaxing music for massage on MP3s, with a two-hour DVD in Spanish that you can watch at home.

For more information contact: Deborah Miller, MA Tel. 418061.

If my life was a movie, my old man would be a featured actor, an important one who only makes a cameo appearance, probably toward the end. Listen, he was absent from my life for years, and when he finally shows up, it's because Mariano, my ex, got a bug up his ass and then he runs off to the cabin to rescue Camila. Rescue is the word he used. I was a druggie, he said, and a whore like my mother. Don't you call my mother a whore, I told him. I didn't exactly pick your mother up in a convent, he told me. I'm taking Camila. I objected; of course I objected. I even picked up the revolver. First I aimed at him. He ignored me. Then I went, like, crazy. Said if he took Camila I'd kill myself. That Camila was all I had in the world. That he couldn't leave me all alone. He picked up the baby and took her out to the car. He had left the motor running. I fired a shot at the ceiling. That piece of shit didn't turn back even out of curiosity. I fired again. And then I heard the car pull away and disappear down the boulevard. What pissed me off most was that he knew I wouldn't have the guts to kill myself. I didn't even have enough strength left to cry. Lucky thing that afterward I met Trabuco, who brought me to the temple. You don't know how he held me together.

It's been said that during the war there was a transmitter where the Hotel Salzburg stands today. That those lights shimmering in the ocean, not too far away, came from submarines. That they unloaded gold from the Reich and took away false passports for the big shots who would flee, following the rats. That quite a few of them secretly disembarked on this beach. That war criminals were housed in the Villa. Nowadays if you bring up the subject, the one thing you'll be assured of is that the only ones who arrived here, as pioneers, were three shipwrecked sailors from the *Graf Spee*, as Nazified as the guys who died on the *Belgrano* were friends of the junta. Nonetheless, some tourists who were renting at Sarita Günther's house, while going through a locked dresser, came across swastikas, documents, and photos from the camps. According to members of the German Club, it was a pack of lies. And they not only defend Sarita, but also anybody who tries to defame the Villa's origins. It could be argued, however, that Crazy Heinrich, son of the departed Inge, went around with his grandfather Klaus's notebook. Because the grandfather kept a diary where he entered everything he had done during the week. And there, in the diary, they say, there are entries mentioning the transmitter, the submarines, the two gray wolves—as they were called—that later surrendered in Mar del Plata. Since the grandfather had a telescope, too, there are also notes about lights in the night sky, sparks coming closer and moving farther away. If the grandfather planted so many trees, Crazy Heinrich believes, it was to hide us when whatever was going to come from the sky inevitably came. When his relatives locked Heinrich up for a while, after the electroshock treatment, he stopped talking about it. Don't try to find out more, either. If you get the idea to ask, no one will have seen that notebook.

El Vocero publishes the speech given by our mayor Alberto Calderón on May 25:

Your Excellencies Señor Provincial Vice-Governor, Señor Minister of Federal Public Planning, Ladies and Gentlemen of the Honorable City Council, Municipal Authorities, Neighbors from the Industry and Commerce Union, and other public service institutions of our dear Villa: I will be brief.

My dear friends: It seems to me that this national holiday should hold a double reason for us to celebrate. The first, of course, is to honor the memory of those illustrious citizens who left us a moral legacy of civic respect. The second is to celebrate this day with the announcement of a key project, an endeavor that our beloved Villa has desperately needed, a work that will bring credit to us all because it responds to the common need of those of us who value our community and celebrate what it represents, a harmonious community where nature inspires the visionary spirit of our founder, who, following his dreams, designed this reality that is our Villa today. Because that is what we are: a vibrant community that extends its hand in friendship to all visitors, to the tourists who are the lifeblood of our economy. The pioneers, those who were born here, and those who later chose our Villa to stake their place in the world, all know what this great project and its

future outlook signify. Because we all needed it. To the Minister of Plan-
ning, here with us today, we express our thanks for your support in this
simple act, simple like our town, for a project that our Villa, vibrant and
joined in solidarity, looking steadily toward the future, has demanded of
us. I would like to present to all of you, ladies and gentleman, a work that
will bring countless benefits to us and our children, a vital need: the sewer
system.

On sunny winter days Marcos and Alicia drink their *mate* in a restored
area of the cabana rentals. *Tano,* Marcos reads from *El Vocero.* There's
a photo of El Tano. He looks dapper in the photo. Beneath the photo
it says: *It's been one year since you departed this Valley of Tears. You taught*
me to smile. You taught me many things, but you never taught me how
to live without you. I will miss your forever, Alicia. Marcos stares at
her: You didn't sign your married name, *Flaca.* It wasn't necessary,
Alicia replies. Who doesn't know that I'm the widow. And she passes
the *mate* to Marcos: Everybody knows I was his girl. Marcos retorts:
Everybody also says, well, you know what they say. Alicia dares him:
Say it. Tell me what they say. That I poisoned him.

Unemployed, without any possibility of finding a job, Marcos
can't even think about up and moving: leaving the borrowed shack
on the beach, the wife of his dead friend, her jealous outbursts. But
he can't do anything about it. He has to put up with it. And, to top
it all off, now, this notice:

This notice, he says, you put it in the paper to end the suspicions.
But they'll never end.

You suspect, too? Alicia asks him.

You never taught me how to live without you, he reads aloud. And
asks: When I'm gone will you also publish a notice to wipe away
suspicions?

You're thinking of leaving me, Alicia replies. For another woman,
no doubt.

Marcos looks at the thermos, at the *mate*. Last time, Alicia stabbed him in the arm with a fork. Now he's worried she'll stick the metal *bombilla* into him while she's drinking her *mate*.

The same thing might happen to me as to El Tano.

If you're a whoremonger, Alicia says, God will punish you.

And it just so happens that God's a woman and is named Alicia, says Marcos.

Now there's a cold breeze. From the southeast.

A storm's coming, Alicia says. And she points to some dark clouds advancing over the sea. Then she touches her belly.

You think I'm capable of killing the father of my child, she asks.

Marcos is silent.

Some kids were playing hide and seek in the forest when one of them was bitten by a snake. Miraculously the hospital had an antidote. Just what we needed, snakes. Crazy Heinrich, who never stops going on about Indo-European religions and their revelations, offered an interpretation of what happened: the Serpent is the origin of all that's evil, the death of the soul. What happened was a sign. We are damned. Attacks keep occurring. Some say they're cobras. And several others think they hear threatening rattles. But what you hear most are sirens: ambulances come and go along the streets of sand, tunnels of shadow in the night. The hospital phone lines are constantly busy. If you're bitten, the best thing to do is call a taxi to take you directly to the ER, though the ER is overflowing and the three doctors and five nurses can't keep up with it because it's July, too, and wouldn't you know it, bronchiolitis is knocking the kids flat. Evil is among us. We don't know which is more toxic, the snakes or our paranoia.

And then we discover that the one responsible for the snakes was Moure, the veterinarian. He had set up a breeding station behind the campground. *A scientific experiment,* he apologized through *El Vocero.* Crotoxin is an advance in fighting cancer. I'm the victim of a conspiracy by the labs that used the forces of religious mumbo jumbo against scientific progress. I've been the victim of a plot, Moure declared. But the truth is something else altogether: Alerted to the fact that he was about to be inspected, he set the snakes loose in the forest and from there they spread out toward the poplar groves and dunes.

Evil is near, said Crazy Heinrich. There are more and more signs. While we worry about the snakes and keep watching the earth, we're losing sight of heaven.

This Saturday the Volunteer Firefighters rushed to put out a blaze in a chalet at Calle 110 and Avenida 5. Four crews of firefighters battled the flames that completely destroyed the property. When they made their way to the interior of the building, they found the bodies of an elderly married couple, naked and tied, with signs of having been tortured. The bodies also revealed multiple burns. The victims were Manuel Nogeuira, 74, and his wife, Jesusa Puertolas de Nogueira, both originally from Galicia. Initial investigations indicated that the fire was caused by thieves who entered the building searching for money from the sale of a property belonging to the victims. Local police have devoted all their efforts to the investigation. During the week many operations have been carried out and, according to police sources, the criminals, youths from this area, have likely been identified.

When a person dies in childhood, adults weep for the life he'll never live. As if reaching old age were such a great thing. What they don't know is that by dying young, a person comes back, like a flash of lightning, reclaiming what he didn't live, but suddenly, when he sees what he missed, the shock makes him wise up, because we kids are wise, but wisdom doesn't bring us any comfort, and neither does coming back. Why come back, I ask myself. You can't rely on love or passion anymore. Or peace, or rage. Or parents or siblings. Blood, even words, don't matter anymore. Now you're your shadow's partner. And then eternal life is seeing, because from Over There you can see Over Here, you can see everything. All the time. Because now everything is all the time. That's probably the worst part of this life: not sleeping, seeing all the time. And I see, I see everything others don't see. And they don't see because they don't want to. Me, for example, they don't want to see me. But they know I'm here. It's not that I follow them around. It's that they won't let me leave. I can see them mating, giving birth, killing one another. And also, afterward, digesting. Most of them pray I won't appear to them. They miss me, a few of them. I'm everywhere. I'm made of fog and memory. I'm the one who doesn't dare shake off this suffering, and when day breaks, the light blames itself, and the beat goes on. I am justice, revenge. I'm the spark of the southeaster. I swear, you people deserve a rest. But it's not me, it's you people who call me, those who can't rest in peace. And you don't let me sleep a wink.

Our Villa is a generous place, declares Dr. Alejo Quirós in El Vocero. *The Villa has maintained the founder's tradition: it receives anyone who comes here with open arms, without asking them where they come from and what their history is. How many times have we had to put up with insults to our pioneers, how many times have they been accused of a Nazi past? Many. And no one could ever prove a thing. And the spirit of the Villa emerged stronger than ever from these attacks that attempted to stain it. Because what matters is to look ahead and act. In this spirit we have received our Latin American brothers and sisters. It seems to me unfair to blame Anita López and her three students for what happened with the baby from the Andean Highlands. Commissioner Frugone and his people are investigating and will soon find those responsible for that heinous act. I advise the community to keep calm and adopt an adult attitude, not believe in vicious superstitions, and trust in justice. Meanwhile, everything that's being said just clouds our Villa's reputation. To disagree is like saying we're all guilty.*

One morning, who would have imagined it, we see them advancing toward the center of the Villa. First just a few, then several more.

Finally, a crowd. Men, women, kids. Unmistakable, those Bolivians. We never figured their community would be so huge. A compact, silent mass, advancing along the main street. Noiseless, the Bolivians, as they march. Also when they stop in front of City Hall. If there's a murmur of voices, it belongs to the shop owners who step out into the street and the people passing through the downtown area at this hour on their insignificant daily errands, shopping, and so on, because this stealthy mob suddenly renders all urgency and worries irrelevant. From one corner to the next, the entire block is Bolivia. And there they stand, mute, expectant, waiting for Cachito to show his face. But Cachito doesn't come out.

Soon the TV station van arrives and with it reporters from the local radio stations. And they, the Bolivians, remain there, ecstatic, silent. The media can't get a single statement from them. Cachito can't stay holed up in his office anymore. Later someone will relate that he felt dizzy, his heart racing, in a cold sweat. That his blood pressure shot up above 200. A call from Alejo goads him on. A long phone conversation, filled with cursing, finally convinces Cachito. Do something, asshole, Alejo yells at him from the other end of the line. And Cachito steps outside.

We know that no matter how much Cachito shows off, he's no Bruce Willis. But this time he has to summon up his nerve and hit the street. He emerges, pallid and with a smile that he must wipe off his face at once. Some people applaud his gesture. They applaud to boost his courage. But the applause lasts about as long as the flight of a flock of startled seagulls.

One of the Bolivians steps away from the crowd and walks up to Cachito, who extends his hand. The Bolivian doesn't shake it. He hands him a piece of paper with the community's demand: they want a thorough investigation.

Then, just as it appeared, the demonstration recedes. We watch them walk away. And we ask ourselves how far this business will go. If it disturbs us, it's because that Bolivian brat could ruin the season for us. We mustn't forget that. We live from tourism. And tourism means forgetting about problems, pleasure, amusement, quality of life. And now the Bolitas have come to screw things up for us.

Why don't you go back to your fucking country, says Edith. She yells it out in a loud voice. She's full of herself, that Jew is.

Just what we needed. Now they're coming out with the story that El Muertito is a baby that the military swallowed up and dropped from one of those death flights. The tide brought in many dead in those days. And all of them got buried around here. Those that weren't destined to end up in the cemetery wound up buried in the dunes. No use stirring up those times again. No one will bring the dead back to life. Stop screwing around. Decades have gone by. You can't live in the past. You have to keep going. That's what I say, but how can the Villa keep going with so much superstition, because, besides the pastors, believers in El Gauchito Gil and Umbanda, there are the ignorant who believe in ghosts.

It's been said many times, this land once belonged to the wild pigs. And so our myth of origins is one of wild pigs. Which helps to clarify our nature, why we are like we are and why we live as we live. Like pigs. Wild. From which you can conclude that the Villa is a pigsty. Look at what happens if a baby falls into a pigsty. The pigs devour him. This is what's happening now. While I'm telling you this story, the Villa is devouring a little girl, a little boy. At this very moment.

Rebirth is a group of parents who have lost their children to death. Next meeting Sunday, July 17, at the UCI (Union of Commerce and Industry). Admission is free and open to all. Friends, family members, or anyone who has lost a loved one. For information, phone: 464942.

That morning when the Bolivians marched on City Hall, that morning when none of us imagined there could be so many of them in the

Villa, advancing so stealthily that the only thing you could hear were their footsteps, their sneakers and shoes, a clicking on the asphalt of the avenue, a whisper more audible than a shout. That morning, when the Bolivians handed Cachito a piece of paper with a call for justice, demanding an investigation of the murder of the burned baby. That morning Crazy Heinrich had come to the supermarket to buy sardines, bread, and butter. We found out what he was carrying in the supermarket bag because, when he saw them advance, so many Bolitas all together, he froze for a moment and then, startled, he backed up toward the corner of Calle 105 and bolted, and as he ran his plastic bag broke. He barely had time to grab the can of sardines, the bread, and the butter, and keep running toward the campgrounds.

They're among us, we would hear him say. The ones from the Andean Highlands. Those creatures. It's late; they're already among us.

And there would inevitably be one of those drug-addled hippies who seriously believed Crazy Heinrich's argument, a hodgepodge of Indo-European religions and those beliefs in spiritual power, the origin of the swastika and its magnetism. Those stories are fine and dandy, they're all very nice. But from that to believing the Bolitas are Martians, give me a break. They may be different, have their own customs, they're a little enigmatic, but they don't bother anybody. Besides, who do you call when you have to make repairs in the house, fix the bathroom, huh?

Apostles of the Faith, reads the headline in El Vocero. *The traditional ceremony of the Apostle Santiago was well attended by the faithful of our Villa. Although the Bishop of Mar del Plata was not able to make his usual appearance, the procession was led by parish priest Joaquín Azcárate and our mayor, Alberto Cachito Calderón. Many brotherhood members and officers participated in the Mass. At 5 P.M., the incense-burning ceremony took place, followed by astronomical and artistic displays as night began to fall over the Villa. The local church representative thanked the Fiesta's organizing committee and its supporters, especially the mayor's office, for their financial contribution. One noteworthy aspect of the religious ceremony was the presence of our mayor, dressed in the religious garb of the Apostle's devotees, thereby reaffirming the religious vocation of our highest municipal authority.*

Cachito, astonished, regards the pistol Beti is showing him. It's a Beretta. She found it under Gonza's mattress, Beti tells him. Cachito doesn't say a word. He takes the weapon. He sticks it in his waistband and heads for his son's room. He's sleeping, Beti warns him. He came home at dawn, she tells him. Cachito walks into his son's bedroom and locks the door behind him. I'm gonna bust your balls, you little bastard. He lifts him by the hair and yanks him out of bed. He grabs his testicles and squeezes. With all the force of his rage he squeezes his son's testicles. You're going around armed again, asshole. Let me explain, Pa, Gonzalo groans. For protection. I got it for protection. In case any crooks try to break in, he says. But Cachito doesn't loosen his grip.

You think I'm an idiot, Cachito says. That's not a question. I had to bend over for the cops so they wouldn't nab you on drug charges. You know what Frugone cost me on account of your fucking dope. And now this, Cachito says. Cachito shoves him, slaps him, shoves him, corners him, shoves him, hits him, and shoves him again. Gonzalo bounces against the surfboard he hasn't used for ages and clatters to the floor. Gonzalo weeps. He picks up the surfboard to defend himself from the blows. You think a diplomatic claim can be fixed just like that. Because there's a claim over that Bolita business, you dumb asshole. Cachito clams up. For an instant he seems to calm down: it's hard for him to believe that this kid is his son. Then, trying to get hold of himself: You have no idea, asshole. No idea. What it cost me to go from being a mechanic to being somebody. Skipping technical school. I did it. Without a fucking degree. And you know why I always wanted to be somebody, he asks. Because I was ashamed of my old man shoveling cow dung in some German's stable. I always wanted any son of mine to feel proud of his father. But what the fuck do you care, what do you know about shame.

Among the many services offered by the Club Atlético, in addition to the soccer field, basketball, tennis, and paddleball courts, and the gym, they also provide a sauna, a Jacuzzi, and an Olympic-sized pool for children of all ages and all social backgrounds. You should see the littlest ones learning to swim in the pool. If there are so many of them, coming from all the schools, it's because of a proposal by "Harpoon" Salvi and Red García, two veteran lifeguards. Never let it be said that all lifeguards are a bunch of lazy potheads. Harpoon and Red were the ones who initiated the proposal: that all the children in the Villa learn to swim, even the poor kids from La Virgencita and El Monte. And that the City finance the project. Cachito wasn't about to miss out on a project with such a public image and quickly got in touch with its prime movers. Dante gave considerable space to the item in *El Vocero*: a double-page spread, color photos and all. Of course the most important photo was of Cachito, standing on the diving board, Peronificating and evoking the Evita Championships. You should have seen Cachito on opening day, arms flung wide, as if he wanted to scoop up all the kiddies in their bathing suits. Children are the only privileged ones. *Mens sana in corpore sano*, et cetera.

Now, in the middle of winter, while outside the southeaster shakes the trees surrounding the grounds of the Club Atlético, it's a pleasure to see the kids jumping into the heated pool, their shouts, the splashing, little boys' and girls' laughter, the lifeguards, the lifeguards' instructions, teaching them to dive, to play with plastic balls, to swim through a plastic hoop, to reach the deep end.

My son emerges from the pool so happy: he pulls up his goggles and waits for my approval.

Did you see me swimming underwater, he says.

That's what writing is about, I think. Swimming underwater.

You suspect you're depressed. You feel sad, apathetic, desperate, energy-depleted; you have difficulty with memory and concentration. Maybe you're hypersensitive and have lost not only your interest in personal relationships, but also your sexual desire. You read self-help books, consult friends and try to follow their advice, but nothing restores your will. You don't know what to do. Depression is an all-too-common illness and can either have a known cause or be of uncertain origin. And it wears down the brains of the afflicted. The first step in recovering meaning in life is to seek help through psychotherapy.

A person is more than just cognition, conduct, and emotions. Above all, he's a complete being who suffers because along the way he's gotten lost and doesn't know how to find himself. The perspective provided by psychotherapy is essential to create a warm, affective framework that does so much good for someone who's suffering. To accompany, protect, and admire unconditionally are, in and of themselves, curative actions.

Deborah Miller, MA 418061. Mention this ad and receive a discount on your first consultation.

The four of them meet for tea at La Casa Suiza. The four of them: Jackie, Susi, Adriana, and Beti Marconi, who doesn't use her maiden name, but rather her husband's, Calderón. Although they don't consider her a Kennedy, she feels like one. Small kids, small problems, Susi remarks. Big kids, big problems. Jackie corrects her. Ours aren't exactly small, but they're not big, either. They're just tremendous assholes. Beti, for her part, reflects: The thing is, problems, I mean real problems and genuine suffering, you only get from your kids.

More than a friends' get-together, this is a mothers' get-together, Jackie says. And she adds: Thank God we have Alejo, who may be whatever he is, but without a lawyer like him, what would become of us all if something happened with the kids, Jackie says. I remember when we were kids, Susi laughs. To think that we wouldn't even give him the time of day. Remember when we used to go out at night to La Almeja Roja. He had to toss a few bills our way for a blowjob. And now look how far he's come and who he is, Susi says. But admit it, girls, without Cachito, Alejo wouldn't have come so far. And Jackie replies: I could say the same thing. Without Alejo your Cachito would never have become mayor. Susi intervenes: Girls, we're not going to argue about this now. Jackie: You're right. That's not why we get together. Beti relaxes: Okay, let's accept the fact that Alejo and Cachito have been thick as thieves forever. Getting back to the subject, Susi interrupts. What's worrying us now are the kids. The usual pieces of shit in this Villa, the same old envious bunch, says Beti, spread the rumor that our kids are the ones who burned the Bolita in the pine grove.

It's true, the kids are awful. But to accuse them of the Bolita business is too much, Susi says. And Jackie, thoughtfully: This is what we get for giving them everything they want. Now try and stop them. Because they're not kids anymore. Susi: We've got to rein them in. Beti: Cachito scared Gonza. If they arrest him again, this time he won't get him out. It's the fathers, not the mothers, who have to set limits, Susi cuts her off. That's what I told Braulio. They'll end up in reform school. Easy, calm down, says Jackie. Nothing's gonna happen. Like Alejo says, what the kids need is a little discipline. And that's that.

Even in the early days of the Villa, if you laid a German chick, you were somebody. Look at Brunetti the Dago. He fucked Bloch's daughter. And he did all right for himself from the start. Member of the Beer Festival Board of Directors. Now all that's fallen apart. Anyone can fuck a blonde. Even the half-breeds fuck 'em. If you want to be somebody, you have to aim higher, screw an upper-class chick, but watch it: if you knock her up and the family doesn't like you, you might end up in a ditch.

Among those who swear they've seen El Muertito is Moni, our poet. Says she saw him near the cemetery. She was picking wildflowers to spread on the graves in the *Angelitos* section when she saw him, she says. But nobody takes Moni seriously. Because she's a poet, and everybody knows: if she writes those things she writes it's because she's got a screw loose. But it's also because she drinks. She hits the Fernet. Another one who swears he's run across El Muertito is Moure. But ever since Moure made those excuses for spreading snakes around, we all believe him less and less, and soon there'll be no one left to take their cat to the clinic. Then there are the Montenegrins from the farms out past the Aeroclub. They come from the Carpathians, and everybody knows that the legendary Count hung out around there. The Montenegrins talk funny. They call El Muertito *Vrucólaco*, which means vampire.

And there are those who claim that El Muertito is Quirós's orphaned nephew: Camilo. That when he lets out one of those screams you can hear throughout the Villa, he has visions and is transformed.

Imagine, how could the boy not see ghosts. Cami barely escaped being killed. Like I told you: when the army burst into the house after wiping out his parents, with the gunshots still echoing in the air, they heard a baby crying. He was in the closet, wrapped in blankets.

Don't even think of going to Auntie Porter to complain about her twin daughters, the ones from Heaven's Branch Santería, that place beneath the birches, around the corner from the chapel. A local Englishwoman, Auntie Porter, sixtyish, a drunk, although when you get close to her, her breath always smells of mint, always with some gum to cover up her gin breath. No one really knows what became of the parents of those girls that Auntie raised. They say the parents were part of a sect and died in a plane crash in Tibet. They also say that the plane disappeared in the Bermuda Triangle. Anyone who asks the old woman will always hear the same story: Heaven took them. And the twins came from that same heaven, on a flight from Heathrow, where some hippie relatives had put them on a British Airways plane to Ezeiza Airport. And so, as they say, that's how Auntie Porter got them in Buenos Aires, where she lived. The descendant of a whaler who managed to set up a factory in the Falklands, and don't even dream of saying Malvinas instead of Falklands if the subject comes up with Auntie; well, like I was saying, Auntie's father had been a railroad worker when the railroad system was English and worked properly, and out of all that past history, Auntie acquired a modest fortune and was living in a house in Coghlan when those two devils, who, according to her, are angels, descended from heaven. The city wasn't an ideal place to raise those two creatures that the Lord had sent her when she least expected it. A miracle. Or rather, two miracles. A spinster, religious, a believer to the point of hysteria, Auntie was convinced that those two creatures were a gift from heaven. So she sold everything, left the capital, and took them to Dolavon, in Chubut, where she had some cousins. But that Patagonia of chapels and farms soon began to seem inappropriate to her. The twins, at age twelve, had already started causing a commotion below the Welsh boys' belts, and at any moment they would have rolled them in the hay, that is, if they hadn't rolled them already, when Auntie, once more, decided on a change of geography and brought them here, as if this were a piece of paradise. The combination of gin and Scripture can be fatal. The consequences are easy to see. And here we have them. The three of them sometimes tending the Santería store. But the one who's really into that stuff is Auntie. The nieces, once in a blue moon. And when they *do* go, it's with that evil little smile, more appropriate for standing behind the counter of a porn shop.

Like I'm telling you, "heaven" gave its name to that Santería store where the two red-haired, aquamarine-eyed little girls were raised, and it's impossible to tell them apart. They were raised among candles, incense, holy cards, and rosaries. One's called Millicent and the other, Mildred. A Biblical curse. And if you don't think so, let Crazy Heinrich tell you, that is, if he ever can. They drove him even crazier than he was. One rainy afternoon the Porter twins walked into his storage bin, drenched and naked. Imagine Crazy Heinrich seeing that apparition, against a background of thunder and lightning: red-haired adolescents, rain sliding down their little white tits, dripping from their pubic hair. Crazy Heinrich leaped between them and dissolved under the water, disappearing into the forest, howling: *Nein, nein, nein.* He didn't stop till he reached the dock. And if a couple of fishermen hadn't stopped him, his destiny would have been the breakers and a bunch of bones broken against the concrete pillars. Two bedeviled Bolita girls had attacked him, he later said. Two Bolitas disguised as redheads. He could tell what they were by their hair. Valkyries from heaven, he said. And if they'd come looking for him, it was because he's the only one who can identify those beings. I'm not crazy, he stammered through chattering teeth as they put him into a straitjacket to take him to Clínica del Mar. Because now he was to be treated by Dr. Uribe, who in those days was testing the effect of electroshocks.

We had no idea of what possibilities electricity holds for the mentally unbalanced, Dr. Uribe maintained in *El Vocero.*

Where do you think Adriana got the cash to set up a business like that, asked someone at Moby. Adriana Pilates, and look at the corner where she put it: Avenida del Mar and Alameda 306. The place, of course, belongs to Braulio Ramos's real estate agency. But in order to set it up, she needed some serious cash. And these days, besides. With some kind of bribe by her husband, that's how she did it, someone else said.

Dante, not a word. And when we looked at him to see if he had any comment, he rattled the ice cube in his glass of whiskey, looked up, and focused on each of us, one by one. What do you expect me to say, he asked us. That Pilates stuff isn't exactly the most important thing in my life, he said. And he patted his belly. We weren't exactly referring to working out, someone else replied. What Julián steals as Municipal Advisor, that's what we're talking about, Dante. Some time ago Berardi the Dago went to the city to ask for an extension on the cabana rental concession, and Julián told him that it was a tricky business, that it was out of his hands, but if the Dago was prepared to collaborate with the administration, he could resolve his problem. You guys know what "collaborate with the administration" means, asked the one who was telling the story. What could the Dago do.

Why don't you talk about this in *El Vocero*, Dante, someone else shot out, emboldened by whiskey. Proof, said Dante. Proof, and let the Dago stop by the newspaper office for an interview. But he'll chicken out, like they all do. Lots of blah-blah-blah, but when it's time to put their ass on the line, they disappear. Nobody wants to be associated with a complaint, get sucked into a trial, and worst of all with the Kennedys in the middle of it, because everyone, some more than others, has a file somewhere in their law practice, from litigation about the neighbor's construction to their divorce, every-one, some more than others. Come on, show of hands: which one of you doesn't have a file at Quirós's law office with your name on it? Nobody, not one person, raised a hand.

Your place is here. You chose it. And when a person chooses a place to live in, they also choose a place to die in. Osvaldo, the construc-tion site foreman, tells me this earnestly. A gray winter morning, gentle breeze in the branches, a muddied Jeep in front of the site: the Bolivians are laying brick. This area was an empty field when I came here as a kid, and here I am. Here I arrived, here I fell in love, here I stayed, here I formed a family, I built. I put up walls, roofs. My own and others'. I've lost count of the houses I built. I like to build. If I'm appreciated in the Villa, it's because I like what I do and try to do it the best I can.

To those who come and decide to stay and build a home, I tell them what I'm telling you. But I abbreviate the statement. I skip the dying part. Or that a house is, really, a place to hide in, because, to one extent or another, we all came here running away from something. Anyway, with the same material you use to build a house you can also build a grave.

The alarm clock rings. Dante opens his eyes: time to get up. On the radio, the FM host, Silvina Prieto, announces the time, temperature, humidity, and the next musical number: *Today can be a great day*, sings Serrat. Cachito Calderón must be getting up now to rehearse his defense of the rigged bidding for the sewer system before the City Council. Alejo Quirós is already on his stationary bike. Father Azcárate is brewing his first *mate* of the day. Commissioner Frugone inspects the jail cells and looks at the clock, counting the minutes till he's off duty. Dobroslav, our Speer, starts up his 4x4 and heads for his masterwork: Paradise Towers. Pedroza is the first to arrive at the cement works and honks his horn for the night watchman to open up. Old Neri pours himself a cup of black coffee, puts on his black suit, adjusts the knot in his black tie, and then leaves for his funeral home. Pedroza, from the Nueva Pompeya Cement Works, is in Poker, the bar opposite Banco Provincia, with Cabrera, the supermarket owner, two truckers, carjackers. Norita yawns and stretches: she still has half an hour to get to the sawmill. No sooner does the cock crow than Malerba leaves for the shopping mall and observes the red sky, remembering his nights of partying when, at this time of day, he would decide which Tropicana girls to bring home to his bed. Even though there hasn't been a flight in ages, Martínez is at his post in the Aeroclub tower before dawn. Dr. Uribe hasn't even emerged from the shower when his cell phone starts to ring: there was a shootout in La Virgencita; two injured kids are waiting for him in Intensive Care. As she didn't get a wink of sleep all night, Moni lights a joint to see if now, with the energy that comes with dawn, she can find that verse she's been seeking for days. Dante sits up in bed, looks at the clock, pees, and goes back to bed, a little more time to loaf. Campas tries to keep Anita in bed for a morning quickie, but

Anita pushes him away: she needs to hurry to get to middle school. Orellana revs the engine: he doesn't like dawn to overtake him on his dope deliveries. In La Virgencita there's still a party going on at the Reyes' place: they're celebrating the holdup of a jewelry store on 3rd. They split before the plainclothes cops arrived. Fournier drinks his strong coffee, loads his backpack with watercolors and drawing pad, and leaves his cabin. Rosita awakens from an erotic dream that turned into a horrible nightmare: she was in an Arab palace, had a harem of several men, was enjoying them all together and one by one when a curtain was drawn aside and there was a baby, staring gravely at her. Rosita disentangles herself from her lovers, runs toward the baby, and when she picks him up, he's dead. She wakes up, embraces Dicky's hairy back and cries silently. What's wrong, darling, Dicky asks. Nothing, she says, nothing. This waiting just makes me so sensitive, she says.

It seems that Crazy Heinrich has been locked up in the loony bin again. That he'd gotten the idea of burning his grandfather's notebooks, the ones where they say he talked about the Nazis. They say a neighbor caught him just in time, as he was lighting a bonfire in the woods, and notified the cops and the firefighters, avoiding a forest fire. The fire will come and purify everything, Crazy Heinrich said. He'd taken ayahuasca, they say. And was in the middle of a psychotic breakdown. He had visions. Ayahuasca, my ass: Crazy Heinrich was born that way. It took four cops to grab him and shove him into a police car. They, the ones from the Andean highlands, the Bolitas, were chosen by the heavenly hordes to put an end to us, the Aryans. Now they're among us.

Never let it be said that we Quiroses aren't humanitarians, says Alejo, when the subject of his nephew Camilo comes up. Without resentment, he says, we raised a child of the enemy. Since he was late in speaking as a child, we consulted a speech therapist. But he wasn't mute. With those bomb-throwing parents of his, no way the kid could've turned out normal. All those explosions left him practically deaf-mute. Everyone knows the story. The parents? Subversives. The army had them surrounded. There was a shootout. When the military entered the house, they were dead. And the baby, wrapped in a mattress, was bawling in a closet. His sickness is in his blood. Around thirty years gone by and still, it grabs hold of him like some kind of madness. Suddenly, for no reason, he starts to tremble, until he screams out so loud they can probably hear him in Madariaga.

It's not necessary for Alejo to describe that scream. All of us in the Villa have heard it at one time or another. After screaming, the boy quiets down. Sometimes, before he screams, he says he has to see El Muertito, that it's calling him. And nobody can restrain him when he has to go see it. Before, when he was a boy, Alejo could hold him back. But he's no boy anymore. And besides, he has that strength crazy people have. If you tried to tie him up, it would take several people to contain him. Besides, it's useless to tie him up. Nothing is accomplished that way. Then Alejo leaves him alone so he can go away and scream his head off somewhere if that helps him get rid of the trauma. Camilo disappears for a few hours and then a kind of sleepiness takes over. He can lie down on a sand dune or in the pine needles in the forest and fall asleep right there in a fetal position. With any luck, he returns home, goes to bed, and snores like a chainsaw.

My family and I have gotten used to it, Alejo says.

If your husband had AIDS, how would you react to the news that your partner had given you the virus? Because almost certainly he contracted the infection by being unfaithful to you. Would you complain that he didn't take precautions? Would you seek medical help? Would you try to begin treatment as soon as possible? None of these is a typical reaction for Argentine women, according to a study made of women who have been infected by their own husbands. After receiving the news, the women enter a period of depression, "freeze" their sex lives, and delay medical attention, like having an HIV test and requesting treatment. And they stay with their husbands. On discovering they had HIV, at first they felt great confusion, then fear, anxiety, and shame. Only after their partners died were they able to feel anger and fury at what had happened, especially when they had to recognize the possibility of infidelity. In our country new HIV/AIDS diagnoses tend to be more frequent among women than among men. If this is your situation, don't hide. Free medication is available to you at the hospital. No one dies of AIDS today. Don't hide from life just because your husband has AIDS. Try psychotherapy. Consultations. Absolute discretion guaranteed. Deborah Miller: 418061.

For the past few years the same announcement has been published in *El Vocero* several times every Friday. Some Fridays a dozen announcements, all the same, appear:

Prayer to Saint Expeditus

Pray 9 Hail Marys for 9 days, make three wishes, one for business and two that are impossible. On the 9ᵗʰ day publish this announcement and your wish, even if impossible, will come true.

The announcements are always signed. The only difference in each one is the signature. Sometimes it's just a name: Elsa. Or maybe: Luis. Lately there have been more announcements signed by men than by women. There are also many who sign with their initials.

It's 3 A.M. And Campas is pissed at Anita: What do I care about your insomnia and your nightmares, he yells at her. You know what riles me the most about this whole business—no matter how much you may deny it, it's a mess *you* made. Education through art, what bullshit. They're half-breeds, get it? Darkies. I warned you. Don't say I didn't. I told you. But oh no, not you. You had to go and get all fucking involved with them, acting like a kid, getting them all wound up. You think we're in Woodstock, idiot. And now I'm the one who has to go stick my nose in it, because your darling students, those druggies, shaved their heads and stamped a swastika on their drum set. Let's see if you can get this through your head: We don't live on your teacher's salary. We live from Campas Sanitary Services, a tradition that started with my old man's hardware store. I don't give a shit if you lose your job. But if I stop selling toilets because of you, we'll be royally screwed. And now, to top it all off, that Bolita-on-a-spit.

Call me Duchess, baby. Don't be shy. That's how the Duchess talks to the kids she manages to pick up on Saturday nights at the Comanche. The Duchess is the Villa's most important loan shark. And she never misses a Saturday at the Comanche. On your way into the Villa, practically on the main road, is the Comanche. That's where the old-timers, men and women alike, get together on Saturday night. And when I say old-timers, I mean over thirty and into their forties. Single guys and gals, separated, widowed. Whoever comes to Comanche on Saturday is on his fucking own and with only one objective in mind: to get laid. The problem is that all the men and women know one another and there's no excitement in what you might pick up. Though the Duchess goes way beyond being an old-timer, there isn't a Saturday she leaves the Comanche alone. Call me Duchess, darling. She always picks up some young guy in her 4x4. And she says goodnight with a wink to the bouncers at the door. Once upon a time she picked up the bouncers, too. No one knows exactly how old she is, but she's closer to seventy than to sixty, that's for sure. Silicone, Botox, hair transplants, the gym, and an over-the-top dress that not even a young chick would wear, all of it, instead of knocking the years off her, piles them on, but she doesn't seem to—or want to—notice: she has faith in herself. The confidence you get from paying for what others try to carry off for free without realizing that always, no matter what you take, no matter how cheap it may seem, always, I'm telling you, always, you're going to end up paying something. And don't even dream of putting one over on the

Duchess. No way. Any kid who goes home with her knows that, after the tumble between the sheets, he'll find some cash under the glass of water on the night stand. When he walks into the Duchess's bedroom, the cash is already there. If, in addition to his macho vigor, the kid also displays a certain chivalry, the Duchess just might toss him another bill before he leaves. She'll compensate him for his hard work. The Duchess realizes she's not Pamela Anderson and she also understands, like a mother, if a guy can't get it up. But it's better for him if he can. Because if he can't, at daybreak, when he slips into his jeans to leave, he'll find that the cash under the water glass is gone. Annoyed, he'll think of turning the place upside down looking for money, something of value. Then he looks at the night stand and changes his mind. He thinks of a better kind of revenge. In the glass of water there's a set of false teeth. And the Duchess is snoring.

Dobroslav pretends to be a nationalist and boasts that he's a patriot. He says he regrets having to give jobs to foreigners, and by foreigners, of course, he means Bolivians, Peruvians, and Paraguayans. But he sure keeps it to himself that because they're illegal, the foreigners work for him for two cents and without receipts. That's our Speer.

Oh well, Dante remarked, every town has its ghosts. And here in the Villa, we have El Muertito.

Moure, our veterinarian, brings to us at El Vocero *an article he found in the* Proceedings of the National Academy of Sciences:

"Kindness and solidarity are gratifying not only to humans. A CT scan has revealed that when a person carries out an act of generosity, he increases the activity level in the gratification centers of his brain. Empathy, which is the satisfaction experienced when someone rejoices in another person's good fortune, is a characteristic that also affects monkeys. Primatologists carried out an experiment with these animals. According to the scientists, monkeys experience gratification when another monkey in the

same social group receives food. It has been proved that social behavior is based on empathy, which grows in human beings and in animals through social proximity.

"From now on I plan to bring in monkeys," announced Moure, the renowned veterinarian. "And by the way, they also set an example."

The one who really knows how that business of the Twin Towers came off is Dante, but he's not telling. Much less publishing it. Let's not forget that Quirós is the real owner of *El Vocero*. Besides, he'll know how to shut up anyone who gets the bright idea of airing the company's secret dealings. If some crooked deal to facilitate the extortion didn't go through at his office, he'll certainly send out his henchmen: Don Carneiro and Gancedo. Malerba, too, although bringing El Capo Malerba into the picture depends on the seriousness of the case. They keep Malerba in reserve for extreme cases. If it's a question of putting the squeeze on someone, Don Carneiro. They only burned down three or four Bolita shacks in Mar Azul; to hell with the settlement that was blocking the housing development. In the event that someone conspires against Quirós's interests or those of his men, if a lawsuit gets hairy and the law practice runs the risk of losing its influence, even in the Dolores courts, Malerba steps in. Let's not forget what happened to the guy who gave Pedroza's daughter AIDS. The gunshot that the kid supposedly fired into his own mouth was Malerba's doing. If Dante's not talking, it's more a question of skepticism than of cowardice. He could go to the media in Buenos Aires or La Plata, and if he recovered, let's not say his courage, but a certain confidence in the human race, then yes, then he'd be capable of investigating and pointing a finger. You have to take Dante's skepticism seriously. We can knock down Quirós, Mendicutti, Ramos, and Cachito, but then who'll come along to take their place, eh? You tell me. Other respectable folk, because they'll pretend to be respectable, as usual, the same famous old moralists, members of the Rotary Club and the Police Association, sponsors of the Fiesta de la Raza and parishioners of Nuestra Señora del Mar Church, the same ones who patrolled the Villa in their 4x4s looking for a scapegoat during the scandal of *los abusaditos*. They're the same ones who later go around bragging that this is the place where nature has its place. What the fuck, nature is us. And nature, bro, has no morals. We think to ourselves: Lots of talk about nature and look how Dobroslav has cut down the forest and given himself permission to build two huge masses where there used to be eucalyptus, pines, birds. We throw out the ones who run the show today, and then what. Pure cosmetics. Something changes so that everything can remain the same.

Red Acosta took the Duchess's dentures to night school. His great revenge against her cheapness: the tight-ass old bitch had tried to pay him off with a couple of pesos. He could have swiped some dough from her, dug around in her bedroom for jewelry. But no. Taking her teeth, Red thought, was a better way to get even. And bragging about it. Just wait till the Yeti finds out, he was warned. The Yeti, the Duchess's son, a giant who looked like a sumo wrestler. The Yeti, a beast that one night, riding his quad, ran over his own father, Squinty Miranda, a hard-core gambler. Let's consider this pair: the usurer married to Miranda, the high roller. They had him under strict control. True enough, neither the Duchess nor the Yeti was sorry about the death of old Miranda, a drunk with DTs. You remember how the old man shed tears from his crossed eyes because scorpions were crawling up his legs and how he danced a malambo to shake them off. No one mourned old Miranda's death when his son, the Yeti, hit him with the quad as Miranda crossed Avenida 3 totally wasted. And, under similar circumstances, no one would mourn the death of the usurer, the Duchess, either. Many are those who hock their things—and themselves—with the Duchess. And if you put up collateral in exchange for a loan, you'd better pay back on time because she'll keep your stuff. Whether it's a store or a home.

The Duchess has no mercy, not even when it's your own home. The day after the loan comes due, the Yeti shows up at your house and, in addition to breaking your bones, he smashes everything to pieces. And he'll show no mercy, either, no matter how much your wife or your kids may cry. So when Red began flaunting the Duchess's dentures, we warned him: don't screw around, we told him, or the Yeti would get him. But the Yeti didn't come after him. It was the Duchess in person who stood outside the entrance to night school. There she waited for Red, smoking, calm as could be. As he walked out, one sidelong glance at her was all it took. Ignoring her, he slipped his arm around his girlfriend's shoulder. And before the girl could climb on the motorcycle, the Duchess smacked her out of the way. Then she grabbed Red by the back of the neck. She didn't even give him time to defend himself. She landed two punches, followed by a kick in the balls. Red managed to pull the dentures out of his pocket. He thought it would calm the Duchess down. But it didn't. The Duchess started kicking him. The girlfriend, a high school junior, latched on to the Duchess's neck. But she couldn't take her down. The Duchess knocked her silly with a couple of smart slaps. Red was still lying on the sandy ground, clutching himself. The Duchess picked up her dentures from the sand, blew on them and looked at all of us, one by one, and asked if we had a problem. She popped in her false teeth. She spat to one side of the road. She climbed on Red's motorcycle. She took off. And disappeared into the night. No way was Red about to go after his cycle. Fuck no.

We heard it at Josema's barber shop:

No woman is really yours till you fuck her in the ass for the first time. The only virginity that counts: the asshole. But then, man, you'll have to put up with her because you'll never get her off your back again. Then the best thing that can happen is for her to get married. And you keep on balling her. Married women are less of a pain. Being a lover is a different status. More positive. The lover always does more for the family than the husband does. Because the lover helps the marriage last. The chick goes back home with jism dripping from her asshole and you can't imagine how guilty she feels. The first thing she does is screw her husband. Then, at dinner, while she serves the cuckold and the kiddies their roast beef, she compares. The kids in private school, the car, the clothes, the vacations. She'll never ditch all that for a romantic like you, no matter how big your dick may be.

Here in the Villa, in the 70s, Vicky's father, Claudio, fell in love with Lili, a comrade from Peronist Youth. They had a little girl: Vicky. She, Lili, was kidnapped by the military. Claudio left the little girl with some cousins. And managed to escape. When Claudio returned from exile, Vicky had already come to the Villa and didn't want to have anything to do with her father. She hated her folks. She hooked up with Turco, the dealer. In order to get clean she took off for Buenos Aires, met a nice boy, Mariano, a car salesman, who tried to help her through rehab. She became pregnant with Camila. The treatment failed. Just like the marriage. And Vicky returned to the Villa with Camila. When she could no longer support herself and the child, her old man, Claudio, came to rescue his granddaughter. The old man did her a favor. He rescued her and took her back to Mariano, the father. But Camila couldn't stay with her father, Mariano, because now he had a new partner, a nice girl, pregnant, and they lived in a one-room apartment. So Camila stayed with her grandfather Claudio for a while, for as long as it took for the tumor to do him in. Because he had a tumor. When her grandfather was on his last legs and the chemo had knocked him out, the father, Mariano, and his new wife had no choice but to bring her into their home. By then Vicky had hooked up with El Negro Trabuco, the nurse. Trabuco brought her to the temple, and Vicky began to recover. Then she called her ex, asked his forgiveness, and begged him to return the little girl. That was how Mariano brought Camila back to the Villa.

Before taking the bus back to the city, he invited Vicky, Camila, and Trabuco to dinner at the Hawaii. Mariano took it as a good sign that Trabuco didn't drink a single glass of wine at dinner; he was the sort of man Vicky needed, practically a pastor. But things weren't as good as they seemed between Trabuco and Vicky. Trabuco kept a jealous eye on her, told her that a sinner never gets rid of the vice in her soul and that the Lord must have had some reason for infecting her, because let's not forget that Vicky has AIDS. Vicky went back on drugs. According to Trabuco, following the temple's recommendations, it was in the child's best interests to live with a healthy couple, two youngsters who had given up drugs and couldn't have children. But Vicky wouldn't hear of it. And she kept Camila.

Generous reward for the return of two toy poodles, a female with a scar on her belly and a male with a bald front paw. Female is insulin-dependent. Wearing pink and blue sweaters when they went missing. Contact: 412873.

I was coming back from the doctor's office with the tumor diagnosis when Mariano called. Would I please pick up Camila in the Villa, he asked. He couldn't go. His pregnant new wife and his fear of losing his job if he missed a single day were reason enough to shift the problem away to Grandpa. Besides, Claudio, you're Victoria's father, he told me. And you're Camila's, I was about to retort. The child gets on better with you than with me, Dad, he said. I'm not your father-in-law anymore, I reminded him. But Camila is still your granddaughter, he said.

The doctor's diagnosis still had me reeling. He couldn't guarantee how much time I have left. It could be a few months or years. And what if I go under the knife, I asked him. The doctor made a question-mark face. I thought about Camila. She was more important than my cancer. I had to rescue her from the Villa.

I put on my overcoat and got into the car. As if she didn't have enough problems with AIDS, Vicky hadn't stopped using. According to Mariano, the best thing would be to take the child away from his ex. Camila gets along better with you, he kept insisting. You're her grandfather. It's not that the child is a burden to us, he said. But understand, he went on, we're about to have a baby in a one-room apartment. Kids don't ask to be brought into the world, I was about to tell him. But I didn't. Vicky had said the same thing to me to justify the gripes she had with me. I didn't ask to come into this fucking world, she said. You and my mother, that cunt, should have given it more thought. Her, a drunk, and you, a coke-head. And I could go fuck myself. Vicky had been raised by Lili's sister. When I came back from exile it was already too late. Vicky had planted roots in the Villa, already had AIDS, and was messed up from all the dope.

It was just past four when I parked in front of the cabin in the poplar grove. A hovel, really. I didn't even turn off the motor. Vicky was awake. I saw the plate, the blow. The empty vodka bottle. I tried to convince myself: she wasn't my daughter. Her breath stank.

I'm here for the girl, I told her. I'm her mother, she said. And I'm her grandfather, I shot back. I'm her mother, she insisted. It doesn't seem that way, I said. You know that if they take away my baby I'll kill myself, she said. She had a gun. I wasn't frightened. I'll kill myself, she repeated. You're already dead, I thought, but didn't say so. I packed a bag with some of Camila's clothes. I wrapped her in a blanket and picked her up without waking her altogether. The shot rang out as I was settling the child on the back seat. Camila was so sleepy that she hardly blinked.

I threw the car into first. The sky was beginning to grow light.

Right around noon. The southeaster was ending. It was cloudy. A hazy, gray light. And sand. A kid in a school smock, wearing a backpack. He was walking along the wooden boardwalk, alone. The beach, deserted. Not a soul. Just that kid, a schoolboy, and me. He didn't see me: I was quite far behind. We were the only two in that solitude. I felt the wind, the sea, the waves. Suddenly I realized: that kid was me.

The one who told Yoli, the beautician, was Tina, a neighbor of Vicky's. It seems the grandfather came to rescue Camila. Vicky, her mother, completely wasted, tried to commit suicide, but in the end she misfired. That's how it went. Vicky was totally strung out. Drunk out of her mind, too. And she couldn't look after Camila. So she called her ex, who's in Buenos Aires, but the guy's expecting a baby with his new wife, so he asked his ex-father-in-law, Vicky's father, the grandfather, to come and get the granddaughter, Camila. And the grandfather, even though he's all fucked up with cancer, just out of chemo, came here. But Vicky refused to hand over his grandchild. And she threatened to kill herself if he took her baby away. She tried. She grabbed a gun. But she missed. When she was alone, she started to wander back and forth, like a sleepwalker. No one would have given five pesos for her when they found her lying along the road. And yet she took off.

El Negro Trabuco, besides having a huge you-know-what, as many of us girls can testify, also has a huge heart. And he forgave her.

Moni repeats some verses by Mark Strand: *To stare at nothing is to learn by heart / What all of us will be swept into.*

The Provincial Police found the Taunus one morning by the side of the road, near the Tropicana. The windshield had been shattered by a bullet. Bignose Riquelme, with lead in his head. Even though he had a pistol in his hand, nobody believed he had killed himself. Given the shattered windshield, you didn't have to be a ballistics expert to figure out that the suicide label was bogus. The Provincial Police rushed the paperwork through and attempted to close the case. And in their hurry to provide a summation you could smell Cachito's influence. But the marches began. And Cachito's plan was thwarted. Old man Riquelme, heading the protest marches, held up a sign: Pedroza Murderer, it said. You should've seen the Shell station owner's eyes. As a sign of mourning, Riquelme crossed the hoses on the gas pumps.

Pedroza, of the Nueva Pompeya cement factory, the Radical Party's top man, combined all the essential characteristics of a *caudillo:* he was a slacker, a gambler, and a gaucho all rolled up in one. He always used to say: One hand shouldn't know what the other is doing. But whatever his hands did always relied on the Kennedys' support. Like the time the ecologists who worked in the dunes reported him for stealing sand. Because the Kennedys supported not only Cachito, the Peronist boy, but also his rival. They always hedged their bets. As soon as Pedroza won the next election and got Cachito out of the way, he would put Julián in charge of the call for bids for the beach cabana rentals in Mar de las Pampas. But it drove Pedroza nuts that his daughter Luz had gotten AIDS. Infected by Bignose. Pedroza went kind of crazy. As crazy as old man Riquelme over his son Bignose's alleged suicide. The old man knew what his kid was involved in. He had beaten the hell out of him and kicked him out of the house. Everyone remembers: his son ended up with a deviated septum, like a boxer.

Can you believe Pedroza had the gall to go to Bignose's wake? He went with his wife and Luz. It was because of Luz, for their daughter's sake, that they went. Luz was madly in love with Bignose. Behind them, Malerba, watching their backs. When Pedroza stopped in front of the casket, Riquelme lunged forward and grabbed him by the neck. They had to pull him off. If they hadn't, old man Riquelme would've strangled him on the spot. Malerba let him go.

I won't stop till you're all in jail, cursed Riquelme. Can you believe that while Riquelme was holding him down, Malerba told him right to his face: You think Pedroza's not suffering, he asked. His girl's days are numbered. You're even. He's gonna lose his kid just like you lost yours. Think it over, Riquelme, when your anger fades, because your pain never will, but your anger will—then, with a clear head, you'll understand. Stay cool, Malerba warned him.

But old man Riquelme didn't stay cool. And he organized the first protest march.

I'll burn down the Villa if I have to, Riquelme said. It wasn't an empty threat. Hardly, considering it came from the owner of the gas station.

No one who hasn't done it has the right to judge me. You have to have done it, feel what I feel, to understand. It's easy to judge; it's easy to accuse. But those men and women who didn't do it have no right to an opinion. You can only talk about certain things when you've lived through them. And felt that pleasure, because it *is* a pleasure. Good and evil have nothing to do with this. I'm talking about feeling. Before you try it, the first thing you feel are scruples, and then comes remorse. That's the before and after of it. But at that moment, what matters is the moment. You feel the moment coming. You feel it all through your body. It's an internal sense of urgency. The body is stronger than the soul. When you judge, when you accuse, you're imposing other people's opinions. Our soul is just other people's opinions. Don't ask the soul for sincerity because you won't find it: the soul always lies. The body, on the other hand, doesn't. The body doesn't listen to reason. Or rather, the body *is* the great reason, the great wisdom, the hidden truth of what we are: a need for purity, for returning to the original state of purity, a state we started to lose as we turned into what we are, not the real us, but rather what others made us be. And there's no way to go back to being what you were, to that state of innocence, a transparent gentleness that we recapture only when we look at children. You'll tell me children aren't innocent, either, that they have desires, and that evil is already lurking inside them, hidden. Even though the serpent may have bitten them, the poison of reason, of what's good and what's evil, hasn't conquered them altogether. That's why they still reflect purity. And that purity makes you dizzy. I've been told that before a seizure epileptics have a vision that encompasses everything: the universe and each one of its beings, a kind of logic that eludes common mortals. I tell you, that instant is accessible if you have the courage to act in spite of the consequences. And then, once you've tried it, other people's opinions and the remorse that comes later won't matter anymore. Nobody knows what it's like till they try to fuck purity.

Mustachioed mayors, Josema says as he trims Dante's high-and-tight. Here in the Villa the last four mayors wore a mustache. Just like the military, see. I wonder what a mustache symbolizes, what kind of respect it hopes to instill.

Suicides begin with the end of the season and the beginning of fall. Then they continue, with greater frequency, from May on. By June it's unbearable. It's best to think of other things. Luckily there's still time until August. Just the same, if you don't have a family or a broad, don't stay home alone. Go out, get together with friends. Or go get your emptiness drunk at the only bar still open at this time of night. Don't stay home alone. Listen to me, go out.

We're approaching the end of June. The time of accusations, the scandal, the hunt for suspects, the parents' march, is over, but the abuse investigation isn't moving forward. There's no proof, they say. While the investigation grinds to a standstill, the school makes reforms. They rebuild the kindergarten rooms. Classrooms get painted. And there's even talk of putting cameras in the classrooms, the patio, the gym, everywhere. When it comes time to reconstruct the events, the setting will have changed.

Someone who was in Buenos Aires saw Fragassi the priest walking along Santa Fe one Sunday night, hand in hand with a boyfriend.

Now there's a new priest, Father Joaquín, who's replaced him as parish priest and substitute principal of Nuestra Señora. Father Joaquín seems like a good man. He looks a little like Jeremy Irons. We'll have to keep an eye on this one, says Moure, because he's going to fornicate the devout ladies. We discover that only one of the charges could be proven by the investigation. The lesions: one vaginal injury and one anal. It looks like the police's hypothesis was correct: there was only one act of abuse. And it was an inside job. A grandfather. But there's also a diagnosis that contradicts the abuse hypothesis: the child might have had some inflammation that later became infected. If that's the case, one might well ask if all that happened was a case of collective hysteria. Still, the majority would rather think about abuse. We infer: nothing will happen. Nothing ever happens here. We also conjecture: the forces of the Church conspired so that it would all come to nothing. Better not to stir things up anymore. Tonight the temperature is going to dip, the cold will freeze you; tomorrow we'll wake up to one hell of a chill. Tomorrow all the kids go to school. And the parents go to Mass on Sunday.

A country that's had concentration camps is rotten to the marrow. We are all worms.

This afternoon it's drizzling and cold, and Moni is walking through the cemetery. She doesn't mind the drizzle. Or the cold, either. I'm burning up. Menopause. The sprinkle on her face, her hair damp. They must think I'm corny, but what do I care. She walks among the headstones and reads the names. Then she writes a poem: *The name /*

on the tomb / identifies / nothingness. She moves her lips as she writes; she talks to herself. She argues with herself over whether the verb *to identify* is the right one, or rather, if it sounds better. In any case the verb should be *to name,* even though *name* is repeated. When it's repeated it produces another effect; it reads differently: *The name / on the tomb / names nothingness.*

Dante writes the article: *Elena Mateo, owner of a rickety shack in La Virgencita, indicated that the situation began with a robbery that she and her companion, Roberto Ferrarotti, experienced in their home on Sunday morning, when a gang of eight minors burst into the house, threatening to harm their children if they didn't hand over money and valuables. Later, after charges were filed, during the siesta hour while the family was resting, the accused minors set fire to the home with the family inside. It was Sunday night by the time firefighters and three police units arrived. The little house was in flames, and the assaulted couple and their children suffered serious burns. Meanwhile, the delinquents became embroiled in a struggle with the police, a melee joined by other area youth. Around twenty neighbors, most of them young and intoxicated, were arrested. As a result of the pitched battle that lasted until late at night, two police cars were destroyed and four agents suffered serious injuries. One firefighter, struck in the head, clings to life in Intensive Care. Our local media report that the couple and their children are literally out on the street, for which reason we are asking for help for these people, who have been temporarily lodged at the local parish.*

A cow. The worst thing that can happen to you when you're driving along the road at night in the fog is to wind up with a cow draped across your windshield. There aren't too many cows around here, but a horse, on the other hand, might cross your path. On Friday night the couple was heading for Mar de las Pampas for the weekend. Near El Palenque, where Don Argüello rents out those scrawny, emaciated, starving old nags, it must've been around 10 p.m., the man, over-confident, wasn't wearing his seat belt. With her eight-months-pregnant belly, she could hardly buckle hers. They couldn't wait to get to the cabin and relax. He hit the gas; he wanted to get there once and for all. And that's when they saw it. And when they saw it, it was too late. The horse draped over the engine. It smashed the windshield, its forelegs inside the car, crushing the occupants. The car flipped over and rolled till it came to a stop upside-down off the road, against a wire fence. The man died on impact. She was dying. She held on till the ambulance arrived, through the trip to the hospital, and the birth. She died in the struggle. The baby, a little boy. A total orphan.

The Villa is changing. When I arrived at the Villa some thirty years ago, there were twelve thousand inhabitants. And one family of thugs. Now let's say there's a population of around forty thousand. And more than six families of thugs, all of them recognizable, because you run into them on the street. If you get called to the DA's office because you've filed a complaint and they show you the mug shots full-face and in profile, you'll be surprised. You'll recognize a few mugs, for sure. Because there's a little of everything: old broads and young chicks, old dudes and young ones. You've got it all: pickpockets, shoplifters, abusers, violent criminals, dealers. Not just young thugs. You know what the DA told me: Around here, one percent of the population has a record. Figure it out: an army of four hundred dispossessed. But, even so, this is still a quiet place. No matter what people say, nothing happens here. And if it does, it's no big deal. We're peaceful people. Most folks here are still quite traditional.

Tuesday nights are sacred for those in the Villa who take an interest in community problems. Because Tuesday is the night for "Get Connected," the news show where topics of concern to us all are discussed. This Tuesday night on "Get Connected," a topic of importance to everyone: child abuse. A panel made up of distinguished figures from our Villa will present their ideas about a drama that is shaking the town. Participants will include: Dr. Alejandro Quirós, psychologist Deborah Miller, Commissioner Diego Frugone of the Greater Buenos Aires police force, businessman Atila Dobroslav, and council members Adalberto Bisutti of the Justicialist Party and José María Giacomino of the Radical Party. Don't miss "Get Connected" this Tuesday night, because no one is alone. "Get Connected," hosted by Luján Barbeito and Javier Miralles.

If you turn on the TV and watch the news or read the paper every morning, you'll see how many massacres there are in the world. Think of Rwanda. Or, if you prefer, right here, on a smaller scale, the eviction of striking oil workers in Patagonia, the expulsion of protesters in the North, and look at the victims, because here, in our country, we have those, too. No protest ever ends without repression taking someone down; no matter how much the government talks about human rights, there are always a few corpses left behind when the protesters leave. Then, if you compare what's happening in the world with what's going on here, which in fact is what's *not* going on, we realize that we're living in a different world; we're living in the best of all possible worlds, we're living by the sea, we're living in nature, we're living among familiar faces, and in spite of our problems, because everyone's got problems, this is a place where those tragedies they show on TV and publish in the papers aren't happening yet. Then, think about it, every morning when you get ready to begin your daily routine, you have to thank God for this piece of earth where it's your good fortune to live. And, if you'll excuse my saying so, if you consider the paradise we live in, you have to be grateful. Unfortunately, what's lacking in our Villa is just that: gratitude. Because, think about it: if someone fucks a couple of kids in the ass, it's not the same as Bosnia. Give me a break. There's no comparison.

Look, kid, says Malerba. And then he clams up. Outside, the German Shepherds are barking. The Dominican woman he brought back from the Tropicana went to bed a while ago, and now it's just him and Fito sitting at the table. It's not about the dough. I don't need the dough. And if you try to tempt me, no matter how much dough there may be, I won't bite. Malerba takes a hit of crack. When I caught Missy, you remember Missy, maybe not, because you were a kid, though you must be the same age as my kid, Matías, a pretty boy motherfucker, the one who's on TV, the story is that I caught Missy banging Matías. A shock for me. I put Matías on the bus and sent him to his old lady. As for Missy, I beat the shit out of her. For being immoral. You've come to hire me because you lived through something immoral; what the Croat did to you is immoral. Your old man, no less. Hold on for a second while I see what's going on. Tonight the dogs are on alert. The cops pester me every so often because I'm under house arrest. Fito's alone now; he looks at the crack pipe. Outside, barking in the night. A shout from Malerba, a gruff shout. The dogs fall silent. Fito would like to touch the 45 on the table, but he doesn't dare. Malerba walks in with the cold of the night. There are sea sounds in the distance, but not so many. Where were we, Malerba asks, and answers his own question: Your immoral old man, Malerba repeats, as if he's savoring the phrase. Your problem is a family affair. You can understand that, I hope. If you want, I'll lend you the piece. A 9 millimeter, with the serial number filed off. A 38, if you'd rather. You choose. But to do it for you—impossible. It's not my place. If your old man had relations—excuse the expression—with your little girl, you have to take care of it yourself. In my humble opinion. I put myself in your place and I understand. Life is about understanding. There are some matters a person has to deal with himself. They can't be delegated. Even if you don't come out of it with your ass clean. I recommend the 22. Besides, it's a double number for good luck.

Later, Saturday. Nightfall. Don Argüello, armed with his shotgun, walked into Quitapenas, the bar near the place where the last shacks in La Virgencita end, by Circunvalación. To call Quitapenas a bar is to give it class. There's a grill in a dark corner, some charred sausages, a chunk of flank steak. There's a small counter that barely seats three or four. Two wobbly tables. You drink whatever they have: cheap wine, beer, and gin. The same crude drinking glasses for everything. On Saturday the Osorios were there: Shaggy, the Hare, Sausage, the Louse, and Poison. Don Argüello challenged Poison: You stole my horses, Don Argüello said. And one of them got away, the one those people killed along the road. From Poison, not one word. He shrugged, smiled, made a gesture, tried to reach for something. The hail of buckshot cut him short. Left him without a face. Don Argüello stepped back, aiming at the others. And he left. By then it was night. Poison cried, that is, if you can call that bloody groan, more dead than alive, crying. Soon he was dead altogether. The other Osorios didn't move. They didn't have the nerve.

Maybe she was carried away by her maternal instinct, but what can't be denied is that her conduct was humanitarian. We're referring to China, a stray dog who saved a newborn's life. Last Tuesday, in the middle of the night, when the fog made our Villa practically invisible, the animal heard the baby's cries and dragged it to her den, sheltering it with her six little pups in an abandoned shed. The enlightening event took place on the deserted outskirts of La Virgencita district. The infant, discovered next to the pups, which were keeping her warm, had a few abrasions on her mouth, some bruises and scratches. Emergency physicians, after examining her, declared that "the chubby little girl, born at 39 weeks of pregnancy, weighs almost nine pounds and is out of danger." On Thursday morning police found the baby's mother. Commissioner Frugone described her as a thirteen-year-old who will remain anonymous and who had

171

given birth to the child one day earlier. The case was categorized as "abandonment of a human being."

Bebé, bebé. Bebé Rocamadour.

Suddenly, at funerals, the memory comes to me. And yeah, maybe I forget what I tell. Maybe I tell what I tell in order to forget.

Dobroslav lost it with Luján and Javier, the directors of the program. They had to call for a cut. You saw it on "Get Connected." The Croat was out of control. We all know the guy's not exactly a humanitarian. But from that to going wild like he did. It happened when Commissioner Frugone said that in sexual abuse cases like the one at Nuestra Señora, a situation of collective hysteria can occur and that sometimes it all starts with an act of abuse in a home, that is, the abuser is a member of the young victim's family. Although it's painful to believe, it's not uncommon for grandparents to be the abusers, Frugone maintained. And he was getting back at him for his beating. That was when Dobroslav lost control. A grandfather could never commit such a depravity. Then that Miller woman, the psychologist, chimed in: denial is often more harmful to society than accepting perversions. Dobroslav tried to go for her jugular: You're a Jew like Freud, and you think we're all like you. Only a twisted Jew's mind could have thought up that stuff about sexuality in children. You're a Nazi, Miller replied. And if you people don't remove this madman from this discussion, I'll get up and leave. Go, go to Israel, Dobroslav told her. Freud was Viennese, you animal, the Miller woman retorted. Then Luján called for another cut. When the argument calmed down, Commissioner Frugone went on to say that investigations of abuse cases are delicate, that justice must proceed with extreme caution. It's necessary to use all available methods, from interviews with specialists to a Gesell Dome. Then Alejo said that the abuse wasn't the Villa's biggest challenge. The abuse business was over-hyped, he declared. There was a lot of exaggeration. Rather than focusing on that collective hysteria, he said, more attention should be paid to another serious problem faced by decent people. And I'm referring to safety, possibly the gravest problem of all. The Croat went back on the offensive: With all this fanfare about human rights, now criminals go free and we family folks have to lock ourselves in our homes. When Giacomino called him authoritarian, the Croat nearly exploded. This never happened under the military, Dobroslav yelled at him. Javier tried to take control of the situation, but couldn't. Bisutti, the councilmember, requested permission to speak. And Dobroslav went on the offensive again: You Peronists have no right to talk. Perón had orgies with the young girls of the High School Students' Union, he said. You're a bunch of perverts, spat Dobroslav. What we need here is an iron fist. Castrate the guilty parties in Plaza 25 de Mayo. And let them bleed out in front of the whole Villa. Let's castrate one of them, and you'll see—this won't happen again.

It didn't take long for all the Osorios, a horde of them, to get together. It must have been midnight when Assistant Commissioner Balmaceda picked up the phone. A neighbor woman from Circunvalación was reporting a brawl in El Palenque. Balmaceda thought he could handle it by himself. The Osorios were about to set fire to Don Argüello's hovel. The Louse, the youngest of the Osorios, carried an oil drum. Sausage, Shaggy, and the Hare were armed. Balmaceda fired twice into the air, grabbed one of the flock, the Louse, and stuck the barrel into one of his ears. Holding the Louse by the neck, with the 9 millimeter against his head, he managed to stop the others. Without letting go of the Louse, holding on tight, he entered the shack, where Don Argüello lay on the brick floor, his head shattered, blood and brains strewn everywhere, a filthy puddle. They had smashed in his head with clubs, disfiguring his face. Outside: screams, the sound of breaking glass. As he stepped out of the hovel, still holding on to the Louse, Balmaceda saw the patrol car, its windows destroyed and its tires punctured. The Osorios, escaping in the distance, crossed from the other side of the road, passed beneath a street lamp, and disappeared into the night. He let go of the kid. They stood there for a moment, eyeing one another. Staring into each other's eyes. Balmaceda aimed at his forehead. What are you staring at, you piece of shit, he said. Then he hit him with the 9 millimeter, knocking him unconscious. He couldn't get him to react. Out of pure rage he peed on him. And he couldn't help having regrets. The Louse was unresponsive. And now he had to take him to the hospital.

I walk along the beach for over an hour, away from the Villa, till I come to this place, where there is only the sea and the deserted beach, stretching out, immense. Then I choose the highest dune. And when I reach the top I feel like a god. From this perspective, beneath a blue sky, the Villa is a wide green stain against the horizon. A few red roofs, three or four tall buildings, shimmer beneath the blinding sun. But just as the blue of the sky is deceptive and we know that it's an optical illusion, so too is the Villa an internal illusion for those of us accustomed to living here. You might think that if a hiker lost his way and spotted a town on the horizon, and if that town was the Villa, just as you can see it from this dune, it might seem like his salvation: hospitality, refuge, a plate of food, rest for his exhausted body and his tormented soul. The Villa as salvation, you might think. But we all know this is just an illusion. The Villa is perdition. We're all lost here. As lost as someone like me, who, looking from this distance, deceives himself by thinking he's an outsider and different on account of the simple fact that he's far enough away to take in the entire view. Nobody, no matter how much of an outsider, observer, or superior type they consider themselves to be, really is. Whoever came and stayed is lost. Because the Villa itself is lost.

Last Saturday, August 27, opening ceremonies were held at the Paradise Towers complex. In attendance were the provincial governor, officials of provincial and community tourism boards, and an elite group of our power brokers. According to estimates, the sizeable throng consisted of as many as 200 people. The local firefighters' band participated in the ceremony, accompanying the chorus of Niños Sarmientinos de la Villa, which sang our national anthem. Then our mayor took the floor. Here are some excerpts from his speech:

We all know that Atila Dobroslav is a man of strong opinions. But we also know that he represents the construction of a successful future for our beloved Villa. We also know that creating and implementing a project causes controversy. But, when the project becomes a reality—and today these two towers are our reality—all doubts and discussions are put behind us. The present is what counts, and all you need to do is lift your eyes to appreciate the magnitude of a construction that, by offering the epitome of service, will attract more tourism to our beloved Villa. Many of Dobroslav's detractors claimed that he was undermining ecology, the ideal of our founder. Many objectors believed this was an undertaking in which money was the primary concern. They were wrong. Because thanks to Adolfo Dobroslav, that is, Fito, Dobroslav's son and his modern design, his enormous creativity, these two towers have envisioned a cultural and recreational space where there will be a permanent exposition hall dedicated to the artists of our beloved Villa. Besides, let us not forget, ladies and gentlemen, my dear neighbors, that these two towers represent an invaluable source of employment. And, with those who will comprise the service wing of this venture in mind, Dobroslav Construction is crowning its work with the creation, in the rear of the buildings, of a day care center for the female service employees' children.

It's like a Hieronymus Bosch painting. You can't look at it. You have to *see* it. Because when you see, you understand. When you understand, the painting is different. And so are you.

Nobody can say that the Pereses didn't love Felipe, but you could tell they had to work at it. Or rather, how hard they tried. Besides, who am I to criticize. No matter how hard you try, a mongo will always be a mongo. On the other hand, he's really smart, Sergio used to say. And Edith: He's no dummy, not one bit. They struggled to convince themselves that what was unchangeable could be fixed. I don't blame them, really. You've got to admit that they did absolutely everything. Except put him in an institution, because putting him away wouldn't have changed anything. Hiding the drama doesn't get rid of it. When Feli turned four they couldn't take it anymore. They thought it over. Feli might find their gun and, in a moment of carelessness, playing, shoot himself. Poisoning him was another option, but slower. Then they came up with the idea of the accident. One night Feli escapes, gets lost, wanders into the road, and a bus, a truck, a car, runs him over. They're asleep. They don't find out till the police come to notify them.

Tonight it seems as if Felipe can read their thoughts. They feed him *milanesa* with French fries and fried eggs for dinner. Flan with lots of *dulce de leche*. But his favorite foods don't make him happy. Feli senses the phoniness of his parents' apparent happiness. Edith dresses him in his pajamas, brushes his teeth. Sergio loads him into the car and takes off.

It's past midnight. Sergio brakes to a halt at the side of the road. He lifts Feli out of the car, gives him a Fanta and a Suflair chocolate bar. Feli complains. He's cold. He's in pajamas and shivering. Sergio deposits him in the middle of the road. He sees headlights in the distance. And he walks away. Feli looks around, confused. The headlights blind him. Papa, he yells. There's no Papa. Headlights from one direction. Headlights from another. A bus, a truck, another bus. They pass by Felipe like gusts of wind. They miss him. A long horn blast. Dizzy, Feli screams. He drops the Fanta. A truck passes. From somewhere in the blackness, Sergio cries. He can't take anymore. He runs toward Feli. And he doesn't see the bus.

At 3 A.M. a policeman rings the Pereses' doorbell. Edith takes a while to open up. When she opens the door, she sees the boy. Feli, crying, embraces her.

Another poem by Moni. She called it "Accounts Due." It goes like this: *As night falls / It dawns on me: / The best place for reckoning / is one's own pad.*

The Falange was about to shoot Don Vázquez, the owner of the general store, but he managed to escape. Here he met Carmen. And got married. From the time they arrived in the Villa at the end of the 40s till now, Don Vázquez and Carmen have spent their lives behind the counter of their store. Don Vázquez and Carmen led a life of deprivation. They never emerged from behind the counter. Not even to look at the sea. They never went down to the beach, people say. They were saving up to return to their country, they said. But they never returned. Not even after Franco's death.

At the end of last summer Don Vázquez was diagnosed with liver cancer. And now it's metastasized. *Morriña, saudade,* says Don Vázquez. It's eating my soul.

This morning Don Vázquez asks Carmen to take him to look at the sea. He doesn't care about the wind or the polar cold. This morning you can see them coming along the dock. The fishermen turn around, regard them. Don Vázquez walks, leaning on Carmen. And Carmen, her arms around him, holds him up by his overcoat lapels. It draws people's attention to see him going down to the beach on a morning like this. Someone tells him so.

To look at the sea for the last time, says Don Vázquez, is to see it for the first.

Who said Don Argüello didn't have a family? Two sons, their wives, and a niece showed up. Crippled, the niece was. They'd come from Chacabuco and were waiting for his body at the hospital door. Also the Osorios: Sausage and the Hare, were waiting at the hospital door; the Louse, taken there by Balmaceda, was still unconscious. Those who were missing arrived: the relatives of the couple who died on the road. A few fiftyish rugby players, two upper-class ladies, a young couple. The three families converged at the hospital door. They began to argue. It all ended in blows. Rugby players, bums, and gauchos, all tangled together. An Osorio brother, Shaggy, pulled out a homemade piece, one of Argüellos's relatives, pulled out a little knife, and a socialite wannabe pulled out an automatic. The wannabe's shot knocked Shaggy down the front staircase. Shaggy, lay on his back, shaking, wounded. The red gash spread along his chest. The wannabe aimed at the other Osorios. Kill those motherfuckers, yelled one of the upper-class ladies. Kill those half-breed bastards. The wannabe was more than willing. The police—late, as always. The hardest part was dragging the crippled woman away from kicking Shaggy, who, at this point, was bleeding from the mouth.

María calculates, plans. If Beti cans her, it's a sure thing her sister-in-law Valeria will end up canning her too. She knows that Beti is going to can her sooner or later. All it'll take will be the slightest excuse, like finding a hair in a corner, grease on a plate, a cup of tea she didn't quite scrub the brownish ring from, not remembering where she put some little thing and imagining that María stole it. Beti will find the perfect justification. For nearly a week now María has been carrying the DVD in her purse when she goes to work at the Calderóns' place.

God gives bread to the toothless, María thinks. Cachito seems like a good-natured guy, charming, like all politicians. Nobody makes *milanesas* like you, María, he flatters her. Leave some of them for me in the freezer. That's why she votes for Cachito at election time. María is a Peronist and votes for Cachito. It's also true that she votes for him because Cachito promised her a house in Circunvalación, and if Cachito loses, he'll surely leave the Villa, Then, goodbye house. She's heard him say so: If I don't win in the next election, we're going to La Plata. But Cachito keeps winning one election after another. He's been mayor for eight years now. And he'll certainly win the next one. I'm sure it's clear to you why María votes for Cachito, says Dante.

The fact that Cachito likes María's *milanesas* and not hers drives Beti wild. Cachito never lets up campaigning, not even with the servant. But Beti's not canning María on account of the *milanesas*. It's because she's missing a few dollars. And now, yes, she's about to can her. And then comes the part about the servant's revenge, a plotted revenge: In a closet, hidden in Beti's clothing, she leaves the DVD she found at the Marconis' house.

María leaves the Calderóns' place. And as she walks away, she thinks of how much she'd love to be there when Beti discovers the DVD, how she'd love to watch it, to have her watch her sister-in-law sticking the dildo into Alejo while they do coke.

At night, if it's clear, you can see the lighthouse from the Villa. And don't tell me its light doesn't seem like a sign from God. A light that comes and goes, and in its comings and goings doesn't lose sight of us. So no matter how much we may think its light doesn't reach us in the depths of night, it's still shining, watching us even though we can't see it. From a distance it watches over us. And don't think it's an impossible distance, either: barely twelve miles. From there it remains alert all night, its single eye blazing, winking at us as if to say: I am above you.

Belén Yanina Remero, age eleven, disappeared one Wednesday afternoon. Her parents, Victoriano, a roofer, and María Adelia, a clerk at Detalles Haberdashers, showed up at the office of *El Vocero* on Thursday. Unfortunately Dante had already put the issue to bed and couldn't include the notice about Belén's absence. We'll pay for it, Victoriano said. I publish these notices for free, Dante replied. Don't write *disappearance*, the father told him again. Absence, he emphasized. Absence, Dante repeated. And he stared at the photo that the mother put on the desk in front of him.

Cute little half-breed, he thought. She looked older. He didn't want to speculate about her disappearance, sorry, her absence. We want it to say missing and not disappeared, the mother also insisted. It's an ugly word, disappearance. Dante asked them if they'd stopped by the police station. No, we're not going to file a report. We don't believe in the police. But you have to file one, Dante said. It's the law. If you don't want to publish the notice, we'll pay you for it. It's a free service, Dante repeated. A service to the community. But I can't publish it till next Friday. We'll wait, the father said. We have faith. You have to see Captain Frugone, said Dante. No, we're not going to the police. To the radio stations, yes. But not to the police. Dante tried again: But the police can conduct an investigation. Victoriano didn't answer. Friday, don't forget, Victoriano said. Next Friday. I won't forget. I know you won't forget, the woman said. You seem like a good man. Dante didn't know what to say: I try. Like everyone, he said. No, Victoriano corrected him. Not everyone.

The man and the woman left. And Dante stood watching them walk away down the middle of the passageway, on a cold, cloudy morning.

They say, they say, they say. Lately what they've been saying is that Fito Dobroslav went to entrust the job to Malerba. But El Capo didn't bite. Instead he put a 22 in Fito's hand. The next morning Fito needed a few whiskeys to face our Speer. He found him in the usual place, the office at the Towers. The workmen could see the scene from outside. They couldn't quite manage to hear what father and son were shouting at one another. The weapon shook in Fito's hand.

He had to use both to hold it still. No way would the workmen get involved. Fito, drunk, hesitated. It gave the Peruvians time to place their bets—would he, wouldn't he, two weeks' salary says he won't. Fito lost his nerve. Instead of backing down, Dobroslav spoke to him sympathetically. Where had he gotten that idea, who had put it into his head that he could be capable of acting inappropriately with Mili. If he had doubts, if he so much as suspected that he had abused Mili, Dobroslav told him, he shouldn't hesitate. Just pull the trigger. Fito began to cry. He fell to his knees. Dobroslav walked over to him. He took away the 22 and stored it in a drawer of his desk, next to his Luger. Fito sobbed uncontrollably. Like a child. His nose was running. Till our Speer picked him up and gave him a couple of slaps. To get some reaction out of him, he said. He was just stressed. He needed to get away with his wife to Miami. A week in Miami wouldn't do him any harm. Heil, Papa, blubbered Fito. Heil, Daddy.

A few days ago, a fishing boat burst into flames off our coast. If it was quite a spectacle to see the column of smoke ascending from the horizon in the daytime, by night the flames emerging from the sea were impressive. As if it were possible to light a bonfire on the ocean's surface.

We didn't learn about it through Remigio. Remigio, Dante's faithful watchdog. He didn't give away a thing. It doesn't matter: it's the sin, they say, not the sinner. As we usually do around here when we discover that someone is hiding something, we started digging and didn't stop. When we found out that Dante had a history with Chiquita, one of the girls from the Tropicana, we tried to uncover everything that he, with his tight-lipped sarcasm and that elusive, guru-like way of responding in proverbs, was never going to tell us. So, if he ever decided to talk about his romance, and we called it romance to give his horniness some respectability, if Dante ever decided to open up and talk to us, we would simply listen and pay careful attention to whether or not the details of his story jibed with what we'd already heard from the other girls, particularly Irene, the owner, who'd told Natale, the guy from the Pasta House, that Dante had something going on with someone on her staff. That's what Irene called her girls: the staff. In the afternoons, we heard, Dante went to the Tropicana. After having a tenderloin sandwich and a beer for lunch at Poker, he would get into his Fiat and head directly over to the Tropicana for his siesta. But that information we already had. We wanted to know more. Not about the acrobatics in bed, because, it's a fact, we guys are discreet about these things. We're not like women; we don't get mired in the details of shapes and sizes. No, we wanted to know what sort of relationship this was. Because, we chided ourselves, how was it possible one of our Moby night group could have a secret? Correction: How was it possible for someone's secret to escape us? And in this, in our curiosity, it must be admitted, there was a chick thing. Deep down, if men and women have something in common, it's just this: the mote in someone else's eye.

Dante looked at the photo again and again. Belén, run off with a boyfriend. Belén, raped, murdered, and hidden in some thickets in the south. Belén, drugged, kidnapped by a ring of slave traders. Belén might have met any one of these fates and other, worse ones, too, even though her parents were Evangelicals and didn't bother anybody. They were well-regarded in La Virgencita. Victoriano was never short of work. People said he was slow, but the best. His tin roofs never flew away in the wind, the neighbors remarked. And that was because of the serenity he projected. It's God, he said. Faith. María Adelia, just as beloved: besides working at the haberdashery, she was a seamstress and dressmaker. When she left work, after she had served dinner and while Belén studied and Victoriano read the Bible, she made cakes to sell for all sorts of parties. On weekends the three of them dutifully attended church. They emerged with an enviable expression of peace on their faces. After that morning when they went to *El Vocero*, Dante could see them on the street, putting up flyers with Belén Yanina's photo. There wasn't a store that didn't have one in its window. Every year you can see similar flyers everywhere; time goes by, the flyer fades, and then, during tourist season, it vanishes. By the next year nobody remembers. Now there's a different flyer, a different face. Dante could see Victoriano and María Adelia going in or out of radio stations and also at the local TV channel. To the question that reporters always asked, Victoriano invariably replied: We don't want the police involved. The police have enough work without dealing with Belén, he said. And in his "enough work," you could hear the irony.

After the Bignose incident, even though he's under house arrest, every so often Malerba escapes and goes for a walk. One night he went into Poker and found Fito drinking alone in a corner. Alone. Because nobody would go near him. Nobody, not after what everyone already knew. Fito lowered his head when he saw Malerba. But El Capo didn't play dumb. He went directly up to the bar, to the corner where Fito was sitting, grabbed his glass, spat into it, stared right at him, and then turning his back just like that, walked away. It's not just me telling you. There were witnesses.

They should drown in their own cum, thinks María, the cleaning lady, as they call her at Cachito's house, the cleaning lady, as she identifies herself when no one is home and she answers the phone. After slipping the DVD into Beti's—her employer's—closet, María thinks: those damn hypocrites. She'd love to see Beti when she watches the DVD and finds out that her little brother, that stuck-up asshole, Marconi the pharmacist, the one who's convinced he's so respectable, such a big shot, with his eternally white, starched smock, like a scientist, acting like he knows it all, doesn't know the main thing: that his dear wifey, Valeria the Jew, who puts on airs like a great lady, is nothing but a druggie cocksucker. And Dr. Quirós, that oh-so-respectable son-of-a bitch, high as a kite and with a dildo up his ass. Let's see what kind of face Señora Beti will put on then. And Don Cachito, he'll be left speechless. Even though it's unusual for a politician to have nothing to say. When he sees. When he sees his sister-in-law sucking Quirós's dick. If I were to make copies of the DVD, I'd love to spy on them after, watch them try to look one another in the eye. Your legal advisor, Cachito, Beti will say to him. Just imagine if somebody else sees this, Cachito will sputter. And Cachito imagines: Alejo, his legal advisor, no less, fucking Valeria in the ass. And letting her stick a dildo in him, besides. The copied DVD circulating throughout the Villa. Well, the drugs wouldn't be a big deal, because anyone can sniff a line of coke, but that pink vibrator up his ass. How am I going to look the voters in the face, Cachito will say to Beti. And all because of that cuckold, your little brother.

Wallow in your own shit, María thinks. Let's see who'll clean up your filth now. Not even an army of Marías will clean up your name. They'll wonder how the DVD got there. Beti won't understand a thing. And Cachito even less. But before going to find his brother-in-law and telling him, Hey, Valeria is cheating on you with Alejo, he'll confront her, Valeria, and he's going to ask her, not to explain what's on the DVD, but rather how it ended up at his house, and then. And then. And then. The only one who it could've been, the only one who had her hands rummaging through my panties before you tore them up and so did I. María. Forgive me, Lord. I didn't do it out of meanness. I was carried away by anger. Overcome by rage. Our Father who art in Heaven.

Three headlines, three articles, one below the other. *Tragic accident*, reports *El Vocero*. This is how Dante wrote the first article: *On Friday*

184

night a young couple traveling in a Honda toward Mar de las Pampas struck a horse belonging to Rudecindo Argüello, owner of The Stockade. Fabricio Capucci, 33, died on impact. His companion, Sofía Escalada, 27, pregnant, gave birth to a son before dying en route to the local hospital.

Horrific crime, the second headline. *Rudecindo Argüello, Argentine citizen, 64, was shot on Saturday night by a gang of young hoodlums. The owner of The Stockade, gravely injured, died several hours later at the community hospital. Don Argüello, a beloved figure in our community, a country dweller and award-winning horse trainer at many of our regional festivals, spent his last years renting out horses to tourists. This tragedy has provoked the indignation of the power brokers of the Villa, who are once more demanding a safety policy to put an end to danger and violence.*

And the third: *Confusing incident at hospital. A confrontation between relatives of Don Argüello and the 18-year-old minor accused of the former's death took place outside our hospital. Joining in the melee were members of the Capucci and Escalada families, relatives of the couple who died on the road after hitting a horse with their car.*

The only photo on the police report page of *El Vocero*, a picture of the Honda on the side of the road, without wheels, without seats: *Vandals strip crashed vehicle*, the caption says.

Deborah's practice has changed addresses at least three times in the past few months. With fewer and fewer patients, and considering the cost of rent, lately she's been moving, at first away from the downtown area, then farther from the popular boulevards, and now, down south. This is the second time she's moved to a drywall-partitioned room in a damp, cracked building by the wharves. At least you can see the ocean through the window, she consoles herself. Deborah has hung blankets and tapestries on the walls, not only to create a cozier atmosphere, but also to cover up the mildew stains. She's also hung a Teatro por la Identidad poster and another of Freud in which his profile looks like a naked woman, his eyebrows her hairy crotch. In her library, always the same, built of cement blocks and boards, she's arranged the volumes of Foucault, Suzuki, Galeano, Mario Benedetti, Khalil Gibran, Anaïs Nin, Simone de Beauvoir, Erica Jong, Susan Sontag, Virginia Woolf, Isabel Allende, Marcela Serrano, Laura Restrepo, Gioconda Belli.

The first thing Rosita asks her when she comes in is if she's read all those books. And Deborah replies that she loves to read. Rosita scrutinizes the apartment, sniffs the myrrh-scented incense, listens to the hushed Tibetan music interrupted by the splash of the waves. What brings you to me, she asks Rosita. I saw your ad in *El Vocero*. Is it true you give a discount if I mention the ad, Doctor, Rosita asks. Not Doctor. Just a master's in Psychology. And you can call me Deborah.

I have a problem, Rosita says. I'm listening, says Deborah. And she invites her to take off her shoes and sit on the carpet. My husband, she says. We haven't had relations since I got pregnant. I understand, says Deborah: he's grown distant. No, Rosita replies. Just the opposite. He spoils me more than ever, but he's on some kind of spiritual kick. The problem is me. I'm so horny I'm exploding. Your desire makes you feel guilty, Deborah ventures. I don't know, I don't know if it's guilt. I went to church. If you went to church, it's because of guilt, Deborah says. You're trying to punish your desire. Rosita isn't going to tell her what happened with Father Joaquín. I was looking for advice. Deborah in the lotus position: I don't give advice. But I can help you think about what you're feeling. I know what I'm feeling, Rosita says. What I don't know is what to do. Right now, for example, I'm so hot I could die. Burning up.

What do you feel like doing now, Deborah asks. I'm embarrassed, blushes Rosita. You have lots of clothes on, says Deborah.

Do you want me to undress, Señora Miller, she asks. I told you, call me Deborah. If you want to. Should I get undressed? Whatever you feel like doing. Do whatever you want. You're free here. I'm free. You're free. Can we speak freely, Rosita asks. You can, Deborah replies. And then: You have a lovely belly. Take off all your clothes. First I'll rub you some oil on you. And then I'll give you a Mayan massage.

The police paid a visit to the Romeros, Belén Yanina's parents. First Commissioner Frugone went. Then Deputy Commissioners Renzo and Balmaceda. Victoriano and María Adelia received them graciously, invited them in, offered them water. The officers tried to get information out of the parents; they asked to see the girl's room. The parents didn't stand in their way. They looked here and there, without touching anything. They acted interested in the computer. If you want to bring in a technician, go ahead, Victoriano said. But the computer doesn't leave this house, he objected. If Belén comes back and it's not here, she won't like it. Then you folks think she's coming back, Renzo said. If you keep up this negative attitude it won't be possible to help you, Balmaceda said. No one called you, said Victoriano. You came here on your own. Just doing your job, said María Adelia. And her irony was the same as Victoriano's had been in the news article when referring to police work. Even if you refuse to cooperate, we're going to investigate, Renzo said.

Do as God commands you, María Adelia said with a gesture inviting them to leave.

Family constellation workshop. What do I do with these parents? What do I do with my child? What am I doing wrong? Systems Theory takes a deep look at daily issues that arise within families as well as institutions, and addresses them. This workshop is designed both for health care professionals and those who seek solutions to problems connected with family and workplace relationship issues, grief, illness, etc. Contact 418061 and ask for Deborah Miller, MA.

If you've got to believe in God and miracles, Santi Rovira is one. Santi doesn't come from a family; he comes from a tribe. And, to be sure, calling that pack he was born into a tribe is an anthropological refinement. Because you can't use the word family for that assembly of degenerates, layabouts, and druggies, a den of iniquity with delusions of la vie bohème, created by old man Pucho. El Pucho baptized this tribe a "community." And it was the ramification of shared beds between this one and that one, all the hims with the hers, the hers with the hers, and the hims with the hims, and not because of any lack of rooms and mattresses in that shack on the edge of the Villa, en route to the cemetery. His partner, Santi's mother, Tacha, a real Jane Birkin when she first arrived at the Villa, ended up a wreck, fat, crazy as a bedbug, and croaking in an open-door psychiatric ward. A shame, when you remember how hot she was when she first came here, before El Pucho arrived. Like so many upper-class girls, she showed up one summer playing hippie. That same summer El Pucho knocked her up. And in the spring she had Santi. Rumor has it that early one morning, full of symphonic rock and gin, Tacha fucked Santi when he was fourteen. After that night, the kid took off, to Patagonia, they say.

Until recently we would still see El Pucho driving that broken-down station wagon, earning a living as a gardener. Landscaper, he called himself. Though his thing was always growing and selling cannabis. Until recently, I say, because his ticker started to fail and suddenly there he was in intensive care.

We had forgotten about Santi. He was somewhere in Patagonia, Caleta Olivia. No one thought he'd come back. But when we told him his father was fucked up, he returned. Healthy, tanned, a grown man. What he hadn't lost, though, was that innocent expression. He'd become a pastor, he told us; it was an illumination, or rather, a glow, the vision of divine light, and it happened one night when a meteorite fell like a flash from heaven and everything trembled, when he was working in the oil industry in Caleta and a tile came flying off a roof and split his forehead open.

That tile showed him his path: the temple.

Now he was coming home to the Villa, having learned that his father was in intensive care. I've come back to forgive you, Papa, he said. So you can go without guilt.

Who told you I feel like going, El Pucho replied. My paradise is Earth. And the last thing I feel is guilt, you idiot. Get lost.

So the poodles appeared. Some kids from La Virgencita found them. The youngsters called the phone numbers that were in the paper. They wanted to know how much the reward would be. They had no idea who the owner was. They called the number published in *El Vocero*. When they figured out that they belonged to El Capo Malerba they lost their interest in the reward. Just the same, Malerba rewarded the good deed with blow. Toy poodles. Malerba rushed them over to Moure's veterinary clinic. It's just that the male has an injured paw and the female is insulin-dependent.

Gonza Calderón rifled through the closet in his parents' bedroom, looking for money in the pockets of the clothing. Carefully, slowly. He always did it. And he always found some. Once he found dollars. When his mother grew tired of looking for them, she concluded that it had been María, the maid, and she threw her out. After twenty years. She blamed Gonza a little. Because when María left, she told his mother: To think I helped raise your son, señora. But it doesn't matter. God always punishes the guilty party. And it wasn't me. I swear by my seven kids. Every time Gonza rifled through the closet he remembered María and was touched by a brief wave of guilt, which lasted until his hand came upon a few coins, a few bills. But now what he's come upon is a DVD. Curiosity gets him. He goes up to his room and pops it in the machine. Valeria diligently helping

Alejo get it up with her tongue. Gonza never imagined that his aunt could suck dick so professionally. The image turns Gonza on and he starts jerking off. Valeria and Alejo snorting coke. Valeria smiles, licking her hand. She's holding a dildo. And she sticks it into Alejo. Panting, Alejo ejaculates, but less than a porn actor. Gonza hears the new maid running the vacuum in the hall. He shuts everything off.

The phenomenon took place at the end of July. Sub-zero temperatures like never before, I recall. It froze your bones. A black night. A huge fire nose-diving from the sky. The darkness began to light up and change color. From green to orange. And then the explosion. A phenomenon, that explosion. It burst, launching gigantic sparks. It wasn't lightning. And the noise, louder than a thunderbolt. Like a jet plane crashing. No, it wasn't a UFO, either. It left us stunned. Everything trembled. An earthquake, thought those who were inside. Furniture, walls. Shattered windows. It seemed as if the roofs of the Villa were about to fly off. The end of the world. The flames fell behind the dunes, exactly between the dunes' water supply and the road. The next day helicopters began flying over the area. There was an ash-filled crater. They said the ashes were volcanic.

The atmosphere protects us from so-called *Near Earth Objects*, Martínez, the director of the Aeroclub explained in his Cambridge-inflected English. There are as many wandering asteroids as comets. And every so often they collide with the earth. Some can be miles wide. They can cause atmospheric damage on a global scale. For example, the extinction of the dinosaurs millions of years ago may have been caused by an asteroid. In the fourteenth century, thousands of people in China died in a rain of flaming stones. In 1900 one of these objects fell in Siberia and thousands of forests burned. A real expert, that Martínez. Big reader of *National Geographic*.

But Father Joaquín didn't agree with the scientific explanation. It was the sins in this place that brought about this warning from heaven. A sign, said the priest. The Lord is warning us. That's what Father Joaquín said a few days before escaping to Tandil for a couple of days with Solange, the wife of Salvi, the manager of La Confianza Insurance.

Erectile dysfunction is not the same as impotence. It's important to distinguish between occasional dysfunction, sometimes caused by an emotional upset in a relationship like insecurity, timidity, or a block, and persistent or chronic dysfunction, which affects 7% of men between the ages of eighteen and thirty, 20% of those in their fifties and 60% after age seventy. Many physical factors that cause this dysfunction stem from diabetes, hypertension, high cholesterol, and obesity. Habits like smoking and a sedentary lifestyle are also contributors. Although in our Villa we enjoy a quality of life favorable to well-being and health, statistics suggest that while cases of erectile dysfunction have not reached alarming levels, they should be taken seriously and without prejudice. This problem, which generally embarrasses those affected, is a common ailment and can be cured. Before taking medications on your own initiative or becoming overwhelmed by thoughts of male menopause, talking about the problem is the first step to reaching a solution. Talk to us. At Clínica del Mar we offer confidential service, with the privacy gentlemen require. Insurance plans accepted. Avda. Del Mar 3587. Phones: 463524/28/39.

One night, after putting *El Vocero* to bed, Dante told us that everything he knew about journalism he had learned from Walsh. We asked him to tell us about Walsh. And he told us a story. Knowing Dante and how every so often, as he speaks, a silence slips in and you can't tell if it's to create suspense or to give him time to think about where his invention will go next, a silence that he sees as intriguing. I mean, knowing him, you guys tell me if you think the story is true.

The military takes over. The guerrillas are cornered. One of Walsh's daughters dies in combat. He writes a letter to his *compañeros.* One night he and his *compañera* have nowhere to stay. There's no place for them anywhere. They decide to sleep on a bus. They take one here, to the Villa. The night of the journey it's impossible for him to fall asleep. The bus plunges into the darkened countryside. He tries to remember the last time he saw the sea. All night long he doesn't sleep. The bus travels through his memory. By the time he finally manages to nod off, the bus is entering the still-dark Villa. There's some time yet before dawn. He and the woman walk toward the sea, toward dawn over the sea. They watch the sun come up. And they take a bus back to the city.

There are those who wonder why Malerba didn't take the bait when Fito the albino tried to put up the dough for him to eliminate his father, our Speer. Let me tell you why: Malerba never liked our Speer. His anger started that winter when he discovered Missy, his girlfriend, in bed with his kid, Matías. Malerba beat the hell out of Missy. And she took off, practically butt-naked, wearing nothing but a poncho, and since no one dared pick up El Capo's filly, it was our Speer, another thug, her savior, who hooked her and set her up in a cottage in Mar de las Pampas. Of course Malerba wanted our Speer's head, and even though his cancer was very advanced and he insisted he was out of the picture, he waited for an opportunity to get even.

And then, like a gift of fortune, Fito showed up to hire him. Malerba found the kid just as disgusting as his old man. A Machiavellian scheme of his, refusing to finish off the father, like the kid asked. He decided instead to put a 22 in the kid's hand. It's not manly to delegate what destiny hands you, he told him. Fito fearfully took the pistol. Then, gathering his composure, he stuck it in his jacket. Malerba patted him on the back: Be brave, boy.

Dobroslav, our Speer, the one who had stolen Missy, murdered. And his offspring, in jail for parricide. Don't tell me it wasn't an elegant vengeance scheme. But Malerba didn't reckon on the Dobroslav kid being such a wimp that he'd chicken out when it came time to pull the trigger. So Malerba will have to keep waiting to get even for that Missy business. Or dream up some other kind of revenge before the cancer drags him off to hell, that is—if there's any hell besides this one.

There was a meeting at the Public Welfare Association in La Virgencita. The neighborhood was prepared to demand more security. What do you mean "more," what we need to demand is security, period, because there isn't any here. Belén Yanina's disappearance is a good example. What we should have done was to organize a march. Even though Victoriano and María Adelia had been invited to the meeting, they didn't show up. They're destroyed, one of the women said. Besides, with that religion of theirs, they don't react, said someone else. The problem wasn't the temple, somebody argued. I go to the temple, too, but I'm here. We have to be the ones to take the initiative. For Belén Yanina's sake and for our own kids.

If the parents of Nuestra Señora had gathered to go on the hunt for the abusers, they could do it, too. More than one had a weapon at home. They would organize patrols. If necessary they would turn the Villa inside out like a glove. And it would be no surprise if the Romero girl's disappearance turned out to be some kind of prank by the snobby kids from the boulevards. They agreed to meet again the next day, but first they would speak to the Romeros. It was essential for them to agree to head the march for security.

Although our Villa offers a quality of life that big city dwellers envy and our landscape is ideal for raising and educating children in a privileged natural environment, many children are nonetheless affected with asthma. This illness compromises the lungs through bronchial obstruction and inflammation. Asthma is very common, and its incidence is increasing daily throughout the world. The latest national polls reveal that it affects

20% of the population, most of whom are unaware that there are simple, harmless treatments that can help sufferers lead a normal life. Childhood-onset asthma can be treated with appropriate medications to prevent lifelong suffering. Medications, inhalers, psychotherapy, and the advent of alternative therapies provide us with different approaches to its prevention and cure. Stop suffering. Here in our Villa, Clínica del Mar offers a first-rate professional team that guarantees every patient a search for the immediate solution to their problem. Health insurance plans and credit cards accepted. Avenida del Mar 3857. Phones: 4635243/28/39.

It's almost dawn. And Dante ambles along slowly after the last whiskey at Moby. For a while now he's been finding it hard to leave the bar; he's the last to go. The last, and the last whiskey. One for the road, he says to Bruno. It won't get light for a while yet. As he approaches the main drag he sees them. Young girls and boys. Not one of them looks more than fifteen, Dante thinks, but there are bigger ones, too. What happens is that poor kids grow old faster. But those who are coming out and joining the march aren't just poor kids from La Virgencita and El Monte. There are also blondies from Pinar del Norte. They lag behind, the younger ones. And even farther behind, those who just recently learned to walk. And yet they join in, silent, serious-looking, assuming a grown-up expression. They emerge from their houses, responding to a call that only they can hear. They come out of shacks, they come out of chalets, they come out of mansions, they come out of apartment buildings. From everywhere, they come out. And they join the crowd. More and more of them. Dante thinks this is one of those opportunities for a great article that comes along just once in a lifetime. He rummages in his pockets but realizes he has nothing to write with. He must make note of the details, he warns himself. He can't allow a single detail to get away from him. Especially now that the kids are heading toward the police station. A cop at the door tries to block them. Cornered, he attempts to draw his weapon but can't quite manage. The swarm of kids traps him, silently, because everything happens in silence. They tear him to pieces. Then they enter the police station. Without so much as a scream or a shot being heard, they take over the police station and all the weapons within their reach. When they go back outside to the street, the bigger ones, who probably initiated the attack, are spattered with blood. The ones with weapons are now in the vanguard. He recognizes some of them. He knows which ones come from rich families and which from poor ones. The kid of a whore from the Tropicana. The daughter of a limo driver. A Kennedy kid. There are also the half-breeds, those descended from natives, and those with immigrant roots. Dante sees what they're about to do. And he can't stop it. He can't. Suddenly he realizes that he always knew this would happen one day.

And today's that day.

The day has arrived.

Blood doesn't count, one of them said. And here in Moby, at this time of night, there's a drunken argument. Let's look around, let's see how many in this town don't give a shit about blood. I can name whole families for you. Fathers against sons. Sons against fathers. Nephews against uncles. Grandparents against grandchildren. Grandchildren against grandparents. Not to mention brothers against brothers. Mothers, daughters, granddaughters. No one escapes here. Not even those who right now are lingering over their last drink before Bruno locks up. Dante lashes out: He who is free from sin, he says, and stops. The topic under discussion is that the Quiroses adopted their wayward sister's son. And especially Alejo, who had his nephew before he had his own offspring. The least he could do, someone retorts. Why do you think the kid's mother got involved in revolutionary violence. Why did the daughter of the most powerful family in town get mixed up in heavy stuff like that and get hold of a machine gun. The room grows silent. Go figure. Every household is a world of its own.

Zanoni the electrician and Cabrera the gasfitter offered to go to the Romeros' place. They were received like Frugone, like Renzo and Balmaceda. The couple invited them into the kitchen. María Adelia brought a pitcher of water and glasses. We're organizing a march, Cabrera began. A march, María Adelia repeated. And what for. What do you mean, what for, said Zanoni. To demand security. Go out into the street, Victoriano, Cabrera said to him. There's not one working streetlamp. The gangs of thugs do whatever they fucking want. We're not the type to march, said María Adelia. If we organize, Zanoni went on, we can change things. We have the means, Cabrera said. We have weapons and we have cars, he said. We've got balls as big as the parents from Nuestra Señora. They took turns speaking, egging each other on. The Romeros' silence inflamed their passions. They couldn't remain so unemotional after what had happened to Belén Yanina. We don't know what happened to her, said Victoriano. What do you mean, you don't know, Cabrera said. She's not here, María Adelia said. The only thing we know is she's not here. But what happened to her, we don't know. Only God knows.

If God hasn't returned her to you yet, Zanoni told her, then it's time for us to do something. We're going to turn the settlements upside down, the shacks in El Monte and La Virgencita, kick in doors, whatever it takes, Zanoni said. We all know where the hoodlums live, Cabrera went on. We're going to clean up this place, Zanoni joined in. Belén Yanina is our daughter, too, he said. No, said María Adelia. We're against violence, said Victoriano. We appreciate your concern, but no, said Victoriano.

At its meeting the next day, the Public Welfare Association discussed how to organize the march. Without the Romeros' participation it would lose its impact. If the parents didn't want to participate it was because they were hiding something. Deep down, they must be afraid of being found out. They would have to go ahead with the march, regardless. We're going to bring posters with photos of the girl. What if it was the parents, a woman asked. Impossible, interjected somebody else. The Romeros were a perfect family. The person standing beside him blurted out: The Pinar del Norte snobs act like they're perfect, too. Those perfect types scare me, said another woman. The temple, the temple, all the time, and then something happens like in the States, added yet another. And he began to tell a story about a documentary on the Mormons. They practiced polygamy, committed abuse, horrific crimes. The Romeros aren't Mormons, a woman corrected him. It doesn't matter, said another. What matters is that they're not Christians. We didn't come here to argue religion, said someone else. We came to figure out what we're going to do. Nothing, said somebody else. We're not going to do anything. Because if the Romeros aren't with us, it can all backfire. And if it turns out they were responsible, then what. Who knows what they did to the kid, someone said. Or what the girl was into, said somebody else. There are so many pious little hypocrites around. Another commented: Nobody looked at the Tropicana. The girl wasn't a baby, someone said. You just had to look at her. She was already a woman. We can't go on with these fantasies, said Cabrera. We'll end up believing she was carried off by a UFO. Another, very somberly, remarked: Don't make fun of UFOs. Let's have the protest and that'll be it, said Zanoni. We can't just do nothing, said Cabrera. We agreed to organize, Zanoni continued. We did, said someone. But now, in the light of the discussion, everything has changed. Tell me what will happen if things aren't as they seem, if the girl hasn't vanished, if the parents were abusing her and they were afraid she'd report them. I have to go home, somebody said. And I've got to get up early tomorrow, said somebody else. You folks go on and tell me tomorrow, said another. Before they realized it, Zanoni and Cabrera were left by themselves.

The march came to nothing. And the rumor began circulating that Belén Yanina's parents had something to do with her disappearance. The parents knew, people said. From more than one window the flyer asking Where Is Belén Yanina was removed.

Couple masturbation is healthy. And we recommend practicing it with the new Play Vibrations. It consists of a silicone penis ring that adjusts to size. It offers a pleasant vibration, stimulating the penis but especially the vaginal area, including the clitoris. Play Vibrations comes equipped with a small switch to turn it on and off as desired. The drawback is that this wonderful scientific invention lasts only twenty minutes and is not rechargeable. It's fun because you have to find the position that allows maximum stimulation. One great plus is that it can be used with or without a condom. Sold in pharmacies and beauty supply stores. Information: 467890.

Fox, heron, owl, gnatcatcher, partridge, shark, goldfinch, weasel, hake, hare, *teru-teru*, sparrow, sea lion, lark, armadillo, swallow, corvina, lizard, hawk, snake. Let each man, each woman, choose one of God's creatures that best represents their being.

This Sunday marks the feast of Saint Raymond Nonnatus, patron saint of children and pregnant women. The Ladies Auxiliary devoted to the Saint asks everyone in the community who plans to attend the 11 A.M. Mass to please bring baby clothing or diapers for donation to Nuestra Virgen de la Merced, Avenida 10 and Boulevard at 9:00 A.M.

That's the way it is here: even if you don't provide the wool, they'll knit a sweater for you.

A tough guy doesn't retire, says Dante. He gets retired. And he clarifies: I'm talking about Malerba. In the 70s, in the mid-70s, Malerba came to the Villa. He came and bought a little place in the south:

the Bora-Bora. He paid cash for it. No one asked him where it came from. No one was about to, either. His reputation might be one answer.

They say one morning that winter the police surrounded the hut. That he was hiding some guerrillas who escaped after the battle of Monte Chingolo. It's possible, why not. We'll never know the truth. And least of all from Malerba himself. I don't go to bed with nobody, Malerba would say. Everybody comes looking for me, he laughed over a whiskey at the bar in Poker. Because Malerba wasn't one to frequent Moby. He was more attracted to Poker's whiskey vibe than to the hippie pub atmosphere at Moby. But I don't want to get off track here. And he continues: They say Malerba worked for the right-wing unions and also for the Navy at the base in Mar del Plata. You can be on God's side, Malerba likes to say, but don't forget that God invented hell, so don't act so high-minded if it makes sense to come to terms with the devil. When democracy returned, the cops came after him again at the hut. They found weapons on him as well as coke. And he was supposed to be out of the game. Retired, he used to say. I'm retired. Before they let me go, I retire. That's what he used to say, but like Dante said—and he also heard Malerba's words—a gangster doesn't retire, and then there was that Pedroza business. Pedroza's girl, I'm talking about Luz. Bignose, the dealer, gives the girl the plague. And Pedroza hires Malerba. No one believes the story about Bignose's suicide. And nobody's gonna ask Malerba either, if he had anything to do with the kid's murder. These days it's impossible for a retiree to survive without an odd job or two, Dante quotes Malerba as saying.

Always, whenever you hear a row, whether in a house or outdoors, there's a silence. Always. And you hear better in the silence. After the last curse Campas hurled at Anita, there was silence. One of those silences where the only thing you feel is the stillness. And within the stillness, in the distance, the sea. A long time went by, interminable.

More than half an hour, for sure. An hour, maybe. Then we heard the car motor. From the slamming of the car doors we understood that both of them had gone out. To the hospital, we later found out. It was late. We went to sleep. Usually in the morning I get up early to bring my husband a couple of *mates*. By six he's already up, opening the kiosk.

Dante published the notice about Belén Yanina for a few weeks. Until one afternoon he ran across Romero leaving Banco Provincia. They said hello. But Romero kept on going, toward the Jeep. Wait, Dante said. And he asked him how he was. I'm all right, Romero told him. Any news, he asked. Nothing, said Romero. Take out the notice if you need the space. It's no problem for me to keep publishing it, Dante told him. Whatever you think, said Romero. I'll leave it in a while longer, Dante said. Don't go to any trouble, Romero told him. It's no trouble, Dante said. God bless you, Romero said. And he shook his hand.

Dante stood there watching the Jeep pull away. He asked himself the same questions the entire Villa was asking. But he resisted thinking as everyone else did. I'm not like everyone else, he said to himself. Maybe Romero's attitude was a quiet, obedient acceptance of his God's will, he thought. His God had endowed him with superhuman pain tolerance. Romero wasn't like everyone else, either, he thought. It wasn't so much the other man's resignation that exasperated him as the fact that it imposed the same resignation on him. He wouldn't just give up. That Friday in *El Vocero*, you could read it again: *Where is Belén Yanina?* That Friday and a few more.

Till Alejo caught up with him: Cut out the crap about that girl. Like we didn't have enough bad press with the sexual abuse shit.

As I was getting up to go to work at the supermarket—it was still dark—I found Lorena awake at the computer. She hadn't slept all night. She couldn't go to junior high without a wink of sleep. She wasn't going to be able to perform in class like that. You can't spend your life on the computer, all shut in, without friends, I told her. I have friends, Nidia, she answered without taking her eyes off the screen. Don't call me by my name, I said to her. I'm your mother. Call me Mom. And you'd better tell me where your friends are, okay? They're right here, she said, still not taking her eyes off the screen. Here, where? We're alone here. You and me. Alone. What kind of friends are they, I said, getting angry. Your friends are imaginary. Leave me alone, Nidia, she said. I told you to call me Mom. They're very close friends. And she kept scrolling through the photos on the screen. And what do you write each other, I asked her. We don't write each other, she said. We chat. And then: don't be such a cop, Nidia. Don't you talk to me like that, Lorena. She provoked me. Turn that thing off. You want me to be bitter like you, she said. Look at that face of yours, like you need a good fuck. I couldn't take it anymore. And I smacked her across the face. That same morning, while Lorena was at school, I sold the machine to a computer store. They didn't give me much for it. I figured when Lorena got home from school and didn't find the machine she'd make a stink. I was ready to knock her teeth out if she sassed me. But no. Not a peep. Nothing. She stopped talking to me. She took her revenge through silence. We were two mutes in the house.

Lorena started going to a cybercafé. As soon as school let out, she ran over there and sat down at a computer until nighttime, when the place closed. And she still didn't say a word to me. Till that night when I dragged her home by the hair. Then she spoke: I'm running away with my boyfriend, she threatened me. What boyfriend, I asked her. Because I didn't know she had one. He's virtual, she said. I'm running away with him. I'll beat the shit out of you, I said. And it won't be virtual.

And what happened, happened. She ran away from home and went to her virtual boyfriend's place. How was I supposed to know he was a kid from around here. As soon as she got to his house, she told me later, Mr. Virtual was waiting for her. With three friends. The mayor's son, one of them was. That piece of shit, Gonza. And Facu Davide, Santiago Luciani, Juanma Quirós, among others. Turns out those guys were her Internet friends. Snooty rich kids, all of them. She came back all beaten up, crying, my sweet baby. What those degenerates did to her. Or rather, what they didn't do to her. I had to drag her to the police station. But she refused to file a complaint against them. She was terrified. She spent all her time crying in her room. It made me feel so sorry for her that I went and bought her another computer. She can't live disconnected, poor thing.

A sixteen-year-old girl was raped in a downtown apartment by four youths who photographed the assault. The girl was lured there under false pretenses by one of her attackers, with whom she had been maintaining a virtual romance, chatting from a cybercafé. When the girl arrived at the designated location, she hesitated to enter the apartment, but the youths grabbed her by her arms and feet and brought her inside. The forensic doctor who examined the victim verified the presence of vaginal abrasions and anal tearing, in addition to hematomas on her arms. Sources connected with the investigation reported that the attackers were under the influence of alcohol and narcotics. It was determined that they belong to prominent middle and upper-class families in our community. Apparently the young man who acted as lure in this act of brutality, posing as the victim's virtual boyfriend, refused to participate in the aggression and left the location when he saw that the situation had escalated. Authorities have decided to withhold the identities of the victim and her assailants as all of them are minors.

Rosita is nuts, says Eusebio the limo driver. When I'm fucking her, with her big belly and all, she asks to let her call me Dicky, like her husband. Does it bother you that I call you Dicky, she asks me. Not at all, I tell her. That way I don't feel so much like I'm cheating on my husband, she says. What really gets her hot is when her nipples leak milk on my dick and then she sucks me off. Well, she also gets me hard you-know-how. I love you, Dicky, she screams when she comes. And it's not just her tits that drip. You should hear how that cunt screams. Sometimes I'm afraid she'll have a heart attack.

Another one of Moni's poems, one of those she likes best.

I say, says / the other / although sometimes / it's me, only / sometimes / but not now, not / when she writes: I.

That night, after Anita appeared in the paper participating in the Forum for a Non-Violent Villa, Campa's shouting could be heard up and down the block. He was beside himself. You think people are fucking stupid, Anita, he yelled at her. You think they've forgotten the mess you stirred up by supporting those kids, those rockers. Everybody remembers the swastika, and now you stick your nose in that forum, as if nothing ever happened here. And no matter how many pretty little pacifist speeches you give, people remember on account of the Bolita baby that turned up burned. While you're going around defending the poor, my sales are dropping. Sure, sure, the only thing that matters to the lady is being in the paper and on TV. You won't stop till you get on the Mirtha Legrand show. Because being low profile isn't enough for you. Get it straight, girl, while you go around thinking your shit don't stink, I'm the one who keeps this household going by selling crappers. Quit playing the big shot. The big shot here is me. The one who pays the bills is the big shot. And don't put on that innocent face. Don't take me for an idiot; I'm not one of your little half-breeds.

No, you couldn't hear Anita. She's not the type to raise her voice.

The next day, when Anita walked into the school with her arm in a cast, she said she had fallen again. It was a miracle the cast didn't break. Down the stairs, from the top floor. She hurt all over, she said. I've just been under a lot of stress lately. Don't know where my head is.

She had come to turn in her resignation, she said.

Ever since then she's felt guilty; ever since *that* happened to her, as Nidia calls Lorena's rape, *that* happened, as if by saying it like that, avoiding the word rape, what happened to Lorena hadn't really happened, as if they hadn't done what they did, and then she might also avoid feeling guilty about what took place, because Nidia feels that if she hadn't forbidden Lorena to use the computer, if she hadn't induced her to go to the cybercafé, that wouldn't have happened to her daughter. In the same way, whenever Nidia thinks about what they did to her, she feels like she's part of the subject, that third person plural: she's one of the ones who did what they did to her little girl. She feels all these things. And she feels them more every day, every night, but especially at night. During the day Nidia works at the supermarket, straightening up the storage room, the carts, handling the cash register. She concentrates on her work. And the work distracts her. Her co-workers realize that. At first they asked her about Lorena. Nidia's face blanched at the question. Her eyes filled with tears. Her co-workers stopped asking. And it's gotten better. But even when they don't ask, Nidia knows what they're thinking when they look at her out of the corner of their eyes, spying on her, that it's a way of finding out how she feels. If Nidia catches a couple of girls looking at her, she gives them a tiny smile. Or she winks at them. It's a kind of disarming. Nidia pretends she's made of iron. She has to be made of iron to keep on going. And she often wonders: what if the thing that happened to Lorena had happened to her instead. She would have swallowed her rage. She wouldn't have gone to the police. She would have found some way to get even on her own. Because the cops, she knows, are on the side of those who did it, the kids from good families, the social climbers. Like Gonza

Calderón. They didn't throw him in jail when he was dealing, so why should they nab him now for fucking a little half-breed. And yes, for them Lorena is a little half-breed. It calms Nidia to think about revenge. What happened to Lorena happened to her. What they did to Lorena, they also did to me. I *am* Lorena. Nidia! Her supervisor, Claudia, summons her. Nidia doesn't respond. Nidia! the other woman persists. Suddenly, as if yanked from a dream, Nidia answers her: Sorry, Clau. I was thinking about something else. I am Lorena, she's thinking, but doesn't say it. Give me a hand in the dairy section, Claudia orders.

Here, too. The tide brought them in. They washed up on the beach. Bodies. It was so long ago. More than thirty-five years have gone by. What, are you going to dig up the dunes? Give me a break. Why do you want to know, anyway. That's over. Who cares. All right, I'll tell you who knows, but don't say I told you.

Even though Zambrano shut down the hospital on him twice with claims from the union, Cachito sort of admires him. But the mongo's abortion was too much. No one came forward with a formal complaint. But that fact, if proven, would be a time bomb in the hands of the opposition. That Zambrano is the abortionist of the poor of La Virgencita. That he secretly practices in the hospital. And no, he doesn't charge them. No speculation about what he does. Solidarity, they say.

Dark, short, beetle-browed, looking more like a boxer than a surgeon, Zambrano is one of the most beloved physicians in the Villa. Although he was in the Malvinas War, he doesn't look his age. We half-breeds don't show our age, he says. Or our suffering, either. If he has to take a risk, he takes it. Like that woman from La Virgencita and her girl who showed up at the ER. Down syndrome, the girl. Pregnant. And bleeding to death. She couldn't have been more than twelve. I couldn't do it, Doctor. You get it out of her. Get that thing out, the mother begged him. Because it had been the mother, with a knitting needle, who had tried to do the D&C. But she failed. God is really punishing us, Doc. First he made her slow, like. And then he filled her with evil.

Zambrano did the impossible to finish up what the mother had begun. He never found an explanation for what happened. Despite the anesthesia and tranquilizers, the girl went into cardiac arrest. And there she stayed. Or rather, there she went.

A little while later, Cachito called him in. And now Zambrano is in the mayor's office. Cachito invites him to have a seat. The doc refuses. This time you've gone too far, Zambrano, Cachito tells him. He wants break the other man's will: You know what you're doing is illegal. Zambrano glares at him: *You're* talking to me about illegality? Cachito tries to lighten up: You know I appreciate you, Zambrano. You're essential to the hospital, people love you, and I'd like you to continue in your position. Zambrano: I didn't know my job was in danger. Cachito: It isn't in danger, but this abortion business stings. And to make matters worse, the mongo goes and dies on you. If nobody hit the roof, it was because I calmed the beasts. You owe me; I just wanted to let you know. Remember: you owe me.

Zambrano turns his back and walks out of the office without even closing the door.

I'll never bring a child into this world, Zambrano thinks. Never. He climbs into his Fiat and returns to the hospital. He has reason to think that way. Besides the Malvinas, many other reasons. This life, for example. Peace is the continuation of war by other means. Et cetera. The butchery never ends.

You know how there are days when you feel worn out, and not necessarily because of your period. Those days are more common now; they start at the beginning of autumn, when besides the cold, sadness sets in. You let yourself go, you don't wash your hair or go to the beauty salon. You can spend an entire month in the same jogging suit. Well, I'm exaggerating: not a month, but maybe a week. And speaking of jogging, you don't wear it for what you're supposed to anymore, because you stop running and going to the gym. Then you stop caring about what you eat—pasta, stews, or smoking, and let's not even talk about your splash of wine, if you don't start tippling in secret. Inertia gets hold of you. It's not laziness, it's not sloth. More like paralysis. And if your man wants you ready and willing, since it's more trouble to convince him that he's not getting any tonight, you open up, so he'll hurry up and pull it out and let you sleep because tomorrow the one who has to get up at seven to take the kids to school and then open the kiosk is you. Before you know it, it's already winter, eternal winter. Cold, rain. Nothing to do but huddle up inside. Unless some Friday, some Saturday, it's a girlfriend's birthday and she throws a party and then you have to dress up, you go to the beauty salon, you buy yourself something to wear, but the fashion show feeling lasts as long as a sigh. And you're worn out again. It's not just a feeling. It shows in the way you look. You let yourself go: you don't shave your legs, don't dye your hair, don't use perfume, and you even stop worrying about cigarette breath. Don't even talk to me about spring: one sunny day, two windy ones, three of rain, and then again, one sunny, two rainy, three windy. It's true, nature speeds up the seasons here. And a girl's got to speed things up too and get caught up with the situation, bloom, so then you make up your mind to go back to the gym, your diet, cosmetics, but it's too late, first because we've had it, and second because who's gonna notice us, as disheveled as we are, gray hair, bags under our eyes, double chins, rolls of fat. The most we'll do is fix ourselves up a little for the season. That's when you've got to be presentable if you have a business, if you have a job at a hotel or work as a waitress in a restaurant. Luckily the season flies by quickly. And soon we'll be going around in that comfy jogging suit again. So, give me a break: if we came here to live it was so we'd be comfortable.

Have you heard the latest? Early Tuesday morning Fabián, the astrologer, argued with his sister Gladys, the acupuncturist. After plunging a scissor into her, Fabián put on one of her bikinis and went off to the beach. It was below freezing. Regardless, he headed for the water. The tide brought him in a few days later. Poor dude. Saturn was misaligned.

You're gonna shit green, says the voice on the telephone, a hoarse voice, a drunken voice. Faked, of course. Ten thousand greenies in cash. A cumbia plays in the background. Cash, asshole.

Ten thousand, in exchange for the video where you can see him with a dildo up his ass. It isn't that much money, Alejo thinks. He must be a novice, he thinks. The voice tells him he's to leave the money in the forest, under a marked eucalyptus tree, that same night. If you notify the pigs, everyone will see you on TV with a dildo up your ass, shithead. Alejo could have told him that nothing comes on the local channel without his permission. But he keeps quiet. He keeps quiet and listens. He listens and waits for the voice to continue: A eucalyptus in the forest, the voice says to him. I'll tell you which one.

Silence. You can hear the cumbia at the other end of the line. It can't be the Reyes or the Vicuñas, he thinks. And surely not the Osorios. They're not smart enough and they wouldn't be so bold, either, he thinks. And he listens: Once the deal is completed, the next night he'll find the video in the same place. Alejo asks the voice what guarantee there is that the exchange will take place. The voice laughs in his face: The guarantee you won't look like such a dick.

He has no choice but to trust him.

Just like all those poor wretches who trust him when they come to his law office so he'll free them from some mess that later on will turn into a debt to be collected, not necessarily in bills. More than once Alejo has acted high and mighty with those who come to see him: I'm gonna make you an offer you can't refuse, he imitates Corleone. It's an offer you can't refuse. And now this voice. He must be a kid, Alejo calculates. Pay attention to the instructions, asshole. Pay attention, asshole.

Why the fuck had he agreed to Valeria's crazy idea of filming a fuck. The stupid whore told him it was so she could get hot when he wasn't there, so she could watch it while she jerked off. Jew bitch. But even more than Valeria's, it was the fault of the blow. Blow fucks you up. He promises himself that he'll never snort again. If I get out of this, dear God, I swear: no more blow. Although now, even as he swears, Alejo realizes he doesn't altogether believe he's capable of giving it up. Suddenly he asks himself what fucking good does it do him to go to Mass every Sunday.

Here in Pinar del Norte, let's be honest, no matter how casual we may act, nobody wants their kids to go to middle school, the same one where the kids of custodians and darkie thugs go. Lots of us aren't religious or believers, but some are, though a minority. You can count the devout on one hand. What I'm trying to say is that a person doesn't have to be Catholic to choose Nuestra Señora as the best school. Even the Jews send their kids to Nuestra Señora. Obviously Nuestra Señora isn't of the same caliber as the private schools in Buenos Aires, but it's the cream of the crop around here. The scandal will pass. But the tradition of Nuestra Señora will continue. Because people like us need it.

They were having dinner. Alejo was the first to notice that it wasn't one of Camilo's typical outbursts, one of those where he would scream and zip out the door. This time it was a different kind of attack: his eyes rolling up, the tremors. Camilo began to buck like a horse. Shaking, he fell on his back. Jackie and the kids backed away, terrified. Alejo grabbed a dish towel and stuck it between Camilo's teeth. He held him. For a long time. For as long as the attack lasted, he held him. And when it was over, Camilo looked around, returning from far away, and started to cry like a child: Everything's all right, everything's all right now, son. You're with us. You're with your family. Don't be afraid. Nothing will happen to you. Then, turning toward Jackie, Alejo changed his expression: Get moving. Call Zambrano.

Zambrano arrived at Quirós's chalet in a flash.

He doesn't need to be admitted. I'm going to medicate him.

Why does this happen to him, doc, Alejo asked. Now, in Zambrano's presence, he was someone else. The fact that Zambrano hadn't toadied before Cachito inspired not only respect, but also a certain affection in him. Just as his past as a former militant did. Two of a kind, Alejo thought they were. Only in different corners of the ring.

Zambrano stared him down. Intently. He didn't like it when people tried to suck up to him, calling him "doc." Least of all Alejo.

Just like my sister, Alejo said. She had these attacks. Later, when she got involved in what she got involved in, they stopped. We realized she was up to something strange because the attacks went away. Until she did, too. She went away and so did the attacks. And she disappeared off the face of the earth. Maybe the boy inherited that sickness. Maybe he takes after his mother. And what's happening to him is hereditary.

Camilo was asleep now.

Zambrano said he was leaving. Alejo asked how much he owed him.

Nothing, he said. And he handed him a prescription. This is the medication.

Alejo stuck out his hand. But Zambrano didn't take it.

It was a cold, clear night. Sleet was falling. The doctor's car was slow to start. A Fiat 1500. With that hunk of tin, and he feels like a big shot, Alejo thought.

Jackie awaited him with a question:

Why did you call your nephew "son?"

Alejo, quick to reply:

I'm not in the mood to chat.

We live on the same street as Anita and Osvaldo. We've known Osvaldo since he was born. He met Anita in La Plata, when he went there to study Economics, but he had to drop out. His father died, and he had to come back and take over the store. Anita arrived shortly after that. A very well-liked couple around here, both of them. You should've seen how Anita took care of Osvaldo's mom when she got sick. They probably have their disagreements, like everyone. We have them, too. Marriage is patience. Sometimes you lose it. It could be that Osvaldo slapped Anita. These things happen sometimes. I don't want to judge. Those of us outside a marriage aren't the mattress. But I don't want to give out misinformation. I didn't overhear that fight. And if I had, I wouldn't go around airing somebody else's business. Besides, all that stuff people are saying about the Campases doesn't do anyone on this block any good. We're tactful people. Not gangsters, druggies, and whoremongers like the half-breeds in La Virgencita and El Monte. You saw what kind of faces those guys have. And to top it all off, it seems there's another township down there now. That's why we lock up everything at night and let the dogs loose.

On starry nights Martínez from the Aeroclub observes the sky through his telescope. Every so often he spots a shooting star and his hopes are raised. When he thinks he's seen a UFO, which Martínez pronounces *oo-fo*, he wonders if one night, in spite of the potholes in the road, one of them might land and save him from this hell.

If we jog our memory, Dante proposes, we'll see that every year there are three or four protests in the Villa. Every year. Let's jog our memory. There was a huge one for the Veira kids' crime, the one from Los Álamos radio-taxi service. Another, the Romina case, the girl that was knifed in the forest. Granted, the chick was a danger; she went from being Beer Queen a couple of years ago to bar girl in Mar del Plata. According to the autopsy, she was pregnant. And let's not forget the march they organized for more police reinforcement during that wave of robberies that ended with the shootout at the door of Banco Nación; the retired couple that was caught in the crossfire, and, according to what people say, it was police shells that killed them. Another massive protest was the one that was organized for García, the gas deliveryman, shot one stormy night as he finished his rounds. On a smaller scale, the one for the gay lottery ticket vendor, shot in the head as he came out of his agency. All the cases we're naming came to nothing. And missing from the list is the Bolivians' march, even though we'd rather forget that one.

Nothing could be proven for those who were suspicious of Romina's crime. The investigation of the cops who were involved in the Banco Nación gunfight also came to nothing. Condorito's death was blamed on some Peruvians from La Virgencita, but after a while they were set free. Nothing ever happens. And nothing, as we all know, is going to happen with the Nuestra Señora del Mar business. And nothing will happen for several reasons. First of all because the whole Villa is happy that this time the shit's splashing on the big shots, too. And also because it's a religious school: the priests will cover up everything. Let no one be fooled. Nothing's going to happen. And since nothing's going to happen here, everything will keep happening.

You think you're going to get kicked out of town for writing this novel. Like hell you are. What'll happen is that everyone will think they're fictional characters, and even when you've taken pieces of one to build another, à la Frankenstein, they'll all want to be in it and discover themselves in there. Because even when the shit splashes on them, nobody will want to be left out. And that won't have anything to do with your literary merit. It'll be pure vanity. Vanity is our downfall. Who doesn't like to be in the picture.

If nothing good can be expected of those four, Gonza Calderón, the mayor's son; Juanma Quirós; and the Ramos brothers, Nico and Matías, then even less can be said of Santiago Luciani, the appointed heir of Velox Transportation. To his father's bitter disappointment, there's no rehab that can bring Santiago, his brain fried by drugs, back to reality. Now, at nineteen, he speaks in a twangy stammer sprinkled with expressions from Tolkien.

The four kids amble through the forest, smoking a joint. They're talking about that crying you can hear at night. Maybe we're gonna have to lighten up on the weed, said Matías. It's not the weed, Gonza replies. It's the Bolita baby. Its spirit is after us.

You sure none of us opened his trap, asks Nico.

No fuckin' way, says Gonza.

What about you, Santiago, Matías asks.

Me, neither, he replies. I'm into other stuff.

After a while, as they roll another joint in a beach cabana, Santiago says he's got a secret. They smoke. They watch him.

A gnome, Santiago says.

He found it in the woods and keeps it in his house, stored in a closet. The others look at each other, wondering whether to laugh or feel sorry for Santiago.

Get a new dealer, Nico orders him.

And Santiago: Your choice. You'll miss the gnome, he says.

They want to see, they tell him. They don't believe him.

Okay, but first I have to buy him dog food, Santiago says. Doguis brand. And he explains: Because gnomes really go for Doguis. It's their favorite food. They arrive at the Luciani house, that California-style mansion at the end of the poplar groves. Santiago leads them in through the back door. Because the gnome thing is a secret, he says. No one at home knows his secret. On tiptoe, he requests. And they tiptoe upstairs to Santiago's room. They haven't been to his house in a long time. The first thing that catches their eye is the fact that he's exchanged the Nirvana poster for one of The Lord of the Rings. Shhh, Santiago says. He's probably asleep. And he slides open the closet door. Sometimes fear and laughter go together. Gonza, Nico, and Matías take a step back when they see Felipito, the mongo, naked and tied up inside the closet. He's been gagged. And he stinks. If my old man and old lady find him, Santiago says, it's electroshock. No kidding.

Selva Malbrán, family judge of this coastal jurisdiction, yesterday rejected a mother's petition to have an abortion performed on her fourteen-year-old daughter who became pregnant after being raped by youths from this city. The victim's identity is still being held in strict confidence for her protection and emotional welfare. Her assailants' identity also remains anonymous while the legal investigation is carried out. The judge has ordered the provincial government to guarantee effective medical, psychological, and social assistance for the patient and her baby. The judge's decision was influenced by the minor's expressed desire not to damage the fetus and to assume the challenge of being a mother to the greatest extent possible. The judge said that she had no doubt that the girl might have suffered an irreversible psychiatric disturbance had she authorized the termination of the pregnancy.

The mystery is in the light.

Almost midnight at the hospital. Except for the ER waiting room, the hospital is asleep and seems to be empty. Zambrano and Nidia walk down a corridor. Zambrano accompanies the woman to the exit. But the woman doesn't want to leave; she sits down on a bench.

This part of the hospital looks like a graveyard. The silence forces you to lower your voice.

I've been told that you do it, Nidia says. You've got to help me. I know two people you've operated on.

Zambrano might have corrected her: there weren't just two and they weren't operations.

I've talked to your daughter, señora, Zambrano tells her. Lorena has made up her mind to continue her pregnancy. My daughter's a minor, doctor, she insists. And she doesn't know what she's doing. She's a baby. You give me a prescription, I'll make her take the medicine, and when she's doped up you do it for her. Your daughter's body doesn't belong to you, señora. I'm her mother, doctor. I know what's good for her. I'll be responsible for whatever may happen. I'm sorry, señora.

You know that if Lorena sees this through her life will be shit. Her life and the baby's, doctor.

I'm sorry, Zambrano repeats.

As a mother, I beg of you.

I'm sorry, señora.

I hope this doesn't happen to a daughter of yours.

I'm never going to have a daughter, Zambrano might reply. Or a son, either. I'll never be a father. He would prefer not to feel such pleasure thinking about it.

In the warm, traditional salon of Hotel Danubio, heated and located right on the seashore, with its Munich beer hall ambience, the German Society invites all fun-lovers to sample our wonderful family atmosphere. It's the twentieth anniversary of our Villa's traditional Winter Festival. Thousands of tourists enjoy and recommend this special event, combining a typical German dinner-show with a night of dancing to a top-flight orchestra and with guaranteed entertainment for all. Families especially— grandparents, parents, children, and grandchildren—gather to enjoy an incomparable evening. The home-style event begins with typical appetizers

and entrées, frozen dessert, and all-you-can-drink beer on tap, followed by
German folkloric dance groups. Later the dance floor will be opened to the
public with two of the finest German orchestras, and the party continues
with joyous abandon, interrupted only for the customary raffles and prizes.
In addition to having the pleasure of welcoming representatives of German
institutions, the event is honored to be sponsored by the Ministry of Tour-
ism of the President of the Nation.

Those are the faces. With those faces thuggery has spread in the
Villa. With guns, now. More and more guns. Ever since those faces
showed up. You've got to see those faces. You can't walk through the
Villa at night anymore. On account of those faces. They look at you
in a certain way, calculating whether or not you have a peso, what
they can get from you. When those faces close in on you, it's a good
idea to have a peso because if they don't get anything, they'll destroy
you. With terror. You can't make out what they're saying. Those
faces blend into darkness. Me, they'd better not mess with. Because
besides the pit bull, I bought a 357. As soon as I see one of those
faces near my house, I don't ask questions. I let the pit bull loose.
And I shoot, too. Suppose I make a mistake and it's not a gangster
but a bricklayer—the hell with him. It's not my fault he if he has that
face. Besides, who are the cops gonna believe, that face or me.

Addiction is a bio-psycho-social disturbance that first destroys the sufferer,
then his loved ones, and later the entire environment, eventually causing
a dangerous social drama that often ends in prison or death. It makes no
distinctions of age or social class: we are at risk and should give serious
thought to prevention. Psychotropic substances, marijuana, cocaine, opi-
oids, stimulants of various types, designer drugs, as well as socially accept-
able habits like alcohol and tobacco, are lurking in our daily lives. Food or
work addiction can also undermine health and destroy personality, causing
anxiety and stress, among other disturbances. Looking addiction in the eye

is everyone's responsibility. Don't be in denial. Seek help. Protecting our-
selves implies caring for our neighbors. To help another is to love oneself.
Deborah Miller, MA. 418061.

Cristina has no right to criticize others. Least of all Anita López, who's an angel. Always was a bigmouth, that Cristina. Now she acts like she's hot stuff, but when Tito the Dwarf used to beat her, she lowered her eyes whenever you passed her on the street, in the super-market, or at the beauty salon. All us girls knew what was going on. You should've seen the kids' little faces. If we didn't hear them when Tito was beating Cristina, it was out of fear. They were scared out of their minds of that dwarf. No, we never heard Tito. The Dwarf didn't raise his voice to her. He beat her. Nice and quiet, he beat her. What I never got is how the Dwarf could do it to her, with her being so big and all. Remember: in the summer Cristina never set foot on the beach. And not because the cookie business kept her so busy. Because when summer comes the Dwarf always hires a few girls. Sure, he bangs them, but that's not why. Cristina didn't go down to the beach because she was embarrassed that people would see the marks that the Dwarf left on her. Till one day she hooked up with Gancedo. The afternoon she hooked up with Gancedo, that very same day, she grabbed the kids and some clothes, and she moved out. Later Gancedo confronted Tito. The Dwarf didn't say a word. He was shitting his pants: If you two are happy, he said to Gancedo, I'm not about to get in the way of a love story. After Cristina dumped him, Tito never found another woman to rebuild his life with. And Cristina, for her part, didn't fare much better. You'd have to be an idiot to think a cop will get you out of a mess and can protect you. Sure, Gancedo's retired from the provincial police force. It makes no difference. Last Tuesday I ran into Cristina at Banco Provincia. Dark glasses and a scarf around her neck. She acted like she didn't see me; she was trying to avoid me, but I went over to her. You fell again? I asked her. It's just that I'm so absent-minded, she replied. I didn't say a word. Between us, I think deep down she likes it.

After Frugone's disgrace and his transfer, Balmaceda was promoted to Police Commissioner, and together with his partner, Deputy Commissioner Renzo, they took over the police station while the scandal at Nuestra Señora was settling down. Just like the Church switched priests in the Villa, the police changed officials. Balmaceda seemed like the toughest one. Maybe because he was sallow. Short and sallow. He intimidated you with that way he had of studying you. With that expression he was able to look cleverer than you. Or like an idiot. Renzo, on the other hand, was nice: blond, blue eyes. He called the old folks gramps, granny. And the kids pigeons, little pigeons. I always say, don't let appearances fool you. Balmaceda would turn out to be less sly and crooked than the other one. But Frugone didn't trust him anyway. And he wondered how much time it would take the two of them and Balmaceda to get into a fight. He didn't have to wait long to confirm his suspicion.

What those two did, Renzo and Balmaceda. They loosened up on the patrol in the south, on the strip that goes from the southern part of the Villa to Mar de las Pampas. They wanted the Vicuñas and the Reyeses to think that the area was a no man's land, a liberated zone. The Vicuñas fell for it. One night they were cleaning out one of the many empty houses, the ones that get rented during the season. When they walked out of the house, the younger Vicuñas had no idea they were surrounded—they put up a fight. The older Vicuña brother emptied a magazine at the police cars. That was how he covered up his brothers' getaway. Renzo and Balmaceda let the kids get away. Then the cops pulled out their guns. Renzo fired first. He got one of them in the leg. The older Vicuña brother was wounded. The two cops approached him. Balmaceda shot him in the other leg.

After that episode, partially covered by *El Vocero*, the Reyeses and the Vicuñas stopped fucking around for a while.

Nacho asked himself why he hadn't finished them off. He could have done it. But he didn't. Why. Simple, Alejo said. You've got to give a wild animal a way out. They don't do the cops any good dead. The message must've gotten out to all the juvies. From here on in they're gonna have to work things out with Renzo and Balmaceda, Martínez remarked. They'll work things out and everything'll be cool. Everything but those assholes who are still patrolling the boulevards to see if they can find an abuser. Grownups playing cowboys, he said. If they'd just leave it to Renzo and Balmaceda, the case would be solved for sure. Of course, they're not gonna put an end to the abuse with a soft touch. But mark my words, they'd solve that fucking mess.

We knew the southeaster was coming; it unleashed all its force in the afternoon. And exactly at midnight, the hour arranged with the blackmailer, the hour when he has to leave the money in the forest, the storm is a gale of water and wind, thunder and lightning; it bellows in the trees, snaps off branches and threatens to knock down trees. Alejo grew up playing in this forest. He knows it. By heart. Malerba follows a few yards behind. El Capo: another shadow. Alejo uses a flashlight. It's hard for him to find the tree with the hole in its trunk. It takes him a while to pinpoint the tree. He removes the supermarket bag filled with dollars from his jacket and steps back. Then he begins the return trip, which he will not complete. He switches off the flashlight. And turns around. Half-hidden by some bushes, from here he can see the tree, now illuminated by a flash of lightning.

A kid, Alejo now sees. It's a kid. And he's got a piece. But he doesn't move from his spot. He waits for Malerba to spring into action. Don't blow the kid away, he says to himself. Malerba circles around, taking the kid by surprise. He disarms him, grabs the gun. And smacks him with his 9 millimeter. He smacks him in the face.

The kid falls and lies still on the ground, blood splashing in the mud. He's crying. Malerba whistles. And Alejo peers out from behind Malerba. The kid groans. His cheekbone is bleeding. Alejo doesn't need to turn on the flashlight to recognize him.

It had to be you, asshole, he says to him. You felt like screwing around. Screwing your old man, screwing me. I ought to blow you away.

Gimme the DVD, he says to him.

Should I finish him off? asks Malerba.

Beside himself, Alejo kicks Gonza in the kidneys.

Gimme the DVD, motherfucker.

Gonza cries, implores. Alejo grabs him by his clothes, lifts him up, shoves him against the tree. He knees him in the groin. And Gonza falls down again. Curled up in a ball, clutching himself.

I didn't mean to, the kid snivels. And he hands over the DVD.

He cries out loud:

Forgive me. Forgive me, Alejo. If you kill me you'll destroy my family.

Alejo looks at the kid, studying him:

I'm gonna make you an offer you can't refuse.

When the pregnancy of the teenager who was recently raped by four youths was made public, the victim began to receive urgent messages, reaching a total of 300 emails. They implore her to reject the possibility of an abortion and to think hard before committing murder. The Rotary Club and the Rebirth Society, among other institutions in our Villa, deny having sent these messages or having provoked their members and supporters to do so. The Parish Association, after similarly denying charges of harassing the victim, declared that in its judgment life and death are Divine, not human, decisions.

Flor carries two glasses in one hand and a bottle of red wine in the other. Fine wine. It looks like a scene from a commercial. She walks toward him, embraces him. Zambrano reacts clumsily to the embrace. She hands him a glass. I am, she says to him. We are, darling.

Anyone who was in the war, lived what they lived and saw what they saw, doesn't talk about it. After the Malvinas, Zambrano finished medical school, married Florencia, his girlfriend since age fifteen, and they came to the Villa. Zambrano has been working at the hospital for nearly twenty years. And she's been a teacher at middle school. If they invite him to the ceremony on April 2nd, Zambrano won't go. And Flor understands. He has nothing to celebrate. Now his war is a different one, he explains. Here, every day. In winter, when all the plagues carry off the inhabitants of La Virgencita, the poor folks fill up the waiting room and the heat turns the air into a warm, cloying, thick, nauseating smell. Because a smell can be all that. The poor folks expect relief from their suffering. And they expect it from him. There aren't many medications to offer them at the hospital. And even fewer consolations. Despite his skepticism about the destiny of these creatures, Zambrano attends them, always willing, always pleasant. Almost servile. As if he were serving God. As if God existed. Sometimes the sufferer gets more relief from talking to someone than from an injection.

And the poor keep multiplying. And as they multiply, so do their hopeless destinies. As a kid Zambrano was an altar boy. He no longer believes in God, but his pity and that love of his fellow man remained with him. A miserable feeling, pity. When they come for an illegal abortion, he secretly performs it. Besides, when he gets home, Flor will be there waiting for him. As is the eternal subject. No, I don't want to have kids. I don't want to see those I love suffer. It's decided. One more time: no.

Now, the moment he walks in, he smells the meat in the oven. The fragrance of rosemary. Garlic and rosemary. Zambrano realizes he's hungry. But he needs a glass of wine more. Before going into the kitchen and pouring himself a glass, Florencia meets him halfway. She brings a bottle of a label he doesn't recognize, expensive wine.

How much did this wine cost us, he asks.

Night. Lightning. It's raining. It's raining buckets. Thunder. A real downpour. It might be the downpour many of us are waiting for, a storm to drown our sins. Nidia tosses and turns in bed. She prays. She doesn't want to hate. She doesn't like plotting revenge. But she thinks about it. Not just one. Four acts of revenge. One for each of the motherfuckers that raped Lorena. And she multiplies: one act of revenge for every sister, brother, mother father. Nidia wants to shoo away the images that come to mind: dicks cut off, balls amputated, nipples squeezed with pliers, teeth yanked out. Also: lit cigarettes, boiling oil, electricity. An endless list of tortures runs through her head. And she prays. She prays, but she can't chase those visions away. It calms her a little to see that there's a faint light in Lorena's room, a blinking light. The computer. As her pregnancy begins to show, Lorena has once more started to spend sleepless nights sitting at the computer. A flash of lightning. Nidia prays for Lorena. A thunderbolt rattles the walls. She prays for herself. The downpour is a burst that explodes against her window. Water's getting in. Fucking leaks. She has to get up and look for the bucket and mop. Let the whole world flood, she thinks. Let the whole world flood once and for all and drown everybody. And Lorena, she asks herself. Maybe Lorena too. The poor thing is a child of sin. One night at the dance, a quick love that lasted as long as a sigh. One November a Chilean bricklayer, Pedro, was passing through. She doesn't even know his last name. Just one night. Nidia gets up, looks for the bucket and mop. On the way she peeks in at Lorena. She's still at the computer. Those pills they prescribed for her at the hospital have no effect at all. It's almost four. And in a couple of hours she needs to be up because she gets up early for work. She considers stealing one of Lorena's pills. Maybe half would be enough. Then she changes her mind. If the pill knocks her out she'll oversleep. Better to keep praying. Because at seven she has to be at the supermarket. Our Father Who art in Heaven.

When he's not plagued with insomnia, Dante likes to fall asleep listening to the sea. But now the sound of the waves showers him with voices. Of children. A chorus. Again, he says to himself. They don't leave him alone. He gropes for the blister pack of Valium, but Valium has no effect on him anymore. Just as his eyelids are about to close, he hears the chorus again, closer by. Them again. They're singing as they approach. They're coming for him. Dante wants to wake up. He knows it's a dream and he struggles to awaken. He rolls over, tries with difficulty to rouse himself out of bed. When he falls, he detects murmurs on the other side of his apartment door. There's light in the hallway. And the voices are the children's. He can hear their laughter. They're coming.

This week two formal complaints were filed against the presence of settlements in the southern part of our Villa. Both the municipal government and the city council complained to the police about the appearance of new settlements around Calle 140 and Avenida 6. Up until now this has been an area of very precarious wooden dwellings occupied by individuals from Paraguay and from the interior of the country. Minister of Safety Carlos Tornelli visited our city and promised to send six patrol cars that will arrive in the next few days.

"These local safety reinforcements are in response to the community's great fear of contingents from the shantytowns arriving here," declared our mayor Alberto Cachito Calderón.

After 3 A.M. Suddenly Dante interrupts the article he's writing, another one on the prevention of child abuse. He drinks his cold coffee. And he wonders what would happen if it was proved that there had never been a single case of abuse, not even the case of Mechi

Speer. If there never was a single act of abuse, what happened was even more serious. Because what was revealed through the collective hysteria was evil, and Dante thinks about evil. He doesn't think about perversion; he thinks about evil, evil pulsing in all the minds of the Villa. If we all believed the case of *los abusaditos*, then we all harbor a fantasy that makes us even bigger shits than we thought we were.

Don't give me that crap about Manal and *Una casa con diez pinos*. Around here it's not so hard to get to the house and the pine trees. What nobody can figure out is how to escape. Because there's nothing worse than a dream fulfilled.

Last Wednesday, the 15th, during the morning hours, forces from the First Precinct patrolling the central zone of our Villa for illegal acts and irregularities in general, intercepted and identified, at the intersection of Calle 105 and Avenida 12, four youths who, at the time of identification, were stumbling around with clear signs of alcohol on their breath. The youths started hurling all sorts of insults at police personnel, generating disturbances while refusing to be taken into custody, thus provoking the personnel to fight. All four were charged with infraction of Articles 35, 72, 74, and 78 of Penal Code 8031/73. Another similar case occurred early Thursday morning at Calle 121 and Avenida 31. On the public thoroughfare five youths were arrested who, at the time of their detention, were also stumbling and inebriated to the extent that their speech was impaired. As they were disturbing the peace and refused to show identification, they too were transported to police headquarters and processed.

This Friday Alejo takes a walk over to the *El Vocero* office, taking Dante by surprise. He throws the copy of this Friday's edition, opened to the police blotter page, onto Dante's desk.

Record number of armed robberies, the headline says.

Since when does the police blotter page have headlines in red, Dante, Alejo asks him. As if all those articles about the abuse weren't enough of a pain in the ass. Think of the tourists who come for the weekend. They come and they buy our paper. And what image of us will they take away. You think they'll come back for high season, huh? This is a town journal, Dante. Not even. A newspaper. And it has to emphasize what's positive about the community.

Nidia can hear her from her bedroom. Poor thing, the medication they prescribed for her girl has no effect. Nidia wonders if all those drugs won't affect her pregnancy. But she has no other option. At least with the drugs she sleeps for a few hours. Every night, after dinner, Nidia gives her the pill. But tonight they had an argument. Don't pay attention to those messages, Nidia told her. If we're going to have the baby, those fucking people don't have any reason to get involved in our lives. It's not our lives, Ma, Lorena replies. It's mine. Then, uncharacteristically obedient, with a meekness that broke her heart, Lorena took the pill, went to the bathroom, brushed her teeth, gave her a kiss, and went to bed.

But after a few hours, like every night, she got up and switched on the computer. Now Nidia is tossing in bed. The sound of the keys wears her out. Every night. Every single night.

Tonight, when Nidia gets home from her job at the supermarket, a neighbor woman comes over to see her. Before what happened happened, Lorena and Sol, the neighbor's daughter, were friends. But ever since that happened, they stopped seeing one another. Sol told Nidia that Lorena had cut her off. Not just her. Lorena had cut off everybody. And now the neighbor has come to her with this sheet of paper. It's a printed-out email. A mass mailing sent by Lorena. The day is coming, says the email. She's sent out hundreds. The emissary is on its way, she wrote in others.

Nidia can't believe that her daughter sent that email. The neighbor woman tells her that Sol wasn't the only one to receive an email like this. She wrote to all the girls in middle school. And to all the boys, as well.

That same night, as they're eating dinner, Nidia asks Lorena whom she sends emails to. Lorena doesn't reply. Don't I help you, Nidia asks her. Tell me, aren't I watching out for you all the time. Tell me, what does this mean. You're trying to drive me crazy. I've got enough problems of my own, you know. And soon I'll have three mouths to feed. Three. Lorena stares at her without responding. Three? she finally asks. Yes, three, including the one that's in your belly, says Nidia, crying. And Lorena is moved by her mother's tears. Lorena grows silent. She finishes her dinner, goes to the bathroom, brushes her teeth, and goes to bed. Nidia waits till her bout of sobbing passes. She goes to bed a while later. She tosses in bed. Lorena has gotten up again and is at the computer. In the night, in the quiet of the night, she can hear the toads and crickets, and also the keyboard. Then she cries again. Like every night, she falls asleep crying.

Even when they removed the cast from her arm and she had begun her rehab, Anita still had pain. At dawn, when the pain became unbearable, Anita begged Osvaldo to please take her to the hospital, that she wouldn't tell how it had happened. An accident, she'd lie. The truth embarrassed her: how Osvaldo had lost control and, suddenly, grabbing her by the arm, had started knocking her around. Anita slapped him back. It shocked Osvaldo that she, the pacifist, the defender of the poor, had reacted to the blow. Anita tried to escape from the house, but Osvaldo intercepted her, blocking the door. Anita had never before seen that look on Osvaldo's face. And he, for his part, had never seen that expression on Anita's. Anita took a step back, grabbed a piece of pottery, and hurled it at him. Osvaldo ducked. Anita ran toward the staircase, trying to reach the second floor. The first thing Osvaldo thought of was the 38 in the night-stand. Anita wouldn't dare go that far. And he ran toward the staircase, too. He reached Anita before she could run into the bedroom. He grabbed her by the arm again. He shook her. Anita cried, cursing at him. Osvaldo was taken aback. The situation had gotten out of hand. Anita took a couple of steps backward. Then she lost her balance and rolled downstairs. Her head smashed against the floor tiles. The first thing Osvaldo thought was: I'm going to jail. Anita took a while to stir. Forgive me, love, Osvaldo said to her. Forgive me, he wept. Blood trickled down Anita's forehead. Osvaldo brought a roll of paper towels from the kitchen. Then peroxide. He helped her get up. Take me to the hospital, she asked him. It was nothing, love. It was nothing. Here's some ice. Have a drink of water. And he didn't stop thinking: I'm going to jail. It infuriated him to think that if he'd lost control, it was his wife's fault. If it hadn't been for that need of hers to be noticed, he thought. It wasn't enough for her to be the wife of a well-known businessman: Campas Plumbing Supplies, a real institution in the Villa.

What Osvaldo couldn't even conceive was that she also felt ashamed. How will I cover this up at the non-violence workshop when I ask the kids to think before they act, she thought.

Take me to the hospital, Osvaldo. And help me lie. You do the talking. Say I fell down the stairs.

The Cultural Encounter, also known as the Festival of Cultural Diversity, as the traditional Día de la Raza is called nowadays, will take on a new dynamic this year. The announcement was made by a spokesman for the city, declaring that the celebration, as usual, will count on the support of the Villa's various communities: the German Club, the Spanish Club, the Unione e Benevolenza Society, among the most prominent groups in the community. Our mayor, Alberto Cachito Calderón, our dear Cachito, also announced some news that affects us all: the traditional festivities will enjoy a significant contribution from the Lebanese community, which will sponsor the appearance of popular music figures. The Lebanese community plans to settle among us and also generate financing for public works through a contract with Dobroslav Construction. On the one hand, this act is in recognition of our hospitality, and on the other it means a capital investment in projects that are being discussed in the highest municipal

circles. Although Engineer Dobroslav refused to provide details about the
scope of the project, he let slip that the investment will surprise our Villa.
The city Financial Department likewise said it should be emphasized that
the Lebanese community's support and investment will help defray the loss
suffered this year by the cancellation of the traditional Maccabean Festival.

Missy embellished the story to suit her convenience. According to her, Malerba was jealous because his kid, with that cool way about him, just like his father's when he was young, wanted to bang her. We know who Missy is: Inesita Morano, the daughter of old man Morano, the Ford dealership owner. You must know him. His son Tito had a hunting and fishing store down by the dock. Well, Inesita was Miss Springtime a few years back. That's where the "Missy" came from. What they say about old man Morano is that his wife, the late Doña Adela, put the horns on him like he was a deer. One winter night when the wife had bronchitis and was burning up with fever, Don Morano gave her an overdose of sleeping pills. The next day Doña Adela was already on the Other Side. The kids were little. And he wanted them to be somebody, that's what he said. My heirs, he called them. He put them in boarding school. He sent Inesita to a convent school in Junín. He put Tito in a school run by Salesian priests in Patagonia. And when they finished high school, they came back to the Villa. Neither one wanted to go on to university. They disappointed the old man. Tito, a slacker who was full of himself, set up that hunting and fishing store near the dock. And it went belly-up. The girl, who was already quite a filly, a complete surprise to the old man, looked like her mother. Man, did we have the hots for Inesita. She gave us all hard-ons. The apple doesn't fall far from the tree, like the saying goes. A whore like her mother, the neighbor ladies said. One time old man Morano beat the living shit out of Inesita with his belt. Maybe this will cure your fever, he told her. You could hear her begging for help. But nobody came to her rescue. Not even her brother. Everyone was afraid of Don Morano. Since he liked to hunt, he always went around armed. He bragged about hunting wild boar with a knife. If you saw him coming along drunk, you'd cross to the other side of the street. Who was going to step in to save Missy.

And then, Malerba. Then, when we least expected it, one morning we woke up to the news: Inesita, Missy, that hot babe, with lashes from a riding-crop, had taken off for Malerba's cabin.

At age fifty-two, after a lifetime and having built a family, Estela now felt lonelier than ever. And even lonelier when Tincho called her *Vieja*. Tincho, who was in his first year at middle school, was the only one of her three kids left at home. And not for much longer. Pablo and Juan, since they'd started studying in La Plata, one of them medicine and the other engineering, came to the Villa less and less often. Eugenio didn't count. Although they still lived together, she couldn't count Eugenio as company. The only thing that turned Eugenio on was his surveying job. What turns me on most is being out in the fresh air, he had told her when they met. If you love me, you have to give me air. To be honest with herself, Estela now thought, Eugenio was turned on by anything but her. Eugenio had never been a real companion. If they had put up with so many periods of shouting and also silence, especially silence, she now reflected, she mustn't fool herself, it was for the sake of the kids. It was no comfort, either, to accuse Eugenio of being too conservative to consider a separation. She herself was terrified by the mere thought of a divorce. Divorce, that was the word. And it frightened her with its legalistic echo. Separated and with three little calves at her heels, where was she going to find another man in the Villa. Well, sure, she ran across guys, but men, real men, would be hard to find. Like so many other women she knew, she'd end up dancing at the Comanche on Saturday nights and going to bed with anyone at all. She'd end up like the Duchess, that loan shark, paying young men to do her the favor. So many women did it out of physical need or boredom. She wasn't going to roll in the hay with just anybody, because, among other reasons, *she* wasn't just anybody. Though it was fine for Eugenio. And he never gave up going to the Tropicana on Fridays, not even when they were newlyweds. The *asado* dragged on, he would lie, and then we played a round of poker. And then another. And by the time we realized it, it was morning. At first that was the excuse: the Friday night *asado* with the boys, or the soccer game every Wednesday night at the local club had gone on too long and that's why he'd returned home at dawn. Deep down Estela had always thought it was better that he went to the Tropicana instead of having a steady lover, though whether Eugenio ever had one or still did was something she preferred not to find out. Sometimes it's better to be in the dark, she thought. And in more than one way, she was in the dark. She was in the dark when she got married. When she had her first child. When she had the second one. When she had the third. And now that the third one was walking beside her, she felt she was still in the dark. Fifty-two years of being in the dark, she thought. Especially if she compared herself to Beti, the shop owner, who called herself a feminist, was aligned with socialism, opened her home to Party meetings, but wouldn't sell you as much as a ballpoint pen on credit. And even though this afternoon Tincho, the only son she had left, was with her, Estela felt alone, more so than ever. More in the dark and alone than ever.

What're you thinking about, *Vieja?* Tincho asked her.

That I'm tired of you calling me *Vieja*, she replied.

Old age is a state of mind, Tincho said to her. It depends on how you face it. Estela looked at him out of the corner of her eye. And where'd you get that from, she asked. Everybody knows it, said Tincho, bored. If you let go of yourself, you're finished. An organ that isn't used atrophies. What do you mean, baby. You know, Ma. And I'm not a baby anymore. Tincho was twelve, but he was a giant who looked like a teenager. Suddenly Estela was afraid of losing him. And suddenly, too, it occurred to her that she'd already begun to lose him.

If she hadn't lost him already. She wondered if Tincho was still a virgin. She didn't dare ask. Eugenio was the one who should discuss it with him. But since he and Eugenio weren't on speaking terms, this, too, like so many other matters, would be met with silence.

I understand, Estela said. Like my mother used to say: It's never too late to set things right.

Gramma's awesome, said Tincho.

But the expression didn't relieve her desolation. In fact, it made it worse instead. Fifty-two years was too late for everything. Except suicide.

This morning Cachito and Alejo got together at Poker for coffee and to discuss the matter. Alejo noticed the bags under Cachito's eyes. Insomnia, Cachito says. I'm going through a bout of insomnia. Alejo scrutinizes him. Cachito gazes back soberly. And asks him the same question: You too?

That's all we needed, says Cachito, the Bolivian Consulate's complaint. It'll fall on our heads in a few days. Our kids are in up to their necks. I talked to Gonza and he told me everything. Take it easy, Alejo calms Cachito. My kids told me, too. Relax, Cachito. I've consulted my contacts and they're going to throw us a line, Alejo says. Cachito frets: Besides, if that business about the burned Bolita baby gets any more press, we'll blow the season. We'll have to move quickly and carefully, Cachito says. Some idiot will have to pay for those dumb kids' fuckup. Because you've gotta be really dumb.

I've thought of a plan. It's foolproof. It's got no downside. There will be a guilty party.

Who, Cachito asks.

Someone who's sick in the head, Alejo says. Someone who's not responsible. Does "electroshock" mean anything to you? Just leave it to me to deal with the cops. They're gonna prove that Crazy Heinrich stole the baby and then burned it. For Heinrich the baby wasn't human, get it? The last time they took him away, when he was about

231

to set fire to the forest, he had that poem about the Andean Highlands and the Bolitas. The Bolita wasn't a Bolita. It was from another planet. We can even get Crazy Heinrich to admit he offed the Bolita baby in self defense.

It's a tragedy about the Pereses. In the blink of an eye, poor, heartbroken Edith lost her husband, had to put Felipito in boarding school, the Del Mar Academy for Special Children, and drive the limo. They say she's saving up to take Felipito with her to Israel. She's fed up with the Villa.

Let her go, once and for all, says Moure. She'll have a blast in Israel.

We'll have to put up with a few days of this. Especially the gray Sundays of late August. Today, for example, a Sunday at the end of August, and alone. It seems like winter will never end. And if you're alone, get hold of yourself so you won't lay into the booze starting first thing in the morning. This is going to be an uphill day in the void, walking without the law of gravity, something like that. You look out the window at the sea. The remains of a southeaster, the remains of your life. Where did your people end up, that is, if somebody ever was yours in the way that you were never anybody's, and when you reached the end of your rope, that was it. Family: Sunday is family day. Hours of gazing out the window, the white, furious breakers. But wasn't that what you were looking for? Weren't you seeking this solitude in order to write? Who did you think you were? Happy are those who can live up to their dreams: a nice little house, the kids, a car. Today you envy them while you suffer your desire for the bottle. You have to write that article, which is a comfort. Something to do. Something to kill time. But time isn't killed. Time kills you. You go around and around, and at last you sit down and the first sentence, the second. The last days of August, this hollow, cracked Sunday, the everlasting southeaster. The southeaster's taking its time in leaving. Two or three more days, at least. Because now that dark sky is giving signs that it's not going away so soon. And yet, in some tree, chirping. You're alone. Illusory moments. At least just hold on till the video rental place opens, check out a film, and then yes, at sundown, the first whiskey and a crime flick, identifying with the solitary hero. No, better hold on. The temptation of the bottle. Now it's closer to tomorrow. Tomorrow's Monday. Tomorrow's another day. You shouldn't mix alcohol with pills. It's just that it's such a long time till tomorrow. Maybe there *is* no tomorrow. Then you remember that fisherman named Charon who baptized his boat *I Muddle Through*. Muddle through till tomorrow. That's what it's about. Muddling through.

This time of year, when dawns are frosty, Alejo thinks, there's no greater pleasure than to light the fireplace while your family is still asleep. There are still embers left over from last night. You push away the ashes, add a few dry branches, some sheets of newspaper rolled up in a ball, and a couple of logs. Little by little the fire begins to take shape, quickly burns the newspaper; everything that was scandal, corruption, tragedy, crime, burns in this enclosed inferno that takes over the branches, burns hard, crackles, and begins to consume the logs. It's pleasant to stand there looking at the fire without doing anything else. You're overcome by the desire to do nothing today, not go to the office, not fulfill any of your daily obligations, and just stay indoors, gazing at the flames. It's true what they say: Fire has a hypnotic power. But it's not only the fascination of the flames that have now grown stronger. It seems as though the fire is saying something that's hard to decipher, transmitting a message in code; it's telling me something, something about me, and if I can't figure out how to translate it, it's surely because it makes me feel ashamed. Just as we all tend to hide a document that implicates us and would be better for us to burn, we hang on to one that implicates someone else and can, under the right circumstances, bring us revenge. Don't I know it, Alejo says to himself.

Slowly the heat radiates throughout the entire house. He throws on another log. And then another. The flames lap at the edges of the fireplace. The sparks fly in all directions. One single spark is enough to cause a conflagration. Suddenly he realizes what the fire is trying to say to him. That perhaps the time has come for everything to burn down once and for all. Instead of continuing to endure this wait for hell, better to take a shortcut. Someone once said: Waiting for punishment is more unbearable than the punishment itself.

After a grueling, top-secret investigation, local police have at last arrested the person responsible for the murder and burning of six-month-old Cristian Valderrama, a Bolivian national, who was found half-buried in Pinar del Norte last May. The perpetrator of this horrifying act was a well-known young man who suffers from mental disorders and has been hospitalized for electroshock treatments on several occasions. As Christians, our community expresses its deep sorrow both for the deceased infant and the unfortunate dementia of the young murderer, who will be remanded to a neuropsychiatric institute for personality disorders.

Like everyone, some more than others, without regard to age, including children, because as Dante once wrote in *El Vocero*, even minors contemplate suicide, Estela had thought about killing herself, and every so often, when she heard about a suicide, for days and nights she could think of nothing else. To make the idea go away, she thought about a magazine article she had cut out, folded, and saved in a Bible, because even though she didn't attend Mass regularly and wasn't much of a believer, she had a Bible tucked away on a shelf in the dining room. At home that Bible was used as infrequently as the library, four modular shelves laden with vases, ceramic pieces, miniatures, and picture frames, standing in front of an encyclopedia and classics published by *La Nación*. The article stored in the Bible declared that suicide was hereditary. And she wasn't about to leave her children with such a burden. She couldn't imagine Eusebio and her son Tincho without her. Though maybe it was time. If it's never too late, Estela began to think, as the famous saying goes and my mother used to repeat, why did that silly woman put up with my father, a gambler and whoremonger, for sixty years. Maybe, she told herself, it would be best *not* to commit suicide. Better to pack a bag and take off without letting anyone know. She imagined herself in a city in the interior, Córdoba, for example, first finding herself a room in a *pensión* and looking for work. Although she had a high school degree in business, she wasn't going to use it. Too old to apply for a secretarial position. But she could clean houses, offices. There was so much to clean in the world, and really, that was what she had done all her life: keep a clean house, have a clean education, a clean family, and clean morals, too. If her friends teased her it was precisely on account of her mania for cleaning: her house gleamed. Everything gleamed, except her. And now, at fifty-two. Not to mention these outbursts that came with the hot flashes. Because the idea of suicide and of moving out were flashes that, to tell the truth, would never amount to anything.

Pig, Rosita tells me when I pull my dick out of her, as if the goo on the glans wasn't hers. And then she tells me to turn down the music. I've got to call my husband, she says. And she pats her baby bump. Today's our anniversary, she explains.

In this Villa more than one woman, more than one man, fantasizes that tomorrow he or she might be a character in one of those crime documentary series on cable, like *My Neighbors' Drama*, one of those. Just imagine, tomorrow you could be Russell Gardiner and be married to Janet Bullock. Or you're Janet Bullock and you're married to Russell Gardiner. Both of them were married before. But their previous marriages were disappointing. Russ is divorced from his first wife, Margaret Campbell, an alcoholic and compulsive kleptomaniac. Now he's in a relationship with Janet, whose previous husband, Brian Rochelle, a violent individual with a history of gang membership in his youth, died tragically while cleaning a gun when the couple was living in Lawson. The death was registered as an accident. From Janet's marriage to the late Brian there were two children, Laurie and Glenn. Now, married to Russ, Janet has become the mother of another girl, Shelley. Russ and Janet seem to have exchanged their bad luck for a happy life. The Gardiners are a respected family in Toynbee Rock, Virginia. They attend religious services twice a week. Russ coaches the kids' baseball team. Janet works half-time at the local radio station. But soon this peaceful, small-town domestic happiness will be altered by fatal deeds. Janet announces that she is writing a novel about the death of her first husband, Brian Rochelle. In the fictionalized work, she states that he was really murdered on account of a debt associated with his troubled past. Doubleday, Janet gushes, will pay them an advance of $400,000 for the rights. One Sunday she walks into church flaunting the contract. The announcement shakes the community of Toynbee Rock. Janet begins to change her look; she buys expensive clothing in stores, claiming she'll need to look elegant for her book presentations and signings. She also swaps their car for a Mercedes Benz. The couple moves to an affluent neighborhood and joins a country club. Happiness, however, will not last much longer for the Gardiners. We will return with *My Neighbors' Drama*.

The Prozac generation is unseating the disciples of Freud. Every day psychotropic drugs win more supporters, displacing the couch. This phenomenon is largely due to the cost of traditional psychoanalytic treatment, which may require two or three weekly sessions. With a smaller investment, mental health professionals are leaning toward psychotropic drugs, which, in a short period of time, combat and relieve exhaustion, anxiety, and sleep disturbances. Another explanation of the triumph of psychotropic drugs over psychoanalysis can be found in the times in which we live, where tolerance for crises has been reduced, and what is valued most in all activities is efficiency. The array of tranquilizers and antidepressants is vast. Even for the slightest conflict, the tendency is to request a prescription or resort to self-medication. And every day there is evidence that this tendency is gaining ground throughout the Western world. Prozac, in this regard, marked a before and an after in treating psychological problems. It's true that states of mind have become merchandised in this way, but equally true is the fact that everyday discontent is growing alarmingly in large cities, and not only there. This phenomenon, as a way of combating frustration, anxiety, and loneliness, is taking place in small communities, as well. Thus, psychopharmaceuticals become the most practical solution. Deborah Miller, MA. 418061.

Estela couldn't bear to see Miumiú like that. The poor cat was getting worse and worse. And she wasn't an old cat, either. What's wrong with this little critter is depression, Vivi the veterinarian told her. Vivi was a homeopathic vet. She couldn't have been more than forty. Short, grayish hair, petite, and with that gentle demeanor that came from yoga and which you could read in her blue eyes, in the soft gaze she fixed on Miumiú as she scratched the cat's head. How old? Vivi asked her. Fifty-two, said Estela. Not you, the cat, Vivi laughed. Estela liked her laugh. She wasn't laughing at her. She was laughing at the situation. Seeing herself from Vivi's perspective, she laughed at herself too. Miumiú's losing her hair, Vivi observed. Like me, Estela said. She's copying you, said Vivi. What are you, a psychologist or a veterinarian, Estela asked. I got my degree in psych, but then I went to veterinary school. Sorry, said Estela. It's not that I don't trust you. It's just that I got tired of taking the cat to Moure, the Mengele of the pet world, who was killing her with shots. And she's getting worse and worse. Animals somatize, Vivi interrupted. Like the adults close to them, their loved ones. If you don't feel good, neither does Miumiú. And if you're in a really bad way, forget it, Vivi explained. Maybe I'm the one who needs a homeopathic vet, said Estela. Who knows, Vivi smiled. She had an understanding smile. Bach Drops for both of you, she said. Starting today, Bach Drops.

It was almost eight. Vivi was about to close. Do you want to grab a coffee, she suggested. What about Miumiú, Estela asked. We won't be allowed in a bar with her. Sure we will, Vivi told her. She liked that about Vivi, too. That she was a sure-we-will type. And so it was.

My Neighbors' Drama. The Gardiners are facing a matrimonial melt-down. But Russ is a good man, dedicated and understanding. He believes he can educate his wife, just as he trains the young folks on the baseball team. Russ doesn't want a divorce. He consults Pastor Timothy Cannin, the flock's spiritual leader. You can do it, Pastor Cannin tells him. The couple will seek help through the church. But the Devil seems to be exerting more influence on Janet than the words of the Lord. For Russell Gardiner the worst hasn't happened yet.

No, they don't attack. Attacks are very unusual. In general, the few cases we've had were by large sharks. They're farther out, about 150 yards from shore. And closer, too. But you can't tell that to a tourist because the rumor spreads and it could ruin the season. When a boat comes in loaded with catch and there are lots of dogfish, people look at them with respect and revenge. Respect, because even when it's a question of small sharks, you look at them and can't forget about their reputation. You should see the fascination they cause. Besides, they have those teeth. But it's not just their teeth that people admire: the design, the shape, the style is what's impressive. In summer, when a boat comes in loaded with catch, the tourists always sur-round it and whisper, astonished to see such a specimen. The respect they have for it. And that taste of revenge in your mouth on seeing them dead isn't so much the satisfaction of having escaped danger; it's something else. Because these are the same sort of people who ask for protection, who ask for more police and a firm hand. And the taste in their mouths is the same as what they feel when a newspaper article reports that a neighbor blew away two kids who tried to rob the kiosk. Yes, they're the same ones who want the minimum age for delinquents to be lowered. If it were up to them, they'd lower it to ten.

You've got to try shark meat. Tender, delicious. Like ours must be for them.

Full moon. An owl. The murmur of branches. Another night of eyes wide open, Nidia thinks, and the gentle tap of the computer keys. The branches in the window, outlined by the moon, are skeletal arms, bony hands. She prays until her will gives out. She tosses in bed. The owl seems to be telling her something with that whistling. The only thing I need now is to start thinking strange thoughts, Nidia thinks. She's got enough problems with Lorena in her room, pecking away at the computer, like every night. Every night. Because even though the psychiatrist at the hospital upped her dose, nothing helps. Pregnant and all, Lorena spends entire nights on the computer. And now when it's beginning to grow light, like a vampire, shielding herself from the light of morning, she lowers the blinds, closes the door, and goes to bed. Every night. That owl. Another turn in bed.

Until Nidia can't take it anymore and gets up. She's knows it's useless to talk to Lorena, to convince her. And yet, one more time, Nidia will try. She sidles along, a shadow among shadows, to the room, illuminated by the glow of the screen. Nidia spies over her shoulder to see what she's writing. On the screen she can see the email she's sending to the city. Her daughter is writing to Cachito Calderón. Nidia can't believe that girl's bravery, writing to the mayor. Last night El Muertito spoke to me. The Emissary is near. The day is coming.

Nidia doesn't know what to do. To scream or to cry. She confronts Lorena. But Lorena doesn't see her. Lorena's eyes are open, but she's not looking at the monitor. Her head high, looking past the monitor, and her hands over the keyboard, the fingers moving by themselves. She's possessed. Nidia stifles a scream, leaps backward, terrified.

Then she moves away. Slowly. Toward the front door.

And she runs out, along the street of earth and sand. When she cuts her foot on a piece of glass, she doesn't even feel it.

Russ Gardiner's descent into hell has begun. And he'll have no way back. Family friends decide to throw a party in honor of the local literary star, his wife, Janet. Friends of the couple phone Doubleday, asking when the novel she wrote about her first husband's supposedly accidental death from a gunshot wound will be released. The neighbors from Toynbee Rock are confused. Not only will Janet *not* receive a $400,000 advance that could pay off everything she's squandered lately—she hasn't written a novel, either. The publisher has no knowledge of any writer by that name. Russ Gardiner begins to distrust Janet, his second wife. He then hires a detective, the former sheriff of Toynbee Rock, veteran Michael O'Reilly. The detective discovers that Janet has written checks with her husband's forged signature. Meanwhile, in the basement of the house, in a drawer of an old piece of furniture from his grandparents, Russ discovers a huge number of bills, the result of the acquisitions his wife has made by falsifying his signature. A call from the Virginia Bank of Toynbee Rock confirms Russ's worst suspicions. Now Janet is in unimaginable debt. She'll never be able to pay off what she owes. Meanwhile, veteran detective O'Reilly discovers that Janet's lies were not limited to defrauding stores, a bank, and most of all her innocent husband. Janet has been cheating on him with other men. Detective O'Reilly shows Russ photos of his wife in various motels and apartments. Photos with one man. Others with two. And even more. Teenagers from neighboring Madison County aren't left off the list, either. Janet, the good mother, sweet wife, and promising author of a non-existent novel, is now revealed for what she is: a swindler and serial adulteress. Detective O'Reilly believes that Janet is an insatiable, incurable nymphomaniac. The couple faces its meltdown. We will return with *My Neighbors' Drama*.

On Wednesday morning Matilde walked into Garra Cross and asked for Dicky. He was on the back patio, taking apart a Kawasaki. I want to talk to you, cuckold, she told him. Dicky looked at her from below, kneeling, oil-stained, the monkey wrench in his hand, wondering where this maniac came from. Because it was clear she was a raving maniac. Dicky stood up slowly.

When he was standing, the woman reached his chest. Sort of short, broad-hipped, and tubby. The woman extended her hand. I'm Matilde Rodríguez de Carrero, a betrayed wife, she introduced herself. Dicky shifted the monkey wrench to his other hand. The woman's hand was icy. What can I do for you, Dicky inquired. I love my husband, you know, the woman told him. Like you must also love your wife. Dicky didn't understand. Fogging over, he realized he didn't want to understand. He felt the sky clouding over the patio, over his life. I think you're confused, Dicky began. My wife is pregnant, he said. So what, replied the woman. Pregnant women don't fuck? You don't know who my wife is, señora. Now, by calling her señora, he imposed distance, superiority, Dicky thought. And she: The little blonde from Winterfest. The Queen, Dicky corrected her. So what, Matilde laughed. You think queens don't fuck? she asked him. Now you know: there's one more cuckold in the Villa. And it's you. If you want to talk to my husband, go to Remismar and ask for Eusebio. The woman turned her back and crossed through the store. Matilde tripped on a Suzuki, which, in turn, fell against a Honda and another one and another and the motorcycles kept falling while Dicky watched the woman walk out to the street and climb on a rusty Zanella and take off. She's gotta be a lowlife, he thought. He felt like crying. But he couldn't.

Moni wakes up startled at night. The only way she can calm her heart is to jot down some verses: *In the silence of the night, / the cabin in the woods: / the voice of the owl / in the icy breeze / tells / the drama behind every blind window / Tomorrow's another day / so far from here.* Then she comes up with a title: Owl, she writes.

One afternoon they called Estela from the hospital. Tincho was in the ER. Anita López, the one from Language and Literature, was waiting for her. Her son was out of danger, she told Estela. It had been an unfair fight. Five against Tincho. In the bathroom at middle school. In your defense, he fought. Someone cursed someone out, asked Estela. No one cursed anyone out, Estela, Anita said to her. Tincho can explain it to you better than I can. Poor kid had his face smashed in. A black eye, with blood in the white. An eyebrow split open, a broken nose. He lost two teeth, and he's got a broken arm and two broken ribs. Estela couldn't understand the reason for such violence. And Tincho didn't want to talk. He had never been a violent kid. Cautious, rather. Prudent, yes: Eugenio had taught him. A wimp, never. Eugenio showed up at the E.R. later.

The issue came up at home. Anita said you got into a fight over me, Estela told him. Well done, champ, said Eugenio, moved, feinting against the void. Nobody messes with your old lady. Besides the other guys didn't get away with it, I suppose. No, *Viejo*. Don't call me *Viejo*, Eugenio said, jokingly threatening him with a right jab to the jaw.

What happened, Tincho, Estela asked him. Please, tell us. Tincho looked away. What, he replied in turn. Why did it happen, asked Estela. Because of you, don't act like such an asshole, said Tincho. Hey, hey, watch your language, Eugenio intervened. What do you mean because of me, Estela asked again. You know, said Tincho. It can't be, Estela thought. And she thought of Vivi. Of course it can be, she thought. Miumiú walked over to Tincho. And he kicked her out of the way. The mewling sounding like something from a horror film in an empty house. I'm gonna smash that dyke cat, Tincho said. Whoa, Eugenio interceded again. What's going on. And besides, the cat has nothing to do with what happened.

She does, said Estela.

The Gardiners move to a more modest section of Toynbee Rock. While Russ takes out a mortgage to finish settling the debts contracted by his wife, Janet gives the impression of having changed completely. Not only has she lowered her aspirations of being someone important, she's also given up her job at the radio station and dedicates all her time to raising her children. The storm is behind them. The Gardiners, with help from the church, have saved their marriage from capsizing. But tragedy awaits the family, especially Janet. One night in May, Carolyn Gardiner, Russ's mother, receives a desperate phone call from Eileen Bullock. Her son has been admitted to the hospital in Toynbee. There's been an accident. During the night Janet shot at Russ, thinking he was a burglar. With a bullet lodged in his head, Russ dangles between life and death. Four hours after being shot, Russ dies. The investigation is carried out swiftly. The case is filed as an accidental death. There is no reason to suspect Janet Gardiner, currently a woman of modest means, mother of three children, now overwrought by widowhood. But Detective O'Reilly hasn't forgotten that Brian Rochelle, Janet's first husband, also suffered an accidental death by firearms when the couple was living in Lawson. O'Reilly travels to Lawson and pores over the files of that case. Two accidental deaths are too much of a coincidence for a woman who, till a few months ago, was scamming banks and deceiving her husband. The case is re-opened. The defense attorney and the DA present equally solid arguments. Public opinion is divided 50% in favor of Janet and 50% against. Until something unexpected occurs. A high school student, a member of the baseball team Russ coached, has found a cassette in the deceased coach's locker.

We will return with *My Neighbors' Drama*.

Tita liked the word progress: progress in love, progress in life. For Tita, the daughter of Doña Herminia and Nazar, the lame *criollo* who sells raffle tickets and organizes healing excursions to an Umbanda spiritual leader in Curitiba, and his wife, who sells lottery tickets, like I was telling you, for Tita to marry Ariel, the butcher from Villa Rica Supermarket, represented real progress. She wouldn't have to keep praying to Saint Expeditius and Gauchito Gil and remain poor like her sisters, even though all three of them, Emilia, Mariela, and Claudia, had nabbed husband—drunkards, gamblers, and druggies, but husbands nonetheless, because her sisters had always been cowards and conformists who had offered up their assholes to catch a husband, and their souls, too. Her Ariel, in addition to being a hard-working boy, was saving to build on that lot he'd bought in La Virgencita. When she became pregnant with Germán, Tita imagined that being a mother also represented a kind of progress. Ariel invested all his savings into putting up a pre-fab. Surely Ariel, as a father, would try to become independent, have his own butcher shop. But no. Ariel wasn't ready yet. Time's flying, Tita grumbled. And we're not progressing. Ariel asked her to be patient. In order to progress you need patience, was his motto. Meanwhile, in the afternoon, he began taking Germán to the butcher shop. To progress you need a trade, he said to Tita. The word progress had gotten stuck in his head. When Germán turned ten, Tita felt she'd already been too patient. And she decided to progress on her own. One night this winter, returning to the house they were renting in La Virgencita, father and son found the place empty. Except for the double mattress on the floor with two blankets and the TV. When I've progressed, I'll come back for you, Tita said in the letter she left them: Ariel, take care of Germán, she had written. And then: Germán, take care of Ariel. They never heard from her again. Nobody in the Villa did, either. Tita must have progressed. And like all those that leave and progress, can you imagine her coming back? No fucking way.

After Quirós and Malerba caught Gonzalo trying his hand at extortion with the DVD, it dawned on them that it would be of some benefit to have the mayor's kid in their hands. God's designs are inscrutable, Alejo joked. So when Malerba, imitating Alejo's imitation of Don Corleone, and squeezing his neck, told him he was going to make him an offer he couldn't refuse, the blubbering Gonza accepted. You're better off under Malerba's control than pretending to behave with your old man. Gonzalo was still lying face down in the dirt in the forest, with one of Alejo's shoes on the back of his head. Alejo was enjoying it: And get this straight, if I don't spill this load of shit you did to me to your old man, it's because he'll knock all your teeth out. And I know what I'm talking about; I'm his friend. From now on your fate is in my hands, kiddo, Alejo pronounced. And he wondered if he hadn't gone overboard with the spiel. Sometimes less talking made a bigger impression. He gave him a kick in the side: Get up, asshole, he ordered.

Just think it's like you've been adopted by the devil, Malerba told him. That smile of Malerba's inspired fear.

What he told Gonzalo was no joke. The idea of adopting the kid tickled him. And of teaching him. Although the boy came from an upper-crust family in town, he had demonstrated an inborn inclination for evil. Malerba found that trait quite acceptable. And he wasn't lying when he said:

I'm going to treat you like a son.

After all, a son was like a dog. It made the loneliness in this world more bearable. He knew it through experience. Because he had lost one.

Vivi knew that it would happen sooner or later. It didn't surprise her that Estela showed up with Miumiú at her house in La Virgencita that same night. The fact that Estela had come with the cat didn't amuse Frida, Vivi's feline. If it was true that animals expressed their humans, as Vivi said. Frida expressed a surliness that Estela hadn't noticed in her till now. Estela couldn't stop crying. It's unfair how they treated me, she said. It's unfair. Vivi could understand her tears but assumed they wouldn't last forever. Because Estela would have to discover the positive side of things. It was fine for her to fret about Tincho's injuries, but if the boy refused to see her, he'd have to learn to manage on his own. Same for Eugenio. Now that they didn't have her there, they would appreciate everything she represented in the management of the household. But they would still make a scene for her, Vivi warned. Wounded machismo, she told her. You don't know Eugenio, Estela said. He's a rock.

Instead of being intimidated, waiting for the next scene gave Estela a boldness she didn't know she possessed. Even better, she hoped that the scene would erupt once and for all. Not only did she want to prove to herself that she was up to the situation, she wanted to prove it to Vivi. Sure I will, she promised herself.

I'm not great at living with people, Vivi had told her. The times I tried, it didn't work out. And when was the last time, Estela wanted to know. Just before I met you, Vivi said. In fact, I was still involved when we hooked up, but I didn't want to say anything to you so I wouldn't scare you off. Do I know her, Estela asked. What difference does it make, Vivi retorted. Maybe it makes a difference, said Estela. No, it doesn't. And, after a silence, Estela had to accept: You're right, it doesn't matter, she said. And then: I love you. And once she'd said it, she asked herself how long it had been since she'd said, "I love you." That night in bed they did it a different way. One Estela hadn't known about. Just like all the things she hadn't known about Vivi. And about herself.

Despite Vivi's prediction, there wasn't a scene, as expected: there were several. It wasn't just Tincho who refused to see her. When she called La Plata, Pablo and Juan hung up on her. It was as if she'd never had a family. On weekends Vivi traveled to Buenos Aires to see her daughter. Because Vivi had an eighteen-year-old daughter who was studying cello. So on weekends: depression. Besides, she had to make sure Miumiú and Frida didn't kill each other. The way they glared at one another, sizing each other up and every so often attacking each other furiously, reminded her of Eugenio. One night, on returning from the veterinary clinic, Vivi found her crying. What did I do wrong, she wept one afternoon. What did I do wrong. Family, Vivi replied. I've already explained it to you: It doesn't work anymore. Family destroys you. Like the Mob. Why do you think mobsters talk and talk about family all the time.

The mewling came from the kitchen. The cats were at each other again. They're killing each other, the two of them, said Vivi. You shouldn't have brought Miumiú. Estela, sadder than ever, said: Maybe I shouldn't have brought myself. Quite possible, Vivi said to her. And that was the first time Vivi didn't say, Sure we will. Maybe, thought Estela, this was the scene that would prove her mettle. I'm going to find myself a place, she said. Vivi didn't say yes or no. But her silence was an affirmation.

What finally made her decide to look for a place occurred one stormy night. If Eugenio had been a screen idol with a mustache and a raincoat with lapels turned up against the rain, with those thunderbolts, crossing Vivi's garden, rapping on the door with his knuckles, the scene would have been perfect for a Mexican melodrama. But Eugenio was no screen idol, just a big, clumsy, bald guy. Besides, instead of a raincoat, he was wearing a garish jacket with Boca Juniors colors that Estela had always detested. And he was drunk.

It's for you, Vivi said when she opened the front door. Eugenio's untimely arrival embarrassed Estela. Go away, Eugenio, please, she told him. You've got no business being here. Eugenio was wobbly: Yes, I do, he said. I came to sit on the nightstand and watch. If you don't leave I'll call the police, Estela said. Go ahead and call, Eugenio dared her. The cops'll enjoy it, too. The nightstand, the grandstand, everyone applauding. Aren't you ashamed, Estela asked him. Look who's talking about shame, Eugenio said, the old lesbo. Even more than ashamed, I feel stupid. And he smacked her. The blow caught her off guard. Estela fell backward on her ass. And as she fell, the door opened all the way and Eugenio saw the pistol aimed straight at his face. Get lost or I'll shoot, Vivi told him.

And Eugenio obeyed.

I didn't know you had that, Estela later said.

Where do you think we're living, girl, Vivi replied.

That same night the cats got into it again. It was hard to separate them. After putting Frida in the bedroom, which was her place, and Miumiú in the living room, as she made tea, Estela told her that she wouldn't give her any more trouble, that she had decided to look for her own place. Even though she expected Vivi to protest, she said it: I think the time has come for me to leave. It'll be better for everyone. And as always lately, Vivi's silence was her reply.

Toward the back of the cemetery beneath some poplar trees, they say, lie the dead that the sea brought in during the time of the military. But nobody wants to discuss the matter. There are those who claim there weren't so many. Three or four, maybe. The one who can remember is Don Gauderio, the gravedigger. But with the amount he guzzles, who knows how much of what he says is truth and how much is gin. That was in the days of Vidal, the military mayor. There are times when Don Gauderio points in a different direction, toward the south; he thinks he gave them a Christian burial down there. If he didn't put up a cross it was because Vidal forbade it. Though he might have buried them farther away, he hesitates, beyond the wire fence around the cemetery, where the land turns into countryside and a few cows peacefully graze. If I'm not mistaken, Don Gauderio might say, they'd been shipwrecked, eaten by fish. In those days you could also hear voices at night. You can't get much else out of Don Gauderio. Besides, who cares about all this. It was so long ago.

On this side is the *Angelitos* section. Lots of wooden crosses. You can tell it's tough for the relatives to come up with the dough for a marble tombstone. The one that has fresh dirt, a new cross, belongs to Cristian Valderrama, the Bolivian baby that turned up burned in the forest. If you ask Don Gauderio if he believes in El Muertito, he'll say those kinds of things have always been around. It was around when the sea brought them in. And it'll be around now until justice for the Bolita baby is done. There will still be those cries coming from his grave, keeping everyone awake at night.

Just as the master will sometimes try to win over the slave or extract some bit of information from him, every so often, like on this stormy morning, Alejo shows up at the office of *El Vocero*.

Death is female, he says after he walks in. And sits down. And if death is a woman, he says, like love, it weakens you.

Dante observes him. Intently, smoking. It's been raining for a long time now. After a few unusually warm days, it starts to rain. You could see it coming. Every time winter regales us with an illusion of summer, sun and temperatures that will allow you to go down to the beach and dive in, every time these sudden tropical days come along, right after that—bam!—a storm. First, the wind. A wind from the southeast that starts with a gentle breeze under a sky that's suddenly dark. After a while, the wind grows stronger. And an abrupt change in temperature: the cold returns. Then come the first drops: fat, dense. And finally the thunder: the sky releasing a furious downpour. Dante thinks maybe Alejo has ducked into *El Vocero* headquarters, a place that reeks of tobacco and humidity, because the storm caught him by surprise on the street and he's looking for shelter. But judging from the way he walked in, greeted Dante, poured himself some coffee from the thermos, swore at the brewed dishwater and stayed anyway, sitting in an uncomfortable plastic chair, and tilting it against the wall, Alejo seemed to have come to offer him some of his monologues.

It wasn't exactly the first time Alejo had come to the newspaper office, sat down, hemming and hawing at first, and then, as if diving beneath a wave, suddenly blurted out a confession straight to his face. Some choose Father Azcárate, it was said. Others, Santi, the little preacher. And others, maybe, choose me. They choose me because they figure a journalist comes pretty close to literature. More than once they've said to him: If you weren't so lazy, you could write a novel about my life, they tell him. And Dante, impassive, utters the same reply: No, thanks. Someone else is probably writing it. I'll pass. Alejo belongs to this category, with the difference being that he's not so obvious; he'll never suggest that Dante write a novel about his life. Just the opposite: he'll tell him his story just to get it off his chest, knowing that the other guy won't write it, and not because he lacks talent, either. What he lacks is perseverance. Like everyone here. For every season there's an excuse to let things be.

What are you writing, Alejo asks him.

Your newspaper, Dante replies.

Anyway, if you were writing that novel, you wouldn't be so relaxed. Besides, there's another reason you don't write it: you're comfortable like this. I finance the paper for you. And you're not about to risk losing your gig by airing your personal sponsor's woes.

Alejo keeps his mouth shut.

The rain brings her back to me, he says then. I remember her most when it's raining, Alejo says. Why did she have to die when she was better than me.

And there's no need to explain who he's talking about.

Last Tuesday night changes were put into effect at the police stations in our Villa. Police protocol dictates that when a department chief is replaced, changes take place at the police stations under that chief's jurisdiction. A few months ago in Mar de las Pampas, Police Commissioner Osvaldo Nicolo replaced Jorge Baltiérrez, who had been in office for less than a year as head of the Pinamar Department. This change, as was reported at the time, was due to an investigation in which Baltiérrez was implicated in the kidnapping of businessman Jorge Villalba, who in turn was implicated in the murder of three Colombians, members of the ephedrine Mafia, at a shopping center in the northern zone. Following this replacement in Pinamar, District Headquarters also decided on a change of cast at our location. Therefore, Commissioner Frugone and several of his subordinates will be transferred to other locations. Meanwhile, Officer Armando Balmaceda will be promoted to Chief of Police and Officer Walter Renzo to Deputy Commissioner to act as his second-in-command. It should be noted that both men are familiar with the Villa and have an impressive résumé, having fulfilled their duties in critical districts like Berazategui and San Martín. In an address to the press, Frugone emphasized that the transfers are not based on any Internal Affairs investigation, but rather on operational factors. Besides, he pointed out, their respective service records are unblemished. In the next few days they will be assigned greater responsibilities in high-risk urban areas. "We believe we contributed to improving security in the Villa during our time there," said Frugone. And he added: "Of course there are still aspects that can be improved, but this is always the case when our motto is 'High Standards of Service.' The Rotary Club, the Swiss Club, the German Club, and the Beer Lovers' Association organized a farewell banquet.

A few days later Estela landed a job taking care of the cabins at Los Tulipanes in Mar de las Pampas. The salary was nothing great, but she had a little bungalow, and, best of all, she was living in the heart of the forest. Miumiú adapted right away. It seemed like she'd always lived in the forest. It was more than she might have expected for someone starting from square one. Because, she thought, in her case it was a question of starting from square one. Right around that time Vivi phoned her to see how she was doing. I've learned so much lately, she told her. I've grown. Estela was afraid to admit that she wanted to see her, invite her to see her bungalow. It was a weakness she didn't want to allow herself. She couldn't do it. Do you want to come, she asked her.

Silence, always the silence of Vivi's negative response. Estela was about to apologize. She shouldn't have spoken to her in that cringing tone. She hated herself for inviting her. But what really killed her: now she knew, it was that hunch she had. It had already come on before that night with Eugenio. It wasn't so much a hunch as a stab of fear. And fear, she well knew, was the scary scenario, the one she had to be prepared for. Vivi had spoken to her about the scary scenario. There's no one who doesn't have a scary scenario, Vivi once told her. Intelligence is a matter of getting your heart and mind prepared to face that moment, to step out onto the stage and act. Be the person you dreamed of being. Step out onto the stage and tell yourself: Sure I can. And so it will be. That was what Vivi had taught her, but it was clear she still had a way to go to reach sure I can. She couldn't hold back, so she asked her: Tell me the truth, Vivi, she said. And she asked: There's someone else, right.

Vivi's silence was shorter: Yes, a story that wasn't exactly over. If I didn't tell you about it, Vivi began to explain. But Estela cut her off: I understand. You didn't want to hurt me. Vivi's instant reply: Exactly, I didn't want to. But I can stop by during the week, anytime, Vivi said to her. Of course I'd like to see you. We can be friends. Friendship is healthier than love. Now Estela was the silent one. Are you there? Vivi asked. Yes, I'm here. And then: If you're planning to come over, no offense, but call first. Quick to react, Vivi: Why would I take offense? Estela realized she had gotten to her. Another one of Vivi's silences and then: How's Miumiú. Estela didn't hesitate: Fantastic—you should see how she's adjusted to the change.

Then, after hanging up, Estela dried her eyes. Those weren't tears of sadness, she told herself. She went out into the forest. She walked. It was pleasant to hear her footsteps on the pine needles. Miumiú followed her. The two of them walking toward the sea. As the sound of the waves grew louder, a feeling began to overtake her. She had the sensation that her lungs were expanding, that more air was getting into her. She took a deep breath. And, climbing a sand dune, with Miumiú still trailing behind her, she saw the sea. She felt like she was seeing it for the first time. A feeling many people have when they haven't seen it for quite a while. Then seeing it again isn't seeing it again. It's seeing it for the first time. And this was one of those first times. Her first time.

At daybreak, when the countryside begins to take shape, trees, lakes, weeds, a lagoon, the whorehouse and its red lights look different. The building, whose purple lights hold out the promise of sin in the nighttime, at daybreak is a stripped-down shack with blue walls. A few cables in the wind, the little red lanterns dangling, swinging back and forth, still lit. The light has a gentleness at this hour. The shack by the side of the road looks sad. You can read the sign: Tropicana. Drinks 24 hours. There's a yellow car parked at the door, the latest model. Someone who stayed on too long. Someone from around here, no doubt. Someone who doesn't care if his car is seen in front of the whorehouse, someone who's got power. You can hear a guy's voice shouting: Blow me, mamita. It's Borelli, from Borelli's Auto Parts. Through Chiquita, the Dominican, we found out that it turns him on to come to the whorehouse with a pair of red panties. Chiquita's panties. That turns him on. Sniffing her panties, putting them on her. Now there's silence, calm at the whorehouse. Every so often the windy rush of a bus going by. You can hear a rooster. At the whorehouse the only thing you can hear is the sound of a faucet, a toothbrush, gargling. Chiquita rinses her mouth, and now, with minty breath, returns to her room. Borelli is sleeping. Silence. It's already daylight. Chiquita lowers the blinds. She aches all over. How she loves the sunrise over the sea, she thinks. She can't remember the last time she saw the sunrise over the sea.

Borelli snores. Chiquita looks for his pants, his car keys. She finds money, but she doesn't care about money. When she finds the keys, she throws on jeans, a sweater, and sneakers. Then she tiptoes out. Stealthily, she opens and closes the door to the room. She gets into the car. And when she reaches the main road, she hits the gas. To the sea.

We all want to get into heaven; we're capable of doing anything to get in. Including screwing those who are ahead of us in line. And then, when we're pushing at the gate, if it's closed, whether by ringing the bell or kicking the gate down, we're determined to try. Until we figure out that the door opens outward. And it's too late.

That night when poor Nidia saw Lorena at the computer, the shimmer of the screen trembling in her face, her eyes blank, she felt the fear of the unknown, ran outside and through half the Villa till she reached La Comadre's shack. You might say La Comadre is accustomed to hearing clapping in the little garden outside her house at any hour of the night because, according to her, that's why God brought her into the world, to fight evil. You know who I'm talking about, Yoli says. The folk healer. How desperate Nidia must have been: not only did she drag La Comadre from her shack at this ungodly hour of the morning, but she also shoved her into a hired car and rode back with her. The girl was still at the computer. Lost.

La Comadre crossed herself and made the sign of the cross on the girl's forehead. Lorena still didn't react. After studying her for a while, La Comadre clapped her hands in front of Lorerna's eyes. And the girl came out of it.

Come on, sweetheart, La Comadre said to her. We're going to bed now. You have to rest.

And she managed to put the girl to bed.

Later, to the mother:

She's in a dream world, my dear, La Comadre told her. That's what's wrong with her. A dream world. She's somewhere else. I'm going to recommend some herbs. Bring something to write on and I'll jot down an herbal tea recipe.

Nidia obeyed.

What day is today, La Comadre asked.

Tuesday, the woman reminded her.

On Friday you'll come with her to my healing center to see how things have worked out.

Because La Comadre calls her shack a healing center. After all, what La Comadre does is heal.

Then La Comadre took a good look at Nidia:

I'm also going to prescribe an antiseptic and a cream for your feet. Just look how your little paw is bleeding.

Only then did Nidia notice the trail of blood she'd left, the piece of glass that sliced into her foot on the road, when she was running along the streets of sand and earth of La Virgencita.

The widow Janet Bullock, formerly Rochelle, formerly Gardiner, is brought to trial on suspicion of two murders, that of her first husband, Brian Rochelle, and of her second, Russell Gardiner, both presumably killed by accident, with firearms. As the defense and the prosecution debate, and public opinion regarding her guilt divides her neighbors of Toynbee Rock, just when it seems Janet will go free, a student and player on the local baseball team presents evidence that will turn the trial around. In the late Russ's locker, student Randolph Crowley found a cassette. Russ had taped it two days before he died. Russ's anguished voice blames himself for his homosexuality, which caused sexual relations in his marriage to deteriorate. Russ tells how a few days earlier, when he couldn't sleep, his wife Janet gave him sleeping pills. He pretended to take them, but instead stuck them in his pocket and the next day took the medicine to a lab. David Kaminsky, a chemist, informed him that they weren't sleeping pills, but rather poison. Instead of a psychotropic drug, they contained an anesthetic made of tropical snake venom so powerful that even the tiniest dose would have killed him instantly. Russ's trembling voice reveals that he has been afraid of his wife for a long time. She won't stop till she kills me. The only thing she cares about is my insurance policy. As soon as she gets that money she'll look for a way to get rid of our kids. Janet is as smart as the devil. And no one will ever be able to prove anything. I hope this recording will be helpful in case something terrible happens to me. The pills, together with the cassette, were found in Russ's locker. Two days before he died, Russ told the student to look in his locker if anything should happen to him. And he gave him an extra key. Asked about his relationship with the deceased, the young witness broke down and wept, admitting that they had been lovers for a year. We will return with *My Neighbors' Drama*.

Working class girls, boys, and women are not the only victims of domestic violence. There are also victims in families that still consider themselves middle-class. And often among those belonging to the elite, as well. Zambrano instantly recognized the sort of "accidents" the women and children had suffered. Their faces, a combination of terror and shame, spoke more loudly than the injuries and words that attempted to explain the accident. When Campas brought Anita to the hospital, Zambrano didn't need to look at the woman's wounds as carefully as her husband's face, his nervousness, to realize what was going on. Anita needed another cast, in addition to bandages. Zambrano gave Campas the cold shoulder. Didn't even speak to him. He took Anita to an examining room, leaving Campas to wait outside. Do you want to file a complaint, he asked Anita. She looked at him. It was an accident. Zambrano asked her: Did your kids see when he hit you? Anita: We don't have any. And then: I found out from Flor, Anita changed the subject. She's so thrilled. She really wanted a baby. Anita had caught him off guard. We work together at the school, she told him. Congratulations. She told me. Zambrano, silent. Flor asked me to be discreet, Anita went on. I didn't tell anyone. Zambrano was still reserved. Sorry if I said something wrong, Anita apologized. I swear I didn't tell anyone.

After applying her cast, Zambrano walked her to the waiting room. Campas got up to meet her.

With what you must have seen in the Falklands, this is nothing, she said to him.

Zambrano turned toward Anita.

You're sure you don't want to file a complaint.

A communicating vessel connects the Calderóns, Marconi the pharmacist, Valeria, and me, Dante thinks. And he thinks of María. María. A linguistic problem, calling María a girl, he thinks. María's no girl, he thinks. She must be over fifty, easy. And that passel of kids she has. And grandkids. And great-grandkids. María comes to clean his apartment once a week. And once a week she takes home his dirty laundry. From underpants to sheets. María calls him sir, though sometimes his first name slips through. But it doesn't bother Dante. On the contrary, he likes it. He has warm feelings for her. And he gets a naughty thrill, a sick pleasure, whenever María confides intimate facts about her other bosses. But you're not a boss, María tells him. You're different. A friend, Dante. And Dante feels less of a difference between him and this woman who comes to wrest some order out of the chaos of this one-bedroom apartment half a block from the beach. Why refer to her as a girl, this woman who's practically an old lady. No, not practically. María *is* an old lady. To call her a girl is a euphemism that covers up more than her old age. It also marks the nature of this relationship. I'm her boss, he thinks. Some time ago Dante realized that María steals from him. But it doesn't worry him too much.

A few months ago he deliberately left some ten-peso bills on the table and went out for a walk. When he got home the bills weren't there. He didn't dare say anything to María. He asks himself why he didn't say anything to her. And he realizes that it's a payment for those intimacies she brings him. Deep down, he doesn't want to lose her. Firing María wouldn't mean just having to wash his own dirty laundry. It would be losing information about other people's. Besides, he says to himself, it's cheaper than having a wife.

You can find out if your little one was abused by paying attention to the following signs. With preschoolers: repetitive and inappropriate games for their age; compulsive masturbation; restlessness; irritability; crying for no apparent reason; sleep disturbances; excessive fears centered on certain people, places, or actions; regressive behavior, like delayed language or bed-wetting. In school-age children: hypersexualized behavior and precocious sexual knowledge; changes in eating habits; mood swings; troubled relationships with parents; disturbances in sleeping patterns, learning, and body image. In adolescents: isolation; lack of confidence; poor relationships with peers; running away from home; self-directed aggression; anorexia and bulimia; drug and alcohol use.

Gonza is dealing. Don't ask me who the boss is. He's dealing. They say Malerba covers him. He's Malerba's gofer. His little errand boy. The kid's become untouchable. Even Don Tito Souza, the trade unionist, respects the kid. It seems Gonza's going to have an FM radio station with rock and reggae and a disco during the season. Bengala, he says he's gonna call it. Very hip. And backing all of it, no doubt: Quirós.

My Neighbors' Drama. The widow Janet Bullock, formerly Rochelle, formerly Gardiner, can no longer claim innocence. The tape that a student member of the Toynbee Rock baseball team has presented in court is sufficient proof to convict her. The jury reaches a swift, unfaltering decision. Janet Bullock is found guilty of the murders of her two husbands. She is sentenced to the maximum penalty: death by lethal injection. But while she remains in prison waiting for her sentence to be carried out, her lawyers find a legal loophole to set aside the sentence. Janet Bullock is now condemned to life in prison. Her children have never stopped visiting her regularly in prison. Shelley, the youngest, is the only one who agreed to testify in *My Neighbors' Drama.* Shelley is an advanced law student at Cornell University, planning to specialize in criminal law. My mother is a well-meaning person. My siblings and I have nothing to criticize her for, since she's always sacrificed to look after us. Her only problem is that in stressful situations she's overcome by an uncontrollable urge to make up for the lacks in her own upbringing on a Mormon farm in Ohio. There her father practiced plural marriage and also had sexual relations with his daughters. Poverty, and the relations her father subjected her to, explain my mother's behavior.

According to state law, if she keeps up her excellent conduct behind bars, Janet Bullock can go free. I don't care what that miserable wretch went through in her childhood, says Carolyn Gardiner, Russ's mother, says. That bitch is some actress. Just like she's conned her kids about her maternal feelings, she's conning the prison authorities. It burns me up to think that phony can go free in 2012. I'll bet the witch'll go back to her old tricks. If she doesn't commit another crime in Toynbee Rock, she's capable of doing it in a neighboring town. In another country. In South America. And some mother will end up crying over her son's death just like I cry for my little Russ.

Eusebio pulls his gray Sienna up to a house in Pinar del Norte. He stops in front of some flower beds. He gets ready to help his passenger, an old Hungarian woman he picked up at Disco. A pack of dogs surrounds him. They lunge at him. But Eusebio ignores them. When a dog growls at you, he thinks, ignore it. Just as the old woman is paying her fare, he sees Dicky sitting on the Harley on the sand road. Eusebio isn't afraid of dogs, but that dude in the black jacket, sitting on the cycle, staring right at him, intimidates him. Seeing and understanding happen in one second. The Sienna backs up, full speed, nearly grazing the Harley, and shoots through the poplar grove toward the asphalt. The Harley follows it.

Then comes the part about the cows, which is what we like to talk about the most at Moby. Even though he wasn't there and is talking on behalf of Martínez, the one from the Aeroclub, the person talking is Rafa, the teller from Banco Provincia. Everyone saw the chase: the Harley behind the Sienna, speeding down the avenue at a thousand miles an hour. Barnet the councilman saw them as he was leaving a council meeting. Mercedes the teacher saw them through a window of the middle school. Nazar, the one who sells lottery tickets, saw them. They almost ran him over. Mirna, the woman who sells costume jewelry in Galería Soles, saw them. Giménez, the one from the Co-op, saw them when they were about to turn onto the diagonal road. Mariela saw them as she was coming back from the temple. Cruz the street sweeper saw them as they entered the roundabout. Borelli from the auto parts store saw them as they headed for Circunvalación. Eugenio the surveyor saw them. The whole Villa saw them. But the one who saw the business about the cows was Martínez, the guy from the Aeroclub, from the tower. The Sienna was tearing along the road with the Harley right on its tail. Eusebio passed a Rápido Argentino bus coming from Buenos Aires. But while trying to dodge the bus and finding himself into the wrong lane, he couldn't avoid the cattle truck that was coming along in the other direction. The Sienna plowing into the truck. And the Harley behind it, at full speed, crashing into the Sienna, and Dicky flying through the air and landing on the shoulder, head first. The truck, overturned, the cows trampling one another in their escape from the pen, stampeding toward the countryside. Some of them ran over Dicky. Eusebio was trapped inside the Sienna, with the wheel nailed into his chest, his face bleeding.

The woman walks into the veterinary clinic just as Moure is about to close. Her hair is disheveled; she's breathing heavily, holding the Pekingese in her arms as if it were a baby. Although it's late, Moure treats the little dog anyway. The dog is frightened to death. More terrified than in pain. It has a broken hind leg.

How did it happen, Moure asks her. The woman doesn't answer him. An accident or a kick. Because it's injured here, too. These were kicks, señora. I'm a nervous person, very nervous, but I never take it out on Fifí. Who kicked her, Moure asks, applying a splint. My husband, she finally answers. He was fired from the co-op and he got drunk. He took it out on Fifí.

Moure looks at the woman. She has a black and blue mark on her neck. What happened to you, he asks. A branch, she says. I was pruning a tree.

This isn't pruning season, señora.

It's just that I'm absent minded.

I'm gonna bring you up right, Malerba thought to himself. Gonza obeyed him with fear in his gestures. He was on alert, ready to jerk his body backward at any moment, anticipating a blow. In the months that he'd been doing odd jobs for Malerba, he worried about making a mistake. Any misstep, the smallest slip, was enough to earn him one of Malerba's slaps. Once in a while he thought about rebelling, but Malerba terrified him. Advanced in years though he was, El Capo still had the strength of his earlier days. You could tell from his expression how much pleasure it gave him to instill fear. Gonza concentrated all his efforts on not letting him down, because even if fear and extortion had turned him into Malerba's slave boy, he'd begun to notice that, despite the harshness of Malerba's treatment, beneath it flowed paternal feeling.

I had a teacher too, kid, he told him one night. It's a long story. Now, you're gonna take your old man's 4x4 and go to the port at Mar del Plata. You'll pick up the package and come back. Because it's in your best interest to come back, I'm telling you.

That's what Malerba's errands were like. Picking up a package in Mar del Plata, making deliveries in Madariaga, Pinamar, and Mar de las Pampas. Pickup and delivery. Lots of houses. Also some stores, 24-hour kiosks, gas stations. Drugs. But not only drugs. Some guns. Cell phones. More than once he'd carried a briefcase, which he wasn't supposed to open, from Quirós's office. The less you know about certain things, the better off you are, Malerba told him. Look, learn, and keep your mouth shut.

One night, as he was getting ready to do a line, Malerba stared at him hard:

I'm gonna tell you something very important. Don't give up your studies. Finish high school. Law, that's what you need to study. To fuck with the law you gotta study it, know what I mean?

Then he took a hit.

There were times, like now, when Gonza made him feel something between pity and tenderness. If he thought he could get by in life because he was the mayor's son, of high social status, the little jerk was fucked. In life you had to have street smarts. And, if possible, a way out. A real way out.

He hoped his lessons would get through to the little punk.

Last Wednesday just before noon there was a dramatic, not to mention catastrophic, accident on Route 11 near our Aeroclub. According to mechanic Juan Carlos Martínez, manager of the facility, who witnessed the circumstances leading up to the ill-fated event, a Sienna from Remismar Limo Service, driven by Eusebio Carrero, who was attempting to pass a Rápido Argentino bus in an unfortunate maneuver, struck a cattle transport vehicle coming from the opposite direction. Following the car at full speed was Ricardo "Dicky" Garramuño on his Harley Davidson. Our local motocross champion was unable to avoid the crashed vehicles and literally flew through the air, losing his life as he hit the asphalt. Carrero, the driver of the Sienna, was critically injured and remains in the ICU at our Villa's hospital; his prognosis is guarded. Meanwhile, Gabriel Cifuentes, driver of the cattle transport vehicle, also sustained serious injuries and was hospitalized. As a result of the film-chase-like collision, the truck trailer overturned and the cattle escaped from their pen, heading for the sides of the road and fleeing toward the open countryside. A head count of recovered cattle revealed the absence of three cows, which, according to reliable sources, most likely have been captured by residents of the settlement in El Monte.

A vigil for our dear Dicky's remains was held at Neri Funeral Home; he received a Christian burial yesterday. A dramatic loss for our community and its athletic reputation, but an even greater one for his dear young wife, Rosita Müller, Winterfest Queen, who is pregnant. This newspaper extends its condolences to the widow.

Last night, thunder. The world seemed to be coming down. Then, the deluge. This morning the storm continues. Calmer, lazily. Look how it's raining. It'll probably go on like this all day. All day and through the weekend. Saturday, and still this rain. Fine, persistent. It won't stop. Occasionally a bird trills. And it's the only thing you can hear. Because the sound of the sea, in this rain, becomes a distant echo; every so often the splashing of a wave. City offices and co-ops are closed today. Law and accounting firms. A few real estate offices remain open with the futile hope that some tourist might drop in to check on pre-season rates. Supermarkets and stores will be open till noon. We could see the water coming; it had been forecast. Now a heavier downpour. It has its charm, the rain. But after a while its attraction is that of an abyss, a dark hole. The few people who are working today start out late, and by the time they open they're already waiting for noon so they can close. After midday the Villa will be deserted and shrouded in rain. It makes you want to stay indoors and never go out again. Though staying indoors can be dangerous. What loser invented that home sweet home stuff. A loser, for sure. Because a loser longs for what he doesn't have. And whoever does have it knows it isn't sweet. After the siesta, which will be deep, a few businesses will re-open. Cars for hire parked in front of the home office or waiting at a service station for a call. No one thinks of going out. And if someone does, it's to rent a video and buy a heat-and-eat pizza. We're going to stay in. We're going to wrap ourselves in bitterness, boredom, and vexation. If you listen closely, you can hear the shattering of a dish, the crack of a belt, a slap, crying, doors slamming. A woman, a child, will dart out, trying to escape, crying for help into the darkness and the rain. After a while, drenched, stifling their tears, they'll retrace their steps, return home. With luck, the man will be sleeping off his drunk. If God exists, he'll have shot himself and his brains will be scattered on the kitchen floor tiles, in the dining room, the garage, the shed out back. And it's not so long till tomorrow. We'll go to Mass. We'll pray for the storm to end.

While Eusebio the limo driver and Gabriel, the driver of the cattle truck, are in intensive care, separated by a floral-print curtain, at Neri Funeral Home, surrounded by a few friends and relatives, Rosita, five months pregnant, unable to cry, listens to everyone's comments: she'll get over the pain, she's in shock. While Father Joaquín walks over to Rosita and touches her face, brushing her hair aside as she looks up, at the hospital Matilde talks with Laura, the truck driver's wife, and recounts her own tragedy: who knows, if her husband comes out of this alive, he'll be practically in a vegetative state, and Laura, in turn, her eyes red from crying, wonders what will become of her and the three little ones if Gabriel ends up an invalid, to which Matilde tells her that she's not worried on that account because they have no kids, but the fact that this mess was caused by a knocked-up whore seems like an irony of fate, a bad joke. As Father Joaquín leads Rosita to a corner, slipping an arm around her shoulder, speaking to her in a hushed voice, she feels warmth; now her warm hands, her soul returning to her body, her body once more a body, she tells him that all the men and women who came to the funeral think it's all her fault and that she's a whore, and they'll never understand how much she loved Dicky, more than anyone else in the world, and if the baby she's carrying in her womb turns out to be a boy, he'll be named after his father, while in the hospital Matilde sighs and tries to comfort Laura: The two of us should go and look for that whore and stick a knife in her belly, but since God doesn't exist and they'd throw us in prison for doing what the Bible says about an eye for an eye, we have to control ourselves and be strong, especially you, a mother, with your little ones, you have to be stronger, though I'm telling you, if my Eusebio stays a vegetable and never gets to tell the tale, I swear by the light that shines on me that I'll do it, I'll grab a knife and go after that whore.

At Moby, Dante launches into a spirited defense of maids. And he reminds us that he speaks with authority, that he has upper-class roots, a family from Coghlan. Yeah, even though I might not look it, a broken-down scribe at a small town rag, I was a Coghlan kid. We had a maid. And I remember the days of Evita, La Perona, as she was called. The maids worshiped her. And the employers feared the maids. For the first time they feared the maids, not the ignorant immigrants from Galicia, I'm talking about the half-breeds, descendants of the Indian hordes that Roca exterminated, those captives rounded up by civilization to serve the aristocracy of the Port City, Dante says, animated by whiskey. How those ritzy families feared that their sneaky, clever servant girl would rat them out. For the first time, the ladies of the house respected their slaves. What's this preamble all about, Dante asks us. I'll try to make it short.

Getting back to María, the Calderóns' and Marconis' maid. With relations as strained as they were between her and Beti, Cachito's wife, María saw it coming: she could tell that they were going to give her the boot. At that time, when she saw it coming, as she straightened out one of the señora's closets at the Marconis' chalet, and remember, the señora in this case is Valeria, who some of you called the Jew, Valeria had a DVD hidden in the closet among her panties. María's attention was drawn not so much to the DVD as to where it was hidden, between the Victoria's Secret and the Caro Cuore. Let's say she was overcome by curiosity. And taking advantage of the fact that she was alone in the house, she went over to the home theater and popped in the DVD. It didn't shock her to see a porn video. It shocked her to see that it starred Alejo and Valeria. Frightened, she turned off the equipment. But her fright disappeared as she started thinking about what to do with that thing. What to do.

Why Dante knows all the details of what happened is all too obvious.

Fede was kind of timid, a shy type you had to pull words from with a corkscrew. Everyone said that if he seemed to be getting more and more introverted, it was because of the weed. The thing is, Fede's a darling, a total sweetheart, Ceci defended him as she nursed Bautista. He needs a chance. He knows how to get along.

Fede and Ceci had moved in together in a house in the South when she became pregnant. We'll get through this, Ceci would say. And Fede agreed with a *hmm*. Ceci still worked at the Electrical Co-op, but her salary was barely enough for two, let alone three. Then Blanco, Ceci's father, intervened and gave him a job at the supermarket warehouse and distribution center. We all wondered how long Fede would last at Superblanco. The first argument he had with his father-in-law was about the weed. Though it wasn't so much an argument as the fact that Blanco caught him stoned. The second and last time was when he found out that Fede was stealing from him. One afternoon Blanco marked a bill. And that night, when he closed up and went over the day's receipts, he grabbed Fede by the throat and made him empty his pockets. He had the marked bill. Blanco beat the living daylights out of him. Even if he had tolerated that pothead when he knocked up his daughter, now the tolerance had ended.

Ceci moved back to her parents' house. She gave no signs that the separation was a sacrifice for her. It's just that the baby makes me think about practical things, she said. I'm starting to forget Fede. Truth is, she'd hooked up with Merlino the Toad, her boss at the Co-op. Merlino, a married man. Twenty years older. He promised her he would get a separation soon. But soon never came. Gimme time, baby.

What happened was that Paula is a nice girl. The proof is that when Ceci ran into Paula, the wife, because around here all of us are always running into each other, Paula greeted her affectionately and always asked her about the baby. How lucky you were to get rid of that bum, she once told her. What you need is a man, honey. Someone to be a father to this adorable little creature of yours. A darling, Bautista.

God metes out punishment, but He's also kind, said Santi the pastor to the people of El Monte when they invited him to the celebration of the birth of Milagros Vicuña, daughter of Eric Vicuña and Marilyn Arroyuelo. Hardly people of limited resources like it said in *El Vocero*, someone remarked. Dante shouldn't play Progressive now with those euphemisms he puts into the news. Family, gimme a break—more like a good-for-nothing bunch of half-breeds who never stop reproducing. Because the way they live, all jumbled up with grandparents, parents, uncles and aunts, cousins, nieces and nephews, nobody can tell them apart or how many of them there are. And you should see how they inbreed, how the defective and retarded ones reproduce. No census can deal with them. A plague is what they are, living off government aid. They've got nothing to eat, but they go out and steal so they can prance around in those fancy-ass sneakers. Man, they were lucky, no matter what the pastor says about Divine Providence: bullshit. When that mob saw the cows charging through the countryside, they drove them into their shantytown. Some *asado* they had. All of El Monte had a free meal that day. Milagritos's birth and the Lord's generosity were a good excuse. They also held up Bayona Wholesale Supermarket to get the booze. Cartons of fine wine, beer, and cider. The party lasted till the alcohol ran out. And, predictably, it ended with a shooting. It seems Johnny Vicuña wanted to bang Julieta, Marilyn's younger sister, but the father wouldn't let him. So Johnny blew him away with the Magnum 357 that a cop from Pinamar had given him. Johnny's at large now.

Till one fine day Paula asks Merlino the Toad for a divorce. The papers have already been drawn up at Quirós' law office, and all Merlino has to do is sign. There's nothing to discuss. Merlino was surprised by Alejo's phone call informing him of the divorce. He asks for time; he wants to think it over. Give me time, Paula. There's nothing to think about. Just go and sign. Is there someone else, Merlino probes. Tell me if you have a lover, he asks Paula. That's my business. I don't stick my nose in your life, so don't go sticking yours in mine. And the kids, Merlino asks her. What's gonna happen to the kids. Nothing, what could happen, Paula said to him. Daniela and Ramiro were already grown, each of them doing their own thing, studying in Mar del Plata; they dropped by less and less often. Besides, the separation wouldn't be a huge surprise to them; they were well aware of the Toad's affairs. So you can just go to Alejo's and sign, Paula insists. The guitar instructor, Merlino takes a stab. The guitar teacher is screwing you, admit it. Stop being an idiot, will you. Go and sign. I promise you I'll leave the girl, Merlino tells her. And he confesses his affair with Cecilia. Paula stares at him fixedly: Don't involve the girl in this. It could have been her or anybody. I hope you don't make her as unhappy as you made me. It wasn't thirty years of unhappiness, Merlino says. Go and sign, I'm telling you. I don't deserve this, Merlino says. I invested in us. I invested in a family. It's like investing in a co-op. You have no right, Paula.

Son, reads the headline on the Society page of *El Vocero*. And the letter: *On a day like today in 2005, a cold month, an adorable, but more importantly, adored little boy was born. He was our pride and joy, a dream come true, such happiness to be able to look at you, see your eyes, your tiny hands. When we looked at you, we wondered how a carnation with that glow, with that charm, had sprouted and been born, as if from a garden. We remember how you cried when you were born, dearest little son. It frightened us to pick you up; we were afraid we might hurt you, break you.*

Today you are our great companion, the light of eternity in our eyes. With great affection, with high hopes, we wish you a happy birthday.

And with all our faith, we beg God to always keep us together. And may the Lord always keep your heart pure to love and forgive.

Your parents, Aurelio and Cristina Cuitiño.

Dante publishes these letters nearly every week. When he publishes them he feels that all is not lost. Sometimes, when it's been a while since he's received one of these letters, he makes them up.

If I had to make a movie with all these stories, I'd set it to Dylan's music. All the stories sung in Dylan's voice.

After they told her at the hospital that Eusebio would remain in a vegetative state, Matilde, shaken, walked into Huerta Accounting Services a few days after Dicky's burial. Her eyes popped out when she found Rosita sitting at his desk, drinking *mate*. Eusebio is going to be a vegetable because of you, you fucking whore. And she pulled out a 22. God knows where she got the pistol from. That doesn't matter. Around here those who don't want guns don't have them. Matilde held the pistol in both hands. But nothing happened. She hadn't released the safety. Malena, the accountant, and Tini, the secretary, jumped on her and wrested the gun away. Rosita's contractions started; her water broke. The police arrived at the same time as the ambulance. The police cuffed Matilde and dragged her out to the police car. The nurses put Rosita on a stretcher, loaded her into the ambulance, and drove her to the hospital.

At last Rosita had her baby: a little girl, dark like her deceased father. We wondered if the Müllers were going to love her just the same, as Indian-looking as she was.

Then we found out that Eusebio had been admitted to the Fleni Institute in Buenos Aires. That Matilde, her neck in an orthopedic brace since the struggle at the accounting office, had sold the kiosk and followed her husband. That Gabriel, the truck driver, was taken to the Interzonal Hospital in Mar del Plata because there's no CT scanner here. And, just like in Eusebio's case, that was the last we heard of the poor guy.

Father Joaquín accompanied Rosita in her most difficult moments. Ever since then Rosita's been a regular church-goer.

Forgiving and forgetting are very much alike. And so let's leave Rosita to rebuild her life.

A black frying pan with the remains of Bolognese sauce. A big pot with spaghetti stuck to the bottom. A strainer. An aluminum tray. Seven china plates, also with remains of sauce. Eight forks. A large knife. Three Tramontina knives. Five tablespoons. Four teaspoons. Six sturdy glasses. Five with the remains of red wine. Four cups with the remains of coffee. A coffeepot. A strainer. A teapot. Three tall glasses. Two full ashtrays. And let's not even count the number of empty bottles next to the trash can. That's what was leftover from last night. And that's what's left of us: remains. Better clean everything up right away.

How is it you haven't heard, Flavia. Lorena, that dopey kid, the daughter of Nidia, the one from Los Médanos supermarket, the girl who was raped and then went crazy, well, Lorena lost the baby. I'm telling you what I heard. That it was born dead.

On this gray morning, Dante walks along the dunes. He goes down to the beach, the oil-stained sand. The sea is brown. The foam on the crest of the waves is ocher. Farther out, a bird flies over the water. Dante can't tell if it's a duck, a seagull, or a cormorant. He adjusts his glasses. One of these days he must go to the optician and have the prescription changed. The bird slips over the current. It navigates the tide with majestic grace. They must be biting down there, Dante thinks. The bird dips its head in. Then its whole body. Some time goes by. Dante waits for the bird to come back up to the surface. But no, the bird remains under water. He waits. When he checks, more than half an hour has passed. Nothing. The bird's disappearance hits him in the chest with surprising angst. The sighting of the bird, the wait, its definitive absence, he feels, are a revelation he can't quite manage to decipher. Maybe the message is that sometimes you try to plumb the depths, and the depths swallow you up. He'll have to think this thing over, he says to himself as he returns, crestfallen, to the Villa.

Flor thought it was unfair not to announce the joyous news to the family. Zambrano was close to telling her about his vasectomy. But to confess it would mean facing a discussion he was in no condition to deal with. He felt like thrashing Flor. Of pressing her: Tell me who it was or I'll beat the shit out of you. But he held it in. He asked himself what made him better than Campas, laying into Anita. It was true: he had never raised a hand to Flor, but he had concealed his vasectomy from her, and this lie was a greater betrayal than adultery. He asked himself if it might have been his refusal to have children that had provoked Flor to look for a lover. He asked himself what love was. And he also asked himself if love, even more than forgiveness, didn't consist of possessing a high tolerance for humiliation, the ability to swallow shit as if it were saliva and put on a nothing-happened-here smile.

The Villa was growing. But most of the buyers were tourists. And so the majority of kids were descendants of Germans or *criollos* from Madariaga. English promised to be the language of the future. But there was no English teacher here. German, of course; you could learn it in many houses, but nobody studied German because it wasn't necessary. After all, lots of people spoke it.

Nobody would've bet five cents that things would turn out as they did for Simone when she put the little sign up in the bakery, the grocery store, the hardware store, the auto repair shop, the pharmacy, the post office, and everywhere. Simone D'Orvigny, French classes. And yet, students started to come. Man, was she hot. Quite a few of us would've signed up if not for our wives' jealousy. So we had to be satisfied with sending our kids, playing the nice guy, and waiting for summer to ogle her in those low-necked sundresses she wore, or else strolling, as if by accident, through the dunes where Simone sunbathed in the nude. She made the boys read Radiguet, Mauriac, Camus, and Sartre. For the girls, Sagan, Beauvoir, Duras, and Leduc. More and more boys wanted to learn French till a guilty conscience spilled the beans in the confessional. And the Sunday after El Negrito's confession, the priest threatened us with Divine wrath. France was the lost sheep of the Catholic Church, he shouted. And he lectured the parishioners, guaranteeing hell for the Enlightenment and all those who, under its influence, descended into the sin of the language that turned youth away from the path of righteousness. And we found out. She had initiated more than one boy. And more than one girl, as well. There weren't so many in either group, and it wasn't all that serious because the boys already sported the shadow of a beard and the girls were old enough to date. But doing it wrapped in the French flag was too much. In my opinion, they went overboard. But who can say.

The only way to show the wind is through its effect on things.

Everyone goes to La Comadre for help: the rich go, and the poor go. And La Comadre receives them all. She makes no exceptions. Money doesn't bring happiness, she always says. And the fact that someone is poor doesn't mean they should console themselves with the idea of going to Heaven. Nobody's satisfied with their luck. Some because they're victims of harm. And others because they cause it. God is just and makes no distinction between rich and poor people's shit. Many's the time I've come across people here who were on the outs with one another, and I brought them together, I got them to make up and even be friends afterward. The most important thing in this life is to shut up and listen. You learn by listening. And you teach by shutting up. Most problems can be solved by listening. And then looking for the right advice. But with those two mothers, I failed; there was no way. And, the fact is, I tried hard to apply all my learning. Until that night they had never been to my healing center. I knew about the problem between those two. Beti, Calderón's wife, whose boy, a great lug of a kid with that goofy expression on his face, had taken the wrong path. Even before the drugs. And then he'd crossed the line with the dope, too, and he and his buddies had fucked up that girl's life. And the mother of the girl who, for her part, had turned into a sleepwalker after what happened. I saw them separately, of course. Both of them brought their kids to see me. I saw Gonzalito and Lorena separately because it could have been a disaster if they met. I won't tell you all about their treatments, as they weren't that different, anyway. Because it's a fact that the hangman and his victim complement each other. Besides, in this case, Gonzalito broke my heart. A wonderful boy, ruined by his parents' lack of understanding. And Lorenita, with that fierce mother of hers, bugging her all the time about how she doesn't want her to be a loser like her. But sometimes the angels aren't on your side. And they ran into each other here. The mothers came to blows. Two lionesses baring their claws. How they laid into each other! With nails and teeth. They tore up my waiting room. Left one wall spattered with blood. And their cubs, on the sidelines. They didn't get involved. Didn't even try to separate them. I had to step in. I still have this arm bandaged. Spaced out, those kids were. Totally indifferent. Gonzalito, in his own world. And Lorena, a sleepwalker. I lost them as patients. But, to tell you the truth, I came out the winner.

Right you are, *flaca*, everything that rises, falls. But why does it fall so quickly.

All of us women have had a slip sometime, a fall like Anita's. Whoever says she never fell on her face is lying. If you're married, for sure you've had an accident like that. And if you haven't, just you wait. That's why it irks me that they're skinning poor Anita alive. As if they were saints. Not one of them is a saint. And neither are the guys. Them, even less than us. Sooner or later a girl can't take it anymore and does something. I'm not talking about cheating. You don't have to go as far as cheating to find yourself in a situation that lands you in the Emergency Room. Then it's happened to you. An accident. And you've gotta watch where you're going. I ask you: Isn't life itself an accident?

You'll understand me, Don Malerba, Nidia says to him. Because if I did what I ought to do, they'd throw me in jail. But you're different. Nobody would dare throw you in jail because you're a respectable, influential man. But if I go to jail, what will happen to my Lorena. I'm not afraid of those degenerate kids and I don't care that they're snobs. Here, I wrote down their names, addresses, and phone numbers for you. I'd like to do it myself. You understand me. You know what I want. All I'm asking you for is justice. Justice for my Lorena and punishment for them. Because there's got to be some justice in this world. I'm more than willing to punish those bastards, but I can't. Look, I know what I've brought you, my savings, it isn't a lot. If it's not enough, just tell me, Don Malerba. I'm prepared to hand over whatever I can from my paycheck from Los Médanos; let's say I pay you on credit. I'll collect part of my Christmas bonus this month. Please, I'm asking you to accept my money. I'm begging you. Don't turn me down. You don't know how grateful I am for whatever you can do. God, Who's watching us, will reward what you did for my Lorena.

Yesterday morning the children of Pía Soldán testified at the Dolores Courthouse in the case of their mother's death. Judge Obarrio had requested

the children's testimony following a psychological examination, when one of
them, Ignacio, the youngest child, related that he had heard his mother beg,
"Please, don't burn me." As minors, the children were interviewed with the
aid of a Gesell Dome.

The children arrived accompanied by their father, Gustavo Camargo, a
city government surveyor, who later was detained. Dr. Alejandro Quirós,
representing the victim's parents, testified that the children, while locked
in their room, had literally heard the blows that their father delivered to
their mother with a slipper, and later, they heard their mother beg not to
be burned with an oil can. Later, during the declarations, the children suf-
fered what appeared to be a block. The children were excluded from the
sworn statements that followed, but Luciana agreed with her younger
brother Martín that "Mom was burned to death." And later, after the
mother's pleas, they heard the shower running.

No doubt about it, Missy got involved with Malerba to piss off her
father. Don Morano and Tito, the son, decided to rescue her and
clean their family name. They climbed into the F100. Tito had a gun.
They say Malerba didn't even flinch when father and son showed
up at his place in the country and Tito shoved the barrel of the gun
against his forehead. Missy tried to get between them. But Malerba
pushed her away calmly, and then, with a smile, looked at father and
son, spat to one side, obligingly lowered the son's weapon, and went
on to give both of them a hard smack. He didn't even let them get
back in the pickup. He kicked their butts off his property. And he
kept the pickup for himself. He kept it just as he kept Missy. Till
Malerba, like I said, began to suspect her and Matías. One afternoon
when he went to the casino, his Fairlane broke down on Calle 11 and
he had to hitch a ride back. His daughter Fabiana was waiting for
him at the fence. Don't go in, she said to him. What's wrong, girl.
Better not go in. Malerba pushed his daughter aside and headed for
the room. He found them in bed. Missy and Matías.

Some questions shouldn't be asked, Moni thinks. For example, how she ended up in this place. If a woman asks herself that at this age, on the heels of seventy, it's because she did something wrong in life. And many are the things that Moni blames herself for. Though not as many as those her kids blame her for. This is what she thinks as she realizes that this pair of boots is done for. A pair of ankle boots from time immemorial. They must be from those days when that song, "These Boots Were Made for Walking," was popular. Moni can no longer remember how many times these boots went in for repair. As many times as she changed therapists, more or less. Poor things, their time had come. Just like mine won't be so very long from now, but it's better not to think about that. Instead, a poem. Then, sitting in front of her dresser, she looks at the boots and writes in her notebook: *Boots*, the title. Then: *While my grandkids / chase little birds / on a patio in Oslo / I throw away / my old boots, / the ones that walked / up and down the whole of Patagonia.* A poem, she thinks, doesn't solve a thing, but it helps let off steam. Then she sticks the boots in the garbage can, pops on the lid, and doesn't look back.

Gonza was frightened by the way Malerba asked him to come over that night.

I have a heart, kid, Malerba tells him now. Even though I might not seem to, I have one.

Gonza doesn't much like his expression when he says it, either.

Malerba lays a revolver down on the table. He lays it down looking him straight in the eye. Maybe you think I'm made of stone, Malerba goes on. I treated you like a son. But I'm not your old man who forgives all your bullshit. Here, things have a limit. There are rules. And there's no forgiveness for what you did. A lady came to see me. A lady from La Virgencita. Some degenerates raped her girl. What do you think of that. And since the ones that screwed her girl are the cream of the Villa, nothing's gonna happen to them. Justice, that's what the lady came to ask me for.

Gonza looks at the revolver. Malerba is testing him. He wonders if he'll have the nerve to pick up the weapon.

She cried, begged me for justice. It broke my heart. She wanted to pay me with what she doesn't have, poor woman. She reminded me of my old lady.

Malerba doesn't take his eyes off him. What do you think, kid, Malerba asks him. Forgive me, Gonzalo trembles. It was a joke. Besides, I didn't touch her. It was the others.

Drop your pants.

Gonza obeys.

Then Malerba grabs him by the back of the head, pushes him down on the table and shoves the barrel of the revolver into him.

Gonzalo screams.

Malerba pulls the trigger. And the hammer makes a dry click.

Russian roulette, he laughs.

Look, all the people here are such money-grubbers that right now, in the middle of winter with so much time till high season, if a film company came to make a movie about *los abusaditos*, the parents of the kids who were harmed wouldn't hesitate to rent them out to collect a few pesos. Not only that, suppose they don't want to use doubles for the film, but instead they'll pay for kids to be deflowered on camera for real: you can't imagine all the mothers and fathers who'd already be bathing and grooming their little ones so they'll look pretty and get picked.

With Malerba you'll never talk about those topics he considers personal. Don't even dare ask him about his kid, Matías, who's building a career on TV. Unless he brings up the subject to brag about the kid's success. Sure, Malerba'll discuss that part, about the present, the kid's success. But see if he'll tell you about before, when he was raising the kid after the mother ran off with a commissioner. The mother split after a beating, leaving him alone with the kids, Matías and Fabiana, the girl who hooked up with García later on. But that was later. And then it seems Malerba took up with Missy. And after that, after he kicked her out of his place in the country, she started spreading rumors about what happened. Correction: First Malerba kicked Matías out; he sent him to live with some aunts in the Capital. And then he threw Missy out. Or rather, he didn't exactly throw her out. Because when he returned from the Terminal that night, after putting the kid on a bus, she was gone. No fool that Missy: she could predict the beating Malerba would give her when he returned home.

Weeping, repentant, she went back home. No matter how hard she banged on the door of the chalet, nothing. From inside came the sounds of an argument between her father and her brother. Don Morano refused to let her in. He felt that it wasn't his daughter, but rather the ghost of his dead wife coming to haunt him. He wasn't about to open the door. But Tito convinced him to give in, to be able to forgive, he told him. Reluctantly Don Morano let her in. And then, resigned, he said to Tito: If she turned out to be a whore like your mother, I hope you won't turn out to be a cuckold like me.

That week Don Morano had a heart attack.

Missy didn't even make an appearance at the hospital. She was at Quirós's law office, very busy trying to find out how much she would inherit when her father died. They say in those days Missy and Quirós . . . They say. Which isn't hard to believe, because, incidentally, Missy covered her ass, considering that Quirós was the lawyer who had succeeded in getting house arrest for Malerba.

Merlino the Toad signs the divorce papers. I'll keep it short and sweet. He signs the papers. And Paula goes to live with Rita, the one from Rex Tourism. Just like I'm telling you. Now they're a couple. Merlino is in the throes of a deep depression. He can accept that Paula's asked him for a divorce, but not that she's hooked up with a dyke. He doesn't even go to Moby anymore. He's all locked up inside himself.

He grabs on to whatever's closest at hand. He brings Ceci and the kid, Bautista, to live with him. We're not exactly a family, but almost, Ceci tells him. Sure, Merlino says to her: We're an extended family. But it sounds phony. It hurts Merlino that his kids, Daniela and Ramiro, don't even want to hear his name mentioned. They visit their mother every so often. It doesn't seem to embarrass them so much that their mother's a lesbian as the fact that their father is living with a woman their own age. Merlino looks older. Besides, Ceci's getting more attractive every day. Merlino had never been jealous before. But now he's consumed with jealousy. If this girl looks so hot, it's because someone's giving it to her. Someone younger than me, he thinks. For sure. He looks at himself in the mirror. I have to get in shape.

Saturday soccer at El Atlético is a must. Just like the *asado* afterward. Soccer keeps me in shape, Merlino thinks. But not the *asado*. I have to stay in shape. One Saturday Merlino skips the *asado* and returns home early. And there he finds Fede, the pothead, on top of Ceci. I'm the boy's father, after all, Fede says to him, ducking the blows. I have a right to see my son, he says. Merlino corners him. Fede gets the brunt of the fight till he bites one of Merlino's ears. And rips it right off. Blood is everywhere. As Merlino writhes in pain, grabbing his mutilated ear, Fede grabs Bautista, picks him up, and runs out the door. Ceci doesn't know what to do—run after her ex-lover or help her current one. She hears Bautista crying. And then the motorcycle. The sound of the cycle masks the baby's cries. But not those of Merlino, in a pool of blood.

They've been at the newsroom of *El Vocero* for a while now. And the rain doesn't let up. Alejo tells Dante whatever he's telling him. Faltering, he talks about Alba. And Dante wonders why he's chosen him as a sounding board. He hesitates, then asks Alejo:

Why are you telling me.

Alejo takes his time. He looks at the pack of cigarettes on the table. He grabs it. He takes one out. And replaces it in the pack.

If you have some filth to confess, you don't go to a priest. You tell it to somebody no one will believe if he repeats it.

Dante doesn't know what to feel: anger, hatred, compassion.

The rain will keep up for a while, Alejo says. And to make things worse, the fucking sewer system. One day we'll be all covered with shit. Who says that day isn't already here. And then, as if nothing had happened, he asks: You still have that bottle of whiskey in the drawer?

Citröen 3CV, Valiant 4, Jeep IKA, Renault Gordini, Jeep with Valiant engine, Graciela Sedan, Dodge Ram 1500, Volkswagen, Jeep with Chevy engine, Scooter, Fiat 1500, Rambler Cross Country, Ford Taunus, Jeep with Falcon engine, Lada, Arenero with 128 engine, Mehari, Peugeot 404, IKA Estanciera, Kaiser Carabela, Rastrojero pickup, Silverado, Falcon Rural, F100. And the motorcycles: from Siambretta to Suzuki, with Gilera, Kawasaki and Zanella to Yamaha. This is how we get around.

Although they both belong to the same low social class and the same middleweight class, years aren't the only thing that separates Monra "the Cannon" Santoro and Sebas "the Beast" Bermúdez. The Cannon must be almost fifty, and being our local hero, he was always a well-balanced boy; outside the ring he never took advantage of his position as a prizefighter. If a fight was brewing, he preferred to step back; he avoided confrontation. He even defended his title in Germany, that memorable match in Berlin, remember, against the Ukrainian Ivan Malenkov. It wasn't easy for him, as you'll recall: the Siberian Butcher, they called him. However, the Cannon, who was sort of against the ropes that night, knew how to deliver that impeccable straight punch to the Soviet: he knocked off his mouth guard and just stood there, waiting alertly, calmly, watching the muzhik crumble. Here in the Villa we pulled out all the stops to celebrate. We greeted him with a procession, fanfare, banners. And afterward an *asado* at El Atlético; over two hundred people. Proceeds went to La Casa del Abuelo. Cannon, Cannon, how great you are, we serenaded him. Our champ, you're gonna win. The Cannon could've kept on fighting; he still had plenty of fight left in him. But no. It's too much, he declared. He had come too far, farther than he'd dreamed when he was a kid, the only child of a humble couple, the father a ranch hand, the mother a servant. Never in his life had he imagined he'd come to know so much of the world, so many good people, because Monra "The Cannon" Santoro was always grateful, and that's another difference, maybe the biggest one, between him and Beast Bermúdez. I've come this far, boys, Cannon Santoro used to say. I've brought my old man and old lady from the country, I've built them a decent house here in La Virgencita, I've built a chalet for myself right next door, and now I'm going to devote myself to my two dreams: my family and the gym. And so the Cannon retired and devoted himself to training at El Atlético. Every so often, for old times' sake, he said, he put on gloves again and organized a fight to benefit the Malvinas Argentinas Hospital. The Cannon fought countless benefit matches. Against "Tiger" Luna to benefit School #5 in La Virgencita. Against "Bolt" Mamonde to benefit La Casa del Abuelo. I fight for love, he declared in an article for *El Vocero*. Dante gave him a two-page center spread in *El Vocero*. The thing is, the Cannon wasn't just a pop idol. He represented the best of us. And he won the whole Villa's affection with that good-ol'-boy smile of his. At forty-six, he would say, I'm complete. The Lord was generous with me, and now I want to pass on everything He taught me. I want to give back what life has given me. I want the kids in the Villa to have a future with healthy minds in healthy bodies. Starting with the promising new star, Beast Bermúdez. My successor in the ring. And in the photos, both of them, teacher and disciple, looked like uncle and nephew. We saw them: the Cannon, smiling paternally, with one arm around the Beast's shoulder. But the Beast's grimace wasn't quite a smile. And his expression, suspicious, lying in wait from afar, as if from underneath, waiting for a chance to hurl himself against his opponent and destroy him. This kid's got more ambition than me, Cannon said. And he wasn't wrong. More than ambition. A thirst for revenge, as someone said.

They saw them at two o'clock one morning, at the terminal, boarding the 7:30 Rápido. The girl, with a blank face, poor thing. And the mother, shrunken, baggy-eyed. Nidia, the mother, had to take her to Mar del Plata, Dante tells us. For her insomnia. They sent Lorena to the psychiatric wing of the hospital. To see a neurologist.

We're in Moby around midnight, listening to Dante tell what he knows about the rape of that girl. At this point he's on his third whiskey and we're here, the regulars, listening to him at this time of night, because it's better to be here than alone, each one of us in his own company. Other people's misfortunes always help to minimize one's own.

The diagnosis coincided with La Comadre's opinion. Somnambulism is what the girl's suffering from. But not just any somnambulism. A kind that's on the threshold of consciousness. Lorena, sitting at the computer, was mentally on a different plane, but she was writing on this one. The neurologists took a great interest in the case. And they contacted the hospital in the Villa so that the psychiatric wing could follow the girl closely. Said there were similar cases in the U.S., where they've been investigating the phenomenon for a while, but never on our continent. Said it was a non-violent cognitive behavior. Until now, somnambulism had been considered a phenomenon in which the mind was asleep. A person would raid the refrigerator, go out, and even take a walk, but their mind was asleep. The North American neurologists were interested in the case, the first of its kind in Latin America.

And so the girl went from being a poor, raped, pregnant chick to become a scientific phenomenon.

When Ceci reacted and saw Merlino the Toad lying in a pool of blood, growing paler, shrunken and trembling, she called an ambulance. And when the ambulance arrived, she picked up the ear and gave it to an orderly. At the hospital they attached the ear to his stomach. Don't ask me for details, Dante goes on. With the ear sewed to his stomach, the tissue will regenerate, and then they'll put it back in the right place. Nobody will even notice what happened. Merlino was given a special leave of absence at the Co-op. He knew that while he was lying in bed at home, looking at the ear on his stomach, at the Co-op they'd be rolling on the floor with laughter.

It goes without saying that after everything that happened, Ceci vanished from his life. It's not that I don't love him; it's just that seeing him like that upsets me. It kind of nauseates me.

Fede had fallen off the map. And Bautista with him. He's gonna let the baby die, Ceci said. And you, you have no idea where he might be, charged Blanco, the supermarket owner. You fell into bed with the first stranger who came along, and here are the consequences. He should've kept you on a shorter leash, like Don Morano with his kids.

Ceci, with a vacant expression, had let everything fly right over her. Once more ensconced in her parents' home, she just cried in the corners. Bring the boy back, Blanco ordered her. Bautista can't be safe with that druggie. Fede loves him, she said. When I feel stronger I'll ask for him back. Blanco couldn't take any more: Even if you're no good as a mother, I can do better as a grandfather, he told her. Tell me where I can find Fede. He might be in Mar de las Pampas with some friends, she said. Where in Mar de las Pampas, Blanco shook her. He was beside himself.

Without wasting time, Blanco grabbed the gun he kept in the nightstand, climbed into the van, and went there. It wasn't hard for him to find the cabin. Above the front door, carved into a beam, was a sign: The Community. Zither music came from within. Blanco entered without knocking. It was difficult for his eyes to adjust to the semi-darkness. Seeing the shimmer of the gun was enough for the Community. It fell silent. Not even the zither could be heard now. There might have been ten or more boys and girls inside. They stared at him as if he were a ghost. Incense and marijuana smoke mingled with the steam from a teakettle in which some weeds were boiling. Bautista was asleep on a mattress on the floor, surrounded by cushions.

Blanco picked up his grandson, carrying him in his arms. Fede didn't even have the nerve to grab him back.

Look, nobody has an accent. Like I told you, we all come from a past. And when we get here, we slap makeup on it. We work on it so much that we end up believing we were somebody else. And after being somebody else, now, by being the same, we feel different.

Hopeless, hopelessly in love, Anita felt swept away by passion. Zambrano had rescued her from the dullness of her marriage to Osvaldo. Between being the wife of the owner of Campas Plumbing Supplies and the lover of a popular hero, because Zambrano was a popular hero, there was no question about whom Anita would stay with. But she couldn't rush Horacio. Anxiety had always been her worst enemy. When she supported that rock group, she hadn't taken the proper precautions with the kids, and then there was that mess with the swastikas. And the same thing with the Forum for Non-Violence: she had exposed herself too much with her pronouncements, she had appeared in the paper and on local TV stations, she'd managed to make everyone notice her and make a large number of women she didn't know greet her on the street, and—it should have occurred to her—that popularity set off Osvaldo's jealously and then there was that beating. Even though she wanted to leave Osvaldo, she felt sorry for him. But at the same time she reproached herself for being so distracted and putting up for so long with a guy who never, for example, had read a book and who fell asleep when she put on *Europa Europa*. How different from Horacio, who, besides being a real man, knew Machado poems by heart. Because not only was Horacio a macho, Anita thought—and she thought about him all the time, she couldn't think about anything or anyone else—he was a romantic like her. He had brought her to orgasm with the same tenderness with which he'd removed her cast. He had also brought to light the Ana who was hiding in Anita. Now Anita was Ana and Ana was all giddiness. She knew this by the way she paid attention to every detail of reality, always finding some sign of this love. Like what happened to her yesterday at Disco. She was in the refrigerated section with the chickens when she noticed that background music: a powerful male voice was singing a song about a world of sensations. That was what her life was like now. A world of sensations. And it was like living in a dream. The problem was that every time she opened her eyes, there was Flor. And besides, Flor was pregnant by Horacio.

What does it matter that the Beast is from a humble background; don't give me that. Not everyone who rises from below gets dizzy from the first run of good luck. And to be fair, you have to admit that the Beast didn't know how to take advantage of the good vibes the Cannon sent his way. And nobody understood him like the Cannon, because he also came from down below, the parents "employed" on a ranch, the father a ranch hand and the mother a servant, both of them slogging away from sunup to sundown in order to feed their offspring. Nobody better than the Cannon to understand the Beast when he wasn't yet the Beast, but Sebas, to show him the way in life, lend him a hand. How could the Beast's story not move the Cannon. Up to that point, the firstborn of a thug who was doing time in Batán and a mother who broke her hump cleaning houses in Pinar del Norte to feed her whole brood; what had marked his fate was that he might follow the father's example. You must know the old lady, Doña María, a self-sacrificing *criolla* who works for the

Calderóns and the Marconis. The same one who cleans Dante's room and washes his clothes. Sebas, like I told you, is the oldest. Martín, the one who works at the Dago Di Lorenzo's auto repair place. Then come Claudia, Verónica, Marcela, and Cynthia. And those grandkids of hers—Facundito, the drug addict, who's always getting booked at the police station, and Augustito, who's in psychiatric treatment. Of course there are hundreds of families like that in La Virgencita. And the way things are, there'll be more. But sometimes, even with the odds against us, we all have a lucky star. The Beast, too, imagine. Just look how the Cannon took him under his wing. Tell me he didn't have a lucky star.

The kid worked at El Atlético. He swept, mopped, cleaned the bathrooms, did a little of everything. Sawdust, bleach, ammonia, brush, scrub rags, mops, that was his thing. Once in a while the kid would bang some old bag. He made a few pesos that way. For a while he was a regular at Moni the poet's place. The kid had been her student when she was a teacher at School #1. Moni explained it by saying that the kid mowed her lawn, kept the flowerbeds in shape, the whole garden. He doesn't want to charge me, she said. But I give him a few pesos anyway. What's for sure is that the kid was fucking Bellini, the gay lottery ticket vendor, you remember, who was shot last year by two juvie thugs from La Virgencita. They blew him away with a shot to the forehead. People said the Beast ratted him out. They say so many things around here. The Cannon looked the other way. Like when he caught him massaging the old fag with oil. The kid was helping out his family. If he made a few extra pesos without bothering anybody, it wasn't the Cannon's business. And seeing the kid like that made the Cannon feel sorry, not just for him, but for his own childhood. Attached, he'd grown attached to him.

Till that theft in the locker room. Wallets, watches, credit cards. Mauro, the bouncer, found the haul hidden in a garbage bag in the broom closet. And he told the Cannon. Leave it to me, the Cannon said. That night, before closing, he caught the Beast, who was still Sebas and not the Beast. He caught him and he pressed him. The kid dug in his heels, it came to blows. Imagine, taking on the Cannon. At that moment, the Cannon said, he had an impulse. He challenged the kid: to see if he could provoke him with the gloves. And Sebas didn't back down. Mauro tied on their gloves. The Cannon and the kid, the two of them alone in the ring at the deserted Atlético. The ex-champ and the little crook. The Cannon's anger had passed. He had fun testing the kid. For the kid it was no joke; he was dead serious. The Cannon decided to put an end to the whole thing, while still teaching him a lesson. He hit him with a cross punch that landed the kid on his ass. Stunned, groping the canvas, he tried to stand. You want more, you little beast, the Cannon asked him. And that's where his nickname came from, according to Mauro. If I take you down to the station now, the cops'll leave you black and blue. Use your head. You're not gonna get very far by stealing. With boxing, who knows, maybe to Luna Park. What do you say. I didn't mean it, Sebas sobbed. It was desperation. Forgive me. It's just that what my old lady earns isn't enough. The Cannon saw through his crocodile tears. He pulled him up by the hair and whacked him a few times. You choose, he told him. The Beast blew his nose. Suddenly he was the Beast. Because "little beast" would be too small on him. Boxing, he said.

Dante heard the conversation early one morning at Moby. They were talking about Zambrano's baby. It had been born suffocated, they said. There was no neonatal treatment to save it, someone said. If it had been born in Mar del Plata, it might've been saved, said another. This hospital isn't prepared, added someone else. It's a backwoods hospital, they said. And if not for people like Zambrano, it was agreed, more people would be victims. Not to mention the women victims, they said, referring to those who had abortions. It wasn't fair for a guy who broke his hump saving lives to go through this drama. And also: To think that he helps so many pregnant women from

La Virgencita and it happens to him, of all people. God is unfair, someone reflected. God doesn't exist, pronounced another. And yet another: Poor woman, because that girl, the teacher, she's an angel. She'll get through it, Dante heard them say. If Zambrano knocks her up again, the girl will get through it. Zambrano seems to be keeping it together in spite of everything. And, of course, someone added: After what he must've gone through in the Malvinas, this must be nothing. Don't be an idiot, someone else piped up. Losing a child isn't the same thing. And the other one replied: A little thing that doesn't even have a name isn't a child. It's nothing. Dante paid for his whiskey. He was tired. Not sleepy, but tired. The next day he had to write up the weekly police reports: three robberies, a car crash, a murder, a rape, and a suicide. Before leaving he heard: If Zambrano seems to be keeping it together, it's because he's got someone to comfort him. One nail pulls out another. Dante stepped out into the night, leaving the voices, the laughter, behind. The sky was filled with stars.

Learn from the silence that is always listening to you.

Moure, the veterinarian, says:
    More than a Villa, this seems like an African reserve where the hyenas are a protected species. We're all scavengers. And, besides, we laugh.

They've been together for months now. As usual they meet in a hotel in Valeria del Mar. Ana smokes. The cigarette annoys Zambrano. But Ana doesn't stop smoking. Till she explains her anxiety to him: She'll leave him. She can't stand hiding anymore. We're all played out, she says to him. I told Osvaldo. I told him everything. And he didn't hit me. He picked up a bottle, and I thought he was gonna break it over my head, but he didn't. Poor guy went down to the beach. And he came back drunk when it was already daylight. He keeled over in the living room armchair. I talked to Flor, too. We went for coffee to the café next door to the school. And I also told her that I'm in love. With your husband, I told her. I made the decision, Ana says to him. Pablo, I broke it off. You're crazy, Zambrano says to her. I broke it off, Pablo, I broke it off. Breaking up is easier than you think. Don't make a big production of it. When you get back home Flor won't make a scene. She understood everything. She made less of a deal than you'd expect. Besides, she's gotten over the miscarriage. This is all crazy, Zambrano says. How could you go and do this without consulting me. Because I love you, she says to him. I'm expecting a child, too, she tells him. Yours. A child of this love. How do you know it's mine, Pablo asks her. Because I know it, a woman knows. It was the night you gave me the Bethania record. That night you got me pregnant, Pablo. I know all this is crazy. I've made up my mind to have it. What I've always dreamed of: a child by the man I love. And I love you, Pablo. You're crazy, Zambrano says. No, I'm not crazy. People can't live a lie. I understand you, I understand what you feel, I understand that for you it's a tsunami. That child might be your husband's, Zambrano says. It's not Osvaldo's, it's yours. Osvaldo hasn't even touched me since. Don't lie to me. I'm not lying to you. It's Osvaldo's. Well, one time, just once. But I know, I feel it, this child is yours. A woman knows. A woman always knows. You're pregnant, Ana. Do me a favor and put out that cigarette. I'm gonna quit. Don't ask me to give it up all at once. It's enough that I gave up my husband. First him, then the smokes.

The Cannon took to heart that business of saving the Beast. So much so that he brought him to El Atlético to sleep. When the kid wasn't scrubbing floors, we would see him working out with the punching bag, jumping rope, lifting weights, and in the mornings and afternoons, just after sunrise and right before sunset, running south along the beach from Parador Extremo, the last beach-cabana rental place in the north, passing by the dock. In a few months, such agility in his legs and a punch like a lightning bolt. He blew us all away in his first preliminary, we recall, against Robertito "The Fearsome" García, a respected fighter from Pinamar. The Beast didn't leave him alone. From the first round on, he never stopped attacking him. Soon the Beast was winning one preliminary after another: Chacabuco, Dolores, Madariaga, Trenque Lauquen, Villegas, Maipú, Ensenada. A meteoric career. In less than a year he took a Federation cup. He didn't lose a single one. And if he didn't get his opponent with a knockout, he amply won by points. His power was the unrivaled kind. It wasn't just a matter of reflexes, speed, or instinct. The Beast didn't fight for sport or for ambition, or at least not *just* for ambition. There's a rage in him, according to Dante, which came over him in the cradle in the hospital where he had been in an incubator from the time he was born in the Villa. The rage came from resentment, and the resentment demanded revenge. It no longer mattered to him what he might achieve in the future, whether to buy himself cool clothes, wear expensive sneakers, drive a flashy car, fuck the hottest girls in La Virgencita and El Monte, or, why not, even a snobby chick. More than once the Cannon had to drag him out of Acid and the Tropicana in the early hours of the morning. Stop thinking like a half-breed, he scolded him. Because he scolded him like a father. If he wanted to be a champ he couldn't spend more time letting a pussy hair draw him in than the title. But nightlife and chicks were his downfall. And yet, they proved no obstacle to his putting on one hell of a fight when it was time to get into the ring.

And when the Cannon realized that the Beast had slipped out of his grasp, it was too late. Even though the Beast heeded his instructions, even though there wasn't a single piece of advice he didn't pay attention to, because he was no dummy, no sooner did he start showing signs of becoming our local promise than it became obvious no triumph would ever satisfy him. Because what the Beast had between his eyebrows, that thing his dark eyes stared at intently as though from below, from a pit nobody could reach, the thing that might have been his secret objective was a secret even for him. No matter how much the Cannon might have thought he had him under control, the Beast had slipped his chain. He wanted to aim high. Very high. And from the highest point he could fly to, from that sky he studied out of the corner of his eye with his cunning gaze, he would never manage to grab it altogether with his hands. He would nosedive and crash. Harder than canvas, asphalt.

Yesterday, like every morning, I went walking on the beach with my German Shepherd. Suddenly the dog charged after a butterfly. The butterfly fluttered, provoking him. The dog chased it and barked at it. A gust of wind carried the butterfly off. And the dog stood there with his tongue out, panting. Then, still not defeated, he gave one more bark. I had a sudden insight: The butterfly was the novel and I was the dog.

As he drives back home, Zambrano wonders how it is that Flor isn't going to make a scene. Zambrano wonders if Ana knows about Flor's lover. He also wonders why he hadn't told Ana that he knew the baby Flor was expecting wasn't his. He didn't tell her, just as he hadn't told Flor about his vasectomy. He wonders how Flor could have taken Ana's confession calmly. He thinks about Flor, more about Flor than about Ana. If Flor didn't tell him she had a lover, it must have been because it wasn't important. Flor's lover didn't matter to him anymore. He'd also concealed the affair with Ana from her just as he'd concealed his vasectomy. And if he hadn't told her about Ana it was because, despite everything that had happened, he still loved Flor. The loss of the baby made him feel less guilty than he'd anticipated. He'd been sure that after the miscarriage they could return to an earlier stage of their love. It was a question of time. Lately he'd been thinking of making Flor go through a series of tests, which he'd be in charge of, and which would result in the news that she couldn't have children. Of course it would be a hard piece of news for Flor, but Zambrano was confident that Flor would get over it. It was a matter of time. But now, with Ana's confession, by white-washing the relationship between them, the scenario became more complicated than he had ever imagined. I was the one who started the lie, he blames himself. I lied from the beginning. And one lie produced another. And another. It's impossible to turn back now. He wonders if by telling Flor about his vasectomy, going back to the first lie, he might be able to reshape his whole history with her from that point on. But Flor, he knows, will not forgive him. Once more Zambrano feels that he doesn't want to lose Flor. That if he had to choose between Flor and Ana, he wouldn't hesitate: Flor. He parks in front of the house. He takes his time getting out of the car. If he didn't and doesn't want to lose Flor, he tells himself, it's because he loves her. And if she didn't tell him about her lover, it was because she loved him more than the other one. As he gets out of the car he asks himself what love is.

At night is when you can hear it most. But after hearing it for so long, we stop listening to it. Some nights it's impossible not to feel it. On calm nights, when the air is frozen. Then, even if you're not close, it comes to you anyway, gets into your room, comes over to your bed, and you can hear it like you hear your breathing. If you turn on the radio very softly, to mask it, you know it's there anyway. Waiting for you to turn off the radio so as to make its presence known, lying in wait. And if you don't turn off the radio, you can hear it too. Because the radio is a subterfuge, the host's voice, the solitary, nocturnal men and women who call asking for romantic advice or a song, and *nada*, neither the voices nor the music distract you from its invasion, just like those who are on the radio can't be distracted, either, and that's the real reason they made up their minds and impulsively, hiding their nervousness, called in to the program. It's a lie that they call the radio because they listen to the program. They call because they listen to the sea. And, like you, they can't stand the sound of it anymore. Because there are nights like this one when, no matter how accustomed you may be, you can't get it out of your head, just like you can't silence those corrosive thoughts it inspires, no matter how hard you try to bury them by sticking your head under the pillow. And to think that tourists collect shells. Because, when they're far from here, they like to place them against one ear and listen to it, listen to it as we listen to it here, crouching, like tonight, hoarse, with contained fury.

For over an hour Zambrano has been sitting in a chair at the foot of the marriage bed, looking at Flor's corpse. Every so often the phone rings. But he doesn't answer. Pills. When he got home he knew by the temperature of the body: nothing could be done. A note from Flor was on the nightstand. I couldn't take it anymore. Forgive me. And in the signature, like she's done since she was a little girl, she's added petals to the "o," turning it into a flower. Always so correct. So attentive to detail. She even put on a black blouse, with a matching sweater and shoes. She was trying to blend in with the ambience of the funeral. The suicide always wants to kill someone else, Zambrano thinks. In general the people of whom they ask forgiveness. Suicide is a dirty trick, he thinks. Besides, someone who commits suicide always takes their deepest shame, their secret, with them to the grave. And this is the case here, too: he'll never know who Flor's lover was, the father of the dead child. They took their own life, people say. More like they take their own death. They take their own death off their backs once and for all, burdening others with a contest of questions and answers. And the phone. He ought to pick up. He hasn't cried since the Malvinas. He can't. He can't bring himself to go near the dead woman. Maybe he ought to follow her, he thinks. The phone keeps ringing. He answers. An emergency, in the ER, a girl from La Virgencita. She tried to do it herself. With a knitting needle. I'm on my way, Zambrano says. He leaves the house. He gets into his car.

293

No, for me, music has to be a *Stabat Mater*.

El Vocero's headlines this week: *Apprehended and arrested; Four-wheeler stolen; Minor apprehended; Auto and motorcycle collide; Weapon in the street; Window stolen; Kiosk ransacked; Tourists robbed; Home burglary; Business held up; Roadway injury; Brushfire;* and *Unfortunate loss.* The last headline refers to the suicide of a middle school instructor, respected and beloved by her colleagues, students, and the community. Dante left out the woman's name and the cause of death, suicide, from his article. He felt bad about Florencia's death. Pretty girl, he thought. And also: Suicide is contagious.

We die of cancer and AIDS. We die of pancreatic disease and we die of a heart attack. We die of asthma and we die of an overdose. We die of a stab wound and we die from a gunshot. We die of angst and we die of love. But what we die of most is boredom. If one person doesn't die every day we have nothing to talk about. Every death is an enigma, whether you're run over by a bus or carried off by the current. And that enigma is what keeps us alive. And, by the way, it reassures us because this time we were passed over, because it wasn't our turn yet, so we can go on gossiping about why the neighbor, who was the picture of health, woke up dead this morning. They say last night, before he went to bed, he couldn't take it anymore and swallowed some pills. His book and school supply store was going well. He had no debts, his wife wasn't cheating on him, his kids were already grown. Imagine: he had named his store "Smiles." We're dying to know why he did it. That's what we're dying of most: to know.

Even if nobody believes it, Dante likes to write birth announcements for the society pages of *El Vocero*. For example:
   Welcome, Federico, Dante titles it. *And he writes: Last Wednesday the stork visited Campas Plumbing Supplies, bringing a present from Paris. Osvaldo Campas, a dear friend in the Villa, and Anita López, middle*

school teacher, welcomed their firstborn, Federico. For García Lorca, the happy father added. And he explained: Federico García Lorca. You know, his mother teaches literature. We greet him: Welcome to the Villa, Fede.

Hope is the last thing to be lost, Dante thinks.

Speaking of Zambrano: Poor guy, one woman says. What lousy karma to live with a suicide.

Not so poor, honey, says another. That widower's one hell of a catch. Women die for him.

Lots of people fantasize about the sea. And they think that by living here they're men and women of the sea. Not even the "BORA" kids, born and raised here, the fanatics who get out their boards and surf even in winter, are altogether of the sea. Neither are those who take their boats out at dawn and come back with corvina, a manta ray, dogfish, whiting. Not one man or woman here belongs to the sea, but rather to the shore. I'm not even talking about the beach. Because to say "beach" is to fool yourself by embellishing the true sense of what it means to belong to the shore. We all belong to the shore: we get as far as the edge, a limit. And here we are, not daring to cross it, to test ourselves in whatever lies beyond. Because even some men and women who feel like they've left everything behind them haven't risked it; they just didn't have the nerve to keep going, to conquer the breakers, to dare to go on, to plunge in. It's not a question of knowing how to swim. Most of us who live here don't know how to swim. And don't tell me they're afraid to leave the shore behind because they can't swim. Not even those who've won a championship risk going any farther. Not in a kayak, not in a rowboat. What I'm saying is: We take pleasure in living on the edge. We peek at whatever might be out there but we never quite take the plunge. Whatever's out there. In the depths. What lies beneath. It's not about krakens. And if it is, let's admit it once and for all, the kraken is the Villa, and we, all of us, are the krakens, at once tentacles and victims.

The one who confronted the Cannon, because they thought that first they had to talk to the Cannon, his manager, was Julián, one of the Kennedys. On behalf of Cachito, he told him he wanted to talk to him. Imitating Alejo, giving him a wink as though it was necessary in order to enter into collusion, Julián told him they were going to make him an offer he couldn't refuse. There was this investment that the City wanted to make in sports. They had already discussed it with Lanari, the manager of Banco Nación. The City was prepared to invest in El Atlético, he told him. To update the facilities, bring state-of-the-art equipment to this sports center. The investment wasn't just about modernizing the gym, Julián told him. Because, in addition, the community was especially prepared to support the Beast's career. A sponsorship, let's say. These days you can't get anywhere without a sponsor. A special interest in the Beast, that's what they had. They wanted the Beast to become the symbol of Cachito's management style. His fierce management style, Julián smiled.

I get it, the Cannon replied. What you guys are trying to do is to distract people, cover up the whole mess, the shit that hit the fan, that business of the sewer system, to restore confidence in Cachito, and while you're at it, build up his image with an eye to next year's election. Because, if I'm not mistaken, there's going to be an election next year.

You got it, Julián said. Cachito's the best thing for the Villa. There's nobody else. With all his faults, Cachito's a great guy. Didn't he talk to Lanari, the manager of Banco Nación, so he'd give you the loan to buy yourself some land?

But I settled the debt, the Cannon told him. To the last peso. And all of it on the up and up. I don't owe anyone a cent.

Don't be an ingrate, Cannon. If not for Cachito you'd still be waiting for the dough from the bank.

I don't like politics, the Cannon said. Nothing personal. But I'd rather go my own way. And let the kid go his.

The Beast's father is in Batán Prison, Julián reminded him. And he'll be there a long time. Think of it this way: We want to put the finishing touches on the education you're giving him. The kid wins, El Atlético wins, we win, the Villa wins. Think of it as a community project, if you like. An act of public service.

I'll think about it, the Cannon said. But he knew he'd already thought it over. If he didn't tell Julián his decision right away it was to avoid an argument. And also because he'd end up kicking his ass out of El Atlético. Not that he wouldn't love to do it. But he knew the risks of going up against the Kennedys. Besides, Braulio, the Kennedy drunkard, was the type to come around let off steam by hitting a bag whenever that chick from the boutique closed her legs to him. That's how he wore out his horniness.

Think it over, Julián said as he walked away.

As if to remind the Villa that he hasn't forgotten, Dante writes in an editorial for *El Vocero*:

According to international statistics, one out of every six children is the victim of sexual abuse. In ninety percent of cases, the abusers belong to the circle of those closest to the child, those from whom he expects protection. As demonstrated by recent cases, it's a democratic phenomenon that crosses social classes and cultural lines with equal dramatic intensity.

But no one claims to have read it.

Around here lots of people boast that they live in the sea. But they're lying. Go ask how many of them even have crossed the ocean on a cruise. Those who have, people in high positions, with more than a couple of coins in their pockets, when pressed, will show more pride in the fact that they're from inland and have managed to buy a little property. Because being from inland carries its touch of *criollo* pride. Just think, the Pampa has so often been compared to a sea, but nobody sees it the other way around, nobody thinks of the sea as a prolongation of the countryside. Why do you think the Indians didn't go near it, not even to fish? More than respect, it filled them with terror. Pure instinct: they knew that the sea's nature, if it has any, is illusory: it always promises an adventure that we'll never have the courage to embark on. Courage, that's what I'm talking about. And when I say courage, I also mean fear. Because if we recognize ourselves on land more readily than on water, it's not just because what the sea possesses is hidden and what the countryside has is visible. Just look how far that feeling extends: we live at the seashore, but nobody serves as much fish at their table as meat. If you offer someone a choice between a steak and a hake, he won't hesitate. It's because of our temperament: a human being has more in common with a cow. Don't tell me how the gaucho, a bloody, meat-eating type if ever there was one, is known for being ballsy. Not only will that big coward never dare go to sea, to the unknown, but out of pure laziness he'd rather skin a calf than cast a fishhook, wait for a nibble, the waiting as metaphysics, meditation. No, don't talk to me about the gaucho, a horseman as he likes to call himself, someone who, if his empty belly ached enough, would roast his own mount. Tell me, what resistance does a cow offer? Docile, it lowers its head and marches off passively to the slaughterhouse. The blow to the head, the knife blade, like a destiny without protest. On the other hand, try to take on a shark. Even harpooned, it resists, it drags your boat, it does whatever it wants with you, and when you least expect it, it turns around and goes for you. It knocks you overboard, and while you're flailing around, desperately trying to climb back on the keel, it chomps off your leg in one bite. Around here, in the countryside, just one animal can compare to the shark's beauty and style, and that's the cougar. But there's not a single cougar left around these parts. Its sinuous stride, its eyes penetrating the night, have instilled so much fear in us that we've exterminated it. But with the shark, we're still at a disadvantage. There's no firearm we can use to conquer it because to pursue it we have to defy the waves, the depths, the threat that comes from what's hidden, and even so, it just might attack us from behind.

A good pair, those two, Bignose and El Pulqui. One was the strongman and the other the smart guy. When they were in middle school, more than once Bignose came to El Pulqui's defense. Those who went to school with them say that El Pulqui did the homework for both of them. And that Bignose guaranteed that nobody would touch the other one. But it wasn't exactly like that. El Pulqui had a knack for playing pranks. You could already see that girlish naughtiness in him that fags have. Because in those days El Pulqui was already effeminate. Raised as he was by dressmakers at the Paris Shop, a single mother and a grandmother, it seemed likely they would end up turning the kid into a queer. But El Pulqui wasn't one to back down if he was picked on. Even if he knew he was going to get thrashed, he stepped up. Fought like a madman. And just when it seemed like he was about to be demolished, that's when Bignose would come to his aid. And nobody dared to mess with Bignose. Not only because he was a massive guy—at twelve he already had hair on his chest—but also because of his reputation, a reputation for pulling a knife and cutting you without a second thought. They said that if El Pulqui acted like a big shot, it was because the other one had his back. They also said that Bignose would send the other one to start trouble so he could go and clobber someone afterward. That's how they worked.

And we wondered how two such different personalities, from such different families, Bignose's bunch of Radical River Plate fans and Pulqui's Peronists and Boca fans, ever managed to pair up. Though if you think about it, it's not hard to find that kind of couple in life. They complemented one another, let's say. One had what the other was missing, and the second one had too much of what the first one lacked.

Until Bignose got involved in drugs, and, according to what they say, kept the change one time. He was found dead in a car on the highway. Nobody swallowed the story that it was a suicide. They also say the hit came from Mar del Plata, because Bignose, pressured by the cops, had ratted out some capos. Others say it was because of Luz, Pedroza's kid. Some say Bignose gave the girl AIDS. They say Pedroza had him whacked. They say. I'm only telling you what they say. Don't mention my name. Don't get me involved. Remember, I come from here.

For many people Fournier, the painter, is just one more nutcase who destiny washed up on this shore. For others, he's a madman who shouldn't be contradicted. And even if it's true that Fournier has strong opinions, and that when he talks, it's more a pronouncement than a dialogue, you've got to admit that, in addition to his vast knowledge, he has a special gift for finding everyone's essence, the thing that makes up the secret heart of their story. A special being, Fournier, says Moni. Let's make it clear: Moni was in love with him. And still is. Because every so often she goes over to Fournier's cabin and asks him to read her poems. Most of the time Fournier throws her out. If you don't know anything about life, don't write poems about human beings. Look at nature. It's harder to write a poem to a tree than to a dead baby who, according to ignorant fools, is a little angel that went to heaven. Born as we are from the basest of passions, we're not innocent. There is no innocence. There's not even a heaven. They also say Fournier's a virgin. The fact that Moni claims he was an outstanding lover, the most sensitive of her considerable collection of guys, doesn't mean they ever slept together. A damn lie, like so many others. To believe Moni, she's gone through the entire Villa. According to Fournier, those are just Moni's inventions. If that's the case, we have to ask ourselves why Moni invented that outstanding lover story. According to some, she tells the story not only to remind us that she was irresistible forty years ago, but also because she thinks that the reputation of being a virgin, in such a machista society, is damaging to Fournier. Though Fournier is more bored than outraged by the whole business. The only thing that concerns him is to finish up his daily work as an electromechanical technician and return to his cabin in the southern forest, like we've said before. As soon as he gets off work, Fournier hops on his bike and heads home. The two or three people he likes and who have been allowed into his cabin say he has no boiler or heater. A cot, a chair, piles of books in a corner, an easel, a weather-beaten table with his oil paints, tempera, and water colors, and a clearly visible Primus stove, a teakettle, and a *mate*. It's a miracle he survives, bathing in cold water. The body is not the prison of the soul, Founier says. It's the fortress.

A study carried out among more than 1800 youngsters between the ages of 13 and 18 by the Center of Public Policy Implementation for Equity and Growth (CIPPEC), which covers five very distinct areas of the country, reflected some concerns faced by adolescents today. The interviewees claimed they had felt discriminated against on occasion, and, according to the investigation, the primary locale of the conflict, even more than streets or other places like bars or discos, was the school, most often the classroom. Physcial characteristics were identified as the primary cause, followed by economic status, skin color, and age.

The adolescents revealed that they were also concerned about sexual and reproductive health, violence, and eating disorders.

Like I was telling you, El Pulqui and Bignose grew up together, a hedgerow between them. Together. Inseparable. No matter that they were night and day; they never split up. Although nature hadn't smiled on El Pulqui, you should've seen how he went in for sports. A real health nut. Whereas Bignose, who had an enviable physique, messed himself up with drugs. And yet they were joined at the hip. Which explains the brawl at El Español.

It takes guts to sit down at that poker table at El Español. Thugs, all of them. Ramos, Martelli, Barbeito el Gallego, and Pedroza. El Pulqui walked into the bar and went straight to the table and challenged Pedroza: Motherfucker, murderer, he said. Malerba was there, too. But he didn't interfere in the fight. Since Malerba was still under house arrest after Bignose's murder, it's not a great idea for him to get involved in shit like that. Even though they say he was the one who offed Pando, the right-hand man at Di Lorenzi's distributorship, he walked right past Malerba without looking at him and challenged Pedroza directly. Pando's death, though it may come up later, isn't what matters now in the story about the brawl at El Español. Because of that, I'm saying, because of Bignose's death, Malerba didn't get involved when Pedroza went after El Pulqui. For that and because getting involved would have made his boss lose face. Besides, he thought, it wasn't necessary. How could Pedroza not have pulverized El Pulqui? A bull, that Pedroza. Imagine, with all those muscles he developed while he was in the slammer. He killed himself working out when he was in Batán. He lays one hand on you and he buries you. Look, how could he not have flattened El Pulqui, little and skinny as he is, though he's pure nerve. Because you've got to admit that El Pulqui is pure nerve. If you've ever seen a madman fight, you know what I mean. You can't beat a madman. Even if you're Cassius Clay, the madman'll get you. You can't stop a madman. And El Pulqui turned into a madman.

If Fournier's paintings are landscapes, when describing them you should take into account that he is part of the poplars, the eucalyptus, the pines, and the acacias. He wanders absent-mindedly through the forest, and suddenly, you see his motionless form blended among the trunks and shrubs, sitting against a trunk, drawing. When someone passes by he doesn't even look up. Unless that person greets him. And only then, after taking a while to scrutinize the greeter, he returns his "hi." Nothing more than that: "hi." He waits for the passerby to disappear. A human being interrupts his vision of the landscape. Maybe we've said it before: his landscapes are deserted. Even when he paints a house, there's nobody in it. One observation:

his paintings seem pre-Impressionist. His landscapes contain so much detail: in the trees, the branches, the treetops. His eye, in a sense, is that of a naturalist. He could be Rugendas.

Fournier's around sixty, graying brown hair, green eyes, medium height, slow gait, slightly listing to the left; he's limped ever since he injured himself repairing the water tank. As a result of the fall, he has a screw in his leg. There are times when he lets his beard grow. When he shaves it off, he leaves the mustache. Fournier is an anchorite but not a derelict. Moni once remarked that not only does he bathe every morning and night in cold water, but when it rains, he strips naked, takes a bar of laundry soap and leaves his cabin to bathe under heaven's shower. He always goes around in mechanic's overalls and workman's boots. In winter he wears a checkered thermal jacket. Typical of his asceticism, he doesn't wear a watch. He doesn't need one. Other people's time is not my time, he pronounces. And when he utters one of his phrases, with a dogmatic emphasis, you ask yourself where the hell he got that from, if it's from Swedenborg, Thoreau, or Wittgenstein. All those phrases come from a notebook where he copies ideas or thoughts he finds in books. Also typical of him: when he rides his bicycle past the chapel or past one of those many temples that have popped up in recent years, he spits.

If there's one activity Alejo can't resist watching, it's horse breaking. Gauchos galloping along, cracking their leather whips while the horses buck, wildly trying to throw them off. The horse falls and lands on top of the *paisano*, who gets up limping, battered, trying to make light of his aching bones. Breaking a horse is like life. You've got to know how to mount it. Just as he never misses one of the *criollo* festivals, if for some reason his trip to Areco, Madariaga, or wherever is canceled, Alejo follows the horse breaking competitions on the Rural Channel.

And if there's a singer who brings him to the edge of tears—though he holds them back—it's José Larralde. If he's had one too many at a nighttime *asado*, when he gets back home he hits the Chivas and puts on Larralde, the "Ballad for a Gaucho Son." Then he looks for Camilo, and, speaking to him in a countrified way, he asks him to *Listen, m'hijo*. My sister, your mother, liked Larralde; she knew him practically by heart. Listen and learn:

If there was no "no," we wouldn't need "yes." / Sin was invented. / But what's it for? / To string these words together: / "Mustn't do that." / Punishment was invented. / But what's it for? / So someone else can do / what you mustn't do. / And forgiveness was invented. / But what's it for? / To ease the conscience of the forgiver. / It's a good way to forgive ourselves. / So now we're good and can go on breathing honesty. / Yes, man, what a lovely word. / Too bad it's kind of long. / Maybe that's why sometimes it's so hard to find.

Camilo listens till Quirós falls asleep in the chair. Then he leaves the house, walking and walking. He walks toward the forest, slips in among the trees, and howls at the moon.

We're at Moby, as usual. Around midnight. The topic is garbage. Quite a topic in the Villa, garbage. Somebody ought to do something about it. Tell me, how many times have we talked about this garbage dump business, someone grumbles. And another pipes up: Now the wind is carrying the smoke this way. A fire along the roadside is dangerous, interrupts another. And Cachito ought to do something before the fire burns his ass, someone adds. But Cachito's got enough to do now with the fuckup his kid caused. What'd he do now, asks the one who's not in the loop. The kid gets away with everything because he's the mayor's son, someone says. Confidence kills, says another. When the kid goes too far, a cliff or a wall will be waiting for him. And no matter how many contacts his old man may have, they won't do him any good.

But soon we leave off the subject of Cachito and his boy. The burning garbage dump worries all of us.

Let each and every one of us burn in our own garbage, Dante laughs. Tonight he's had too much whiskey. He sounds like a Biblical plague.

The nighttime fog blends with the cloud of smoke.

One morning we woke up and the sea had receded, forgetting us. The beach extended farther than usual. About three hundred yards, someone estimated. More, said another. The sand drift it left behind reached practically to the horizon, a brownish stretch of sand, denuded. But the distance wasn't as important as the fact that it happened in the first place, the retreat of the water, a low tide that at once produced surprise, melancholy, and an understandable fear. Surprise, I say, because we had never seen a low tide like that before. For the kids, that endless beach was an unexpected source of fun. For some, melancholy, because we could only think that the change represented the loss of a familiar landscape. Because nothing troubles the spirit more than the loss of the familiar. When the face of the beach changed, revealing that interminable sand drift, the sadness made us think of happier times, though nobody here knew, or ever will know, what happiness consists of. In truth, what disturbed us most was that the landscape had changed, and we felt that the sea, in its withdrawal, was rejecting us. Another thing we felt was fear. The sensation of dread was spreading. We knew that the sea's retreat was temporary, that it would return, and when it did, it would come back with a vengeance, overtaking the dunes, upending the rental cabanas, covering the boardwalk, the wooden walkway, and invading the Villa up to Calle 1. Which was what happened. Then we realized that the disdain it made us feel had been a sign, that when we least expected it, it would mow us down, punishing us, drowning our sins once and for fucking all. If life was born in the sea, we didn't seem to deserve it. And that same sea which had given us life was warning us with its retreat and sudden, violent rise that it regretted having given it to us, and that at this stage there was no possible redemption, and just as it had bestowed the grace of this world upon us, it would soon snatch it away. Let us pray, someone said. And more than one woman, more than one man, knelt down, and gazing at the sky, imploring the steely clouds, that deafening storm, began to pray.

Ever since the cloud of smoke settled onto the Villa, more and more faithful have been attending Sunday Mass. The parish priest takes out a copy of this week's *El Vocero* and makes good use of the head-line: he refers to Dante's article. Sodom, he says, as he starts his sermon. Soon the chapel isn't big enough to hold everyone and Mass will take place in the open air of the Sports Center. This very Sunday, while the hydrants and firefighters are about to give up in the fight against the flames and are calculating how long it will take before they consume the pines and poplar groves, a few clouds close in over the faithful. At noon a southeaster comes up. The first drops fall at siesta time. Fat drops. After a while the downpour begins. It rains all week. End of danger. As usual with every storm, the dirt and sand streets are flooded. Even in a 4x4 it's hard to plow through the poplar groves of Pinar del Norte. Unlike on other occasions, no one curses the storm. On Friday, when the rain lets up, we feel like different people. The wind persists on Saturday. But Sunday dawns blue. The garbage dump fire, that nightmare, is behind us. Our faces all look newly-scrubbed. We're clean. And this Sunday, when Father gets ready for Mass, the faithful are the same old candle-suckers. Then, energetically, Father returns to his task with the copy of *El Vocero*, launching into his sermon with ill-concealed fury. Sodom, he shouts. And so he begins.

We could imagine the Beast sitting across from Cachito at the City Office. The Kennedys, Alejo and Julián, were also at the meet-ing. They accomplished nothing by cursing out the Cannon. What mattered now was his former pupil, the kid. To open his eyes. If resorting to contacts was called for, Alejo would take care of it. The Beast would train in Mar del Plata. And that's how it was. They set him up in a country house in Camet, assigned him two veteran trainers, Marcelo Grisolía, from Junín, and Federico Murcia, from Bragado. They would keep the Beast on a tight leash. No screwing around—just pure, hard training. In a few weeks the Beast would beat his own record. He'd be like Monzón at his peak.

All the same, no matter how carefully Grisolía and Murcia watched over him, the Beast ran off on them one night. When he returned at dawn the two of them shoved him up against the wall. They got into it. The Beast pushed both of them off. When it looked like the training was going to hell, Alejo intervened. He asked the Beast if he wanted his old lady to keep scrubbing houses all her life, not to have enough money to buy medicine for the nutcase, for his brothers to end up stealing and dead, and his sisters turning tricks. The Beast bowed his head. He seemed to be listening to reason. And for a moment Alejo thought he had managed to get him under control. Besides, he told him, think about what you stand for, Beast. You're an example for the Villa's youth. A real example. Cachito and I want the kids in the Villa to have a better life. You can't let them down, Beast. You can't let yourself down. Think it over.

Suddenly Alejo felt emotionally overcome by his own words. He was ready to believe in what he was saying. He was so skilled at speechifying that sometimes, like now, he ended up convincing himself.

It won't happen again, Dr. Quirós, the Beast told him. I give you my word of honor.

That's what I like to hear, Alejo slapped him on the back.

If you tallied it up, it was better not to think about how much the kid's word of honor was worth.

You know why more than one kid is tempted to try his luck studying to be a chef. Because this is a town of starving motherfuckers, my boy. Name one person here who doesn't think with his stomach.

Look what I found in a book by Michelet: *A brave Dutch sailor, a steadfast and cold observer, who spends his life on the sea, frankly says that the first impression one gets from it is fear. The water, for every terrestrial being, is the unbreathable element, the element of asphyxiation. Fatal, eternal barrier that irreparably separates the two worlds. Let us not be surprised if the enormous mass of water that one calls the sea, unknown and dark in its profound density, always appeared dreadful to the human imagination.*

Camelot, don't tell me the Villa isn't Camelot. Because a kingdom is like a big family. As long as harmony reigns, of course. Till a betrayal destroys the peace. Like what happened to the Mamas and the Papas. Mama Michelle, Papa John's girl, and Papa Denny were lovers, but they couldn't keep it a secret. While on a trip to Mexico, crossing the border and driving through Tijuana, smoking, Papa Denny couldn't take the guilt anymore and told Mama Cass he was in love with Mama Michelle. Mama Cass was furious. She started punching him while he was driving. They went off the road, nearly overturned. Shortly after that, Papa John caught Mama Michelle and Papa Denny screwing in a motel outside of Sacramento. And he split. From the house and from the band. Later on Michelle and John made up and bought a house in Bel Air. For a while the four of them were back together, but Denny started drinking to forget Michelle. Mama Cass, for her part, decided to go solo. Meanwhile rumors of drug abuse and alcoholism spread. Not to mention Mama Cass's weight problems. The group fell apart as she swelled up. But she died on her own terms. After singing at the London Palladium, in a musician's tiny apartment. Pure envy and spitefulness, the myth that she died choking on a sandwich. It was her heart that killed her. Because Mama Cass had one this big. Not even she could fill up that heart.

According to Dante, Fournier, that ascetic, pretending to be a lone wolf, has a real conflict about purity. Like everyone, he drags along a past he never talks about. But Dante's found a way to dig up some clues. Fournier's father was a Vichy Republic collaborationist. After the war he sought refuge in our country with his wife and two children, Claude and Gervaise. His wife threw herself under a train. The man put his children in boarding school with the Silesian monks in Patagonia. And he came to the Villa and worked here for a while. Later he went to Chile. And he never came back to see the kids. Now Gervaise lives in a chalet in Pinar del Norte. And her brother, the complete opposite, in that shack down south. Dante suspects that underlying that conflict Fournier has about purity, which makes him pass for a mystic, is a still greater, indecipherable pain.

A mystic in his own way, Dante says.

Last Sunday, unidentified subjects made off with a 2700-liter water tank from a construction site at Circunvalación and Calle 100. That same day a washing machine disappeared from a house located at Avenida 13 and 110. Both incidents were classified as thefts.

Sources close to police authorities suggest that these crimes are connected to the marginal groups that have taken over remote lots on the outskirts of our Villa.

This business with the marches does the Villa no good whatsoever. It's a well-known fact that Bignose was an addict and a dealer. His death is no loss. I'd even say that the Villa is a better place now, breathing cleaner air. It's all politics, shameless deal-making. The Riquelmes were lifelong Radicals. And now, with the kid's death, they've made a deal with the damn Peruvians to fire up the marches. I don't believe any of them. If the kid turned out to be a delinquent, it's their funeral. Like the saying goes, you reap what you sow. The Kennedys, on the other hand, have their dirty dealings for sure, but I don't see why they'd be interested in the case. As far as Pedroza's concerned, he may be a gambler and a whoremonger, and no doubt he's got his arrangements between Nueva Pompeya Cement Works, our Speer, and the City, but you can't deny he's given credit to more than one poor slob who needed to build a roof over his head. His daughter Luz was a model child, an honor student at Nuestra Señora, first lady-in-waiting at Winterfest. Till she fell in love with that delinquent. Go figure what she saw in him. I think she did it to bug her parents. Those rebellious stages young people go through. That's why I say you shouldn't stand in the kids' way when they date someone you don't like. Because that makes it worse. That was Pedroza's mistake. Opposing it. Now, sure, if your little girl, the light of your life, gets infected with that shit, what do you do. If Pedroza had him killed, I'm not telling you I support it. The only thing I'm saying is that all this crap about marches doesn't do anybody any good. Look what kind of image we're projecting. We live from tourism. And tourism, I'm telling you, I studied this stuff in school, is all about image. They don't do us one bit of good, those marches. We're not Catamarca.

The man walking along the deserted beach stops, picks up a shell, and puts it to his ear. And he hears his own name.

Around here the day will soon come when all of us fat girls will be legion. All of us, Mama Cass. We'll take up more space than we do now. And you know why. Because we have no shame. Genius has no prejudices. Take a good look at us; we have our style. We don't turn up our noses at beer, burgers, pot. And we're as smart as our idol, Mama Cass. A genius, Mama Cass. So get ready, dudes. 'Cause we're forming a group. The Mama Casses. We don't need no Papas. Fuck 'em. Mamas, just Mamas. *Dream a little dream of me,* asshole.

A total lie, forgetting. No love story is ever forgotten. Even if it didn't have the right bed or was a total platonic jerkoff fantasy, it'll pursue you. It'll slip between your sheets, throb on your pillow, become the most terrible sleepless night, remorse for not having made the gesture that might have changed your life, and now, instead of being with some other girl, some other guy, under a shared roof that deadens your soul, you'd be with the one who walked into your dream when you least expected it. And don't think the same thing couldn't be happening to the one who's sleeping beside you. She mumbles, talks in her sleep, pronounces a name you've never heard from her lips before. It could also happen that tomorrow, over coffee at breakfast, he'll ask you: who was that guy whose name you repeated in your dreams last night. She's trying to write a poem on this subject, a sort of romantic autobiography, according to her, and an essay on falling in love, a sentimental education. Sometimes the woman who never wet the sheets is the most persistent pursuer. You assume you left her. And maybe she assumes she left you. Each of you with your backpack. You tried to put miles and miles between you. Or else she was the one who got on a plane. One fine day a postcard arrives from Reykjavik. It says, simply: You're still in my orbit. Nothing more. A short little phrase. Signed with an initial. Then you realize that you're still orbiting in her sky, just as she was in yours. For an instant the Earth stops spinning, it stops, the story doesn't start over: it continues. The trick is how to continue. By accepting, Moni says. Moni wrote a poem about it: *No one is altogether forgotten, forgotten, / no one / regardless of their exact traits / no one, no woman, no man / is ever left behind / and when you least expect it / there they are / waiting / at the corner / of a nightmare, / staring into space.* If you ask Moni, who prides herself on being a good advisor, she'll tell you: No one ever leaves anyone. We pretend to leave one another so we'll feel the illusion of freedom for a while. Still, in spite of all the years and all the men I've fucked, I still miss one of them, don't ask me who, the one who'll show up in my next nightmare to make my life miserable. I thought I'd forgotten him, but I haven't. And he hasn't forgotten me either. Because when someone gets into your dreams, it's not so much from desire, tenderness, the surrender there might have been in that story, but rather because of what was lacking: we dream of what was

311

missing. Still, what we didn't know when we thought it was missing, was that it wasn't missing and never would be, that it would resurface the night we least anticipated it, in the calmest dream, turning first into surprise and then waking us with a frightened, suppressed scream. I could tell you stories that would make your panties wet forever. I loved without considering who, says Moni. Men, women. To some men I was a big whore. To some women I was a hardcore dyke, a real lezzie. What do I care. I don't hold it against them. From all my loves, male and female, I keep one unrepeatable moment, one that tends to come back in dreams, damaged, with details that don't quite fit: the little street that winds down from Saint Michèle, passes through San Telmo and finally ends up in Puebla, and there's the person you least expected, they seem to have always been in that place, waiting. Tell me I don't sound like Chavela Vargas: *Touch me here, Macorina. Touch me here.*

Noctilucas, or sea sparkles, that nocturnal phosphorescence in the sea, have a scientific explanation. They're algae that possess an enzyme that produces light on reacting with oxygen. But that doesn't convince me. Those sparkles are proof of the existence of God.

It annoyed the Cannon that the Beast had gone off on his own. When someone asked him if what annoyed him the most was being pushed aside, the Cannon bristled: I've got enough with what God gave me, he told him. I have a gem of a wife, three kids who are a treasure, and I earn a living doing what I love, managing El Atlético and pulling kids off the streets whenever I can, rehabilitating them through sports. I don't need more than that. I've got all the love a human being needs and more, the Cannon told him, because he had a habit of talking like that, like a believer. What hurts me the most is the human part of that boy, the part that was damaged. He didn't even mention the Beast's name: he had become "that boy."

Let me tell you about the wind from the sea. By which I mean the southeaster. The others, like the north wind, are nothing compared to the one from the southeast, and when it comes it seems like it'll stay forever. And it always arrives with a downpour that whips the Villa, floods the streets of earth and sand, turning those that go down to the sea into torrents, and then both the downtown streets and those beyond, the streets of Pinar del Norte and the ones back in La Virgencita and El Monte, become torrents of sand, mud, and garbage. Like a foretaste of the Flood. And to think that when it happens, the Flood, I mean, we're going to end up floating in our own waste, another kind of waste, the life we've wasted. But I don't want to go Apocalyptic on you. Wind, I was talking about the wind. About the southeaster that corners us and drives us into hiding. The ocean rises and knocks down the rental beach cabanas. It wraps around them and shakes them like boats on the high seas. More than one of the guys in charge make a run for it as soon as they see the black clouds, that terrible storm, gathering. Though for dreamy, romantic types, the southeaster has its charm. Especially if you have a refuge, some shelter in the forest, a good roof and firewood for the Franklin stove. Then the southeaster is pleasant. Because it's pleasant to listen to the wind whistling outside, the branches shaking, the noisy crackling of the leaves, the sensation that the grove, the poplars, acacias, pines, and eucalyptus are protecting the chalets and the cabins from the sky's fury. And these sensations, which others might find poetic, for the masses, the half-breeds, Bolitas, Paraguas and Perucas, the laborers, the unemployed, the juvie thugs, and the wretched who live in El Monte or La Virgencita, in their dwellings, cottages, shacks, the huts of the poor, which are always half-built, with windows whose missing panes have been replaced by a sheet of plastic or cardboard, the tin roofs held down with bricks, and inside, warming themselves with a charcoal burner or a carafe, families that eat their stew in front of the TV, for them the roar of the southeaster, its power, offers nothing wondrous at all. Rather it's a punishment from heaven, more proof of a God Who yet again puts them to the test and never stops fucking up their lives, and every so often, they look out of the corner of their eyes to make sure the roof won't fly off, that the water's not getting in, and that, with any luck, the southeaster, its fury, won't leave them without electricity this time because that means no TV, their only consolation to distract them and keep them from thinking about the tragedy the deluge might bring. And if the lights go out, tough shit for them. The poor will always be with us.

Beppe and Nicola are from the same town in Piamonte. They landed at the port of Buenos Aires at the end of the war, one month apart. The first to come to the Villa was Beppe. And he got a job as a bricklayer for old man Gesell, the German. One month later, Nicola climbed out of a truck. When they ran into one another here in the Villa, they didn't say hello. Nicola, too, got a job as a bricklayer for the German. When they worked on a job together, they didn't talk either. Both bought their own lots. The German decided they'd be neighbors, one next door to the other. Neither one protested this vexation. The years went by. They didn't marry, didn't have a family. When they occasionally ran into one another at the Tropicana, both of them, sometimes one right after the other, they always had the same whore, Beti. Neither one asked Beti about the other. And if Beti ever asked one of them about the other, they brushed her off. Not only weren't they big talkers, but neither said a word about the other. No one ever knew what was hidden behind the rancor that united them. Beppe built a hotel, the Stella. Nicola built a chalet, and in back, a few rooms that he rented out in summer: Mare Nostrum Cabins. They never spoke to one another. Never. They must have been the same age, or almost: over eighty.

Yesterday Beppe died. They say Don Beppe left papers bequeathing the hotel to some Italian nephews. And that his body was buried there, in the town in Piamonte. When Don Nicola finds out about his countryman's death, as he walks by the Hotel Stella, he spits. Then he crosses himself and keeps on walking toward his house. He enters, closes the door. Then we hear the gunshot.

One Saturday afternoon, Fournier, lurking behind some shrubs in the forest, is painting hurriedly because the last afternoon light is fading. When you keep still, in silence, that's when the sound of nature comes to life. You can hear the birds. The breeze gently skimming over the branches makes a different sound. If you look up, you can barely see the sky. The atmosphere exudes melancholy, but this calm weighs on your chest, too: it seems like something terrible is about to happen. You're overcome by a sort of fear. And soon the fear turns into terror. Fournier realizes that this presentiment of an imminent, frightful event comes from this light.

Then he hears the crying. He pushes some branches aside and sees the child. He can't be even five years old. He runs along, limping, without pants. There is blood on his buttocks.

Fournier's first impulse is to leave his hiding place, run toward the child, pick him up, take him to the hospital. But he restrains himself. Calm, mute. He's paralyzed.

The child disappears among the trees.

Fournier trembles. He trembles and cries.

And this might be an explanation of why there are no human figures in his paintings.

With the purpose of honoring the shipwrecked victims of the Graf Spee *who were pioneers in the Villa, eighteen young people unfurled red flags with swastikas and Nazi banners at the local cemetery. They wore black jackets with swastikas, combat boots, and relevant tattoos. "Since they behaved peacefully, there was no need for police intervention," declared Mayor Calderón.*

The protest marches over Bignose's death became more frequent and each time had more participants. The Riquelme case, as it was called, came out in newspapers in the capital and on TV. The Federal Police intervened. Pedroza and Malerba were arrested, tried, and sentenced. Light punishment. Both were soon released on probation. Quirós got them out. You can believe that when they returned to the Villa, a welcoming committee was there to greet them. They fêted them with a lamb barbecue.

Old man Riquelme showed up at the festivities. He brought a gun. But he didn't get to draw it. They stopped him.

That same night he shot himself.

All I need now is to be charged with his death, too, Pedroza said. Supposing I *had* been responsible for Bignose's death, which I wasn't, I wouldn't be stupid enough to whack his father, no matter how much he wants to kill me.

Though lots of people think it was out of frustration.

What can you expect from justice.

That's what I think too, Pedrone said. What can you expect from justice when they send two innocent men to jail.

You don't have to go into the forest at night for an owl to screech at you. Sometimes when you're walking through a poplar grove, you can hear its screech. It seems like a warning, but of what? Let every man, every woman, draw their own conclusions. An owl knows what you've done, what you're going to do, what you're hiding. An owl is wise. That's why it can see in the dark. If it's supposed to be bad luck, it's precisely because it knows about our dirty doings and it knows that sooner or later we'll end up paying for them. You walk along, you hear its footsteps on the pine needles, and suddenly the screech. Or else, like last time, one of them flies over you in a nosedive. You thought it was going to attack you. That it was coming toward you. But no, it was just a nosedive, heading straight for a rat. You hadn't even seen the rat, but the owl had. Don't tell me they don't scare you:

not only are they wise, they eat rats, too. And we, you tell me now, what are we.

Who among us doesn't have a whore or a fag in the family. Who doesn't have a thug. Who doesn't have a gambler. Who doesn't have a druggie. Who never stuck his hand in the cookie jar. Who never looked the other way when a dirty deal could implicate him. Who never lied to a jury to get off. Who never was tempted when a friend's wife gave him the eye. Who never sought an advantage in a deal even if meant screwing over an acquaintance. Who never forged a signature. Who never ran over a dog and kept on going. And now you give me this shit about how the Villa is rotten. Tell me, where do *you* come from?

No, what happened at El Español wasn't like they told you. Here's the real story. El Pulqui had just started working at El Español. Behind the counter and waiting on tables. He was wiping glasses when the five of them walked in: Piñeiro, Martinelli, Braulio, Julián, Pedroza, and finally Malerba, watching Pedroza's back. While Martinelli was dealing, Piñeiro asked El Pulqui for a whiskey. He served them, one after another, generous shots. He skipped over Pedroza. Hey, kid, said a finger tapping on the rim of an empty glass. El Pulqui turned his back on him. You're pissing me off, you little asshole. El Pulqui kept walking toward the counter. Pedroza stood up and followed him. He caught up with him just as El Pulqui was placing the tray on the bar. He laid a hand on his shoulder. He didn't expect the kid to gobsmack him with the bottle. Pedroza stumbled. And that's when El Pulqui gained the advantage over him: one, two. Without stopping. Later we found out he had trained at El Atlético. He had prepared for this moment. His moment. And he didn't stop. Because he knew that the minute he let up, Mendo would cream him. Malerba could've stepped in, but he didn't. Who would've imagined that that kid, who would never be anything but a nobody, no matter how

317

much he trained, El Pulqui, I mean, who would've thought he'd end up rearranging that thug Pedroza's face? Malerba tried to step in. But Pedroza stopped him. It would've been embarrassing if his sidekick intervened. He had to take on the kid himself. But he was already on the floor. And before kicking him in the balls, El Pulqui, with that squeaky little kid voice of his, said to him: This is for Bignose. That's when Malerba got up, ready for action. "No," Pedroza, crawling, stopped him. He tried to stand. Don't touch him. Pedroza was spitting blood. El Pulqui had broken his teeth.

We all heard it.

You'll pay for this, Pedroza said to him.

Unflinching, El Pulqui made his way between the two of them, between Pedroza, whose face was a disaster, like a squashed plum, and who was leaning against a table, and Malerba, struggling not to lose control.

El Pulqui didn't turn around. And he walked right out.

It's a total lie that we live off the sea. We live off the surface and the shore. I'll have to get back to that shore thing. And how it also includes the human livestock that comes to spend the high season. I'll try to explain it to you. Tourists, that herd of domestic animals that arrives during the season, don't come to the sea. Don't kid yourself: the sea is a lie. No matter how much some of them claim they come for water sports, it's a question of surface activities, just as the beach, for those who go there, doesn't mean the sea or the sun, but rather the vain exhibitionism of the surface of their bodies, nearly all of them deformed by fat, workouts, or surgery. Lovers of the sun and the open air, they claim to be. And they lie. If they care so much for the sun, it's to get a tan, to acquire a skin tone that will conceal their natural, sickly pallor. If they care so much about the open air it's because it lets them show off their tan, the weather-beaten look of their skin. Superficial people look for surfaces to show off their superficiality. Because nobody, male or female, is what's inside them, a complicated system of internal organs and plumbing, the circulation of blood and excrement, and in their soul, whose whereabouts nobody knows, because the soul is not that beating, pulsing muscle, their soul, I say, is inhabited by fear, pure fear. Just as we've chosen to live at the seashore, those men and women, and their offspring, too, have chosen it, but by deceiving themselves, fantasizing that in two weeks at the beach they can become someone else, that body, that shell, two weeks without thinking about needs other than those of the body: eating, digesting, copulating. And we who live at the seashore live from them, those who idealize an existence here, those who don't have the guts to give up their little cockroach lives, to look out at the shore, step on the quaking earth, the cracking surface. If we're terrified by what lies beyond the shore, they're worse: they're not even capable of reaching the shore. And they think we live off the sea. They like to believe it. Because it gives them hope that they'll be able to do it, too, maybe tomorrow, the next day, next year, when they save up a few pesos, never. No, we don't live off the sea. But let the seasonal tourists believe that. We feed their illusion. And by feeding it so much, we end up believing it. That's how we are, people on the edge, living on the edge.

A baby's first year of life is a time of great happiness and great change for the family. But during that first year of life, parents should pay attention to the most frequent health problems that may appear: fever, respiratory infections, colic, vomiting, diarrhea, and constipation. It's equally important to be aware of the child's monthly growth guidelines as well as accident prevention in the home.

Nonsense. That girl hasn't got the plague. Luz doesn't look like she's got AIDS. What I think is that if she can't find a guy it's because they're afraid of her old man. Remember what happened to Bignose, and then tell me if you feel like screwing Pedroza's daughter.

Unlike what tourists prefer in the summer, to watch the sunrise or sunset on the beach, for us the sea loses its attraction during this season and becomes a source of depression. The steely winter sky begins to dissipate into a sea mist; the deserted beach acquires an oppressive aura. It's strange how the sea swell, which from afar and by night is that intimidating rumbling, now sounds muffled, a repetitive, monotonous crackling that makes you think of the automatic gestures of our lives, the same old habits with which we make the same gestures every day. We've come this far. And it's hard not to think of the void and the absurdity of our existence. We've always believed that by coming to live at the shore we could be other people, feel self-important, and even when we've finally made it, when we've managed to earn a peso, we've imagined we could bed the neighbor's wife who really turned us on, when we've achieved a certain amount of social standing, that we could become outstanding members of this society. Even when we believe our fingertips have touched that dream fulfilled, when we observe the swell, one wave after another, one wave the same as the next—despite what some optimists say, that no two waves are alike, that each wave is unique, singular, and different—the repetition and monotony of the spectacle darkens us, just as the landscape grows darker, and then, like a revelation, though devoid of enthusiasm or surprise, like the confirmation of an idea we've always had but which just now, at this very instant, in this succession of one rolling wave after another, pops up with inexorable logic: this sea, which has always been here, is an inducement to flight or to suicide. The idea begins to coalesce. Flight is no longer an option. The flight was in coming here, to the shore. And you could go no farther. It's too late to turn back. So suicide is all you have left. But it's winter and below freezing. The very idea of leaping into the sea gives you chills; you tremble. If you're going to do it, much cleaner and less troublesome for your loved ones, that is, if you can consider them loved ones and they, in turn, can consider you the same, the most practical and tidiest thing is for you to go get the gun and fire the shot here, facing the sea. It's not such a bad idea: for your last vision from the shore to be the starry night over the sea, for the end to consist of leaving the shore behind and seeing what, if anything, lies beyond. But when you go back for the gun, when you walk into the house, it's possible that your loved ones might be there, that at that moment, an unexpected wave of attachment might overcome you, and then you hesitate, you postpone your plan. Attachment and guilt are always easy to confuse, and in the midst of this confusion, you let yourself be. Of course, by remaining in the heated house at the dinner hour, with the TV going, there's reconciliation with habit. An armistice with your depression, which, now, in a forced smile at your wife and kids, closely resembles cowardice. And what I've just outlined for you is one example. It explains why in winter nobody commits suicide in the sea à la Alfonsina Storni. More common is the rope hanging from a beam, three blister packs, the gas valve, the Gillette, or a shot on the back patio. Homespun deaths, if you like. Which, after all, in statistical terms, aren't so many. Not even a dozen. Which shows that we're all resigned to remaining as we are and that we'd rather stay put. Really, it's not essential to dwell on the matter; we've chosen to stay at the shore, and no one wants to leave it.

Like we said, after Malerba, on Pedroza's orders, liquidated Bignose, the dealer who had given Pedroza's daughter AIDS, who would have wanted to go near that girl? Luz, Pedroza's girl, was a broken soul. The only one who talked to her was El Pulqui. He and Luz had become real close friends. He convinced her to go with him to the evangelical temple. While Pedroza and Malerba were locked up in Batán, El Pulqui was Luz's shadow. He comforted her, he told himself. Besides, the virus came between them. It didn't go beyond friendship: they were joined by Bignose's memory. They were also joined by their hatred of Pedroza: Luz didn't visit her father while he was in prison. And when he got out on parole, she never spoke to him again. After the trammeling he gave Pedroza at El Español,

El Pulqui's friendship with Luz was dangerous. For a while no one heard anything about El Pulqui. He'd finally taken off, we thought. And shortly after that, Luz fell off the map as well.

Despite the presence of drunk driving checkpoints, more than twenty drivers were stopped along the routes leading to our Villa. Authorized sources declared that this figure is considerably lower than the actual number, and that the authorities preferred to play down a figure that is viewed as alarming. Among those stopped were the children of a well-known provincial deputy, an employee connected with a government department for minors, and two stars of the revue, a comedian and his entourage who were on their way to present a hilarious show.

Unforgettable, last Saturday night. El Atlético was bursting with people. Of course, hardly anyone from the poplar groves up north. No one expects to see anyone from the Rotary or the Beer Lovers' Club. El Atlético's warehouse encloses a haze of *choripán* and burgers; soft drinks and beer make the rounds. And, of course, wine cartons, too. In the intervals between one fight and another, lots of cumbia and folk music. The basketball hoops have been pushed aside, and in the center of the warehouse stands the ring. There are bleachers for the cheaper seating in the grandstand, and plastic chairs on either side of the ring make up the stalls.

Boxing night is a night of celebration. Two species whose paths never cross: the power brokers and the denizens of La Virgencita, El Monte, and Circunvalación. The darkies, as they're likely to be called by any one of the snobs who think of themselves as big shots because of their ostentatious roles in Winterfest. Boxing attracts another zoological spectrum, according to Moure the veterinarian, who never in his life stepped foot in El Atlético nor will he, least of all when there's a boxing match on. This is where laborers, masons, kiosk attendants, lifeguards, electricians, plumbers, gasfitters, mechanics, waiters, maids, and gardeners come, the farm workers from the lumberyard and all those who survive as best they can, by scavenging, scratching out the end of the month to the best of their abilities. Families and couples come, sweethearts, girls and boys, strays from the public elementary and secondary schools, as well as vagrants, male and female, pickpockets, thieves, and, as one might expect, the families of thugs who clear a respectable place for themselves in the bleachers and command a view from there. If anyone's absence is noteworthy, it's the Cannon's. His absence escapes no one. It's so palpable that it's a presence—as is his disdain for his ex-pupil. One who always shows up is Dante, leaving his seat, wandering, greeting people here and there, without missing a detail, taking mental notes. Our scribe is crazy about boxing and never misses a match. As Dante always says: Boxing is a noble, gentlemanly sport. And more humane than chess: there's nothing more perverse than intelligence in the service of evil. Boxing, on the other hand, is as human as it is bestial. And it doesn't pretend to hide the animal in us.

When the lights go out, when there's only the lamp in the ring, the theme from *Rocky* bursts forth, echoing, deafening, making the walls shake and your stomach throb. The spotlights focus on the contenders, surrounded by their assistants, making their way through the crowd. El Atlético explodes. You can feel the emotion in the air. Those with the highest expectations for the show are the women. The chicks are dying for the Beast, just as they once melted for the Cannon, till the Villa's ex-champ retired to devote himself to his wife and kids, to El Atlético, and also to declare that he'd hung up his gloves with respect to the ladies, but those of us who know him know that wasn't exactly the case. Among us, among the women, it's said that the Cannon has one the size his nickname suggests and that the Beast's lives up to his, as well. That the Cannon's is thicker and the Beast's is longer. That the Cannon can't get it up like the Beast, and that's because the Cannon, *mens sana in corpore sano*, refuses to take Viagra. And that if the Beast lasts longer it's because nowadays it's the young people who abuse Sildenafil, as shy types call it when they ask for it at the drugstore. Quite an event, Saturday night boxing. The bleachers and chairs aren't enough to accommodate such a huge crowd. Authentic popular zeal, says Quico Marengo of Villa FM broadcasting, in a joint production with the TV station. Live and direct, the two most important media outlets in our community. An unforgettable pugilistic encounter. Because Cachito asked the TV station to air the fight. With Quirós's support he got the Villa's most important businesses together as sponsors and offered them the broadcast for their business. No other program on the channel has had as many sponsors as this transmission, which, aside from being great business, as we know, contains quite a bit of political campaigning. Because with this move, Cachito Calderón is giving an early sign of being on the campaign trail, anticipating the launch of his candidacy for a third term. Today, this event brings joy to every home, Quico says, nearly voiceless from all the exertion he's put into speaking. A night of sport for the entire family, Quico goes on, while Dicky, the cameraman, pans the room, pausing for a few minutes on the Virginias, twin hookers who've shown up tonight dressed to kill. And the lights go out.

First we see him arrive, punching the air and with a face like a dog's, the challenger: Lucho "the Puma" Roldán, from Tandil. You wouldn't want to get into an argument with this kid. Pure sinew. You should see the agility with which he hops into the ring, and, shrugging off his robe, greets the throng. They applaud and whistle at him. And when they whistle at him, he grabs his balls in an unmistakable gesture that amplifies the explosion of whistling. Even though they're a minority, his fans make their presence felt. Tandil is here, they shout. Till the chords from *Rocky* grow louder, and then the spotlights linger on the figure of Sebastián "the Beast" Bermúdez. It grabs everyone's attention, provokes whispers, is disturbing, and in more than one way, comical that the Beast is a walking ad, with the slogan stamped on the back of his robe in bright, fuchsia letters: Cachito Administration. When he takes off his robe, there's a tattoo on his back: Cachito Administration. And on his pants, too: Cachito Administration. The TV cameras close in on Cachito Calderón, who, standing in the stall, raises his arms, his fingers in a V for victory. Glorious, confident of the Beast's triumph, Cachito is already celebrating his re-election next year. Who remembers the business of the sewer system now? The Beast steps over to the ropes, extends his hand to Cachito, an unforgettable moment. Our mayor, our champ. United. No man, no woman, will ever forget that image of the successful local athlete greeting the most charismatic mayor our Villa has ever had. A real photo op.

There are times when misfortune is like a southeaster. Just look at Bignose, a kid from a good family: he gets into drugs and gives AIDS to his girlfriend, Luz. Pedroza, the girlfriend's father, sends Malerba, his hit man, to liquidate the kid. They want to make the murder look like a suicide, but it doesn't work out for them. Old man Riquelme, Bignose's father, even though he's a Radical, organizes protest marches with the aid of dissident Peronists and the Greens from the Humanist Party, calling for justice. Pedroza and Malerba spend two years locked up in Batán. When they're released, they're greeted here with a welcoming committee and a lamb barbecue. Old man Riquelme shows up at the barbecue. With a gun: he wants to avenge his son. But they stop him. Sometime later, he shoots himself. Two months later his wife dies of a heart attack. El Pulqui, Bignose's best friend, hates Pedroza as much as Luz, his own daughter, does. One night at El Español, El Pulqui gives Pedroza a walloping that leaves him black and blue. El Pulqui and Luz split, leaving the Villa. One night Malerba appears at the little house belonging to the Leivas, El Pulqui's parents. Malerba asks for the son. The old folks are destroyed by his absence. Malerba doesn't believe them: the old folks are playing dumb to save their son. Malerba puts the squeeze on them. At their age, a broken hip is no joke. The old folks throw him out. Later on their house burns down. They go to live at La

Casa del Abuelo. Pedroza pays them a visit. He tells them he holds no grudge against their son. That if they'd like, he'll help them find a new house. All he wants to know is where his daughter is. Luz, the light of my life, cries Pedroza. But he doesn't convince the old folks. One night, when the old lady is coming home from the supermarket, someone hits her in the hip with a stick. She doesn't see her attacker. The old lady is taken to the hospital. And the old man files a complaint against Pedroza. But who's going to prove anything.

Everybody smokes. In the morning, beginning in fall, women come out of the shops and smoke in the sunshine. Sales clerks smoke. Women from phone centers. And from supermarkets. And from shoe stores. Boutique owners and hairdressers. Kiosk saleswomen and artisans. They all smoke. As soon as the sun beings to warm up the morning, countless women come out to bask on the sidewalk, like bitches in the sun, and smoke. And if there is no sun, they come out anyway. It's not so much because smoking in shops is forbidden. It's more because indoors, their loneliness is unbearable. So they step outside to smoke. They smoke, as if they're waiting. Old women smoke, forty-somethings and thirty-somethings smoke, the young ones smoke. Widows, married women, the separated, and the single. Sometimes they smoke and chat. The greengrocer and the pharmacist, sitting in the sun, smoking. When someone goes by, they stop talking. And then they make remarks. Since nothing's going on, they talk about the people going by. They smoke silently, pensively. Embittered, taking deep drags. You wonder what the talkers are talking about and what the solitary, silent ones are thinking about. They talk about men. They think about men. They light up a Jockey. Their husbands, their lovers, their children. A Derby. Their frustrations. A Le Mans. Their hopes. A Lucky. They say that. A Philip Morris. I heard that. An L.M. They gossip. They talk about last night and tomorrow. Give me a light. A Marlboro. Some cough, others clear their throats, but this doesn't stop them from having another cigarette. Both the talkers and those who are alone look at whoever's passing along this sidewalk and the one across the street. They smoke. They look at the sky, which is now cloudy. They don't care that the temperature has dropped and a cold breeze is starting to blow. They smoke till noon. Then they lock up and disappear till after siesta hour. Then they're back again, in front of their businesses, smoking, in company or alone. They smoke as night falls and shop windows begin to light up. Many of them stay out on the street until closing time. The day never ends. They smoke till it's time for them to go home. Today I didn't make a cent, one complains. I'll have to wait till the next long weekend. Got a cigarette, girl?

It seems that Gonza Calderón, who sometimes went around teamed up with Bignose, received an email from the kids a while ago. They also say that Malerba pressured Gonza to find out where Luz and El Pulqui were. Neither Pedroza nor Malerba, one out on parole and the other under house arrest, can leave the country. But Pedroza, as we know, has his contacts.

If you pay attention you'll hear how the neighbors' gossip travels through the plumbing of the building.

Nature is against her children. Look at that nice couple who, this Sunday, while having a picnic in the woods, laid their two-month-old baby down in the shade of a pine tree. While they were making their sandwiches, a pine cone came loose from a branch and fell on the baby's head. It hit him right on the soft spot. No, at the hospital they couldn't do a thing.

Those kids, children of the crème de la crème of the Villa's high society, heirs to a notary office, a real estate office, stores on the main street, descendants of prominent members of Nuestra Señora del Mar Parish Association, distinguished Rotary families, all members of the Police Co-op, the power brokers, as Dante often calls them in his articles in *El Vocero*, a term that, when he says it, makes you think of power lines: you barely graze them and yet they wound you. Those kids, as we were saying, the snobs, not one of them over twenty, except for the Vega kid, the son of the Vegas from Bazar del Mar, who's still repeating his fourth year of night school, and if the principal hasn't kicked him out yet it's precisely because he's one of the band of snobby kids. Mess with one of them and you're done for. Unless you're Malerba: remember how he got justice, in his own way, but justice after all, with Gonza Calderón. And it didn't matter to him that Gonza was the mayor's son. He really messed him up. Remember how we all saw him limping after Malerba got through with him. With Gonza and the other two, Clavo and Facu, the ones who raped Lorena, that girl from La Virgencita. It turns out that the mother, a poor, helpless gal, knowing that justice wasn't going to intervene, tired of begging at the police station, fed up with consulting *La Comadre*, knowing there'd be no punishment for those who raped her girl, made the best choice: she asked Malerba to bring her justice. She moved Malerba. And, for the record, it's not easy to move El Capo. If he didn't touch Mati Quirós it's because Alejo found out just in time about the revenge Malerba was carrying out. Just in time. The only one who escaped Malerba. We also know: for Alejo, there are no secrets. He knows everything. And sometimes he knows before it happens. So Alejo stopped Malerba in time and avoided having Mati meet the same fate as the others who went around limping. Someone said that they were going to get together and take care of Malerba. But not even all of them together had the balls. What we didn't doubt was that they'd pull one of their stunts again. Not on Lorena, the raped girl, anymore, in part because her mother wangled a transfer to another supermarket in Madariaga, and mother and daughter moved away But they would find some other girl to fuck over.

One morning Pando informs Di Lorenzi that some cash is missing. It had to be last night, Pando tells him. He can't figure out how. They look at each other, they ask each other who. Pando's been working for him for over ten years, so Di Lorenzi can't suspect his second in command. But it's true that Pando is always the last to leave, the one who sets the alarm connected to Telefónica del Mar's security system. They ask themselves who else knows the code, who has access to the cash register. Two trusted employees: Silverio and Eulalia. Silverio is an old-timer at Di Lorenzi Dairy Distributors. It's hard for Di Lorenzi to imagine it might be Silverio, the foreman. And Eulalia, even less likely. Pando would stake his life on her: she's his lover. Quite a lot of cash was stolen. The cops and Co-op security determine that the alarm was connected all night. The theft happens again. Three, four more times. Without triggering the alarm. Di Lorenzi wises up. The only way to explain how they got access to the distributorship is to find out if the alarm is disconnected at any point during the night. Di Lorenzi talks to security. Early one morning the alarm is disconnected. Security guards are posted in front of the distributorship. Just then Malerba arrives. Without getting out of the car, he flashes a pistol. Di Lorenzi shows up a few minutes later. Pando, hunkered down in his car, resists arrest. The security van blocks his way out toward the beach. Di Lorenzi exchanges words with the security guards. Malerba stands apart. You can go now, Di Lorenzi tells them. He'll speak to Pando. He'll take care of the matter himself. Malerba nods.

Pando is sitting at the wheel with the motor running. The lights from the security van shimmer in the night. He's been his right-hand man all his life, Di Lorenzi says. He'll settle the matter by talking. And no one will get hurt. Convinced, the security guards leave.

Then, various versions: That Pando was so ashamed to have Di Lorenzi look him in the face that he fired the shot himself. Di Lorenzi couldn't stop him. When the Provincial Police arrived, he was already dead. That's one version. The other: That Di Lorenzi made a deal with the Provincial Police. A suicide. Just like with Bignose.

I watch the sea. I watch it from the shore. As I watch it, I see the immensity I never was, am, or will be. When I die, set me on fire. Throw my ashes into the sea.

Sporting the Cachito Administration tattoo on his back, our young local champ is coming out to fight. "The Beast" Bermúdez goes out to meet his challenger, Lucho "the Puma" Roldán, the champ from Tandil. The Latino champion of the World Boxing Council, our champ, after months of preparation, displaying extraordinary physical form, thanks to the collaboration of his managers, Mario Grisolía and Federico Murcia, and under the supervision of ex-champion Cannon Santoro, is now about to face Lucho "the Puma" Roldán in ten rounds. Remarkable, the enthusiasm, the encouragement, the support provided by our mayor Cachito Calderón and his aides. The Beast is ready for a fight; he provokes, flings his arms open before his rival. Hit me, he seems to be saying. He feels sure of his strength. Defiant, he doesn't even put up his guard. The Puma hesitates, the audience roars. The Puma's punch comes as a surprise, a clean hit, devastating. The Beast staggers backward, affected. Another punch by Puma Roldán. And another. The Beast stumbles. Our local champ can't quite recover. The Puma lands another hit, a real killer punch. The bellowing of the crowd. Our champion lies on the canvas. Now the clamor turns to booing. The Tandilero, Lucho "the Puma" Roldán, winner by a knockout, the new middle-weight Latino champion of the World Boxing Council. Less than two minutes into the first round, the most anticipated fight of the year has ended with the defeat of our beloved Beast.

A girl offers a baby up to the new champ. The Puma lifts his little daughter into the ring and dances with her. The Puma kisses the baby and leaps around with her to a true cumbia beat. Cachito, our mayor, can barely conceal his bitterness. His smile is starched, more political than ever, as he hands the trophy to Puma Roldán. Then he goes over to talk to the Beast, who's shaking his head, still stunned and slow to recover. The winner, Quico Marengo repeats over the loudspeaker, by a knockout in the first round, Lucho "the Puma" Roldán. The trophy goes to him, ladies and gentlemen. The Puma holds the baby in one arm and in the other hand, held aloft, the trophy. He salutes his public. Cumbia music shatters the atmosphere. The Tandileros in the audience jump up and down euphorically. The Puma looks at the trophy, notices something, argues with the presenter, the referee, and the judges. I want to give it back. What's going on in the ring, Quico? What's going on? It seems there's been a mistake. Angrily, the Tandilero champion returns the trophy. He puts his baby on the floor. He threatens to charge at our mayor. It can't be, it can't be, more respect, oh, they're telling me what happened. An innocent mistake, a misunderstanding: the trophy has the Beast's name engraved on it. His victory had been taken for granted. A tense moment. Locals and Tandileros hurl rebukes. There's commotion in the stands. No shoving please. No shoving. Please, guys. They're about to grab one another, but the police intervene. The Tandileros are carrying their idol on their shoulders, his baby still in his left arm and his right fist on high, waving.

But you can breathe defeat in the air, in the silence that takes over El Atlético. Crushed, our mayor, Cachito Calderón, leaves, followed by his team. A real popular heartbreak for the people, the unexpected defeat of Sebastián "the Beast" Bermúdez. An unprecedented occurrence in a rising career that was the joy of our Villa, which today, now, tonight, is plunged in a gloom saturated by the drizzle of a cold, inclement winter that freezes our spirits. The sky over the Villa is weeping tonight, and those of us who still can't accept this defeat, our hearts infected with frustration and gloom, are weeping too. It doesn't matter: we still love you, Beast. And as Almafuerte, the great poet of the humble, once said, "Don't embrace defeat, even defeated."

That foggy early morning when the Costamar bus jumped the low barrier and the train split the bus in two, Lito, at the wheel, aside from being drunk, was high. Luckily the bus was nearly empty. Lucky is just an expression. It was only carrying ten passengers, though three of them died and seven sustained injuries. Still, it could have been worse. Imagine what the same accident would've been like in high season. Old man Neri went to Quirós, asking him to use his influence in the court in Dolores. In a few months Lito was out on parole. This time he couldn't run away. He had to bow his head and help his father at the funeral home. I'm depressed, Lito complained at night in Moby. This gig is deadly, he said. Not bad for someone who's brain dead, Dante retorted. More compassionately, Bruno recommended: What you need is a woman. A real woman, he told him. Not a whore from Madariaga. To make a home with, settle down. Lito looked so defeated that even Dante took pity on him: You ought to settle down, Lito. After what happened to you, no one's gonna give you a job. Be thankful you've got your old man's funeral home. What more do you want. Dante felt sorry for him, too: Try it, Lito. Settle down. Start a family. Trying costs nothing. A family will lift your spirits. You've got nothing to lose by trying. After all, if you change your mind, you can split. Alejo, who was also at Moby that night, slapped Lito on the back: What you need is emotional stability.

You have to realize that Lito was a good catch. When the old man died, Lito would be the only heir to Neri Funeral Home. Though it didn't seem to please Neri at all. Neri the Sicilian would have preferred a different son instead of this dark-haired, dark-skinned giant who took after his late mother, a *criolla* from Ayacucho, not only in his features, but also in his tendency to laziness. I'm no deadbeat, Lito defended himself. What I've got is sadness, from being around stiffs so much. If I look at dead people all day long, what am I supposed to feel like doing, the cumbia? Love, Dante insisted that night at Moby. All you need is love. Love changes you.

Nobody loves me, Lito blubbered. Who's gonna love me if I smell like death, no matter how much cologne I put on. He cried like a baby: At night I dream of stiffs. You're gonna be lonelier than we are, they laugh. I go to the Tropicana, get laid, fall asleep, and right away there they are in my dream, on the Costamar bus, dead, asking me to wake up. And then I wake up. I wake up and I can't sleep a wink the rest of the night.

You fuck her too? Braulio asks him. No, she's not my type, Alejo lies. Too big a whore. Kick her out; she's gonna give you problems, he tells him paternally. She gives good head, but it's not enough. How do you know Mimí's good at sucking dick, Braulio asks him. Nothing in this community is alien to me, Alejo slaps him on the back. That chick is with you for the money.

You have to be at a store from 9 to 12 and from 5 to 9 without anything happening. There's Mimí at her clothing store, Mimí's Fashion World. In the front window, off to the side and at the bottom, the flyer still remains: Where Is Belén Yanina? Today is Thursday and no one's been in since Monday. Annoyed, she closes before noon. She hops on her little motorcycle and goes over to Ramos Good Faith Real Estate.

You have to call first, Braulio says. My wife might be here. Your wife knows, that's for sure, but she plays dumb because it works out better for her. I came because I don't have a cent. Nobody came to the store today. Here neither, Braulio tells her. You're shitting me, she says. You're from the Kennedy family. The cream of the crop. And I'm a nobody. Separated, with a kid. Don't I pay Jere's tuition at Nuestra Señora del Mar, Braulio says. You have any idea what a teenager eats? A lover has obligations. I have to support the other one, you know. I'm the other one: Pleased to meet you, Mimí Borowicz, the one who sucks your dick. Calm down, Mimí, Braulio begs. How do you expect me to calm down if I didn't ring up a fucking cent this week. Braulio hands her a hundred-peso bill. It's all I've got, he says.

Braulio clears his throat, grumbles. Alejo's right, he thinks. He pulls out another bill. Mimí walks around the desk, leans over the chair, and grabs his fly. At siesta time my kid's at the Sports Complex. I don't like to pay for blow jobs, Braulio says.

I'll expect you at three, darling. She blows him a kiss. This is final, says Braulio. Sad, lonely, and final, he says. And he wonders where he got that phrase from. At three, okay? Mimí says. She walks out of the real estate office. Braulio watches her get on the cycle.

And he knows that at a quarter to three he'll be looking at the clock.

When her aunt informed her that her father was in the hospital and there wasn't much time left, Marina said she was sorry, but that dead guy wasn't her father. She remembered all the letters she had written him when she was a girl. He never answered one. Before she turned ten, she stopped writing him. If her father had forgotten her for thirty years, the hell with him. And zero remorse.

Now she *really* was an orphan, she thought. Just the same, she was overcome by remorse. It was then that she decided to enter the little shed in back. She wanted to find some photos. Before she died, her mother had stored a ton of things in boxes. And there they were: in a large bundle, all the letters she had written to her father. In another, all the letters he had written to her. Which her mother had also hidden.

While he was doing time, Lito hardly slept at all. Just as his eyelids began to droop, the dead came looking for him. Lito found himself behind the wheel again, his companion snoring beside him. Lito took a hit and took a swig from the hip flask. The dead were approaching the cabin. Murmuring, they drew closer.

In the yard the house has a little neon sign that used to light up at night with blue and red letters: Graceland. And not because anyone in the family was called Grace. The house dates from the sixties, a chalet with a gable roof, a screen door, and a wrought-iron gate with a zinc overhang for the car, a white 1961 De Soto. The dwelling is surrounded by a yard that, up until a few months ago, was a gardener's dream with its multicolored floral adornments. Now the house is faded and dirty; the weeds and undergrowth try to smother it, and the windows and doors, always closed, contribute to its ghostly appearance with the glow of the neon Graceland sign. Add to this the De Soto, which will end up ruined by storms and saltpeter. The De Soto looks like it's been there forever, abandoned, like a part of the house, an essential. Graceland wouldn't be Graceland without the De Soto.

Don't even think about going to the Tropicana this Sunday. You won't find one girl on duty. Sunday's August 6th, dude. Day of the Child.

To give you an idea of how stories come about in this place, a good example is the Costero, the bus that goes from one end of the Villa to the other, and which Bedford Arturo drives: an old hunk of tin that's always breaking down. The other night—cold, foggy—the Costero was on its last run. Arturo couldn't wait to stop at Ruli's place, buy himself a gram of blow. But out of the fog emerged two shadows: a Bolita couple—the woman pregnant, about to pop. For a moment Arturo nearly continued on his way, but he's got a heart. He helped the husband get the woman into the bus. He hit the gas. He cursed: it meant passing Ruli's cabin without stopping for his gram. Just then his headlights shone on another woman, Titi, with a gun to her head. I got off track with my story for a second. Titi had threatened Ruli, saying that if he didn't stop dealing she would shoot herself. It was his fault that their kids, Tina and Lucio, were druggies, too. Just imagine Ruli giving up dope and his business. People come to his house, and I say "come" because this part is present tense, they come from as far as Mar de las Pampas to buy. The thing is, Titi didn't convince him with her threat; she went and got the 22 and stepped out into the night. She was planning to shoot herself just as the Costero went by, so that if she missed the bus would run her over. When the headlights hit her, Titi pulls the trigger. But she doesn't off herself: Arthur maneuvers the Bedford and crashes against a pine tree, and the impact sets off the Bolita woman's labor. Arturo has a suicidal chick on the road, a bloody head, and another chick giving birth on top of the bus. He asks the Bolita guy for help. They load Titi on the bus. The Bedford takes off, smoking. And that's how they get to the hospital. With one chick giving birth and the other dying. I'll tell you how the story ends. The Bolita girl had twins. Titi wound up sort of brain dead. But it didn't end there. Now Ruli's gonna keep dealing more than ever because he needs cash for Titi's treatments. And since he's real grateful to the couple, he hired the Bolita guy as his delivery man and the Bolita gives Arturo coke for free. You should see how fast the Costero runs now.

Mimí Borowicz, like all of them when they're kind of cute, thought she was too good for us. And she hooked up with Brandsen, the one from La Marea theater group, from Casa de la Cultura. Or rather, the one who hooked her up was Brandsen. Every afternoon, when he passed Mimí's Fashion World on the way to his classes and rehearsals, he eyeballed Mimí and Mimí eyeballed him. They started exchanging hellos. Brandsen didn't waste time. He walked into the place and came directly to the point. He asked her if she was planning to spend her whole life waiting on customers in a third-rate boutique, or if she'd rather aim for a more secure future in the dramatic arts. With a single glance, Brandsen knew how to recognize a temperament suited for the art of the stage. And Mimí dreamed of making her debut in a theater on Avenida Corrientes.

It didn't take Brandsen even two classes to get into her pants.

Graceland is Elvis's house. Elvis's name isn't Elvis. His name is Elbio López, but all of us in the Villa know him as Elvis, just like we also know him for his white '61 De Soto. Elvis, the illegitimate son of Crazy Trixie, the daughter of the late Hellers, remember, those Germans who got fed up with their daughter, a lost cause, they said, and moved away from the Villa. Trixie would hook up with one guy for a while, then another, and that's how she got along. Till she split for the U.S. and came back pregnant. She had spent a night of unbridled passion with Elvis, she said. The baby would be called Elvis, like his father, she promised. Because Elvis was responsible for her pregnancy. She was mentally connected to Elvis, she said. All she had to do was softly hum a ballad and Elvis would reply from North America. Trixie died drunk one winter, I recall. They found her lying near the dock with an empty bottle of gin. She had a photo of Elvis rolled up inside the bottle, which, we imagine, she had planned to throw into the sea as a message to the father of her child. It was a photo of Elvis, her son. She named him Elbio because the court didn't recognize the name of the King of Rock. Elvis Junior was raised by an aunt and uncle from Quilmes. There he started out as a sound technician for a group no one remembers, the Mad Dogs. It took the group less time to dissolve than to set up on stage. The Villa is my Memphis, he said. While he was making plans to form a new group and produce it, he set up an audio/television repair service: he called it the Heartbreak Broken Appliance Hotel. It was a sort of homage, he said. He played Presley all day long at his booth in Galería Soles. Meanwhile he set up the new group, and again he called it the Mad Dogs. They performed three times. Once at their opening, in the Villa. But the sound was bad. Just the same, we encouraged the group and gave them good press. Another time in Pinamar. And again the sound system failed. But you saw what those Pinamar snobs are like. The Mad Dogs had to call it off. The third time in Madariaga: the sound system bombed completely and the show ended up in a fight.

Bottle-throwing, broken heads, the usual in these cases. And that was it. Elvis had driven himself into debt with the sound equipment, in addition to the cost of setting up the business. If my place was out on the street, he said, I'd have better luck, but stuck in a strip mall, who's gonna know I'm here. But the debts he contracted didn't worry him too much. Because when he collected his father's inheritance, he'd save his skin. Elvis maintained that he'd filed a lawsuit in the U.S. for the Presley inheritance and that he was one of the King of Rock's thousands of illegitimate children. The moment had come to claim his rights, he said.

Impressive is the word for the operation carried out in our Villa by the Dolores Brigade and the Federal legislature. It happened that another one of those involved in the shameful case of the abused children at Nuestra Señora del Mar School was a friend of the institution's kiosk owner. An abundance of pornographic material, items acquired at porno shops, and 400 grams of marijuana were discovered at the suspects' respective homes.

It breaks your heart to see El Criollito in a wheelchair. Juan was his given name, which, with the surname Del Campo, promised he would turn out to be a full-fledged *criollo*. Ramón and Elisa had no other children. As superintendents of a building, they lived in a space that wasn't big enough for more than one. When Ramón turned on the Rural Channel on Saturdays to watch the horse breaking competitions, he missed Maipú. Elisa missed it, too. They drank wine and waxed nostalgic. We'll go back some day, Ramón consoled her. As soon as we save a few pesos, he said. And Juancito will grow up to be a real gaucho in Maipú.

Like so many *criollos* in the Villa, they didn't miss a single folklore club meeting. They instilled country traditions in the boy. By three he was already tap-dancing. At four his *malambo* was quite the hit at Uniendo Lazos. After he appeared at Tierra Adentro, he was invited to perform at Pago Querido. El Criollito was his stage name. By the time he was five, wherever there was a gaucho festival, there was El Criollito, earning cheers and applause. What a respectful silence he commanded with his boots to the rhythm of the bass drum. Those legs, those feet, had a life of their own, independent of his body, his arms dangling relaxed at his sides. Then the bass drum fell silent, and the *malambo* became so possessed that you were afraid El Criollito's ankles would break. Suddenly, unexpectedly, he would come to a perfect halt, imposing a hush, an awed hush. And the applause and cheers would explode. His parents entered him in a program on Channel 7, *Federalísima*. The prize was ten thousand pesos, a trip to Iguazú Falls, and a carved wooden trophy in the form of a soldier, to be presented by a veteran of the Malvinas War. The Del Campos were dreamstruck. The ten thousand pesos would go to buy them a piece of land in Maipú.

Early one rainy morning, while it was still dark, they got off the Rápido Argentino at Retiro Station. Del Campo took in the city with a sweep of his arm:

Our future depends on you, he told his son. With your *malambo* you'll have the people of Buenos Aires in your pocket. And the money, too.

But as soon as they left the station, El Criollito was hit by a car. Disabled for life.

Another apartment-house gaucho, like so many around here. But don't let Ramón hear you call him that because he'll kill us.

Who's who in this Villa, who's each one and who's the other. And the biggest question of all: who am I, who's telling this story, who's writing it. So many empty houses. And yet, sometimes you can hear voices. But you still haven't answered the question: who's writing this page. And you can't give an answer. Maybe you could, if you knew who "I" is. You walk into those empty houses, pass from one to the other. From one room to another room. Nobody's there. Sometimes I don't even feel my own presence. But the voices of those missing are there. Those voices dictate to you. They, the absent, write to you. Each key on this machine has the initial of the name of the one who'll come into being in the next story. On the surface, none of them is the story of the one who's writing. But all of them are that *who*. The "I" who's not aware of being. Because he or she chose to be someone else, the one who listens to the voices on the wind, in the murmur of the trees. *I am from here, yet a foreigner. When the day comes to stop being or existing / here, perhaps, /maybe, / for all we know / then / these words might be / your voice in my voice / on a morning like this / blue sky, seagulls / calm sea and warm breeze.*

A saint, that Norita. She always figured out a way to get by, and, what counts most in the Villa, without bugging her neighbors as is the custom here. Her parents were among those who came to the Villa in the seventies. Norita's parents were older. The old man worked as a brick mason, and the mother as a maid for the German women in Pinar del Norte. An accident took the father: a southeaster knocked him off a scaffold when the Brigantis were expanding the Hotel Jónico. The widow and daughter had to manage for themselves. Norita started working at the Bazar del Mar. Norita was always tall, but at that time, and we're talking about the seventies now, man, was she ever scrawny. She had anemia, asthma, and to top it off, diabetes. But then she went for treatment. Disciplined as she was, she also started practicing tae-kwon-do. In the morning, no sooner had the sun come up than she would put on her sneakers and a jogging suit and go out for a run. She took the main drag, the road that leads into the Villa, passed the roundabout, the totem pole, continued straight and followed the route toward the cemetery. Every morning, rain or shine. She looked like she came out of one of those shoe commercials: "You can do it." And Norita could. She was cured of everything.

Since she couldn't be content doing nothing, it wasn't unusual to see her carrying boxes at the bazaar when necessary. At the same time, she talked constantly to her clients about New Age, about being oneself, and when her work day ended, she devoted herself to giving massages and healing muscle cramps. She kept it up till she was able to quit the bazaar and do her own thing: massage. Also manicures and electrolysis.

That's why it was so sad when Norita fell in love with Lito, the son of Neri from the funeral home. She deserved better. A gambler, a whoremonger, a bum, Lito, old man Neri's only heir, had always avoided breaking his hump working. For me, work is death, he used to say. When old man Neri threw him out of the house, he got a gig as a bus driver on the Costamar line. It's more fun to drive a bus than a hearse, he said. Till one day at a railroad crossing near Conesa, the bus he was driving became a hearse. Lito nearly didn't make it. And old man Neri had to make a deal in court to keep Lito from being thrown in jail for negligent homicide. As if he wanted to settle down, Lito decided to get married, have a family. And he chose Norita.

Determined to find correspondences between his father's biography and his own, Elvis persisted. Presley, too, had been born as one of a pair of twins. He was born in a city in the South, though Cañadón Huelche in Santa Cruz, Patagonia, wasn't the same as Tupelo, Mississippi. He, too, was of humble origins. And his father, like the King's, had also gone to jail for a mess involving bounced checks. The fact that he'd named his daughter Lisa María, like Lisa Marie Presley, was a gesture that would surely touch his father when it came time to recognize him as his son. The lawsuit to be recognized as heir had been going on for several years now and had consumed every peso he could scrounge up. At one point, in order to keep the lawsuit going, he thought of trying his luck at Bingo. It was a terrible time for Elvis. But the greatest tragedy still remained to be seen.

Where will his funeral be, Moni asked when she found out. Because the Beast had been a student of hers in those prehistoric days of the late eighties, when the Villa was no longer a village, summers were no longer so hippie-ish, and the leftist militants, now professionals, were buying land and building. The Villa began to grow till it became this thing we are now, more than forty thousand strong. In those days, like I was saying, there was only one school, and it was more than enough; and it was around that time when Moni, who had come for the summer, decided to stay and was one of the first teachers, and Sebastián Bermúdez, like nearly all of the Bermúdez family, was her student. One of her favorites.

At Neri's, they told her. And in a closed casket. He was unrecognizable. After the failure of the first assault, and by assault we're referring to that first round he fought against Lucho "the Puma" Roldán, he left the Villa. Don't give up the ship, my ass. The morning after his defeat he took the first Rápido to Mar del Plata. When the Cannon found out that the Beast had left the Villa, he prophesied: He's gonna end up drinking *mate* with his old man in Batán Prison. The little we heard about the Beast was that at first he made a living as a male escort and then moved on to holdups. Muggings. People coming out of banks, shops. A failed jewelry-store heist. The police caught him off-guard. The Beast got into a shootout with the cops. He managed to get himself a car, a Corsa. The cops took him by surprise while he was driving it. As he fled, he crashed head-on into a truck. It left him unrecognizable.

Since the Beast's mother, María, cleaned house for Marconi the pharmacist, his wife, Valeria the Jew, intervened so that the city would lay out the cash for the kid's funeral. It was also said it was Alejo who suggested to Cachito that the right thing was for the city to take care of the funeral, a way of showing that this administration did not abandon its people; and if that's the way things really happened, if it was Alejo who suggested to Cachito that the city pay for the funeral, it logically evoked an earlier scene: Valeria, trying to help out her servant, María, and then telling Alejo, her lover, that the city should cover the costs. So by putting all the pieces together, we arrive at the conclusion that María had come crying to Valeria, her employer, and Valeria, in turn, had told Alejo, and Alejo, on his part, proposed to Cachito that the dearly departed and would-be local champion's funeral had political value, and that was how the Beast got a proper burial. María, running her fingertips across the lid of her son's casket, in a pause between bouts of sobbing, regretted having stolen that recording in which her employer and Alejo were snorting coke and fucking, and then slipping the DVD in among the clothing in a closet of the house of Cachito and Beti, sister of Marconi, the cuckolded pharmacist. How strange that the mess she had planned never came off, she said to herself. Surely Beti, on finding the recording, had hidden it and covered everything up, because that's how these snobs were: they covered everything up. What María had no way of knowing was that Gonza, Cachito's druggie kid, would be the one to find the DVD and try to blackmail Alejo, as if it were such a simple thing to extort a Quirós, as if Quirós wouldn't have called El Capo Malerba to grab that little twit by the balls, hard, once and for all. But I'm getting away from what I wanted to tell you: When she found out about the Beast's death, Moni felt awful. And she decided to write him a poem. A poem doesn't solve anything; it wouldn't bring the Beast back to life, or the son back to the mother, or anything. But at least a poem was a gesture. And there was something poetic, so Pasolini-like, about the way the boy ended up, Moni thought. Real Pasolini. The poem Moni wrote for him was short. It was called "Gladiator," and it went like this: *The gods / toyed with your fate: / You were chosen, / special, Icarus, / but the sun burned your wings / and you were / a fallen angel.* Moni slipped stealthily into Neri Funeral Home. The Beast's sisters, nieces, and nephews were there. Moni had lost count of how many Bermúdezes there were. There were neighbors from La Virgencita and El Monte. A floral wreath from the city: Cachito Administration, the banner said. Another: Quirós Family. Also a floral spray: Friends from El Atlético. Moni slipped in stealthily, practically a shadow. She wore a black head scarf. Not only was it appropriate for the situation, it concealed her gray hairs. She walked slowly over to María. María didn't budge from her spot beside the casket. Moni handed her the poem. She had written it in cursive, in purple. María took a long time reading those verses. She didn't understand them. But she didn't want to offend Moni. His name was Sebastián, Moni, she said. Not Icarus. Moni explained to her who Icarus was. Then leave it like that, said María. Thank you, she said. The poor woman had just about used up all her tears. She hugged Moni, blubbering. You were so good to him, María told her.

The Beast had a marble tombstone. A photo of him, in a bronze frame. Defiant, on guard, with gloves on, provocative. On the metal plate you could read: Sebastián "Beast" Bermúdez. Below, his dates of birth and death. Twenty-two years had gone by between one and the other. And below that, a bas-relief, also in gilded letters: Fallen Angel, it says.

Ramiro, the kiosk owner from Nuestra Señora, the one with dyed hair and an earring, and Gabriel, the athlete, were more than friends. Not only that, Gabriel had been going with Floreal Bellini, the gay lottery ticket vendor who was offed by some kids from La Virgencita two years ago. Remember how there were always protest marches calling for security. The kids were released from prison and are back around here, but that's another story. What you've gotta wonder is if, as homosexuals, they could be dumb enough to risk abusing the school kids. According to Deborah, the psychologist, sometimes those who commit this kind of crime can't stand the weight of guilt and eventually try to get caught. That they're now trying to involve Betina is totally crazy. Betina likes men. And women, too, it seems. The fact that she was close to Ramiro and Gabriel doesn't make her a degenerate. Besides, what proof did the guys from the Brigade find where they went looking. Nothing that's not tucked away in any family's dresser. A couple of dildos, some porn flicks, and weed. Besides, after all this time, *now* they come along with their search warrants.

If you ask me, politics is behind all this. The opposition that wants to kick Cachito out of office. Like we don't know that Cachito is on the board of Nuestra Señora. Of course, his name doesn't show on the membership list. But his sister's does. She's on the board of directors. Always the same story. Politics rots everything. And the ones who pay in the end are the innocents. Two little fags and a nympho.

For some time now, Malerba has been talking to himself. When he realized he wasn't talking to anybody, he felt alarmed: I'm an old coot. He had survived the wear and tear of prison life. But it wasn't going to be easy for his body to dodge illness. Cancer, diagnosed Dr. Uribe. Masking it with crack wasn't going to change things. After a while he decided not to make a big deal of the business of talking to himself. Because if he turned it into a big deal, it would be worse. He knew himself. He had always been fanatical. But now his obsessions were getting more intense. A guy has feelings, he says to his shadow on the wall. Don't get upset. A guy remembers his first dead man. Not the ones who followed. But also, over time, the memory of the first one remains in the past, and you remember him only when you have to carry out another assignment. Time takes care of fading his features. You start confusing them with the ones who came after. Then you're not remembering the dead man anymore. You're remembering what you felt for him. But this memory is tricky. Because what you think you're feeling now, now that you're about to do it to someone else, that thing you think you felt back then is what you ought to be feeling for the deceased now. The best way to stop driving yourself nuts with remorse over the first one is to take on another assignment, right away. One after another, you rack them up. Till it feels natural to you. Sometimes when I'm traveling out in the country and I find a dead little bird, I think about these things. What's a life without a little bird in the storm. You think that if God really cared, He wouldn't let them die. But what God really cares about is just keeping the population of His creation stable. In order for some to be born, others have to die. You think of a guy who does what I do as a cold killing machine, like the detective novels say. No, a guy has his feelings. And I've thought about this lots of times. I've thought to myself, I didn't choose the work I do. God put it in my path. And if I'm good at what I do, it's because God wants His will to be done. And if God decides that I've got to go, I'll go, even against my own will. No one escapes God's will. We're like little birds. Every time I find a dead one out in the country, I think about these things. Those little birds knocked down by storms break my heart.

Tell me the truth, Mimí, Braulio begged her, looking like such a loser that it broke her heart. Admit that you're fucking Brandsen, that theater guy.

You've started early with the whiskey, Mimí said to him.

Around here everything gets found out sooner or later.

It's early for whiskey. You've started laying into it early, darling.

The truth, Mimí. It's bad enough being cheated on by your wife, but by your lover . . .

I'm his student, just another one. And we're just friends.

The actor's married, you know.

So what. Yeah, Norbert is married, but he and Sol have an open marriage.

So now it's Norbert.

Well, in the theater you've got to use your body; a kind of intimacy develops. It's a matter of artistic experience, Braulio. Expressiveness, you know?

What I know is that for a month now you've been playing Meryl Streep in Casa de la Cultura, and it's been a month since we last fucked.

Don't exaggerate. Not a month. Less than that.

Look, maybe the whiskey is fogging up my head, but my dick's got a better memory than me.

Mimí closes the store. She takes Braulio by the hand. She leads him into a fitting room, loosens his belt, unzips his fly, pulls down his pants and his briefs, and blows him. This'll calm him down for a while, she thinks. Norbert drives her crazy, but she's not stupid enough to toss aside what a Kennedy can give her.

After swallowing it down, she's going to ask him to lend her a few pesos. She's got to pay Jeremías's school tuition.

We made bets on how long Lito's rebirth would last. It was hard to believe that a big old player like him, after marrying Norita and getting sucked into that New Age-y crap, had become a spiritual being. How long will it last, we wondered at Moby. And we kept on betting. Dante bet the most. And if several of us followed him in kind, there was an explanation: no one saw other people's weaknesses like Dante, no one. Dante: the editor of our dirty laundry.

Rafa arrived with the first hint of Dante's victory. Rafa works at Banco Nación. And, according to him, between the computer and the clients, they're going to ruin his back. He consulted Crespi the orthopedist. Crespi found that he had a crooked spine. What you've got is a posture problem, he told him. And he sent him to Norita for massages. Since Norita was at the gym, Lito took care of him. Rafa said it was funny to see Lito shaved bald, in a white kimono. He looked like the Japanese chef on the Gourmet Channel. And with that Vangelis type of music. He asked Rafa to get undressed and lie down on the massage table: I sleep here now, Lito said to him. The witch makes me sleep here. She closed her legs to me and threw me out of bed. Rafa asked him why. She caught me in the act, Lito said. And he told him: Here, on the table, just like you are, face down, I was banging the chick. I did it when the witch wasn't here. I was so horny for that broad that I forgot to lock the door. Just as I was giving it to her, the witch walks in, looking for some Chinese ointment. You can't imagine the scene. She killed us with tae-kwon-do.

Rafa was slightly daunted by lying on that table: Don't get upset, Lito. He stood up. And, as he dressed, he said: Nothing against you personally. But the doc told me to see Norita.

Elvis had Lisa María with Azul Estrella, that rocker who used to sing at La Cueva del Blues, a wooden, tin-roofed building where all the summer lowlifes hung out. The Rotary reported them several times for making too much noise. Once, the cops showed up, found dope, and hauled a few of them away—nearly all of them except Turulato, the owner of La Cueva. They didn't nab Turu because he had an arrangement with the cops. But not with the Rotary. And the cops couldn't avoid doing something after the fuss the Rotary made. The thing is, Azul sang at La Cueva. She had her style. But even better than her style was her bod. You've got to admit that Elvis was a hunk in those days. Well, that summer they conceived Lisa María, who was born at the hospital seven months later. As soon as she was born, Azul moved away. Your children are not your children, she quoted Khalil Gibran; they are the sons and daughters of life. You saw how everybody here quotes Gibran. When it's time for them to wash their hands of the kids, Gibran. And on to something else. Azul also told him that she had to follow her Tao: the path of rock was her Tao, infinite. And so Elvis became responsible for Lisa María, and he was as good a father as he could be, though if he had spared the child a few scenes of sex, drugs, and rock and roll, she might have turned out different. Less rockabilly and more religion—she would've been different.

Heaven is a bribe from God.

The Villa District Police Headquarters confirmed finding a fetus in the liquid sewage purification system on Calle 113, between Avenidas 1 and 3. The discovery took place yesterday afternoon, when an employee who was doing maintenance of the filtration systems found the small body. The fetus, whose sex could not be determined, measures 25 cm. long and is fully developed.

The discovery was filed as a cause-of-death investigation. The remains will be analyzed by a forensic doctor, who will call for an autopsy to determine the cause and date of death.

After Norita discovered Lito with a female patient and thrashed both of them, they didn't talk for weeks. One morning she broke the silence and announced that she had initiated divorce proceedings: she gave him twenty-four hours to find another place. Lito should have given it some thought before he cheated on her. Now Lito is once again driving the hearse for Neri Funeral Home. I'd like to go off on my own, he says. But I've got no choice, I've gotta work with the old man. There's no getting away from it: death is my thing.

You know how Elvis's sideburns turned gray after Lisa María disappeared. No, Lisa María's not his wife; she's his daughter. She's seventeen and was queen of the Villa Rockabilly Festival last year. Ever since Lisa María disappeared, Graceland has been falling apart, and when it collapses altogether, it'll fall on Elvis, and that'll be the end, almost certainly the end he's expecting. And there's nothing to be done. The Lisa María thing is killing him. And nothing comes out of his house except the music of "Can't Help Falling in Love."

Even though she was diagnosed with emphysema this winter, Doña Herminia still walks up and down the streets selling lottery tickets. She wheezes, but she won't stay indoors. She'd rather walk back and forth in the drizzle with her red plastic purse than stay at home. Seventy-ish, skinny and shriveled, in spite of her sick lung she still has the energy to walk quickly and flash an optimistic smile whenever she enters a house or a store. The first thing she asks when she arrives is: What's new in your life, *vidita*? She calls everyone *vidita*. Tell me what you dreamed last night and I'll give you your lucky number, *vidita*. She even calls the cops *vidita*. And not only do the cops turn a blind eye to her illegal trade, they bet their own lucky numbers.

Some say that Doña Herminia stays out on the street because she has lots of debts. That her little shack is in hock. And that if it weren't for her, old man Nazar and the kids, who aren't such kids anymore, because Mariana is around twenty-four and Jorgito twenty, the three of them would be out in the elements, freezing to death. It's also true that Doña Herminia doesn't stay at home because she's afraid of Nazar, her husband. Though he hasn't beaten her for a while, not since the sons grew up and stopped him once and for all with a thrashing that cost him a few ribs. They also say that Doña Herminia is out on the street because she hates seeing her husband blitzed and her sons high. They're always half gone. But it's not the drugs, some say. They've been slow since birth. Jorgito, the younger one, the dumber one, turned out that way because Nazar kicked the shit out of Herminia while she was pregnant. Their daughters, Emilia and Mariela, Claudia and Tita—the one who did all right for herself by marrying Ariel, the butcher, till one fine day she dumped him—well, like I was telling you, the four girls have been married for some time. And they say that, even more than getting married, what each one of them did was save her own hide. That's how mean Nazar is, worse than his pit bull.

This winter Doña Herminia is rushing off to Beto's butcher shop. He offers her a *mate*. Doña Herminia feels dizzy; the floor collapses under her. She falls. Beto comes to her rescue; he's about to call an ambulance.

Forget the ambulance, Doña Herminia says to him. And play number 48—it's due to come up, *vidita*.

On a Friday or Saturday after midnight, always Friday and Saturday, if there's a southeaster, it's quite a show to go down to the dock and watch the tide come in. The waves rising over and covering it. The cars parked sleepily at the shoreline, one next to another. A drive-in movie, I'd call it. But the southeaster is where the film would be. When someone rolls down a window you can sense it, you can sense the stink of weed and music: *Shine on, you crazy diamond.*

We've all got contradictions, Mimí explained to Norbert. You know I'm a Yid—only you and no one else. I tell everyone I come from a Polish Catholic family. And since Jere's father's name was Ramírez, I was able to register him at Nuestra Señora. You're a real bohemian, and as an atheist you won't understand. Besides, Jere needs a father. And you'll never leave your wife to commit to a serious relationship and all that. You might think I'm the one who needs a father for him: think whatever you want, Norbert. What's so terrible if they teach him religion? After all, like it or not, religion teaches you what's right and what's wrong. I want the boy to turn out right. And no matter how much I love the theater, I admit I'd rather have him be a doctor or a lawyer than a failed actor directing a little bunch of clowns in a small-town theater. And I'm telling you nicely, straight out. Because I adore you and I know I can't be this direct with anyone else. I adore you.

Dante recalls the afternoon when Elvis came to ask him to publish the announcement of his daughter's disappearance. Where are you, baby, Elvis wanted the caption over the photo to read. I can't put "baby," Dante told him. Why not, Elvis argued. Because I can't, Dante said. Nothing else: just that caption and the photo? What's it to you.

You, me, everybody, we all know Elvis is nuts. You have to include facts, Dante told him. For example, where she was last seen. Coming out of the temple, Elvis replies. Lisa María used to go on Tuesday and Thursday afternoons to Jesús de la Revelación. She taught gospel. Dante repeated: Gospel. Yeah, what's wrong with that, can't a seventeen-year-old kid be a gospel teacher. She loves the temple and she loves rockabilly. A star is born, Dante said. Elvis didn't get the irony. Wasn't the King of Rock called Aaron, didn't he have a Biblical name? Does rock somehow go against God? Dante tried to cut him off: Agreed, Dante said, tired of arguing. We'll put in Lisa María's photo with no last name, no facts, just: "Where are you, baby?" You got it, Elvis said. Where are you, baby. Tell me one thing, Dante asked. What, Elvis stood up. Did you file the police report, Dante asked. Get off my back with the damn cops, Elvis replied. She'll come back when I collect the inheritance. Because it's gonna come out everywhere: "Elvis, son of the King of Rock in Argentina." An inheritance worth millions, he said. With conviction, he said it. They'll see when it comes out on the front page of *Clarín*.

If Lisa María didn't matter that much to Elvis, Dante thought, why should he worry?

Tonight, as Cachito takes out the garbage, a black dog comes along. Cachito wants to touch it. The dog backs away, growls at him, bares its teeth. Cachito stares it in the face, growling back. I'm your mayor, too, asshole, he tells it. And he growls again. The dog lowers its head and walks away, frightened. That's the way I am, Cachito thinks. No one messes with my garbage.

According to the dictionary, *cave* comes from the Latin *cava* and is related to hollow. It's also related to *cavity*, an empty space or hole. Around here, when autumn comes, especially after Holy Week, when the last tourist goes home, even though it might still officially be autumn, for us it's the first day of winter lethargy, and not just because here the seasons arrive too soon. That's when we hole up. Each one in his own cave, whether it's an imposing California-style chalet, an unpretentious one-story house, or a shack. Although we may think we know everything about everyone, it's not true. People think they know who's screwing who, who's doing drugs and who they buy from, who's offering bribes and who's taking them, who's about to kill himself, who's about to kill someone else and who his victim will be, though it might be the other way around, the victim might really be the assassin. People think they know, but deep down, nobody knows. Because each one stays holed up in his cave in the depths of winter and the depths of his soul, since the soul is the real cave where people hide the shame they'll never reveal, not even to their own shadow. On these drizzly mornings, afternoons, and nights, when the fallen leaves rot in the dampness of the forest and there's not even a street dog to be seen, if it weren't for the smell of firewood emanating from some chimney, you'd say the Villa is uninhabited. Not even the thugs are around. You've got to take courage against the cold, the forecast of falling temperatures and below-zero weather. Silence intensifies the desolation that weighs on the chest of anyone who goes around alone at night, scurrying, the only pedestrian, crossing a deserted street. No one looks out a window if something happens, a scream, a gunshot. What was that, honey. Nothing. Turn up the TV, Beto. It's drizzling.

More than once Moni has thought of suicide. Then she jots down things like this: *To arrive at a place without a name. What I find will not be in the realm of words. It will not be language. At last I will be a non-being.*

Why did Brandsen throw Mimí out of the La Marea theater group, you ask. According to his version of the story, it was because of her lack of talent. One night at Moby he explained how the girl was more qualified to be a model than an actress, although she had a few too many years on her to be a model. Keeping in mind how hot Mimí is, with that dick-sucking face of hers and that amazing bod, I don't believe the old girl left the group just because she thought she could become the new Graciela Alfano. Don't shit me—that's not why you kicked her out, Dante said. You could predict it would cause big trouble to steal a chick from a Kennedy.

One morning Barbeito el Gallego showed up at the place: Look, man, I got nothing against your sideburns or against rock or against Elvis. I like Julio Iglesias, too, but I'm not a fanatic. The rent you owe me, cough it up. Have a little patience, Gallego. I'm gonna collect my inheritance soon. You know who my old man was.

Barbeito's understanding was all used up. Your goddamn inheritance, my ass. Look at me, I'm the fucking heir to the Spanish throne, see? But I don't stop paying my taxes. And if you don't move out, the next step'll be a lawsuit.

There were two of them. Wearing hoods. Waiting for me. As soon as I walked into the house, they came out of the darkness and pointed a gun at me. Keep your mouth shut. Once we got inside, they started giving it to me. They kicked me while I was down on the floor. One hit me in the head with the pistol. I couldn't see through the blood. The other one took my Rolex, my ring. Tied me up with wire. My wrists and ankles. My circulation was cut off. Where's the safe, they asked me. They went through everything, the drawers; they took stuff. One of them grabbed the frame with my daughter's picture. He looked at Luli. She's a tough kid. If she shows up, you'll see. I told them I only had two thousand pesos in the house. We could go to La Tranquera, I suggested. To my store, I told them; I've got four thousand more there. They kicked me again. It's just that I usually deal with credit cards, I said. More kicks. Please don't let Luli get home early, I prayed. Luli had gone to a birthday party and wouldn't be back till dawn, for sure. Go find an iron, said the other guy. This guy could use a pressing, a nice, nice little pressing. I couldn't see through the blood. I heard the other one rifling through stuff, opening drawers, turning them upside down. Don't let my wife or my little girl come now, I prayed. Here's the iron. If they lay one finger on Luli and they don't kill me, I'll get those two motherfuckers if I have to go to the ends of the earth, their families, their kids, their dogs, I'll kill 'em all. I prayed my wife wouldn't come, either. You'll change your mind when we iron the girl's tits. I couldn't speak; my mouth was dry. Where's the cash. Just then the car engine, the headlights. It was Celina. But she could see the hooded guy's shadow and she backed up. One of them left the house. I heard Celina screaming. She was crying for help. All the dogs in the neighborhood began to bark. Celina told me later that the hooded guy grabbed her by the hair, trying to pull her out of the car. He yanked out whole clumps of it. Celina hit the gas with the guy hanging onto her hair. She crashed into a tree. Then one of them yelled: Let's get outta here; it's fucked. Before he left he kicked me in the back of the head. And I don't remember anything else. When I reacted, Celina was grabbing her head. Look at my hair, she cried. My new extensions. Can you believe that?

Did you notice that nowadays they don't say kid, brat, or squirt. They say youngster. Faggoty, old-world talk. Well, whatever, I heard that just recently one of them, like four or five years old, a little blond, limped out of the forest crying, no pants, his bloodied little butt exposed. All we need now is for them to blame the gnomes.

You know why this place will never progress. Because of cross-breeding. Here we've had the worst kind: gauchos cross-breeding with hippies.

The investigation of the cases of abuse at Nuestra Señora del Mar Institute once again has changed direction. Following the resignation of district attorney Salcedo, the last DA in charge, Dr. Diego Arocena, DA of the Decentralized Office of Tuyú, will now take over. The case has already gone through the hands of three district attorneys; this is the fourth time such a change has been implemented.

On this torrentially rainy morning, before opening his office, before downing a breakfast consisting of three double-espressos to clear up his hangover, before shaving and showering, before getting out of bed, with Lourdes between him and Susi, because there's not a single night when Lourdes doesn't crawl into the marriage bed, before he's fully awake, realizing that he was dreaming of Mimí, that she wasn't fucking him, but rather Brandsen, and he was sitting on the nightstand, watching Brandsen giving it to Mimí in the ass, and he laughed at Braulio jerking off, and then he woke up with his dick like a tree trunk; as he stirs himself awake he figures that if he carries the child to her room, she'll surely wake up, and even if she doesn't, by the time he gets back to bed, Susi won't even want to think about a morning quickie, and so he slowly begins to whack off. And, as usual when he fucks Susi or jerks off, Braulio thinks about Mimí. What worries him most as he jerks off is that Lourdes might wake up, but the child is sleeping like an angel, or rather, like a fairy. Lourdes is a fairy, Braulio thinks as he jerks off. And he closes his eyes, concentrating on Mimí. He finishes with great effort. Too much effort for a mere trickle.

He gets up, tiptoes quietly to the bathroom, shaves, showers, makes his coffee; already on the second cup, he's overcome by uneasiness. He doesn't recognize himself in the house, the silence weighs on his chest, he feels guilty and doesn't know why, sadness overwhelms him, and he discovers Susi standing at the kitchen door.

Why are you crying, she asks.

I'm not crying.

It's not fair, Braulio. It's not fair at all for you to suffer over that bitch. She's consuming you.

What are you talking about.

You know who, that chick from the boutique.

You're crazy. There's no chick.

Susi grabs the roll of paper towels, peels one off, wipes her husband's tears and makes him blow his nose.

Elvis had to close the Heartbreak Broken Appliance Hotel after receiving several official letters sent to him by Barbeito el Gallego, the property owner. We, his friends, took up a collection for his air-fare to North America. He was prepared to go all the way to claim his inheritance, he said.

And it was then that the greatest tragedy, the final blow, the kidney punch, the fatal bullet, struck. He received a document from the United States informing him that his lawsuit had been dismissed and that he had to pay costs for libel. The document was issued by the law firm representing Lisa Marie Presley. Our Elvis had turned out to be one of so many thousands of guys who go around bragging that they're the sons of the King. Though we tried to dissuade him, even when he'd hit bottom, Elvis was prepared to travel to the U.S. He would sell the De Soto, if necessary. It broke our hearts to see him crumble and scream all at once, because Elvis was up and down all the time. Then we took up the collection. I still wonder if we didn't give him the dough just so we wouldn't have to see him anymore. And we didn't. We never saw him again. The house, Graceland, became the property of Quirós Realty and is up for sale. The De Soto is still there. Rusty piece of junk. Someone spread the rumor that he was in Quilmes, that he had gone back to his roots, that he once more had set up an appliance repair shop, audio and video. But he never came back here, to his Memphis.

Nobody ever heard a word about Lisa María, either.

There are so many who disappear one day and are never heard from again.

Cachito swore to me up and down that he would make every effort. That he would get them, he gave me his word. Cachito Calderón is one of La Tranquera's best customers. What do I care if he's with the Peronist Party. It would be the same to me if he were with the Radicals. Barbecues have no ideology. Family dinners, birthdays, anniversaries, celebrations—Cachito asks me to organize them all for him. Once a week he comes to the grill to eat. Along with the members of the City Council. For me, solving your problem is a matter of State, he told me. I give you my word of honor. I'm even bringing in the forensic police for you, Luciano. The thing is, a week after the robbery the Brigade nabbed one of them. He had been in the joint for eight years. There was a murder pending. They hunted him down in La Virgencita. They found my Rolex and the ring on him. The other one's still at large. But they've got him, Cachito told me. They've got him. No matter how many hoodies they wore, we've identified them, Cachito said triumphantly. The ones they didn't catch were the real hoodies, I said to him. Those responsible.

Cachito looked at me with that angelic face he knows how to put on when it suits him.

The shysters, I said. Or are you going to tell me they're not in cahoots with a legal firm around here. And you know who I'm talking about, Cachito.

You can't do everything, Luciano, he told me. Sometimes settling a little is even good for your health.

Sitting under the overhang of the beach-cabana rental office, the man picks his teeth, digging out bits of food and spitting them out. If only we could do the same with the past. Clouds are rolling in from the southeast. And he keeps on picking his teeth.

People love to tell of their own misfortunes, and especially those of others. Luciano shows up and says: You'll never guess what happened to me. When someone comes out with "You'll never guess what happened to me," nowadays you rarely expect it to be something good. Then he tells about the robbery, the guys in hoodies, and to keep from crying, he laughs at his wife, at the hair she lost when the thug yanked it. But what happened to him, happened, and it sucks.

The scene takes place off-stage. La Casa de la Cultura Theater is deserted. Except for Brandsen and Mimí. They begin by speaking softly, but then the conversation grows louder. It's not a conversation. They're arguing. From the way they act, it might seem like they're rehearsing, but it's not a rehearsal and it's not voice training, either. And if it's not yours, whose would it be, Mimí asks him. I haven't fucked anyone else in over a month, Mimí says. Annoyed, Norbert smiles, a nervous smile, a smile halfway between cynical and frightened, if, in fact, a smile can be all that at the same time.

What about Braulio, he asks her. Or are you going to tell me you only fucked me. Don't be a bastard, Mimí says. Ever since I hooked up with you, I've stopped sleeping with him; I called it quits. I'm almost sixty, Mimí. And if I haven't had kids till now, he starts to say, without finishing the sentence. 'Cause you're an egotist, Mimí interrupts him. Sol didn't want any either, Norbert says. Another egotist, she says. You didn't want any because you only thought of yourselves. Norbert tries to stop her: And what about you? he asks. You'll try to tell me you had it for love. Kids aren't born out of love. They're born by accident. We're all children of fate. Stardust. Nice monologue, Mimí says. But I'm the one with the baby bump. Now Norbert's smile is neither nervous, cynical, nor frightened. It's a hard, sarcastic smile. A smile can be these two things. It won't make any difference to Braulio to pay two tuitions, he says. Mimí stares at him intently. A long time. And then she kicks him in the balls.

The other day Teddy, Susi's cousin, came to visit us. The pilot. He's living in Hong Kong now. He works for a third-rate airline financed by British capital. He told us that, unlike us, the Hong Kongese never start a sentence with the word no. They consider it impolite. They'll always start with a yes, even if later they tell you, politely, that they can't or don't want to or they won't whatever it is they're doing, saying, asking for, or receiving. Look how we talk, look at all the times we say no like a catchphrase.

Don't tell me I'm wrong.

Déjà vu can happen to anyone. And anyone it's happened to can recognize it instantly. It's more than the sensation of having lived something before. It's the disturbing sensation that history is repeating itself and, at the same time, that it's impossible for this to be happening. You don't need to finish telling me what you're saying or what's going to happen to me. It already happened. And I've been in this place before.

It's hard for Braulio to look him in the eyes. Julián speaks to him in a soft voice: Look, little bro, he says, there's only one way to get out of this mess. And it's for you to give up booze. You've got to accept it. You can start from scratch. Others have. You've got a wife who loves you. Matías, Nico, and Lourdes are precious children. Your family's here for you. Alejo's here, I'm here. We're gonna help you, Julián says to him, wanting to sound convincing.

Braulio considers the glass of whiskey he has before him on the table in the corner of Poker. Booze, probably, I can give up. But Mimí: doubtful. Mimí, I don't think so. And less now than ever. I love her, Julián.

Did you talk to Alejo, Julián asks.

I didn't have the nerve, Braulio says. And Julián notices it: his brother is at once ashamed and afraid. I don't want Alejo to find out.

Alejo always finds out.

It won't be from me, Julián says. I give you my word.

A baby bump isn't something you can hide very long, Braulio says. He downs his whiskey. He orders another. And, after a silence: Everyone knows that Mimí and I have been a couple for a long time.

Brandsen's fucking her, too, Julián says. And he quickly regrets being confrontational. But it's the best thing: confrontation. Nothing like a good scare to make a drunk react, he thinks. And he hopes now Braulio will react.

It's mine, Braulio says.

How do you know.

Because I know.

My ass. Yours, my ass. You want to believe it's yours because it suits you. That way you feel less like a cuckold.

You sound like Alejo.

Luciano can't stop talking about the robbery. And when he talks about it, he shows the scar that was left on his head. If I woulda had a piece on me that night, he says. But it won't happen to me again. Just let them come now. He winks. I'm waiting for them. And he shows his friends at La Tranquera a pistol, a Glock, which he keeps in the cash register of the store. And at home, another Glock. And also, like in *The French Connection*, he smiles and rolls up his pant leg, because in his leg holster is a 38. Let's see if they'll try anything now. I'm not the kind to go out and fire a few shots to alert the neighborhood. No, now I'll wait for them quietly. No way am I going to take the pills Moure gave me. You're suffering from post-traumatic shock, he told me. I don't want to be tranquilized, I told him. I don't want to get a wink of sleep. I want to be awake, Luciano says.

Then what had to happen, happens. Early yesterday morning he hears someone at the door, gets up, see a shadow, shoots at it. And he kills Luli. He lets loose a scream that terrifies the neighborhood. Then, over his daughter's body, he shoots himself.

It was last night.

If you want to go, the funerals are being held at Neri's.

The Virignias, the two of them like to be called. You've got to have a contact, but it's not complicated. The Virginias have more than one contact. You call a cell number and they answer right away. If Pancho Dotto gets them, he makes them model for him. Of course, first you've got to clean them up. They're half-breeds, you know. If they're that hot in their natural state, just imagine what they're like all cleaned up. You call, and they come right away. Like us. Friday night. The three of us were there: El Cholo, Andrés, and me. We were at Migue's apartment; he's a pig. For him, every hole's fair game. But it wasn't his idea. It was El Cholo, who's married. C'mon, Moro, he said to me, don't be a pussy. We had just finished putting the sweetbreads on the grill when El Cholo came up with the idea for the party. We called them. They showed up. On a Kawasaki. Real biker broads. We ate. Finished all the tripe. We drank. Five bottles of Don Valentín, because Andrés likes to drink fancy wine. We chit-chatted. Two ladies, those girls. They asked for Cokes. We didn't have any. Water, then. Darkies, but ladies. Sisters, at least that's what they told us. We asked them how much. They said two hundred apiece. Six hundred total. One hundred a head, we told them. A hundred fifty, they said. The haggling began. Fine. One hundred, we stood firm. Three hundred for all three. Without a rubber, they explained, the price is different. Without a rubber the price went up. And what about the *asado*, we asked. The *asado* counts for something. Three fifty. Andrés brought over some champagne. Okay, we said. They drank champagne. I'll use a rubber, Andrés said. I'm engaged, he explained. Ooh, faggot, we said. Four hundred and it's a deal. All three of you. Fine. And so, after the *asado* we got down to business. Never with two of us at the same time. We're not fags. One at a time. We tossed a coin to see who would go first. I came in last. When we were finished with all that, we popped open another bottle of champagne. And after a while, in less than two hours, they left. We stood there looking at each other when we heard the cycle take off. Real pretty girls. Nice. One Virginia cleans houses and goes to middle school at night. The other Virginia works at a kiosk down south and also goes to school. Computers, she told us. First rate, the Virginias. They almost had us falling in love with them, I'm telling you. I'm not kidding, they're good enough to marry. But if you marry one of them you have to leave the Villa. Not me; no way, man. The quality of life here is something I won't give up. Here: I'll give you their number.

It was almost one. Who could it be at that time of night: a car stopped in front of her chalet. Mimí wasn't even expecting him. She had just been helping Jere with his homework, and now she was glued to the TV, watching *The Bridges of Madison County*. That movie really got to her. The same parts always brought her to tears. And Mimí liked to cry during those parts. Because that way she could cry for what she couldn't cry over in real life. She was capable of getting knocked up and kicking a jerk like Brandsen in the balls, but not of shedding a tear. She'd always gotten along on her own. And she would find a way out of this disaster, too, she thought, touching her belly. Jere was sound asleep. She wondered what the hell Alejo was doing at her house. They had fucked before she hooked up with Braulio. Out of respect for Braulio, Alejo had said to her. We've got to knock it off. But you're the one who turns me on, she'd told him. I don't care what turns you on, girl. What I care about is my family. And Mimí stayed with Braulio. Maybe that's why she had no respect for him. Because she'd settled for the tuition payments at Nuestra Señora, the taxes, and the credit card. For a moment Mimí fantasized. Maybe now after so many years had gone by, Alejo was finally fed up with screwing the pharmacist's wife and would come back to her.

The black Mercedes braked silently. A black Mercedes. The only person in the Villa with a black Mercedes got out of the car. He didn't need to knock on the door. Mimí opened it for him. Alejo entered with the cold night air and a whiff of Hugo Boss. She noted that even in his choice of cologne, Alejo was a higher roller than his younger brother, Braulio, who never got beyond Colbert Noir. Hugo Boss, right? Mimí asked.

He wasn't there to waste time: You and I know each other, Mimí. I'm gonna make you an offer you can't refuse, kid, he said to her. First, you get rid of the fetus. Second, you get the hell out of my Villa. And third, you stop seeing Braulio. And if I find out you've come back looking for him, that kid of yours could have a bad time of it. A traffic accident, imagine. His whole life with a prosthetic leg. It's not fair. Think of a number. There'll be no problem with the amount. Tomorrow you'll come by my office after ten; I'll be there by myself. In dollars, he said. Euros, if you prefer. Spain's a good place. And that's that.

You're a son-of-a-bitch.

Think, Mimí. For once in your life, think of your kid.

The kids were getting out of school and, like always, when they passed by Rouco's place, they teased the pit bull. They threw stones at her, yelled at her, eliciting terrifying barks. Rouco went to the middle school to complain. But you know what kids are like. They never learn till there's a tragedy. And that noon, Rouco had let the dog loose on purpose.

Owners end up resembling their dogs. And the pit bull was the canine incarnation of Rouco. So many things have been said about Rouco. What we know for sure is that he collected a pension from the army. It happened like this: When the kids went by the chalet, the dog attacked. One kid's throat was torn open immediately. Relentless, that pit bull. She grabbed another kid by the back of the head. Neighbors came out to see, men and women. With crowbars, knives, one ridiculous lady with a broomstick. Miguez with a revolver that didn't work. The men sent the women back inside. But they didn't go near the pit bull. Minetti had the guts to try. When the pit bull jumped him, he barely had time to cover his face. Laureano tried to grab her by the collar. Impossible. They said that Rouco was enjoying the show from behind a window. He emerged only when Otero showed up with an ax. The pit bull lunged angrily at Laureano. Otero's ax missed, splitting Laureano's head wide open. Then the dog went for Otero. He fell with the bitch still latched onto him. Just then a shot was heard. And another. The second one killed the pit bull. But it was too late for Otero. Rouco said he had tried to hit the dog. So much blood, all over the place. We surrounded Rouco.

Aiming at us, he retreated into his house. Someone brought gasoline. We were going to set his house on fire. Then we heard another gunshot. The explosion paralyzed us. Silence. We thought Rouco had done himself in. But no. He took us by surprise. The 4x4 zoomed off at full speed. Some people headed for their cars, trying to follow him. Of course, by the time the cops showed up, as usual, it was too late. The tally: Not counting Laureano and Otero, two dead kids and three in intensive care. And their prognosis doesn't leave much room for hope. We never heard of Rouco again. You remember the pit bull's name: Eugenia. He named her after his ex.

One Thursday morning Dante read the news in the "No" supplement of *Página/12*: Lisa María and the Gospel Heartbreakers, the group led by new female rock sensation, was about to launch its first album at the Hard Rock Bar in Vicente López. It wasn't hard for him to recognize the girl's photo. He thought of Elvis. That morning, though it was still early, he went over to Poker and ordered half a whiskey, straight. And he toasted. Alone.

After the night of the tragedy, Celina looked like her own older sister. She aged ten years in a few days. Although not pretty, at age forty-plus she was sexy and pleasant, charming. She always had a sharp retort to any snide remark. Besides, she was always very courteous to each one of us who came to eat at La Tranquera. She'd always ask about our kids, our wives, our jobs. And she always had a saying, a proverb. In fact, when La Tranquera closed down, we missed Celina as much as Luciano, who had the habit of giving a discount to locals. What we would miss the most, let's be honest, was the best barbecue around.

Don't be a dickhead; there are more and more people in the Villa with the plague. Don't be surprised if one morning we all wake up with the virus. And yet we still keep screwing non-stop like someone who walks along, trying to go unnoticed.

Three dangerous minors escape from Batán and guards are charged with dereliction of duty, *El Vocero* reported today. The great escape took place at the Batán Receiving Center for Minors. This time there were three dangerous hoodlums who fled. One of them has been charged with murdering his father, another with sexual abuse and battery, and the third with several aggravated armed robberies. As for the parricide, the Police report that he can be recognized by his tattoos. The most notorious of these, on his forehead, is a tiger. Following their escape, the three youths may have chosen separate hiding places. It is suspected that the tattooed parricide may have sought refuge in our Villa.

We thought that Celina would fall apart after Luciano and Luli's deaths, that the psychiatrist, Dr. Bloch, and the church, even with Father Beltrán's assistance, wouldn't be able to get through to her. Neither drugs nor prayers helped Celina recover.

You know what happens with mourning. As is often the case in these situations, at first everyone commiserates with you. Then the parade of well-wishers starts to dwindle. Lots of women surrounded Celina. Later there were fewer and fewer. Even a sister who came from La Plata to stay with her for a while finally left. And we don't know what would have become of her if not for that agreement between Dr. Bloch and Father Beltrán. The psychiatrist insisted that she go to the beauty parlor to spruce herself up a little, to give herself something nice to look at in the mirror, unless she wanted to let herself die. Unless you want to kill yourself like your husband did, he said. Maybe that doctor was right, the priest thought. No one has the right to take his own life. And what she was doing was taking hers away. Father Beltrán thought Dr. Bloch's recommendations were a good idea. That she should go to the beauty parlor.

Celina took him up on his suggestion. She went to the beauty parlor. She had her head shaved. Sinéad O'Connor style. And she disappeared off the face of the map. Later we found out. We heard it from Alejo Quirós. She had left him a power of attorney See how crazy broads are? It's understandable: what happened to her was enough to drive anybody nuts. But you really have to be off your rocker. We might've bet that she'd sell everything and take off for the Caribbean. But no: with what she collected from the sale of the house in Pinar del Norte and from La Tranquera, she went to Pakistan. She looks after beggars in Lahore. Anyway, if she wanted to play Mother Teresa, she could've started around here. With all those sick kids, dying of hunger, in La Virgencita and El Monte.

Police sources report a raid on a house in the neighborhood of La Virgencita where Umbanda rituals were being practiced. There they apprehended Pai Egidio Gonçalvez, accused of having sexual relations with at least six women, who, according to testimony collected by this newspaper, after having their hair literally washed by Gonçalvez, were forced into prostitution and threatened with inescapable harm. Commissioner Balmaceda of the Regional Police Force denied that any human remains were found at the back of the house or that the hair washing was performed using human blood. The ceremonies, he declared, were carried out with animal sacrifices, especially chickens and goats.

The one who was connected to the Umbandas was Lidia, the wife of Vignatti the Dago. The Dago, you know who I mean: the master builder, the one who put up who knows how many little houses in the south. That's how the Dago made a pile of dough, by building on the cheap. His wife, Lidia, or rather his ex, got involved with Pai Egidio. After nearly ten years of dating and nearly thirty of marriage, the Dago and Lidia hit bottom. All because of what happened with Víctor, the kid. He was studying architecture in Buenos Aires. One time the parents go to visit him, and they find him sharing the apartment with a darkie. It was a blow for the Dago. Besides dropping out of school, his kid turns out to be a fag. It's your fault, the Dago blamed Lidia. You always spoiled him. If you'd have left him to me, tough love. But that didn't happen. I should've brought that faggot up the way my old man did with me. Now the Dago recalled his father, a pig-headed Calabrese. The father hammered nails into a piece of wood so that they'd poke out the other side. Sort of like a fakir's board. And when one of his children disobeyed him, he made him kneel on the nails. The kids had to kneel there for a long time. The Dago can still show you the scars on his knees. Vignatti and Lidia argued fiercely. One night she pushed him away: My desire is gone, Lidia said to Vignatti. And who told you you've got to have desire, he replied. He turned over and couldn't sleep all night. Contritely, the Dago told the story.

She accused me of being an animal. Besides, I couldn't sleep a wink, thinking about the kid. You know what it is to think how you fed him, brought him up, how you busted your ass so he'd have a better life than yours, and he goes around sucking dicks, offering up his asshole. I could picture him, I swear to God, with his mouth full of jism. And I cried to myself. You don't understand him, Lidia said to me. You're a materialist. If being spiritual means eating cock like your son, I said, I thank God for the father I had, with all his defects. That's when she closed her legs to me. Not even Yemanyá will save you, she told me.

You ask me why they all come here, those who come and those who keep on coming. I'll tell you—they come for what they want and can't have somewhere else: easy cash and a good time. They think they can live from tourism, two months of ripping people off and ten of scratching their asses. Of course, the majority fail. And the minority, those who say they've succeeded, are lying to you and to themselves. Because their little dream fulfilled is a deformed imitation of what they wanted. Rough drafts, that's what we are. And then if you ask me why those who come for what they want and don't get stay here anyway, I'll tell you: they stay, we stay—I include myself—because we get used to being what we are. And we even get a little kick out of failing. Resignation has its advantages. It forces you to accept your limitations, to settle, and to blame the next guy. Deep down, failure is a consolation. Those who accept it most are the ones who tell you that at least they tried. It's that simple. The thing is, nobody wants to admit it.

Dante titled the article: "Gunman brought down." He was careful to avoid making the article look like he was sucking up to the police. Succinctly he wrote: *Gabriel Oviedo, 29, identified as one of the two hoodlums who broke into the house of Luciano Ferrando, a dear neighbor from our community, attempted to escape from the police vehicle transporting him to Dolores. Agents took down the delinquent, preventing him from fleeing.*

Dante owed the headline to Commissioner Balmaceda.

Don't put "shot" in the headline, Dante. Put something elegant, for example: *Brought down while attempting to flee.* The main thing is to make it very clear that we were fulfilling a general wish of the whole Villa.

Ah, I forgot. You missed the mark with the Umbandas, Dante, Commissioner Balmaceda now says. Do you really want me to tell you what we found?

Early this morning a gang of unidentified minors, presumably residents of La Virgencita, broke into the Pinar del Norte home of Norberto Brandsen and Sol Vargas, our celebrated promoters of the theater group La Marea. The vandals were especially brutal with Brandsen, beating him fiercely with blunt instruments that disfigured his face. His partner, Sol, received a vicious cut on the right side of her face, which will require a complex plastic surgery procedure unavailable in our country. Before leaving the home, the group of approximately ten attackers ransacked the house, making off with the equivalent of five thousand U.S. dollars in cash, jewelry, and other valuable objects. Just moments before escaping, one of the attackers, a minor, fired a 357-caliber pistol at the theater director's legs.

A deplorable act of violence that occurs repeatedly in our community and which, in this case, especially affects our image. As is well known, for the last few weeks the La Marea theater couple has been rehearsing a free adaptation of A Midsummer's Night Dream *by British playwright William Shakespeare, which was to be our Villa's entry in the annual Latin American Theater Festival in Córdoba.*

Sadly but understandably, La Casa de Cultura announced that theater classes and other activities have been suspended until further notice.

That's what I say, someone pronounced. Weapons are the devil's work. Now, just between us, my humble opinion on the matter, and I'm almost convinced of what I'm about to say, is that if instead of shooting the daughter, Luciano had shot the witch, he wouldn't have offed himself.

It wasn't just because the kid turned out a fag that Lidia and I stopped getting along, Vignatti the Dago says. The Umbandas had a lot to do with it. They filled my wife's head, he said. Lidia was different before she went to that Pai Egidio's macumbas. Suddenly my house filled up with candles and incense. Everywhere, candles. Who died here, if I may ask, I said to Lidia. My love, she said. One night in May, very cold, Lidia gets it into her head to dress all in white, puts on some crystal necklaces with little blue stones, grabs some candles, and leaves. I don't ask her where she's going. I follow her. She goes to the sea.

Deathly cold. But all the girls are dressed in white, loose and flowing. All of them around a bonfire where the Pai is making signs to the stars. The guys, too. And they're singing, like Indians around a campfire. The wind whips the flames. Vignatti the Dago, from a sand dune behind some tamarisk trees, spies on the ritual. They looked like they had epilepsy, he recalls. There were some darkies, too. They were playing bongos.

But what got me the most wasn't seeing Lidia dancing the macumba. What got me was that, like her, there was a bunch of familiar faces. Some from the Rotary, others from the German Association, from the Spanish Center. A councilman and his wife. Two of the Kennedy women, as well. And that Pai dude, working them like a capo puppeteer.

I went back home crying. At what point did my kid turn queer, I asked myself. At what point. At what point did Lidia start to go nuts. Where had I been, that I just found out? At the construction site, from dawn till dusk, working like an animal. And while I was building houses for others, I thought, my own was falling down. A queer kid. A crazy wife. Without a doubt, I was cursed. Someone had cast the evil eye on me.

I've made up my mind. I've gotta see a witch. They tell me La Comadre is good.

What do you guys think.

I don't remember who told us that Julián initially accompanied Braulio to the little school. He took him there, like a kid. For a few months Braulio laid off the booze. But then he started hitting the bottle again. Now he was going to the Tropicana. According to him, the hookers came out cheaper than a boutique clerk.

The last we heard of Mimí was through Barbeito el Gallego, who goes to Spain every year. Mimí was in Barcelona. It seems she had tracked down Jere's father, the son of Spaniards, and had applied for citizenship. She'd gotten a job at Zara. It was hard for Jere to adjust. But he was going to turn out all right, she said. Although she had found a job, Mimí wasn't satisfied with her situation and kept going to auditions.

Although it came out in *El Vocero* that the bones found in the Umbandas' house were from animals, the rumor that they belonged to human beings, specifically babies, settled over the Villa like a fog. People also started saying that they were Bolitas, Bolita babies. Babies had disappeared from Copacabana, the Bolita neighborhood. So those baby bones might well have been from Bolitas. The rumor lasted a couple weeks. Not much longer. Because it wasn't a big deal. You're not gonna tell me that Bolita babies are more important than the kids from Nuestra Señora. It's like, after that mess about the burned Bolita, people became more sensitive to these things. C'mon, man, if *El Vocero* says that they were animal bones, it has to be true.

Falling in love, passion, all the things that concern love, are always in motion, changing. Like the dunes. That's why they're called living dunes. And the reason: because they change location and shape with the wind. In the same way, we go from one bout of horniness to another, and what we feel changes appearance all the time: today you might get it up for the chubby, big-assed supermarket checkout clerk, and tomorrow for that skinny chick who works in the kiosk at the bus station. The same thing happens to them: they might be hot for the lifeguard at the beach cabana rental station around the corner, and the next day they're madly in love with a greengrocer. And married or single, it doesn't matter. No one's responsible, bro. It's because of the wind. Tell me, does it ever occur to you to judge the wind, the dunes. They're a part of nature. And it's a known fact that the force of nature is uncontrollable. From autumn on, it's been proven, the winds start up. And in winter, the cold enters the picture along with the wind. Then not only do the dunes change their shape; so do we. No one is sufficiently protected from the wind. And when the first signs of warmth arrive, they're followed by consequences: the first baby bumps. Who could this one or that one be from. Knocked up by the wind.

Malerba says he was already a capo before his military service. That year I spent down south only made me depressed. Everything reminded me of reform school. The hookers at the whorehouse were pathetic. Just as well I started fucking a young dude. In exchange he asked me for protection. To shield him from the others. One day I'll pay you back, he told me. His name was Gorriti. A kid from a good family, a law student. He loaned me books. Thanks to him, I'm a pretty cultured guy. Gorriti became a judge. And he paid me back the favor from the military. He managed to get me a reduced sentence.

Last Monday afternoon police carried out a spectacular deployment to arrest members of a family of delinquents in a residence located at the intersection of Calles 115 and 15. The family is known for having racked up court cases and for enjoying the benefits of being out on parole. The legal category under which they were finally arrested was "concealment aggravated by recidivism." This means that several robberies have been committed, and no matter how sure we are of who might have done them, we have no evidence to detain him, declared Assistant Commissioner Balmaceda. In the case of this family, when we raided the residence we found, in addition to fugitive individuals with outstanding warrants, a number of objects from several robberies. Another suspect in this case is a minor, a fifteen-year-old female, arrested some time ago, when a brawl broke out at her birthday party, resulting in the murder of one of her suitors. The minor is considered to be extremely dangerous and is suspected of various violent crimes, including four murders.

Seagulls, sparrows, larks, hummingbirds, ravens, crows, parrots, frigatebirds, vultures, doves, cardinals.

Before, Dante often came to the Chess Players' Circle. Before. He even managed to qualify for a championship, representing us in a tournament in Mar del Plata. At night, after closing up the newspaper office, he would come. He smoked, drank tea. He didn't budge from the chessboard. One cigarette after another, one cup of tea after another, and on to the next game. They say chess can become a vice.

That seemed to be his case. One time Pedroza challenged him to play for money. Dante refused. Pedroza goaded him. Dante accepted. Reluctantly, unwillingly, he accepted. We remember that night. He cleaned him out, even his house. When he got up from the table, at daybreak, Dante said to him: I don't want anything of yours. I don't want to have anything to do with you or with guys like you.

And Pedroza stopped coming. Dante comes less often, but he comes. To watch. But he doesn't play anymore.

Once we asked him where he learned. And he talked to us about his father. There was a bar on Avenida de Mayo. It had a long basement. He would go downstairs with his father. Dante remembered the fog of tobacco. The silence cut by the slap of hands on the timers on the tables. He remembered hands supporting chins. He remembered their expressions. He remembered their eyes, glued to the chess pieces. His father was a regular there. One night he beat Najdorf. That night was remembered long afterward as the Night of the Englishman. They used to call my old man the Englishman. His father, he said, imported English porcelain. A good job. A big, old house in Devoto.

My old man got stoked up. He started playing for money. One day he threw himself under the subway train. He left us out in the street. I was a student at an Irish school. Where I met Rodolfo Walsh. He was a few years older than me. I played a lot of chess with Rodolfo.

But this part of the story, we realize, is a ploy by Dante to change the subject. And forget the previous story. Anyway, who knows if what he says about Walsh, as we believe, isn't just another one of his lies.

The thing is, Debi busts my balls because she's an intellectual. If I want to ream out the kids, I'm a fascist. If I want to watch the game, I'm a dumb fuck. If I want to fart, I don't give a damn about ecology. I swear to you, if I leave her, I'll find myself a girl from Paraguay.

On the coldest, grayest days, you can see Moni wandering around among the tombstones in the Angelitos section. She goes around and around. She stops, jots something down in her notebook and starts wandering around again. There are moments when she pauses at a tombstone to read an epitaph. It's no use: she can't find the right turn of phrase for the poem she's trying to write. Until Don Gauderio, the gravedigger, informs her that it's closing time. It's getting dark, señora. Moni resists leaving. But she obeys. When she leaves, Don Gauderio lights the first lanterns. Some tombstones, the ones that have a bronze plaque, a photo protected by glass, give off reflections. Moni can't stop thinking about Santiago and Paloma. How long has it been since her kids called her or sent her an email. Nothing. As if she were dead to them. Surely that must be what's blocking her inspiration for the poem. Suddenly she has an idea. Maybe if she tries on a sunny morning, her mind will clear.

So she goes to the cemetery on a warm, bright Sunday. She arrives early, before the first relatives begin to show up. They come by car, by bus, by jeep, on motorcycles, and bicycles too. Quite a few arrive on foot. Because it's only about a mile from the Villa to the cemetery, and it's a nice walk.

Moni observes the faces of the mothers and fathers, the grandmothers and grandfathers, the brothers and sisters and uncles and aunts; she observes their features and their expressions, their gestures. And as she observes them, she thinks she notices signs of unspeakable sins in all of them. She tells herself that if God snatched away these people's tender, brief lives, He must've had a reason. He snatched them away in order to save them.

Today, she realizes, isn't an auspicious day for that poem, either. Maybe, she grudgingly admits, that poem will never be, just as the lives of these babies. And she'll never get beyond this notation, either:

Here the angels / have old folks' faces, she writes.

And she returns to the Villa.

It was just before nightfall. And the wind was coming from the southeast. A strong wind. Regardless, Facu, the Dago, Lucas, and Martín put on their wetsuits, determined to take out their boards. We watched them passing the *mate* and the weed. Those guys were totally nuts.

Then we saw him. The kid wasn't more than fifteen. He wore a green jacket, raggedy jeans, and sneakers with no laces. He was on top of the dune. Calm, staring at the sea. He didn't even notice us. He appeared to be seeing the sea for the first time. He didn't even flinch when he heard the police sirens.

Camila put out the joint. The sirens were getting closer.

The kid had a tattoo on his forehead: a tiger. He walked down the dune and started running toward the sea.

The cops appeared on the dunes. A whole bunch of them. They shouted at him to halt, to give himself up. But the kid didn't stop. He ran, pulling off his clothes. He was tattooed everywhere. He plunged into the water. He swam past the breakers. Till he disappeared into the sea.

The cops stopped short at the shoreline. One of them aimed at him but didn't fire. The kid was swimming far out. The others started yelling into their cell phones. They called for a helicopter. It wouldn't have done them much good. It was almost night by now, and a southeaster was coming. Cursing, the cops turned back.

The sea brought the kid back in. After five days. We found him in the north, beyond the cabana-rental stands. He washed up after the southeaster. He was swollen, deformed, nibbled by fish.

Lucas, who knows about tattoos, said that those hadn't been done on Bond Street. They were from jail. They showed up better on the dead flesh. Darker, they seemed.

Every memory, a cage. Memory, all this I'm telling, spoken fictions, lies that can convince us of the truth of what we said and even of whom we said it to, and then I wonder: is it true what happened, what others lived, or is the only possible truth the one I think they lived, a truth that isn't real. Are they, I wonder, the protagonists, the *what* of what I'm telling? Or is it me, the *who* that's telling it, what counts? Memory is always suspect. We remember what we don't want to, prisoners of an impossible amnesia. And, as we remember, the past is a variation of mimesis. Memory is always the past. We live in the past. In the past of what others did. A past that, in the telling, has already become ours. Fleeting, like the sparrow. Because let's not kid ourselves: no matter how caged we keep him, the sparrow thinks only of escaping; he just waits for a chance.

But this is also the place where, at midday, bald Weisz plays a Schoenberg recording performed by the Tokyo Symphony on an FM station.

They say that when Don Tito receives you in his office, he snorts a line, takes a slug of whiskey, lights a cigarette, and every one of his gestures has a slowness that wears you down. It's even worse if you had to see him because you messed up and, as we all know, if there's one thing Don Tito doesn't forgive, one thing that can cause you big trouble, it's for somebody to let him down, and if you don't believe me, just look at Gimpy Domínguez. Tell me, why do you think he walks like that? He walks like that because he decided to draw up a list to oppose the Central Labor Union members, under the wing of the rival union. Don Tito was waiting for him, straddling a chair and smoking, with a glass of whiskey in his hand. There's more: Don Tito was waiting seated under a lamp. They pushed Domínguez, who fell to his knees before Don Tito. You crossed the line, *gordo*, he said. You forgot Perón's Twenty Truths. For a Peronist, there's nothing better than another Peronist. Treason, what you did. Don Tito winked at one of the boys. And they gave Domínguez a beating he wouldn't soon forget.

To the workers in his union, the municipal workers, and not just them—indeed, to all the workers in the Villa—Don Tito Souza is more than the regional representative of the Central Labor Union, a father. We're a great family, he always tells his *compañeros*. A Peronist family. And I'm the father of the Peronist family in the Villa. We Peronists are happy because we have the Twenty Truths. We live happily with them, and if need be, like the General said, we're ready to die happily for them. And Don Tito stares at you, hard. He snorts a line and stares. If he offers you some, you'd better accept. Be careful, though, to get one thing straight: forget about calling him *compañero*. You call him Don Tito.

Whatever you need, Don Tito will get it for you. A house, a job at the Co-op for your kid, a loan from Banco Provincia, even Quirós to defend you in a lawsuit, whatever you need. And if Don Tito calls you, like now, you've got to be there. But it's unusual for Don Tito to come looking for you if you've never asked him for anything or screwed him over. Though maybe not all that unusual, because not owing Don Tito anything can be pretty fucking bad. Not owing him anything can be worse than owing him. If I were you, Juan, I'd be scared shitless.

Not even the Seven Samurai can save this Villa.

The problem isn't the years. I don't go out on the road on account of my family, Héctor still says. Over sixty, he keeps repeating that his job here as a brick mason is temporary. Because I'm not selfish, and I don't want to leave my missus stuck with the kid in a wheelchair. Especially not the kid.

Héctor arrived at the end of the seventies, one January like this, with a guitar and a harmonica, trying to be Bob Dylan. But as he found himself a local girl, Lina Benedetti, the daughter of Franca, the one from Marechiare Pasta House, Héctor stayed on. What a babe Lina was. By March she was pregnant. Luckily that Dago, Benedetti, the construction foreman, lent him a hand and brought him in to work on the building job. The Benedettis gave the young couple a house they owned in the south, which they rented out during the summer. The Benedettis looked on Héctor with a mixture of pity and disdain. Héctor thought only of getting the hell out of the Villa. One of these days I'll hit the road, he used to say. But he was in love with Lina. And even more so after the kid, Mauro, was born. He was crazy about that kid. In the winter Lina went back to the Pasta House. Héctor tried to break free from his father-in-law and started driving a limo. As soon as I earn a few pesos, I'm blowin' in the wind, he said. He went back to working as a brick mason.

Forty years have gone by since then. Lina, that little Italian girl who was so hot, has replaced her late mother as the matron at Marechiare's. After Benedetti died, Héctor inherited his profession and his customers. Mauro, the boy, turned out to be a walking disaster. He didn't finish grade school. All he cared about were motorcycles. He's gone Hell's Angel on me, Héctor would say proudly. Till he ran into a Río de la Plata bus and ended up in a wheelchair. Now he helps Lina out at the Pasta House.

If you need to do some remodeling, build an addition, change a bathroom, call him. But be careful not to talk about rock, because he'll pull out his harmonica and start playing "Like a Rolling Stone."

The spider came from Misiones, like my mother and that wood. We had bought the wood for the house at the sawmill. Good wood, Misiones wood. And in that wood was the spider that bit her, may God keep her in His glory and forgive the sin that tormented her and which she wouldn't tell me till the day, or rather, the night she died.

Because my mother came to the Villa in the seventies. And here she started a new life. She got married. And had me. Trouble, of course I gave her plenty. I didn't finish high school and here I am, a limo driver. And her, a laborer. My father wasn't like that. He had a weak character and was a barfly. But he sure was loving. He had a big heart. How I cried for him. Till my mother stopped me short: Don't cry so hard for him 'cause he isn't your father. I did the math.

I wrote down the dates. Not that it was necessary. She'd come to the Villa with me in her belly. And I was her sin.

She didn't even notice the spider bite till her arm swelled up in no time at all. We got to the hospital too late. They didn't have an antidote. And what if you cut it off, I asked. No use. My mother was delirious. Then she told me: I shouldn't even think of going to Misiones to see which of the two, her own father or her brother, was the one who had knocked her up. Because both of them were already dead when she left. The night before, she had put a spider on each of their cots. Then she climbed into the rowboat and rowed away. She hitchhiked her way to the capital. At a *pensión* a woman from Santiago told her that there was always work here during high season. And like so many other women, she came for the season and ended up staying.

God doesn't forgive, she said before she died. A sly old fox, God: He sent me a punishment from my own homeland.

I feel melancholy over what never was, someone said. And he hit the nail right on the head: all of us here feel the same.

This morning, with the sky still dark, when Juan Melitón gets up, the kitchen reeks of wine. As usual. Because ever since they didn't renew his contract at the lumberyard, he goes around all day loaded and in a funk. Can't even pick up an odd job. Really, who's gonna offer him an odd job with that booze breath of his. He gets up, takes a shot of gin, puts the teakettle on, prepares the *mate*, lights a cigarette. He tiptoes back to his bedroom. He watches his wife and son sleep. Mariela, on her back, her hands bandaged, snores, drooling a little. Kevin, like his mother, sleeps on his back, but with that one eye half-open. He's slept with that eye half-open ever since he was a baby. As if he'd known from the beginning that it was a misfortune to be born of a drunken laborer and a servant.

Last night the three of them argued till after 1 A.M. Their shouting could be heard throughout La Virgencita. The neighbors came to bang on the door of the Melitóns' pre-fab. All because Kevin doesn't want to keep going to school; he hates school, and now that he's already been expelled from three of them, now that Mariela's enrolled him at the double-shift technical institute, he hates school even more. Juan grabbed him by the neck and pushed him into a corner: You wanna be a laborer like me, you fucking little snot? he asked him. Is that what you want, asshole? No, Kevin shouted back. I want to have money. Stupid kid. Mariela, in the middle, seized his arm before the blow struck her son in the face. Kevin took advantage of the move to shove his father. Juan fell on his back, knocking over everything on the table. What really pissed Juan off was that the bottle of wine had rolled to the floor and shattered. When he tried to grab his son again, Kevin eluded him with a kick. But the kick landed on his mother, who had gotten in between to separate them. Both of them, father and son, ended up crying, standing over Mariela, who was rolled up on the floor, her hands bleeding from shards of broken bottle.

Till recently Juan and Mariela used to fight like crazy, and the thing was just between them. But since Kevin started bringing home report cards with lower and lower grades, they've joined forces against him. This morning, still in darkness, Juan sidles up to Kevin's bed. He feels like hugging him. Clutching his pillow, one eye closed and the other half-open. Juan reaches out his hand to caress him, like when he was a little boy. He's still a boy, he says to himself. But he doesn't quite manage to touch him. Because Kevin, eyes wide open now, pulls out a 38 from under the pillow and aims it at him.

I'm aware of all the problems in our community, declared Alberto Cachito Calderón in an informal chat with this newspaper. And he said it in his dual capacity as mayor and leader of the Neighbors' Justicialist Union. "I'm in the habit of walking up and down the Villa like I did when I was a militant. I'm aware that this administration still has a way to go. I was able to accomplish quite a bit in two successive terms, but not everything I wanted to achieve. The study of the beaches, opening the doors to private investments, and in this regard, the Paradise Towers have been a good sign of the mutual understanding between our city and the business community. Now let us try to take one more step, to bring to fruition a long-term desire of the people, which has now become an urgent necessity: the new sewer system. That's where we are right now."

Now they're saying that in his handwritten letter, Fito stated his original intention was to kill Dobroslav, his father. And here's where we have to recall the time Fito went to the police station to file the complaint of abuse of his little girl, Mechi, which then confirmed a previous theory from Police Commissioner Frugone, in charge of the case at the time. Of the eleven reported cases of abuse, assuming that they could be proved, at least one had been committed within the family environment of one of the victims, and that was the Mechi Dobroslav case. In effect, it was said that the grandfather had been the abuser. How could Fito have put up with it all this time, from the discovery of his four-year-old daughter's abuse through the grand opening of the Twin Towers; all this time, I say, putting on his best dumb-ass face. A coward: I agree. And you also have to take into account that it concerned his own father. Two nights ago Fito wrote that letter; then he climbed into his Audi and headed south. He parked the Audi in front of the dock, and right there he stuck the barrel of the gun into his mouth and pulled the trigger. With such rotten luck that he missed and ended up paralyzed and an idiot. The letter was in the glove compartment. He accused his father of abusing Mechi. But nobody saw the letter, which, according to some, remains in the hands of his wife, Mausi, who refuses to make a statement. Between Mechi's abuse and Fito's suicide attempt, the family's had enough tragedy, without adding the accusation of sexual abuse by the grandfather, which, lacking firm proof, was character assassination. In this amoral society of ours, there are bitter people with dark motives who try to create sensationalism out of other people's pain, declared Federico Jürgens, Mausi's father and Dobroslav's relative by marriage. To sling mud at Dobroslav, our Speer, Jürgens maintained, is to sully one of the Villa's leaders and the honor of a respectable family. All I can say, responded Dante, is that the letter to the father, if it ever existed, can't be found anywhere.

Once, when he was eleven, El Perro rebelled against Don Tito. Without saying a word, Don Tito tied him to a walnut tree out back and beat him with his belt. No one dared interfere. Not even Doña Domitila, his wife. Now, although they say he's getting old, all it takes is a single look from Don Tito to straighten out any family member. You've got to put yourself in his place. With that huge family. I don't have a family, Don Tito likes to say. I've got a town. On the female side there are Ethel and Virginia, aside from Doña Domitila. And Ethel's daughters with El Loco. El Perro, as we know, can't stand his brother-in-law, and as soon as Don Tito says the word, he'll bring the brother-in-law down. El Perro is merciless when he gets mad. Every chance she gets, Paola gives him hell, asking him to give up drugs. Then Pedrito bursts out crying and no one can stop him. Pedrito is El Perro's son, the one he had with Paola, who's pregnant again. El Loco and Ethel are also going down the tubes. Ethel turned out to be one hell of a whore. And El Loco, watching every move she makes. How can I not be a slut if they gave me a cabaret singer's name, Ethel defends herself. But watch out if El Loco raises his hand against her. Because if he even touches her and the father or the brother finds out, El Loco'll end up just like Rodolfo, the one who was Virginia's husband. One day Rodolfo took them to the sea. The kids didn't know how to swim, they went in the water, and the current swept them away. Rodolfo didn't know how to swim, either. Many people say that after that tragedy, the couple broke up. And Rodolfo disappeared. He was never seen in the Villa again. But those closer to them believe that after the kids' burial, Don Tito and El Perro took him out for a ride, and adiós, Rodolfo. After that, Virginia got on a religious kick, became devout, and started helping out at Rebirth, the organization for parents with dead children. Virginia organizes raffles, collections, and even charity bazaars. Quite a family, the Souzas. And there you have them, stirring up trouble: Marianito, Alejandra, Fernanda, Paulina, Martín, all children of Ethel and El Loco; and Pedrito, the son of El Perro and Paola. You've got to handle all those destinies. And Don Tito, who knows Perón's political leadership handbook by heart: one look is all he needs.

Julián, the Kennedy, says Dante, was Secretary of Planning, Political Secretary, and Secretary of City Government, in that order. Now he works as an advisor. And to that end he also relies on Alejo's invisible advice, all the experience behind the Villa's oldest law firm. Various shady businesses are attributed to Julián: trash collection, contracting a builder for the bus terminal re-design project, the coastline pedestrian walkway. The last great business deal will be the construction of the sewer system. The call for bids was prepared by his brother Alejo at the law firm.

No, stop screwing around with that book; leave it alone. If I had all the shit that you have going on, the last thing I'd do would be to toss those coins. What if it throws it back on you, tells you to cut it out, says that the answer is within you. I swear, I'm afraid of the *I Ching*.

Edi explains why he stopped working as a bouncer at Comanche and became a limo driver: three mouths to feed, three boys: the oldest twelve, the middle one seven, and the youngest, four. Three mouths to feed besides that bitch of his, Selva. Don't think that me and the witch didn't try for a girl. But we had no luck. All boys. It's the witch's fault. Because they say it's the mother who chooses the kids' sex. And all of them are just like her, all darkies. What a witch, Selva. What I'm trying for now is to get the company to send me to Buenos Aires at least once a month. I'll get paid well and use it to buy some cute toy for my little girl, because I've got a little girl there; she's gonna turn six. Lives in Lugano. With her mama. Let me explain. Around two years ago some chick I don't even remember calls me and tells me I'm the father of a little girl. I didn't even remember the chick. I picked her up when I was working security at Comanche. The chick called me in January. I didn't even remember her. It took me a while to refresh my memory. Nela, her name was, a sweet little thing. Now she's older, but she's still hot. She had come on vacation with the little one. And she found me. Even though I don't work at Comanche anymore, she found me. Said I had to know; the girl was my daughter. If I didn't want to take responsibility, it was okay, she said. Everything's cool. Sabrina, she named her. A little blonde. Sabrina looked at me with those pretty blue eyes of hers, and I melted. The chick told me that if I didn't believe her, I should go to Buenos Aires, have a DNA test and all that stuff. Everything by the book, everything above board, through the court and all, I did the DNA test. Sabrinita, my little girl. And blonde, can you imagine. Here's a picture of her. I carry it hidden. Always with me. When I'm driving the cab, it's in my wallet. When I get home, I keep it in a secret place I've got. It's one thing for the witch to find a photo of another chick on me, and something else for her to find a photo of a little girl. Imagine, with all the shit that's going on, what if she thinks I'm a perv.

Those clouds, I wonder: do they mean water or cold.

No one is innocent, Dante thinks. There are no innocents in the world, and not in this town we pretentiously call the Villa, either. Pape Satàn, Pape Satàn, aleppe. Every one of us; we are the Inferno.

Some more than others. Somewhere I read that the way to survive in hell is to stay close to someone less hellish. Opportunism, I say. In the blink of an eye, this dark jungle is going to burn. And like that guy who quoted a poet while he set fire to a city once said: Let us let the wind speak. Let it whistle hard till it turns this place into a garbage dump. Burned to a crisp, smelling like garbage. A flaming abscess, swept away by the gale. You think we deserve a better fate, huh?

Next Saturday, the 28th, the Waldorf Education Civic Association begins a monthly series of training seminars on the Waldorf pedagogical approach, designed for educators, parents, and families interested in learning about various perspectives on the education of our children. The proposed series is called: "Expression of the Senses and Their Treatment." As the title of the seminar indicates, it will deal with the recognition of sensory problems, how they are manifested, and what kinds of therapy may be effective.

The seminar will be taught by Austrian educator Hannah Lagersfeld.

The suggested donation is 20 pesos. A delicious home-made buffet will be available, with proceeds to go to Caracolitos Kindergarten.

We will meet at Soleado Beach Apart-Hotel.

So often, the fog. From dawn on, from the edge of the horizon, it buries the sea, rendering it invisible, barely a calm, continuous breathing, devoid of nuance. Then one can imagine that this is how the departed breathe, those who are there, concealed in the fog, waiting for us to approach, waiting with the conviction that even though we may deny it, we are drawing nearer every second, blending in with them, becoming one more of them. There are days, if, in fact, you can call them days, when the fog, unsatisfied with growing denser over the sea, advances this way, climbs the dunes, wraps itself around them and approaches the nearest constructions, the houses and buildings that rise opposite the beach, at first silently surrounding them, and then, just then, as if in a single gulp, devouring it all.

And it doesn't remain there, it's not content to take over this zone, the coastline, but rather it keeps going, it comes toward us, a cold, clammy vapor that filters through the trees, swallows up the forest and consumes it, making the trees disappear and silencing the first morning songbirds. Perhaps, with any luck, you might hear an owl, but it could be just an illusion. Because you may think you can hear something in the fog, but you can't. The calm it casts over the landscape is deceptive: it's more the desire to feel a presence than the possibility of someone daring to penetrate the white, blinding mass that envelops everything. Besides, if you feel a presence insinuating itself, who can say for certain that it isn't the dead, who this morning, instead of waiting patiently out there in the sea, have decided to leave it behind in order to come for us, and what better opportunity to absorb us than the fog that has already overtaken the eucalyptus, pines, and acacias, the streets of sand, and which now unhurriedly slips along, because there's no reason at all to hurry. Now reaching the downtown pavement, it spreads to the south and even beyond, extinguishing the remaining lights of the night before, the lanterns of the chalets, and farther on, wrapping itself around the metal-and-cardboard roofs of the warehouses, barracks, and shacks, passing over all the rooftops, covering them, crossing Circunvalación, slipping densely, compactly, toward the cemetery. Then who can swear to you that we, too, have not already departed. All of us, in the fog.

Dante didn't want to express an opinion about the project. He said his function is to inform. And that publishing Cachito's speech in *El Vocero* and providing the news was enough. The sewer system: a necessity, it read. Let everyone draw their own conclusions, he said. It's true that he said it with a touch of irony, but he could've taken a risk and said what we neighbors are thinking. At night we talked it over at the counter in Moby: You know it as well as we do, Dante. It's a shady deal. Cachito and the Kennedys managed the bids. And who got the contract? What a coincidence, huh—the construction firm belongs to a cousin of Cachito's wife, Beti. All in the family. With what Cachito pockets from this set-up they build another hotel in Spain, because rumor has it they already have one on the Bay of Biscay. Dante's not the type to get upset. He rattled the ice cubes in the glass and looked at us. Proof, he said. Bring me proof. Who's seen Cachito's hotel in Spain. Proof, as my master, Walsh, used to say. You can Walsh us around all you want, Dante, but you sure sit on your hands, Miranda the optician challenges him. You and your master, said Giménez, the guy from the Del Mar Electricians' Co-op. Enough already with your master. You know where you can stick your master. Dante, silent, bowed his head. Don't mess with Walsh, Dante said to him, still rattling the ice cubes with his finger. So what if I mess with him, Giménez provoked him. No one thought that the unflappable Dante, the imperturbable Dante, would be capable of reacting with a punch. He swung at Giménez. But the other man ducked, and the blow hit him in the shoulder. What a brawl there was. We had to separate them. And in doing so, some-one else landed a punch. It's true: instead of resorting to fists, with the same irony he put into the headline, Dante could have reminded Giménez what *vox populi* is, that for a few bucks he'll wipe out your debt to the Co-op. He could have, but he didn't. Because sooner or later all of us have a shred of dignity in us that rises to the surface. And that makes us feel better, even if the satisfaction is short-lived. After the altercation, Dante stopped coming to Moby. But just for a while. Because we also know that there are so few of us in the Villa and we all know one another. To prove what others are up to is easy. But so is proving what a person wants to hide. Who is guilt free, tell me. Think of it this way: you have to go on living.

Tell me one thing. Do you know who killed Laura Palmer.

Things between the Cobra and Betina went from bad to worse. Betina kicked him out of the house again and again, but there was no way. I've grown attached to your colts, he told her. First of all, Betina replied, the kids aren't horses. And secondly, they're *my* kids. Not your nags. Whoooa, Bessie, the Cobra said, trying to slip his arm around her. But Betina pushed him away. She was in debt. She'd discovered some money missing from the cash register as she was closing Las Camelias, her little barbecue place at the roundabout. It wasn't the first time. She should never have hooked up with the Cobra, let alone bring him home with her.

Now Betina was fed up with the Cobra and his gambling debts. If she doesn't pay tuition this month at Nuestra Señora, her kids will be out of school.

One night she throws his saddle out the window. She doesn't need her kids to help her lift it. Alone, without assistance, with the force of her rage, she throws it. Whoa, Bessie, he yells. Betina whinnies back at him. The kids copy her.

That night the Cobra sleeps in the stable that he hasn't finished building in the paddock. He sleeps on some horse blankets. He hears thunder; a storm is coming. In spite of the thunder, the Cobra can make out the gunshots. Three shots. He steps out into the night. And finds El Capo Malerba. He's just liquidated his nags.

You leave Betina alone, he orders. And get your ass out of the Villa.

You mounting my mare? the Cobra asks him.

I worked out an exchange, Malerba replies.

He hits him in the face with his 9 millimeter. And leaves.

The last one to see the Cobra is Braulio. He's on his way to Mar del Plata when he sees the Cobra walking along the berm in the same direction. Walking along with his saddle over his shoulder. He looks like a down-and-out cowboy. He walks like a loser. Braulio hits the brakes. He gives him a lift. When they reach Mar del Plata, the Cobra asks to be let off at the Bristol. I know a guy who likes horses and he'll give me good money for the saddle, for sure.

Braulio doesn't say a word. The casino's right there.

Moni wakes up in the middle of the night. She wakes up more and more often. She wakes up and writes. She writes and hesitates. She doesn't know if what she's writing is a poem or a story: *Once there was / a tall tale / death was alive / and told the tale / but the living / couldn't believe it: / they were dead, too.*

In winter, especially when it's below freezing, gray sky, we all have days of crying out a sadness that we can't blame on anyone else. Because it's sorrow for ourselves that we're feeling. At times like that it's best to go down to the beach and walk into the frozen wind. And if you run into anyone, it's not embarrassing. With the wind in our faces and below-freezing temperatures, the cold makes all of us cry.

Look, I know about it, and it doesn't matter where I got the word from because what counts is the proof, and I've got plenty of that. You're sleeping with my wife. Stop, don't put on that face. It's no big deal. Happens here all the time. It doesn't matter to me, really. And try to understand. It's not about fucking, it's not about jealousy, it's not about possession. The only thing that interests me is not losing our friendship. Go, screw her as much as you like. It doesn't upset me to be called a cuckold. I don't give a damn about other people's opinions. The only thing I ask of you is that we don't cut off our friendship. Because girls are a dime a dozen. But a friendship like ours, you know, isn't so common. And if you fuck her, look, even that shows a double difference between people like us and the others. We can say we like the same things, and among them, the same girl. Which explains one more coincidence. So, no worries. Give me a hug now. C'mon.

Come and get acquainted with the Seventh Day Adventist Church. This week we will share the Biblical story of God's fascinating call to His children at different stages of history. From Noah to our times. See how these valiant men of God responded to what God expected of them . . . and what

God expects of you. Don't miss it; it's an opportunity for you and your
family and friends. Admission is free. Music. Gifts.

Speaker: Yuri Brasov.
Monday the 20th: Call to Noah.
Tuesday the 21st: Call to Abraham.
Wednesday the 22nd: Call to Moses.
Thursday the 23rd: Call to Elias
Friday the 24th: Call to John the Baptist.
Saturday the 25th: Call to the Faithful Remnant

At the second door there's another half-breed standing guard. Juan
crosses the threshold. An anteroom overflowing with men and
women. Although Juan thinks that since Don Tito called for him,
he'll get in sooner, he's wrong: he'll have to arm himself with patience
and wait his turn. One more among all the wretches waiting silently,
as if in the anteroom of a faith healer. Though it embarrasses Juan
to admit it, he's afraid. What he was told, that not owing Don Tito
anything can be more dangerous than owing him, remains etched
in his brain. Don Tito leaves him for the very end. He's the last
appointment.

Juan takes off his beret and walks into the office. No drugs, no
whiskey. No evidence of what they told him about Don Tito. A sixtyish country type, a *criollo*. Portraits of Perón, Evita, San Martín,
and Rosas. Also one of him with Lorenzo Miguel. You know who he
is, Don Tito asks him. Juan doesn't know. But he ventures a guess: A
patriot, he says, wriggling out of the predicament. That's what I like
to hear. Don Tito invites him to have a seat. You know why I sent
for you. Juan bows his head, plays with the beret. Honestly, no, he
replies. You're a step ahead of me, Don Tito. But since you're always
busy, I didn't want to bother you. The thing is, Mariela and me,
we've already got one calf, our Kevin. And now she's pregnant again.
With what Mariela makes as a super and me at the city lumberyard,
we can't do much. Things are very tight for us. Maybe, I thought,

you could get me an odd job. I mentioned it to a buddy. And it looks like he went and told you about it. And then you sent for me. And here I am. At your service. And only then does Juan lift his head. He searches out Don Tito's eyes.

Exactly, I sent for you about an odd job. My son, El Perro, and my son-in-law, El Loco, need someone to give them a hand with something.

Now there's a different gleam in Don Tito's eyes. He's not a good old country boy anymore. He's an old fox, sizing Juan up. Then, hand on his shoulder, he walks him to the door: I see you've got good references, Melitón. We'll get along fine.

Practically in his ear, Don Tito says:

Because for a Peronist there's nothing better than another Peronist.

When we lose our parents, we're called orphans. When we lose a spouse, we're called widows or widowers. But when we lose a child, there's no name for it.

Rebirth, a support group for parents who have lost their children to death, announces its next meeting on Sunday the 19th at the Beer Lovers' Club Headquarters at 8 P.M. The group is free and open to the public. Friends, relatives, or anybody who has lost a loved one can attend.

For me it's never *dusk*. It's always *nightfall*. Always. And it's nightfall because we turn night-like. Gradually we become the shadows that slowly fog the Villa. It seems slow, but in fact it's just a prolonged moment. The sky clouds over, the sea darkens, you can hear a bird, see a bicycle in the forest, and as you walk through the trees, your footsteps crunch the leaves. Soon it's nighttime. And the same thing happens if you walk on the wooden boardwalk that stretches along the beach. When you take the coastal road you can feel the mist calming the waves. The mist, the grayness, blur the outlines of the cabana-rental stands, the buildings and houses. The street lamps begin to flicker on. A thread of little yellow lights, which, you realize as you walk along the wooden boardwalk for a while, are haloed by total blackness because it's already night, night has fallen. And something has grown darker in you, too. Not even with one of those street lamps can you brighten the night that has invaded your entire body. You pick up the pace. You want to be home once and for all. Suddenly, it's the thick of night. You understand why kids are afraid of the dark. How can you not be afraid, with the things that go through your mind. You're afraid of everything and everyone.

I'm the owner of the My Living Space complex, located at Alameda 307 and Calle 208 in our Villa, where one more crime, of the many that happen to us daily, occurred. Last Tuesday a gang of juvie thugs tried to enter a cabana occupied by guests, but were thwarted by the presence of the caretaker, who suffered the consequences with cuts on several parts of her body and abrasions from a rope they cinched around her neck as they went looking for computer equipment and money. As a result I had a conversation with Captains Renzo and Balmaceda. I am taking the liberty of sending you, via this message, a piece of information that may be of interest to all of you.

According to the police bulletin issued on the August 17th holiday, to use just that one day as an example, there were 25 reports of robberies of various types filed in our area, the majority committed against visiting tourists. One can assume that many more robberies went unreported. Later, other events occurred, which we are discovering day by day and which cause us concern, since, unlike in earlier days, when thieves only broke in and robbed unoccupied places, now things are the other way around, as they enter with weapons while the residents are at home. The loot consists of items that tourists usually bring with them during their stay: these days a family generally brings a notebook computer, and their children a tablet, as well as digital cameras, latest model cell phones, GPS devices, personal belongings, and money, which they keep in a backpack, and in a couple of minutes the equivalent of at least $6000 is gone.

In a nutshell, Renzo informed me that the total number of personnel he has on hand is 15 officers, not counting those on annual or medical leave, taking courses, etc., and that they're making a great effort by increasing working hours. He also informs me of their limited resources for vehicle repair expenses and equipment needs, even including gas, as they are allocated only 15 liters a day per vehicle.

He also told me about a list of certain needs, "unbelievable that they exist," among them the fact that 5 vehicles are out of service for lack of batteries, and the only reason one of them is currently operational is because the Chief had the battery from his own personal car installed in it. It is incredible that neither the Police nor the City can even provide "batteries." If they did we would have more units on the streets. I also found out that the beach, through which many delinquents flee, or where they stash their until a later time, cannot be patrolled, and that there are "now" available, ready for pickup, two quadricycles that were repaired at a private auto repair shop, but they can't be picked up yet because there isn't enough money to pay the $2500 repair bill and these quads would be how the beach would be patrolled.

In accordance with the information collected through personal connections and my career with the Argentine Army, I was able to contact various armories in the Federal Capital. Three of them are prepared to sell us firearms at reasonable prices. Through these contacts I also carried out a survey of security professionals who would be prepared to direct shooting practice-sessions if we create a small artillery range. When consulted about the matter, the police institution informed me that there would be no problem with civilians acquiring weapons as long as the owners hold permits from the National Arms Registry. As this security strategy is still in its embryonic stages, and, as you will understand, requires a certain degree of confidentiality, I ask those interested in acquiring the weapons to kindly contact the undersigned directly.

Thank you.

Manfredo R. Piacentini

Army Colonel, Ret.

011-15 3356-0783

Make no mistake, says Ortega. Chan, the little Oriental chick you see in the porn flicks, the one who gets her face showered with buckets of jism from three dicks while one of them fucks her in the pussy and another one in the ass, isn't Chinese. She's Korean. From the North. In North Korea, if they catch you crossing the border without permission, they torture you and execute you in public, or they give you years of forced labor. The girl escaped with her mother and two little brothers across a river. Fifteen years old, that girl. In winter, crossing mountains and jungles, a sixteen-hour march. Without stopping. They reached a zone at the border, a narrow river. In that zone the army casemates are placed hundreds of meters apart. The distance between them makes crossing easier. But you can't let your guard down, Chan told me, because the army guys are so camouflaged in the jungle that they're invisible. With bloody feet they made it to Seoul. Fast forward. When they arrived in Seoul, her mother got a job in a Chinese chopstick factory and later selling fruit on the street. Her brothers, as farm workers. The girl sold fruit on the street. A guy picked her up and offered her a job in a computer factory. It was a trap: she ended up locked in a pigsty, selling sex. As soon as she had the chance, she took off. Fast forward. She moved to Bangkok. She wanted a better future. Since she already had experience, she got into the porn business in Thailand, but with higher ambitions, in front of a camera. Fast forward. I found her at the Orléans on San Martín and Córdoba. Strung out on drugs. And now, without going into detail, she's here, like me. We're gonna set up an awesome studio here in the Villa. I've talked it over with Cachito Calderón. Alejo—your know him—put us in touch. With the Dominican chicks from Madariaga, it's all cool. We'll test them, of course. Now, check this out: for all the dumb hicks out there, this'll be a completely new experience here in the Villa, a sound and image studio. We're gonna tape weddings, baptisms, socials. C'mon in and I'll introduce you to Chan. She's gonna help with the auditions. Although I think it'd be cooler if she acted in them. Oriental stuff always adds an exotic touch. It's real sensual. And Chan can handle all the jism that comes her way. She'll definitely have no problem. With all she went through to get here, imagine how thankful she is to God. After that, getting cum squirted in your face is like rinsing it with holy water.

There they are, the six of them, aiming at one another. El Perro Souza, Don Tito's son; his brother-in-law, El Loco; and the three Reyes brothers, the toughest members of the Reyes family. The Souzas against the Reyeses. And Balmaceda, the military man, aiming too. And there, in the middle of all of them, afraid of getting shot, is Juan Melitón, the laborer. Don Tito Souza had ordered him to go to the union warehouse: the boys needed a hand with transportation. The cargo arrived at dawn. The small plane landed near Malerba's field. Juan could tell by their accents that the pilot and the others weren't from Santiago or Tucumán or Córdoba. Mexicans, he figured out. Juan had never seen so many weapons all together: machine guns, rifles, pistols. The fact was he didn't so much have to give the boys a hand as transport the packages himself from the aircraft to the 4x4s of the Souzas, El Perro, and El Loco. They were standing watch, armed as well. And Juan had to do the work by himself. Then off to the shed where Don Tito was waiting for them. Don Tito inspected the delivery. Then he patted him on the back: For a Peronist there's nothing better than another Peronist. And he gave him three hundred pesos: To buy something for Kevin and take your missus out to eat, Don Tito said. As soon as Don Tito left, El Perro and El Loco started arguing. One of them took out a bottle of whiskey. And the more they drank, the more they argued. Even though they weren't brothers, when brothers fight, outsiders will devour them, Juan was about to remind them, quoting *Martín Fierro*. Which is the same as saying that for a Peronist there's nothing better than another Peronist. And then it was daylight. The Reyes brothers showed up without anyone's noticing. They wanted to take some packages with them. Juan thinks the first to draw a gun was the younger Reyes brother. But it might've been El Perro, who's always far gone. Everyone yelling and aiming at one another. Renzo, the military guy, came out from one side, aiming too: Put down your weapons, assholes. Juan puts his hands up, takes a step back, walks away slowly, cautiously. They don't even see him. Put down your weapons. And while everyone is aiming at everyone else, Juan moves back, back, to the door, and, hands still in the air, steps out into the street. He starts running. He doesn't stick around to see how the thing will turn out. He runs, never stopping. With hands held high, he runs. He runs and disappears.

Cold, windy morning, overcast sky. Winter light. For days now, Moni has been reading Simone Weil. In her notebook, she writes: *In the summer of 1941, every day at dawn Simone Weil prays an Our Father. I adopted the unusual practice of reciting it every morning with complete attention, the mystic writes. If she becomes distracted or nods off, she starts over again till she attains a state of absolutely pure attention. If she thinks of starting over for pleasure, she desists. She doesn't start over unless she experiences true desire. Sounds, if there are any, reach me only after crossing that silence,* she writes. Moni especially notes that Simone Weil talks about "reciting" and "crossing that silence." Which makes her think that there is a poetic aura to Weil's exercise in unction. Reciting isn't the same as praying. And crossing the silence pursues an end that only words can realize. Or, in any case, music: the word as musical note. That is, Simone Weil inserts prayer in the place where poetry, a religious attitude, and the sacred, revelation, meet. And this must be the reason, Moni thinks, why poetry is written by hand and not on a keyboard.

It's as if the other woman has become me, she thinks. Or perhaps she's found me and is dictating to me.

The wee hours. Everyone at Souza's place was already asleep. It was after three, and the TV was still on in the bedroom where Don Tito and Doña Domitila lay sleeping. They were awakened by machine-gun fire, she recalls. On the Satellite Plus station a blonde was explaining how to make place mats out of willow. As soon as the first round went off, Don Tito wrapped his arm around her and they dropped to the floor while bullets shattered the blinds and window-panes. The kids began to scream. El Perro grabbed two pistols, and crawling along the floor, reached the side of a window. Ethel and Paola, on all fours, hurried over to the children's beds. By now Don Tito had grabbed his revolver from the nightstand. But he couldn't even look out. The gunfire had smashed the windows and the front door, blowing out the glass, and pieces of plaster sprouted from the walls. After the last round they heard a car engine accelerating. Then, silence. A deep silence. The attack couldn't have lasted more than a few minutes. When El Perro stepped out into the street, no one was there anymore. Voices from neighboring houses, barking. Don Tito, in pajamas, went through the house checking to see if everyone was all right. If the women and children were okay. Where's El Loco, Don Tito asked. Ethel looked at him, not knowing what to say. Where's your husband. Ethel didn't know. The kids were crying, all together, endlessly. Answer Dad, you fucking whore, Paola said. Don Tito cut her off: More respect: she's your sister, he said. Doña Domitila went up to her daughter and smacked Ethel in the face: You brought that garbage to this house. Paola gathered up the children and led them to the back of the house. She gave them some pastries and a jar of *dulce de leche* to calm them down. Then she started preparing some Nesquik. Just then the police arrived, too late. Like they always do, when everything's all over. Don Tito sent them on their way. Assistant Commissioner Balmaceda asked him if he had any idea who it might have been. Nothing happened here, Don Tito said, calmly. No sooner had the cops left, El Loco arrived. He was pale, nervous. The kids, he asked. How are the kids. El Perro came up to him, blocking his entry. You and I need to talk, Don Tito told his son-in-law. I had nothing to do with it, El Loco said. Let's take a little stroll, Don Tito said. Somewhere we can talk.

You never forget completely. Moni always remembers *los abusaditos.* Even though the entire Villa seems to have forgotten about the matter and there hasn't been a single line published in *El Vocero* about the investigation, which, supposedly, or so she's been told, was transferred to a court in Dolores, while the wind rattles the shutters and the whistling filters into her house, she wonders what will become of *los abusaditos.* Voices on the wind, she hears. And it's not an illusion. Suddenly a poem comes to her: *After a day of southeaster / today will be the last night of wind / and tomorrow another day / but not of calm.*

According to the *National Geographic,* observes Martínez, the Aero-club director, *yerba mate* is a bitter infusion that fascinates and stimulates the inhabitants of the Southern Cone. Which would explain a lot about what's happening to us. Too much stimulation.

El Vocero published it this week: *Stolen Childhood,* the headline of the article. *Amid the greatest secrecy, the Federal Police yesterday disrupted a ring that had been trafficking in child pornography over the Internet. During raids carried out in the Federal Capital, the province of Buenos Aires, and our Villa, investigators seized a total of over 10,000 electronic files depicting minors in sexual situations. Upon inspection of the material, police discovered that these persons also kept videos in which adults*

engaged in scenes involving children of both sexes between the ages of 2
and 9. According to Article 128 of the Penal Code, this crime is punishable
by two months to four years of prison. The operation, known as "Stolen
Childhood," formed part of an investigation on a worldwide scale. Data
concerning the computers on which these images were observed and from
which they were distributed came from Germany, where agents special-
izing in cybercrimes habitually monitored web links in search of pedo-
philes. More than 58 countries were eventually involved in this operation,
although local investigative sources explained that, in every case, the tim-
ing was determined by the investigation itself, which is why these raids
in Argentina were preceded by others abroad. In principle, there would
be no way to determine that the scenes featured Argentine children or that
they had taken place here. In this instance, the worldwide investigation
went after users who connected to a file exchange service. These are free-
access systems, as they can be used for the exchange of material that is not
illegal and is in the public domain. As for the investigation conducted in
our community, police officials did not reveal the names or addresses of
those involved. It was simply confirmed that pedophiliac materials on hard
drives were confiscated, and abundant additional evidence stored on CDs
and other electronic devices was collected.

Even with his diabetes-related ailments, limping and sometimes
grabbing his middle, Nazar has kept his looks. What remains of
the *criollo* dandy he once was, is a graying man with a bushy white
mustache, who strolls through the Villa with a muzzled pit bull on
a chain, as if a chain were more appropriate than a leash. He looks
dangerous, Nazar says, but he's sweet, like me. Gentle and sweet.
And on top of that, Nazar, in his sixties, has earned a reputation as
a benefactor.

Last year Giménez, from Del Mar Electrical Co-op, and Dorita, his
wife, went to Brazil for winter vacation. One night, on a road that
cuts through the jungle, they stopped at a service station in Misiones.

They were having coffee when an old woman with a bandaged eye came into the bar, followed by a boy in a wheelchair, a guy with a bald pate typical of chemo, and a little girl on crutches. And then a number of lame and sick people, all of whom entered the bar, filling the space. Nearly all of them were familiar faces, people from here, from the Villa. But Giménez and Dorita weren't as terrified at seeing the ailments of those invalids and plague-ridden folks as they were of greeting them. They stammered, grumbled, coughed. They whispered, as if they were in a hospital. Besides, all of them had that smell of poverty and illness. An overwhelming funk. They felt afraid. Those hideous freaks, they thought, had pursued them. They thought about running back to their car. Till they saw him: waiting until all the unfortunate had entered the bar, Nazar, as polite as he could be with the wretches. Nazar had organized a raffle. With what he collected, he paid for a trip to Curitiba, where a white doctor worked miracles curing poor devils who had lost all hope. With that homespun, welcoming tone of his, Nazar told Giménez and Dorita of his situation. The diabetes was giving him nothing but trouble; it was getting worse and worse. And since he hadn't found relief in any treatment, when he heard about Dos Santos, a healing doctor who saw patients in Curitiba, he planned that trip. As he couldn't pay for plane fare, he was traveling by bus, he explained. And while he was at it, he was doing a good deed for all these friends of his. Friends of his, he said. And he made an inclusive gesture that took in all the freaks. I'm doing them a good deed.

Tonight Juan is on his fourth glass of gin at the counter of Defensores when El Perro comes up to him. You're getting tanked, Melitón, El Perro says. Juan doesn't like to be called by his last name. And, coming from El Perro's mouth, it sounds devious, besides. Ever since the last time they saw one another, that early morning with the small plane, that delivery, and then the Souzas aiming at the Reyeses, and Balmaceda taking off. But after that, everything got worse and worse. Because that thing with Kevin happened: the kid was going around armed. Then Mariela blamed him: he hadn't asserted himself as a father, she reproached him. Kevin had slipped his reins. And, to complicate matters, now El Perro was coming after him. He'd been afraid of crossing his path after that early morning at the shed. El Perro ordered a "Jaypee" as he called a J&B, and, talking to the mirror on the other side of the bar, the image of San Cayetano with some olive trees, slid between a bottle of Fernet and one of vermouth, he said to him: Let's say the patron saint of workers sent me, Melitón. How well can you manage a shovel? he asks. Juan remains silent, buying time. He hesitates before saying: I never tried. You never dug a hole? El Perro asks sarcastically. What kind of hole you taking about? Funny guy, El Perro laughs. The old man told me you'd give me a hand. The old man is Don Tito Souza. And nobody says no to Don Tito. Come with me, El Perro says. They get into the 4x4. They drive past Circunvalación, near the garbage dump. El Perro hits the brakes, gets out, and there's the shovel. There's El Loco, too. Unconscious. Juan suddenly sees him. Beaten to a pulp, El Loco. His face a bloody mess. El Perro grabs him by the ankles and Juan by the wrists. They take turns digging. But Juan digs the most. Every so often El Perro goes back to the car, takes a hit, then a swig from a bottle of whiskey. Juan ends up doing the work himself. When El Perro decides the hole is deep enough, the two of them pick up the body again, El Perro by the ankles, Juan by the hands. The body rolls into the pit. And as it does, it moans a little. He's alive, Juan says. So what, El Perro replies. Juan covers the hole. My nephews are grateful, says El Perro. Missing him will do them more good than having him around. How about shoveling in some of this, El Perro says, offering him a hit. No, thanks, says Juan. But he does accept the bottle.

The number of minors involved in serious crimes is growing in our Villa. The point-blank shooting of a 34-year-old man by a minor, which only through pure luck failed to kill the victim, has been added to the list of crimes committed by minors in cold blood and with impunity. Reports circulating at the close of this edition about an assault on a private cab, along with shots fired at a police vehicle, indicate that this offense may also have been committed by a minor. In general these are minors residing in the Villa who, at an early age, have access to weapons and engage in increasingly virulent criminal activity. A serious problem that has no adequate solution, but for which finding one has become more and more imperative. In this regard, judges from all over the country have agreed that courtrooms are absolutely over capacity.

It rained all night. In the morning it seemed like it was going to clear up, but then those black clouds arrived.

Mariela doesn't ask Melitón where he gets the money from even though he's been unemployed for months. He doesn't offer her any explanations, either. A friend, a super from the next block, told Mariela about it. That when Juan isn't at the bar, where he spends most of his time, he goes around yoked to El Perro Souza like his shadow. If it's best for Mariela not to find out, for Juan it's a matter of keeping quiet, and so they forge on. The only thing worrying him is Kevin. He didn't even go to school anymore. A God of his own must have enlightened Juan when it occurred to him to bring up the Kevin issue with Don Tito. If Kevin was hanging around in bad company, who better than Don Tito to advise him and find a way to put Kevin in his place. So Juan goes to union headquarters to see Don Tito. Look, Juan, in Peronism there's only one category of men, those who work, he told him, and it was one of the twenty Peronist Truths. If we want to straighten Kevin out because he's straying from his family, we'll just have to straighten him out. If he doesn't go to school, he has to work. Let me see what I can do for the boy. I'll tell El Perro to take care of it. Don't worry. We'll get Kevin straightened out. What's the union for if not to solve our *compañeros'* family problems. Suddenly

Juan is afraid. He wonders if it had been such a great idea to consult Don Tito. In life we shouldn't wander from the straight and narrow path, says Don Tito. And Juan asks him: Is that what Perón said? And Don Tito: No, that's what *I* say.

Two poems by Moni:
1) *Lightning in the night / in the dark pampa / slashes of blood*
2) *Whinnying in the dark / thunder and rain crying down / dead little countryfolk / galloping along.*

At night, from behind a slope, the headlights of a private cab come into view, one of the three or four that circulate through the Villa at this hour. In winter, none of the four or five limo rental agencies that, with any luck, stay open at night has more than one car. They're the only engines that can be heard at night. Headlights that pierce the mist. At full speed. Because the streets, avenues, boulevards— the entire Villa—are deserted; they become a ghostly dimension. The cab drivers don't dare enter certain areas. They don't pick up or transport passengers to La Virgencita, El Monte, the far end of Pinar del Norte, past the southern limits, or Circunvalación. I'm a crazy fool when it comes to making money, but not crazy enough to let a fucked-up thug blow my brains out for two pesos. And it's not just guys anymore. Girls, too. If you don't think so, just look at what happened to Macho Mama, the one who drives a Sienna. Macho Mama's husband, Big Daddy, is in the hospital and she needs the money. Since she's good with a guitar, she started singing in some restaurants. Boleros, mostly. I'm not saying she's the new Chavela Vargas, but she does okay. When she was done singing, she would get into the cab. Even though Big Daddy didn't want her to work at night, Macho Mama paid no attention. A hard-working gal, that Macho Mama. Like I'm telling you, it was barely dawn Saturday morning, and three girls stopped her at the entrance to Don Bosco

Clinic. None of them could've been more than fifteen. By the time Macho Mama realized what was happening, it was too late. She had a gun barrel at the back of her head. They took her cash and the car, and they kicked the shit out of her. Dyke, they called her. Her, of all people: a total lady. She ended up in the hospital, in the ICU, next to her husband. Another one they attacked was El Negro. A few weeks ago, on a rainy night, he picks up a young couple at the bus terminal. Suddenly the guy sticks a revolver in his side and says: You lose. And don't make me shoot and wake the baby. You can't trust anyone these days. A blink of an eye, and they've got you. You need to keep all your antennas up. Obviously, even though nothing's going on with the missus anymore, I'd like to stay home at night. For my physical and mental health. But I've got five mouths to feed. And in the morning, when I wake them to go to school, how will I look them in the eye if I don't have coins for the corner kiosk.

Dr. Uribe, director of Clínica del Mar, is considering lowering the risk classification of the devices used to administer electroshock treatments, reinforcing what many psychiatrists consider to be a growing acceptance of electroshock in modern psychotherapy. "The procedure has grown in popularity," declared Uribe. For a few seconds and under anesthesia, patients receive an electrical discharge through electrodes, which produce cerebral shock and convulsions lasting up to a minute. Those opposed to this treatment are unaware of the progress electricity can bring to all types of mental disturbances, the expert maintained. "It's a treatment for the most severe form of depression." This change would put electroshock devices in the same category as syringes or surgical drills. Those in favor of electroshock, among them many renowned psychiatrists, say that the treatment is much safer than ever. Opponents, including certain groups of former patients, maintain that electroshock can cause memory loss and brain damage that do not compensate for its short-term benefits. However, Dr. Uribe claimed that none of the patients subjected to this electrical treatment at Clínica del Mar has reported significant memory loss, a phenomenon that might actually be beneficial, Dr. Uribe concluded, since all of us have experiences we would rather forget.

You'd have to ask yourself why Doña Doris Dobroslav, our Speer's wife, stayed out of the scandal of *los abusaditos*—which, according to some, involved and compromised her husband—and vanished off the face of the map. She shielded herself—or her husband and son shielded her, as we said—with a mental breakdown after that whole situation affecting her granddaughter, Mechi, that poor, abused little thing, and later Fito, her son, who, after a cowardly attempt to kill his own father, the grandfather accused of abusing his granddaughter, shot himself so unsuccessfully that he was left a vegetable, confined to a wheelchair. A major tragedy for anyone. Too much for a seventy-eight year old, insulin-dependent woman with a heart condition who, they say, also suffered a stroke as a result of the family drama. If Doña Doris went into hiding, they also said, it was because after her ischemia she was completely out of it, and Dobroslav kept her locked up, afraid that she would get lost walking along the boulevards, a more-than-dubious argument, since no one gets lost in our Villa: we run into one another all the time. Rumor had it that the bitterness and pain of everything that had happened with her granddaughter and son left Doña Doris bedridden, with neither the strength nor the spirit to get up, and all she wanted was to die, that she prayed to God to take her. It was also said that if Doña Doris avoided all contact with the neighborhood, it was not only because of the tragedy, but also out of shame: one of our Villa's most honorable families now disgraced. Imagine: her husband, Mechi's grandfather, might have abused his granddaughter, and Fito had tried to kill his father, and failing that, attempted suicide, another failure, leaving him a paralyzed vegetable. I'm repeating myself, I know, but sometimes it's necessary to recap, or if you prefer, reconstruct, if you want to know the truth. That is, if there is one single truth in a family.

Anyone you ask will tell you the same thing: that they came here because they wanted to start over, that here we have the sea, which is purifying, and that here, in spite of what people say, we all know one another. Our defects can be seen close up. Like with a magnifying glass. But so can our virtues. Sure, we're controlled by a corrupt lawyer, connected to the power brokers, but he's also helped all those who, without his influence and dealings, would have ended up in debt or in prison. Sure, our mayor is a crook, but how many people has he found jobs for, gotten out of a fix, how many has he arranged a business license for, pushed a deal through for, gotten a hospital bed for. You'll tell me that a contractor destroyed the forest to build those towers that were, and are, a shady real estate deal, but consider how many jobs it created for Bolivians and Peruvians. The police we have now aren't any better than the previous ones, sure, but as soon as they arrived, they put a bullet into a couple of thugs and calmed the shantytown darkies for a while. So, the new priest might be banging a lady parishioner. It's possible, but how many souls did he relieve with his forgiveness, a prayer, last rites. You'll tell me that necessity is as ugly as sin, and that's why we look the other way. And I'll tell you that you never know when you'll have to turn to one of those you look down on, and then, if the other guy is willing and gets you out of trouble, what then? You've got to be more understanding. If there's anything special about us, it's this: we're understanding. That's why our arms are wide open to newcomers.

You heard about the three Federal Police raids where they picked up kiddie porn. What happened was, the Feds went over the Provincial Police's heads. If they didn't inform the local cops, they had their reasons. One of the houses involved, no kidding, belongs to Lalo Salgado, the Rotary Club treasurer. The local cops don't report it, of course, because their collaboration with the Police Co-op is at stake. Tell me, if they didn't confiscate his computer, why was Salgado checking prices at Mar Informatic. Because he was left without a computer. The Feds took everything away. You say it's impossible, that if it was true, Salgado wouldn't be parading around the Villa so boldly, acting the part of the obliging neighbor, and I'll tell you, no kidding, no one here is what you think. Not even you are like you think you are.

After sending the issue of *El Vocero* to a printer in La Plata, Dante would drop in at the Tropicana on Thursday afternoons. At first he started going twice a week. And now, more often, at irregular times, with unexpected frequency.

He walks into the room. Chiquita serves him a whiskey on the rocks with a splash of soda. She helps him take off his shoes. Dante sighs. He leans back in bed and watches her undress. Plenty of guys would go crazy for Chiquita. But not him. Not at this stage of his life, he thinks. But he's fooling himself, and he knows it: he's not coming just on Thursdays anymore. Chiquita does her thing slowly, no rush. Dante sips his whiskey and lets her do it. Then they chat.

The one who does the most talking is Chiquita. She tells him about her life in the Dominican Republic, tells him about the poverty, the destitution, her sisters, one crazy and the other a maid at the Sheraton. And her brothers: the fisherman was eaten by a shark. The thief was shot up by a rival gang. Her taxi-driver father, a good man, hard working, died trembling with fever and violent convulsions. Possessed by the devil. Chiquita tells him of a Colombian executive who fell in love with her at a resort, and of an emerald green sea. Dante wonders if what she's telling him is the truth or a soap opera she's invented for herself. Maybe what counts is the possibility; it could be this is what she thinks he's waiting to hear.

Dante tells her of his militant past, of shootouts, of his friend Rodolfo and the bomb he planted in the Federal Police Building. Then he tells her about his son. He must be your age, Chiquita, he says. Chiquita smiles, calls him "Papi." He likes it. Dante melts when he talks about his son. We don't see each other often. Never, in fact.

He doesn't love me, he says. He doesn't even want to see me. Chiquita tells him that the same thing is true of her and her mother. That they're different. She doesn't hate her, she says. But she doesn't want to see her anymore. Chiquita talks about her mother. But Dante isn't listening to her now. He's thinking about his son. Chiquita stops talking. She realizes Dante isn't listening. What's his name, she asks. Your little boy. Juan, says Dante. And he's not a kid anymore. He's already a man. And your little boy. Trini, Chiquita says. She's a little girl, not a boy. Sorry, I got confused, Dante says. And he realizes that neither of them has been listening to the other too carefully. In any case, the other one is a wall on which to project a film that might or might not be real. Tell me about your son, she asks him. Another day, Chiquita. Now let me rest a while. At six I've got to be at a press conference the mayor is giving to announce the sewer system.

With more than 200 motorcycles arriving from various parts of the country, a "moto-lunch" was held on Sunday at noon, organized by our Villa's Bikers Group, known as "Wheels of Sand." The meal was accompanied by videos and musical performances by live bands.

Attention, friends: Never call these intrepid souls "cyclists." Yes, you can call them "motorcyclists" or "bikers." Here's an anecdote: Alberto Cachito Calderón, our mayor, participated in the gathering. He was later seen very enthusiastically trying out one of the motorcycles that had competed in the event.

Why, then, we wonder, did Doña Doris call for Santi Rovira before she died. Why Santi, the pastor, of all people. It might be because he'd earned a reputation in the Villa for being pure, Dante ventures. And we know what being pure means for us: a creature that's kind and slow-witted at the same time. Let's say it once and for all: a dumbass with fleeting moments of saintliness. I'm not saying this is my opinion, but it does represent the majority. Santi inspires more confidence than any priest. Among other reasons, because he forgives you for everything, no matter what. And besides, whatever you might tell him, he'll forget. Some say that Santi forgets on account of that roof tile that smacked him in the dome in Caleta Olivia when he was working on the oil tanker, and the beam was a messenger from heaven that turned him to the temple. As for me, I think he forgets on account of the weed. You know how smoking joints can wipe your brain clean. So Doña Doris, before she took her last breath, asked to see Santi. She wanted to make confession to him. To the dear pastor, she said.

The thing is, Santi has that look, like St. Francis walking on the rooftops of Assisi and scattering seeds to the birds.

And may I know what you're doing at the union office, Melitón, Mariela asks him one night. Management, Juan replies. What kind of management can you do when you don't even know how to read or write, she retorts. Management, Juan repeats. And he lays some cash on the table.

Mariela dyed her hair blonde. Once a week she goes to the beauty salon, buys herself clothes. Her friends envy her. There are situations where you're better off not knowing, she thinks. What matters is that ever since Juan has been working for Don Tito, the Melitóns' situation has changed. Like Don Tito says, Juan repeats, work brings dignity. And if you don't think so, just look at Kevin. He's different since he's been working. Because Kevin agreed to work. And he's got a job at an auto repair shop. Since Kevin's been working, father and son fight less often. Things are going so well for the Melitóns that, thanks to the union, the couple decides to take a trip to Córdoba, an excursion with the retirees. For Juan, who's never seen anything but the countryside, this trip is like a dream. Before getting on the bus, Mariela and Juan ask Kevin to behave himself. Kevin's become more of a man. Even his voice has changed. Deeper, hoarser. Juan doesn't understand how Don Tito brought about this change, No matter, Kevin is a different young man. And even though it's true that Juan

410

sometimes remembers the time they buried El Loco, it's also true that those memories are less frequent. What counts is that, ever since he's gotten closer to Don Tito, things are going better for Juan, and even Mariela has started opening her legs to him again. Like mountains, but lower, a retired lady tells Mariela. That's what the *sierras* are like. Like flattened mountains. Juan can't fall asleep during the journey. His nerves won't leave him alone. Suddenly he realizes that Kevin is on the bus, has a gun, and is shooting the retirees. One by one he kills them. He never runs out of bullets. And now he's coming to shoot them, too. Juan wakes up. The bus advances through the night. Out the window he can see only darkness.

- *Make a list of what we like and dislike.*
- *Concentrate our energies on what we want.*
- *Itemize our strengths.*
- *Write down everything that's unique about us.*
- *Live in the present moment and not in a hypothetical future.*
- *Identify those with whom it's not hard to affirm ourselves, think about what we will say to them, and plan when and how we will do it.*

Deborah Miller, MA, New Age Psychologist: 418061.

Old Nazar still tells that same joke: I'm so sweet that God punished me by making me a diabetic. And he says it while stroking the pit bull's head. I'm talking about Nazar, the father of Mariela, the superintendent of the Transatlántico building, the wife of the late Juan Melitón, that's who I'm talking about. If now, at sixty, old Nazar acts like such a hummingbird, imagine what he must have been like when he was young, when he went to dances in Madariaga and Ayacucho. At a folk music club meeting he met Herminia, who would become the mother of Emilia, Jorgito, Mariela, and Mariano. Herminia was married. She had three children. I was told that when he met her, she was living with a ranch hand, a good man. Mother of three children.

Someone told the hummingbird to be careful, that the dove had a nest, a mate, and chicks. Nazar didn't care and flew off with her. More out of pride than affection, because what interested that arrogant man was getting attention, showing people what he was capable of. The husband went looking for him. He tried to murder him and nearly did. But they got him off their hands. Nazar brought Herminia to the Villa. Alone, without the kids. Because the husband wouldn't let her take them. She was already pregnant with Emilia, the oldest. Jealous, and with good reason, Herminia soon realized there was no turning back. If she made a scene with Nazar, he would beat her, just like the baby, with his belt. One time he kicked her in the belly. Jorgito, the youngest, was in there. The first to escape was Emilia, who went to live with a certain Agostino, a Dago builder. Don Nazar didn't have the nerve to take on Agostino the Dago. Then Mariela slipped out from his clutches. She went to live with Juan Melitón. Around that time Juan was working as a butcher. And when Nazar went looking for his daughter to bring her home to his shack, Juan was waiting for him with a razor blade. Over time, Herminia built a little room out back. And she moved there with Jorgito and Mariano. The boys were bigger then, and Nazar wouldn't risk raising a hand to Herminia anymore. In those days she sold raffle tickets. Till she died of cancer. Since then Nazar's been living in a front room with the bullmastiff at the door and the pit bull inside. He'll never admit that he keeps it out of the fear that, when he least expects it, his kids will show up and take, not just his life, but also the money from the raffle tickets, now that he's living the sweet life. The one most determined to do away with him is Jorgito.

You've gotta remember Teo Olsen, the cartoonist. In '76 he split for the U.S. and worked at King Features. Later he went to see Stan Lee, the one who did Captain America. And Lee hired him for Marvel Comics. He drew all the characters, all the superheroes. But something happened. I think it was his lover in California, a millionaire who invited him to go to Tibet, the one who turned his head around. Turned Teo into a Green. It's been years since he broke up with her, but he's still as Green as can be. Plus, over the years he's become more radical. He must be seventy by now. You can't recognize him; doesn't have a tooth left. No, Teo doesn't do email. A fanatic ecologist. No running water or electricity or phone. He buried himself in his trailer on a southern dune. And he doesn't want to be moved from there, either. Of course, he gave up the comics years ago. He's against all forms of violence. And he survives on a few dollars he gets from an ecological magazine in San Francisco. Death is part of life, he wrote me. And not the other way around. That he thinks about death a lot. According to him, death comes at a very high cost. And he's not just referring to the cost of a burial. He's talking about the environment. Some U.S. scientists revealed the high level of pollution on earth that's caused by cemeteries. It seems the dead are like batteries; you can't just toss them anywhere after they're used. Luckily, he tells me, the Greens became aware of this problem a long time ago. And they use biodegradable materials for shrouds, caskets, and crematory urns. The burial site must also be considered. There are already cemeteries that have been cleared of headstones and mausoleums. He's left instructions for when he dies, he wrote me. He wants to be wrapped in an ecologically-friendly shroud and buried in a forest. The trailer, he says, he's leaving to me. You don't know how much good it would do me. My housing problems would be solved. And I'd never spend another winter in some dump at the beach.

There are nights when you can hear it. It's a childish ballad, a little ditty, like a Christmas carol. You can't really understand the words, just the tralalalala. They say that when El Muertito sings nearby like that, it's because a child is suffering. Many people can't stand the little ditty. Among them Ramírez, the guy from the locksmith's. He's tough on his kid. Someone said that when Keith acts up, he ties him to a tree out back and lays into him with his belt. It's no picnic to raise a boy by yourself, he grumbles. Lila, the hairdresser, dumped him for being abusive. If she didn't take Keith with her, it was because she took off with a dude, and the kid was in the way. She's the one who named him Keith, for Keith Richards. A real Rolling Stones fan, that Lila.

Tonight Ramírez is about to whip Keith when he hears the tune. Ramírez goes for his 38 and walks out into the night. He starts firing at the sky. But the melody grows closer, louder. When he walks back into the house, Keith is waiting for him with a knife. As soon as Ramírez steps inside, the boy plunges it into his stomach. He leaves him bleeding on the floor. "It's only rock 'n' roll," Keith laughs. And runs out the door. Ramírez manages to drag himself to the phone and call the hospital.

The melody is gone.

At 7:30 P.M. Sunday evening, Julio Martínez, 34, left a friend's home on Calle 102 and Avenida 6 together with his wife and some of her friends. No sooner had they exited the house, the women were assaulted by two minors, determined to snatch their purses. Following the usual pattern, while one of the youths attacked, the accomplice waited on a motorcycle. Martínez, who at that moment was closing the front door, leaped on top of the assailant to prevent the robbery. But the minor was armed and fired at Martínez, who received a bullet wound in the abdomen, affecting his stomach, liver, and intestines. Despite his injury, he was able to hold on to his attacker while the second crook beat him. When several neighbors, alerted by the noise, came out to the street, the second thief tried to escape. He then fired at a young woman, Linda Morando, 17, who died instantly of a head wound. Meanwhile, neighbors sought revenge on the youth held by Martínez. Police rescued the young offender from the fury of the neighborhood, and he was subsequently taken to the hospital and later arrested.

Martínez, meanwhile, underwent surgery for over five hours, as doctors had to remove part of his digestive tract and reconstruct several sections. At

the time this edition went to press, the man was lucid and in stable condi-
tion, although he will remain in intensive care for several days to avoid the
risk of infection.

The minor, only 15 years old and a local resident with an extensive
criminal history, was booked for aggravated armed robbery. This Monday
the boy was transferred to a maximum security correctional facility for
juvenile offenders. The fugitive accomplice responsible for Morando's death
was also identified as a native of our Villa. His parents, it was determined,
are currently on vacation in Córdoba, and authorities are attempting to
contact them in order to inform them of their offspring's deplorable action.

Gilles de Rays had it all. He belonged to the nobility; he was a
marquis. A handsome guy, with a jet-black beard. And that's where
his nickname, Bluebeard, came from. He was educated, a reader of
St. Augustine, owner of a castle. He was ill-tempered and a fag. He
fought against the English, drove them out. I'm talking about the
fifteenth century here. Gilles liked young boys. They drove him
crazy. Not only did he rape them, he decapitated them. After chopping them up, he would go into a rapture that made him pass out.
The more ramped-up he was, the greater the tortures he inflicted on
them. He hung them from a hook, he sliced them up. Afterward he
threw the pieces into the gutters. Till one day he got into alchemy,
went looking for a pact with the devil, and got into some rituals that
annoyed the Church. And that the priests did not forgive him for.

You don't fuck around with the devil. The Inquisition locked him
up. He was judged and condemned to hang. Before dying, he asked
forgiveness of the parents whose children he had slaughtered. More
than two hundred, it was calculated. He asked them to let him sing
a *de profundis*. He sang it. Then they hanged him.

Dante takes a break, orders another whiskey, and then:

Just between us, let's be objective, he says. Comparing what Bluebeard did with what happened to the kids at Nuestra Señora is
bullshit. Which proves that man has evolved. We ought to celebrate.

415

Very short, their vacation. Mariela and Juan came rushing back from Córdoba. Because of what happened with Kevin. He had killed. He was in jail. Incommunicado. Juan went right over to Don Tito's.

And Don Tito seemed to be waiting to tell him:

I think you were too late to straighten Kevin out. Besides, the devil carries weapons. As the General said: You can't give weapons to someone who can't yet grow a beard. Although he's a minor, Kevin murdered a pregnant girl. He tried to steal her purse. The woman put up a fight. And it happened. Think of the media frenzy. They're stirring up the wasps' nest, bringing up all the latest police cases in the Villa. They've dredged up the business of the abused kids at Nuestra Señora again. Cachito Calderón is going nuts over how things like this are going to ruin the season. The only thing I could do was talk to Quirós so the police don't club him to death. And that's doing a lot. A privilege. I'm really sorry, Juan. You know how much I worry about kids, who should be the only privileged ones. But, hey, the General's not here, and we are the way we are.

And, for the last few years, while Nazar picked up a few pesos with his raffles, Herminia also did her part selling lottery tickets. Store after store, house after house, Herminia went up and down the entire Villa, from Pinar del Norte to the South, and especially among the poor folks of La Virgencita and El Monte, the shantytown that's started sprouting up lately. When she started getting backaches, she tried not to pay attention to them. Until one day last autumn, one of those drizzly days that seem like it's already winter, she fell getting off a bus. Emilia and Mariela went to the hospital. Mariela already had her hands full with Kevin in jail. Now, on top of that, their mother was in the ICU. They listened to the diagnosis. A tumor. Herminia didn't have much time left. She was so good that she'd turned the lottery business over to Nazar. She thought of Nazar till she closed her eyes. Not good, stupid, Mariela said. That old fucker never deserved her. Because of the grief he'd caused her, Nazar should die, they thought. All that suffering had caused the cancer. And Nazar was responsible. Jorgito spent days and nights at the door of the ICU, waiting for news. He wouldn't leave, no way. He was the one who felt his mother's suffering most. Maybe because he had been in her womb when Nazar beat her. It seemed as if Jorgito was withering away while his mother was dying. Mariela was the one who said they'd have to keep an eye on Jorgito when their mother died. There was no doubt that Jorgito would get even with his father. Herminia died. The two daughters didn't let Nazar come to the funeral at Neri's Funeral Home. And after the burial, when Jorgito returned home, he was greeted by the bullmastiff and the pit pull. Nazar had gotten there ahead of him. You don't know how much I loved your late mother, he told them. He was crying. Since I had been a ladies' man, the poor woman kept a close watch on me. I didn't cheat on her for pleasure. I did it out of fear she'd dump me for someone else and I'd be left alone. I've always been afraid to be alone. Nazar was crying. And the pit bull kept Jorgito the avenger at a distance. Slyly, Nazar said: If you've come to cry for your late mother, you're welcome here. Make yourself a couple of *mates* and we'll cry for her together. But if you're here for some other reason, better turn around. Jorgito went away. He'd fuck up the old man another time. One of these days, when the pit bull wasn't around.

Local police broke up a group of Nazi teenagers. The names of the youths have been withheld because of their status as minors and in order to ensure a thorough investigation. From the confiscated leaflets and documents, it could be determined that they were attempting to spread anti-Semitic propaganda. The organization, known as Alba Thule, was dedicated to recruiting youths ages 15 to 17 over the Internet to indoctrinate them in white supremacy, xenophobia, and anti-Semitism, explained Police Commissioner Renzo. "We cannot rule out the possibility that this cell may have contacts with others abroad," he declared. Among the confiscated documents there was also a wide assortment of reading material, CDs, a computer

containing a great deal of information on the Third Reich, books on esoter-
ics and mysticism. Deputy Commissioner Renzo affirmed that this organi-
zation worked to indoctrinate these children, who unfortunately ended up
sympathetic to the Nazi movement. "What surprised us were some of the
items we found," the officer declared. In a home in Pinar del Norte, there
were brass knuckles, knives, extendable metal clubs, two fire extinguishers
connected with adhesive tape and a walkie-talkie type of communication
system joined by a cable, which was not an explosive, but rather was used
for intimidation.

It would be unfair to believe that everything here is human misery.
There's plenty of kindness, but kindness doesn't get press. Barely two
pages, the last two of *El Vocero*, the society pages and acknowledgments. On these two pages, next to the horoscope and the tide chart,
the 24-hour pharmacies and the video club's new releases, that's where
you'll find kindness. The brick mason and the baker lady embracing,
cheek to cheek, and underneath, a caption: We've been together for
an eternity, and we've still got another eternity to go. In this eternity,
which has lasted twenty-three years, God has placed three wonderful
human beings in our hands. This is what being soul mates means,
and that's how we'll stay till God fuses your soul and mine in a single
light. A brief note: The Volunteer Firefighters' Association thanks
its neighbors for their donations, which will go toward the purchase
of a new truck. A very brief note: Happy birthday, Tamara: Long-
distance hugs and kisses. We're proud of your athletic successes. Your
Mom and Dad. This page also expresses concerns for one's fellow
man. There are different sorts of expressions of thanks: for recovering from pneumonia, for the return of a lost bicycle, for family support in building a house. There are birth and death announcements.
And no shortage of notices by Alcoholics Anonymous and Al-Anon,
announcing their meeting times and locations. There is also the tenderness of someone who lost his dog, expressed in the photo of a fox
terrier and a little accompanying note: "I got lost following a bitch

in heat in January. My name is King. Please phone 417893. Reward."
All these men and women, young and old, display their noblest feelings on these two pages. And there are others, many others, like them, because every week familiar and unfamiliar faces come to *El Vocero* headquarters and ask Dante how to place an ad. If there is so much kindness and gratitude in this Villa, it's because publishing on these two pages is free, Dante reminds us. It's true that Dante's a skeptic: What they want is to look better, Dante says. But that doesn't guarantee they can. Vanity, what they're putting on display is their vanity. They want to shine in the paper like kindly souls. Later, when the season arrives, the announcements dwindle. They're less concerned with gratitude than the blind hope of lining their pockets during two months of tourism.

Twelve eight-balls of cocaine confiscated, Dante writes. *An operation carried out at noon last Tuesday by members of the Dolores Narcotraffic Delegation and the First Precinct ended with the confiscation of 12 eight-balls of highest quality cocaine at a kiosk located at Circunvalación and 112ᵗʰ. The operation began around 11:00 A.M. yesterday and lasted until past noon. It included the confiscation of a 22-caliber weapon and the arrest of a 40-year-old woman. It is estimated that the approximately 150 grams of the drug could have been converted into more than 450 grams on the street. Assistant Commissioner Balmaceda told* El Vocero *that in the short time he has been living in our Villa, the battle against drugs has made considerable advances. "Although ours is a slow, constant task," he said, "perseverance week after week brings about favorable results in the end. And if we have to cross rough waters to put an end to drugs, then we will cross them."*

One Saturday night Mariano and Jorgito drank some Fernet, did a few lines, and decided to settle the debt. They would avenge Doña Herminia, their mother. And make some cash in the process. They went over to Nazar's place. But with the pit bull there, it wasn't going be a piece of cake to off him. They poisoned a couple of steaks and took off. They were determined to make him spit out where he was hiding the cash from the raffle tickets. They shit a brick when they entered Nazar's shack. Now, along with the pit bull, they ran into the bullmastiff.

We woke up at daybreak. A deep sound, a gurgling that seemed to emerge from the depths of the Earth and which, combined with the stink that was starting to come from the bathroom, left no room for doubt. Something was going on in there. Excrement and its stench were coming up from all the plumbing connected with the sewer system project. It was still long before dawn, but the lights in all the houses had been turned on. There were voices and shouting, as well, because everyone had gotten up and was doing the best they could, with buckets and trash cans, to carry out the shit that was invading their homes.

It was bound to happen sooner or later, someone said. We're gonna be covered in shit.

And, on top of that, the sky clouding over in the southeast. A big one was coming.

I don't know why people judge Mariela. For being practical, they judge her. You need to understand that—not only was she my friend, she was an example. I wish I could be like her, so that if you croaked, I could start over, with a real man. Juan Melitón wasn't so much a poor slob as a miserable bastard who didn't know how to treat her like a woman deserves to be treated. That's why she threw him out in the street. And it wasn't because of the business with Kevin. It was because he wasn't man enough for a woman like her. Don't let anybody come around telling me Juan fucked his life up because he couldn't stand that Kevin went to prison. Sooner or later Kevin was gonna go wrong and end up like his father: drunk, frozen to death in the doorway of the lumberyard. But instead he chose to become a juvie thug and take his chances. Imagine what you'd do in Mariela's situation, I'm telling you, because you don't have far to go to end up like that, sloshed and frozen stiff. But Mariela didn't sit around crying like some old-time widow. When she went to visit Kevin at Marcos Paz Jail, she met Ernesto, the prison guard, who fell for her from the moment he saw her. And she fell in love. At last, a good man, it seemed, who didn't drink and went to temple, besides. Very religious, he was. It's true that everything happened really fast, that she should've been careful and not gotten pregnant so soon after so much misfortune. But life knows what it's doing. Ernesto proposed that they live together. That she should quit her job as super in that building and go to work cleaning houses. Because he wanted her all for himself, he said. He has four kids, three boys and a girl, from a previous marriage. And with this other one on the way, he'll have five. Besides, he says that as long as Kevin's in jail, where he'll be for a good long time, he'll look after him as if he were his own.

I'm not gonna tell you again, babe: you keep on hitting the booze and you won't see hide nor hair of me again. What'll you bet that if I throw your skivvies out on the street, you'll end up like that useless piece of crap, Juan, clutching a bottle, dead of cold in an abandoned shed. You think I can't find me someone like Ernesto. Or even better. And don't tell me to stop yelling because the kids are asleep. I'm not yelling. And if I am it's because what I'm saying is true. The kids know perfectly well who both of us are. They know who I am. And who you are, you hopeless drunk.

Around that time the southeaster arrived. The streets of sand that lead down to the sea carried along torrents of filth. Every so often the lights went out. Lightning, thunder, downpours. And then what happened with the sewers, remember? It seemed like the world was going to end. The Apocalypse.

It was hard for Santi to recognize the voice of that old woman with a German accent on the telephone. When the voice told him it was

Doris Grünewald de Dobroslav calling, he got dizzy. She wanted to confess, the voice said. Why had she chosen him, he was about to ask her. But he didn't. He felt so upset.

The memory Santi had of Doña Doris didn't tally with that voice or, now, as he arrived at the mansion, with that enormous, bony woman, tanned like leather by the Villa's climate. His memory was one of a living statue, blonde and powerful, whom everyone made way for and greeted with an affection that bordered on fear. It wasn't because she was the wife of the Villa's most powerful builder, our Speer. Or because she sympathized with his ideals of racial superiority and all that crap. In Doña Doris there was, because at that time, when Santi was a kid—he must've been around twelve and lived in the hippie community, and she was in her late forties but didn't look it—there was in Doña Doris, I tell you, already a kind of self-possession and strength in her gestures, a strength that didn't eclipse her femininity. She might have been a peasant, but she was also a goddess. And when Santi saw her walking through the Villa together with Fito, her albino son, he was gripped with envy. That woman who strode through life like a tank accompanied by her son, never holding her hand, always a certain distance from his mother, as if he were her guardian rather than her offspring, I tell you, when Santi saw Doña Doris and Fito go by, he wondered why, in the distribution of lives, he hadn't been assigned such a woman, a haughty mother, her nose in the air, a woman like that, instead of being the son of a languid, depraved, randy tribeswoman, because El Pucho and La Tacha hadn't established a family or even, as they asserted, a community, but rather an encampment where the only rule was to run around butt-naked while LSD, mushrooms, and weed circulated, and it might have happened, of course, as it did, that La Tacha, his mother, had climbed on top of him one conga-filled morning, whispering that she wanted to merge with that child of God. The next morning, just after his fourteenth birthday, while everyone else was sleeping it off, Santi split for the main road, the road to hell, that is, to Patagonia. And now, nearly ten years later, back in the Villa, that woman whom his younger self, fascinated, would have wanted as a mother, had come looking for him: she had chosen him. For his purity. For being someone who, having lived through what he lived through, and it was practically *vox populi* in the Villa that the little pastor had been deflowered by his mother and stood firm in the face of evil, finding a path to purification, as I was saying, for being who he was, Doña Doris had chosen him. And now he was walking into the house of his ideal mother. A little blonde maid let him in.

But Doña Doris was not alone. Next to the marriage bed, a bed she occupied by herself, was Fito, drooling, zombified, in his wheelchair. Suddenly Santi felt guilty for his childhood envy. Guilty for having coveted the mother of this paralyzed vegetable. He couldn't understand why God had destined such a punishment for that imposing woman. Neither could Santi understand how that agile, albino child, with his precocious military bearing, had ended up slobbering, motionless, in a wheelchair. Perhaps he, Santi, as a boy, when he didn't yet imagine he'd be a pastor someday, in his childlike resentment, in his envy of Fito, had wished the curse upon him. If what he was witnessing now, the old mother and the paralyzed son, was the fulfillment of one of his wishes, then his entry into this house was the guilty suffering with which God had punished him. No, Santi said to himself, he couldn't have wished for such a terrible thing. It was difficult for him to believe that, as a boy, no matter how much he may have despised his family and coveted another mother, he could have wished such harm on someone: now people in the Villa were saying that the grandfather had abused his own granddaughter; the son had gone looking for revenge and didn't succeed in pulling the trigger; and later, he had tried to do himself in, but the shot missed, and he was left paralyzed. Santi, deeply affected, looked at the invalid in his wheelchair, circling round and round the bed, where illness and rot consumed the mother, because now, as Santi drew nearer to them, he could smell it: Doña Doris gave off a sweetish stench.

Every Friday Moby sponsors a regular fishing forecast in *El Vocero:*

Very good fishing this weekend, both oceanfront and deep-sea. Oceanfront: large quantities, if not quality, of corvina. Also plenty of dogfish and angelfish. Best fishing spots: past the sand mines and the marina. For deep-sea fishing, good quantities of sea bass, whiting, and Patagonian smooth-hound, all of good size. Tuesday's southeaster has affected fishing conditions. We hope they will change by the weekend as the weather forecast predicts.

Cachito Calderón stormed into *El Vocero* headquarters. An emergency's not the same as a catastrophe, was his first reproach to Dante. You should have called it a sanitation emergency, fuckwit. Dante stared at him silently, waiting for the other man to unload his rage and his arguments, always so political. Just look at the image you give of my administration by calling it a catastrophe, how bad you make me look. Not to mention what the media will say as the news spreads. Did you think about the tourist season? Cachito asked. Did you think of the fact that we live from tourism? And you headline it "Sewer Catastrophe," as if nothing was wrong with that. Sanitation emergency, you should've put, Dante. Emergency. An emergency is a predicament. And you can get out of a predicament. A catastrophe is a tsunami, for example. Do you think what happened was a tsunami? It was a storm. The storm drains got clogged up, that was all. Not a sewer catastrophe. What I think, Dante said finally, happily, is that we're all up to our ears in shit.

One might wonder why Doña Doris sent for Santi, Dante goes on. There are those who lean toward last rites. But it might also be surmised that if the elderly woman chose Santi, it was because, like everyone else in the Villa, she knew that Santi had been abused by his mother. And no one would understand her like the little pastor, just as she understood what he must have gone through. If the elderly lady, and Dante called her an elderly lady to give his story a more literary flavor, but as I was saying, if the elderly lady had sins she wanted to repent for, without a doubt the most serious one had been her union with Atila Dobroslav, our Speer, whose vilest deed hadn't been the destruction of the forest. What Doña Doris had to tell Santi, says Dante . . . and then stops. Here Dante digresses: We make confession not so much from guilt as from shame. It's not that we repent for some despicable act we've committed, some loathsome thing that reveals our own baseness, nothing like that: we make confession, just like Doña Doris Grünewald de Dobroslav, because we're ashamed to recognize ourselves in what we've done. Or what we've put up with. Keeping our mouths shut, being accomplices, is as embarrassing as the crime that was witnessed. This, Dante says, always from the perspective of someone with a conscience. At the last minute, Doña Doris turned out to have one and told Santi about her shame; she told him in front of her son, the wheelchair-bound vegetable who, listening to what his mother was saying, started to squirm, groan, and dribble like a terrified kid. While the mother was confessing, Dante says, for Fito it was like the story was happening all over again.

Dobroslav had fucked the kid. Back when Santi would see him walking next to his mother, safe, his head held high, the model Aryan child, an albino with clear blue eyes, his gaze fixed on a future that, without a doubt, he would bend to his will with the same rigor as his father. And now, sitting on the edge of the bed, holding Doña Doris's hand, Santi listened to her tell in a hoarse whisper about the time she had discovered the father sodomizing his son. And she had kept it quiet until now.

A suspicion fell on Dell'Oro, a teller at Banco Provincia. A few months ago, Dell'Oro was the same teller who gave Natale, the one from the Pasta House, fifteen thousand dollars. Resorting to an M.O. similar to the one used in Salvatore's robbery, two assailants entered Natale's home. And though he's kind of a stutterer and seems like a dummy, Dell'Oro, the teller, is being investigated.

But what intrigues Dante most is that in both robberies, Natale and Salvatore have totally ruled out their kids as suspects. Mustn't forget that Gastón Natale and Roque Salvatore are partners in more than one crime. Dante recalls: Gastón Natale and Roque Salvatore were implicated along with Gonzalito Calderón and the other snobby kids in the rape of that girl. Lorena, her name was. Daughter of Nidia, the woman who used to work at Los Médanos discount supermarket.

If a cop had suggested this second hypothesis to Dante, he might have published it. Just to screw around with those kids a little. Someday those fancy-ass kids will have to lose their impunity. Someday. And I'll be at Moby, smoking, with my glass of whiskey. How I'll enjoy that.

A group of local bus drivers, concerned about the bad behavior of the crowds of youngsters who use public transportation during school hours, have launched an educational campaign in the schools. "We're gonna go from classroom to classroom, from child to child, dropping off leaflets and explaining the dangers of bad behavior on buses," those responsible for the campaign asserted.

A storm was approaching from the seaside as Santi left the Dobroslavs' house. The wind shook the poplar branches. And he felt like a sleepwalker. He walked away slowly. With his measured step he tried to meditate on what had just happened to him: the slobbering invalid, the old woman's confession. But then he picked up his pace and, by the time he realized it, he had started running, and not because of the rain that had come unleashed. Anyone seeing him run through the poplar groves would have thought he was trying to protect himself from the downpour. But no. Santi ran, trying to escape from that story, from his own, from everyone's, from the entire Villa, but when at last he entered the temple and fell to his knees before the pulpit, he regained his bearings. He would never leave the Villa. The

Lord had placed it in his path. And He had entrusted him with the comforting of souls. It was not by accusing his fellow man or revealing his abjectness that he would redeem us. It would not be him, a minister of God, who would assume the role of the righteous. Each person had to take charge of his own conscience, he thought. Doña Doris hadn't called him just to make confession. The task Doña Doris was assigning him was to punish. Like I'm telling you, Santi didn't believe in the effectiveness of punishment. Rather, he trusted the awakening of each conscience. If God had brought him back to the Villa, it wasn't so that he could play the avenging angel. His task, always, must be to understand. Only through understanding was forgiveness possible.

Soaked to the skin. He was crying. Like a child, he was crying.

Gimme a break, Micki interrupted him. In the 70s I came to the Villa with lots of intellectual yakkity-yak under my poncho; I yakked and yakked and yakked, and just when I was about to get the girl, along came a jerk with a guitar and fucked her three times.

The thing is, we didn't see Doña Doris after that time when Fito, her son, tried to kill himself. And when we remembered her existence, hidden away in that big house in the forest, it was the day they carried her out in a casket from Neri Funeral Home.

And later, another version, coiled up like a viper, began to slither through the Villa. It seems Doña Doris didn't die of any of the illnesses she'd suffered from. That it was Dobroslav, our Speer, who had done her in. And that it wasn't euthanasia, as in the case of Alejo Quirós with his father, the late Don Evaristo, but rather the way to keep a secret secret. A secret that was inconfessable even to a priest, because Doña Doris, though she had participated in collections and charitable works for the parish, had never been one to go to Mass regularly, to confess, or take communion. Not because she didn't believe in God, Dante thought. In any case, it was because she didn't

427

even trust the discretion of His ministers. But she had sent for Santi, the little pastor. Which suggested that, although Doña Doris didn't trust the ministers of the official God, she had faith in Santi's piety.

And who's gonna be interested in your novel about this place, they tell me. Nothing ever happens here.

As soon as the business with Kevin happened, Ernesto told Mariela about it. The kid had hanged himself. It was the night after the afternoon when Mariela had visited him in jail to inform him that she was engaged, pregnant, and going to live with a good man, Ernesto, the prison guard. If God took him, Ernesto consoled her, it's because the kid would be better off in heaven than in jail. Just think: you have a new life, a life that belongs to us. And he asked her to go to temple with him one more time.

What was the poor thing supposed to do after such a tragedy. She couldn't stand the pain. And so she went to temple. When God takes something away from us, He gives us something better in exchange, they explained to her. Just as God had taken Juan away and given her Ernesto, now a new life was growing inside her and had come to replace Kevin. And it was proof that she shouldn't lose her faith.

Mariela went to live with Ernesto in Marcos Paz. That life kept growing inside her, the life that God had given her in exchange for Kevin. Some women friends from the cult taught her how to make cakes. And now things were going great for her. She was in the sixth month of her pregnancy. Ernesto encouraged her to make pastries, too. She considered opening a bakery, but Ernesto was opposed. He told her that a woman should be at home or in the temple. Mariela told him she couldn't spend all day locked up with her ghosts. Because the ghosts had followed her to the new house. If she had something to do, she said, she'd dwell less on the past. Ernesto told her that if she wanted to free herself of the ghosts, she had to go to temple more often. They argued. Till Ernesto slapped her. Mariela asked him if that was why his ex had left him and taken the kids. If you open your mouth, I'll cut out your tongue, he said.

The fights continued. She miscarried. It would have been a girl. The fights grew worse. Till one night, while he was sleeping, she grabbed Ernesto's regulation pistol. And fired into his head. Then she wrote me the email she wrote me. And shot herself. While I was reading her email, Mariela was already dead, may she rest in peace.

Though everyone thinks that being the mayor makes him feel like a big shot, like the owner of the Villa, it's bullshit. Sometimes in the morning while he's shaving, trimming his mustache and staring at himself in the mirror, Cachito levels with himself and wonders who he thinks he is, imagining himself the leader of everyone's destiny. He's not above Renzo and Balmaceda, the cops, who have already made a deal with Don Tito Souza and his sons for getting into the coke business. He's no better than the Croat Dobroslav, who bribed nearly the whole Legislative Council in order to chop down half the forest and build those two towers. He's no better than Santi, the pastor of the poor and hopeless, who undoubtedly has some hidden weakness. And he's no less of an animal than the barefoot wretches he allowed to set up camp in some empty lots on the fringes, or more respectable than the stuffed shirts from the Rotary. If he thinks about his family, Beti, for example, he asks himself what, in her case, being clean means. Beti doesn't ask questions. She doesn't want to know. As long as she's got cash in the ATM, she doesn't ask. And if they stay together, it's because, more than a marriage, they're a partnership. The Esteemed Mayor and his Lady. At this stage, as Alejo said to him, half the Villa knows that he, Cachito, is screwing Ayelén, the Second Winterfest Princess, and in exchange he's given jobs to her whole family, a bunch of lazy half-breeds. For sure the rumor's reached Beti. It wouldn't be the first time Beti found out about his adventures. And if she sticks with him it's because she's no better than him, either, and where is she going to find someone else who can offer her comfort, vacation trips, money. Then there's Gonza. He'd rather not think about his son: always getting himself into trouble. And if I was elected mayor by the community, Cachito thinks, it's because I represent it. Like Alejo says, if no one's hands are clean here, no one is spared here, why should we be any better. Stealing's no big deal, Alejo has told him. What's a big deal is not doing something important every so often. Cachito tells himself that he's no better than Alejo, either. Even though having a conscience, he thinks, doesn't make him any different. Who can guarantee him that the ones who abused the kindergarten kids at Nuestra Señora don't have a conscience. Having a conscience means admitting there's a limit, that if a certain line is crossed, there's no turning back. And yet, what's so bad about the arrangement Fatty Oviedo proposed to me to get himself the bid for the sewer system, Cachito thinks. I don't need to get re-elected if I seal the deal with Fatty Oviedo. I'll finish this term and I'm outta here with my pockets lined. Someone else, anyone in my place, would do the same thing. I'm no better than anyone else, but at least I don't fuck little kids. The Cachito in the mirror winks at this one, the flesh and blood Cachito, who suddenly loses his smile and curses: he's cut himself.

At first it goes unnoticed. One night you realize you haven't bathed that day. And the next day you don't shave. Well, you don't plan to go out, anyway. Why not stay indoors staring out the window at the sea. The third day you're still wearing the same undershirt, the same underwear, socks, the same shirt, same jeans, same sweater. I say sweater because generally this happens in the winter. Who cares about elegance here. You're not gonna bathe, shave, or change to go buy cigarettes. Besides, you can do without cigarettes. And it all happens in a single day, the fourth, with the temperature below freezing and sleet, and then on this day, the fifth, you also stay indoors. In the turned-off refrigerator there are some leftover sausages, hard-boiled eggs, old bread. You can get by without going out. Soon you'll be out of *yerba mate*, but it's not that important. And the gin—well, when it's gone, it's gone. Today, you realize, you've spent the whole morning staring out the window at the sea. When your cable was cut off you didn't care: you had, you have the sea, you thought. Hours, looking at the sea. Hours, hours, hours. The light keeps changing. Some clouds appear, drift over your head, it clears up for a while, more clouds appear, and still more. In the afternoon a feeble sun peeks out, but just for a little while. Then it clouds over again. And goes on like that till nightfall. You don't turn on any lights because your electricity's been cut off for days. And you don't turn on any heaters because they've also cut off your gas. Now you go around in three sweaters. And at night you sleep with your clothes on. One morning, when you wake up, you stay in bed. Just as you can no longer remember how long it's been since you've left the house, you also can't recall how long you've been lying in bed. You don't even get up to go to the bathroom. How long? The first time you peed on yourself, it worried you a little. Just the first time. Not after that. You close your eyes. And just as you never left the house or got out of bed again, you'll never open them again. In the darkness you can barely hear the sea. Barely.

I sing. Even though the grown-ups can't see me, I can see them. And I sing. Even though they don't believe I exist, I'm here. Even though they don't want to hear me, I sing. I sing about the bruised skin, the broken little bones. And all the children hear me. They hear me on windy nights. Because the wind carries my song between the trees and from rooftop to rooftop. My voice filters through the shutters and the closed doors. Heal, little one, heal, my ass. My song is a howl of rage. And Camilo's not the only one who hears me, like some people say. Lorena hears me and Kevin hears me. Adrián hears me and Mechi hears me. They all hear me. Girls and boys. Those who are afraid at night and with good reason. Because the grown-ups are going to hurt them. There are times when I sing all night long. Then the children open their eyes in the darkness and quietly repeat my song. Some want to get up and do it now. But I tell them, singing, not yet, that it's still a while till the full moon. And that when it's like a blue day in the nighttime I'm going to call them all together. It won't be long now. I'll let them know. That night, silently, on tiptoe, while the moms and dads, grannies and grampas, aunts and uncles are sleeping, you'll all grab a kitchen knife, a pair of scissors, a hammer, a gun, a can of kerosene, and you'll do what my song says. Listen. Listen to my song. The song of El Muertito.

The new people are strange. Those who bought the house across the street, the one that was abandoned. Ever since the old lady died, it's been a dump for trash and rats. Besides, the half-breeds were about to take over at any moment. That's why at first we thought it was a good thing that the new people were buying it. I'm not saying the newcomers had anything special about them that would draw your attention. That was exactly why they were strange from the get-go. Because you got the impression that they wanted to go unnoticed. He must be around sixty, and same for her. They have a last name that's hard to pronounce. Full of consonants. We found out their last name when the mailman brought us their mail by mistake. They're Jews, for sure. They arrived in a red Renault 21, greeted us, and started unpacking, sanding, painting. Just the two of them. From dawn till dusk. All day long. It took them a few long weeks to get the house in shape. Without help from anyone. They took care of their business together, went on errands together, to the sea together. Together, like they were afraid. Doesn't seem like they have any kids. Because if they did, they'd have come by already. No friends, either. Nobody's come to visit them since they've arrived. They're polite: they say hi, but they don't go beyond that. No matter how much we give them an opening to talk about the weather, they don't talk. They sort of give you the impression they're okay just with being together. The first thing we thought was that sooner or later they would come out of their shell. But no, not even when the ambulance came from the hospital. We asked the woman what had happened to her husband. He's not my husband, she said. Well, then, to your brother. He's not my brother, either, she said. She cut us off from asking anything else. Since then we haven't said a word to them. More than shy, they seem proud to us. And that attitude of theirs, ignoring us, makes a person look on them with mistrust. There must be some reason they don't have anything to do with anybody. But they won't fool us. Because we don't take our eyes off them. Even though they may not be onto it, we're watching them.

Almost 6 P.M. And in August, at this hour, it's already getting dark. A sad time of day, when silence and darkness begin to sift over the Villa. If you walk along the shore road, you won't even come across a dog. If you walk around downtown, hardly anyone on the street. And yet the everything-for-two-pesos shops stay open, along with some boutiques and kiosks. A few supermarkets, too. There are some girls and boys smoking in front of the e-game parlors. It's the time of day when we hole up in our caves. On account of the cold, they say. But also because there's no dough. Just like every other year, the same complaint: it wasn't a good season and it's still a few, long months till the next one. And so we shut ourselves in. Even though we may not feel like it, we shut ourselves in. After all, where're you gonna go. Eating out is a luxury at this point. And going to bingo means losing the ten pesos you've got left. So: stew, wine, and indoors. We eat while watching *Showmatch*. How'd it go today, she asks. Good, you answer. And you? Normal. We laugh at Tinelli. We see those incredible broads and compare them to what we've got. The women compare, too, they compare the studs to us. And you end up making your peace with the comparisons. If we fuck, we'll be thinking of some other girl, some other guy. With our eyes closed. When nothing happens for a long time, we rent a porn flick. And we also compare. We always lose by comparison. Sometimes we wonder who we're fucking when we watch porn flicks. Better not to answer that question. It's like when we compare the life we're leading here with the one we might live somewhere else. For example, in the city we left behind. Then we convince ourselves that there's nothing like living here. Everyone's nuts in the city. Alienation, money, violence, insecurity. We've got lots of reasons to prefer the Villa to the city. Quality of life, we say. Nature, we say. The sea, we say. You fall asleep with the TV on. At dawn you're awakened by barking, a gunshot, screams. Your dog is barking, too. The police siren. You roll over and go back to sleep. Tomorrow is another day. It's a question of making it to tomorrow. What happens is that no one pays attention to what Serrat says: Today can be a great day. We listen to a lot of Serrat here.

We, the hotel room suicides, are special people. We're discreet, pleasant, and we don't create inconveniences for the loved ones with our endings. It's true, it's even less inconvenient if you commit suicide on the beach. Killing yourself out of doors has its advantages. But, let's think about this: the beach lacks intimacy. To commit suicide there, exposed to birds of prey and stray dogs, in plain view of anyone at all, is an act of aggressive exhibitionism. Like those who throw themselves under a train, letting others contend with putting the pieces back together. We abhor public suicides. The person who chooses to end his life chooses to end a farce. Doing it has its touch of heroism. If what you're after is to demonstrate a rejection of others, why aim for an opera that will emotionally affect everyone. Those of us who choose a hotel room know how to appreciate silence, the modesty this sort of farewell requires. Because, you know what, it's a matter of avoiding the sentimentality of teary goodbyes.

We call Bermúdez the gardener "Cyclops" because he has only one eye. Or rather, he has two, but he can only see with the left. The right one is a gray slit. If you ask him what happened to make him look that way, he'll tell you it was a highway accident. And he'll start describing it to you in detail. As if he were reliving it. And yet, the truth is different. Dante knows it. The Cyclops's eye got fucked up in a military prison. He was a militant in the Workers' Revolutionary Party. With all the years that have gone by since then, you'll ask why he hides the truth. No, it's not out of shame. It's because he's afraid that the snobs in Pinar del Norte won't hire him because he's a Lefty.

At the request of the Committee of Parents of Abused Children of Nuestra Señora del Mar Institute, Señor Norberto Zamudio, child and adolescent psychiatrist and Vice President of the Argentine Association for the Prevention of Infant and Juvenile Abuse, will present an informative talk on child mistreatment and abuse this Saturday the 30th at 9:30 at the Hotel Gaviotas. The talk is designed for professionals in the fields of health care, education, and justice. The topic is: Diagnosis of Childhood Sexual Abuse, the Revictimization of the Child, and Childhood Sexual Abuse and the Judicial System.

Admission: 100 pesos. For information and registration: 408954.

We didn't know Dante was in love. He'd kept the romance a secret. If someone hadn't been passing along the road in front of the Tropicana one day at noon and seen him all swanked up in suit and tie, with a bouquet of flowers and a box of candy, we never would have found out that Dante, our chronicler, Dante the skeptic, the solitary, reticent one who watched us with a distant, half-clinical, half-merciful eye, Dante, of all people, was in love. Then we asked Jennifer. Jennifer, always so discreet, wouldn't tell us. In this business—she was talking about the Tropicana—privacy is essential, she said. The girls aren't about to go blabbing about their clients' predilections. It's like church: you can mention the sins, but not the sinners. None of the girls wanted to tell. But Nati, stoned out of her mind, did tell. Dante came twice a week to see Chiquita. He sure kept mum about it. We knew that Dante despised Borelli, the guy from Borelli Auto Parts. And that Borelli was with Chiquita every night he went to the Tropicana. His baby, that slime ball called her. He never stopped talking about the Dominican chick. There was no one else like her, he said. He had trouble believing that such a young chick could have the experience of an old-timer. And without any shame whatsoever, he went into detail. He described her prowess in bed like an indoor soccer match: he was always the one to score a goal. Every time Borelli started talking about it at Moby, Dante glared at him. The boastfulness of the impotent, he said to him one night. Borelli gave him a dirty look. Dante got up and left. The encounter seemed to end there. When we found out about Dante's love, we thought we understood. Nacho was the one who had the nerve to offer him advice: Jealousy demeans you, he said. It's not like you think, Dante replied.

But, we could tell: Dante had lost. Love, so what, someone said. He's begging her to leave the Tropicana and run away with him. You want to know a secret, says someone else. He doesn't call her Chiquita. He calls her by her real name, which nobody knows.

Lately Fournier had been hanging out only with dogs. He didn't even talk to Moni anymore. He's going through a spiritual crisis, she said. Besides, all artists are misunderstood, she told us. Any stray dog that crossed Fournier's path ended up in his cabin in the woods. Now it wasn't unusual to see him walking through the woods with a pad of paper and his watercolors, followed by a pack of lame, dirty, mangy, destitute dogs. If Fournier went deep into the forest, set up his easel, and laid into the oil paint, the dogs would surround him, preventing the curious from getting too close and spying on his work. If Fournier was once a loner who only rarely stopped to chat with someone, when he began collecting dogs, he cut off all contact with us. We wondered if he was still painting those solitary landscapes, without a single human figure. He already had quite a reputation as a nutcase in the Villa, because of what people said, the rumor that he'd become a hermit because he was a virgin. The one who spread the rumor was Brandsen, the director of La Marea, the theater group from Casa de la Cultura. Brandsen had asked Fournier for a set design for *The Seagull*. Fournier painted him a seagull with a slit throat. Brandsen asked him to fix it, to make it subtler and less expressionistic. It would've cost Fournier nothing to repaint the head. Fournier grabbed him by the neck: Nobody tells me what to do. Least of all, you. It was around that time that we started to see him, first with two dogs, then with three, and later with the pack. Dogs, those domesticated wolves, are more human than we are, he told Martínez. Someone said that now he was sleeping surrounded by them. Which explains that smell you noticed when you ran into him at the supermarket. If you looked at him and he realized you were watching him, he would challenge you: What're you lookin' at, he once said to Beti Calderón. Never saw a dog, huh? And he walked away between the shelves, holding a bag of bones.

Brawl at the dock, reads the headline in El Vocero. The event took place early in the morning of Thursday the 7th at the fishermen's wharf. At 7:30 P.M., after the wharfside concession stands close, the place is visited by hundreds of people who come to fish and have a good time. According to habitués, the place turns into chaos, and the use of drugs and alcohol is not uncommon. In this context, on the aforementioned day, a fight involving five individuals broke out, a fact that has not been officially confirmed but which was corroborated in several accounts by those present. One account maintains that a man was wounded with a knife and states that this individual has been admitted to the Inter-District Hospital in Mar del Plata. The second version confirms the fight but denies the use of a knife. The third reports that police received no official complaint and began an ex-officio investigation after a request for information by a radio station. The fact is that the event triggered doubts about police information that describes only those cases that have been closed and not those that remain unsolved. On the other hand, the theory that the perpetrators have taken an oath of silence to avoid consequences cannot be dismissed. There is one

crucial piece of data: that any knife-wound victim admitted to the hospital
must be reported.

If you ever walk into a nuthouse, you'll find yourself greeted by an
affable, bright, jovial loony who'll gesticulate and spin around inces-
santly while spewing out a constant stream of clever remarks. This
loony will act as your tour guide. And he can guide you through the
workings of the nuthouse, explaining the function of each area, each
room, who's living here and who's living there, what their particular
craziness is, their manias, their obsessions, why they laugh all the
time or burst out crying like a baby. The tour guide introduces you
to the inmates and their stories, their habits, and the hidden corners
of their pasts that could bring a person to this imprisonment. Neither
the psychiatrists nor the nurses know as much about the crazies as
this guy, who, for a few cigarettes, because the crazies never stop
scrounging cigarettes off you to chain smoke, I mean, for a few cigarettes, he'll introduce you to the secrets of the place and its inhabitants. At first you'll be disconcerted by their gestures, tics, compulsive
movements, blank or intent stares, because blank stares have that bit
of concentration in them, an obsession over a place that's not here,
because even when it seems like they're fixating on you, they're really
watching something else, a person, an object, some scenery, a memory they're stuck in and can't escape from because madness might just
consist of not being able to escape from a memory. The most astonishing part, when you walk out of there, when you leave the nuthouse
behind, when you're walking along the streets of sanity once again,
is how disconcerting it is to note that there is no difference between
those left inside and those who are strolling through life without
a care in the world: they wear the same expressions, the same gri-
maces of joy, sadness, or desperation, they have such a strong family
resemblance that you don't understand what distinguishes one group
from the other, when the line that separates them is invisible; you ask

yourself why they've installed bars, grilles, walls, heavy doors, locks, hasps. And the same is true of us, those of us from the Villa. Let me explain: there's no difference between those of us who belong in the Villa and those who come from outside, even just passing through. Those who come for the season are no better, and neither are those who, in an act of boldness, decide to try their luck and stay. No difference. I'll give you an example: look at Dante, taking such pains to play the guide to our depravity.

The howls came from the forest. Fournier's dogs, we figured out. The first to go over and try to see what was the matter was Moni. She tried to approach the cabin, but the dogs wouldn't let her get too close. They growled at her in an ugly way. Moni called out Fournier's name a few times. And the dogs responded to each of her cries by howling. If she attempted to move closer to the house, they growled at her. If she shouted his name, they howled. Moni ran to the fire station. The police intervened, too. It was hard to scare the dogs off, and, after pounding on the door a few times, the firefighters decided to knock it down.

He was lying there, naked. The dogs had protected the body from the rats. Fournier had been dead for at least a week. He was lying naked. What was most shocking to those who entered first, Deputy Commissioner Renzo and Zambrano, the doctor, was the ritual suicide Fournier had inflicted on himself. He was lying in a pool of dried blood. Zambrano wanted to keep Moni out. It was useless. Contrary to what they had imagined, Moni didn't faint or vomit or scream. She simply observed the body and then crossed herself. And we, who had always thought our poet was a Jew. His work, she said. Be careful with his work, she said. Pointing to the paintings, she said it. But no one noticed the canvases that were stacked against the walls. They couldn't have been worth much. Then Moni went away, muttering some prayers. One of the dogs, the husky, followed her.

The husky moved in with Moni. He goes everywhere with her, like he used to do with Fournier. Some nights he howls and howls. And there's no one who can comfort him.

In spite of the massive tourist onslaught over this long weekend, our many commercial bookkeeping ledgers showed mediocre balances. "Only food and lodging," many business owners confirmed. According to the Chamber of Commerce and Industry, invoices for these two categories were also insignificant, which indicates that this winter will continue to be a long one. Councilman Horacio Barnet declared that the long weekend was a flop largely because of the incompetent installation of the sewer system. The stench could be detected the entire weekend. The weather observatory had predicted winds from the southeast, but they never came. As a result, the stink was noticeable both in hotels and dining establishments. The real guilty parties in this situation are Mayor Calderón and his network, who at this point have given a strong whiff of their seat-of-the-pants management style.

The obituary Dante wrote reported that Fournier, our talented visual artist, committed suicide following a period of depression. His sister Gervaise, the artist's only heir, has decided to donate all his work to the City. It's what my brother would have wanted, she said. Because even though he was a difficult person, my brother loved this place and its people. And so his work, by order of the City Council, ended up in a vault in Casa de la Cultura. Amalia Donato, secretary of Casa de la Cultura, organized an exhibition. More by accident than through Amalia's initiative, an art critic from Buenos Aires, César Mantovani, visited the exhibition and wrote a long article in *La Nación*. Dante, evil-minded as ever, came up with an explanation: It wasn't so much the value of Fournier's work as the critic's need to raise his slumping prestige by discovering an unknown genius. What can you do: Dante will always be a skeptic. He argued with us: He knew Mantovani, an old fag from the Buenos Aires gallery circuit. A secret artist, Mantovani called Fournier. Nobody had ever paid any attention to Fournier. And now our landscape artist was a misunderstood genius whose work was just now coming to light.

I always said he was a genius. Always, Moni repeated, with the Siberian Husky following her everywhere. Cachito Calderón and the Kennedys kept a few paintings. *A way to expand the esthetic patrimony of our Villa*, Cachito declared in *El Vocero. What I've done was make an investment. Because Fournier's paintings are part of our identity, the passion for nature professed by all of us.*

Architect Carlos Gonzaga, Secretary of Planning, Public Works and Services, accompanied by Julián Mendicutti, advisor for community issues in our City, gave a press conference explaining the projects faced by the city: a cultural center, a health center in La Virgencita, running water and gas pipes. Our mayor, Alberto Cachito Calderón, also stopped by later to participate. The most important thing, he pointed out, is to fulfill a long-postponed desire, the project I announced a few months ago, which consists of new, modern sewer lines, with the needs of our inhabitants in mind. It's a well-known fact that the sewer system has encountered certain difficulties related to the area's groundwater, but these unexpected and unpleasant problems are on their way to being solved. We're moving ahead with this at full speed. And I can assure you that I lose sleep worrying about when the Villa will be able to fully breathe the spring air, the fragrance of our nature, the stimulating breezes of our sea.

If we all sleep with—or rather against—one another, get drunk, get high, roll high, it's out of boredom. Tedium starts to appear in the fall, and, like the drizzle, envelops us till we get lost in it. In general what we do is screw somebody over: put the horns on a partner, betray a friend, take it out on our kids. Since we don't have the nerve to off ourselves, we screw our neighbors instead. The months remaining till summer loom large. One southeaster follows another. The temperature keeps dropping. Icy mornings. One day is like another. A whole week below freezing. And another. Not even the perspective of a long weekend and the arrival of tourists to bill changes the mood. Because the holiday lasts as long as a dream, a mirage. Then we go back to business as usual. Many say that the advantage of living here is that you have time, time to enjoy nature, time for sports, time to read. Time for yourself. It takes them a while to understand that the most unbearable part of living here is having time. You have so much time, you don't know what to do. You think about reading a book, but you don't. You think about renting a flick, but you don't do that either. You turn on the TV, channel surf, turn it off, and you sit there in front of the dark screen, hypnotized by your reflection in it. Time paralyzes you. You've got to kill time, they say. And time ends up killing us if we don't have the guts to do the job first. I've already mentioned this to you; I've already told you about my suicide fantasies. Tell me one person who doesn't have them. Gestures become slow, so slow that you can feel your hair and nails growing. That's how the dead must feel. They feel, but they can't do anything because they've got all eternity ahead of them. So it's better not to think. We can't stand it anymore. The only thing that can take our minds off the void is spying on our neighbors. Because other people's lives are always more interesting than our own. Until we know the tiniest crevices of their days and nights. That's a distraction. Like crossword puzzles, sometimes. Five-letter word for boredom: ennui.

With these lines I want to publicly express my thanks and send warm greetings to the whole community: to Mayor Alberto Calderón; Dr. Alejo Quirós; Father Beltrán; Señor Gutiérrez, Director of Banco Nación; Señores Salvatore, Martínez, and Rinaldi, Directors of the TV station; to the Rotary Club; and to all the businesses that donated gifts for the lottery. Thanks to them it was possible to hold a dinner on the 14th for my colon surgery. In addition I would like to thank those in charge of making the asado, *Tachito Ludueña and Catriel Ramírez. Thanks also to my parents and brothers and sisters, who sacrificed so many hours to meet their goal of collecting money for the operation and to my grandmother who traveled here to be with me. Thank you with all my heart and all my love. A thousand thanks.*

Adalberto Barragán

When it starts to rain hard, like now, water flows down from La Virgencita and El Monte. A few hours of nonstop, heavy rain is enough to make the current bring in all the filth, overflow the streets, and, if the deluge doesn't let up, flood the streets leading down to the sea. Soon the current will drag along everything it finds. Imagine if the storm lasts three days in a row. Besides the garbage, the current might carry dead animals, a child, an old man. The last gale knocked down trees, posts, roofs, blew off corrugated metal sheets and cables. As usual, the TV channel and the radio stations reported the weather alert. A neighbor woman from La Virgencita who was coming home with her kids after buying wine at a grocery store started to cross 107th right there, where the current forms a kind of whirlpool. Electrocuted, all three of them. You've gotta be a dumb half-breed to go out of the house with kids. Along with the thunder and wind you can hear the sirens of ambulances and fire trucks. Indignant neighbors start calling into the radio and cursing. Cachito has already inaugurated the sewer system, but most drainage channels will overflow. Fury erupts on the radio stations. Politicos from the opposition add fuel to the protest. But as this storm is stronger than the previous ones, Cachito's declarations don't appease the rage and desperation of those who have been isolated for three days. A helicopter flies over the Villa, and the camera shows us the scene. Predictably, where the storm has produced the most destruction is in the poorest neighborhoods, around La Virgencita and El Monte, which border on Circunvalación. The poor wretches resist leaving their shacks for fear they'll be robbed. Last night there was a shootout between two rival gangs: juvie thugs from El Monte and La Virgencita were at each other's throats. A dead kid was carried by the current to the sea. Because the current flows furiously toward the sea. Maybe it's not such a bad thing if this current sweeps up all the darkies and feeds the fishes. Pure ecology. Nature is wise.

Below freezing.

The last southeaster was the most disastrous of recent times. The sea washed over the rental cabanas and the wooden boardwalk, and reached the first row of buildings. The force of the swell partially destroyed the pier and knocked down some beach cabanas. Anyone walking along the beach these mornings will be able to appreciate the strength of the gale in the ruins it left in its wake. But the most dramatic aspect of the tempest are the victims: eight dead and more than fifty injured in various accidents, most of them residents of La Virgencita and the shantytown in El Monte, neighborhoods leveled by the storm. Malvinas Argentinas Hospital was over capacity with cases of childhood pneumonia and an indeterminate number of children with bronchiolitis. Dr. Carpio, director of the hospital, admitted that the institution has ground to a halt and that the scene is overwhelming. To date there have been no child fatalities, but the next few hours will be decisive if the hospital does not receive aid from the Province.

Meanwhile, families that were left homeless have been provided temporary shelter at the airport. Councilman Federico Jürgens's opposition to offering airport facilities as temporary lodging for the victims has caused controversy. According to Jürgens, president of the Beer Lovers' Association, the victims lodged there are largely marginal types with an underestimated potential for danger. Indigent, undocumented families constitute a risk for the airport facilities, which even before this crisis were in urgent need of repair. We all know that these types of people harbor the lowlifes who have been assaulting our Villa of late, Jürgens declared. By the time we get these delinquents out of here, it will be more expensive to fix up the airport. Jürgens's assertions set off a swift reaction from the human rights sector of the Villa, which recalled Jürgen's past associations with the dictatorship, of which he was a officer during the last military government. I'm not going to argue with a bunch of losers, the councilman responded. If I were so insensitive I wouldn't be one of the active members of Animal Protective Services.

Adding to the tragic scenario was the unfinished construction of the sewer system, which, in areas where the pipes have not yet been installed, expelled an overflow of excrement. This crisis will be relieved shortly, as soon as we have finished installing the sewer system, declared Mayor Calderón, responding to challenges by those who blame him for the flooded streets and the resulting streams of excrement, all of it a source of infectious disease. I am in a position to announce that Oviedo Construction is already on the job. This bit of news should help keep spirits calm.

Suddenly my memory comes back to me at funerals. And, yes, there are times when I forget what I'm telling. Maybe I'm telling what I'm telling in order to forget.

On Saturday my ex came to pick up the kid. By law I have to take her, Gus said. But Abril refused to go. She hid and refused to go. I had to force her. When she came back on Sunday, the poor little thing was out of control, wild. Mama, it hurts me, she said. I gave her a bath. And I asked her. Then Abril told me: He touches me with his finger.

And what I did was go to the Quirós law firm. I talked to Alejo and he told me to forget the whole thing, that it wouldn't happen again. I'll get you your divorce as soon as possible, Delia. But first I'm going to send an acquaintance of mine to have a little talk with him.

Afterward, you must have read about it in the paper. It came out in *El Vocero* that my ex, Gustavo Dionisio, emcee for Olas FM Radio, had a terrible accident while he was repairing the roof of his house. As a result of the impact he suffered a fractured spine and a concussion.

Dante persists in writing those articles in *El Vocero*:

Through seductive stratagems and forms of blackmail, which include gifts and promises, or simply through physical or psychological violence, the minor is used as a sexual object. The abuser steals the victim's childhood and initiates him/her in perverted sexual practices that leave indelible marks, even though these may not be detected in the medical exams to which s/he is subjected so as to confirm deeds s/he can rarely reveal in words.

Because they feel threatened, because they are asked to keep the facts concealed as a shared secret in order to preserve family integrity or to receive something desired in return, or simply because they have no parameters to describe what has happened, abused minors remain silent.

After the period, Dante thinks: As if anyone still cared.

Thirty-four years in Entel were enough to make me feel second-rate. It was when they canned me that I met Elena. You're not second-rate, Darío, she convinced me. You possess a force you don't know how to use. The book told me so. You have the Power of Greatness. And she suggested: Why don't you take a look at the book to see what to do with the severance pay. I took her up on the suggestion. And the book replied: Change, which means moving. The book never fails, she said to me. You're in a period of change. I was still worried about what to do with the severance pay. Elena pushed me into consulting the book again. Creativity, it replied. Creativity is the sky. Elena explained it to me: All beings are creative, she said. Only we don't explore that part, which is the sky part. The book says that creativity is the sky. What does the sky suggest to you, she asked me. Kites, I said. Where do you see them, she asked me. How should I know, in the sea. It would be cool to sell kites on the beach. You have to follow the oracle, she told me. And I'll follow you. In a wholesale toy store on Constitución, I bought a bunch of kites. Elena and I loaded them into the Citroën and we came to the Villa. It was November. We rented a little chalet for the season, which was a big expense. But I didn't have to get worked up about it, Elena told me. Because the oracle's message couldn't fail. The season was a washout. By the time we figured things out, winter was upon us. Elena worked at a real estate firm for a while. The kites that we'd stored in a little shed behind the house had been ruined by humidity. I put them out in the sun, but it didn't help. Elena consulted the book again. And the book replied: The Clan, it said. Family. One month later she was pregnant. See how the book's never wrong, she said to me. Then Tao was born. And I started working for the limo company. Now the doctor's given me some pills for depression. I swore never to pick up the book again. But Elena insisted. Ask it about your situation. I didn't want to argue with her. I obeyed. The Abyss, the book replied. I didn't even want to read it. And on Sunday I used the book to light the fire for the *asado*.

I don't need to leave my desk to find out what they're saying about us, and especially what they're saying about me. Not only that we're a Mafia family, which is what people think, but they also say that if Julián is Cachito's advisor in the city government, it's because I put him there to take care of our real estate businesses. That if he could, Julián would push me aside and manage all the Kennedy's businesses, but they don't credit him with the brains or the balls. Just a front man. All for show. They say I keep that drunk, Braulio, at the real estate office out of pity, because it's the easiest job. And that if someone gets in the way of our interests we get rid of them without scruples. That more than one crime here in the Villa, even if it involves drugs, has to do with us, and that's why, from my legal office, I manage the jurisprudence, moving the Villa one direction or another. They also say—I know they do—that I'm the brains, the cold-blooded one, and that just like I killed my father, I don't back off if we've got to erase somebody from the map, even if it's a family member. Because I know they even say that: that I killed my father. Some say I did it to spare him a slow, terrible death. That's what Braulio thinks, I know it. He said so one night at Moby when he was hammered. Fucking

447

asshole, always shooting off his mouth. And Julián, for his part, said I killed the old man so I'd inherit the practice sooner. He said so to some bar girl he was fucking in Mar del Plata. Rumors reach me even from Mar del Plata. Now, Valeria, be honest with me: do you really think I'm capable of offing my old man? The truth, tell me. If I were such a turd, do you think I would've adopted Camilito, my guerrilla sister's son? I see that boy and my heart breaks. And, you know, it's strange, of all the kids in the family, including my nieces and nephews and even Juan Manuel, my own son, Camilito is the one who looks most like me. My spitting image. When he has those attacks and screams like that, I realize he's got my personality, only reversed. He screams out what I keep inside. But some day Camilito will learn the value of silence. Who can say he won't be the successor to our humble empire.

People take poor Lisardo for a crackpot, but between you and me, there's nothing poor about him: he's a millionaire. But in ideas. Just look at his ideas: meteor-ideas, asteroid-ideas, planet-ideas, cosmic ideas, galactic ideas, though many of them seem like satellite-ideas from a single, distant, unreachable star. Lisardo, the kid who looks like a humanoid, and in keeping with his appearance, that's what he named his booth at Galería Soles, where he sells used novels and magazines, comic books, mysteries, a bunch of science fiction, especially science fiction, and that's why he called the store Humanoid Booksellers. Lots of people might think that the kid's half gone: skinny, hair disheveled, with that expression like someone who just got out of bed, a vacant stare, all of him sliding around inside a black sweater, always silent, keeping to himself, mulling over those things he mulls over, though if we think about it, his ideas aren't so weird. Look at what he came up with the other day, when Martínez from the Aeroclub, a great sci-fi fan who swears every so often that he's seen a UFO, walked into the place looking for something to read, because Martínez is a loyal customer of the bookstore, and he remarked to Lisardo: Sometimes I wonder what God must think looking at us from up there.

Lisardo took his time before answering: We're all mutants from a Philip K. Dick historical novel. Martínez retorted: Dick never wrote a historical novel, kid. Of course not, Martínez, said Lisardo, the humanoid bookseller, but if Dick ever got reincarnated in the future and wrote one, the characters would be like us, mutants forgotten in the past tense. Here all of us think we can change, but we're kidding ourselves; we believe in tomorrow, but there *is* no tomorrow. Static, always here, in the same place, convincing ourselves we can be different and we're always the same. Sometimes not even that, we're not even the same. Worse, rather. And stuck in the past, besides, because no one can escape his yesterday. There's no spaceship that can get us out of here, Martínez.

More of the same in the new article in *El Vocero: Unlike rape, which generally is committed by a stranger and on a single occasion, abuse comes about as the result of a slow, gradual, seductive process that occurs within a framework of trust. The abuser leaves signs along the way that can be detected beforehand. He prepares his victim, sexualizing him or her through ploys disguised as paternal care, like sleeping with the minor or sharing a bathroom as if it were an innocent hygienic activity, exposing him or her inappropriate images of his own body, or, through videos that are not necessarily pornographic but which do contain erotic content, exposing him or her to information that disregards the child's developmental age under the pretext of offering him or her sex education classes.*

Eleven whales, over eighteen feet long, and weighing approximately four tons, washed up on our beach early Wednesday morning. While rescue workers were busy trying to save the victims of this massive foundering, Pastor Santiago Carlos Rovira of The Faithful of the Revealed Light congregation prophesied that man should not change something that, in his view, was a sign from God. Greenpeace

Militants and members of the Save the Planet Foundation clashed with the pastor's pronouncements. The whales are innocent, said Alejandro Bombal, Secretary of Flora and Fauna. As innocent as children. The pastor would recruit more people to his cause if he'd come out and give a little push. This theological discussion of the environment had broad repercussions and the debate occupied several of our local FM stations.

Without silencing or implicating himself, Pastor Santi Rovira declared that the whales are a message: God is showing us our fate if we continue to wallow in sin.

I caught last night's episode of *My Neighbors' Drama* in the middle.

It was, it is, the story of two sisters. One morning the younger one, who's now twenty-four, goes to the police for help. There's an old detective who at one time investigated the death of her older sister. The parents said that the child had drowned. And that afterward they had dressed her. The detective always thought the parents' attitude was suspicious. Contrary to what usually happens in such cases, instead of clutching the dear departed and crying, broken-hearted, they stayed away, allowing the police to do their jobs. But even though the police suspected the parents, they couldn't find sufficient evidence of a crime. Now, fourteen years later, with the girl's accusation, there was an eyewitness to the event. If she hadn't reported it earlier, it was out of fear. The parents had kept her terrified. If she so much as pointed a finger, they threatened, they would cut her up with the chainsaw and throw the pieces to the dogs. Years went by. The parents separated. The younger sister stayed with the mother. Shortly after being left alone with the girl, the mother started pimping her out. The girl had her first abortion at twelve. Only now had she worked up the courage to fulfill the oath she made to her dead sister.

The mother lived in a trailer on the outskirts of town. She was interrogated, and the recording that was made using a Gesell Dome showed a Satanic whale who responded by screeching and sometimes smiling a sheepish smile, denying everything. The father lived in a religious community. In the video you could see the sniveling toad: now he'd found religion and spilled everything. The memory, he said, was tormenting him and he wanted to come clean. The guy pleaded guilty, was tried and sentenced to life in prison. The woman, on the other hand, was released for lack of evidence.

Every Sunday the girl, now this twenty-four year old woman, chubby and sweet-faced, polishes the marble on her sister's grave. She always brings her sister's favorite doll to the cemetery. Sitting in the grass, she makes the doll talk to her sister. After a while she bursts into tears. The girl and the doll both are afraid the mother will reappear in their lives.

If you wanna talk about a real twisted son-of-bitch, let's talk about Don Peyrou, the foreman at the lumberyard. He had it in for Daniel because he had knocked up his daughter, though later it all came to nothing because she had a miscarriage. Then Daniel hooked up with Cati, who at one time was fucking Moure, the veterinarian. And they had Maxi. But Don Peyrou still was out for blood. If Daniel showed up one minute late to work, Don Peyrou would dock him for the whole day. Don Peyrou played a thousand dirty tricks on him. Till Daniel decided to try and pull the rug out from under him and went to the City Council with information about Don Peyrou's bribes: what he asked for to send out the street sweepers to clean a street or clear out a vacant lot. And also for the laborers to construct parks and gardens on their own. It cost Don Peyrou an indictment. But he didn't lose the job. Because Castañón from Maintenance was always in with Peyrou. We all knew that Don Peyrou would get even, that he'd wait for the right moment. And it came when Daniel's kid died in an accident: a car ran over Cati, who became paralyzed; the baby carriage went flying through the air. The car was doing ninety; it didn't even stop to look. The driver was never caught.

Even though you may not know it, you're always prepared for the death of anyone but your child. Imagine, poor Daniel. After taking bereavement leave, when he came back to the lumberyard, still a mess, he was unaware of the surprise that awaited him. They had transferred him to the cemetery. And the one who arranged the transfer, who else could it have been.

Don't complain, Danielito, Don Peyrou said to him, laying a hand on his shoulder. Now you'll be able to spend more time with your kid.

We thought Daniel would react. But no. Guess what he said to Don Peyrou:

Thanks, he said.

And he headed off to the cemetery.

Family Therapy Seminar based on The Orders of Love.

Bert Hellinger provides a new vision for understanding human relationships through the family constellation system. When a person in the system suffers a tragic fate, is excluded, dismissed, or forgotten, in generations to come there will be systemic identifications and implications. This means that in a generation a member of the family, unknowingly moved by family conscience, will play the role of the person who was excluded, taking on a destiny that is not his own. He will live his own life with feelings that don't belong to him and which he cannot control.

Hellinger teaches us: Peace begins in my soul when all the things I denied, rejected, judged, regretted, repressed, and projected can find a good place and rest within me beside those things I approve of, when they can be loved for their meaning, for their consequences, and their contribution to my growth.

Coordinator: Mario Raymundo Spataro. Individuals: $30. Couples: $50. Personal Growth Work: $120 (includes participation).

Saturday, August 15, from 2:00 - 7:30 P.M. In the Beer Lovers' Association Lounge.

Moni worked up the nerve to go over to Fournier's cabin just recently, several weeks after his death and burial in the local cemetery: a plot at the far end of the cemetery, where it becomes open countryside beyond the last wooden crosses, the most recent graves, extending along the wire fence toward the cow pasture. Because you've got to admit, Dante said, it's not that more people die in this place. It's that every day more are born. The more who are born, the more who die, he then pronounced, sententiously, playing the sage, but without managing to lend a *criollo* tone to his urban accent. Moni, like I was telling you, took her time visiting Fournier's grave and laying some lavender on it, just like she took her time going into the abandoned cabin. Or rather, it wasn't Moni, but her anguish, her desolation, that took its time, everything Fournier had meant to her and was now called absence. She entered slowly, timidly, maybe fearfully. For an instant Moni thought that Fournier must be painting and that, as usual, he'd put on a grumpy expression; why was she coming over to mess around when she knew he was concentrating on his painting, that obsession of his for retouching his landscapes up to the last moment, that obsessive retouching that turned each landscape, each corner of the forest, into an identifiable place, a place that seemed accessible: a person could walk right into the landscape and through those acacia tress. I'll love you till I die, Moni thought as she walked into the cabin. But Fournier wasn't there. That's it, she said to herself without much conviction. A pestilence: cat piss, dampness, confinement, and a weasel she heard on the roof overhead. Fournier had two bookshelves with books, some boards on which Kierkegaard, Swedenborg, Dostoyevsky and Nietzsche stood moldering. Moni picked up *The Wanderer and His Shadow*. She peeked at the underlining, recognized those phrases that Fournier would whip out in order to win an argument with her. Then she saw the photo. In black and white. The boy in the photo was Fournier, in his Salesian Brothers uniform. A sad-eyed boy. Behind him, around him, framing the boy, the Patagonian steppes. Wind, dust. Looking at the photo, Moni thought she understood. She didn't exactly know what, but she understood something, something she couldn't define. The weasel on the roof started moving around again. Instead of feeling afraid, she felt less alone.

Around this time of year, suddenly, without our realizing it, in September, you can feel a change in scenery and in spirits. The sun comes up earlier, draped in mist. But after a while it clears up. And from the sea there comes a sparkling clarity. The waves seem transparent and the foam is whiter. The green acquires an intensity, the red of the rooftops is purer, and in the calm of the day that's about to begin, you can unmistakably hear the sea. Later you'll hear the soft warbling of sparrows and larks. In the forest the magpies make a racket and, if you walk among the pines and eucalyptus, the fragrance of humus rises from the soil and cleans your lungs. It's glorious to get up early at this time of year. You feel joy. You feel like living. In spite of everything, you feel like it. And you become hopeful thinking that today no one will burn a kid with a cigarette.

But let's not fool ourselves. There are still some southeasters, some cold spells, awaiting us.

Swelled with vanity by the advances of science, men boast of wisdom but have grown stupid. Their faithlessness to God has resulted in impurity, slavery, and base passions. Hearts pursue unnatural relationships. Sexual abuse is one of the consequences. God offers man merciful forgiveness through Jesus Christ. But it is necessary to recognize the seriousness of the sin, repent, and diligently struggle against evil by virtue of goodness. Anyone suffering from this illness must not trust his own resources, but rather seek help in order to enter a rehabilitation program. At the same time, he must distance himself from environments where he may find himself alone with potential victims. If we do not recognize the sin and our need for God, the sin will eventually drag us off to hell. That's why Jesus's call to conversion, Divine Mercy, is urgent. Let us help our sinning brothers and sisters to save their wayward souls. This is the call of Hearts Pierced by the Love of Jesus. Calle 105B and 119th, Barrio La Virgencita. Evangelical Congregation meetings: Tuesdays and Thursdays at 8:00 P.M. Saturdays at 7:00 P.M. Sundays at 10:00 P.M., 6:00 P.M., and 8:00 P.M.

What's wrong with Dante that he won't quit writing those articles on abuse, Alejo cursed. Nobody cares about it. What happened, happened. It's over. And we can't get bogged down by what's already happened. People will think we're all shits. But look, look—just look at what he's publishing now:

When an abuser turns up, everyone says: "But he seemed like such a nice guy." Contrary to what you might imagine, there's no way to establish an identikit for the typical abuser. You can't trust anyone. It could be the music instructor, the priest, the teacher, even the father. However, certain traits can be identified in many abusers: people who tend to make physical advances toward others, who tend to be "handsy" without respecting others' personal space, and are often verbally abusive. You might say there are lots of people who fit that description and have never abused a child. Just as there are also others of this stripe who are socially adapted and keep it well hidden.

What the hell's he writing, what's wrong with that damn fool. He's trying to say we're all a bunch of babyfuckers. You've gotta have a filthy mind.

Others say that the Muertito you can hear some nights is an unborn baby. Nights when there's a full moon, that's when you hear it the most.

With everything that happened to Mausi, I think the best thing she can do is take Mechi away from here and start a new life somewhere else. Distance themselves. Problems look different from far away. They get smaller. Till a person loses sight of them. And around here

455

everyone has an opinion, everyone judges. It's unfair for her and the child to have to put up with the whole Villa's gossip and dirty looks. According to what she's told me, she'd promised the little one that trip to Disney World long before what happened. Her husband's suicide attempt. That little girl without a father, because you've got to admit that the way Fito ended up, paralyzed, retarded, he's not a daddy. Mausi's situation isn't easy. And the trip is the beginning of a new life. Because Mausi told me she plans to go live in Brazil. She says she's gonna open up an inn in a little town north of Seguro. I'm telling you because she showed me a map of where the town is. And, of course, with the income she gets from the apartments in the Towers, plus the help from her father-in-law, because Dobroslav's not gonna stop helping her, she'll have more than enough to start a new life. What do they want Mausi to do? Stay and take care of the poor wretch, huh? I'll tell you something else: the women who criticize her and say Dobroslav paid her off to keep her mouth shut, are envious. Plenty of them would love to have such a generous father-in-law who understands that the best thing she can do is go away and start over. Like the song says, "They say distance is forgetting." And in life you've gotta know how to distance yourself and forget. Like children. Because children forget.

When, on a stormy night, this southeaster, for example, razes the Villa, knocking over trees and poles, the electrical poles fall, too, the high-up connection boxes flash in the wind, cables whip by, whistling as they cross the darkness, street lights go out, streets, houses, buildings, everything, for hours we're plunged into the deepest darkness, you can touch it, and you'll have to wait till daybreak, because only with the first morning light will the three or four repair trucks from the electrical co-op begin to circulate. Even then the darkness will be a long one; it will last as long as a torture session, because this blackness represents the immense, deep, inscrutable night of the soul. As we huddle indoors, there's no choice but to face our own darkness. You might have a lantern, a candle. But that's no longer the sort of light that will redeem you from your ominous thoughts. No matter what efforts and maneuvers you resort to in order to escape, nobody can. Even if you light your way with a flashlight, you won't strip away those thoughts, it's impossible. Because you *are* those thoughts: to do someone in, to do yourself in. The endless night is a perfect opportunity for your worst fantasies to cross your mind. For you to act on them, as well. In the darkness, anyone can justify his confusion, pulling the trigger at a shadow. And end up getting rid of someone he couldn't stand anymore. It wouldn't be the first time something like that has happened. Or the last. An accidental death wouldn't surprise anyone. If you run someone over with your F100, it's because you can't see anything in this tunnel of eucalyptus and acacia trees; what do you expect if it's a black hole. Besides, there's the downpour, the bog. The darkness doesn't just lend itself to a gunshot that blends with the thunder or the revving of a motor. It's also ideal for ditching a corpse. You can take advantage of it to get rid of the body. You load it into the trunk and head for the dump. Who's going to stop and notice a car parked along the road at the side of the garbage dump in this kind of hurricane. No one will stop, for one basic reason, among others: braking under these conditions means risking getting killed yourself. But what we think about most is that this is the opportunity. And the only thing concerning you isn't where you left the candles, but how to do it without leaving a trace.

It didn't take long to learn that the accident suffered by Dionisio, the announcer, was as un-accidental as the abuse his little daughter Abril had suffered. The fact that it was none other than Don Carneiro who found him after he fell off the roof, and the swiftness with which Delia got her divorce, no doubt were due to the intervention of Alejo Quirós. Which makes you think that, no matter what people say about Alejo, in a way, even in a dark sort of way, he punished a crime that ordinary justice wouldn't have exacted with such speed. Now then: what does "crime" mean with regard to the beating Don Carneiro administered to the abuser, and what is meant by ordinary justice, as if abusing a child were an ordinary act. It's obvious in this case that Alejo, by doing things his own way, whether we like it or not, doesn't feel a bit of remorse. Because Alejo, whether we like it or not, is the law. And not just the law. Justice, too. But an extraordinary sort of justice. A righteous dude, our counselor.

Quit hassling me about Paradise Towers. If you want to know who the civil accomplices are of the ecological offense you're so concerned about, check the list of apartment owners in the Towers. See how many units are listed in the name of Mausi Jürgens, the main beneficiary as co-owner, mother of the abused little girl. And check how many are in the name of Beti Calderón, Cachito's wife. How many in the Kennedys' name. And don't think there isn't one listed for Valeria, the pharmacist's Jew, yeah, Beti's sister-in-law. With a unit there, in the same tower, Alejo won't even need to move his car to hop into bed with the Jew.

If they keep getting themselves in a knot over this business of *los abusaditos,* they'll end up claiming the kindergarten was run by Bambino Veira.

These days we see Dante going around in a fog, like he's somewhere else, and while it's true that the Villa might be a sort of somewhere-else for lots of folks, this somewhere-else where Dante seems to be isn't the beach or the forest; it's not the dawn that breaks earlier at this time of year, a time when you can already feel summer in the first morning sun that warms the window, filters into the bedroom, and assaults the eyes that reluctantly blink open. For the past few mornings, Dante's been having trouble rousing himself. The only explanation he can think of is last night's whiskey, but that strikes him as simplistic. The explanation lies in the hypothesis he's begun to develop. A brain teaser, more than a hypothesis, and the name brain teaser is no coincidence, because the matter of *los abusaditos* has wormed its way into everyone's brain. What Dante's been trying to do lately, the result of which are the articles he publishes on child-abuse prevention, has been to try to take the puzzle apart and put it back together again, following the real-life script of the film that all of us, each in our own way, has made of the scandal. He didn't recall where he had read a phrase by the director Robert Altman: A film is a puzzle. Altman's thought lodged in his brain. He wrote it down on a card with a marker and put it next to the computer keyboard. What Dante should have thought of doing was to write the script of what happened. He absolutely never thought of it as a film project. When he thought about a movie script, he thought of a narrative structure with details that escaped him, pieces that eluded him, an incomplete shape, and, by putting a piece here, he had to remove another one there, and then the script mutated; what up to a few months ago had been one reality had now become another. The idea of assembling it, thinking about the research that lay before him, exhausted him before he even got started. He decided to take things calmly. But it was a false calm. Sometimes, like now, as he pores over *El Vocero*'s archives from that April day when the scandal broke and up to this morning, he asks himself if he shouldn't write *Evil* with a capital E, affording it that absolute character typical of the religious mysticism of one possessed. As he rifles through the pages, he has an intuition: Evil is here. That night, in Moby, he's about to mention it. He holds back. But he does ask what would happen if the facts had been pure imagination. What I'm saying is, which is more serious: if "nothing ever happened here" is the Villa's collective response so as to cover everything up, sweep the dirt under the rug, and forget—or if nothing, in fact, really did happen, he said—and if nothing happened and it was all rhetoric of the collective imagination, something has burst like a boil.

On Tuesday afternoon law enforcement agents intercepted an act of tres-
passing in a lot located on Avenida 31 between Calles 115 and 119. A
group of individuals was found trying to occupy the premises by building
a wooden shed. A man who resisted arrest by threatening law enforcement
agents with a firearm was arrested and taken into custody. Another simi-
lar incident was reported that same day at Calle 150 and Avenida 4, also
averted by police personnel. A large group had occupied a block and was
caught in the act of marking new property lines.

Early Thursday morning, another group of people tried to move into
an area at the intersection of Calles 148 and 9. When forced by police to
move along, they reassembled in another vacant lot in the area, from where
they were once again expelled. A open brawl broke out, during which two
policemen were seriously wounded and five men, three women, and seven
minors were arrested.

Through Borelli we learned about Dante, his story, the story of his son. Chiquita told him. Dante was in love with her, she said. And he opened up to her like no other man did. I love that reporter more every day, Chiquita told Borelli. She said it to make him jealous. Because she loved to make Borelli—who was drooling over her—suffer. Besides, she hated it that Borelli, that dirty old man, got off by wearing her panties. And she told him. She told him what she said Dante had told her.

That when there was a civil war here, some secret agents broke into his house early one morning. Dante and his little boy were asleep. Eva, his wife, wasn't home. She had her nocturnal activities, too. Like him, she planted bombs. One night they came for her. Three cars with armed men. They weren't looking for him. They were looking for Eva, his wife. Dante didn't matter to them; he was just a sports writer who worked for a radio station. They were looking for his wife. He meant nothing to them. If he would tell them where to find his wife, nothing would happen to the baby. One of the secret agents removed all the bullets but one from his revolver, placed the gun against the baby's head, spun the barrel. Russian roulette. He had to choose. The guerrilla or the baby. Dante chose the baby. When the men had gotten the information they were after, they left. Dante warmed a bottle, put powdered milk, diapers, and a coat in a bag and took the little one to his parents' house in Patagonia. Then he came to the Villa. He never heard anything more about the woman. And some years later, when he went to visit his son, as the relatives had told him the truth, the boy refused to see his father again. A good man, Dante, Chiquita told Borelli. A good father. I would have done the same thing if my husband had put my baby in danger. I like that man, Chiquita said. Dante has a huge heart. Borelli took off Chiquita's red panties which he sometimes wore to turn himself on. And he left. It wasn't jealousy anymore. Now he hated Dante. Like never before. A silent fury invaded him. That Dante is a liar, a phony: he makes up a different past for everyone. And I'm sure he promised you a different future, dummy. What do you think, you fucking whore, he turned toward Chiquita. That he's gonna get you out of this shithole, that you're gonna run away together, that you're gonna marry that turd. And he walked out of the whorehouse, slamming the door.

That night Borelli ended up at Moby. And he told us the story Chiquita had told him. Nobody said a word. We didn't care how much truth there was in it, how much of Dante's story had survived Chiquita's embellishment. It wasn't the kind of story you blab just like that. Not even in confidence. We'd heard heavier tales before. But this one was toxic to us. It wasn't a story that a person with the slightest shred of dignity would go blurting out. There are things you just don't play around with. There are codes. I think it was Gerardo the lifeguard who grabbed Borelli by the collar, slapped him in the face, dragged him to the door, kicked him downstairs and told him that the next time he ran into him, he'd cut out his tongue. Gerardo pulled out a switchblade, proof he wasn't lying. He's a Calabrese, that Gerardo.

Lucas died of Sudden Infant Death Syndrome shortly after his first birthday. There was a whole argument about whether it was appropriate or not to hold a funeral for him. Children don't have funerals, said Moure, the one from the veterinary clinic. They're still little animals. However, Vivi, the mother, insisted. You're not the father to say what should be done, Vivi snapped at him. The fact that Moure had a past with her didn't give him the authority to express an opinion. Vivi was crazy, declared Amalia, the one from Casa de la Cultura, who had been her friend at one time. She must've been nuts to have a baby when she was single in the first place, said Rafa, the teller from Banco Nación, who had also banged her for a long time. And he added: Luckily the kid wasn't mine. God knows whose it was, with Vivi such a slut, repeated Luján, the one from the TV station, as if it were necessary, as if we didn't already know who Vivi was. She never was an artisan, said Clara. She barely got by. She lied. She quit doing crafts a while ago and was bouncing around from bar to bar as a waitress. Till Cachito found her an administrative job in Tourism. What happened was, before making a final decision, Vivi consulted Pai Egidio, who advised her to close the little casket and throw it into the sea, to let the infant find his way back to the origin of life. Vivi consulted Santi, the pastor, who told her that no matter what she did with the tiny departed creature, she would keep him forever in her heart. And finally she consulted Father Beltrán: give him a Christian burial, he recommended. Lucas's funeral was held at Neri Funeral Home. When we saw the casket, several of us thought the same thing: it looked like a toy. And Lucas, like a doll. He wasn't buried, Amalia recalled. Vivi wanted to have him cremated. And she kept the ashes for a while, till Lucas started coming into her bed at night. He asks me to let him in, she explained. Until one day, Martínez, the director of the Aeroclub, convinced her to scatter the ashes from the control tower. We all picked up on Martinez's interest in Vivi's crazy notion. One very windy morning they went to the Aeroclub. Because Martínez knows a lot about the sky, Vivi explained later. We deduced: Martínez was the father.

You don't know for what reason or at what moment it will strike. In this situation, reason doesn't matter. Out of the blue and when you least expect it, it grabs you, and it won't let you go. It can be for just a little while or for days. It doesn't matter how long in real time. It's always an eternity when it hits you. And exactly how happy you are doesn't count, either. Because it's precisely when you feel that happiness is finally possible and you take a deep breath, then, at that moment, its favorite moment, it takes you by surprise. You can be happy, watching your son play in the woods. Or you've just made love to the love of your life. You've paid off the mortgage on the house. Or were granted the trip you'd been dreaming of. Like I told you, there's no apparent reason for when it appears and grabs you. There's no logic to it, so don't drive yourself crazy looking for an explanation. It grabbed you and it won't let you go: the sensation that something terrible is about to happen, a sensation of dread; an evil whose magnitude you can't even imagine is going to have it in for you and—why not?—also for your loved ones. Especially for your loved ones. Because when it comes, it will take no pity on the weakest and most helpless. Absolute vulnerability, that's what you feel. And, like in a horror movie, you're the victim of a prophecy, because it was written that this would happen to you, that you could see the attack coming, anyone but you would have noticed it, because, as usual, it attacks when you least expect it. Like now. You can't do a thing. Maybe the smartest course of action is not to resist, turn off the light, sit down on the ground, and curl up against the wall in a corner, waiting for it to loosen its grip on you. You hug your knees and tuck your chin. Then you grab the back of your head. You count. One, two, three. You count to a thousand. And it's still got you trapped. No, counting doesn't do any good. You can hear the wind whistling through the branches. You want to get up and run away. But you know that no matter how much you run, no matter where you go, it will follow you like your shadow. Freeing yourself from its onslaught is as impossible as freeing yourself from your own shadow. Because the attack comes from your shadowy side. Suddenly you're relieved by knowing how clever you were to turn out the light. In the dark there are no shadows, you tell yourself. But, no way around it: it doesn't let go of you. Now it's grabbing you by the scruff of the neck. Even in the darkness there are shadows.

Quit that crying. You're too big for that whining now: when's Daddy coming back, when's Daddy coming back, when's Daddy coming back. I've had it up to here with you. You act like a baby, crying like that. You're five already but you act like a one-year-old when you get that way. Enough. Daddy's not coming back. Ever. Besides, he doesn't love us. Not you, not me. And you even less than me. Get it straight once and for all: it was your fault he went away. He didn't want to have kids. But you came anyway. I thought he'd change his mind when he held you. But he didn't. So cut if out already with the when's-he-coming-back. Never. He's never coming back. And if you keep bugging me, I'm gonna fuck off too and you'll have to manage all alone, get it? I won't even leave you the dog or the cat. All alone.

I is someone who sometimes comes to me with the voice of another. At first it's hard for me to recognize that voice as my own. But then, for a moment, I think that voice is mine. Believing it is enough to make it mine. But this feeling is deceptive, it lasts less than a moment. Olly olly oxen free for the one writing this page, writes the voice of the other.

I've told you before and here I go again: What if all this was a curse, the curse of the Land of Storks. Even the name that Father Thomas Falkner gave these parts when they were covered in water was a curse. A curse, the irony of the original name of this place. A curse that fell and will continue to fall like a shadow on the cradles of the children of this land. And since it's a curse, what can we humans do against divine will. Let us pray.

We invite the community to the Second Environmental Encounter, organized by the Environmental Network of Friends of the Villa and the Mar de las Pampas Public Welfare Society, which will be held in our city on Saturday, September 19, at the Center for Retirees and Pensioners, Avenida 6 and Calles 105 and 106, beginning at 7:30 P.M.

Topics to be presented and discussed are: Protected Natural Areas, Organic Waste Treatment with Earthworms, Pet Spay and Neuter Campaign, Aquifer Issues, Provincial Resolution on Trawl Fishing, Coastal Management and Conservation of Deep Sea Fauna, Chemical Protocols, Light Pollution, Legislation on Animal Protection, Native Trees, Dangerous Power Lines, and Native Cultures.

All these topics will be explored by prominent specialists.

He who does not believe in God does not believe in the nation of God, Pastor Santi said last night. Just imagine, this place as the nation of God. And yet we go to church, we go to temple, we believe. Perhaps because we realize that we are lost.

Don't tell me there's no *mate* in my stories. Go on, change the *yerba*.

Let's recap, Dante insisted. This place originally was the Land of Storks. What do storks bring? Babies. So the German suspected of being a Nazi established his little empire here and promoted the Villa as a young resort, an ideal space of freedom where kids would grow up healthy and safe from the poisons of the city, its temptations and its vices, Dante began, and asked: You follow my rhizome? Someone, *sotto voce*, inquired: That rhizome thing, is it a rash? Shall I continue? Dante asked again. Yes, we told him: it was late. Last round, Dante ordered. And he continued: We also have to keep in mind that here there were, and still are, wild pigs. And quite a few make a macho show of hunting them with knives. Let's connect the dots: storks, *abusaditos*, wild pigs, hunting. Because there's a connection between these topics. I'm just formulating questions here: what happened, how, will we ever know. But it's also a certainty, gentlemen, after what happened or didn't happen, that no one, not one of us, can be the same again. No one.

Knowing oneself helps, the article is titled. *Among therapists it is practically dogma that self-knowledge is an indispensable requirement for a good life. Understanding, according to that line of thinking, will free one from psychological problems and promote well-being. That may well be true, but my recent experience makes me wonder if understanding is so important. For years psychoanalysts and other therapists have discussed this subject, which touches the very heart of the way therapy works. Theoretical debates have not resolved the problem, but an interesting key has emerged to the possible importance of self-knowledge in comparative studies of different types of psychotherapy, only a few of which emphasize self-knowledge. In effect, when two different types of psychotherapy have been compared directly, it has often been challenging to find differences between them. With regard to patients, the meaning is clear. If you are depressed, for example, it is likely that you will feel better regardless of whether or not your therapy uses the cognitive-conductual method, which aims at correcting your distorted thoughts and feelings, or psychodynamic therapy, oriented toward self-knowledge. As the common ingredient in all therapies is not self-knowledge, but rather a non-specific human link with the therapist, it seems fair to say that self-knowledge is neither necessary nor sufficient in order to feel good. And not only that. Sometimes it seems like it intensifies a person's suffering. For years researchers have known that depressives have a tendency to recall sad events of their lives. It's not so much that they produce negative stories, but rather that they forget the good ones. In that sense, their negative visions and perceptions can be depressingly accurate, though skewed and incomplete. It even makes us ask ourselves if, in order to be happy, we might not need a bit of self-deception. None of this means that self-knowledge has no value. Far from it. If you do not want to be held hostage by psychological conflicts, self-knowledge can be a powerful tool to free yourself from them. You will probably feel less emotional pain, but that isn't the same as happiness. (Deborah Miller, MA. Phone: 418061. Mention this article and receive first session free).*

At siesta time Valeria, the Jew, comes to Alejo saying she wants a separation from her husband. She doesn't want to die behind the counter of a pharmacy. She's already told her husband she doesn't plan to work there anymore. She wants to work as a decorator, she told him. She didn't study architecture for three years just so she could end up cross-eyed, reading romantic novels. I deserve better in life than being Marconi's wife, she told him. While she was giving him a blowjob, she told him. You want to be Quirós's wife, Alejo asked her. And she, licking him, why not? You'd go to Mass for me, he asked her. For you, whatever you want, she said. And swallowed the wad. And now, tonight, sitting at the family table, he realizes that even though Jackie doesn't blow him like Valeria, he would never exchange her for a girl like Valeria. If he thinks about it a little, Jackie is more ambitious than Valeria. Jackie acts like she's in her own world, and if she doesn't question Alejo about what everyone in the Villa knows, his affair with Valeria, because it's not possible that she, his wife, is the only one who doesn't know, if she acts like she's in her own world, he thinks, it's because she knows a divorce wouldn't do her any good. It wouldn't do either of them any good. Valeria would be faithful to him, for sure. And Valeria would be faithful because, knowing her like he does, she would think twice before putting horns on him. Isabel asks him if the scallops are tasty. Exquisite, Alejo says, approvingly. And to the kids: Who's the best cook, he asks. Mom, Mili and Juan Manuel reply à duo. Camilo doesn't answer. A real leech, his guerrilla sister's son. Camilo, he prods his nephew. The nephew doesn't answer. Camilo, Alejo insists. Old Stinkfoot cooked, says Juan Manuel. Old Stinkfoot is María, the maid. Juan Manuel, Alejo says again, reprovingly. It's the truth, says Juan Manuel. That half-breed smells like dirty feet. He feels like slapping the kid's face. But he controls himself. Show more respect for *criollo* blood, Alejo says to him. The boy defies him: Then her blood smells like dirty feet. It's the truth, he says. Go to your room, Alejo orders. Juan Manuel gets up from the table and leaves. Mili starts to cry. Camilo lets out a shriek, one of his interminable shrieks. When he stops, Jackie looks at her husband. We were doing fine till you showed up, she says to him. I was fine, too, till I showed up, Alejo is about to reply. But he prefers to keep things calm. You went to the hairdresser's, he remarks. That haircut looks very nice on you. I thought you hadn't noticed, she says. Beautiful, says Alejo. But he doesn't mention anything about her last surgery, that little nose job. You look like Araceli González, he says to her. Thanks, she says, loosening up. Tonight he'll fuck her in the ass, he thinks. Because even if she doesn't suck dick like Valeria, she likes it in the ass more than anyone else.

We'll have to wait and see how events unfold, said someone, doesn't matter who, because what matters is what was said, anyone could've said it, and what's said, as long at it's said by anyone from the Villa, is what counts, because it was said about the investigation at Nuestra Señora. How many months have gone by, Dante wonders, and starts to calculate. From April till now, more than six months, they've changed DA's, and still nothing. Besides, since the season is almost here, soon no one will remember the matter and everybody'll say, like Cachito did, that it's better not to stir up the wasps' nest because a case like Nuestra Señora damages the Villa's image just when we're investing in a strong tourism campaign: Full sun ahead, as the slogan goes. Full sun ahead vacations. So the truth about what happened at Nuestra Señora will be known when it has to be known.

Meanwhile, we'll have to wait and see how events unfold. And what are those events: the investigation, which, as we know, includes questions, interrogations, expertise. Lots of pages, too. You have no idea how many pages the case has built up. Let's think. What's an event. Something that's unique for everyone, something that attracts your attention, but about which only the outside layer, and not the essence, is known. If we have to wait and see how events unfold, it's because there's something there that nobody can see. Or doesn't want to see. Because seeing it would certainly cause disappointment, if not disillusionment. And it might well be best to wait and see, but especially to wait, always wait, as people do in a place like the Villa, where nothing ever happens, where we all know one another and we know who's who. Nothing wrong with waiting. I'd even say I like waiting better than what happens when it ends. Because the end of the wait can also be a conclusion that compromises, damages, undermines. And so we'll have to wait, and let's hope the event never unfolds because God knows who will fall when things are turned inside out. Anyone might fall. Anyone, and there are even those who say, as if trying to keep spirits calm, that we'll have to wait and see how events unfold.

After that first time she entered Fournier's cabin, Moni had the courage to keep going back. There had been something between her, the poet, and the painter—two local artists who would never achieve big city recognition but who, at this stage of their lives, didn't care very much, more concerned with their own obsessions: Moni with her poems about dead little *criollo* kids and Fournier with his landscapes. When Moni stepped inside, as usual the weasel on the roof stirred uneasily between the roof tiles and the beams and then quieted down, as if lying in wait. As she entered the cabin, Moni wondered, as usual, why nothing more had ever taken place between them. And also that maybe it had happened, but she, capriciously, had wanted "something more" and hadn't realized what there really was between them. I'll love you till I die, she thought, and then corrected herself: I love you even beyond death. She remembered a story, the one about Sissi Bernhard, the dressmaker. People in the Villa called her Sissi because her bridal gowns looked like they could have been made for Romy Schneider. When her husband died at age eighty-seven, she was seventy-three. That night, instead of reporting his death, Señora Bernhard lay down beside him in bed and wrapped her arms around him. She wanted to spend one last night embracing her love. And it was then, as Moni whispered, as though reciting one of her poems or praying, while she was going over the pads full of sketches, that she saw it. Fournier had never told her he wanted to do her portrait. But there it was, in pencil, in charcoal, in pastels, and in water colors. It was unmistakably her. Why hadn't he ever asked her to pose for him, she wondered. And yet she had posed, she now realized. She had posed so many times without knowing it. Those times when, as they drank *mate*, during a discussion of painting or poetry, Fournier fixed his gaze on her, he was studying her. And afterward he sketched her portrait from memory. Then she went to the bookshelves and dug around to see if, among the dead man's books she might find that black grocery-ledger book with the black oilcloth cover, where Fournier jotted down his thoughts. Moni poked around in the library, without success. Then she opened the dresser and rummaged among the clothing that stank of enclosure and in the drawers filled with papers until she found it. She opened it and read: "It's not the artist who observes the model. It's she who observes the artist."

On Tuesday night another meeting was held in La Virgencita in connection with various registered cases of security lapses. Limiting possession of weapons as a preventive measure was discussed. Although no conclusion was reached, there was unanimous agreement that there is an urgent need to continue discussing the subject. City councilors and institutional spokespersons were in attendance. The head of city government, Alberto Cachito

Calderón, along with police authorities and distinguished representatives of our community were also present.

Of concern to all the community, according to representatives of the Rotary, the Chamber of Commerce, and the All for One Neighborhood Association, is the need to end impunity for certain well-known criminal families, not only from La Virgencita, but also from El Monte. These families have long criminal histories that go unpunished, as shortly after being arrested the perpetrators are set free again.

Calderón agreed that this shared concern deserves a political decision that he is prepared to make.

Don't be sad, says the oracle. You must be like the midday sun.

Personnel from the Department of Security, along with the Verdemar Association, police personnel and neighbors, rescued an apparently wounded sea-lion cub. A net was employed to save it and a cage to protect it. Then the endearing creature was transferred to Marine World. A gesture that defines the positive ecological commitment of the people of our Villa.

It was discovered that Carlos Vicuña, the thug "brought down" by the police, one of the hooded assailants of the Ferrandos, had a record and was considered to be a "dangerous lowlife." He had spent eight years in jail and had a murder to his name. The police apprehended him at the back of Pai Egidio's residence. But no one mentioned this. Just as no one mentioned the fact that illustrious figures from the Villa participated in the Umbanda sect rituals. A dozen well-known surnames would have lent something more than character to the information Dante would publish. It was clear that the Pai provided the delinquent with information about his flock. And that Vicuña, with someone else's help, would then raid them. As is always the case in the Villa, the rumors were closer to the truth than the article published in *El Vocero*. Dante didn't report that the Vicuña guy was living at the Pai's place, nor did he mention the illustrious surnames that would have turned the story into a bombshell. Several of those surnames belonged to business owners who published ads in *El Vocero*. And Dante knew that if he exposed them, he'd be left without certain advertisers who pitched in a few bucks so the rag could keep being published. Besides, even if Dante had risked naming names, tell me, you think this would be a healthier place?

I want to stay with you, Silvita said to him. You can't sleep here, Santi told her. I'm not gonna sleep with you. I'm gonna sleep with Jesus, she said. I feel safer here. I'm sorry, Silvita. You have to go back home. I'm afraid, she told him. I'll walk you home if you like, Santi said. No, it's not walking there that scares me. Please, Brother Santi. It's impossible, Silvita, Santi waved her off at the door of the temple. And before closing it, he looked around. At that hour, Silvita was the last to leave the temple. He didn't want the neighbors to suspect anything: the pastor sending the girl home at that time of night.

And now, at midnight, Santi runs through the forest. It must have been ten minutes since Silvita called him. She knifed her stepfather. He had tried to grope her again. This time Silvita couldn't take it anymore and grabbed a Tramontina. No, she hadn't phoned the police yet. She wanted to talk to him first. Jesus comes before the police, the girl had told him. And now Santi runs, disappearing into a tunnel of trees.

He runs and realizes: even if the Villa is 250 miles from the capital, it's farther from the hand of God than the most remote Patagonian hamlet.

When he arrives at the house, a pre-fab structure surrounded by a wire fence, he sees light in a window. Santi pushes the screen door open. A fox terrier leaps around him, barking. Santi dodges it. The dog bites his pants leg. Santi pushes it away and walks into the house. The man is lying on the carpet. His throat has been slit. Santi can hardly keep from heaving. He looks around for Silvita. He finds her passed out in the bathroom, her wrists bleeding. She's slit her veins. The dog goes on the attack again.

He finds the telephone. The line has been cut. He walks out into the night, the fox terrier still barking at him. Santi yells for help. Now the neighbors' dogs are barking. Santi yells again. No one comes.

Help, he shouts. For God's sake, help.

But the barking muffles his cries.

And yet Dante was never altogether one of us. And you can tell. Like many others, he came for a while, running away from something, stayed, stayed longer and longer, became a friend, but he was never altogether one of us. At best, an observer-accomplice. You might say he was never entirely here. And that the other place where he seems to be, though he may feel like an outsider, is now, definitively, this landscape, us, the Villa. In other words, he's discovered hell. Us.

They say El Muertito is a practical joke of Camilo's, the poor fool that the Quiroses raised, the son of Alba, the guerrilla sister, the one the *milicos* took down in Tucumán. It wasn't in Tucumán, someone says. It was in Córdoba. No, it was in Munro. What does the place matter, says someone else. They say the kid goes around at night howling. It sounds so loud some nights, they say it sounds like he's howling through a loudspeaker. They say it's the dead woman's revenge, that the mother is crying through the kid's howling. They say we'll keep on hearing it till the parents have a Christian burial, which strikes us as unlikely, because who knows what the military did with the bodies. According to his Uncle Julián, the one who works at City Hall, once the military had taken the baby from the wardrobe where the parents had stashed him, wrapped in a mat, they razed the house, hauled off the bodies, and burned them in a mass grave. What I think is, El Muertito's not crying for any of those reasons they say. What I think is, he's crying for justice. I'll never get tired of repeating it.

New charges filed; arrests made, reads the headline in El Vocero. *A violent, pitched battle between members of families residing in the neighborhood of La Virgencita unleashed a reaction by neighbors from Calle 104 and Avenida 18, who defended themselves from the attack and submitted a letter to Mayor Calderón. Accompanied by the Chief City Executive, the protesting crowd held a meeting at the District Attorney's office. The news came out that the immediate cause of the conflict was a standoff in which an 18-year-old was shot, an act of aggression that confirmed a long-standing problem exposed by the neighborhood and which brought about a positive result. The neighbors managed to have the charges changed from "use of firearms and assault with minor injuries" to "attempted quadruple homicide with multiple offenses." The DA then launched an investigation leading to last Saturday's raid, in which police apprehended three brothers, ages 22, 19, and 17, members of a family identified as criminal. It should be emphasized that the members of this family have, of late, become the scourge of our community. They have, further, been accused of making threats, demanding payment of tolls to walk the streets of the neighborhood, and committing repeated robberies and rapes. Today the three delinquents are under arrest. However, the La Virgencita Public Welfare Association has demanded greater police vigilance in the neighborhood, stressing that other delinquent families still go unpunished. A true everyday drama suffered by the working people of our dear Villa.*

They take me for an idiot, Valeria thinks. I know all too well what they think of me. The Jew, the whore. Insomnia, 3 A.M. Beside her, Marconi snores. And he won't wake up, no matter how hard she pants as she touches herself. Thirty-eight years old and 4 A.M. She touches herself. Because every Jewish girl loves cock, they say. That's what they think. That's what Beti told me the *mamitas* at Nuestra Señora say. When Valeria, the wife of Marconi the pharmacist, drops the kids off at Nuestra Señora, when she gets out of her 4x4, there are the street sweepers. They stop working to ogle her. How those horny darkies stare at her. How horny Alejo gets when he fucks me. I like him to give it to me up my ass. To have him leak out of me. And for him to film us. He loves it. Wanker. Because I'm forbidden fruit, he loves it. Because I'm a Jew and I'm married. If we could make it legal, he'd look for someone else. Meanwhile Marconi plays dumb. The mayor's brother-in-law's not about to make a stink and have the whole Villa point to his horns. He's not gonna make a stink because his wifey's fucking a thug like Alejo, either. Alejo's gotten him out of more than one hole, from lawsuits by his pharmacy employees to court cases for selling banned medications. Alejo's gotten him out of plenty of scrapes. Why wouldn't he help him, if Marconi is his mistress's husband. And it all stays in the family. We're a select circle, the Kennedy clan. So let's just change the subject.

Valeria stops touching herself. She didn't come.

She takes a sleeping pill.

Father or pastor, Dobroslav asks. What do I call you. Maybe you'd rather I call you brother.

Strong, leather-skinned, with callused hands, Dobroslav studies him slyly. It's the look of someone who asks for guarantees before puking up his sin. But being the embodiment of purity doesn't make him superior. Before the Croat he feels small, weak. Brother, Santi tells him. Call me brother. And he asks: Why did you come to this temple and not to your church. Santi stares at him intently. Tell me.

Men like me don't believe in any church because we build them. I'm not here to ask for forgiveness, Dobroslav says. Because I'm unforgivable. I need to talk to someone. Someone who'll listen to me. And understand me.

Santi keeps staring at him. I'm listening to you, he says. He's about to say *brother*, but doesn't. It's hard for Santi to call him brother.

Dobroslav hesitates before speaking. Dobroslav tells him what he has to say. I should interrupt him, Santi tells himself. But no, he won't cut him off. Let the guy pour out his soul. At the same time, he feels a sick attraction to his story. It attracts him more than it should. Vertigo. He feels dirty listening to him. After a few minutes, he stops him:

I don't want to hear any more, he says.

Dobroslav's eyes bore into him. He's about to explode. And he does. He grabs Santi by the collar, slaps him in the face. Santi tries to get away, but can't. He hadn't reckoned on the old man's strength. Dobroslav slugs him, leaving Santi sprawled on the temple's tiled floor.

It turned you on, Dobroslav says to him. I know what you felt. If I find out you squealed, you're a dead man, Dobroslav tells him.

Everyone in the Villa owes the Duchess something, or soon will. Even if the winter is long, our loan shark's patience is even longer. The same understanding attitude with which she accepts the deed to a property and in exchange lends an amount that's less than its value without losing her smile. That warmth she puts on when lending money is inversely proportional to her coldness when the term is up and she sends her son, the Yeti, to collect or throw you out of your home, and you'd better pray that the beast leaves you with a single bone in place.

Even though we all know who she is, that morning I don't think anyone in the Villa knew the loan shark's, the Duchess' full name: Clotilde Biaggi, widow of Miranda. The late Miranda, as I think I told you, died under the wheels of the Yeti's motorcycle, which ran right over him in the middle of Avenida 3. Considering how much the deceased drank, the fact that he was drunk when it happened allowed the kid to get off without a jail sentence, though he wouldn't have turned down a chance to wipe out his old man, and some say the Yeti waited, with the patience he inherited from his mother, till Miranda was plastered so he could claim it was an accident. Till the Duchess and the Yeti, Rogelio Miranda, her son, whom the mother called Roger (and Dante didn't know the kid's name either), showed up at *El Vocero* headquarters together, arm in arm, to inform him that they had come with a news item of cultural importance for everyone. Till then, like I was saying, nobody, not even Dante, knew their names.

The Duchess had decided to donate a significant sum to refurbish La Casa de la Cultura, to support La Marea theater group and show the entire Villa that she wasn't a person who was interested only in material things. Standing beside her, still holding her arm, the Yeti, imperturbable. The Duchess had discussed it with Brandsen, the director of La Marea. They would refurbish the auditoriums, reupholster the seats, update the lighting, invest in a new production. Waiting for Godoy, she said. Godot, Dante corrected her, looking at the Yeti to see if the monster would take offense and attack him in his mother's defense. I'm no fool, the Duchess said. I know it's Godot. But the show will be for a broad public. Godoy sounds more *criollo*. And I want even the country people from Madariaga to come. The proposal will be huge. And it will have the city's backing. I'll take care of all the expenses. Because money I've got. They won't badmouth me anymore, because everything they say about me reaches my ears. I'll show those Philistines I've got more sensitivity than anyone. Not just more money. More heart, too.

When the cops entered El Monte in search of Doña Reyes, the family threw bricks at the two police cars. The cops fired back with rubber bullets. In the commotion, Doña Reyes managed to escape: she climbed on her motorbike and headed for the outer boulevards. Her grandchildren disappeared in the fracas. As the battle raged on, some kids, the Reyeses, people said, took advantage of the fact that the reporters were following the action from close by and climbed into the TV station's van to rip off a camera. There was such a hail of rubber bullets that the neighborhood ended up locking itself indoors. According to the cops, when they broke into Doña Reyes's pre-fab, they found plasma TVs, cell phones, audio equipment, various small appliances, weapons, drugs.

A while later, Rody, the TV channel's cameraman, called one of the Reyeses, asking about the camera. We're cool with you guys, Roachie Reyes told him. We appreciate you being here because that way you show how oppressed we are. The guy who did it, and I didn't say nothin' to you, Rody, was Johnny Vicuña. Go that way. I'll give you his cell number, but don't say I gave it to you 'cause the kid always carries a piece.

Dante says that Rody didn't have a clue who the guy was. Johnny Vicuña, the youngest of the Vicuña siblings, steals for a cop in Pinamar, the one who supplied him with the Magnum. Johnny hardly ever steals in the Villa. Like hell it was me, Johnny protested. The Reyeses blame us Vicuñas, but we don't fuck with you guys. *Somos derechos y humanos*, as General Videla said. Righteous and human. We'd never pinch a tool of the trade. It was the Reyeses who nabbed your camera. No lie.

Rody told him he hadn't filed a police report yet. That he'd wait for the thug to leave the camera on the sidewalk in front of the TV station after dark. If the camera turned up, everything would be cool. No police report. That night Rody waited till after the ten o'clock news. When he left the station, there was the camera.

The next day there was a shootout in El Monte. Rumor had it that the Vicuñas got into it with the Reyeses. The one nobody knows a thing about yet is Doña Reyes. They say she's hiding in Ayacucho. The only thing I can tell you for sure is she'll be back. You'll know when she's back by the number of holdups there'll be. The Reyeses are a plague, too.

I'll never know what I did to Judith to make that thoughtless woman treat me this way, Brother Santi. Judith is my mom. But she doesn't like me to call her Mom. She never liked it. She always wanted me to call her by her name. Like she always wanted me to be someone else. I tried everything to please her. I studied dentistry, but since I injured this hand with the saw at the butcher shop, I couldn't continue. The saw belonged to Bernardo, who had a Kosher butcher shop. Bernardo didn't want me to call him Dad, either. Bernardo never loved me much. And even less when I fell in love with Rudi, who was a *goy*. It gave Bernardo a heart attack. And he died of another one when I told him he was gonna be a grandpa. I had a miscarriage. Rudi left me. From that time on I decided not to look anymore. No husband, no kids. Then I started gambling. I would run away to Mar del Plata, to the casino. It made Judith sick. The psychologist told me I was sublimating. That luck wasn't going to help me solve what really was responsibility. That I had to recognize I was sabotaging myself. That I should distance myself from Judith, she advised me. Deborah Miller is the therapist's name; she's a friend of mine. She's lived here for years and sees tons of people. It was Deborah's idea for me to come to the Villa. I left my family, I left Buenos Aires. And I came. Here I made changes. Like coming to this temple, Brother. But I couldn't bring myself to tell Judith. What for. She'd have filled me with guilt. That where I belong is in a synagogue. I thought about it. But there are no synagogues here. I didn't want to feel any guiltier. And yet I never stopped calling Judith on her birthday. Never. Happy birthday, Judith, I say when I call her. And what does she say in return: It had to be you, you wretch. You're calling to remind me that you exist. Don't call her anymore, Deborah told me. But she's my mother, I said. Besides, I believe love can accomplish everything. And I kept on calling her. Every time I called, Judith said the same thing to me: You didn't die yet? Maybe Deborah was right, I shouldn't have called her anymore. But guilt was poisoning me. On Tuesday I phoned her again, Judith turned eighty. She's a Scorpio. I always thought that was why she has that personality. What are you calling for, she said. When are you going to realize I don't love you, stupid. What do I have to do to make you understand, kill myself? she asked. That's what you want. Okay, I'll kill myself. That way you won't have to pay for phone calls anymore and you can spend your money on bingo. Yesterday they phoned me from Buenos Aires, Brother. Judith killed herself. She stuck her head in the oven.

After what happened at Nuestra Señora, more than one mother, while changing her baby's diapers and admiring how well endowed he is, will wonder, for sure, if in this admiration that her infant inspires in her and the tenderness with which she applies his talcum powder, she might not be promoting the development of a future abuser.

There's a store called Nashville, and practically right next door to it, a delicatessen called Kentucky. Those names say something about us, man.

Local news published by Dante: *The local city council announces an important event. The adaptation of a classic play by Samuel Beckett à la criolla for the general public. "Waiting for Godoy," under the auspices of La Movida theater group, will be performed in the Clotilde Biaggi de Miranda Auditorium. The name of the auditorium, at the initiative of our mayor, Cachito Calderón, is an expression of the community's gratitude to the impresaria of the same name, who has made a contribution of invaluable theatrical importance. Renowned director Norberto Brandsen will be responsible for adapting and directing the famous play. Proceeds will benefit La Casa del Abuelo. Please note that our entire community is invited to this singular event, whose purpose, according to its promoter, Clotilde Biaggi de Miranda, is to launch a series of plays within the context of a time-honored theatrical repertory that will help to promote the most select examples of theatrical culture in our Villa. It will no doubt prove to be an evening of unforgettable artistic appeal that no one should miss.*

Quirós isn't the only one who has an in with the cops and can get a juvie thug off with probation. There are other law firms that also have pull at the precinct. There's Dobal, Miglioranza, Suardi, Campodonico, Lóizaga. And I'll give you more names if you'd like.

There's no law firm that will refuse to get a kid off the hook. There's no shortage of shysters who invoke Human Rights to justify the defense of delinquency. Those who ask them for help don't have a cent to their name. And if the shysters agree to represent the accused, it's in exchange for favors. You never know when you're going to need one of these kids. No one will give you a hand for free.

As the juvies are minors, before long they're back out on the streets again. They're sentenced to house arrest, but they don't serve. And they go out and steal. Whenever the police are supposed to verify whether or not the kid is serving his house arrest, in general they burst in, kicking down doors, armed and ready; they can't risk having the kid, or someone else from the family, greet them with gunshots. The family, I say, but in the Villa there are currently quite a few more than half a dozen families of thugs. They hate each other, they shoot at one another, they hang out together, they reproduce. Their names are well known. Besides, they brag about their family trees. And their powerful friends. Relationships between the law and power are nothing new. Or between politics and crime.

There's a close connection between political power, the provincial police force, and dirty business: prostitution, drugs, robbery. When election time rolls around, you can see the thug families perched on the candidates' vans, celebrating and singing partisan jingles. Remember the last elections and the Vicuñas. After Cachito won, the Vicuñas fired shots from the back of a pickup truck. Whether they were drunk or stoned isn't what matters here. Yeah, that close relationship between a mayor, the council members, and the criminal element. The same mayor, the same council members, put on a sorry face when there's a robbery or a murder that riles the town. When the precinct gets their new police cars, they've got their opportunistic speeches ready. The shiny new units, which are never enough to patrol the Villa, will dupe the good consciences in the neighborhood into believing that donating money to the police association has some merit. What everyone forgets is that those units don't have four-wheel drive, and if they have to conduct a chase in the sand, they'll get buried.

An armed battle among neighbors from El Monte turned into a confrontation with the police. The incident took place on Tuesday afternoon, but the initial provocation occurred last Sunday, when members of two families, the Reyeses and the Vicuñas, faced off firing at one another. The conflict most likely arose from an old rivalry as well as from the theft and subsequent return of a camera belonging to the local TV station. As on other occasions, when police arrived at the scene, both groups banded together against law-enforcement agents. The episode involved some thirty people. When the squad car arrived, it was greeted with rocks and gunshots, requiring reinforcements to be called in to hold back the onslaught. Agents took a dozen members of the aforementioned families into custody, including three minors. All were booked for assault and battery and resisting arrest.

It's a fact that our Villa is known for its good vibes. Here everyone gives off a good vibe. Acts of kindness. Hippiedom. Or nearly. Imagine: a supermarket called Beautiful People. And beyond that, another supermarket: The Pines. The produce store: Green Planet. Then the butcher shop: Fat Cows. The student bookstore: Crazy Little People. The open-air market: Gandhi. The optician: Light of Your Eyes. And the booths: Smile, Love, Happy. A barbecue joint: Brothers United. The soda factory: Bubbles. The bakery: Friendship. Earthy stuff combined with New Age. It might seem like these customs make us different from any other town around. But don't kid yourself. When someone does something nice for you, it's for two reasons: first, he knows the time will come when he'll ask you for something, and you won't be able to refuse him. Second reason:

nobody likes to be called bad-natured. On the other hand, playing hippie also has its justifications: gentle and peaceful, you put on your best vegetarian face so you don't have to contend with other people's pettiness, not to mention your own. Let's light a joint, man. Here, if no one challenges you directly and if cutting off another driver is frowned upon, it's not out of pacifism, but rather to avoid the problem. A bunch of chickenshits. By the same token, nobody will report you unless there's bloodshed. Because, in the end, what do you know about the next guy if you're not from here and neither is he. Just because someone's lived here for twenty years, it's not enough to know who he is, because, it's a fact, most of us come from some other place, some other life. You know what this is an ideal place for? For being a protected witness. Deep down, we're all protected witnesses here. And the ones we need the most protection from, besides the neighbors, are ourselves. Honestly, and no offense, I'd rather you hadn't told me what you told me.

When he chose Xime to work for him, Marconi the pharmacist verified that her high-school diploma wasn't a fake like so many other applicants'. It was a good sign. Besides, Xime was married, which guaranteed she wasn't an airhead and would take her job seriously. Another point in Xime's favor was that she wanted to study biochemistry. But it was impossible at the moment: her husband was setting up a business and it was tough for them to make it through the end of the month. Marconi was impressed that the girl wanted to continue her studies and that she'd give it up out of love for her husband. The sacrifice spoke well of her. Don't worry, girl, Marconi told her. With me you'll be able to learn a lot. This pharmacy might not be the university, but you'll be able to get an education.

By her first week at Farmamar, Xime was already starting to like her boss: so discreet, polite, detail-minded, his perfumed hands, his short-sleeved smock, always white, impeccable. The fact that the white-haired Marconi was around sixty, far from distancing her, drew her closer. His experience, all the things he knew, the respect with which he treated her, were an attraction—as she now realized—that she'd already felt during the job interview. But this feeling was combined with sadness, too, and a growing tenderness. It was when Xime discovered that Marconi was a cuckold. The feeling no doubt came from the pharmacist's demeanor, his submissiveness, as though he were always ready to be of service. When she found out what half the Villa already knew, that his wife, Valeria the Jew, was Quirós the attorney's lover, that feeling became tinged with bitterness, as well. Xime thought of her own father. And her mother. That whore had left them when Ximena was three. She offered no explanation, but Xime didn't have to dig too deeply among her father's things to find that letter in one of his jacket pockets. It was an evil letter, in which her mother told her father the names of all the people that she'd slept with. Maybe, Xime thought, the Jew cheated on the pharmacist because it pissed her off that he was so good. There are people like that, Xime thought. People who are so good that they make you feel like slapping them in the face to wake them up and realize that their fellow man, most of the time, is shit and that life is nearly always a pile of garbage. Maybe if she'd had the guts to give her father that slap in the face, it might've plucked him out of his desolation and prevented him from shooting himself.

Marconi was so humble: Don't call me doctor, girl, he had told her. Xime found it charming that he called her "girl." Marconi spoke in an absorbing way: There's a reason the drug ads say if you have any questions, consult your doctor, girl. I could be the best pharmacist in this Villa and in the world, but that doesn't give me the authority to practice medicine. And that gentle smile of his, Xime thought, was the smile of a generous man. Although for some, like her husband, Jorge Pousa, Marconi's Mormon-like expression was that of a coward. If you ask me, your boss is generous because he doesn't have the balls to kick his wife out and lose his status and his connections, Jorgito said to her. Don't forget that Marconi is Cachito the mayor's brother-in-law. And the one who's banging the Jew is a Quirós, her husband went on. Maybe it's not that Marconi's got no balls. It's probably just convenient for him to play dumb.

I think you're jealous, she said. Jorgito replied ironically, Yeah, sure, I'm jealous of the old fart.

To the Police Family, reads the announcement in El Vocero. We would like to announce to all members of the Police Family, active and pensioned alike, that next Saturday there will be a meeting at the Rotary Club. Police officials will be in attendance, along with Commissioner Eduardo Negrete, president of the "Movement for Police Dignity." At this meeting, which will take the form of an educational chat followed by Q & A, various problems will be discussed pertaining to active police personnel as well as retirees and those on permanent medical leave. The main topic of discussion is the growing demand for those retirees and/or pensioned staff, to fill positions as security guards in many businesses, restaurants, hotels, etc. While this demand suggests increased income, in the case of the elderly, it can prove risky when attempting to confront youthful offenders, most of them high on drugs and prepared to kill or die.

Cecilia Camarassa, the one from Miranda Photo Studio, came to the Villa with whatever she could salvage from her unhappy marriage to a second-rate TV-series actor, gambler, and whorehouse regular. It wasn't so much the accumulated gambling debts that did the couple in, she would say, as the saga of infidelities that the guy endlessly racked up. And so she arrived at the Villa with a few pesos that she'd managed to salvage from the debacle and a five-year-old son, Tomasito, with a disability, because the poor kid was practically a deaf-mute. It was tough for her to begin a new life in an unfamiliar place. At first, like we always do, we watched her, to see if she'd be able to meet her rent expenses by herself, without a man at her side. But she managed. You have to keep one thing—or several—in mind: Cecilia was a really sexy chick and had a sweet personality, which, for women, was totally phony, a ploy to snag some jerk with money and save her ass. It didn't take her long to have a bunch of fools drooling over her. And yet, no matter how much we assumed there were certain stories about her, even though around here nobody puts their hands in the fire for anyone else, we couldn't prove a single thing, not one. One day Trini, the chick who runs the Everything for Two Pesos store, got hold of her. We all know Trini's a bigmouth, but she must've had her reasons when she blurted out to Ceci: If you don't use it, it'll dry up. An organ that isn't used atrophies, girl. What are you waiting for. That's what Trini told her, which was as much a gynecological recommendation as it was a piece of older-sisterly advice. But Cecilia paid no attention. For Godot, Ceci told her. Who's that, Trini asked. Don't you know Beckett, Ceci asked her. A perfume? Trini guessed. And for a while the rumor circulated that Ceci had a lover who sold perfumes. But none of that could be proved, either.

Only now, after she'd been living in the Villa for four years, something happened that nobody could have imagined: Ceci ended up falling for Adalberto Bacigalupo, the biochemist. An old bachelor with bushy eyebrows, thick glasses, a crooked nose, those rabbitty teeth and pockmarks, besides. Someone who couldn't even buy himself a girl at the Tropicana. A good soul, though, and that's the truth. One Friday night they both happened to show up at the performance by La Marea Theater Group at Casa de la Cultura. They were the only two in the audience of *Waiting for Godoy*. That's right, I said *Godoy*. Because the group thought that in order to popularize Beckett, they had to make him more *criollo*. No matter how countrified they made the characters sound, that night Godoy wasn't the only one who didn't show up: Neither did anyone else besides those two.

Believe it or bust. That night we happened to be talking about the bodies washed up by the sea during the time of the military dictatorship when we heard the shriek: El Muertito, we thought. And we also thought of Camilo, the Quiroses' orphaned son. The scream could be heard throughout the Villa, and, like they say, it froze our blood.

You heard the latest. Here's the forecast: the first heat waves on their way, we all go around horny, not to mention the kids with their hormones raging. We'd seen them and we could sense it coming: there's going to be a lot of shooting. They were frolicking through the meadows like puppies. Hugging and kissing one another to death. And not only that. In pairs, carrying beer. The youngest Reyes girl, Princesa, had taken up with one of the Vicuñas, BB—for Bottle Blond. The two families, which had been fighting like cat and dog for so long, tried to forbid their love, like the Montagues and the Capulets, you might say. But Princesa got pregnant and BB went to talk to the Reyeses. He wasn't armed. He came in peace. Let's smoke the peace pipe, he said. They gave him a dirty look. He raised his arms, asked to talk to old lady Reyes. BB had knocked up Princesa. I want to give her my name, he said. We'll see about that, old lady Reyes said. It was too late to bitch about how they could've been so stupid and not realized that Princesa was screwing BB. Old lady Reyes, that shrewd bitch, said the mess wasn't such a big deal. The unborn Messiah might mark the end of the war. The women had to meet and come to an agreement, she said. And she went to see old lady Vicuña. What a party they threw. White dress, cumbia and more cumbia, drugs, but then the old, unfinished business came up again. There's always bad blood among relatives. And it's worse between relatives by marriage. Politics, after all, always involves settling accounts, but also negotiating. But when it comes to young people, forget it—they like to shake things up. The settlement turned into one big shootout that could be heard as far as the boulevards surrounding the community. Old lady Vicuña, poking the bride and groom with the barrel of an Itaka, stood in the middle of the crossfire. Not another shot. Only the echo of the reports and the stink of gunpowder. When the silence was complete, she shouted: If you keep fucking things up, I'll blast the bridal couple. What bullshit. And she stopped the shooting. You people don't know what love is, said old lady Reyes, emerging from behind an overturned table. Wise old women. You act like you never had a family, you pieces of shit. And you know even less about business, said old lady Vicuña. You should've seen those two old broads. Pack of animals, one of them said. Haven't you ever heard of marketing strategies, asked old lady Vicuña. No one. No idea. She grabbed the bride and groom's hands and asked them to exchange a kiss. It took a while for Princesa and BB to react. And when they kissed, old lady Reyes blurted out, this is love, people. From now on, we're all family, she said. And her declaration stood, grudgingly, but it stood nonetheless. What're you gonna call the baby, she asked. We don't know if it's a boy or a girl, Princesa said. It doesn't matter. What matters is that, either way, the child will have a double last name: Vicuña Reyes. And proud of it. Lineage.

Old lady Reyes and old lady Vicuña toasted with cider. Wise old women: We old ladies aren't about waging war, said one of them, doesn't matter which. We're about stopping it.

Hold on tight. Let the Villa tremble. Because the Vicuñas and the Reyeses united will never be defeated.

Dante writes this article without optimism:

Yesterday afternoon the Chamber of Deputies of the Province of Buenos Aires approved by a roll-call vote a project proposing the creation of civil and commercial courts in the Dolores Department of Justice, with seats in the districts of La Costa, Pinamar, and our Villa. Welcome news in the process of bringing justice to our city.

But we can't generalize. It's also true that there are some lawyers, both men and women, who listen to the mothers who are organizing to wage a war on drugs and save their children from addiction and robbery. In their law offices, it's not uncommon for an attorney with links to city politics and government to do a good deed by cooperating with those mothers. Not all legal eagles are out for political gain: they can act in good faith, too. That lawyer yesterday might have been an old school-chum of the imprisoned kid's father; they played soccer together, went to dances, and now the lawyer feels sorry for his friend, for his druggie or thuggie son who's in jail.

No, I didn't dream it. Believe me, Brother Santi. I swear he came last night. When I walked into the cabin, he was right there, where you are, in that chair. And old man, in a jacket, a blue jacket, kind of shiny from wear, a white shirt with narrow pink stripes, beat-up jeans, and very worn-out cowboy boots. He had on a bow tie. A bow tie with an ox head on it. In spite of the ravages of age, it was impossible not to recognize him. Sitting there, drinking a glass of water. He hardly looked up when I walked in. He hardly even looked at me. And he talked to me like you talk to a lifelong friend when you're making a confession:

I'm tired, he told me. Now I know, now I've learned. Only now. Wisdom is a question of stopping the cycle.

He said it in Spanish. Spanglish, really. Like he was half Mexican.

I didn't know what to call him, Dennis or Señor Hopper. Mister Hopper sounded fake to me. So then, Dennis. Just plain Dennis. Don't go, Dennis. I went to get a bottle. He put a hand on my shoulder. Thanks, he said, but no thanks.

And before he left:

Remember.

How could I not believe in God. God sent him to me. The only way I would accept His existence and believe in His heavenly word was through a messenger like that.

Nevertheless, Jorgito had proof of Marconi the pharmacist's generosity when he needed a loan to set up his business in front of the house in La Virgencita, a grocery store. When Xime sounded him out to ask for a loan, Marconi didn't hesitate to help the couple. He came through with a loan and also contributed materials for the lot. You'll repay me when you get back on your feet, he said to her. Marconi also paved the way for Jorgito by financing his merchandise with Pedroza, the wholesaler. I'll vouch for the boy, he had told Pedroza. Now Jorgito felt ashamed of having suspected Marconi. The fact that he was such a cuckold didn't take away from his being a great guy. God always figures out a way to test the good ones, Xime said to him.

Above the door of the grocery, in big green, yellow, and red letters, Jorgito painted the name of the store: Everything for Less.

If the actors of La Marea went on with their production of *Waiting for Godoy* that night, it was more out of pity than because of their faith in the power of art. The pity they felt for not only the Duchess and the Yeti, mother and son together, eating candied nuts in the first row, and that other pair: the only ones who had paid for a ticket: Ceci and Bacigalupo. When the curtain came down, they applauded enthusiastically. With an emphasis that showed compassion, they applauded. Someone said they had never seen such a sad show at the Casa de la Cultura Theater. Sad, the pity with which the actors performed for those two. Sad, the pitiful applause of phony admiration those two produced. Their palms sounded like two lost birds fluttering in the immensity of the empty hall.

When they left the theater, Bacigalupo invited her for coffee. Why not, Ceci thought. And that's how they began. Excuse me, Bacigalupo told her, but before anything can happen between us, may I make a confession? he asked. And he didn't give her time to reply. It's true what they say about me, because I know what they say about me. As a biochemist I'm up to date on all the bacteria and viruses that circulate around the Villa. Rumors are the worst plague. They affect all of us. Especially when there's some truth to them. And the truth, in my case is this: I'm a virgin, Bacigalupo told her. Which could be an obstacle in our relationship, if we're going to have one. I'm aware of my ugliness, he said. He stopped short for a few seconds so as to study the effect his confession had produced in Ceci. Then he went on: Less attractive men have found a way to win a young lady. It's an impediment I have. I'm not telling you this so you'll feel sorry for me. It's just that you strike me as a sensitive soul. No one who isn't sensitive would remain in her seat in an empty theater throughout the whole show even when the performance is garbage. I was watching you, Cecilia. And I don't think I'm wrong if I tell you that I noticed how certain passages moved you. Besides, there's your solidarity with the artists. May I ask you something? inquired Bacigalupo without giving her time to say anything. Do you like Beckett? he asked. He didn't wait for a reply. And he went on: He was Irish, but he wrote all his works in French. And I have the feeling that something similar is happening to the two of us. We speak Argentine, but we communicate in another language. I have that feeling, Bacigalupo said. What do you think? Sorry, I'm overwhelming you. I talk too much. We solitary types talk a lot. I love the way you are, Ceci told him. And she thought she saw Bacigalupo's eyes well up. Really? he asked. Really, she repeated. I'm going to tell you another secret, Bacigalupo said. What we saw tonight is my favorite play. No matter where it's playing I never miss it. I always hold out the hope that Godot will appear in my life that night. Godot is what I call love. We're all waiting for Godot. Always. And tonight, he was about to say, but he fell silent. Ceci couldn't believe it, the two of them alone at El Café del Mar, she couldn't believe herself asking Bacigalupo: Can I call you Godot?

Intimate products for men and women. Lingerie. Lubricants. Erotic toys. Tupper-sex parties: exclusive service for women. Absolute discretion. Neighbors, come and enjoy! Open 12 – 6 P.M. Phone: 479654. Email: villasexy@hotmail.com

There's no reason to be afraid of El Muertito. But most people don't see it that way. The problem is that everyone, men and women alike, has a guilty secret. Which of us has never harmed a child? Try to remember. Then, when he appears to us, we get scared. Some women start screaming; others suffer an attack. A few nights ago one ran out of her house and along the boulevards in her nightgown and didn't stop till she reached the sea. They say she drowned. Because just as there are those who have heart attacks, there are others who kill themselves. Taborda the plumber shot himself. Who knows what he might have done to his kids. There are quite a few who go around talking to themselves for the rest of their lives. And even more who go away and never come back.

When Dante returned to his apartment after midnight, he was touched by that young couple in hoodies, huddled in front of his building. He didn't need to see their faces to know they were kids. Even on drizzly nights with a biting southeaster coming in from the sea, there they were, those two, on the opposite sidewalk, sitting under the roof of a bus-stop shelter, oblivious to the cold and the rain. Their passion insulated them from the cold, the drizzle. When he spotted them, Dante was moved. As he passed by them, he tried to act distracted, though he spied on them out of the corner of his eye. He remembered when he himself, in other times, in another life, was that kid embracing a girl. Watching those two entwined like little animals, indifferent to the harshness of the elements, he also felt a mixture of tenderness and rage. From all appearances, the bottle-blond boy and the dyed red-haired girl had come down from La Virgencita or El Monte. They certainly had nowhere to go to do their thing, a roof, a cot, a blanket, all they would've needed for making love. It filled him with tenderness: he didn't think "fuck." He thought "love." He thought: If love can save the world, let's hope it can save those two. And he also thought: What a fucked-up future for those two, loving each other as best they could. And they had no choice but to love each other that way, where they could find a deserted place like this street, the street where his building was, the dark, deserted street that led to the sea half a block away, the street along which gusts of biting wind rose up. As he walked into his building, from the entry hall, he looked at them for the last time, as if saying goodbye, before ringing for the elevator and going up to his apartment. When he arrived, he turned on the radiator. He poured himself a last whiskey. The room warmed up right away. And as he crawled into bed with his socks on, wrapped in the warmth, his feet still numb but growing warmer, reading a thriller, allowing himself to drift into sleep, he realized that he envied those two down there in the street, and that if his feet were frozen it was because the cold came from his heart. One of these nights, he promised himself, he'd lend them his place.

How could he have imagined, as he later found out, that the couple, those poor little lovers, as much in love as they were poor, were marking him.

The name of the grocery, Everything for Less, was the slogan Jorgito had focused on in life: keep his head down, work hard, be satisfied with whatever he might achieve in a tough society like ours, which bursts into flames in the summer and then is extinguished during the other three seasons of the year. That was why Jorgito chose to set up the grocery in La Virgencita, a neighborhood where his customers would be locals and not casual tourists. They were predominantly working people, like his next-door neighbors, Mercedes, the teacher, and Alfredo, the electrician from Tucumán. Mechi had been Jorge's elementary school teacher. They'd grown so friendly with their neighbors that they were going to be the godparents of their son, when they had one. Because Jorge dreamed of having a boy. But not now: first they wanted to establish themselves in life. When we're in a good position, Jorge said. We're not irresponsible like the darkies.

Mercedes advised them not to think so much about material things as about love, not to let time go by and to become parents now while they were young: Jorge was twenty-three and Xime, like I told you, twenty. Mercedes was forty-two and obsessed with being a mother; she tried all sorts of treatments till she became pregnant. Alfredo, more resigned than enthusiastic, went along with her. At fifty, if he had to postpone a job in order to travel to Buenos Aires or Mar del Plata for another test, Alfredo just went. Since science had determined that the problem wasn't his, but his wife's, he accompanied her with pleasure. Till they tried assisted reproduction and Mercedes got pregnant. It was all a great joy.

It surprised Xime that, at their age, Mercedes and Alfredo could show such optimism, such hope. If you guys have one now, Mercedes said, our kids'll grow up together. But Xime and Jorgito, despite Mercedes's insistence, stubbornly postponed having a baby. Whenever she wasn't working in the pharmacy, Xime helped Jorge at the grocery store. They had invested their savings and had fallen into debt with Marconi with Everything for Less. Xime hoped that the store would take hold in the neighborhood, that it would grow into a supermarket and then, yes, she would quit the pharmacy, they'd try for a couple of kids, and she'd take over the cash register at the grocery. Only then would they go for it.

Alcides Nicosia, owner of Temptations Supermarket, was the victim of a holdup by seven heavily-armed delinquents at his place of business. The robbery took place Sunday night. After ransacking the supermarket, the crooks led Nicosia to his home, a chalet next to the store. Entering the residence, they overpowered the family members, submitting them to a brutal interrogation. The thieves made off with a lesser amount than they expected, but they ransacked the chalet, taking small appliances, computers, and clothing. In their flight, one of the assailants, who drove a VW Bora, was arrested. The suspect, whose identity is being kept confidential, has a long criminal record, was recently released from Batán Prison, and belonged to a gang made up of two well-known criminal families, which, according to the police investigation, had merged forces so as to carry out commando

operations. The supermarket owner's wife remains hospitalized at Clínica
del Mar, recovering from the shock sustained from the incident.

A moving funeral, Tuquita the lifeguard's. He hadn't been a lifeguard for long when what happened to him, happened. He worked
as a lifeguard here in the summer, and in the winter he took off for
a Mediterranean summer. He was a swimming instructor at fancy
hotels. He hooked up with a Swedish chick. And came back here
with the girl. She was built, that Helga. With what he'd saved during
those years plus the dough put up by the Swede, imagine, he took
over his parents' bakery. How happy the prodigal son made those old
folks. He'd settled down. Had a serious profession. The noble profession of baker. Tuquita and Helga remodeled the bakery, put a new
spin on the merchandise: flavored breads, cakes, jams. Everything
home-made, they put in the shop window. And also: Established
1950. And Helga was pregnant.

That's when it happened, the argument with the three Paraguayans Tuquita had hired. Evil tongues say that the Paraguayans, besides
being bakers, were dealing pot from their country. Rumor also had it
that they used the pot to make scones that could knock you on your
ass. Which explains all the young customers they had. In high season
the kids stood in line from dawn on, waiting for the first batches
to come out of the oven. Later on Tuquita had that run-in with the
Paraguayans. Early one morning, as soon as he lit the oven, they got
into it. One of them plunged a screwdriver into the back of his neck.

The funeral, like I was telling you. Moving. I won't deny it: more
than one guy wanted to comfort the Swede. Then came the time to
throw Tuquita's ashes into the sea. It was his wish; he always said so.
The lifeguards, in their latex swimsuits, waded out into the sea in
spite of the approaching southeaster, swam past the breakers carrying palms and wreaths. The waves carried the flowers back to shore.
Moving. We were shivering, but nobody felt like losing that emotion. Like a movie. The ceremony broke your heart. It could've been

filmed. Some smartass reminded us that there were no cremations at our cemetery. It was a fucked-up thing to say. Then where did the ashes come from. The bakery, someone said. The oven.

Wonder who's doing the Swede now.

No noise awakened him because they were silent as they opened the door to the apartment. What woke him was the light. And when he opened his eyes, drenched, because Dante always woke up drenched, they were on top of him, the pregnant chick, with a small baby bump, just a few months along, and a 22. The boy, with a 9 millimeter. They wore hoodies, jackets, jeans, and sneakers. She stuck the barrel under his chin. You've made a mistake, Dante said. I've got no money. I get it that you might need money if you're gonna be parents, but I don't have a cent. The girl forced him down to the floor, on his knees. The boy pointed at the books, the overflowing shelves, books on the floor, books on the nightstand, books on top of the fridge, books everywhere. Yeah, right, like you don't have any cash in all these books, the kid said. The girl hit him in the face with the gun barrel. There was no way for Dante to avoid the blow. Then she kicked him in the balls. In his underpants, bent over on the floor, naked, Dante felt even more defenseless. He could feel his heart in his mouth. Go look, he told them. Not a cent. The couple wasn't about to check all the books. His heart beating overtime, his breathing labored, Dante was more scared of his ticker than of being shot. He could feel the night chill in those two, threatening them. Let me take a pill, he said. It wouldn't do you any good to have me croak of a heart attack. Don't be an asshole, she said to him. And the boy: Watch it—if I let her, she'll eat you for breakfast. The chick went over to the nightstand, pulled open the drawer. A watch, a little silver chain with a crucifix, an old Parker pen, a blister pack of Rivotril, a bottle of Losartan, another of Metformin, and one more of Diurex spilled out. Also a gaucho knife with his name on it, a souvenir from some *criollo* fiesta. The girl grabbed the Rivotril first. Rivogil, she said. And she kept the blister pack.

Leave me one, Dante pleaded.

Drop dead, she replied.

And she scraped the pesos together. This is everything, she said. Everything, Dante repeated. You won't find anything else, he said. I'm a poor guy. If I had any loot I wouldn't be living in a one-room rental, he went on. All I have is books. Those who have books have no money. Those of us who have ideas, have books. He needed to talk to them, he told himself. If they were in the mood to talk, he could manage the situation. And so he went on: If I were some rich snob, I wouldn't have books. If I read, if I write, it's so that kids like you don't have to rob and get blown to fucking pieces. You got it all wrong about me. I don't even have a car. The most valuable thing I own is this copy of *The Divine Comedy*, he said.

He was already standing next to a bookshelf, looking for a book. The couple aimed at him: If you pull out a piece, I'll waste you, the boy said.

Dante removed the volume: an edition by Ulrico Hoepli, Editore Libraio, commentate da G. A. Scartazzini, 1914. The boy snatched the book from him. He tried to read: What language is it in, he asked. Italian, Dante replied. Inferno, Purgatory, and Paradise. He said to them: It's priceless, very valuable. And no one's gonna give you a red cent for it.

There's the computer, the boy said. The girl seemed to have forgotten him. She looked at the notebook on the table. The Toshiba had been around for a while. Grab it, the boy said. She obeyed, but first she was going to hit him again. She was distracted by the bottle of Johnny Walker. She passed it to the boy. She rummaged through the things that had fallen out of the drawer. She picked up the watch.

It doesn't work, Dante said. It was a memento, from my old man. The chain and the crucifix belonged to my old lady.

It's all silver, she said. And kept it. Then she grabbed the notebook.

You're pathetic, she said to him.

They stuck the notebook, the watch, the Parker, the little chain with the crucifix, and the gaucho knife into a backpack. And all the meds. That too, she said. She had spotted the blood pressure monitor on a shelf. That too, the boy said. The book, the girl said.

No, please, not the book, he cried.

It's all money, the girl said. We'll see if it really ain't worth nothing, the boy said. And he put the book in the backpack.

Please, Dante begged.

The girl forced him backward, the pistol at his neck. If we find out you called the cops, you're fucked, the boy said. And they took off.

Dante got dressed. He went into the kitchenette. His heart was exploding. He drank more water. In the early morning silence, he heard a motorcycle engine rev.

Later he called the limo service and asked if Remigio was in. He was. They got me, he said. I'm okay. But I need for you to find me a 24-hour pharmacy and bring me what I'm going to tell you—write it down.

He drank even more water. If he could manage to pee, it would lower his blood pressure.

In spite of the hoods and scarves, he had recognized them. Princesa Reyes and BB Vicuña. The newlyweds.

Important figures from our community starred in a lively debate before TV cameras during the broadcast of "Vox," a program dedicated to current events in our Villa. Both the Parents for Security Association and the Southern Neighborhood Commission expressed their concern about the great number of weapons circulating around the streets of our Villa, as well as the numerous attack dogs set loose by their owners at night in the face of a growing feeling of insecurity. Captain Renzo and Dr. Alejo Quirós refuted that information. And our mayor, Cachito Calderón, also present at the round table discussion, said that these complaints are made in bad faith and only serve to tarnish our Villa's image just as tourist season is

approaching and his administration is carrying out one of the most notable
works in the Villa: the construction of the sewer system. If this kind of sen-
sationalism continues to spread, it will ultimately ruin hotel and restaurant
owners, as well as other business people. In this regard, the Industry and
Commerce Union supported the opinions expressed by Calderón. "We must
focus all our efforts on the season and not on a shot in the air or a couple of
bigmouths," Calderón concluded.

But it's also true that there's no shortage of gangsters in the neighborhood. Jorgito's Everything for Less was held up four times. One
holdup per month. After the fourth time Jorgito joined up with the
neighbors who were demanding security. He took part in a march
that ended at the police station. He met with police authorities. It
was Gancedo, one of Quirós's goons, also a security guard at the Del
Mar Telephone Co-op, who gave him the idea: What you need to
do is pack heat. If any thugs come in, you blow them away. And the
cops'll turn a blind eye. It's a fact. Gancedo had been a cop. He got
him a 9 millimeter with the number filed off and explained how to
use it. With the pistol under the counter, Jorgito felt more confident.
Besides, Gancedo emphasized, if there are any complications, just
talk to Dr. Quirós. He didn't tell Xime he had a weapon. She'd be
frightened, of course. And that's what happened.

He was crazy, she said when she discovered the pistol. She didn't
want anything to do with a weapon in the house, she told him. It's
not for the house, Jorge corrected her. It's for the store, he said. It's to
protect our assets, our future. They're not gonna get me a fifth time.

Xime mentioned the matter to Marconi. Jorgito was driving her
nuts with that gun hidden under the counter. The pharmacist listened to her attentively. She didn't have the nerve to ask him, but
finally she did: she asked Marconi if he could talk to her husband, to
convince him to get rid of the weapon. I've got a gun, too, Marconi
told her. Xime was silent for a few seconds. Marconi showed her
that week's edition of *El Vocero*. Pharmacy holdups are a big concern,

read the headline of the Police Blotter on page 5. Following a series of robberies, the College of Pharmacy and police authorities held a meeting to devise preventive measures and attempt to unveil the facts. The Police carried out a series of recommendations for avoiding greater damage, such as a potential exchange of gunfire that could result in collateral victims. Xime didn't know what to say. She never would have imagined that such a gentle-natured man could be capable of using a weapon. This social reality leaves me no other alternative, girl, Marconi said.

Xime fell silent, pensive. If Marconi found out that his wife was screwing Quirós, he might go crazy and cause a tragedy. When a man like Marconi lost control, it could be a catastrophe. The ones who seemed like sheep were the most unpredictable. Take Barreda, for example, that dentist who one fine day got fed up with the humiliation that his mother-in-law, wife, and daughters subjected him to and blew them to bits with a shotgun. Besides, physically, Marconi reminded her of Barreda. Like Barreda, but younger, Xime thought. What happens if one day Marconi wakes up to the news that the Jew is cheating on him and there's a tragedy, she said to herself. It's dangerous to have a weapon in the house.

Weapons aren't the problem, Marconi told her. Men are. We are. You have to keep cool and wait for the right moment to act.

Xime wondered what her boss was trying to tell her. Marconi touched her face. With his fingertips barely grazing it, he touched her. It was a gentle, fleeting gesture, understanding. They were so close. Xime felt that the closeness, those warm fingers caressing her face, were paralyzing her. She closed her eyes. And she felt Marconi's lips on hers.

That same morning, after the robbery, Dante walked into *El Vocero* headquarters and sat down at the computer: *Open letter to two juvie thugs* was the title. And it continued: *I am Dante, the creator of the newspaper. Those who know me in the Villa know who I am and know that I have no personal fortune other than my book collection. They know I'm a supporter of the public schools. I know that teachers have a hard time of it and that many of their students have been through the court system. Maybe it was two of those kids from the alternative middle school, a young couple, who on Tuesday at 5:45 A.M., generally the time I get up, forced their way into my home at gunpoint and took away, among other personal valuables, a notebook computer and a copy of* The Divine Comedy, *a 1912 Italian edition that belonged to my grandfather. I didn't and don't have money, but I do have books. The thieves thought there might be cash hidden among the pages. I don't care about the objects or the small amount of money they took from me. But I do care about the computer and that book, tools of my trade.*

This wasn't the first time I've been robbed. If you are one of those juvie thugs, the girl or the boy, maybe you'll understand what I'm talking about. I'm not one of those who believe that injustice and juvenile delinquency should be remedied with an iron fist. I do believe in building a more just society, with a fair distribution of wealth, without abject poverty or drugs. What you stole from me, I repeat, were my tools. The silent and humble "weapons" with which I earn a living so that kids like you might have a better fate than turning trigger-happy.

Everybody shrugs when you ask about the Villa's Nazi past. The same as when you ask about the abuses at Nuestra Señora. And don't you find it suspicious, I ask you. Isn't it possible that the two situations are connected. We ought to analyze the relationship between these two issues.

Right there, in Madariaga, Dante says, there was a metal-can company that had unusual technology for its time. They say that's where they packed the food rations that the submarines came to this beach for. They also came for passports for officials on the run. And when some people tell you they've heard stories about radio transmitters and lights on the sea, they're not lying. Nor are they lying—though it might be an exaggeration—when they talk about Strauss's house, in whose basement documentation of the camps was found. It's no coincidence that, after the sinking of the *Graf Spee* in the Battle of Río de la Plata, at the end of the war, two German submarines surrendered, not very far from here, at the port of Mar del Plata. And when the German set up his Parque Idaho, a summer sports colony, one might well ask why he promoted it among the German community and so many Osram employees came here. Sure, Idaho is a name with North American associations and he gave that name to his territories because an uncle of his, the painter, had lived there. Let's think: what better alibi than that name. Our dear and honorable Villa formed part of the Ratlines. You won't find proof, Dante affirms. Not one bit. No one will risk giving you any. They assume. Here everyone assumes. Of course: they assume and it's assumed. They report and it's reported. But no one saw a thing here. Same as what's happening with the abused kids at Nuestra Señora. If you're looking for threads to connect the creation of a Nazi town with *los abusaditos*, all right, there is a connection: silence.

And it didn't even occur to you to tell me, Alejo said to him. Not even that, Dante. If you'd told me, the stolen stuff would have shown up right away. In a matter of seconds, Renzo and Balmaceda would've put the computer and your precious book in your hands. That, on the one hand, officially. Unofficially, I would've sent Don Carneiro and Gancedo and you would've gotten it all back instantly. You know how this kind of stuff gets done, Dante, but no, what you wanted was to be the great bleeding-heart liberal: Just look at the newspaperman with his nice little open letter to the thugs, get a load of his good feelings. He might be one of that SOB Alejo Quirós's henchmen, he might be his scribe and the bossman might dictate what the paper has to say, but regardless he's got his good feelings, a pure soul. That's what you were looking for, right? For everyone in the Villa to say: That Dante might be his master's voice but he's not such a dog.

Look how he dealt with the robbery. Who the fuck do you think you are, Dante. You don't fool me. Since you haven't got the balls to be Che Guevara, you play Saint Teresa of Istanbul. You take me for an idiot. Tell me, you think I'm an idiot? I control all the wheeling and dealing in this fucking Villa and you take me for an idiot. This isn't over. It's not enough for you to keep busting everybody's balls with those articles going on and on about abuse and making people feel like perverts; now here you come with your good intentions, this open letter to those fucking thugs, so no one'll confuse you with the hardliners. Your stuff'll show up. As sure as my name is Alejo Quirós, it'll show up. And when it does, you're gonna publish it. And you're gonna publish it to make two things clear: that around here nobody fucks with me. Because you belong to me, is that clear? And whether you like it or not, justice exists. And it's me.

Of Calcutta, Alejo.

What're you talking about?

Mother Teresa. Calcutta, that's where she was from.

Honestly, finding Demián moved me as much as it frightened me. Fact is, I used to fuck his old lady, though he never knew. I hadn't seen the boy in ages. I've known him since he was a baby. I even held him in my arms. What a smile. From the time he was little you could see the nobility in that smile. The old lady was one of us through and through. Ingrid, the voice of The Kingstons. That was in the eighties. I was the runner for the band. Ingrid was screwing the Monkey. Demián's father, the drummer, was the Monkey. And my thing with Ingrid was top secret. Real intense. Ingrid was super passionate but she couldn't break up with the Monkey. Till she took off for Bahia. I saw the kid, Demián, again a few years ago, in the nineties. He told me Ingrid had joined a commune. She was somewhere around Lago Puelo. I don't judge: if Demián became a dealer it's because there are no opportunities in this fucking country. He'd always been crazy about the Villa, he told me. His childhood memories were from here.

He was trying to get me to take him in. But it was useless. In any case I got him a beach cabana down south. And I established some contacts for him. It's just that you see that smile and right away you like the guy. But you can't get anywhere with the pigs if you don't make a deal. He had to flee. I lost sight of him. And look where I run into him again, at the door of the building. I give him a hug. Like a son. And he hugs me, too. Like a father. How old are you, I ask him. Thirty-four, he tells me. Crazy how fast time goes. And your ma, I ask him. She died, he answers. I'm dumbstruck. Yeah, she died. Five years ago. Better not to know of what, I think. Because I never got myself tested. I'm standing there, frozen, when the kid tells me. Five years, I repeat. That long since we've seen each other, I say. Five years, he says. Five. He looks at me sadly. Right then and there I get all paranoid thinking he knew I was fucking his old lady. It's all cool, he says to me. Let's go up to your place, he says. I'm expecting a chick, I lie. If Demián comes upstairs, I know how it'll go. We'll talk about the past, old times. Even though the kid could be my son, he's already got old times. And he'll do the first line. Tomorrow, I tell him. Better tomorrow. He won't find me here tomorrow. I made plans to go fishing with some friends. Tomorrow, I tell him as I give him a hug. And besides, it makes me feel funny to tell him I quit drinking.

Balmaceda turned up at *El Vocero* headquarters with the same backpack the kids had used. First Balmaceda put the notebook on the table. It was a Dell. Not a scratch on it. Brand new. This isn't it, Dante said. The one they took was a Toshiba. Look, this one's nice and new, Dante. It's a good deal, the policeman insisted. They had already gotten rid of the Toshiba. And by now it's probably on sale in Mar del Plata. But this one's not mine, Dante said. Just stop screwing around and take it, Balmaceda smiled. His smile was like a battering ram. It's an offer you can't refuse, he said with a wink. After hearing that well-worn phrase, Dante had no doubt of who was behind all this. You know, Dante, Balmaceda said. You can't refuse. Take the computer.

Then he pulled the book out of the backpack:

Was this the book, Balmaceda said to him. It didn't sound like a question. And it was, in fact, the book. Balmaceda also put the watch, the little chain with the crucifix, the gaucho knife, and the old Parker pen on the table. Then he said: We brought it to your office so you wouldn't have to bother going to the police station. Dr. Quirós told us you were very busy. We didn't want to bother you. We saved you the red tape. And also from having to go to the DA's office. Identifying the thieves could take you all morning. Look, here in the Villa, right at the DA's office, there are files on one percent of the population. You'll find everything there: from grandmothers to their little grandkids. Scary mugs and respectable ones. Everything: old ladies, old guys, men, women, children. Not all crooks, obviously. There are rapists, druggies, dealers, snitches, wife-beaters, hookers, racketeers. A whole zoo. And you know how much one percent of a stable population of forty thousand is, Dante.

Four hundred, Dante replied.

Exactly, said Balmaceda. So, when they ask us for protection, it's a joke. What can a few of us cops do against an army four hundred strong. Now if they didn't tie our hands, we could blow a few of 'em away, and end of story. Not a single fly left buzzing around. But, sure, since we're all righteous and human, we've gotta suck it up. And then what happens, happens. No one gets any respect. Not even you, Dante.

Dante sat there staring at the cop.

What about the kids, he then asked. The girl's pregnant.

Was, Balmaceda replied. She lost it resisting arrest. God is clever: one less little beast. Just think, we conducted an operation. And those people, each time we go after them, they don't make it easy. The girl fought hard. She had a hemorrhage, we sent her to the hospital, and when she gets out she'll be under house arrest, since she's a minor.

The other little shit escaped through the back door of the house. But he won't get very far. We know where to find him.

Dante remained silent. He wanted to come up with an ironic remark, something sarcastic. He thought about those two. He thought about the girl.

I guess I ought to thank you, Dante said.

We don't want you to reward us with money, Dr. Quirós told us. If you could just publish that we, the police of this Villa, recovered what was stolen from you. That we fulfilled our duty. We don't even care about getting our names in the paper. So long as everyone knows we're doing our job, that the community can trust us. It's an image thing, like Dr. Quirós said. And you know about that, Dante. Who are we to teach lessons to journalists. Least of all you, a real capo.

Coincidences don't exist, Dante would say as he collected information to write the article: *Violence in La Virgencita: Armed assault, one robber dead and a shop demolished.* Both the young thugs who had held up the grocery and the grocer had been students of Mercedes Berardi, the night school teacher. That Monday morning, a sunny day, just before noon, the two juvies, middle school students on motorcycles, both of them with police records, parked their cycles in front of the grocery store. Jorgito was slicing ham for an old woman. When he saw the kid walk in, he slid his hand toward the 9 millimeter under the counter. He didn't need to look twice to recognize a juvie thug. It was Eric, the one who had a little girl with Miriam Arroyuelo. But Jorgito didn't know this; he didn't know that the other guy had a family, if you can call any kind of relationship among the Vicuñas "family." And even if he had known that the juvie had a wife and child, it was already too late, and what had to happen, happened. The kid never got to aim his gun at him: Jorgito already had the 9 millimeter in his hand. The old lady, in the middle, let out a scream. Shots were exchanged. The kid's bullet hit the woman in the arm. Jorgito fired three times. The bullets shook the kid, spun him around like a top, and propelled him toward the door. He fell to the sidewalk on his back, bucking. The other kid, another Vicuña, with his cycle revved, accelerated. Jorgito was about to take him down. He fired again. Before the cycle reached the corner, the shot hit the kid in the leg. The cycle turned away, heading toward a ditch. Then Jorgito heard the woman's screams coming from the grocery store. He hesitated between helping her and wiping out the juvie in the ditch. The kid was limping toward the street corner. He considered following him and finishing him off, but the poor old lady was still in the grocery. He stepped over the dead guy and walked into the store. The old woman, more dead of fright than alive, was sitting against the counter, clutching her bloody arm. Jorgito phoned the police station. And the hospital.

Neighbors started poking their heads out. Before the patrol car and the ambulance made their appearance, the entire band of Vicuñas was already approaching, with Johnny in the vanguard. And just behind him, shaken, the widow, Miriam, with Milagros, the little orphan daughter. Seeing them approach, Jorgito aimed directly at them. There were many of them: more than a street mob, it was an Indian raid. They were coming for revenge. But Jorgito was prepared to blow some of them away before they could take him down.

Then the sirens blasted. First the patrol car. Behind it, the ambulance. In the patrol car were Deputy Commissioner Renzo and two agents. They parked the car between the grocery and the attackers. First, curses were hurled at them. Then rocks. Renzo fired into the air. The mob stopped short. More cursing ensued. They were going to blow away the grocer. Jorgito refused to surrender the 9 millimeter. The cops persuaded him. Then they loaded the grocer into the patrol car and the wounded neighbor into the ambulance. As the patrol car pulled away, Jorgito could see through the rear window how the mob was shoving its way into the grocery store. A rock smashed against the window, cracking it. Jorgito burst out crying like a child.

Alejo can't explain what could have awakened him. Was it barking at dawn, the wind shaking the poplars, or Isabel stirring as she slept on her back beside him. Something in the calm, but what. He goes to the kitchen for a yogurt, walks through the house as he eats it, peers into his kids' room, continues toward the living room, turns on the light, and gazes at a portrait of his father. Without a doubt, he inherited this calmness in the face of struggles from old man Quirós. And insomnia is one such struggle. It always frightens him. A fear that keeps getting denser. Suddenly the peace of the household is threatening. Suddenly someone—a father, a mother—walks into Nuestra Señora and fires shots at the principal and teaching faculty. An administrative assistant at City Hall reports to the TV station that the sewer system bid was fraudulent. Valeria commits suicide and it comes out that they were lovers. Suddenly his reputation teeters. His family name, an illustrious name in the area, a name that signifies power, influence, safe haven, is a diamond in a pigsty. Alejo knows that all those who come to him for legal assistance are grovelers, but beneath a gratitude akin to licking his boots lies an attempt to hide their hatred for him for being trapped in a secret debt, more moral than financial.

My conscience is clear, he tells himself. They hate me because they need me. And they need me because I free them from fines or from jail. Ingrates, in the end. Because I could just let them get buried in their shit, but I help them out, I rescue them.

He goes out into the cold August night air, into the frost that settles over the garden surrounding the mansion. How odd, he thinks, that Rex hasn't come to sit at his feet. Rex, he calls softly. But the Rottweiler doesn't come. Alejo walks in the shadows. Till he sees him. The dog is lying on the lawn next to the double iron gate. He's dead. He's been poisoned.

Coca is the principal at the Sarmiento, a school in the southern part of the Villa, near La Virgencita. She's disturbed at what happened to those three kids from La Virgencita. The three of them sniffed gasoline. They were playing at setting themselves on fire with a lighter: Hey, look, I'm burning you, see, I'm burning you. They were playing at scaring each other with a cigarette lighter. Two of them doused the third. And they set him on fire. The hospital couldn't save him. Coca tells me that she declared the day he died a school holiday. The funeral procession was as large as it was moving. The mother led the procession into the cemetery outside of town. After burying her son she went to leave flowers on four more graves. Each one corresponded to one of her sons. Now she has five in the cemetery.

Here's how the news appeared in *El Vocero: Important police operation,* the headline read. *Last Thursday police forces carried out a major raid of a house in La Virgencita, the residence of a young delinquent couple. At the scene they found various valuables, the bounty of their heists. This newspaper would like to express its thanks through this medium for the recovery of a notebook computer, the same one on which this information was written.*

Roland began with one of the Duchess's commercial units near downtown. He put down a year's rent in advance. It was a major risk for someone to set up shop in the Villa during off-season. The guy must've been pretty sure of himself. And he must've also had enough to cover such a dicey bet. He was the first to arrive. Then Delfina, the platinum blonde. They tossed a few pesos to some girls to advertise the store. They distributed business cards with an Aubrey Beardsley reproduction, an androgynous little drawing, advertising Roland Darthes, unisex coiffeur, and the slogan "Dare to be you." He transformed the place, a box, into an white space with clean lines. Can you believe those cards had an effect? Not only because of the esthetic touch, Beardsley. Also because of the prices. Or rather, the absence of prices on the card. It simply said: If you're not satisfied, you don't pay.

Why don't you go ask around in Madariaga. Talk to Valdez, the horse trainer. Because Valdez must remember. There was a gaucho who named his sorrel Führer.

How the story ended? The way most stories end around here: badly.

Besides losing Everything for Less and finding themselves in debt, no matter how much Marconi told Jorgito that now wasn't the time to worry about the money, Xime and Jorgito couldn't put up with the threat, the terror—and they had to leave the Villa. They went to Mar del Plata, to the home of some relatives of Ximena's. Xime found a job at a convenience store, a place that also had internet service, phone booths, and a photocopier. Jorgito worked in a home-goods store in Luro. After they had been sharing the house with the relatives for a little while, the problems began. Xime was away all day and there were nights when she came home late. Jorgito didn't ask questions; he was starting to feel depressed. The relatives criticized Xime. And Xime reproached Jorgito for not stopping them. If they had had any savings, they would have moved out right away. Marconi often came to Mar del Plata to help the couple. He co-signed on an apartment for them, loaned them the money for the deposit. And when they couldn't make it to the end of the month, he helped them, too.

If Jorgito had suffered anxiety attacks after wiping out the Vicuña kid, he got worse after Ximena's rape. Because Xime was gang-raped one Friday night as she was coming home from work. Xime was able to recognize a Vicuña. The gang had traveled to Mar del Plata specifically to take revenge on the grocer. Soon after that Xime learned that she was pregnant. Jorgito asked her to abort that baby, which didn't belong to them, he said. Xime herself wasn't sure. She took a while to make up her mind. But Mercedes convinced her not to do it. After so much death, she said, a pregnancy was a sign from heaven. Heaven is cleaning up the blackness, Xime. You can't reject this message from heaven. If Mercedes, the teacher, hadn't convinced her not to abort, Jorge and Xime wouldn't have had Soledad.

Mercedes was against abortion. Just as she and Alfredo had planned, Mercedes was finally pregnant. Seven months along. She couldn't stop looking at Soledad. She looked at her as though she was a trailer for her own movie: Identical to Jorgito, Mercedes pronounced. I think she looks just like you, Jorgito, she would say. But Jorge didn't even look at her: he rejected the infant, said she was no child of his. Xime, he realized, was upset, always upset. Not only did she not know how to take care of the baby, she didn't know how to pull her husband out of the depression in which he was becoming mired, either. A baby and a depressive were quite a handful for anyone. And too much for Xime, who couldn't look at the baby and at her husband without recalling the rape. The only thing that comforted, distracted, and gave her a little strength was having coffee at the Tío Curzio on the weekends with Marconi. He's like a father to me, she would say. The apartment Marconi had rented for them was on the ninth floor. From the balcony you could see the ocean; at night Jorge would sit out there wrapped in a blanket, staring at the sea. He didn't seem to feel the cold or the southeasters. Till he jumped.

Poor thing, said one evil tongue. Jorgito did himself in, thinking his baby was a Vicuña. But she was no Vicuña. If you took a good look at her, said someone at Moby, you could tell she resembled the pharmacist. That's what finished him off.

As always, Dante found out through Remigio. After spending some time in a safe house in Mar del Plata, BB Vicuña came back to the Villa. After cops raided the pre-fab he had shared with Princesa Reyes in La Virgencita, he wasn't about to show his face around there. His brothers set him up at Doña Elpidia's, a relative who rents rooms down south, near the Terminal. But BB didn't arrive alone.

He brought a chick with him, Rosamonte, they called her. When Princesa found out that BB was back in the Villa and that not only had he not come to see her, but he also was banging someone else, she lost her shit. The thing that enraged her the most was the fact that BB was casing houses with the girl. With the excuse that he was planning a break-in, he went around pawing that fucking chick. Princesa asked herself if it bugged her more that she'd lost the pregnancy during the robbery or that her husband was parading around the Villa with Rosamonte.

Princesa climbed on the motorcycle and started riding through the Villa till she found them. She caught them casing a chalet on a boulevard up north. She didn't even wait long enough for BB to take his hand off Rosamonte's tit. She blew them both away on the spot.

Alejo got involved in the mess that followed. He worked out Princesa's fate with the Reyeses. The mitigating factor was the psychological imbalance that affected her after losing her baby and the resulting temporary insanity that led to the crime of passion against her husband. After spending some time as an inpatient in Moyano Psychiatric Hospital, she would return to the Villa under house arrest.

And don't tell me that this isn't helping the poor, Alejo later said to him. I saved that Reyes girl's ass. If she had gone to jail, she would've had a rough time. When a person is serious about helping others, he doesn't go around showing off. Who were you trying to convince with that open letter, tell me, Dante. Yourself. Just look at the disaster you created with that little open letter of yours. A miscarriage, the girl in the nuthouse, and a couple of kids blown to bits. Your little book wasn't worth that much, admit it.

Dante listened silently.

From now on, just one favor. Don't play the plaster saint again. And stop screwing around with that child abuse shit. Think it over, asshole. It's getting closer and closer to the season.

"Asshole" was a bit much, Dante said.

Right you are, asshole.

In those days of the romance, we thought Bacigalupo seemed more enthusiastic than ever. He walked briskly, even though it wasn't like there was any particular hurry. Rather, he had gained momentum. He wasn't one to frequent Moby much, but once at the bar, Bacigalupo said it himself: It's the chemical reaction to more elevated feelings.

We knew that biochemistry is the science that studies the chemical bases of life. Bacigalupo's enthusiasm on falling in love with Ceci came from discovering the chemical basis of love. There's chemistry between us, he said that night at Moby.

The fact that a hideous guy, because it was undeniable that Bacigalupo's features triggered an instinctive revulsion, and besides, there was that cavernous, grating voice of his, the way he wrinkled his nose and lips when he adjusted the eyeglasses that always slipped off his nose, and also those rabbit teeth in his pockmarked face, I mean, the fact that such a guy, whom we would stare directly in the eye as if to show him that his ugliness didn't unnerve us, that we could handle that unpleasant appearance . . . I swear, his love affair with Ceci was nothing short of magical. Ceci, whose beauty seemed to grow beside the biochemist. To think of them as Beauty and the Beast was redundant. Instead, we tended to spin conjectures that ranged from the most obscene, alluding to the presumed dimensions of that syringe of flesh the biochemist must have been lugging around, to faith in love, because, after all, those two had been together for months and they were all lovey-dovey, two turtledoves.

Love exists, said Malerba one night, perhaps the least likely person to make that comment. The thing is, you guys are rats, incapable of positive feelings.

Hear, hear, said Dante from his corner, whiskey in hand. A toast to love.

You're shitting me, the other guy goaded him.

Not at all, Dante said. Love's a welcome touch in this nest of vipers.

A fake *criollo* is someone who buys his traditional, but hip, clothes at Cardón and says he likes Soledad Pastorutti, but at home listens to Norah Jones.

How could it be someone who looked like him. More than one person here saw him walking along the beach. Nobody saw him get out of a car or a cart, or come along on foot, either. He couldn't have come down from the air because had he landed in a plane, we would've known. Therefore, the only possibility is that he came on one of the nighttime submarines. One day we saw him, from a distance, accompanying the German, who was showing him his forest. From a distance, at first. Later, closer up, in Raimundi's grocery store, buying some seeds. He talked through gestures. The German had put him up in a cabin that stood where the Hotel Danubio is today. Nearby lived the three castaways from the *Graf Spee*. The pocket battleship, as it was called in those days. They said they had been sailors, as if they were telling you they were draftees. Not officers or fanatics. They had been recruited. No one asked them anything more. Besides, you couldn't understand what they were saying. Arno was one, the old drunk who died on the street this winter. The German gave them a place to live, like he later did for the man. Those three, the shipwrecked sailors, now dressed in breeches and canvas shoes, stood watch over the man and his wife, a blonde who liked to bathe naked in the sea. The man didn't talk to anyone. Valdez, the trainer, brought him the horses. And then the man and the woman rode through the dunes. Later on Keno, the Valdezes' second in command, brought them the horses. The man developed a special affection for Keno. And he gave him a little silver cross, one of those that are like a twisted X. Because one morning the Parodis were butchering a lamb when the man walked by. He cursed them out big time. And it wasn't too hard to understand that he was on the lamb's side. Then, suddenly, he clammed up. He looked around, like someone who's just put his foot in it. And went back to where he'd come from. We found out he was a vegetarian. Very affectionate with kids and dogs. Sometimes he also liked to paint local landscapes, when the forest was wilder. Among those who saw him were several country folk who had worked for the German. Even though he'd shaved off his mustache, they recognized him. Look, if you go out to Madariaga and Keno is still alive, ask him, and he'll show you the little cross.

And one fine day he suffered a terrible fatigue of the soul. Didn't even have the strength to kill himself. The stroke saved him the trouble. We found him lying in the southern dunes. One icy morning, partly frozen and muttering unintelligible phrases. We took him away in Tulio the fisherman's little truck. He stank of fish when we dropped him off at the hospital. He was in intensive care. But they couldn't get him out of there. And that's where he stayed. Like so many others.

Because it wasn't, it isn't, an isolated case. Every so often someone comes to the dunes to die. Like an elephant cemetery, the dunes.

No saint ever went through more than Beto, the one from Las Vacas Gordas. It's fine for God to test a person, but He went overboard with Beto. Three operations. Appendicitis, kidney stones, a disk. Then, the holdups. The first one was on a Sunday morning, just as he was opening the butcher shop: two chicks, stoned from a night of partying. They didn't get more than change and they grabbed a few strips of *asado*. The second was at dawn: the thugs got in through the back, jumped the wall, emptied the meat locker, but got zero cash. The third: two dudes, probably the Vicuñas, nabbed two thousand pesos and made off with the knives. The fourth: a young couple with a baby. From how scrawny they were you could tell they were dying of hunger. Aimed at him with a prison-made zip gun. They were pathetic. Beto convinced them they wouldn't get very far. He spoke to them of God, because if anyone's a believer, it's Beto. He convinced them to give up, and he even gave them two pounds of *milanesas* and let them go. But the really bad-ass holdup was the fifth, one night when he was about to close. There were three of them. From the Reyes gang. They were super fucked up, two guys and a chick. The bitch was the one in charge. They threw him down on the floor and kicked the shit out of him. That, after his disk operation. They got away with nine grand. Then they locked him in the meat locker. He almost didn't live to tell the tale. Frozen like a chicken, that's how he was. I almost didn't live to tell the tale, is how Beto tells it now. Luckily, since I was late, my wife had a bad feeling and called the cops. From the meat locker I went directly to intensive care, Beto says. And here I am. Grateful. How could I not be grateful. God tested me. And He gave me the strength to keep going. And I do. Because whatever God gets out of you when He puts you to the test, if you don't turn atheist, He gives back to you twofold. But just to be on the safe side, I also said a prayer to Gauchito Gil.

Mercedes, as we know, had tried endless treatments, but no way, she couldn't get in a family way. Until she did. Now, please, Alfredo asked her, you're not going to keep going to school with that belly. I'm *La Seño*, Alfredo. My students take care of me. Just like that, in her seventh month. You had to see Mercedes as a teacher. If she could walk through La Virgencita alone at night, it was because of the respect she'd earned at the school. The toughest kids protected her. Don't mess with *La Seño*. Alfredo insisted: It's dangerous. You can't walk around there at night with that belly. Mercedes refused to listen: They love me. And they've got nobody else.

In spite of her belly, Mercedes got along till one of the Vicuñas, Luisito, a third grader, hit her. Mercedes managed to get away and shield herself. The other kids grabbed Luisito. The impact of his fists was less than it might have been. Only then did Mercedes ask for a leave of absence and stayed home.

Mercedes was opposed to expelling the boy. That boy belongs to a large family, she explained. He's the fifth of I don't know how many siblings. The father's in prison in Batán. The mother ekes out a living cleaning houses. Two of his sisters became prostitutes. And they don't stop having kids. The older brothers all have records. The only structure the Vicuñas have is school and *La Seño,* argued Mercedes, and that's me. The boy was high on drugs and had an attack of jealousy, she said. Since he feels like I'm his mother, the pregnancy stirred up jealous feelings. Don't give me that cheap psychology, the principal told her. Your dear little kids, pieces of shit, she said. This is my school, and I'm the one in charge. Mechi wasn't about to cave in. My students are like my children. The principal tried to ease the tension. You're pregnant, Mercedes, she sighed. Why don't you worry about your real child.

The next day Luisito Vicuña was expelled. He promised to get even.

The same thing that happens to Nan Goldin happens to me: Sometimes I don't know how to feel with a person if I don't take his picture first.

Roland Darthes, unisex coiffeur. First the girls tried him. And then the boys. Roland was developing a young clientele. Informal, he called it. Innovative and creative. In a short time, the clientele grew. Strange new hairdos. And there was no shortage of those females who were no longer girls. What made Roland attractive was not just that he gave away free haircuts to those who weren't entirely satisfied. Very avant-garde, one customer told him. I'm not so modern, said another. My boyfriend's gonna tease me. But later, when their girlfriends gushed over the haircut, they came back. What made him attractive was the way he treated them: a tender intimacy combined with sarcasm. You can tell by the way he acts that he's gay, the guys said. It was hard for them to admit it; they were jealous. All the chicks melted over Roland. Any doubts about his sexuality vanished when he brought in Delfina, a skinny platinum blonde who looked like a model. The chick's a cover, people said. Roland and Delfina moved to a place downtown. Now their clients included the crème de la crème, the power brokers, all of Pinar del Norte, and, of course, the three Quirós women: Jackie, Susi, and Adriana. On more than one Saturday you could find Valeria, Marconi the pharmacist's wife, there, gossiping with Jackie over a copy of *Caras*. They looked like bosom buddies. They had Alejo in common. Cachito became a client, too. But before him, Beti. And Alejo. The three Quiroses. Even the biggest big shots tried him. Although Roland offered Cachito, Alejo, and some others, Dante included, but not everyone, haircuts in their offices, they refused. Naturally we all drooled over Delfina, but the platinum blonde never went beyond insinuating that underneath her white uniform she wasn't wearing a thing. We were turned on when she rinsed our hair with warm water: her fingers, massaging our hair, also massaged our sexual fantasies.

If anyone had achieved a meteoric career in the Villa, it was Roland. Evil tongues claimed he owed his success to Delfina, who turned on the girls as much as the guys. She was fucking Jackie, they said. But Jackie is a dog, even though Alejo's conned her into thinking she's Araceli González, the actress. And who's talking about love, someone said. She's also doing Betina Moure. Why do you think all the women want her to do their waxing. The guys, because they're wankers, because the blonde gets a rise out of all of them. And the girls because for them it's a novelty.

Here's what I want: When Delfina fucks my girlfriend, I want them to let me sit on the nightstand and watch.

It broke our hearts when Maurito got locked up. Luckily now he's at a correctional farm. I just pray to God that when they send him back to us, our son will be like when he was born. What, you smoking alone? Pass me the roach. I can't stand the anxiety.

And so the day of the wedding arrived, a Friday, a simple civil ceremony. Then a luncheon at the Beer Lovers' Association. Not too many guests. The Kennedys, but not all of them. Adriana and Julián with Felicitas and Luz, their daughters, who were dressed like two fairies for the occasion and kept harassing Tomasito to play with them, but to no avail: Tomasito stuck close to his mother's side, stubbornly refusing to budge. Marzio the ecologist and Santiago, his new partner, were also there. Graziani, from the home décor shop, and his wife. Also Don Barbeito, Mirna, and Weisz, the bald guy who plays classical music on the FM station but now was serving as DJ. And a few more whose names escape me at the moment. There was a cold appetizer, good wine, *vitello tonnato*, followed by chicken, ice cream bonbons and a modest cake for dessert, plus champagne. Felicitas and Luz and Tomasito, Ceci's little boy, tugged reluctantly on the ribbons. Every so often Bacigalupo drew near him and gave him a smile, if you could call that expression of his, with bits of pastry cream on his swollen lips, a smile. We had no doubt that Bacigalupo put a lot of effort into his lovemaking. No doubt, either, that if there was any obstacle in the way of the lovebirds' complete happiness, it was that quiet, silent boy. But better not to think about that now, better not to anticipate events, better to believe, as Dante said, that love might have a chance among us and, besides, now the waiters were bringing around whiskey with the coffee.

We saw the bride and groom leave. We saw them get into Bacigalupo's Renault 21. We had tied tomato cans to the back bumper, but they didn't make much noise on the sandy streets. Then we also saw Tomasito, Ceci's little boy, looking back at us through the rear view mirror, looking at us without understanding what was so funny about cans tied to the back bumper. He wore an expression that—we must admit—dispelled our joy, a joy that included the Bacigalupos, their guests, and especially the deaf-mute child.

You'll see that love conquers all, said Dante. He said it without irony, as if wanting to believe in what he was saying. With those good-hearted observations, Dante managed to take us by surprise.

Night falls. There's a warmth in the salty air. Every so often a bus, a car, shoots past the Tropicana, which has already turned on its neon sign. Dante emerges, chest out, walking erect. He smooths his damp, post-shower hair and, slipping on his jacket and dark glasses, faces the world. He alone. A personal challenge. He lights a cigarette. At least that's how he wants to appear. Tough, the look of someone who's been through a beating. He gets into the limo. Silently. Remigio, too, is silent as he drives the car. Like all the afternoons when Dante shows up at the Tropicana for his siesta with Chiquita, Remigio has picked him up right on time. He spies him through the rear view mirror. Dante's got a dejected-looking mug. Remigio takes his time before speaking. What a face, he's about to say. But he refrains.

Outside the car window the dunes go by, a pine grove, and then more dunes. After that, the cloud of smoke from the garbage dump. Through his dark glasses the sunset looks even darker. There's always a last time, Dante thinks. But he doesn't say so.

Excuse me for butting in, Remigio insists. But something's the matter with you. You don't even need to tell me what.

Always a last time, Dante thinks. And he's not about to tell Remigio this was the last time he came to see Chiquita. He came to say goodbye. For both our sakes, he told her, we should break it off. This thing has gotten out of hand, he told her. I could be your father. At my age I'm in no condition to start over. But who's asking anything of you, Chiquita said to him. Our thing is what it is, and it's fine, she said. And that accent of hers, so Caribbean, Dante said to himself. And he wonders if that wasn't the thing that made him fall in love with her. A manner of speaking. Let's be friends, if you want,

Papi. Why such a fuss, she said. But it wouldn't be good for him to keep seeing her, he thinks. It's best for both of us. And especially for her, Dante thought. But he didn't say so.

You know, I had this idea, *jefe*, Remigio says. We could make a pile of dough. The two of us, partners.

Partners in what, Dante asks.

In a novel, Remigio goes on. A pile of dough. With the secrets I know about this Villa and your flair for writing, we'd make one hell of a novel. I tell you what I know about everybody. And you write it.

A best seller, Dante goads him on. That's what you're thinking of.

But secret, a secret best seller. One that'll never get published.

I don't get it.

Simple, *jefe*. You write a novel about the Villa, one chapter for each character. Chicks and dudes. When the chapter's done, I leap into action. I go see the person and tell them someone is writing a novel about the Villa. And that the person, a chick or a dude, shows up in one chapter. I give them a copy of the chapter to read. When they read it, they're gonna want to kill themselves. Who wants their deepest secrets made public. Imagine the Villa's secrets, the involvements, because here everyone is involved, in one way or another, with everyone else. When the characters read their part in the novel, the first thing they'll think of is how to keep their chapter from coming out. And they'll pay up, for sure. Since everyone here has a price, figure it out. Bingo! Everyone pays up. We'll make a fortune.

A secret text, Dante says.

Call it whatever you want, *jefe*. You're the one in charge of words. My job's just to collect the dirty laundry. Yours is to write about it. And then I go by to collect.

And when the novel's finished, Dante asks. What then.

We're not gonna be dumb enough to publish it. Our best seller's gonna be a secret. That's the cool part. Whadda you say.

We'd have to think it over carefully.

I've already thought it over, Remigio says. The only thing left is for you to make up your mind.

And what about fame, Dante asks. Because every writer is after glory. Let's say I like fame.

Don't give me that fame stuff, *jefe*. Death isn't serious. Besides, what do you expect from posterity, tell me: a street with your name on it. Think it over right here and now. What matters is now, enjoying life.

Now the night envelops the car as it pulls up to the first lights of the Villa. Through his dark lenses, a blink of shimmer. Dante lights another cigarette. In spite of the shadows, Remigio scrutinizes him through the rear view mirror.

Don't tell me it's not a good idea, he says. Look how your face has changed. Imagine for a second what it would be like. We rake in the money and split. Think it over, *jefe*. It's not every day such a great opportunity comes along. And when it does, you can't let it slip away. You could get yourself not one Chiquita, but thousands of 'em, whichever Chiquita you like. You know how many Chiquitas are on the horizon.

If everything is written, so too is the next act. And against that one, we cannot rebel. The most we can do is to read it. In the facts, in the sky, in the wind. But our condition as readers is conditioned. Beforehand. Never afterward. We don't know what we're here for. Sometimes we think we suspect why. But our suspicions can never be confirmed. Among other reasons, because when we think we're sure of a cause, the effect unnerves us: it responds to a different reason. If we are nothing but texts, we are innocent. It's true that these lines of reasoning aim to free us of guilt. As long as we are words, we might reason, let no one be blamed. In any case, the guiltiest party is none other than the author of our days. And yes, to believe that God is the author of our story doesn't free us of guilt, but it does offer some relief. God is our consolation. Though if we really think about it, God is crafty: all He does is deceive us with readings, force us to doubt everything all the time, even His own existence. And then we ask ourselves if any greater evil than that—constant doubt—can be written, a doubt that gradually becomes suspicion, and so we end up suspecting not only everyone else, but ourselves as well. No, I'm not the one who's writing this line.

It's midnight and Mercedes is in bed. Beside her, Alfredo watches a movie. But the phone rings again. Every so often, in spurts, someone calls and hangs up. Alfredo glares furiously at the phone. Mercedes knows it's him, Luisito Vicuña, her expelled student. Alfredo asked the police to take him into custody, but Deputy Commissioner Renzo said he didn't have enough priors. Alfredo borrowed a short-barrel 38 from Don Tito Souza, the union leader. You, too, with a gun, Mercedes said. Look how Jorgito ended up. Look how my students ended up.

And there they are, the two of them, Mercedes and Alfredo, now at dawn, counting contractions. It would appear the moment has come to rush to the hospital. They've left the car out in the street so as not to waste time if necessary. They go out. They get in.

They see shadows approaching. Mercedes makes out the figure of Luisito. In the commotion of the contractions, Alfred left the revolver on the nightstand. He gets out of the car and dashes toward the house. He returns with the revolver. He arrives just as the kids are forcing the car doors open.

Alfredo fires into the air. The kids step back. There's one trailing behind, with a revolver. He shoots. Alfredo fires back. Mercedes screams. The kid falls. The others escape. Luisito, Mercedes cries.

The contractions. Mercedes can't bear the pain. Her water breaks. A police siren wails. Alfredo doesn't stick around to wait for the police. Mercedes bites her lips. Alfredo speeds toward the hospital. The emergency room, dizziness, the orderlies. One of the orderlies notices the revolver in Alfredo's belt. But he doesn't ask. He tells him he can't go in. And Alfredo stays outside in the waiting room.

Minutes go by slowly, endlessly. Till a physician, Dr. Zambrano, comes out.

What was it, doctor.

Is, Zambrano tells him. A little boy.

And the mother, Alfredo asks. Zambrano calms him with a hand on his shoulder.

She's fine, my friend. Go home and rest.

At that very moment Deputy Commissioner Renzo and two of his men walk in.

Alfredo needs to go with them to make a statement about the dead boy: Luis Vicuña.

If Cachito brags about anything, it's that his administration is distinguished by its public works and contractual transparency. An example of the progress it promotes, he declared in *El Vocero*, is the sewer system, an urgent need that the Villa was clamoring for. And who won the bid, let's see. Remember how Cachito broadcasted the news during the southeaster. Oviedo Construction. And know we know who that fat Oviedo guy is, a cousin of Beti Marconi's, Cachito's wife.

You think you know someone, but you don't. You can live your whole life with someone, and when you least expect it, they turn out to be someone else; they plunge a knife into your back. If that can happen between husband and wife, brothers and sisters, and between friends, don't be taken in by the friendly "hi" people give you out in the street, and should the occasion arise, as you walk into Moby one night, they could even invite you to sit down and share a table. Never mind, don't trust them. What we know about the other person is never what we see. Because what we see is fleeting, the tail of a cat that's just rounded the corner. A tiger's tail, too. Or even worse, a dragon's. Don't even think of rushing toward the corner to see the whole animal because it can reach out and scratch you, tear you apart with its fangs, or singe you with a mouthful of flames. It's better to be prudent, move cautiously, keep your distance. We're all guilty until proven otherwise, someone said.

But Yoli didn't give too much importance to the fact that some of her clients had defected to Roland. They left, but they'll be back, she said. It's for novelty's sake, she thought. It was hard for her to accept that the Quirós women, lifelong clients, would let themselves be captivated by that fairy, because Roland was affected, a closet homo, according to her, and that platinum blonde cow who pretended to be a model was more common than dirt. They'd get theirs. Sooner or later everyone would know who was who. And just as the Quirós women would come back, so would all the others. A bunch of ignoramuses, Yoli said. You can tell they're hicks: anyone from the capital dazzles them. Because, in the twenty-some years she's been in the Villa, Yoli has seen a good number of rivals come and go. It's always the young women who come for the season and then stay on for the rest of the year to try their luck. And they don't last. The women go back to the city, frightened, or they find work as waitresses or store clerks. And the guys end up driving limos. Those who come from here, Yoli would say, know who's who. Trendiness gets old fast. On the other hand, what's classic lasts, she said. I can give you a modern haircut, but always in moderation, within the limits of good taste. Modern styles aren't for everyone. You've got to know your client's personality, know how far they dare to go and at what point they'll start feeling ridiculous. Don't forget, around here what everyone fears the most is to look ridiculous. You don't get over that.

But despite all these rationalizations, she couldn't quite stifle her distrust and resentment on seeing how so many of her female clients crossed the street whenever they had to pass by the door of Yoli Hair Design. What hurt her was the feeling that she might get out of touch, not just with the styles, but also with the latest news, the gossip, the information you won't find in *El Vocero* but rather at the hair salon. An empty hair salon, Yoli realizes, feels like a room at a funeral parlor.

Zulma is a police officer. She must be around fifty, and she works at the local police station. She was one of the first female officers to work at precincts devoted exclusively to women and counseling against domestic violence. Zulma works with the mothers of troubled youths. Besides having studied that specialty and becoming certified in it, Zulma has street smarts and doesn't hesitate to get out there when it's urgent to go after a crime. Since when does a police officer change the world, people have said to her. You think you're in a movie.

Zulma doesn't worry about these snide remarks. Sometimes when she's on duty she can go a day and a half or even two without sleep.

I come from La Matanza, Zulma says. I've always liked the coast. I asked for a transfer. I wanted to be near the sea. Now that I'm here, I hardly ever see it. I don't even have time to go to the beach with all that's going on.

If I got this cancer and I'm on my last legs, it was because of the anxiety they gave me. And because I was always one to keep my mouth shut. Always. I never liked to argue. Don't give me false hope, doctor. I know I won't be around much longer. But they're still gonna find out what I think of them. Everything I kept to myself. Especially my dear sister-in-law, the worst of all. I'm gonna do the same thing as Susana, Rubén the roofer's wife. The same as Miguel Santiso. The same as Carlos Ortiz. The same as Norma Brindisi. It was really clever of them to send their messages from the Beyond. Just look at what Susana did, poor thing, with that heart attack that carried her off, may she rest in peace. After she died, on the first anniversary of her death, Rubén, her widower, opened the mail and found the message: "Even though you cheated on me all along, you were the love of my life and a fantastic husband. All I ask you is never to take off your wedding ring." Susana had opened an account at Wishes Beyond Life. Another one that signed up with that website, the late Pinhead Trigo, the guy from the storeroom. And it wasn't so serious for Lena, the widow, as it was for the kids. One fine day, while opening the mail, Pablito, the youngest, opens an envelope and reads: "Don't waste money or time. And excuse me, but I haven't been able to tell you my secret till now: I may have been married, I may have had three kids, and I may have been a good father, but I was gay. Please forgive me for letting you know like this. But I was afraid you wouldn't understand me. And that I would lose you. Don't waste your time or the money you inherited." I know I don't have much longer, doctor. Nobody wants to tell me the truth, but ever since I was taken to the hospital, I know that, even when they send me back home for a while, they'll put me right back in, and I won't be able to take the next round of chemo. So I need to take advantage of those days at home and find out how that business of messages from the Beyond works.

Dante smiled tolerantly when we told him how hot Roland's little platinum blonde was. Wankers, he thought. They're capable of paying double what Josema charges for a haircut just to get a look at that chick's nipple. It never even occurred to him to change his scalper, Dante said. He would stay loyal to Josema and his razored high-and-tight. Even if there were customers ahead of him and a long wait, Dante liked to sit in Josema's barbershop, which was more like a bar than a barber shop, to sit, like I was saying, and eavesdrop on the conversations in which—let's make this clear—he barely participated. His habit was to blurt out a phrase every so often that would sound like an aphorism, an interjection, as well as to goad the one who was now offering his opinion on this or that, a fire among the shacks in El Monte, the money the Kennedys would make with that lot auction in Mar de las Pampas, a knife fight in La Virgencita, the increase in holdups in Pinar del Norte, the whereabouts of Father

Fragassi after the parents from Nuestra Señora rearranged his mug. Always a witness, Dante. He said it one time: the stories at the barbershop reminded him of those of a North American writer. And, speaking of stories, when Josema got nervous hearing about Roland and Delfina, when envy gnawed at his guts as he learned how many customers had been seduced by that Frenchified faggot and his bimbo, Dante calmed him down: Take it easy and you'll see. You and Yoli are both serious types. Don't even talk to me about Yoli, Dante, please, Josema bristled. They had been both man and wife and business partners ages ago. Yoli had said their separation was on account of gambling, that the vice had consumed Josema. In the end it turned out the separation was because of a checker at Océano Supermarket, a darky, according to Yoli. Well, Yoli was no slacker, either, and around that same time she had her affair with Moure, the veterinarian. To get back to what I was saying, Dante made that remark about serious people one afternoon when Josema was cutting a two-year-old kid's hair. Imagine, if you have a little kid, you're not gonna trust his head to just anyone. No way, said the boy's mother. Because Dante's remark had shaken up memories of *los abusaditos*. No matter how hard the entire Villa tried to forget the matter, the memory kept ticking like the workings of a bomb, just as Dante, every so often, wrote articles about child abuse prevention, articles that, like the ticking of the bomb, suggested it might go off when we least expected it. And if it doesn't, Josema asked. If it doesn't what, Dante asked. if it doesn't explode. Maybe it'll be a worse punishment for all of us it doesn't, Dante mused. Maybe a worse punishment is this metastasis.

Now the days are longer. The light is different. And the worst is over.

The Yids shit their pants. Because when the Maccabiah Games roll around, the Mossad agents who try to go unnoticed show up, but we all know that those athletic boys who stay at three or four hotels and start running around the Villa without missing a single security detail are from the Mossad. And afterward, when the darkies arrive, the Falcons of the Provincial Police and the patrol cars go around giving tickets non-stop. Also the helicopters, day and night, that don't even let you enjoy a siesta. And in the sea, right there, two ships from the Border Police.

Who told me, you want to know. You know I keep my mouth shut. Don't ask me how, but I know, and it's more than just a rumor. This year the kikes aren't going to hold their pentathlons on the beach and their dances in the plaza. It's a bummer, because they filled the hotels and restaurants and dropped a pile of dough in the Villa. This year, no fucking way. I'm not a racist. I've got nothing against them. Especially if you consider the dough, because they spent lots of it on the festival.

And now, you know whose fault it is they're not coming back, 'cause the ragheads, the Arabs, aren't dumb. The Arabs kept them from coming. I don't mean because of that attack on the AMIA. I mean because since everyone is racist here and hates the Moishes even though they spend good money, the people from City Hall preferred to deal with the Arabs instead of playing it safe. So we're going to have a festival for the Arab community. I don't know what it'll be like, belly dancing contests, turban competitions, camel races in the dunes, go figure. And so the fucking Israeli assholes aren't gonna come, So now tell me what the fuck I'm supposed to do with a closed hotel in November.

How could we not see it, said Dell'Oro, the teller from Banco Provincia. Why would a terrific girl like Ceci get involved with a monster like Bacigalupo. The fact is we were all a little shocked by how much Bacigalupo disgusted us. A disgust, like I'm telling you, that deepened whenever you stopped by the lab for a test and then, as he drew your blood, as he leaned over you with the needle, that monstrous impression his ugly mug caused got stronger. What we missed, according to Dell'Oro—and not only Giménez and Moure agreed, we all did—is that Ceci, as hot as she was and having been cheated on so badly, so devalued, had looked for someone who couldn't even pick up a girl. A guarantee of fidelity, that's what Bacigalupo meant to Ceci. That's what she figured, for sure, and that explained the romance and destroyed Dante's illusion that love conquered all.

But no, what causes anguish isn't asking ourselves who we are, that quest. Let's not fool ourselves: that thing, the malaise of the mystery, as corrosive as saltpeter, is not our tragedy. It's not the question, it's not the quest that destroys us. It's what we find. And we find it practically without realizing it. Suddenly we realize that *that* was right there all along. So it's neither the question nor the quest that plunges us into this place. It's what we find. It surprises us that we didn't need to search for it in order to produce the discovery. It's within us. It's we ourselves. I advise you not to think too much about this issue. You don't know how many suicides occur among us every year. Of course, there are more than what gets published in *El Vocero*. If I report all those who commit suicide, Dante rationalizes, there'll be an epidemic and there'll be no one left here at all.

Mariano needed help with Spanish, Silvina told her. The last time Moni saw Mariano, she felt it in her guts. Surfer, pothead. Silvina had raised him by herself. With no father, I was always afraid he'd turn out to be a fag. So it doesn't bother me that he's a surfer and a doper. Better a Rasta than a queer. But at middle school, what can you do. He flunks every subject. Wouldn't touch a book with a ten foot pole. You've gotta lend me a hand, Moni. You can help him with Spanish. Just send him to me.

And now here he is, so close to her. Do you like poetry, Moni asks him. From the window you can see the forest. This afternoon the sun seems to be casting a greener glow than usual on the trees. The words to some songs, the boy, who's no longer a boy, replies. An ephebe, Moni thinks. What do you think of this, she asks. And she reads to him: *The nocturnal tide / heaves the silence / nocturnal / like me, nocturnal / music, seasick / without you.* Do you like it, Moni asks him. A pregnant woman wrote it, Mariano says. Why pregnant, Moni asks. Because she's nauseous, he says. Do I look pregnant, Moni asks. Did you write it, Mariano asks her. Tell me, am I so fat. Mariano scrutinizes her. You're cool. Really, Moni asks. Really, Mariano affirms. And taking out a joint: Can I? he asks. We're studying, Mariano. He could be my son, she thinks. No, not my son: my grandson. C'mon, Moni, if you smoke too. Mariano flashes her a smile, so tempting. But we're in class, she says. He's already lit the joint. They smoke.

Later, in bed, she thinks: I should've controlled myself. She's turned on by the scent Mariano left on her. She touches herself, turning herself on even more. It'll be hard for her to forget the kid, she tells herself. Very. Her cell phone rings. The call interrupts her. It must be Silvina, she anticipates. I have to pretend. And she picks up.

It's Mariano. Today's class was great, Prof, he says to her. Thanks, sweetheart, she replies. Tomorrow, the kid asks, can I bring a friend. He has problems with Spanish, too.

Moni laughs. Back to life, she thinks.

You're something else, she says.

She can't refuse.

It's spring, she thinks. Blame it on spring.

We all owe some kind of debt. To others or to ourselves. When there's no way to get out of the debt, we try to change the course of events, find another path, a path of no return and no regrets, where we can feel that this was our destiny and no other. We wonder if Roland and Delfina might have shared these thoughts when they decided to settle in the Villa, if they believed this was the place to start from scratch, like the majority. We didn't ask them where they came from. It wasn't necessary. They mentioned Miami. Someone said they had made their money there. Versace, Lili thought she heard Delfina say.

They had worked on runways for Versace. It was worth wondering why people who had reached such heights would come here, of all places, to live. They'd gotten fed up with the tumult, they said. It was enough to see how they related to everyone and how they garnered, if not exactly esteem, the impression that they had been here all their lives, to understand they were here to stay. It took them only a couple of months to gain the local acceptance that anyone else would have to work a year to get. They were criticized for what we've already mentioned, and we know it, it doesn't bear repeating, that with his classy looks and seductive ways, he couldn't have been satisfied with the platinum blonde alone, and he must have been screwing a few of his clients, though the soreheads insisted he was gay. And since nobody could get into her pants, they said she was a lezzie and was fucking several women: Verónica, the one from Pan Casero, the artisanal bakery; Miriam from Topito's, the handicrafts shop; and Alicia from the chocolate shop, Dulcinea's. Since they were a constant topic of conversation, they were accepted as being from here; they were ours. And Alicia thought so, too, that morning when she went to get a trendy haircut.

That morning. It was early. A black 4x4 stopped in front of the salon. Three people got out. They were scary, said Alicia, who was on her way out with her trendy haircut. She rushed away without looking back.

And one fine day the slut took off once and for all with a hippie who played the flute. My two brothers and I stayed with the old man. It wasn't easy for him to raise us. Two boys and a girl, me. But he managed: he worked in construction, then as a plumber and an electrician. Till he got set up as a gasfitter. Those were tough years for him. Imagine, alone with three kids. With the boys he managed very well. One look from him was enough to bring order to the table. And if they didn't obey him, a slap. He kept them on a very short leash. Me, he didn't know what to do with. And even less so when I grew up. It's not that he was jealous. Caution, rather, was his thing. I think I reminded him of my old lady. Even though I wasn't a whore like her, I resemble her physically. And in all those years my old man—not one romance. Nothing, not even some random woman. If he was invited to a party, a birthday, a wedding, the old man would leave before the dancing started. We couldn't even find out if he went to the whorehouse along the road.

The only time he ever raised a hand to me was when I started going out with Tuti, the druggie who ended up dying of AIDS in Batán. You need to get laid, I said to him when he forbade me to go out with Tuti one night. And that was the time he slapped me. I locked myself in my room. I followed his orders. I didn't go out with Tuti again. That slap saved my life, imagine. If I'd have kept dating Tuti, I'd have ended up with the plague. For months we didn't talk to each other, the old man and me. He was suffering inside, but he didn't show it. A tough guy. And I didn't cave. Till one day, with tears in his eyes, he said to me: Please, Gabi, don't turn out like your mother. I threw my arms around him.

Like I'm telling you, we never knew him to be with anyone but the old lady. But what could he do: she had marked him. His existence was pure work and loneliness. Till he died. Fell from a building under construction. He died working. An example for us, he was. It took us a long time to go into his room. We kept it locked up for over a year. Until we worked up the courage to empty it, clean it out. Nothing, not even one picture of the old lady had he kept. Not a trace of any love affair. What really broke our hearts was when we opened that drawer in the nightstand that had been locked and we found the dildo.

Don Pancho may now be in charge of the Comet Building, a four-story structure with thirty-some apartments, but he's never forgotten the time when, as a young man in Neuquén, on an oil dig, he got into a shootout with some thieves. It was at night, following a robbery of the Del Mar Electrical Co-op. He remembers the gunshots. He fired a revolver. And he hit one of them. Knocked him off his horse. The horse dragged the guy a long way. The overseer congratulated Francisco. Because in those days he wasn't Don or Pancho, he was Francisco. Then they went to look for shovels and together with a few ranch hands they buried the deceased. The tough part isn't killing a Christian, observed the overseer, a tough guy from Corrientes. The tough part is getting rid of him. Later on, because there were some wetlands nearby and because someone must have let the cat out of the bag, the place began to be known as the Dead Man's Bog, and Francisco decided to move on to other territories and came to the Madariaga area. He was a ranch hand on three *estancias*.

The one who is suddenly Don Pancho recalls all this tonight; he recalls as he hears noises in the park behind the building, stands up in his long johns and thermal undershirt, barefoot, goes for the revolver on the nightstand. The same revolver as back then, a 38; he keeps it in mint condition. It looks brand new. The revolver is the same, but he's not. He cautiously goes to investigate those noises. And he sees. A juvie thug is taking apart the motor of the water pump. Don Pancho doesn't even give it a second thought. He fires. And the kid falls without a sound. A clean, direct shot to the head. Somewhere nearby dogs bark. It annoys Don Pancho to have to grab the shovel at this time of night. But there's no way around it. So he goes back to the caretaker's office, bundles up, and grabs the shovel.

In the morning he buys rolls of turf and plants them on top. In December the first owners arrive, ready to set up their apartments for rental. They congratulate him on the park. And they pay him extra. One of these nights he'll take those pesos to the Tropicana. Because at sixty-eight there are times when Don Pancho still feels like Francisco.

No matter how hard Bacigalupo tried to win Tomasito's affection, every week bringing him gifts of little collectible cars, candies, and story books, and renting movies he might like, no matter how diligently he helped him with his homework, took him to the speech therapist and drove him to and from Nuestra Señora, in his way of treating the boy, we all saw, aside from Bacigalupo's efforts and good will, a tenacity that added to the admiration Ceci felt for him. Because in love there's an element of admiration, Dante said. And we thought he was going senile. Chiquita, the little hooker from the Tropicana who Dante had gone crazy over, had been softening up the sarcastic observer of our debasement. It's not his son, we told him. If Bacigalupo does all that for the kid it's because there must be something more complicated than love for his mother. That's what you guys think because you're twisted, he said. Besides, that kid, Tomasito, is a deaf-mute. How could he not touch Bacigalupo's heart.

If you want to confirm a rumor, buy *El Vocero* on Friday. On Friday, the day it comes out, it's the best-selling newspaper, so much so that it steals readers from *Clarín*. In the almost thirty years I've lived in the Villa I've been able to attest to how the police blotter has grown from a quarter page to half a page, then a whole page, and later two. I always noticed that in the police blotter they never published the names of those arrested, regardless of whether they were guilty or innocent. Dante was sincere:

This is a small town. We all know one another. If you think I'm wrong, just imagine I publish the name of someone who turns out to be innocent. He gets burned, I get burned, and I've got a problem. If the person named is guilty, sooner or later he'll come to collect for the humiliation. We're few, we know one another, and there's no need to name names because, when an article comes out, everybody knows who we're talking about.

Without saying a word, the three of them sat down to wait. Roland was giving Alicia a trendy haircut. Roland got nervous. Delfina, off to one side, was looking for a razor. One of them grabbed her wrist.

She didn't scream. She let go of the razor. According to Alicia, the guys hardly spoke. And from the few words they did say they seemed like Mexicans. Or Salvadorans. Or Cubans. Latinos, she said. They sounded like subtitles. Alicia realized, from how hurriedly he finished doing her hair, that Roland was getting her out of the way. And he did, just like that. As she was about to leave, terrified, one of the guys grabbed her by the arm. You forgot this, *mamita*. And he handed her the little jacket. They weren't ordinary thugs. They were more than thugs. Alicia went out into the street, walking quickly. She didn't turn around to look. She thought about going to the police. But no. She had never liked to stick her nose where it didn't belong, she later said. Besides, if she filed a report, if something happened, if they called on her as a witness for whatever might happen, you know how bureaucracy works, it would never end. And she wanted to get back to the beach cabana as soon as she could. A yoga session would get her back in balance.

And when we can't stand each other anymore, when we have nothing left to say to one another, not even to provoke an argument, then on Sunday we invite some friends of ours, a married couple, over for an *asado*. And afterward, when they leave, we have more than enough to talk about. A whole week's worth. And that's the good part about being social. Of course, we're not off the hook, because we still get invited back. And, yeah, we accept. Because just as our hosts need something to chew on, we'll go home with some juicy stuff, too.

Melisa was already skinny when she went off to study design in Buenos Aires. Every time she came to the Villa, she frightened us. I'm a whale, she complained. Just take a look at yourself in the mirror, Delia would say to her. She can't, she's invisible, I would say. A toothpick. We thought she was doing all right in Buenos Aires. Till her girlfriends called us and told us to come: everything was wrong.

And when we got there, she looked like a prisoner in a concentration camp. For weeks she hadn't touched a morsel. She didn't even weigh ninety pounds. She wanted to weigh sixty-five. As though she wanted to disappear.

I still remember when I lifted her up. A feather. In order to have her close by during the treatment, we put her in a hospital in Mar del Plata. Physician, psychiatrist, nutritionist. Delia travels every other day to see her. I'd like to go more often, but I can't close the Pasta House. Of course I'd like to see Melisa more often. But if I close down, I don't bill. And if I don't bill, I can't pay for Melisa's treatment. Or the psychologist. Because I'm going to one, the Miller woman, the one who has an ad in *El Vocero*. I go there to cry. All I do is cry when I go there. I swear, sometimes I think it would be better if what Melisa had was cancer. With cancer you know what you have to do: chemotherapy. The last time I went to visit her, I brought her a Tupperware container with ham and cheese agnolotti. What Melisa used to like before. Get them out of my sight or I'll throw up, she told me. I realize I went overboard when I spilled them on her head. Animal, Delia said to me. The girl has an eating disorder. I couldn't look at Melisa all skin and bone and the agnolotti in tomato sauce scattered all over the pillow, the sheets. I burst out crying. Even though you might not think so, I'm sensitive.

After that I started with the psychologist. A highly skilled woman. The cure, she told me, is astroanalysis. What's happening with Melisa, she said, is that she's an indigo girl. Indigo children have a soul that's hypersensitive to atmospheric pressures, she said. Just like me, I said. And I realized I was sniveling again. Maybe I'm an indigo too. Even though I weigh 285. Could be that Melisa takes after me with her hypersensitivity. And everything that's happening to her is my fault.

What we all know about everyone else, as you might guess, is always more than what we know about ourselves. I'd say we're strangers to ourselves. We look at ourselves in the mirror when we wash our face in the morning, when we adjust the rear view mirror, or look out of the corner of our eye when we pass a display window, but what we see isn't us. I'm not who you think I am. I'm not the one who reported my neighbor's illegal wall to the city. I'm not the one who left that mark on my little girl's face. I'm not the one screwing your sister-in-law. I'm not the one who spilled garbage at your front door. I'm not the one who poisoned your dog. I'm not the one who wrote that insult in the toilet stall at the bar. I'm not the one who drew up the budget and passed it on to a client. I'm not the one who fucked my little nephew. I'm not the one. And we know it isn't us because we don't know anything about ourselves. We know that who we think we are is constructed by others, those whom we think we know everything about. Don't think I'm talking about being curious, about poking around in other people's lives and then gossiping. I'm talking about something different: the way we have of knowing ourselves is through what others believe about us. We resemble the creature invented by others more than you might imagine. Mostly because it's more comfortable, and it saves you the trouble of going around clearing things up. The maddening part is that you can't stand it when others control aspects of you that you yourself are unaware of, whether through ignorance, indifference, or because it's better not to see yourself projected in that person others say you are. But you've also got to admit that it's more reassuring to resemble the person that others have constructed than to construct yourself, to go to the trouble of taking action to destroy the myth, arguing with the others, showing them they have a false idea of who you are. Tell me the point of getting involved in this polemic. I'm not who you think. Come on, do you think I'm a. You thought I was a. Useless, this debate. What does a person gain by being himself. What loyalty to what principles is a person supposed to profess if, in the end, we negotiate, because if you like this place, nature, the forest, the sea, if you want to stay, you have to come to terms. Let's not kid ourselves: it's simpler for all of us to be like what others think we are because that way, it's equally true, we make them feel they're more intelligent than we are. Tell me, who doesn't like to feel like the sharpest guy in the Villa. And if you want to make a good impression here, for things to go reasonably well for you, to be respected, then don't try to put the low-flying fools to the test. Just go with the flow. And if nobody wants to remember the scandal of *los abusaditos* anymore, you forget it, too. Like everyone, you, too, came from someplace else and you came here to forget. Don't get yourself all worked up over a memory that's not yours and eats away at you; don't screw up your opportunity to start from scratch, a new life. Look what a day we have today: blue sky, warm climate, the green of nature, the sound of the sea. Don't drive yourself crazy with memories. And don't pay attention to Dante. He's determined to stand out, thinks he's a hotshot because he writes those articles about the prevention of child abuse. Watch him and you'll see that he's on a different wave length; he's gone round the bend. He's not like us anymore. He's someone else.

The bodies appeared on some dunes in Pinamar, with signs of having been tortured. According to the police investigation, it was a vendetta. Narcos, the paper said. The man's name was Walter Fanelli, an Uruguayan, age thirty-eight. Hers: Samantha Freire. In the photos published in the papers, it didn't look like them, but it was: Roland and Delfina, the hairdresser and the platinum blonde chick.

Look where they came to hide, someone said. Even at the end of the world you're not safe from narcos. There's no place left to hide. Suddenly, when the story broke, some idiots had the bright idea that this would make the Villa important. We're Miami, bro, said one of them. And Barbeito el Gallego stopped him: It doesn't do our image any good. This kind of news doesn't help anyone.

Oh, no, another said. I know someone who came out ahead. The Duchess, he said. The place is vacant before the season and available for rent with all the equipment inside. She's already put an ad in *El Vocero*: "Hair salon space for rent."

But don't think that by reaching October we've left another shitty year behind us. No, this stretch just ahead of us is the toughest. We've got to fine-tune our reflexes, pay attention to the opportunities that may arise, because before you know it, the season's already here, and you'll see that there are always laggards still begging for a loan from Banco Provincia, and if the bank turned you down, better go scratching for the dough somewhere else. And there are also those who start fixing up their shops with the holiday season upon us. There's never a shortage of slowpokes who are still putting up display shelves when January comes and catches them off-guard. This month is critical. True, there are still cloudy, cold days ahead that recall winter and make you feel like staying in bed after a morning quickie in the spoon position. True, other days are blue, sunny, warm, a foretaste of summer, and it's hard to resist the temptation to go down to the beach. But as soon as you look the other way, the season's here. Even if it fucks up your herniated disk, you'd better face the morning, wash off the sign that says "Apts. One, two, and three bedroom units for rent. Inquiries here." Pull the weeds from the garden, mow the lawn, trim the privet hedges, get rid of the anthills, open all the doors and windows, air everything out, put the mattresses and blankets out in the sun, remove the cobwebs, kill the roaches, chase the rats and bats from the roll-up blinds, and get the apartments ready so they can be occupied by other roaches, rats, and bats: humans.

They keep that report on Human Rights and Safety at the TV station. Noemí Casal, of Barrial del Sur, was the one who promoted the project with the City Council. The council members, anticipating that Noemí would wear them down, approved her project from the get-go because even more urgent than human rights was the debate about the sewer system and the opposition's questioning of Cachito about the concession. Once Noemí's project had been approved and put into practice, she called the station,, asking them to broadcast the meeting between a psychologist, Deborah Miller, Deputy

Commissioner Renzo, and some police officers. At the meeting the psychologist suggested a therapeutic exercise. It was like a game. The group members, including Deborah and Noemí, passed around a ball of yarn. Each participant had to throw the ball to a colleague. Meanwhile, all of them were wrapped in the thread of yarn. The connection between them symbolized a network within the community. As each participant threw the skein to a colleague, they had to express what they were feeling. The TV crew was there to film it.

Of course the channel broadcasted some statements in favor of the relationship between Safety and Human Rights. Noemí, Deborah, and Renzo spoke about it at some length. But what the channel didn't have the guts to show was that image of Renzo, with a childish smile, throwing the yarn and saying Love. No one wants to end up buried in a sand dune.

Tonight it's raining again. Toto walks with the whiskey bottle: You know what I think. We were all right by ourselves. The two of us by ourselves. Mirna doesn't answer. She's fixated on the TV. Don't you feel anything, Toto yet again. Mirna turns up the volume. Toto pulls things out of the freezer: pie crusts, Tupperware containers, chicken, *milanesas*, boxes of ravioli. At last he finds an ice cube tray. Don't you have anything to say, he asks. Mirna ignores him. We have to talk, Mirna. Toto feels like he could break the bottle over her head. From behind, a blow from behind. Just one would do the trick. From the TV, laughter. The laughter blends with the sound of the rain, the wind outside. He plants himself in front of the TV. Let's talk, he asks. Explain to me, why another one. I told you, I want it, Mirna replies. And then: Get out of the way, I can't see. Toto doesn't move. Why don't you want to talk, he asks. It's no use, she says. Don't play bipolar with me, he threatens her. Get out of the way, I can't see. And this fucking rain to boot, he says. There's nothing to think about. It's a question of feeling, she says. Mirna. Toto wonders how they reached this point. Guilt. He steps away from the TV, picks up an ashtray, is about to hurl it against the screen. Mirna ignores him. If he doesn't break the set, he thinks, it's because he'll miss soccer. Think about it, Mirna. I've already thought about it, she tells him. I'm almost forty. My last chance. Toto plants himself between her and the TV again: There are two of us in this. Three, she says. You should've used a condom.

Sometimes the sky comes and other times it goes. It doesn't depend on your mood. Rather, it's the attitude you take when you look at it. It's never still, never the same. Its comings and goings are more obvious on gray days, when the shades of gray shift along with the wind. It doesn't matter if you're the one moving. Whether you're walking or keeping still, you'll perceive it: sometimes the sky follows you, accompanies you, passes over you, continues on its way and seems like it's ignoring you. Other times it comes straight at you and seems as though it's trying to carry you off. And if it comes straight at you, don't resist, accept that it will overcome you. Same thing if you feel like it's following you: don't speed up, don't run. Remember, it will catch you. Because no one can go faster than it. Maybe the best approach is to keep calm and not let yourself be frightened by that immensity advancing across the sea from the horizon, stirring up the waves from afar, raising them higher and higher as it carries them toward the shore, ever faster and more furious. And then there's that blinding sandstorm, the wind that lifts the sea toward the dunes. When the sky looks like that, pay attention. Whether it's coming or going, the sky always tells you something. It's up to you to decipher its words, which can be a whistle, a scream or a dull snap. Feel it. It's speaking to you as an equal. Don't get swelled up or let it intimidate you. Don't run away. Stay where you are. Pay attention.

El Día de la Raza, even though we now call it by the politically correct term Festival of Cultural Diversity, is still El Día de la Raza for everyone. Yids are Yids and darkies are darkies. And let's not fuck around. It's a question of skin. And not only that. Also of culture. The Yids may be very intelligent, but they're tightwads and opportunists. And the country folk are lazy, shifty half-breeds. Established by the Spanish Club, the Italian Circle, the Beer Lovers' Society, the Rotary Club, and the German Club, for over thirty years it's been considered not only a celebration that brings the entire Villa together, but also attracts tourists. In this regard, that long holiday weekend has always been considered a thermometer that measures the fever of the season beforehand. Four blocks of Avenida 3 were reserved for pedestrians. Stands selling everything from quince tarts and empanadas to exquisite cakes that represent the most traditional German pastry art. In the early years, pasodobles and jotas, tarantellas and canzonettas, waltzes, and polkas resounded over the loudspeakers. From time to time, so as not to snub the *criollos* from Madariaga, you'd hear a chacarera, a zamba. But regardless of how open the organizers tried to appear to the *criollos*, you could see their diplomatic smiles, their disdain for the natives. *Criollos* disguised as gauchos, different from the ones you find today, who go in for cumbia and beer. For the main celebration on Sunday, they prepared an enormous paella in Plaza 25 de Mayo. It fed up to 500 people. And the portions, on plastic plates served with plastic cutlery, were sold to benefit La Casa del Abuelo and the former Crisólogo Larralde Hospital, later rebaptized Hospital Evita by Cachito, in a demagogic attempt to get Peronist votes. Agreed, the paella was a Galician custom, but I ask you, if it weren't for the Galician conquistadors, wouldn't the Charrúas still be going around barefoot and fishing for bream.

But times change. People evolve. And just as the Villa has grown, this festival that stimulates business and stirs up everyone's expectations without exception has grown, too. The Vicuñas and the Reyeses get drunk in anticipation of the number of cars they estimate will come into the Villa in the drizzle: stereos, DVDs, audio equipment, cameras, cash. Because, as usual at this time of year, like I said, the weather is rotten. You'll see how this sprinkle turns into a downpour.

Then, on top of the thefts, there'll be a storm. And the festivities will go to hell.

This year Mayor Alberto Calderón, our Cachito, had obtained the Lebanese community's commitment to support the Cultural Diversity Festival scheduled for October 12, support that would replace the collaboration usually provided by the Israelite Society, sponsor of the Maccabiah Games. At the last minute it happened that the Lebanese community's intervention may have caused offense to the Israelite Society. From now on, their representatives announced, the Maccabiah Games will be held in Pinamar. It also happened that, due to a rift between both communities and despite the mediation of representatives of the local community, combined with Dr. Alejo Quirós's participation as a consultant, negotiation attempts were fruitless. Nevertheless, Mayor Calderón confirmed his decision to hold this Festival of Cultural Diversity, offering our Villa and its visitors a splendid, unforgettable spectacle with the participation of outstanding tropical musical groups to delight adults and children alike.

You know how there are blank days. Well, yesterday was one of them. I don't remember what I did. I can't recall. As if I'd been someplace else and not here. Someplace else, a place where memory doesn't even exist. Because I can't remember that part. It's also as if yesterday I'd slept all day and all night, and now, on waking up, the blankness grows longer; I don't know where I am. Just imagine how intense it is—this morning I don't remember my name. Not knowing who I am isn't what worries me most. It's that guy staring at me from the mirror. I'm talking to you. Stop looking at me that way. I'll knock your teeth out if you keep looking at me. I throw a punch at him. And now the worst part is that I don't remember why my hand is bloody.

It's just as well, Cachito consoled himself. We won anyway. And let's hope the Arabs and the Yids won't think this is the Middle East and blow each other up. And since we've got no shortage of sand here, maybe they'll confuse the dunes with the desert and start launching missiles. Cachito tried to resolve the mess between them, but he couldn't. The festival has to be for everyone, he said. Regardless of skin color. Money has no flag or homeland. And besides, this festival is a tourist opportunity, said Fernández of the Chamber of Commerce and Industry. We've got to be inclusive. Because inclusivity means invoices.

We're gonna have cumbia, guys, added Cachito encouragingly.

The cumbia beat is the most popular, who can deny it. Throw in some cumbia and you've got it, baby. The first thing Cachito worried about when setting up, despite the rain, because now the drizzle was a heavy downpour, were the loudspeakers. From 9 A.M. Thursday, when the businesses from Avenida 3 open, till 8 P.M., when they close, Cachito's voice can be heard over the loudspeakers, between the chords of a cumbia, promising:

Turn up the cumbia. Villa neighbors, ladies and gentlemen, this is your mayor, Alberto Calderón, Cachito to one and all, speaking. Turn up the cumbia. It's the desire of my administration that nobody be left out of the wholesome merriment and abundant fun in our next Festival of Cultural Diversity. Turn up the cumbia. One goal of my administration is to fill this celebration with benefits for commerce and tourism, and for the characteristic hospitality and warmth of our people to overcome all differences. Turn up the cumbia. We—you and I—all have a single objective to achieve: the happiness and greatness of this Villa, which has always been defined by lending a hand to newcomers. Turn up the cumbia. Once more, all together, let's hear it for the Villa. Turn up the cumbia. And let's hear it for the sun, the symbol of our community. Turn up the cumbia. This has been Cachito speaking. Turn up the cumbia. Over and out.

If you're a local and your parents come for the long weekend, you'll have to put up with your wife's constipated expression. And if your in-laws come, try to keep your plastic smile from becoming facial paralysis. Because, tell me, who can put up with their parents or in-laws in the house for three days straight. And let's not even talk about your sister-in-law and her boyfriend. And you know there's a kind of vibe between you and that little slut. So you've gotta proceed with extreme caution. Then there are the kids. If they're not glued to the TV all day long, you've got them on top of you, bitching that they're bored. Forget about a quickie with your wife. After lunch, when you're logy and feel like taking a nap, along comes the witch, telling you to take the family out for a ride. And you've gotta get them all into the car and take them for a spin. Head toward the beach, they ask you. Till they wear you out, and even though you know you could get trapped in the sand, you let them have their way and look for a road down to the beach through the dunes. For a while you feel like it was worth it to indulge them, driving along the shore. That half-adventurous, half-romantic feeling. Until it's time to turn around and go back, and you realize that the car is starting to get stuck. Everybody out. Get out and push. Hand me a shovel. There's no shovel, asshole. There's gotta be one. Take out the mat and put it under the wheels. Help me dig. And the tide coming in. The tide. Call the Auto Club. It's got no charge, stupid. You forgot to charge the cell phone. I'm cold, Dad. Me too, Dad. Get into the car. I told you, idiot, I told you we'd get stuck on the beach. Now it's raining buckets.

And the tide. The tide. The tide.

Cachito has hired some zaftig girls with plunging necklines and miniskirts to promote the festivities, each one combining the colors of a different flag, all of them standing under umbrellas in the dense drizzle, pale and shivering, handing out flyers with the announcement: Come celebrate free with Cachito, the title accompanied by a photo of a smiling Cachito, and under that the program for the festival, which includes the now classic parade of floats, the procession of those cool giant puppets, the stellar performances of Damas Gratis, los Wachiturros, Ráfaga, Grupo Cali, and for the grand finale, the guest of honor, the elegant star Marcela Morelo. Of course, we all have our doubts that Cachito will be able to pull it off, not only the guarantee of a change in the weather, but also a program like that and manage to pay the corresponding fees. A ridiculous expense if you consider that he still has the sewer system project pending, because Oviedo Construction broke up some streets in La Virgencita and El Monte, and if there's a flood, better not to even think about the consequences of the overflowing, turd-filled gullies coursing downhill toward Avenida 3 and Plaza 25 de Mayo where the stage has been set up.

It's true that in October the nice weather starts to announce its presence. Who doesn't feel like inviting someone over; who doesn't feel like coming to visit. Some families invite friends, grandparents, and it's a pleasure, after a winter that seemed eternal, now, with this warm sun, to walk in the forest, stroll along the beach, get together on nights that are friendlier. Then a person can catch up with friends and family. And they, in turn, feel the same way. They feel they're breaking from routine, that coming for three or four days, taking advantage of the long holiday weekend, is a great opportunity.

And this applies not only to us year-round residents and our relatives. It also applies to those who, without a friend or relative here, decide to give themselves a foretaste of summer and vacation. Those who can, rent a house or rooms in an apartment-hotel. Those with fewer resources go to a cheap hotel. They load the wife and kids into the car and they come. Their bring their jogging suits, sporting equipment, racquets, the bike. They stay a minimum of three days. The more fortunate, four. Determined to milk the experience for all it's worth, they plan everything, every moment of the day, every hour, every minute, every second. From practicing aerobics, playing a little soccer, taking pictures of themselves at the beach, to sitting down at a restaurant and gorging on seafood. Those who come to enjoy themselves know that here they'll have a chance to do everything they like. And more.

Look at that pack of darkies, says Moure, the veterinarian. It looks like Gorillas in the Mist. Our famous diversity now consists of including whites like us, he cursed. Just look at what that demagogue of ours has done with El Día de la Raza, turning it into a Blacka-palooza. If at least it was a festival of *real* blacks, Brazilian blacks, a nice *escola do samba*, mulatto girls with their tits sticking out, I mean, that would be different. But these are half-breeds. What can you expect of half-breeds.

The fact is, around this time of year you always get at least two cloudy days, if you're lucky. That is, if it doesn't rain all three days and the sun finally peeks out on the last day, when it's already time to go home. Then, if you're hit with lousy weather, arm yourself with patience and better bring along a package of sedatives. If you chose to go to a hotel, you're screwed. Tell me what you're gonna do with your wife and the three kids in a hotel room. So you have to go down to Avenida 3 and take them to the arcades. And eat burgers afterward. And after that go with the missus to buy a sweater because she saw one she likes, and when she walks into the store she starts looking at this one and that one and doesn't know which one to get and then, when she finally decides, it turns out not to be her size, while you and the kids stand in the doorway of the shop, watching the drizzle with blank faces, the same blank faces all the idiots like you have, walking down Avenida 3 at a snail's pace. And it's drizzling, driz-zling and cold. And all you want to do is go into a bar and order a double whiskey, and, if things work out, flirt with the waitress, who could be your daughter.

Once there was a sea lion. It washed up on this beach, to the south. For days it was stuck in the sand. It looked like it was dying. Wounds all over, abrasions. Along its flanks the skin was open, its flesh red, purple, dark. Every so often it moved its head. It was dying slowly. The beach dogs came over to it. Although the sea lion hardly moved, none of them got too close. If the sea lion, always in the same place, moved just a little, the dogs would back up, barking. Then came a long weekend. The tourists brought their children to see the oddity. The kids gathered stones. And threw them at it. A fun game, stoning it. The boldest ones, goaded by their parents, went after sticks to poke in its wounds. The parents seemed to enjoy it more than their children. You should've seen how they cheered them on. Till a southeaster knocked over the crowd of adults and children. The rising tide dragged the sea lion back into the ocean. No doubt when they returned to the city, the kids would have a good story to tell. A children's tale. And they lived happily ever after.

Beside the half-breeds, now the festival was an invasion of grubby artisans, pot-smoking Rastas, old hippies selling those tacky knick-knacks. The German pastry booths were crowded out by hot dog and *milanesa* sandwich carts. And countless brands of beer. To top it all off, rain, rain, rain. Since Wednesday, nothing but endless rain. Avenida 3 turned into a bog. The artisans, Rastas, and hippies took shelter in shop doorways and spread out their blankets there, displaying their junk. The storm grew fiercer on Saturday night. More than one shopkeeper, supermarket manager, pharmacist, restaurant manager, almost all the merchants and even the mangiest kiosk owners, swearing and fighting over the space available, initiated what might be described as an attempted sparring match that ended up in a brawl in which brutal punches were exchanged. Friday night suddenly became a battle between the locals and the invaders.

But it wasn't restricted to a few blows. Because the cumbia-fest Cachito had promised was attended by fans of two soccer clubs:

Rosario Central and Quilmes. The battle, which had until then been limited to a few lucky punches, kicks, and rolls in the mud, suddenly took on an epic dimension that would have left Mel Gibson in *Braveheart* crosseyed. Booming voices, shouting, howling. Chains, brass knuckles, icepicks. Broken teeth, ripped-off ears, bloody heads, fractured arms, squashed noses, ruptured testicles, black eyes. Anybody who got knocked down was lost.

Just when it seemed like the Quilmeños had teamed up with the blanket brigade and were trouncing the Rosarinos along with the shopkeepers, the conflict took an unexpected turn. The two fan clubs joined together against the shopkeepers. Because both had more in common with the Rastas, hippies, and artisans, because, you've got to admit it, among these lowlifes there's always a Rosarino and a Quilmeño. The police sirens did nothing to lower the voltage of the battle. The shrapnel of wind and water dissolved the effect of the tear gas. Frightened, stumbling, elbowing each other out of the way, couples and families with children escaped the theater of operations as best they could. It culminated with the surrender of shop owners, the lowering of metal blinds, and the withdrawal of warriors in a barrage of stone-throwing while confronted by advancing police forces. Two ambulances weren't enough to carry off the injured, and police roused the fallen with their billy clubs and shoved them into patrol cars.

The police car and ambulance sirens arrived at the city lumberyard from afar. It was quite a sight: the queens and princesses of each community waiting in the shopping arcade, all dolled up in typical costumes, fresh from the hairdresser's, painted lips, in full makeup. Anyone who hadn't brought a raincoat or an umbrella had put on a borrowed jacket. If at first they were suspicious of one another, the storm made sure they'd band together to seek shelter under the roof of the arcade and later move into one of the sheds where some laborers had lit an impromptu fire and were roasting cuts of beef for the *cumbieros*. The cold they were starting to feel in their bones ensured that the queens and princesses didn't refuse a rib or a *choripán*. Neither could they refuse a glass of red wine or a beer. Their hairdos had collapsed in the rain and their makeup was running. But at least they were warming up. Generous, those *cumbieros*, as gallant as could be, and even romantic. No wonder the party got going. A cumbia sounded, and little by little, at first to shake the cold from their bones and later, enlivened by the wine, the queens and princesses wiggled their hips to the beat, accepted the workers' invitations, and the dance party was under way.

Outside, beneath the deluge, the floats waited in this order: the first, with a snout shaped like a giant sausage, the German community's float. Next, in the form of a gondola, the Italian community's float. It was followed by a galleon representing the Spanish community. And the Bolivians were represented by a condor.

A cell phone rang and Cachito's voice could be heard, imperative. It was one of the princesses, who apparently had a special understanding with the mayor, who took it upon herself to dissuade him:

In this hurricane, sweetheart, no way.

Later Dante would write in *El Vocero*: *Given the intensity of the clash on both sides, police intervention was necessary. Several police units quickly arrived on the scene to try to calm the belligerent spirits. The battle was so violent that agents were forced to resort to the use of tear gas. But the gas had no effect due to the wind and rain. Then the agents were obliged to engage in direct bodily combat against the two gangs until things settled down. Under these conditions, several of the combatants were wounded, and many arrests were made. The proliferation of police vehicles interrupted traffic, which consequently had to be rerouted along side streets. These detours, combined with the heavy rainfall, obstructed the traditional parade of floats of the local ethnic communities.*

Thinking that the giant-headed puppets might distract pedestrians trying to leave the downtown area, Cachito ordered them to congregate in Plaza 25 de Mayo and from there to proceed on their stilts while the loudspeakers blared "When the Saints Go Marching In." The gigantic puppets included: Donald Duck, Daisy, Mickey Mouse, Goofy. The whole Disney gang. They advanced slowly against the wind, hobbling. The gusts from the southeast were more and more intense. The puppets were losing their balance. Rain pummeled the Villa. And to make matters worse, the lights went out, a defect that the Electrical Co-op swore up and down would be repaired in a few moments. But no. The incessant thunder and intermittent lightning, the gale winds, and the downpour, more than a storm, were the wrath of nature gone berserk, which in its fury promised to plunge the Villa into a swamp of muddy sand and shit, because now the current poured torrentially from the poorer neighborhoods and started flooding the downtown area as the tourists attempted to flee, splashing around in that fetid undertow. The movement of cars trying to get away produced a wave of excrement that pushed the thick flow toward the inside of the shops.

The real party belonged to the thugs, who, taking advantage of the concentration of people downtown, sacked more than one chalet in the north. Emboldened, the Vicuñas and the Reyeses marched in, weapons in hand.

To be smeared like that in *Clarín* and *La Nación*, Cachito later said. And he pounded his fist against the newspapers spread out on top his desk.

I'm not God; I can't deal with everything. What more do they want of me. I try to do my best for everybody. Like the General used to say, the people's happiness. That's my objective. And this is my reward. I don't deserve this injustice, Cachito said, pacing around his office. I can organize Rock in Rio, if I set my mind to it. I can talk the Rolling Stones into playing. I can even face Keith Richards and Mick Jagger together, man, but not with the unbridled force of nature against me. And on top of that, those savages, barbarity.

No one ever found out what happened with the artists who had been hired. Maybe the performances were canceled due to the weather and lack of minimal security. There was talk of legal steps taken by the musicians' representatives. Cachito came out and denied them.

The weather and security, my ass, someone said. What happened was that Cachito went too far with the "commissions" he tried to impose on the artists' representatives.

And as if to compound the catastrophe, on Sunday at noon the service stations crossed the hoses at their pumps and stopped selling fuel, speculating with the price hike that was expected to be announced at any moment. So quite a few tourists were stuck in the Villa, fuming, till Tuesday. Marconi the pharmacist was overjoyed because he got rid of nearly his entire stock of ibuprofen and Excedrin.

Finally, on Wednesday afternoon, a pale little sun emerged. What a relief, that little sun, announcing a change in the weather.

What a relief, that little sun.

Lightning victims. During the recent storm, a bolt of lightning struck a Pinar del Norte residence, which fortunately was unoccupied. The structure suffered serious damage and was largely destroyed. The firemen that arrived on the scene, summoned by a neighbor's phone call, succeeded in putting out the blaze after several hours of intense work. When the flames on the roof were subdued, it was determined that the current had penetrated the light post of the house and traveled through the electrical system, causing serious damage throughout the dwelling. Unfortunately, after smothering the flames and entering the charred home, firefighters discovered a dead man and woman inside, alcoholic vagrants who used to spend the night in abandoned houses in the neighborhood.

The Northern Neighborhood Association filed a complaint with the city about the number of vagrants who choose to stay in unoccupied homes in the area until police authorities intervene to remove them. "Quite a few neighbors, honest and upright people, have been complaining about the continuing presence of these marginal types who make undesirable an area characterized by its real-estate potential during high season. Let us hope that in order to get rid of these dregs of humanity, it will not be necessary to appeal to heaven to send down its punishment," concludes the petition drawn up by the Association.

Look at me: if there's one gift I've got, it's talent. I had the talent to come here. Mine was a literary decision. Because there's nowhere as ideal as the Villa if you want to write. No sooner did I get set up in a house in the forest than I got started on a novel. With what I inherited from my old man, who was a judge, since I'm not the spending kind, I could and still can afford art. I gave him the first half of the novel. A combination of Henry Miller and Raymond Carver, my masters, from whom I learned to seek and find my own voice. *Fly, Crazy Heart*, it's called. But I didn't finish it. What happened was, when I was halfway through I got into songwriting. Because I also have talent for music. I wrote twenty-four, all at once. For a double album: *I Surrender*, I was gonna call it. Romantic songs, protest songs, metaphysical stuff. Kinda like a combination of Bob Dylan and Leonard Cohen, with a touch of Bob Marley, too, but with my own personal seal, because I've got a style. I've always played, since I was a boy. First I played piano. Then I turned to guitar. One afternoon when I wasn't thinking about anything, I picked it up and that's how it went, first one, then another, and another. And without weed or booze. I'm not trying to tell you all twenty-four are brilliant, but there's material for an album. They're more like variations on the theme of the novel, which is autobiographical. And there they are— any time now I'll go back to music. What happens is that having talent isn't so simple. For example, when I was about to sign on with an independent label, I started thinking about the album cover and I got into painting. I always had talent for the visual arts. As a kid I won several sketching contests; I went to a painting workshop and even took part in a collective exhibition. A style somewhere between Rothko and Pollock was what my first stuff was like, but with a vibe of my own. I almost had the sample ready: *Fly, Crazy Heart*. Of course, the images I captured had to do with my personal thing. And that's what I was into till recently. Because I hit a dry spell. Sometimes inspiration takes its time. Sometimes it comes sooner, when you least expect it. And this place, I mean, it's ideal if you've got talent. Now I'm taking it easy. You know, inspiration means a lot in art. And around here there are lots of people like me, people with talent, who understand you. Lately I've been thinking a lot about ceramics and I'd really like to set up a little kiln out back, but I don't want to rush things. It's not a matter of going around starting a lot of stuff without finishing anything. It's the risk of having talent, you know. That's why the thing I don't give up on is soccer. And I don't miss a single Wednesday match with the boys. I've been living in the Villa for thirty-seven years and I've never missed a Wednesday soccer match. Because having talent for soccer and being a ten like me isn't easy. You've gotta control talent like the ball. Because talent can result in a goal scored against you. What counts is precision, discipline, staying in shape.

A real uproar took place at the Honorable City Council when the Civic Front, led by Ramón Miguens, entered the chamber to question our mayor, Alberto Cachito Calderón. He was blamed for recent attempts by marginal groups to occupy lots. The unlawful occupations, as reported by this newspaper, ended in brawls and arrests. Calderón was accused of being an accomplice to these takeovers. "This is how he ensures we'll get more votes," declared Socialist councilwoman Mirtha Loprete. "When we talk about insecurity we have to talk about collusion between city authorities and these marginal sectors that have become the scourge of our dear Villa."

In response to the criticism, Calderón pointed out that intolerance is not democratic behavior. The families that tried to occupy the lots did so following a misunderstanding over the assignment of parcels that the city will shortly set straight. According to our mayor, it should be stated that the heads of those households wrongly accused of illegal occupation are part of the work force that is carrying out the construction of the new sewer system.

One night when Dante walked into The Humanoid Bookseller, he found Lisardo writing in a notebook. Tiny handwriting, scrawls as timid as his appearance. Don't tell me you keep a diary, Dante asked. Not exactly, the kid replied. More like thoughts. Anecdotes, sometimes. The anecdotes are also meditations. Things that go through my mind. If I write them down, I can forget them. And they don't bug me anymore. Dante stood there watching him. Lisardo held his gaze. And do you, Dante, he asked him. Do I what, Dante said. Keep a diary, Lisardo asked him. Besides *El Vocero*, I mean. Dante replied, with a touch of sarcasm: I've got enough with other people's hell without writing my own. Give me a break.

What girl could fall for Fabrizio, the son of the Dagos who own the Montefiore lumberyard. It wasn't so much that he was lame as that he was kind of withdrawn. A quiet guy, at age twenty-four he still barely said boo. If you spoke to him while standing in line at Banco Provincia, at most he might reply to your attempt at conversation with a grunt or two. His father was worried about his future, which was also the future of his own fortune. And there was Cardo, the foreman. Or rather, there was Pía, the foreman's daughter, just a stone's throw away. Pía, a real cutie. The fact that Cardo looked after the boss' interests, that he didn't let a single roof tile out on credit even during the rainy season, we also knew. Just seeing the expression on his face when he refused to give the discount a person might ask for was enough to make you realize that in his refusal, in that attention to the boss's interests, was an interest of his own, as silent as his son. And so when the Dago Montefiore suggested to him that Fabrizio marry Pía, the arrangement was mutually beneficial. Pía, following her father's wishes, was studying business administration in Mar del Plata. The Montefiores and the Cardos figured out ways to promote the marriage. In the old-fashioned way, they arranged their children's engagement as well as the marriage. The fact that Pía was a gem and would never have rebelled against her parents suggested that her focus would be on her romance with Fabrizio.

And so the wedding day arrived. Ceremony in the chapel, followed by a huge reception at the Centro Italiano. The Montefiores went all out with the reception. More than two hundred guests, among whom neither the Quiroses nor the Calderóns were absent. Dante published the announcement in *El Vocero*. Next Sunday Fabrizio Montefiore and Pía Cardo, two young lovers who represent the hopes and dreams of our new generations, will be united in matrimony. *Auguri.*

Sunday dawned overcast. As the ceremony began, thunderbolts shook the chapel, drowning out the organ that was struggling to elevate strains of Mendelssohn throughout the nave. Montefiore, in a cutaway, Regina, his wife, in a floor-length pink gown. And the Cardos, also elegantly dressed. Cardo in a black suit, his hair plastered down, looked like someone else. And his wife, Mirna, strutted like a peacock in a pearl-colored dress, less pretentious than the one worn by her daughter's future mother-in-law. No doubt the Montefiores had paid for their future relatives' elegance.

We watched Pía proceed down the aisle on her father's arm. Ramrod straight in his suit, Cardo on the red carpet. And the girl, a second-rate Beatrice in white, Dante would say later, on her father's arm. We saw Fabrizio, black tuxedo, eyes lowered as usual, waiting for her at the altar. The storm prevented us from hearing the conjugal vows, terms of a contract devised by Father Azcárate.

We never expected it. Pía yanked the tulle from her head, dashed her bouquet to hell, and, walking back up the aisle, began to peel off her dress. Elbowing her way through the crowd, she stripped. She left the chapel and ran without stopping, stark naked, disappearing in a downpour that to us seemed like the forecast of an imminent new Flood.

If you're not going to change things, leave everything as it is. Because if you insist, they'll end up changing you. And you haven't got it so bad.

Fatty Oviedo's construction firm was supposed to start laying the sewer system in June. But they started in August: they broke up the streets of the Villa. As it would take a few months for the dough to arrive from Banco Provincia to pay for the work, the construction firm would finance the start of the job in the meantime. The Provinicia's money transfer was delayed. The ditches remained open. Do something, Fatty, Cachito begged him. You've gotta be patient with us, he urged. You know we have as much interest as you do in making this thing run. And why wouldn't Cachito and his functionaries have an interest: the price of the job had been set at a million, of which three hundred grand were to be divided between our dear mayor and his closest civil servants, Gonzaga and Bastiani. But Fatty Oviedo, who never stopped stuffing his face, put away a roast lamb and exploded. For the widow, Fatty's second wife and the mother of two little ones, there was no need for drama because Fatty had prudently taken care of all the details of the inheritance, including the children of his first marriage, who lived in the U.S.

Meanwhile, the construction job was at a standstill. Summer was coming. We wondered how things would pan out. It started to rain. The Villa was gutted by the excavations. And the ditches overflowed. Oviedo's children came from the U.S. And a few weeks later, the check made out to Oviedo Construction arrived. Like vultures, Cachito, Gonzaga, and Bastiani fell upon the children. But they said they knew nothing about that arrangement with their late father. They cashed the check from Banco Provincia in the name of the construction company and went back to the United States.

Rain. Endless rain. And now what, we asked ourselves.

Because it wasn't just waste floating in the ditches. There were those who saw fetuses.

Whom a person may choose as a partner doesn't depend only on his or her preferences. The first experiment to take on this question directly has just produced unexpected results. Desired and actual traits do not coincide either for men or women, although they manifest in very different ways. Men prefer thinner women than the ones they have. Women can prefer either thinner or fatter men. In spite of everything, men tend to get their own way, or to come as close to their goal as possible. For example, those who prefer extremely thin women have partners who are thinner than average. A general conclusion is that the traits normally considered to be essential for attraction have little influence when the time comes to form a couple in real life. Alexandre Courtiol and his colleagues from the Universities of Montpellier and Paul Sabatier have measured people's preferences in height and body mass and compared them with the traits of their actual partners. The volunteers—116 heterosexual couples from Montpellier, France—did not express their preferences verbally, but rather by designing their silhouettes directly on the computer with a special program. The body mass index (BMI)—weight divided by height squared—is a strange formula because the weight of a body doesn't grow proportionally to the square of its height, but rather of its cube. But a tall person isn't simply an enlarged version of a short one—s/he tends to have a more pared-down bone structure—and squaring instead of cubing the measurement partially corrects that complication. If you are about to enter into a relationship and have doubts about your choice, consult Deborah Miller, MA. Tel. 418061.

Yesterday, as gloomy a morning as any, as I was walking along the beach, I came across a blind man. He had the typical dark glasses and white cane. He wore a dark overcoat. The wind ruffled his coattails. It struck me as odd: he was barefoot. He stared at the sea. Or, rather, his face pointed to the sea as if he could see it. Maybe he did see it, I thought. After a while I worked up my courage and asked him what he was looking at.

And he replied:

What no one can see.

A fact is never an isolated event, according to Dante. You have to observe it in relation to others. Although sometimes it seems like everything happens at the same time, randomly, there's a logic to that simultaneity, an order, a dynamic, a movement that in turn generates an action, and that action, another, and so on successively. No matter how hard we may try to separate the wheat from the chaff, here, in this redoubt, everything connects with everything else. To explain an act requires explaining countless previous acts that lead to the one now calling our attention. No fact can be explained in a vacuum. And so we go on, suspicious of our neighbors, because if we're suspicious of ourselves, how can we not mistrust them.

Look at what happened to me. I took seeds from different bricks. Nearly eighty. And I got these plants, whaddaya think of that? It looks like weed, but it's not. When you plant from bricks, other stuff shows up. It might be that there were other seeds in the dirt I used. What's for sure is that they're huge and give you one hell of a hit, different, strong. A nice, long trip. God knows what plant protection law I'm breaking.

For Tomasito's eleventh birthday, Bacigalupo went all out with the gift. On a trip to Mar del Plata he bought the kid a nice, imported camera. He thought he'd earn both ways with that gift. He earned points with the kid, of course, and with the mother, too, the owner of the most prestigious photography studio in the Villa.

Tomasito took a shine to photography. He liked to take pictures in black and white. His mother taught him to develop them. The kid never put that camera down. He brought it to school with him, took pictures of his classmates. And once, when some little monster tried to snatch it away from him, he didn't back down and was able to defend himself with his fists till he broke the other kid's nose.

It seemed like more than a hobby for Tomasito. It was interesting to see him going around the Villa with his camera, making portraits, photographing landscapes, finding subjects to capture, always an alert observer. Nothing escaped him. Neither the movement of branches in the wind nor the crest of the waves. Neither the fishermen returning from the high seas nor the seagulls flying over the breakers. Neither the sun through the pampas grass nor the gallop of a dapple horse at the back of the cemetery. We had gotten used to the deaf-mute kid showing up when you least expected him—click!—and there he was, focusing—click!—as if at every moment, what for us was ordinary, for him—click!—was the materialization of a miracle.

His photos speak, said Dante, moved. And he even published some of them in *El Vocero*. *Precocious talent for imagery*, read the headline of a page he devoted to him in the paper.

A few days later, despite a rampaging southeaster, I was walking along the beach again. And I saw him. The blind man was standing and facing the sea. The wind whipped his coattails. He had both hands on the head of the white cane. The agitated foam licked at his bare feet. It must have been a little below freezing, but the blind man didn't mind the storm or the cold. I watched him from a certain distance. This time I wasn't going to ask him anything. I had decided to observe him, applying all my stealth moves.

But it did no good. He turned toward me. He smiled. Not a friendly smile. Then he turned his back and started walking away.

When his form became nearly invisible in the squall, I went back home. Without knowing why, I started to shiver.

The smell of apples reduces fear-based palpitations. Mint relieves fatigue and fosters a positive attitude. The fragrance of jasmine also contributes to relaxation. Essential oils are extracted from flowers, leaves, seeds, roots, and trees, and are then steam-distilled. They are the basis for aromatherapy, a treatment that dates from 3500 years BC. Revitalizing, purifying, calming, energizing, the oils can be used as ambient scent for massage, as drops on handkerchiefs, in incense, or in bathwater. In addition, aromatherapy

provides excellent, immediate relief of physical and mental slumps. Get in
touch with aromatherapy. Deborah Miller, MA. Tel. 418061.

Though Beti Calderón was reluctant to go out that night because
another southeaster was on the way, her friends, her sister-in-law,
and the Quirós women convinced her. You're a Kennedy, too, Jackie
goaded her. Beti didn't want to leave Cachito and Gonza alone. But
the women insisted. It wasn't so much that they pleaded with her;
they practically carried her. She should leave the guys alone; they
could manage without her. Cachito and Gonza didn't need her.
Beti was about to reply that it was true: father and son would get
along perfectly without her; they didn't need to consult her to get
into trouble. And so Beti went out that night with her friends Jackie,
Susi, Adriana, and Valeria. The wind shook the grove as Beti got
into the car, leaving the chalet behind. She had an uncomfortable
feeling, imagining that the storm might foreshadow a misfortune.
She chided herself for being overly sensitive. And paranoid. Gonza
was in his room, stoned, sleeping. And Cachito was watching soccer. Even though she didn't feel like going out, her friends were her
friends. No matter how much they might badmouth one another,
they had something in common: their relationship with power. The
Pussies of Power, as Dante once called them after too many whiskeys
at Moby. Beti's premonition that something terrible would happen
was borne out.

   In her absence, Cachito glimpsed an opportunity and grabbed the
boy. He was going to have a father-son talk with him, he thought.
He walked into his room without knocking. Gonza was snoring. A
talk about what, Cachito said to himself. He yanked him out of bed
by the hair and started slapping him. Then, as Gonza was slow to
react and pissed off, he began throwing punches. He couldn't keep
on jeopardizing his position, Cachito yelled. You can't, shithead. And
he began listing all the dumb things the kid had done. First, thinking he could blackmail Alejo with the porn CDs with Valeria. Then,

working for Malerba, the biggest thug in the Villa, carrying dope from Mar del Plata and, on top of that, becoming a runner for Don Tito Souza. After that, getting mixed up in Lorena's rape. And as if that weren't enough, getting mixed up in the murder of the Bolita baby that was burned to death in Pinar del Norte. And the kidnapping of the mongo. No, Gonza protested, I wasn't part of that one. Don't lie, you little turd. Besides, it makes no difference. Cachito kept slugging him. Gonza defended himself as best he could. He was bigger and stronger than his father, but he lacked his rage. Shithead, Cachito repeated after each blow. It took Gonza a while to return a punch. He managed to reach the door and ran out, leaping downstairs, and, on the way he grabbed the keys to Cachito's 4x4.

The vehicle was parked in the yard, by the garage door. Cachito followed him. And just as Gonza revved up the 4x4, just as his father stepped out into the night, just at that eternal moment when he saw his son at the wheel, the 4x4 flew through the air. And yet it was a matter of one second.

Then another explosion, this time in the sky. A bolt of lightning flashed a momentary daylight onto the smoking remains of the 4x4; Cachito's horror, on his knees, his mouth open in a scream. A thunderclap made the Villa tremble.

Last Monday an agreement was signed in La Plata between our city and the province for the delivery of ten brand-new mobile police units for our Villa. The mobile units, mostly vans, will be added to our law enforcement sector to guarantee the security required by an ever-growing community.

Of all the funerals we have in the Villa during off season, there are always some that stand out. This year we've already had one, quite moving, for Don Evaristo Quirós, which brought together the community's power brokers and which, as we're all aware, no one failed to attend. It's true, there would've had to be a good reason for anyone to miss it. Don Carneiro, we saw him, remember we saw him, kept a list of those attending. Since all of us, some more, some less, owe Quirós a favor, we took pains to stop by Neri's, pay our respects to his children, my deepest sympathy, that whole ritual sometimes including a hug or simply pronouncing the relative's name, placing a hand on his shoulder. The Bolita baby's funeral was also well attended, though the crowd and the funeral procession mostly consisted of poor folk. Let's tell it like it is: it was a half-breed funeral. There were also delegations from the Spanish, Italian, Polish, and German communities. Let's be honest: they were there just for show, to prove they're not xenophobic. Different from Tuquita's funeral, because whoever went to Tuquita's funeral, may he rest in peace, did so out of feeling for him, one of our most beloved lifeguards, you remember. With the cash he brought back from working on the Mediterranean coast, he set up a bakery and a confectionary shop. I'm talking about Tuquita, of course, the kid who got whacked by the Paraguayans he had hired to knead dough and bake. That's what funeral conversations are like: one deceased evokes another.

Gonza Calderón's funeral was different. It was a blend of compassion and an aftertaste of spite. What nobody failed to whisper was that Gonza was offed. A settling of scores with Cachito, maybe. And, my friend, you don't have to be a genius. Or do you guys think Cachito had no debts with even tougher dudes than Quirós. Who told you that. Miguens, he claims he's got proof. But nothing ever happens. The day he can produce one concrete piece of evidence, the Kennedys and Cachito will have him wiped out. They aren't worried about Miguens. He helps create the democratic climate those assholes need. Fact is, there's never been and never will be a funeral as talked about as Gonza's, not for a long time.

Lots of half-breeds, obviously. Voters. Those Cachito won over with *choripanes* and wine. In spite of this detail, you've got to admit the funeral was a huge success. Impressive, all those floral sprays and wreaths. Reading sash after sash on the wreaths that came pouring in with the names of families and businesses was like leafing through the phone book. But what provoked the most comments were those two wreaths: Vicuña Family and Reyes Family. They drew more attention than the presence of El Capo Malerba. So don't give me that bullshit about how there are no deals made between the politicians, the cops, and the thugs.

On Wednesday a sewer leak was reported on Calle 104. The quick action of a patrol squad allowed the situation to be swiftly corrected. But the possibility of more defects of this type cannot be dismissed.

No way was Miguens going to miss Gonza's funeral. Ramón "Matchboy" Miguens, the eternal candidate of the Civic Front, that ragtag bunch of left-wing Peronists, scattered socialists, progressives of various stripes. Three consecutive elections challenging Cachito. All three lost. Sure, Miguens might've thought that with Gonza's death, a whole array of prospects would open up to blow Cachito off his path to the mayoralty. First of all, after the kid's death, Cachito would be a broken man. And if he broke, because a blow like that could force him into retirement, the next elections would belong to him. Secondly, if Cachito didn't withdraw, the 4x4 explosion would lend itself to speculation that might be harmful to his candidacy, among which the most logical would be revenge. And why not think about narcos. Just a year ago, hadn't Cachito planned the creation of a port a few miles away from the Villa? A port would have been ideal for drug trafficking. Suspicious, that port project. Not only had it inflamed the indignation of the opposition that made up the Civic Front, it had also provoked a certain coolness among Cachito's supporters and voters. The frustration seemed to affect Dobroslav, our Speer, who was to be in charge of the port project, more than it did Cachito. Because Cachito would never lack opportunities. Case in point were the Paradise Towers, the inspiration of Alejo Quirós, a project that had fed Dobroslav's ego as much as the Kennedys' and Calderóns' fortune. What would happen, Miguens wondered, if the rumor were to spread that the port project had been a response to the interests of a Colombian cartel, and that when the venture failed, the narcos had gotten even by blowing up the 4x4 as compensation for the money invested in designs and environmental impact studies. If Miguens had a gift, a gift that justified his nickname, Matchboy, it was his tireless capacity for sparking rumors against Cachito. And his rumors, one after another, caught fire in the Villa. But their fire lasted, as the nickname suggested, about as long as a match flame. And yet this time he was convinced that this particular rumor would ignite and end up defeating his adversary.

Anita López tells the story at Gonza's funeral. She had trouble getting over what happened to her in the classroom. She was teaching *The Slaughteryard*, as she never tires of explaining, when Julián Mayorano pulled out that automatic pistol. She was writing on the board. She'd felt the class's silence, a silence that always makes you think before turning around, because if they're quiet it's because they're doing something. She turned around. It wasn't the kind of silence she'd thought. It was the silence of terror.

Julián Mayorano, standing, poking the gun barrel into his mouth. She doesn't remember what she said to the boy, if she managed to say anything at all. Julián didn't look like he was listening to reason. The silence was all that could be heard. She walked toward the boy, holding out her hand, hoping he would hand over the weapon. Please, Anita said. The only thing that came out of her was that *please*. With her hand extended. She was close to him when Julián squeezed the trigger.

The son of a well-known family, the Mayoranos, owners of one of the important home-goods stores around here, Julián had a car, a motorcycle. He was a good student, not outstanding, but a good, hard-working kid. He was dating the adorable Gabrielita Ferri, daughter of a very Catholic family. Gabi was the one who cried for him the most. That boy had everything, says Anita to anyone who wants to listen. He must've also had a reason to kill himself.

We found out a few months after the classroom suicide, when Gabi started to show. She refused to have an abortion. Julián threatened to kill himself if she carried the pregnancy to term. She replied that if she had to choose between the two deaths, she preferred his. And Julián granted her wish.

No one, not even Dante himself, can say exactly when he realized that writing articles about the detection and prevention of child abuse had become an obsession for him. And at first no one noticed how those articles, documented on the internet, started to become an almost regular section of *El Vocero*, either. At the beginning, a piece every so often. Then, twice a month. Later, one in each issue. Every Friday. How ironic, this space devoted to abuse awareness, while the dossier of accusations of Nuestra Señora, with its almost five hundred pages, languished, buried in a DA's office in Dolores. You didn't have to be too sharp to see that in Dante's obsession, his persistence in cranking out one article after another, there was a sort of official pronouncement, and if Dante had any proof, if it was in his power to accuse anyone, to testify before a jury, we wondered what he was waiting for. Like nearly everyone, the vast majority, we let ourselves be controlled by rumors and gossip, but even though some of those stories came very close to the truth, Dante couldn't give them credit unless they contained concrete evidence to take up with the court. He had, we realized, taken on the situation as a personal crusade. The night of Gonza's funeral we brought up the subject with him.

Now, as we tried to forget the scandal at Nuestra Señora, there were two matters stirring public opinion: one, Paradise Towers, our Speer's pride and joy, those concrete masses rising with impunity where a significant expanse of forest had once been, and also the construction of the sewer system, streets and boulevards gutted with no sign of a single pipe, and thus, the foreseeable debate within the City Council, challenging the bidding because, as Cachito's opposition maintained, it had all been rigged. Now there are other topics, Dante, someone said to him. The business of *los abusaditos* is old news. What was he getting at with those articles, pointing a finger at the entire Villa for its complicity in more than one sense, through silence and indifference, but no one dared tell him so. Possibly because it would imply assuming a responsibility that intimidated us. Besides, another long holiday was coming, a foretaste of the season. Experience has always shown us that these holidays give us an idea of what the season will be like.

Dante replied: Since when are the environment and a few fucking pipes more upsetting than child abuse. Unmoved, he ordered another whiskey.

The southeaster, we hoped it would be the last.

Off in a corner at the funeral, Malerba advised: If they fucked you over once, get ready, he said. Get ready because bad shit always comes in threes. They've tasted blood. And don't give me that crap about how you're gonna buy a dog. They'll blow the dog away. The safest thing's a piece. I'll get you one with the serial number filed off. And you don't tell nobody—get it?—nobody about it. Not even your shadow. Especially not your wife. You keep it well out of the reach of your old lady and the kids. But handy. Listen, bro, having a piece is no big deal. If you want to do it on the up and up, you go to Casa López in Mar del Plata, do the paperwork at the National Weapons Registry, and do the target practice at the shooting range in Pinamar. If I was you, I'd do it the easy way. Any cop around here'll get you a piece for a few pesos. And if not a cop, some security guard from the telephone co-op. Getting your hands on a piece is easier than buying a lollipop. When you have a feeling someone's breaking in, you pull it out. And you use it. Don't pull it out just to show off, hands up and all that shit. Shoot till you fill 'em full of holes. After that, no calling 911. Fuck 911. They say the hardest part isn't killing; it's getting rid of the stiff. Don't let them try to tell *me* that. If it's just one, it's easier for sure. But if there's two of 'em, don't think it's a lot more work. You load 'em into the car. You drive past Circunvalación and bury 'em in one of those dunes with tall weeds. Around there the strays, those starving dogs, will smell 'em first. You don't have to get all worked up about the cops finding 'em. You have no idea how many they find. And you think someone's gonna come and claim them. Just the opposite—the cops are grateful. Though they might get pissed off because they lost one or two that were working for 'em. Why do you think the stuff the thugs steal never shows up. Because the cops themselves are in on the take. So just be cool. Mark my words. Wait, wait for 'em, they'll come. Do what I tell you. You'll see how good you feel. And afterward you can tell me about the great fuckfest you had with your better half: you'll give her quintuplets.

Monday at dawn, after breaking a window, three minors entered a property located at Calle 106 and Avenida 2, the El Pino Building. The residence belongs to a woman from Santiago del Estero who came here to work as a maid for the season. As she was not home, the criminals turned the house upside down, breaking objects and carrying off a bag of 50-centavo coins and a new notebook computer purchased two months ago. When interviewed by this newspaper, the woman was deeply distressed and anguished, shedding countless tears and moaning, "After working non-stop, I'm left with twenty pesos in my pocket."

Identified by a neighbor, the youths were pursued by police, who found them at a residence in La Virgencita. The young offenders resisted with sticks, crowbars, and knives. After wounding an officer, they were taken to the police mobile unit, but family members attempted to stop them, which led to a fierce battle. Reinforcements were summoned to get the situation under control. Meanwhile the juvenile offenders took advantage of the confusion and fled the scene.

Nights at a wake are as long and boring as those at the hospital. Useless, too. Because nights at the hospital offer the consolation that, with any luck, the loved one might recover, stay among us a while longer. Nights at a wake, on the other hand, offer no consolation at all. No matter how long you stay at your loved one's side, he'll never be the same again. That is, he'll never *be* again. During a night at the hospital you can stay till another relative shows up to relieve you. Or remain, watching and waiting till dawn. And with dawn the illusions of the night grow stronger, that hope the loved one will return to this side of life. Where there's life there's hope, as the saying goes. But when the loved one dies, what sense is there in staying. If you really want to keep him company, the only thing you can do is take your own life. Beti's thought about it. She thought about it that night, when, at the height of the southeaster, in the downpour, lightning, and thunder, and despite Cachito's and the firefighters' efforts to keep her from getting closer, she could see the pieces of her son. Gonza's torso lying near the flowerbeds in front. The firefighters collected her son's scattered limbs and deposited them on a stretcher. As they dragged her inside the house, Beti felt her son's features growing dim.

A lengthy hypothesis to explain our sexual preferences—and even our aesthetic tendencies—is that beauty is an indicator of health. A symmetrical face, for example, would be the ultimate outcome of a favorable developmental process. This would explain the human preference for symmetry. However, this idea does not explain some new data. For example, if Rubens's The Three Graces *represents the seventeenth-century standard of beauty, attractiveness at that time would remain outside the limits considered to be healthy by modern medicine. There are, in fact, several recent technical articles indicating that* The Three Graces *suffered not only from breast cancer, but also from scoliosis, swayback, hyperextension of the metacarpal joints, and flat feet. Rather than a sign of Darwinian vigor, beauty in this case seems to be a symptom of illness. It is surprising that while great differences exist between one woman and another as far as preferences are concerned, there is no bias toward "taller" or "fatter" men. With men, that happens only with regard to the height of their ideal girl: there is no general tendency. There is, on the other hand, one regarding body shape. The ideal woman weighs, on average, ten pounds less than the real one, or is 2.5 points lower on the BMI. However, the variability of preferences each woman represents seems to be compensated for when distributed among various groups of women. Thus if we look only at the average of a population, we can see that our preferences coincide with our reality: the traits we consider to be ideal coincide with those of our partners. If your partner is your problem, call Deborah Miller. Tel. 418061.*

As the southeaster grew fiercer, Beti stood beside Cachito with one hand resting on the casket. Staying here all night won't bring Gonza back, Cachito whispered, trying to embrace her. Beti allowed herself to be embraced. She could have retorted: If you stay here, it's not for Gonza or for me; it's for you. So that the Villa can see its mayor suffering his loss, standing beside the closed casket, at the head of the casket, accepting condolences with a pained, automatic smile, that smile Beti was so familiar with, a political, but also drug-induced, smile, because whenever it was necessary to put on an expression for the occasion and keep it up for a long time, as she had witnessed at the funerals of Don Evaristo Quirós and Tuquita, Beti had no doubt, our Cachito had what it took.

During the last southeaster local police were put on alert by a grim incident. A dead body was found in the southern zone next to Circunvalación, where ramshackle dwellings lacking essential services have sprung up. It was near the doorway of a rickety sheet-metal structure where they discovered the body of a man identified as Alberto Montezinos, an Argentine national, age 59. The deceased had no livelihood and was described as a vagrant. His corpse was discovered face-up, with his feet tied and his pants rolled down around his knees. His face was covered with a bloodstained bag. There was evidence of blunt force trauma to the head and lacerations on his lower abdomen. With the intervention of the Functional Unit of Decentralized Instruction of our Villa, the incident was deemed a homicide.

And close at hand, as if guarding Beti beside the casket, more like evil angels than bodyguards, were Gonza's friends: Clavo Martínez Gálvez, Facu Davide, Mati Quirós, Pitu Veira, Santiago Luciani, Gisela Robledo, the Porter twins, Tobi Mendaña, Melanie Ortiz, and Lucas Iriarte. One wondered what sort of sentiments they were feeling—sadness, absorption, a lesson learned from the outrages committed, a sudden awareness of mortality, or more simply: the emotion of a Goth tableau. Because it wasn't just that it was winter and they were pale. They were pale from some sort of applied make-up base. Silent, mute. They had formed a ring around the casket as if the human remains hidden there belonged to them. And yes, why not, no one could guarantee that the explosion of the 4x4 hadn't been another practical joke by that breeding ground of evil. That's what Santi, the pastor, thought, though he didn't dare say so. What's more, the suspicion made him feel guilty. And he preferred to deny it to himself. Without any need to strain his purity, so great was his will to be a good Christian that every thought he had about the vileness of his fellow man struck him as a sin of his own.

Also during the most recent southeaster, police apprehended a 52-year-old citizen in connection with Case #7653-IPP 2088/07, categorized as "aggravated sexual abuse," because it was committed by a relative and caused serious mental harm in conjunction with corruption of a minor. The suspect, who resides in the southern part of the city, was investigated by the Second Supervisory Court of Criminal Proceedings in Dolores on charges of abuse of his minor grandchildren. The man was detained at the police station, where he will remain until his transfer to a supervisory court; a preliminary hearing has been arranged. It should be emphasized that this incident is completely unrelated to the investigation of allegations of abuse at Nuestra Señora del Mar Institute and predates the nationally publicized events of earlier this year.

Each of us deals with pain in his or her own way. The loss of a child, they say, is insurmountable suffering. No one recovers from such a loss. And yet Beti had read a novel about a man who lost his son and soon afterward went back to his routine: he returned to the office, went to the bar, got together with friends, went fishing. The most terrible thing about this pain, people said, about any sort of pain, but more so with this particular kind of pain, was that she would get used to living with it, and after a while, doubtless, there would come a time when her memory would erase it and her life would go on as though she had never carried Gonza in her womb, as if he had never existed. To cling to the pain, she felt, was another way to overcome her guilt, because Beti couldn't stop feeling guilty. She had failed as a mother: she had spoiled Gonza too much. She had looked the other way. Gonza wasn't a bad boy, she thought, looking at his kindergarten photos: Gonza at age five in his gray school smock, blue collar, little red tie, rosette, as standard bearer on Independence Day, one 9th of July. He was a sweet child, obedient, affectionate. At what point, Beti wondered, had that boy turned into a troubled teen. At first she had consoled herself by thinking that adolescence, as Deborah the shrink had told her, was always traumatic and full of conflicts. It was a matter of keeping him reined-in and communicating with him, according to Deborah. And a father figure was fundamental at that stage of development. But Cachito had no time, she rationalized. Besides my son, he had told her, according to the latest census I have nearly forty thousand souls to watch over. And it was the care of those souls that brought her comfort, trips, new cars, surgeries, refurbishing, because Beti was never satisfied with her new house and so she had taken on remodeling and decorating it. She would have made an excellent architect, she was convinced.

So good at figuring out ways to make over the house but unable to provide guidance for her son. As the house grew bigger, shinier, and more comfortable, their son became murkier, sloppier, threatening, the stealthy presence of a dumb beast lying in wait, his eyes gleaming with evil shrewdness, suggesting that he was about to commit a foul deed. It was true, every day Gonza seemed to become more like his father. He was the spitting image of Cachito, but dirty, unkempt, slow, sluggish, and snide. What in Cachito was the immaculate figure of a politician—an elegant sort, emitting a subtle fragrance, healthy, rosy cheeked, and with a nimble, friendly way of extending a pat on the back, an embrace, a handshake, everything that made up his aura, his charisma—in the son was slovenliness, lethargic gestures, filth, and a manner of speech that was a cross between slobbering and stammering. Do something with your life, shithead, Cachito would say to him. Look in the mirror. It infuriated Gonza when his father called him a shithead. And if he reacted when his father started beating him, it wasn't on account of the blows, but because again, yet again, one more time, he had called him a shithead. Gonza might have been many things, but a shithead wasn't one of them. He couldn't stand to have his father call him that.

These were the things Beti thought about at her son's funeral.

The third time I ran into the blind man, he was, as usual, on the beach. It was one of those cold, cloudy mornings when a silvery sun tries to peek out, but doesn't quite succeed. As usual, the blind man was barefoot, with his glasses, cane, and overcoat, looking at the sea. I was about fifty feet away from him.

Suddenly he turned and started walking toward me. I wasn't about to give in to fear. I let him approach. When he was close, very close, I noticed he smelled of sweat and old clothes. Without losing his smile, he raised the cane.

It happened very fast. He smacked me on the shoulder. As the pain grabbed me, he struck me again, this time in the face, from my ear to my cheekbone. He knocked me down. And he began discharging one blow after another. I managed to get away by crawling through the sand.

You people are the blind ones, he said. And he laughed out loud. All of you.

I got up and started running.

One wonders what those silly little stories are, after all, those short-lived rumors, anecdotes that at the time are either told or experienced, but mostly told, because a story can be lived as one's own even if it's not; it can actually be lived in the telling, or rather, the sense of living seems to be no different from that of telling and being told, and so I ask, what do those stories that buzz around here and there turn out to be, with or without us at the center, for as we know, you may not be the central character of the story you're telling, but when you tell it, taking over its emotions, adjusting the details, I mean, it seems like you *are* the central character and this is when it's a good idea to think of what all these stories circulating around our Villa really mean, what their significance is, what there is in each one of those existential bagatelles to make us think of them as jewels, what do we find in that mania, more a vice than a mania, for telling, and we should consider it carefully: We tell other people's stories and live them as our own, I maintain, and by living them, even vicariously, we are resurrected from the lethargy we wallow in. Let me try to explain: Those stories make us live; they bring us back to life. And if they do, it's because we're dead. Think of it this way: It's not the living that live off the dead. It's the other way around.

It's true that every funeral is an occasion that leads to a softening of the heart, the perfect opportunity that no scoundrel disregards in order to show that he, too, has a heart. There was plenty of that sort of feeling at Gonza's funeral at old man Neri's Funeral Home, but it's also true that if it drew a crowd, it was because of its character as a public act. It was a matter of being in the mayor's good graces, of offering condolences, but also of making an appearance. The Kennedys, all of them with their women, were there out of sentiment more than obligation. The tragedy could have befallen any one of the families, a kid blowing up like that. Besides, the size of the crowd attested to the fact that this wasn't just any old death. The mayor's son had died. To be seen, to offer condolences, was not just a compassionate gesture. It was also a matter of self-interest. The poor folks who showed up owed Cachito more than one good turn: a job with the city, a tax deferral, different kinds of favors. That cynical bit of popular wisdom, make friends with the judge, really counted with Cachito, the populist. And among the townspeople standing in line to see him was also Nazar, the cripple, who, in addition to selling lottery tickets, knew how to hoodwink the desperate into signing on for a trip to Curitiba, where a *pai* cured illnesses, freed people from harm, and fixed love sickness, among other maladies. Nazar cut an impeccable figure: a kerchief around his neck, white shirt, corduroy jacket, new breeches, and spit-polished boots. Perfumed, too. He tried to hide his limp when he walked. As usual, Nazar, inseparable from his pit bull. He had to keep it on a tight leash and give it a yank every once in a while.

Before allowing him into the funeral home, Don Neri asked him to please leave the dog outside. Nazar objected. He's gentle, he insisted. There was no way to make him see reason. In order to avoid a scene, Don Neri finally let him in with the dog. No sooner had they entered the room, everyone else backed off. Nazar walked slowly toward the casket. The kids gave them wide berth, too. And Nazar stood there alone facing Cachito and Beti. It might have been a simple act of carelessness. Though knowing Nazar, it was the gin. As he attempted to put his arm around Cachito, the pit bull slipped his grasp. Quick as a flash, front paws first, the dog lunged and sank its jaws into one of Cachito's legs, more like shackles than pincers, dragging him from side to side, shaking him. In the confusion, among those who were scrambling for the exit and those who decided to confront the pit bull, was Gancedo the thug. Gancedo pulled out a gun and fired. In that same confusion, the casket fell to the floor and the lid came off. There, wrapped in black plastic trash bags, were Gonzalo's remains. Some say Gancedo fired three times. Others that he emptied the barrel. The thing is, the pit bull died amid Gonza's remains, an arm here, a leg there, the torso, the head, unrecognizable if we hadn't known who the dearly departed was. Nazar cried like a baby kneeling beside the pit bull. In the corners, delicate stomachs upchucked their dinner.

But most disgusting of all was seeing Gonza's head rolling, the scorched cranium of a macaque which, in its fall, as if summoning a will of its own, began to tumble around, and in an attempt to avoid it, more than one, as if dancing a fandango, nudged it, horror-struck, with a toe, and that movement, too, looked like a dance step. To see the mayor's son's head roll was something we had all desired, who wouldn't have. Though, let us agree, it would have been even more desirable to have the heads of the powerful roll first, and *then* their children's.

The ambulance arrived soon enough. Beti, in an outbreak of shrieks, trying to elude those who wanted to embrace her, almost ended up in a straitjacket. Fortunately a nurse stuck her with a sedative. Cachito crawled over to the head, picked it up, clutched it to his chest.

The paramedics attended to Cachito right there. He asked them to give him pain killers, disinfect the wound and, after bandaging it, to take him home to change clothes.

Beti, drugged, was taken to Clínica del Mar. Poor girl, not even electroshocks would restore her nerves. After a while Cachito was back there, leaning on a cane, standing at the head of the casket, receiving condolences. Drugs are a blessed remedy on such occasions.

577

That week the only topics of conversation in the Villa were the funeral and the southeaster. And many were those who found a dark connection between them.

On Friday *El Vocero* would publish the following: *Southeaster causes disaster*, the headline would read. *Last weekend's storm left in its wake fallen trees, branches, signs, and blown-off rooftops in different parts of the city due to strong winds and the southeaster that mainly affected the coastline, beach cabanas, and Pinar del Norte. To address the damage, various tasks were carried out early Monday morning by the Department of City Urban Services. According to reports, mechanical loaders and municipal trucks were used to pick up light poles, while fallen trees that had been blocking traffic were removed. The sea level rose above the row of rental cabanas and penetrated beneath the concrete structures above the beach, with the tide washing away a significant amount of sand. It was noted that Moby, our historic and well-loved beachfront bar and nocturnal gathering place for friends, sustained broken terrace windows as well as the destruction of its wooden shutters.*

The other headline competing in importance with the southeaster: *Community grieves over dramatic accident. As a result of a vehicular defect, Gonzalito Calderón, our mayor's son, has lost his life. The outpouring of community solidarity demonstrated at his funeral reflected the deep shock of the entire Villa. A promising young life that leaves a gap among us.*

When we met again at Moby, we ribbed Dante: You didn't make much of an effort to cover the crime, someone said to him. And another: You were more than a little cryptic, Scribe. Accident, my ass. An attack, what doubt could we possible have. We didn't need proof. Instinct, pure instinct.

Every night, as soon as Javier comes home from work, Agustina starts complaining that they've raised the tuition at Nuestra Señora, that Martincito got a warning again, and that Belén isn't doing well in math, plus the electricity bill is due, and there's the phone, besides.

Not to mention the cable because today an overdue payment notice arrived. Javier pours himself some gin. Then he says: I'm a city surveyor, not a magnate. And she replies: What you are is a hopeless loser who can't support a family. Don't raise your voice to me, he shouts at her. And that makes Agustina scream at him even louder. The kids, Javier says.

The kids close the door to their room. Martincito turns up the volume on the TV. Belén cries. She sobs quietly. Martincito puts his arms around her. The screams blend with the Simpsons. From the living room comes the crash of broken glasses. Then a blow that makes the house quake. Belén wants to go see. But Martincito holds her back.

Now no more screaming can be heard. Only the Simpsons. His curiosity piqued, Martincito turns down the volume on the TV. The silence is threatening. His sister is no longer crying. She's trembling. A long time goes by. Until the door of their room is opened.

Dinner time, Agustina calls them.

The two young siblings obey. They sit down at the table. C'mon, change your faces, Javier tells them. Moms and dads argue in every house.

Agustina serves *milanesas* with mashed potatoes.

Or do you want us to get a divorce, huh? he asks them. Maybe you'd like to be the children of divorced parents.

Tell me, what greater punishment for Alejo, the Mafioso adopted by his uncle, Don Evaristo, a crooked shyster, than his own nephew, whom he, in turn, adopted: Camilo. Instead of "the apple doesn't fall far from the tree," the saying ought to go "the adoptee doesn't fall far from the adopter." I'm talking about the Dead Little One, El Muertito. Even though he must be around thirty, he is and will always be El Muertito, the Dead Little One, the punishment God sent to those who think they own our destinies, ambassadors of the Lord in this dissolute Villa. And may God also take pity on El Muertito, that poor soul in pain who torments our nights by reminding us of our mortal natures. Let us pray for him. Let us pray for ourselves.

Till that night when Ceci put Bacigalupo's things in a bag and threw him out. And all of us in the Villa know, without exception, we all know that when winter ends, with the spring comes a wave of separations. Those who live together have spent three seasons that way: fall, winter, spring. If it's a lot for anyone who's alone, it's too much for anyone who's part of a couple. You crawl your way along to December, with an aching back, your reflexes on edge, and the desire to say the hell with it all. But in Ceci and Bacigalupo's case, as Deborah the psychologist would say, it wasn't the exhaustion of the relationship.

Looking like a sheep with its throat slit, Bacigalupo picked up the bag. He looked at Tomasito sweetly, almost crying. Don't say anything, Ceci told him. You better not say anything. Bacigalupo picked up the bag. He wanted to say something, but he couldn't think what. He tried to get close to Tomasito, give him a kiss. But the boy walked away from him. He stood next to his mother and hugged her waist. Bacigalupo understood that it would have been pointless to ask for an explanation, to mutter an excuse. He simply looked at Ceci and whispered one word: Thanks, he said. And he left.

That night he had nowhere to sleep. He went to the lab. He sat down in the waiting room, like a patient waiting for him to draw blood. It took him a while to open the bag, to see which things Ceci had packed for him. The first thing he found when he opened the bag was an envelope from Ceci's store, Glances. Inside were a few black-and-white photos. And in all of them he was with a different woman. I won't tell you who they were because it would surprise you to know how many were from the Villa, married and single, young and not so young. All of them compromised him. If he wasn't snuggling up to one in a car, they were smooching in the woods or he was walking into a house, looking off to both sides in case he'd been spotted. The "thanks" he had given Ceci when he left now began to acquire some meaning. Thanks to Ceci he had overcome his monster complex. Thanks to Ceci more than one woman had wondered what she had seen in him that made her choose him in spite of his repulsive ugliness. Thanks to Ceci, Bacigalupo was now a different man.

Sitting in a chair in the waiting room, with the envelope and photos in his hand, he could contain himself no longer and started to cry.

Around here, if you don't take advantage of the season, you have no other option: you kill yourself or you let yourself die.

It was during another southeaster when the old sewer system overflowed again, the pipes exploded, and in the ditches that the Oviedo Construction Company had dug to replace the pipes, gutting the Villa, our excreta flowed turbulently, and then that stench you could detect, said Dante, was the humus of our vices and sins. It was in those days, when Dante decided to continue with his articles on the prevention of child abuse, when he began to bombard us with Alighieri, the ninth canto, where they talk about the infernal suffering of heretics. He would recite it for us: *This marsh, that breathes its foul stench, / circles the woeful city round about.*

Everything we do is for the kids, Alejo says to anyone willing to listen. If we make sacrifices, it's for them. Our greatest concern is to give them a secure future. For them to be somebody, to have a profession, to be able to build worthwhile lives for themselves. That's why we struggle to give them a good education. Education is everything. Say what you will about Nuestra Señora, it's the best school around here. After all, what happened there could have happened in any other school. To keep harping on the scandal, Dante, my boy, isn't just harming the institution. It's screwing up our kids' lives. And the Villa, too. Because the season's already here.

It's a little gang of seven, eight kids, not many more. They always rob at night, always in Barrio Norte. Those kids have style. Their tactic consists of setting off several alarms in several houses, all at once. The cops, with their broken-down patrol cars, don't know where to go first. Even Deputy Commissioner Renzo's getting tired. Those little shits aren't gonna fuck me up with the season about to start. Those goddamn kids aren't gonna get up my ass. And that night, when the alarms go off, he grabs his 9 millimeter and gets behind the wheel of a patrol car. The siren crosses Barrio Norte, drowning out the alarms. Three kids take off fast down a boulevard. The Vicuñas. At the corner of 306th, two of them separate, one going right, the other left. Renzo turns off the siren. He follows one kid silently. When the fugitive starts getting tired, Renzo slows down. Now the patrol car is following him, practically on his heels. If he steps on the gas he could squash him, but no. He's enjoying this. Till the kid runs out of breath. And falls to his knees. Renzo gets out of the car with the 9 millimeter in his hand. The kid's on all fours, panting. Renzo pokes the barrel into the back of his head. The kid's breathing turns into a whistle. Suddenly, he coughs. An ugly cough. A bloody cough. Renzo lifts him by the hair. He looks him right in the eye. The kid's eyes are white now, rolled back. His T-shirt is covered with blood. It turns Renzo's stomach to grab him by the collar, drag him toward the car, stick him in the trunk. Before he takes off he wonders if it he wouldn't have done the kid a favor by shooting him. Finally he turns on the siren again, hits the gas, and drives toward the hospital. When he takes him out of the car in the hospital parking lot, the kid is still coughing up blood, trembling. His T-shirt is red jelly. I should've blown you away, asshole. But I was doing you a favor. Now you're born again, you little piece of shit, he says to him. And you're gonna fuck yourself up. He pushes him toward the emergency room. Go on in.

One November morning you go down to the beach and there they are. They look like they've been there forever: the first skeletons, white, stuck deep into the sand, beneath the sun. They're the wooden frames of the tents, announcing the imminence of the season. It seems impossible, people say. How fast the year went by. The season is already here. And once the season begins it never seems to end. Just as the frames seem to have been there forever, it seems as though it's always been high season in the Villa. Suddenly, one April morning, you go down to the beach and there they are again, the skeletons, stripped bare. Cold wind. That was all. Brief, short, the season. Like life. And the lesson, because there's a lesson in this transition, is that just when we thought we'd learned how one should live, the tricks, the survivors' ploys, the end draws near; it's imminent. Which makes one deduce that the shrewdest tactic consists of living in the present, the here and now. Summer was never anything but an illusion. Never. Here reality consists of those nearly ten long months of solitude and waiting. If there was a lesson to be learned, we would forget it right away, and once again, happiness is something we failed to recognize while we were living it. And now I'll leave you. I have to finish taking the poles out of the little shed at the cabana rental place.

The first to arrive, between November and December, are the ones from Santiago del Estero who come here to earn some good cash by breaking their humps in the hotels and restaurants. They get off the buses with whatever they can carry on their backs, and when they leave, with the pesos they've picked up, they buy themselves aerodynamic sneakers, a plasma TV, audio equipment. Big fat suitcases tied up with string. They take away a bunch of boxes and packages. You should see them in March when they gather in droves to hop aboard those buses where they'll travel like cattle, crowded together, sleeping off the beer in an atmosphere that stinks of feet. But that just happens in March, April at the latest. In January you'll see the men working in cold-storage rooms and in kitchens, sawing a side of beef, peeling potatoes, chopping onions, carrying trays, while the women tidy up rooms, clean bathrooms, change sheets, run the vacuum, and scrub endlessly. The youngsters who can't land a gig make themselves some flannel rags to wave cars into available parking places for spare change. You'd better be sure to have the change. Later, when the restaurants have emptied out and the tourists have gone to their hotels, the Santiagueños go off to dance cumbia and drink *mezcladito*. But don't think they only fuck one another. More than one big, strapping kid bangs an old lady and collects enough for a motorcycle. In the morning there they are again, back at their posts, wasted. You can't imagine the staying power those guys have. Not to mention the women, single and married alike, who don't turn down a fuck because the start of classes is right around the corner: school smocks, supplies, and workbooks are expensive, and that little half-breed chick is just over twenty and has two calves to send to school. Later, in March, in addition to threads and brand new appliances, lots of chicks will have also acquired a baby bump. But now it's January. Look at them sweat. I always say, and not because I'm just another hick from Termas, that if all of this country were like Santiago, it would be a world power.

The section: Police Blotter. The headline reads: *Parricide thwarted* And below that: *Minor shoots father, who remains in guarded condition.* Moving into the body of the story, Dante writes: *The case was reported last Sunday at a residence on Avenida 27 between Calles 117 and 119. Police are investigating the reasons why a 17-year-old youth fired a weapon, presumably a 22 caliber, into his 37-year-old father's abdomen. Police intervened upon receiving a 911 call from neighbors who had heard shooting. When they arrived they found an individual with a gunshot wound in the left side of his abdominal area. The victim reported that his 17-year-old son had fired the shot. The victim was admitted to the local hospital, where he was treated and is currently in guarded condition. The assailant fled the scene, but was detained last Tuesday at noon in the vicinity of the location where the violent incident took place. The case was filed as attempted murder aggravated by relationship and use of a firearm. The Assistant District Attorney's Office of our Villa is investigating.*

After a long hiatus, Oviedo Construction has resumed its work on the new sewer system. The interruption was due to the death of its director, Victorio Oviedo. His passing was the result of ingesting a chicken bone. His death produced a conflict over his successor, resulting in the breakdown of work on the sewer project. With the conflict now resolved thanks to government intervention, our Villa now looks optimistically at the advancement of a project that will soon be a reality.

Imagine that tomorrow there's a nuclear disaster; a radioactive blast wipes out the Villa. Not even a parrot is left standing. Centuries go by. Centuries. Until life begins to regenerate once more. A young goatherd tending his goats discovers a cave. The cave is deep. Lighting his way with a torch, he goes inside to see what's up. Till he trips over some piles of newspapers. Like I told you, the world has been reborn. And it was reborn illiterate, as is all new life. The boy looks at the letters with a blank face: they're hieroglyphs to him. Though maybe he doesn't even get what those marks are. But he can see the photos. And we're in them. It's a collection of *El Vocero*. The kid doesn't understand the headlines: Abuses at a kindergarten. Scandal at Nuestra Señora. And he wonders who the men and women in that photo could be, serious types, one of them with a mustache, suit, and tie. It's Cachito Calderón. Beside him is Alejo Quirós, so respectable. Our little goatherd, whose only garment is a loincloth made of animal hide, is curious about the clothing those anonymous dudes in the paper are wearing, though he has no idea what a newspaper is. Suddenly he gets a pressing urge to take a shit. And when it's time for him to wipe his ass, he grabs the newspaper. With any luck, that will be the destiny of all we've done and do, our spontaneous scummy deeds and our belated redemptions, the memory of our presumed grandeur and the guilt buried in every conscience, what will remain of our shamelessness in the name of violated purity. And with luck, that too will be the fate of the articles I write in this newspaper, Dante says. Amen. If God exists. What do you think, he asks: Does He exist?

Now you can feel it more. Even though it's still November, the season is already here. It gets light earlier, days are warmer and sunnier, skies bluer, groves greener, and roofs redder. You can hear saws, hammers, sprinklers, and the voices of brick masons, painters, and carpenters. The morning light has a transparency that can be seen in the foam that the wind skims off the crest of the waves. Although it's spring, many days are a foretaste of summer. It's pleasant to walk along the beach. And there are days when you can already take a dip in the sea. This time of year is hopeful. We all feel that something important is about to take place. We don't know exactly what, but it's going to happen. And when it does, we're determined to be alert and not miss this opportunity, because what we're all waiting for is that, an opportunity. Then we feel we're better than we are. It's the sea air, someone says. Because at this time of year the sea air pervades the whole Villa. And it imprints its force on us. Look at the doors and windows opening. The buildings, hotels, chalets, shops, raise their blinds, fling open their shutters, and roll up the curtains. From apartments, rooms, businesses, comes a blast of gloomy dampness, and the sun begins to break through the darkness; it crosses a spider web, and as it dusts the atmosphere, the dust motes sparkle. Who cares what happened at Nuestra Señora, or the business of Dobroslav's towers chopping down the forest, the Kennedy's real estate schemes, the complaints against Pedroza, the accusation against Cachito Calderón for misappropriation of funds. No one wants to pay much attention to El Vocero's police blotter, which now occupies two central pages. Of greater—and growing—importance are interviews and photos of the members of the Hotel Owners' Association, the Commerce Association, and the Culinary Institute. According to estimates by these institutions, in spite of inflation, the Villa will be the best vacation choice because our prices are competitive. And since we live from tourism, we'll just deal with the whole mess about *los abusaditos* when the season is over.

My son is three-and-a-half and has a shovel. It's a real shovel, not a toy one. Under the midday sun, between two sand dunes, he scoops up the sand with his shovel and carries it. I watch him come and go, carrying sand, building a mountain. Sometimes after a new load, one of its sides collapses. But it doesn't seem to bother my son. He spends a long time doing this. He keeps loading and unloading sand until the mountain is as tall as he.

I ask him what he's making.

A mountain, he says.

Soon the mountain is taller than he is. But he doesn't give up. Each time one of the sides collapses, without blinking, my son picks up the sand, unloads it once more on the uneven side, arranges it. And he persists. His work is no different from mine. Writing a novel shares some of this vision. My son's dilemma is also mine.

My son hands me the shovel. It's your turn, he tells me.

I grab the shovel; I imitate him. I'm going to shovel sand till I can't do it anymore. And then some more. I'll go on all night, I tell myself. And tomorrow, when he wakes up, my son will find me concentrating on the mountain. This mountain that is a novel.

This novel that you're reading.

Dante gets up at dawn, when the sky is starting to grow light. The blood-red horizon over the tranquil sea. As he prepares a *mate*, he turns on the Del Mar FM station. At this time of day they play tangos. Lucio Arce is singing, the host announces in a tone that attempts to sound like it's from the outlying slums. A young talent, he proclaims. Dante doesn't trust young tango artists. But as he goes for his second *mate* he realizes that this voice is different, that there's something different in the lyrics. And he follows them closely: *They dragged the guy who knew too much / From the bottom of the ditch. / He knew the same things we all know / but only he dared snitch. / They drove him out of town one day / Just like a mad dog running / And folks pulled down their window shades / like when a storm is coming. / Cruel destiny can be a curse, / It's lethal and contagious / It dealt that man a losing hand / His fate was far from what he'd planned / His death, swift and outrageous. / And in the darkness and the cold / Things went from bad to worse. / Now if you're ever in a fix /And don't know what to do / I have a piece of good advice / I'll gladly share with you: / As all delinquent types well know / there's no solution but / to tie a blindfold round your eyes / and keep your big mouth shut. / In dealings with the underworld / It's best to be discreet / and keep your profile very low / when walking down the street.*

What Dante's listening to on the radio is no tango. More like a warning from destiny. Who the hell does this tango singer kid think he is, Dante asks himself. My guardian angel.

That's how it is with justice: when it's missing, you have your suspicions, because when it's missing, it's to someone's advantage. And you're suspicious when it comes, too, because for sure it's arrived just to fuck someone up or to benefit someone who's never the victim. Which makes you wonder why justice would remember to show just up now, in November, and claim its due with search warrants right when the season is upon us. Press coverage of the searches is inevitable, Rinaldi says. And it'll damage all of us. Moure echoes: All of us. Because the TV channels are already here, doing interviews in the streets. And there's always a bunch of assholes who'd love to get some screen time. If the lack of news about the investigation has led the parents of *los abusaditos* to go stirring up shit, well, fine and dandy. But even the parents understand that if they stir up too much shit, the season will be ruined. That's why they're keeping a low profile.

Leave it to me, Paco Barbeito pipes up. I can negotiate.

Barbeito el Gallego meets with the reporters from the Todo Noticias channel. He invites them to lunch at El Español. He talks to them about the season, its imminence. We live from tourism. We're all working people. People around here wait for the season all year long. It's the only chance they'll get all year to collect a few pesos and struggle along till winter's over. In fact, the Chamber of Commerce and Industry denies the abuse. And, of course, we want to clear up this episode that stains all of us. But you, the media, have to understand the Villa's situation and also think about the harm you'll cause to many homes. We members of the Chamber of Commerce and Industry have been analyzing the situation and have a proposal for you all, Barbeito says. At no cost whatsoever to you and your families, service at the best restaurants, the best hotels in the Villa. The entire season, no charge. On condition that, well, you start spreading the news that the season is coming and leave that stuff about *los abusaditos* alone.

That same night we see El Gallego on TV. Hidden camera. We see him talking to four reporters. On the screen, the caption: Abuse: Bribery attempt. And we clearly hear El Gallego offering free food and lodging for the season to all journalists present.

We all know *El Vocero* is partially financed by ads. And that the greatest investment, the strongest support, comes from the City, is an established truth. Also that Alejo Quirós, the City's legal advisor, is the one who establishes the guidelines for the editorial slant of the newspaper, our journal, as we call it, even though it's just a paper. Because on Fridays, the day *El Vocero* comes out, no one in the Villa skips reading it: we're all here, whether we like it or not, in our mirror. Like all mirrors, it's deceptive. Sometimes we see ourselves as worse than we imagine. Sometimes, on the other hand, we see ourselves idealized. What's indisputable is that for years, day after day, Dante has worked out a way to write about what's happening, what's happening to us, sometimes taking pains to protect someone's identity, someone suspected of accepting bribes, a juvie thug, and he doesn't protect them out of decency: it's that he might be mistaken, he knows it; it's possible the suspect is just a suspect and the kid isn't a thug. But it's also true that even if they are, in fact a bribe-taker and a thug, tomorrow they'll cross paths at the co-op, at the supermarket, in the street. Why play the puritan, the intrepid citizen. We are few and we all know one another, Dante tells himself. And that's just the way it is. But, to get back to *El Vocero's* financial backing: the ads and city publicity aren't its only means of support. There's also Alejo's personal interest in the paper as a platform for his power. Every so often, from some article or other that Dante shapes, Alejo dictates to our consciences what we ought to think. Alejo's not interested in becoming mayor. An insignificant post, he believes. His thing is absolute power: the real power behind the throne. Whether it's he or some arbitrary poor slob who occupies the mayor's office doesn't matter to him at all. No matter who it is, they'll follow his orders. Puppets, all those functionaries. Clowns. Dante, meanwhile, seems to maintain a certain independence. Democracy is more business-like than a dictatorship, Alejo once said to him. And I'm the one telling you this, me, a right-winger. Just look at what bunglers the military were. A laughing-stock. Democracy, even though the fussing and fuming can deafen you, lets you do business more freely. And Dante recalls an idea of Lenin's: Democracy is the dictatorship of the bourgeoisie. I do what I can, he thinks. I write what I can. Or what they let me. With respect to certain shady deals, sometimes there's no choice but to broadcast them: the business of the towers and the razing of the forest, that farce of a sewer system. Also publishing the police blotter, always without naming names, because, like I told you, I could really get it for being a snitch. Harping on a lack of safety is a topic that gives the press credibility. Sometimes I think it has its positive side. Fear makes people stay home and keeps them from being a pain in the ass. But the business at Nuestra Señora is something else, Dante, it seems Alejo told the editor and only writer for *El Vocero*. The scandal of *los abusaditos* affected all of us. Because, in essence, what was abused was the Villa. What will the tourists think of us. That we're a town of degenerates. And now that the season's almost here, you keep banging away at those articles on the prevention of child abuse. There are so many topics that could inspire your pen. Miscellany, old man. Distract the readers. And make the tourist who's come here to rent a place and buy my paper, yeah, my paper, feel that this is the best vacation spot, the best place to buy a piece of land, and, while you're at it, give me some recommendations on those properties in Mar de las Pampas that Ramos is dividing into lots. Talk about the scenery, the countryside, unfettered nature. Tourists don't come here so that you'll make them think about their brats' assholes. I ask you: So what if the tourist who comes here to invest is an abuser, what the fuck is it to us. We've gotta be concerned about investments, progress. I'm talking to you about development, get it. So stop screwing around with that abuse shit. Do me a favor. Think about it, Dante. Promise me you'll think about it.

Dante doesn't reply.

What do you say, Alejo asks him.

I don't say anything, Dante says.

And what are you thinking about, Alejo asks.

About Melina. I'm thinking about Melina.

Who the fuck is Melina.

The girl who shot herself in the chapel, you remember. The one who fired two shots into her belly.

And what does that have to do with what I'm saying to you, huh, Alejo spits out.

I wonder why she did it, Dante says.

Alejo is beside himself:

What the fuck does some crazy chick who offed herself in March have to do with this specific time of the year. Who the fuck remembers. The season's coming, Dante. Get with it. And the season will

591

do you good. More ads will get published in *El Vocero*. You win, I win, we all win. And you're wondering about bullshit from the past.

Dante stares at him hard.

Didn't you ever wonder why that girl might've put two bullets into her belly.

No, never, Alejo replies. And then: You think I know it all. No, I don't know it all. I've got enough problems knowing all the shit this fucking Villa piles on my desk. And you're one of them. Do me a favor, Dante. Stop screwing around with those articles.

And before he walks away:

It's in your own best interest.

And while the debate goes on at the Honorable City Council over the increase in municipal taxes triggered by the construction of the sewer system, while the ditches dug by Oviedo Construction Company for that same thwarted sewer system remain open, while Cachito (in absentia due to mourning) is accused of corruption, he walks erect, with the help of a cane made for him after the attack by Nazar's late pit bull, seemingly unexcited by anything except—and with good reason—his flirtation with the first princess of the Fiesta de la Raza, an eighteen-year-old beauty from Catamarca. His supporters maintain that the flirtation is just another rumor circulated by the opposition to cast aspersions on our mayor. The only thing for sure is that ever since it's been whispered that Cachito is going around with Ayelén Verónica Márquez, her father and brothers have started working for the city. Her father in Maintenance. And her brothers at the lumberyard. Ayelén, for her part, has launched her career riding four-wheelers in the northern dunes.

Why should we be shocked, Dante asks after someone reads the story of that attempted parricide in El Monte. And in a soft voice, pensively, he insinuates: Maybe here's the first fact of this kind. We don't need to repeat the story of how Fito Dobroslav went to hire El Capo

Malerba to liquidate his father, our Speer, the one who abused his own granddaughter. That's why I ask, says Dante, why should we be shocked because a kid from El Monte fires a shot at his father. The kid's head rolling around at the funeral. Will more heads roll, I wonder. Tell me, I'm asking. But don't make me talk, okay? Dante downs his drink. Tomorrow he'll continue working on that article on child abuse. And Alejo, Cachito, Dobroslav, and all the power brokers of this Villa can go fuck themselves. He'll continue with those articles until . . . His train of thought is interrupted. Maybe tomorrow, he says to himself, he'll rise to the challenge of this rage.

More than fifty cabana-rental stands within 45 miles. Over 200 hotels. Not counting the hundreds of houses and apartments for rent, or the campsites. In summer, between December and March, over two million human beings will pass through here. The thousand-headed monster, like an alien life form, will reproduce day after day. In January the human tide will be uncontrollable. And after the first week, there they are: the swarm of local Rolling Stones junkie fanatics, snobs, Twitteristas, hipsters, rampaging whiteys and menacing darkies, Lolitas who dream of being in *Gente* magazine and pay off many a limo driver with a blow job. Boyfriends, girlfriends, lovers, one-summer Don Juans and one-night sweethearts, couples made up of the newly-single who collect one brat from here and another from God-knows-where, numerous and mixed families, a torrent that takes over our Villa to a cumbia beat; the beaches, a human anthill. Imagine, we've gotta feed them all. And clean up their shit. The bodies—it's better not to look at those bodies. Or listen to their conversations. To the north, the upper middle class. Toward the south, more plebs. Many of those who look for a house along the northern boulevards, only to discover that the neighborhood is full, have no choice but to head south. But don't think those up north have more breeding. They may have more money, but they lack class. Lots of 90s-era social climbers end up in the north. They think they can distinguish themselves from the half-breeds with a Pathfinder that they don't even know how to drive. They'd be better off with dual traction in their brains. You should see how they bury themselves in the sand when they head toward Pincén, the nudist beach on the road to Última Esperanza Lighthouse. The lighthouse is about twenty miles away. It has 276 steps. I counted them. And its beam has a reach of 54 miles. The 4x4 drivers say they're going to the lighthouse, but what really interests those wankers is exploring the nudist beach. As if they'd never seen bellies, butts, tits, blood-sausage dicks, because what I think is, some guys slap themselves to maximize their assets. And when a 4x4 stops on the sand, Don Faustino, a good ol' boy from Tandil, shows up with his cart pulled by a couple of Clydesdales and fleeces them for over 500 pesos a ride. Don Faustino watches everything, as he lays into his nag with a riding crop. We live from this, he says. But we're also going to die from this. God will punish our ambition.

Well, no, we never found out and never will, who was behind the assault that eliminated Gonza Calderón. Anyone, Dante thinks. Someone who got ripped off in a shady deal, a con victim, but also— why not?—an act of revenge, some debt Cachito might have owed someone powerful. Quirós, we wonder. No, Alejo wouldn't have been so clumsy. Alejo had other methods. Alejo always had an offer nobody could refuse. We thought, we all thought, there might be some dirty business with narcos. And the cops. Who the hell knows. Whatever, no one was going to miss the kid.

Quite an event, the funeral, we recalled. Spectacular, someone said. All those cars. A caravan. Not since the funeral of old man Quirós, the illustrious deceased Don Evaristo, had there been such a throng. From the power brokers to the Bolitas, although, it was said, the Bolitas attended the funeral to make sure that the devil was dead.

No matter, the death of a son is always the death of a son. Irreparable. No one would want to be in Cachito's shoes. But, Dante thought, Cachito, with a few lines of blow in him, would soon be strolling through the Villa, his face starched with grief. How touching to touch others. His pain would be a good talking point for his next campaign. No one like a father whose son was killed can fight against the lack of safety and guarantee us neighbors that he'll do everything possible and more to turn our Villa into a model community. He would put an end to the lack of safety, he promised. And to corruption, as well. Once and for all, forever, the Villa would be the pristine place that everybody, like him, had dreamed of to raise their kids in. In Gonzalito's memory, he'll say, I give you my pledge.

And here we'll be, waiting.

Sometimes you may wonder how we see ourselves. And then you try to take a look at yourself from the outside. As if conscience could create the perspective of distance, of seeing yourself. Your very own self. Ever since that business of *los abusaditos,* Dante likes to think that the Villa, in a spate of guilt—guilt, not conscience—can observe itself from the other side of the mirror of a Gesell Dome. Within the interrogation cubicle we are probed, and when we talk it's not so much our desire to tell that matters as our need to prove our innocence. We want to emerge clean, uncontaminated, without letting any of this shit splash on us. As if that were possible. At the same time, on the other side of that fake mirror in which both questioner and subject are reflected, are those who analyze what we say and our subtlest gestures. A word, a tic, can betray us. They analyze, study, and control us, not letting us get away with a single thing. Those on the other side of the mirror dissect our thoughts and our actions. In fact, not only do they observe us: they judge us. If we consider that our ego is divided and is on both one side and the other simultaneously, that it's a split ego that understands itself to be at once accuser and accused, we will come to the conclusion that no one, no matter how clean he thinks his ass is, can pass the blame on to his fellow man. It's equally true that by positioning ourselves on both sides of the Gesell Dome simultaneously, all of us, without exception, must recognize ourselves as guilty. Let's put it this way, Dante muses: We are all assassins. And here's the mother of all conundrums: if we're all guilty of what goes on in this rotten Villa, no one in particular bears the blame. So you can pull off the vilest shit you like, the depravity that turns you on the most, because you'll never be guilty as long as your vice is generalized and divided among everyone. Conclusion: As they say, it was nobody. The same old song: nobody saw anything, nobody heard anything. That's why Dante avoids rifling through the collection of *El Vocero*, an entire year's worth of issues, organized week by week and stored in folders fastened with string, tied to a wooden stake. Let's check our memory, he likes to think when for whatever reason he needs to review a story from the past. Even if the information is related to this or that municipal ordinance, even though it might be a matter of reviewing a bureaucratic decision made by the City Council, as he thumbs through the newspaper pages, it's not only the old police blotters that sap his nerves. Each and every one of the reports, whether from the society pages or the obits, will make him feel not so much older as more weathered. And weathered is a euphemism to cover up the admission that he's been broken. In general, as in the case of *los abusaditos* or the police blotters, the articles protect the identities of those involved. It's not just a question of looking out for the kids. It's a question of looking out for oneself. You don't know if the father, uncle, grandfather suspected of being a child abuser really is one, Dante repeats to whoever wants to listen. And whether he is or not, he might come and whack you. Same with the juvie thugs. You name one, you've accused him. And the whole family, the gang, falls on you and blows you away. So it's better to play dumb. As if you were on this side of the Gesell Dome, on the side of the person being interrogated. How do we see ourselves, you wondered. I'll try to explain this to you. We see ourselves from one side and the other, but we prefer not to dwell on this question. We have just one life, it's too short, and to go stirring up shit with a spiel about social responsibility and collective guilt when there are so few of us and we know one another so well, doesn't do anybody any good. Neither the accused nor the accuser. Neither the hangman nor the victim. And don't give me any crap, because playing the victim has its secondary benefits. It's obvious that if you keep thinking this way you'll come to the conclusion that we're in hell. Watch it—don't go overboard playing the moralist: we're not evil people. We're human. And like everyone, we have our defects. You can't spend all day thinking about the kids' bloody little assholes, the guts hanging out of knifing victims, the blood streaming out of shooting victims, the wet fetuses tossed into pastures, the black-and-blue marks on battered women, the terror and humiliation of rape victims, the hammer slayings of those mugged retirees, the flame-engulfed bodies of the poor half-breeds in a shantytown fire. If you drive yourself crazy, you're done for. To live you've got to know how to forget. Let me tell you two things: first, that we're not Auschwitz and this isn't the Navy School of Mechanics. Second, this is a tourist town and we have the duty, the moral obligation if you like, to see the glass as half full. But neither from the interrogators' point of view, nor from the perspective of those who keep watch. We choose the positive side. Another factor to keep in mind: these twisted thoughts are typical of winter. Wait a little till summer comes and with the first heat waves you'll see life in a different color. Gesell Dome, my ass. You're talking to yourself, Dante tells himself. And the monologue, as you know, is a symptom of madness.

Judging from the number of anti-stress therapies that will be offered on our beach, one gets the impression that sun and sea are no longer enough to free our tourists of tension. A large variety of treatments are being promoted at rental cabanas and tents: oxygen therapy, electrostimulation, shiatsu, ergonomic-chair massage, foot massage. The offer sometimes includes a free introductory session, plus an additional free session sponsored by leading cosmetics and athletic clothing companies. Relaxation and renewed energy are the slogans. From firmer glutes to freedom from annoying muscle spasms, this summer our Villa presents a full range of services for the tourist to achieve the balance and harmony of a clear mind in a relaxed body, in a session by the sea.

First the smoke was a fog that spread along the road. The lack of visibility caused a vehicle pile-up. A car braked suddenly to avoid hitting a motorcyclist. A truck following behind hit him. And, in turn, a bus rammed into the truck. Behind, three more cars, same thing. Firefighters arrived ahead of the ambulance, the only ambulance the hospital owns. Luckily there were no fatalities. Later the smoke enveloped the pine grove, hiding the construction. But what worried everyone most, at least in the beginning, even more than the visibility was the stench, the stench of the garbage dump. Till we realized that if the fire reached the pine grove, it wasn't going to be just a forest fire. Because the pine grove is right up against the boulevards, and from there, the whole Villa would burn.

Did you hear? It's a fact, the case was declared closed. The case of *los abusaditos* was filed away. I'm not kidding, I heard it from my wife's cousin, who works at the courthouse in Dolores. Tell me it's not fucked up for the case to die in a court in La Plata. Cachito's connection with the governor, you better believe it. A return of electoral favors. A load of dirt that'll get lost in the smoke. And no one will remember. Remember that.

The ongoing purpose of the powerful police operations deployed in the Villa is to offer maximum security to tourists. "We will be everywhere," said Alberto Cachito Calderón, mayor of our city. "The governor and I conferred and reached an agreement," Calderón declared. "We are prepared to launch an all-out war against the criminal underworld. In addition to a plane, six helicopters, and mobile units equipped with GPS, there will be more squads, patrol cars, and permanent vehicle checkpoints. A total of four hundred agents are already in the streets at all hours, and in this regard, the law never sleeps. Drivers must not only have their documents in order but also must submit to sobriety tests. The development of the operation has already begun and its success is guaranteed," Calderón continued. "Groups of adolescents have been arrested, not only as they were leaving discos, but also on the beach and in the forest, a favorite place for the young to get drunk and stoned. I am convinced that security, in the real sense, begins at home. For this reason, those youths who were arrested but did not have prior convictions were turned over to their parents. The family is an institution that must recover its prestige. And we, the elders, must preach by example."

There are no innocents, Dante insists. Not in the world and not in this town we pretentiously call the Villa, either. We are all hell, some more than others. Somewhere I read that the survival strategy in hell consists of choosing who is less hellish. An opportunistic strategy, I say. If you've gotta burn, let everything burn. Like the one who quoted a poet as he incinerated a city: Let the wind speak. Let it blow hard till it turns this place into a garbage dump. Charred, smelling of trash. Do we, perhaps, deserve a better fate?

From Alejo's tone of voice on the telephone and the way he asked him to come to his office that night after closing, Dante realized that he was in for some bad news. He preferred to take his time. Tomorrow, he told him. Right now I'm all messed up from the smoke. He needed to think. We can't wait that long, Alejo said. If you don't come here, we'll go there. Who's we, Dante asked. He felt the warning shoot through his whole body. Us, Alejo said. And hung up.

I saw the squeeze coming, Dante would later reproach himself. It was on account of the articles. That night, before he could lock up the office of *El Vocero*, there they were: Alejo, Don Carneiro, and Gancedo. Alejo in the middle, flanked by the thugs.

A squeeze, what doubt could there be. A squeeze, said Dante, as if demanding an affirmation of the obvious.

Call it whatever you want. You're the scribe, Alejo said.

Then he coughed: This damn smoke.

You're gonna cut out all that shit about abuse, Dante, Alejo said.

Dante looked at Don Carneiro; he looked at Gancedo. Don Carneiro and Gancedo didn't look at him. Rather, they watched him. They were waiting for one gesture from him to jump him. Dante didn't move. He waited, then slid his hand along the desk, looked for a cigarette, because he'd started smoking again, lit up.

You can't keep someone who wants to fuck kids from doing it, Dante. The Villa's being invaded by a paranoia that does no one any good. No one, he repeated.

I protect innocents, Dante said.

Around here the only one doing any protecting is me, Alejo said. The power is me. We're in November and you're still dicking around with those articles. Wise up: the season is coming. Talk about prospects for the season, the possibilities the Villa offers for tourists, nature, the attractions of the place, which are many. Ecology, dumbass. If you want, talk about the smoke. Talk about ecology. Ecology makes people happy, Dante.

It's a squeeze, Dante repeated.

No, it's a negotiation. I'll make you an offer you won't be able to refuse, Alejo said.

I seem to remember hearing that before, Dante said.

Hear it again, said Alejo.

You're gonna take away your financial support of *El Vocero*, Dante replied. It's your right.

No, I'm not about to shut down the paper, Alejo told him. It's an important medium for the Villa. We all read about ourselves in this paper. We like to see ourselves.

You can fire me, Dante challenged him.

No, I don't want to kick you out. I want you to see reason. You're useful: nobody knows the Villa like you. Where would I find someone else so lucid and so resigned. The time it would take. Don't fuck with me. I want you to change your attitude, Dante.

And Dante: Every man, even the biggest scumbag, has a little bit of purity that sometimes rises to the surface, he cited. Maybe that's where I am at this moment. My purity's rising.

Purity doesn't suit you, Alejo said. You really love Chiquita, right.

Dante hesitated before cursing Alejo out. He didn't do it.

Alejo, with a blank face:

What if this Thursday, when you go to the Tropicana, Chiquita isn't there. You know these girls come to a bad end. Yours might end before her time.

Like every year, the newspapers and the TV will report that Retiro Station has collapsed. Throngs of people will pile up at the wharves, waiting for hours for the extra buses to arrive, more than 500 of them, which are mostly delayed while the drivers from the transportation companies threaten to strike for higher wages. Despite the crisis, hotels in the Villa are 90% occupied, as hordes of tourists continue to arrive from all parts of the country in minibuses, cars, vans, on motorcycle, hitchhiking, and even by bicycle. Many of those who come, generally those from Greater Buenos Aires and the interior, think that this is a classy resort for people with lots of money. Just by coming here, any asshole can feel like a big shot. Just look at those who stay in Barrio Norte, nobodies who think they're hot shit because they have a chalet in the pines, a 4x4 and a quad, they think they're Rothschild's sons. Without exception, whether they're upper-middle class or lower-middle, all of them, even the half-breeds who put on airs driving a school bus disguised as a motor home, act like magnates from *Caras* magazine. All of them acting high and mighty even when they're just a bunch of poor slobs who pinch the handful of *pesos* they've saved up to last a whole week on a diet of pizza and hot dogs. The ones with real dough, let me tell you, those guys don't come here, and they don't set foot on sand that after one day turns into a garbage heap of cans, bottles, supermarket bags, *yerba mate*, diapers, and even tampons. And then they tell you they like the Villa because you can breathe nature here; they're all la-di-dah with their let's protect the planet, but then they crap out last night's fried squid under the tamarind trees and leave their shitty toilet paper to float in the wind. Not to mention the charcoal and burned branches that appear in the morning among the dunes, beer bottles, cigarette butts, condoms. And there's no shortage of drunks, either, lying unconscious till well past noon. Life is short, after all, and the few vacation days we have last about as long as a drunken binge. The incredible thing is that many of these losers probably think they're on the Côte d'Azur. What a privilege to come here, they say. And what do we do? We curse under our breath and greet them with open arms, but first we raise prices. Welcome to the Villa.

The City has announced the implementation of its "City under Surveillance Plan," an intense coordinated effort of the tasks of prevention and control to strengthen security during the summer. The Plan integrates the work of the police, the regional government and the Civil Defense, Fire, Sanitation, Transportation, and Municipal Security Departments. In addition to the mayor, participants at the meeting included the government secretary, the director of security, department chiefs, the heads of investigations and of local police stations. Further, guidelines were established for the strict enforcement of permissible hours for alcohol sales, which in the case of groceries and markets will end at 9:00 P.M., as well as policies concerning evening hours, to which end a schedule of meetings was established, to be carried out in the coming days among community members, merchants, and representatives of the restaurant and food industry and dance halls, with special focus on enforcing closing hours for these establishments.

On a related note, it was announced that either next Monday or Tuesday all the new summer security personnel will be introduced publicly, more than one hundred reinforcement units, with their assigned equipment and mobile devices; among these 25 patrol cars and 25 motorcycle backups will be designated. This event will take place at the entrance to the community building.

In an exclusive report to El Vocero, *our mayor, Alberto Calderón, declared that the Plan proposes to guarantee maximum control in order to allow for the healthy relaxation and freedom offered at this time of year by our city, long recognized as a summer resort where everyone, from babies to seniors, can have fun together.*

With regard to the continuous onslaught of smoke our Villa has endured lately, Calderón declared that the disturbance is temporary and that we should not be concerned. According to the weather report, as soon as the wind changes direction, the smoke will cease to be a nuisance.

This hospital, with its Alpine style and tiled roof, was designed by the German in the 50s, and was built only during the dictatorship. It was conceived as a Villa with a maximum of ten thousand inhabitants, and now we're five times bigger, without taking into account the flood of tourists. In a few days, at this early hour of the morning, the ER will overflow with the wounded, O.D.'s, drunks, and morons at death's door, and there won't be a single bed available in the ICU. Don't even think about bringing in your baby, with its case of summer diarrhea, because you'll be stuck in the waiting room along with a mother with her little daughter shaken by convulsions, two kids shot by a tourist when they peed on the privet of his chalet, car crash victims, broken heads, bloody bodies, a poor jerk who tried to resist a holdup and caught a bullet instead, some kids in an alcoholic coma, the bruised victims of a club brawl. And just wait for the morning contingent to appear, the strung-out kids who wage battles. Don't ask the cops why they didn't step in: Deputy Commissioner Renzo will tell you maliciously that all this is because nowadays human rights are in fashion and they can't even touch a hair on the little bastards' heads. So they wait for them to beat the shit out of one another, and then, yeah, they lend a hand by piling them up, unconscious, on the sand. The four or five hospital stretchers will go from one end to another, leaving in their wake the screechy echo of unoiled wheels, broken springs, crying, and moans. When not a single bed is left for inpatients, we'll pull some beat-up mattresses, reeking of cat piss, out of the storeroom and dump them into the hallways. And anybody who's puking had better stay out of our way when surely there's a three-year-old with leukemia in the ICU.

If all is written, so too is the next act. And against that we cannot rebel. At most, read it. In the facts, in the sky, in the wind. But our condition as readers is conditioned. We always read what has been written for us. And we confirm it: it was written that it would be this way. We don't know what we came for. Sometimes we think we suspect it. But we take so long to confirm our suspicions. Because, among other reasons, when we think we're sure of a cause, the effect throws us off: it responds to another motive. If we are nothing but written creatures, we are innocent. It's true that these musings aim to free us from guilt. As long as we are words, we might be able to reason: let no one be blamed. Let everyone be blamed. Because if we are all guilty, no one is. An alibi: in any case, the guiltiest of all is the Author of our days. And yes, believing that God is the writer of our story doesn't free us from guilt, but it alleviates it. God is our consolation. Although if we really consider the matter, God is malicious: all He does is deceive us in our reading, force us to doubt everything, all the time, everything, even His very existence. Then we ask ourselves if a greater evil than that can be written, the constant doubt, a doubt that turns into suspicions, and so we end up suspecting, not just everyone else, but ourselves. No, it's not me, Dante, who's writing these lines that he won't publish.

The bus terminal is a monumental hangar that takes up an entire block. It's located four blocks from the fishermen's wharf and opposite the second police station. Its architecture reflects the typical design of the last military dictatorship, a construction that, in its vastness, looks more like a fort than a building designed to provide a public service. The original idea, the first sketches, were Don Karl's work, they say. And its resemblance to totalitarian architecture is indisputable. Of course, the job was entrusted to our Speer, Dobroslav. And it was inaugurated in the 80s. On days of ghostly, ominous mist, the terminal is a dark gray mass, visible from the main street, from beyond the stores selling fishing gear, *alfajores,* or cheap clothing.

At the northern wing, twelve parallel parking docks for the buses, a newspaper kiosk, windows for parcel shipment by transportation companies, and a mural painted by students from middle school. Seeing all that, you wonder what their creators were trying to prove, what this childlike imagery was trying to represent. If the totem whose meaning is still being debated looms above the entrance to the Villa, here the totem is reproduced, but with the German's image incorporated. Beneath the eagle's head is the head of Don Karl, erect, solemn, gazing at a pale blue sky. Southeasters have dulled the mural's colors. For example, the yellow of a sand dune, once strident, that gigantic red bird, and then, behind it, a lighthouse projecting an elongated beam of light. The artists' perspectives in general are quite naïve. The images compete with one another, like that hand opening up, in its palm the landscape of the Villa, the forest, the slanted roofs poking out amid all the green. At the left margin of the mural, a poem titled "Traveler, You Will Return." And, when you board the bus and look out the window, you can read the poem that's incorporated into the mural: *Traveler, you will return, / thirsting for sun / and when your bare feet / brush the sea foam, / you will become the wings of a gull / Perhaps you will fly / through the acacia treetops / and among the dunes / Torrents of gold will engulf you / as if stopping time's flow / toward vastness.*

At any time of year, there are always two or three dirty old dogs. The bus terminal dogs are as pathetic, old, flea-ridden, sick, and spindly as beggars. Dogs in terminal condition. And the sadness they make you feel can only be compared to the sadness that emanates from the terminal on days when a southeaster rages, when the gale sweeps the docks, and the passengers waiting for their bus pull up their collars, stomping around to warm their frozen feet. And the wind that soaks you through. Inside, dusty, dark, the terminal is cold in summer and glacial in winter. The windows and counters of the bus lines all in a row: Rutatlántica, Zenit, Flecha Bus, El Rápido, El Onda, Brown, Serrano, Micromar, Alberino, Plusmar, Plaza, Álvarez. Several windows display posters of missing children, photos of a little girl, a little boy, their names, a few details. The grayish photo of Belén Yanina is still up in a few of the windows. Seeing them, you ask yourself if each person who stops to look at them will register those details, if he'll pay proper attention to the lost little girl or boy, if he'll commit this information to memory and will take each one of these dramas seriously, and how long their effect will last, which, when converted into a statistic, will become a number and soon thereafter, indifference. There are so many unfortunate kids in this world, he'll say to himself. And he'll continue on his way, turning his back on the poster, walking away with his ticket toward a bus that's about to depart.

At one end there's a bar, El Camello: Delicious mini sirloin steaks, tasty *milanesas*, extra-long hot dogs, nutritious sandwiches, sodas, beer, fine wines. But the most popular offering in this enormous, deserted place is blow. Closer up, on this side, phone booths offering national and international service: Talk in comfort. Right next door, a kiosk called Freeshop. In back, to one side of the bathrooms, mounted on the wall, an altar with the Virgin, Nuestra Señora del Mar, with a spent candle and wilted flowers.

You walk along, looking for a destination. Madariaga, Mar del Plata, Dolores, Chascomús, Castelli, Lezama, La Plata, Luis Guillón, Caseros, Longchamps, Tropezón, Grand Bourg, Llavallol, Burzaco, Solano, Retiro, Adrogué, Avellaneda, Bariloche, Ciudadela, Choele Choel, Villa Tessei, Florencia Varela, General Belgrano, San

Miguel del Monte, Villa Regina, Liniers, Ramos Mejía, Haedo, Ituzaingó, Vicente López, Olivos, San Isidro, General Pacheco, Wilde, Quilmes, Tapiales, and also combinations with the provinces. Cipoletti, Jujuy, Misiones. You choose, from Buenos Aires to Pedroza. And from La Quiaca to Tierra del Fuego.

The farther the better, you tell yourself. Where no one can find you. Not even you.

Religion Today, Dante puts as his title. *An attitude that highlights the Christianity of our Villa is the trip to Lourdes planned by our mayor, Alberto Cachito Calderón. Accompanied by his wife Beatriz, the couple has taken on a project that enhances the community: to build a replica of the Cathedral of Lourdes in our Villa. "By doing this we will be the only place in the world to have this architectural miracle, and that is why we hope to sign an agreement to stimulate the arrival of believers from all corners of the national map. This construction will not only aim to strengthen worshipers' religious fervor. It should also be considered a significant contribution to the tourist industry insofar as our Villa may obviously be considered a privileged place for the pilgrimage of those who, in addition to believing in God, believe in us."*

And it's finally the night, this night, the season is here, it's now. Like every year, the opening begins at nightfall with a religious ceremony at the pier: Father Beltrán blesses the waters and then, the great fireworks show. We may not all go to church, but no one misses the fireworks. Maybe a lot of folks arrive just when the priest, at the end of the jetty that extends into the sea, blesses the waters, the waves, the whole ocean. A spotlight surrounds him. His actions, his gestures, the way he crosses himself, brings his hands together in supplication, murmurs a prayer, it all contributes to giving the religious service an operatic quality that inspires, if not faith, the desire to have faith, to believe. That's why nobody arrives so late that they miss not only the religious service, but also the start of the fireworks, that moment when you hold your breath before a sputtering in the dark, the lighting of a wick, and then, crackling, the phosphorescence explodes and the first flare is fired, a dizzying, multicolored line that rises toward the sky, obscuring everything around it, the moon and the stars. The night is an explosion of lights that trace everything from golden globes to the launching of a firework that rises slowly, overtaking the tops of the flares and the globes, and, tracing a rainbow-hued pirouette, another flare follows its rising path till it stops, hovers levitated in one place, and then, for an entire second, both fall in a nosedive, disintegrating in an iridescent cloud. And there's a collective *Oh*, a noisy exclamation that arises from the depths of every one of us. There's always some asshole who comments that in the commotion of the firecrackers, anybody could take advantage of the deafening bangs, the din of the explosions, to blow someone away with a bullet. The asshole's right. What better conditions for getting rid of someone you've always hated: everyone deafened and staring fascinated at the sky, mouths agape. You won't get another perfect opportunity like this till next year. Go on, right now. Who will notice the difference with all the explosions. No one.

The fireworks illuminate faces. Profiles look bluish and can barely be differentiated or identified in the rapid alternation of darkness and brilliance, a brilliance that sometimes lasts a while, surprising us on an equally artificial day. Holding our breath, we let out a sigh, a laugh, a scream every time a firecracker explodes, the clamor of a burst of colored lightning. The crowd—and we are all the crowd— sometimes emits a unanimous murmur of astonishment, a sound that's a little like a breeze passing over the faces that emerge from the shadows, brighten, and dissipate once more, the open mouths of men and women, adults and children, the old and the sick and even the disabled because not even those who get around with canes, crutches, or in wheelchairs are about to miss a spectacle like this one, which, with its crackling, endless light show, has come to confirm that it pays to muster up our courage in the fall, withstand the corrosion of saltpeter, winter with its storms, the onslaught of spring downpours, and now, at last, defeats and frustrations, personal Calvaries and this collective inferno. The entire collection of misery that we are remains behind us, and we convince ourselves that a better life is about to begin, that the hope it was so hard for us to sustain, so very, very, very hard that it finally wore us out, we now see, we all see, that hope had meaning. We recognize one another in the intermittent, fleeting sparks. All of us.

We are the creation of the German, Don Karl, our mythical character, the founder of the Villa. Here they are, the guests of honor, the German's two daughters who live in the Villa: Christa, the aging hippie, who filed the insanity lawsuit against her father, and Elisa, the confectioner and pianist, who refused to participate in that conspiracy. Of course, since then they won't even say hello to one another.

We also descend from the late Salo Katzman, his foreman and a Treblinka survivor, and we recall what people used to say: if the German hired a Jew to be his foreman, it wasn't because he had stopped being racist but rather because he preferred a blond Ashkenazi to a *criollo* from Madariaga. Other special guests, as if to prove we're not racists, are the descendants of the late Katzman: Diana, the dentist, and David, the cardiologist. The two of them, their airfare paid by the city, have come from Tel Aviv.

Standing at the display table is Martínez, the operator of the Aeroclub, on this occasion serving as fireworks expert. Next to Father Beltrán, who's gazing at the sky with a beatific look on his face, we see Alberto Cachito Calderón, our mayor, with his wife Beatriz Marconi, both of them in strict mourning. Standing tall, his forehead high, leaning on his handcrafted cane with a theatrical expression, Cachito, holding Beti's arm. You'd think she's helping him walk, but he's play-acting. And behind them, the Kennedys, all of them: Alejo, the capo of the law firm; Julián, the city official; Braulio, the one from the real estate office. All their wives and all their children, the heirs: Jackie flanked by Mili and Juan Manuel; Susi with Matías, Nico, and Lourdes; Adriana with Felicitas and Luz. With one of Uncle Alejo's hands on his shoulder, without missing a detail of the smallest crackle of the fireworks, Camilo, the orphan, son of the late Alba, Quirós's guerrilla sister. Contrary to what we had expected, Camilo doesn't issue the shriek we've all become accustomed to, the shriek that paralyzes the entire Villa, because Camilo remains silent, rapt, perhaps because the din of the firecrackers reminds him of when the army burst into his parents' home, shooting. Which would explain why every so often, when a rocket lights up, he covers his ears, and if the bang is more powerful, he covers his eyes. Josema the barber watches the kid out of the corner of his eye; for sure it'll be a topic of conversation at his shop.

Marconi the pharmacist, and Valeria, his wife, the one who's fucking Alejo, are there, too, arm in arm. As if protecting the Kennedys and their circle, not very far away, Don Carneiro, the old capo, keeping an eye on those kids who are likely to make trouble, even on a special night like this: Clavo Martínez Gálvez, Facu Sergione, and Tuti Vega. Making sure they don't get out of control, Don Carneiro says. No way would María, Quirós's maid, miss the party. She and her whole tribe: Claudia, Verónica, Vanesa, Augusto. Although Marzio the ecologist thinks the fireworks are a bunch of pagan nonsense, typical of the petty-bourgeois, he couldn't help bringing his twins. For the kids, he says he's making the effort and tries to go with the flow. Beside him is Dr. Uribe, owner of the Clínica del Mar, together with his daughter, Catalina, and his son-in-law, Graziani the accountant. When they first arrived, we looked at them in surprise, but at this point nothing can surprise us as much as the fireworks; that's why we didn't even pay attention to Mabel, the teller from Banco Provincia, her husband, Mario, Marianito, the baby. And with them Elvira and Daniel, the other swinger couple. Fact is, nobody's missing here. Look, there's Irene, the boss at the Tropicana, and some of the girls, how elegant they look even though you can tell what they are. A few feet away, keeping her distance, is Chiquita, on Borelli's arm. It's impossible that Chiquita hasn't spotted Dante, impossible that their eyes haven't met. She pretends to be distracted. She's ignored him on purpose, that's for sure. She's better off with Borelli, Dante thinks. He's right for her, he says to himself. She's out of danger. And he realizes that this isn't the resignation of someone lucid, but of someone defeated.

Then Natale, the one from the Pasta House, with his kid, Gastón. And Montefiore, from the lumberyard, with his wife, Regina, and Fabrizio, the son whose bride ripped off her clothes at the altar, leaving him jilted at the church that Sunday when we thought the Flood was coming. We also see the pioneers Friedrich Stegman, the one behind the first water pumps, and his wife, Doña Tea. In back of them, their daughter, Gisela, and Freddy, her husband. It's obvious that the family cut off relations with Rosita, the Winterfest Queen, daughter of Gisela and Freddy Müller, who committed the worst offense against the Aryan community by getting involved with Dicky Garramuño, the motocross champion, may he rest in peace. Everyone from Huerta Accounting Office is here: Malena, the accountant; Tini, the secretary; and Rosita Müller, who's been an assistant there for a while now. Nearby you can see Remigio, the limo driver, with his wife, Daniela, that cutie. Also Dr. Pausini, the gynecologist from Clínica del Mar. There's not a chick who doesn't give him a friendly greeting. Or a guy who doesn't make a remark as he goes by. Look: Simone Orvigny, the French professor, is here. Farther down, stiff-backed, without letting himself look impressed, Retired Coronel Manfredo. Piacentini, owner of the Mi Espacio Vital complex in Mar de las Pampas. The bankers couldn't miss the occasion, either. Gutiérrez, manager of Banco Nación, and Rafa, of Personal Loans. With them, Dell'Oro, the teller from Banco Provincia.

Balmaceda and Renzo have chosen to remain behind, keeping watch, from three patrol cars in a row. Nazar, a few yards away, with his mastiff. Behind him, Emilia, her husband, Don, and her siblings,

Mariano, Mariela, and Jorgito. The Giménez family, from Del Mar Electrical Co-Op, all of them. Malerba, the gunman, coughing constantly but not about to give up smoking, a toy poodle under his arm, has joined in, also, with the Pedroza family, who lately, ever since Malerba's lungs got fucked up with crack, have taken him under their wing. If anyone had hired Malerba tonight, with rockets quaking everywhere, would be the ideal moment. But no: tonight Malerba is just another neighbor, and his expression as he watches the fireworks is that of a child. Don Morano, from the dealership, was one of the first to arrive. For La Comadre, the healer, the whole celebration is an auspicious abundance of white magic: that's what she says. The lights in the sky will cure souls.

You've got to move aside and let people through. Here comes Dobroslav, our Speer, pushing Fito's wheelchair. And Blanco, the supermarket owner, too, with his daughter, Ceci, and his son-in-law, Fede. They've come with Merlino, the one from the Co-op, and his wife, Paula. There are VIPs, too, Villa big shots. Look: Salvatore, from Hogarmar Appliances, and Roque, his son. Of course, El Gallego, Manolo Barbeito, owner of Galería Soles, is here; he's pitched in with a large check for the celebration.

The staff from the TV station don't stop filtering in among the people, annoying them with their cameras, recording comments that will barely be heard, because when the volume of the explosions goes down, the theme from *Chariots of Fire* blares deafeningly in your ears. Even Bermúdez, the Trotskyite gardener, the one we call Cyclops, is in attendance. He's standing near Mirna, the pregnant forty-something who sells costume jewelry at the handicraft gallery. For a while Mirna's been fucking Berto, that kid whose arm is around her shoulder. Weisz, the bald guy from the classical FM station, wouldn't miss it, either: Handel, he says. They should've played the *Royal Fireworks Music,* the baldy says. If they'd have asked me, we wouldn't have to put up with *Chariots of Fire.* Beti, the owner of Las Camelias Grill in the rotunda, tries to make her way toward the dock. But from below, from the beach, you can see better. Deborah, the shrink, goes around greeting everybody. You'd think she's seen the whole Villa professionally, because to one extent or another, we've all set foot in her office, I mean all of us except Dante, because that one keeps himself off to one side, lying in wait to detect some human weakness that will confirm the skeptical, merciful notion he has of us. Now Andrés the surveyor and his wife, with Belén in her arms, are greeting Dante. As you walk through the crowd, you'll encounter more and more familiar faces: Jacobo the kinesiologist and his daughter, Perla, with Pinhead Soria, the boyfriend Jacobo can't stand for two reasons: for being a half-breed and a goy, but more for being a half-breed. Norita, the New Age masseuse, is bedazzled. As is Beto the butcher from Las Vacas Gordas, who's brought his wife, Elba, and Vane, their little girl. Macho Mama, the limo driver, who became a widow in November, has come with Taborda the plumber. We wonder if there's something going on between them.

Don Tito Souza, the union leader, with Doña Domitila and all the women in the family, who are from the Peronist Feminine Wing, don't stop applauding. Though he might have his differences with Cachito Calderón's administration, Don Tito can't stop singing his praises. And coming with his whole family is a way to mark turf: Ethel, El Loco's widow, with her kids, Marianito, Alejandra, Fernanda, Paulina, and Martín. They've also brought along Virginia, the widow of Rodolfo, who was carried off to sea, which was a relief to the family. In back, timid El Perro, together with Paola, and Pedrito, the little boy. Don Tito's sworn enemy, Ibáñez, a Workers' Central Union delegate, is also there with Lidia, his partner, and their children: Agustín and Eva. The boy was named for Agustín Tosco, the murdered left-wing union leader, and the girl, obviously, for Evita. Doña Domitila and Lidia, the two union representatives' women, barely said hello.

Of course Ayelén Verónica Márquez, First Winterfest Princess, the one they say Cachito's banging these days, was going to show up, With Ayelén is the entire Márquez family. They say Cachito's given all of them jobs with the city. Carlos Gonzaga, secretary of City Planning, tries in vain to approach Cachito: he was left out of the Honor Guard, and it's going to be hard for him, with such a mob, to get away from the Virginias; let's hope no one thinks he has anything to do with those girls. Because the Viriginias, the two little whores, are also here, simple and without makeup, looking like two *criolla* fairies.

There's more, just look: Mayorano the shopkeeper, with his son, Julián, and Gabriela, Julián's girlfriend. Pertini, from the real-estate office with his two children: Andrea the architect and Diego the designer. Don Peyrou, the supervisor at the lumberyard. The Parentis have also come: José Luis and Lidia. Castañón, from Maintenance. Martínez, the guy from the Aeroclub. And Brother Santi, with the Romeros, Victoriano and María Adelia, in between the two of them, arm in arm. Santi watches the fireworks without blinking, as if hypnotized, murmuring who knows what, a prayer, maybe, thanking the fireworks as if they were a gift from heaven.

Because the fireworks make us feel better than what we are. You'll tell me it's not a matter of holy flames, just rockets, firecrackers, and flares, but it's enough to renew one's spirits, to make people kinder, bless their hearts. Moure the veterinarian wouldn't fail to come with Betina, his daughter, a kindergarten teacher at Nuestra Señora. Sitting in the sand, Moni jots down in her notebook: *The seasons pass by in turn / they pass us by / extinguish us in turn / and we remain alone / glowing / in the fireworks.*

Rinaldi, from Los Médanos Supermarket, seems to have gotten over his son's suicide. He's here with his new woman, the little *criolla*, and the baby. At least this is not a night to let yourself be overcome by sadness. The Duchess, the money-lender, is here. She's with Dr. Carpio, the hospital director. Also with them, Doc Zambrano. And Mirtha Loprete, the socialist councilmember, has come with Cuchi the electrologist. Best not to ask what Ruli, the dealer, is up to, slipping through the crowd. Look who's over there: Anita López, the literature teacher from middle school, with Osvaldo Campas of Campas Plumbing Supplies: they had a baby, Federico, not long ago. Gervaise, sister of the late Fournier, has come, too. But the fireworks don't seem to brighten her spirits. My brother was crazy about fireworks, she remarks. But he's not here anymore. Maybe he's watching from above. And from above he paints them.

If you like, I'll go on and name more of those who came: René, from Paprika Restaurant; Martelli, the public auctioneer; Mike and Paula, the artisans who make incense. And Noemí Casal, from the Southern Neighborhood Association. Nearby, Adalberto Barragán, Tachito Ludueña, Catriel Ramírez, the *criollo* grillmasters.

At a distance, from atop a dune, Dante watches. Melina, Dante thinks. And says to himself: What if this were the answer to the forgotten question. And if it was, what then. What if the question is God. Maybe this is His answer. Stars, he thinks: the three cantos of *The Divine Comedy* all end with the word "stars."

All institutions are represented tonight: the Nuestra Señora del Mar Institute, the German Club, the Swiss Club, the Malvinas Argentinas Hospital, Clínica del Mar, Clínica Don Bosco, the Beer Lovers' Society, the Rebirth Society, the Rotary Club, the Waldorf School.

You don't have to be mistrustful to infer why, in this massive congregation of the Villa, it's not possible to spot either the Vicuñas or the Reyeses. Not to mention the Osorios. How could they forfeit this opportunity, where everyone is looking up at the fireworks in the sky. The Vicuñas and the Reyeses, while we're all sky-gazing, have their feet firmly planted on the ground and must be ripping off houses and shops like crazy. You'd better have remembered to set the alarm before you left the house. If you didn't, kiss your new plasma TV goodbye.

A genuine popular fiesta, the opening of the season. A star-filled sky, the mesmerizing fireworks that illuminate us, making us imagine that the radiation of that light doesn't come from the flares, Roman candles, skyrockets, but from within us. And so tonight we've all come together at the wharf once more, all of us, the entire Villa. Another bang and another explosion that rises up to the night sky. After each flare, applause. A skyful of luminous radiance. Firecrackers again. They sound like gunshots. And I'll tell you again: any motherfucker could take advantage of this moment to exterminate someone. And don't tell me this idea hasn't crossed several people's minds. The firecrackers would muffle the sound of a shot. The idea can occur to more than one of us. There are always reasons why this might happen in the midst of the flashes and bedazzlement. And this is the ideal moment.

And yet it doesn't come to pass. Not yet, at least. Because those lights come from all of us. Agreed, our light, the one that comes from each of us, might be artificial, but it's ours, it's the light we've got, a borrowed light, and this isn't the time to have twisted thoughts, but rather to applaud, laugh, celebrate. Life is so short, someone says. Let's enjoy it. *Carpe diem.*

The celebration lasts for more than an hour. Having awaited it for so long, it seems shorter to us. Like happiness. Which, by the time you take notice, is gone. And when it ends, we are others. We return to our cars, vans, jeeps, motorcycles, bikes. And those who have no vehicle stroll along the beach by the light of the moon. We walk away from the wharf, filled with a strange happiness.

The season will be our salvation.

Author's Acknowledgments

Ángela Pradelli, Ricardo Arkader, Patricia Muñoz, Juan Boido, Soledad Barruti, Paula Pérez Alonso, Antonio Dal Masetto, María Inés Krimer, Cristian Domingo, Eduardo Belgrano Rawson, Rodrigo Fresán, Orlando Balbo, José Roza, Carlos Cottet, Jorge Portas, Martha Berlín, Adriana Lestido, Elisa Calabrese, Oscar Finkelberg, Miguel Paz, Analía Belén, Liliana Escalante, Miguel Berger, Francisco Gamboa, Carlos Guarnieri, Miguel Molfino, Juan Ariel Gómez, Juan Forn, Enrique Guastavino, Adolfo Adorno, Patricia Richie, Lucio Arce, Eduardo Spiner, Aníbal Zaldívar, and Hernán Mlynarzewicz.

Also to my sister Patricia.

Guillermo Saccomanno was born in Buenos Aires in 1948. Before becoming a novelist, he worked as a copy writer in the advertising industry and as a script writer for cartoons and other films. Saccomanno is a prolific writer, with numerous novels and short story collections to his credit. He has won many literary awards, including the Premio Nacional de Literatura, Seix Barral's Premio Biblioteca Breve de Novela, the Rodolfo Walsh Prize for non-fiction, and two Dashiell Hammett Prizes (one for *Cámara Gesell* in 2012). *Gesell Dome* is the first book of his to be published in English.

A ndrea G. Labinger, professor emerita of Spanish at the University of La Verne, holds a PhD in Latin American Literature from Harvard. Labinger has published numerous translations of Latin American fiction, and is a three-time finalist in the PEN USA competition. Her recent translated titles include Ángela Pradelli's *Friends of Mine* (Latin American Literary Review Press, 2012) and Ana María Shua's *The Weight of Temptation* (Nebraska, 2012). She received a PEN/Heim Translation Award for her work on *Gesell Dome*.

OPEN LETTER

Inga Ābele (Latvia)
  High Tide
Naja Marie Aidt (Denmark)
  Rock, Paper, Scissors
Esther Allen et al. (ed.) (World)
  The Man Between: Michael Henry
    Heim & a Life in Translation
Svetislav Basara (Serbia)
  The Cyclist Conspiracy
Sergio Chejfec (Argentina)
  The Dark
  My Two Worlds
  The Planets
Eduardo Chirinos (Peru)
  The Smoke of Distant Fires
Marguerite Duras (France)
  Abahn Sabana David
  L'Amour
  The Sailor from Gibraltar
Mathias Énard (France)
  Street of Thieves
  Zone
Macedonio Fernández (Argentina)
  The Museum of Eterna's Novel
Rubem Fonseca (Brazil)
  The Taker & Other Stories
Juan Gelman (Argentina)
  Dark Times Filled with Light
Georgi Gospodinov (Bulgaria)
  The Physics of Sorrow
Arnon Grunberg (Netherlands)
  Tirza
Hubert Haddad (France)
  Rochester Knockings:
    A Novel of the Fox Sisters
Gail Hareven (Israel)
  Lies, First Person

Angel Igov (Bulgaria)
  A Short Tale of Shame
Ilya Ilf & Evgeny Petrov (Russia)
  The Golden Calf
Zachary Karabashliev (Bulgaria)
  18% Gray
Jan Kjærstad (Norway)
  The Conqueror
  The Discoverer
Josefine Klougart (Denmark)
  One of Us Is Sleeping
Carlos Labbé (Chile)
  Loquela
  Navidad & Matanza
Jakov Lind (Austria)
  Ergo
  Landscape in Concrete
Andreas Maier (Germany)
  Klausen
Lucio Mariani (Italy)
  Traces of Time
Amanda Michalopoulou (Greece)
  Why I Killed My Best Friend
Valerie Miles (World)
  A Thousand Forests in One Acorn:
    An Anthology of Spanish-
    Language Fiction
Quim Monzó (Catalonia)
  Gasoline
  Guadalajara
  A Thousand Morons
Elsa Morante (Italy)
  Aracoeli
Giulio Mozzi (Italy)
  This Is the Garden
Andrés Neuman (Spain)
  The Things We Don't Do

**OPEN
LETTER**

WWW.OPENLETTERBOOKS.ORG